D0930466

EVERYMAN,
I WILL GO WITH THEE,
AND BE THY GUIDE,
IN THY MOST NEED
TO GO BY THY SIDE

# R.K. NARAYAN

## MR SAMPATH – THE PRINTER OF MALGUDI,

## THE FINANCIAL EXPERT,

## WAITING FOR THE MAHATMA

WITH AN INTRODUCTION
BY ALEXANDER MCCALL SMITH

EVERYMAN'S LIBRARY
Alfred A. Knopf  New York  London  Toronto

THIS IS A BORZOI BOOK
PUBLISHED BY ALFRED A. KNOPF

First included in Everyman's Library, 2006
First published in Great Britain in 1949 by Eyre & Spottiswoode Ltd.
*Mr Sampath – The Printer of Malgudi* – © R. K. Narayan, 1949
First published in Great Britain in 1952 by Methuen & Co.
*The Financial Expert* – © R. K. Narayan, 1952
First published in Great Britain in 1955 by Methuen & Co.
*Waiting for the Mahatma* – © R. K. Narayan, 1955

Introduction Copyright © 2006 by Alexander McCall Smith
Bibliography and Chronology Copyright © 2006 by Everyman's Library
Typography by Peter B. Willberg

US website: www.randomhouse.com/everymans

ISBN: 0-4000-4477-4 (US)
1-85715-294-8 (UK)

A CIP catalogue reference for this book is available from the
British Library

*Book design by Barbara de Wilde and Carol Devine Carson*

Printed and bound in Germany by GGP Media GmbH, Pössneck

# CONTENTS

---

# INTRODUCTION

_A novelist of little things_

India has long occupied a special place in the imagination of outsiders. It is in every sense an astonishing country – a country which is immensely rich in history, which is inhabited by the most remarkable and engaging people, and which holds within its boundaries virtually every type of landscape one might care to contemplate, from Rajasthan deserts to high Himalayan snowfields. For those who are smitten by India – and their number is legion – there is a rich body of literature in English with which to nurture this passion. One might pass a lifetime in a library of Indian memoirs, topography, history, religion, and philosophy, and, of course, fiction. And on those fiction shelves one would come across, in pride of place, the novels of R. K. Narayan, all well-loved short books with beguiling titles (how could one resist a book called _The Vendor of Sweets_?), and each of them a delightful window into the world that is India. Who was he, this scholarly-looking man with his heavy-framed spectacles and his air of intense concentration? Why are his books so cherished and admired by enthusiasts in so many countries?

R. K. Narayan is one of those novelists who commands universal affection. The cult of twentieth-century best-sellerdom created many writers who were far better known than Narayan and who consequently commanded much larger audiences. It also produced those who were much better rewarded in the financial sense and who moved on an international stage amongst the glittering and successful of this world. Few of such writers, however, have been loved in quite the same way as Narayan was. And few of those to whom literary success came succeeded in remaining much the same people at the end as they were at the beginning. Narayan, however, did just that. He led a relatively simple, family-oriented life, and he died more or less where he began, a member of the same community which he so lovingly recorded in his novels. And when he died, a whole world came to an end – the world of Malgudi, the town he created and peopled with a cast of characters who remain so utterly memorable.

Narayan was born in 1906, and his life more or less spanned the century. The India into which he was born was the India of the British Raj, part of an empire that bestrode the globe and which had complete confidence in its place and its mission. To be born an Indian at such a time involved being part of a somewhat complex and contradictory society. At the same time as being a citizen of a world-wide empire, with all the cultural baggage that went with that, one was also a member of a nation that had been conquered (and not for the first time, in India's case). That gave rise to a particular form of cultural identity in which one was part of a metropolitan culture yet peripheral to that culture, a semi-outsider. But then there was one's own culture – in Narayan's case, Hindu culture – which gave a very strong and a very complete identity, much stronger in many respects than the imposed culture of colonialism. This mixture of Hindu and British cultural influences meant that an educated citizen of the Raj had at least two great and subtle languages upon which to draw; two world views; two aesthetics; two souls, perhaps. This was cultural pluralism before the term had come into common usage.

Rasipuram Krishnaswami Narayanaswami (simplified to R. K. Narayan, at the suggestion of Graham Greene) was a member of a comfortable Brahmin family in Madras. His early life is well documented in his entertaining autobiographical memoir, *My Days*, published when he was almost seventy. In India, family background and caste could then, and still may, entirely determine what one was to do with one's life. Narayan's caste was one noted for its intellectual distinction and high culture. His father was a headmaster, whose work required that he be transferred from time to time, and for this reason, amongst others, Narayan's upbringing was largely entrusted to his grandmother, a redoubtable character who took it upon herself to supplement what she saw as her grandson's inadequate education at the local school. She instructed him not only in the more mundane subjects, such as arithmetic, but also in mythology, classical Indian song, and Sanskrit literature. If one looks for the early influences in his life which set Narayan off on the course of being a writer, then surely it must be these afternoons at the feet of his grandmother that played a vital role in producing the gifted and creative story-teller who eventually emerged.

Narayan's early education is amusingly described in *My Days*. He went to a number of schools, some better than others, and ended up studying in Mysore, at the school where his father was headmaster. Reading today his account of his life in school, one is struck by the colourful nature of the education meted out to children in those days. Teachers were as often as not eccentric, lazy, or brutal, and, although Narayan does not discuss the syllabus in any detail, one suspects that much of it was unimaginative and dominated by rote learning. Certainly, Narayan appears not to have enjoyed the academic side of his schooldays, and reveals that this emotional antipathy to formal education continued into his later years; even as a grandfather his sympathies lay with his young grandson when he showed a disinclination to go to school.

Not surprisingly he failed to get into university at his first attempt, and this gave him a year during which he could read at leisure before making another attempt at the entrance examinations. He spent this year in Mysore, which he thoroughly appreciated as a city, passing his time in taking walks to places of interest and reading widely. To the modern mind, with our insistence on the parcelling out of time, a year of reading seems an almost unattainable luxury, redolent of the simpler, less-hurried world which we have now lost. Narayan details some of his reading of the time, and tells us that he revelled in tragic endings. He was particularly fond, he says, of stories in which the heroine wasted away from consumption. But melodrama was not his only fare: he also discovered Wodehouse, Arnold Bennett, Thomas Hardy, and, he says, almost every English writer of any significance. In this way he immersed himself in a fund of stories, to which he was later to contribute so generously when the Malgudi novels began to stream from his pen.

His early writing efforts stem from this period of waiting and were guided by a book which he found called *How to Sell your Manuscripts*. Every author will recognize the hopes and disappointments of that stage of a writing career and will remember the role played by the mailman. Narayan sent off manuscripts of his juvenilia to London, and was, of course bitterly offended by the cold rejection slips. Like one of the characters in his own novels, he believed in his vocation – against all the odds that are stacked against the neophyte writer – and he felt sufficiently confident, after an indifferent university career, to set himself up as an author. There had been a few half-hearted attempts at a more conventional career, including a spell as a teacher, but these never amounted to very much. Fortunately for Narayan, the Hindu family system was sufficiently supportive for him to set out to live the life of a man of letters well before a penny had been received for anything he had written.

The story of the publication of Narayan's first novel, *Swami and Friends,* is typical of the struggle which so many successful writers have to go through at the outset of their career. The manuscript of *Swami* was sent to London, where it was rejected by publisher after publisher. Narayan became accustomed to this, and ceased to smart with each rejection. But then, in a last throw of the dice, he asked one London publisher to send the manuscript, when rejected, to a boyhood friend who was then studying in Oxford. Narayan instructed this friend to tie a weight to the manuscript and throw it into the Thames. Fortunately he did not comply with this request, but instead gave it to Graham Greene, who used his influence with the publisher, Hamish Hamilton, to secure the book's publication. *Swami and Friends* appeared in England in 1935, and the career of Narayan as novelist began.

Narayan's early novels are very clearly autobiographical in inspiration, and one of them, *The English Teacher,* deals with a tragedy which he himself experienced – the loss of a young wife. Narayan's marriage had been a love-match, though one which had taken place in the context of all the complicated family negotiations and consultation of horoscopes that accompany Hindu marriage. His wife's death from typhoid was movingly described on the pages of *The English Teacher* and again in *My Days.* He was devastated, but he came to an acceptance of what had happened, and, as his friend Graham Greene had predicted, after a time he began to write again. The novels now moved into a new and more mature phase – a phase in which the personal experience and concerns which sometimes clutter up a novelist's early work were replaced by proper fictional discipline and objectivity. It is this second group of novels which are featured in this collection: *Mr Sampath – The Printer of Malgudi*, *The Financial Expert*, and *Waiting for the Mahatma*. These show Narayan maturing as a novelist, and starting to fill in the canvas on which he was to paint his masterpiece, the picture of Malgudi. The three novels were published between 1949 and 1955 – a period of great importance in twentieth-century history, which not only saw the emergence of independent India but also the birth of a completely new world order. A strong sense of being caught up in change pervades all of them, even if history is observed from a very particular perspective – that of a perfectly imagined town peopled by a cast of colourful and eccentric characters.

Narayan's central concerns as a novelist are clearly present in these three books. He was not a great exponent of plot as some writers understand the term. His novels often have a rather rambling feel to them, and there is little sense of urgency in identifying a unifying theme. But therein lies their charm. Although the modern reader is used to much tighter plotting – and indeed tends to expect it of novelists – these works exhibit a delightful sense of ebb and flow, which in fact reflects the nature of the characters' lives. Narayan generally writes about people whose lives do not always follow a clear direction. They may be striving for some goal, but they are not always sure what this goal is. As a result the novels sometimes have false starts and shifts of direction. There may also be a lack of resolution. Such characteristics may strike some as faults – and indeed many critics have taken that view – but they give to Narayan's stories a delightful organic feel. Because we know that our own lives may often be a bit directionless and vague, Narayan's characters seem very real and true-to-life.

*Waiting for the Mahatma* is the most overtly political of the Malgudi novels. It is an important part of the Narayan oeuvre because it dwells upon a theme which is to be found throughout his novels – that of a society in transition and the effect which this transition has on individual people. It also shows us that Narayan was not really a politically engaged novelist, a fact for which he has sometimes been criticized. How can one write about a society in which great issues of poverty and injustice are present and not address these issues more directly? How can one dwell on small dramas in the lives of middle-class people when the lot of so many is a grinding struggle to survive? Other authors have been criticized for writing about the middle classes, and there is no room for a full discussion of the issue here. However, it is worth remembering that writers usually feel most comfortable in reporting the ways of their particular social milieu – and Narayan was no exception. Sriram, the central character in *Waiting for the Mahatma*, is a typical Narayan character – comfortably-off without being rich. His world is bounded by the borders of Malgudi; beyond that is the world of village India which he barely recognizes when he encounters it with the politically-conscious girl who takes him under his wing. The world of the untouchables, forced to scavenge on the edge of the town, is also present in this novel, but it is peripheral. The people from that world, and the villagers too, are not ignored, but the book is not about them. This is not to say that Narayan is unsympathetic. It is just that the book's main thrust is personal, rather than political. The great causes – the cause of Indian freedom, the cause of social justice – are present in the book, but they are handled in a different way from that of a more determinedly political novelist.

*Waiting for the Mahatma* is one of Narayan's more memorable books. What is most striking about it, perhaps, is the portrayal of Gandhi, who appears in Malgudi to speak to the people, an event which we see from a number of widely differing perspectives. For the authorities this is potentially awkward, as India is at war and the British are anxious about the tide of feeling which Gandhi is provoking. At the same time, even those who represent the State are aware of the importance of this man and the resonances of his message of Indian freedom and of love. Narayan's description of the Mahatma reminds us of just what a remarkable man he was – how direct, how honest, how insistent on the power of love to conquer arms.

His portrait is a truly arresting one because it is painted in exactly the same way in which Narayan portrays any of his characters – by showing us the minutiae of their lives, the little acts, the ordinary conversations that are the stuff of a life. Gandhi walks into the book as anyone might walk through a door: suddenly he is there and we believe unquestioningly that we are in his company.

There is much to move, and even to amuse us in this book. Sriram may not be a particularly attractive character – there is a terrible scene in which he bullies a shopkeeper whom he accuses of selling English biscuits, a scene which rings frighteningly true of the psychology of the political thug – yet most readers will sympathize with his grandmother, who has a remarkable escape from premature cremation (her toes twitch as the funeral pyre is lit). Of course she cannot return home, as that would be most inauspicious, and so she goes off to await death on the shores of the Ganges, where she leads a comfortable existence 'in good company'. This is a feature of Narayan's genius. The comic possibilities of an argument over English biscuits or a rising from the funeral pyre are combined with a much more serious point. Comedy, which abounds in Narayan's books, is frequently poignant. When Ghandi visits Malgudi he is whisked off to a local official's imposing residence and invited to sit on a beautifully-covered seat. He spots a small boy, the son of a sweeper, who has insinuated himself into the compound and invites this boy, this dirty little boy, to sit beside him on the clean seat. In the background, the official bristles with indignation, the very picture of municipal pomposity. Gandhi talks to the boy sweetly and invites himself to go and stay, there and then, in a simple hut in the boy's lowly community. This is masterfully handled by Narayan. It is a very funny scene, and yet it is a passage in which utter integrity and nobility of soul shine through. It is difficult for a novelist to portray goodness and innocence without preaching or tripping over into sentimentality. Narayan avoids these pitfalls and presents spiritual values in the clearest but most delicate manner.

The theme of the young man on a journey – the innocent abroad, the ambitious dreamer – is also present in *Mr Sampath – The Printer of Malgudi*. Although this is a highly enjoyable novel, with some intriguing pictures of typically colourful Narayan characters, the looseness of structure referred to in complimentary terms above does become a bit problematic here. William Walsh, one of Narayan's better-known exponents, described the shape of it as 'oddly hump-backed', and he is right. It really is two separate stories, the first one focussing on Srinivas, the self-published editor of *The Banner*, a crusading paper with great ambitions, and the second one largely concerned with the film industry and Mr Sampath's experience of it. Ambitions of stage and screen are notoriously unlikely to be fulfilled, and in many of Narayan's novels you can see disappointment looming well in advance. Here Srinivas takes himself very seriously in his writing and yet, like so many of the young men in Narayan's Malgudi, he is doomed to failure. He is trying to do too much; the world that he lives in is inevitably going to bog him down in its morass. This process of gradually being brought down to earth, of rising up only to be cut down again, is a metaphor, perhaps, for the struggle which the individual faces in India. India is such a complex, crowded country that it is often difficult for a person to achieve what he wants to achieve. There is an immense weight of history, there are just too many people wishing to do the same thing, or something else, for any one person to get anywhere – or that is how it must sometimes feel. At the time when Narayan wrote *Mr Sampath*, that feeling must have been strong. India was saddled with a creaking bureaucracy and the dead hand of an ancient social system; the economy was closely regulated; there were many complicating layers to life. Of course conditions are very different today, and the immense and impressive talents of the people of India are being at long last released. But it must have been very frustrating to be somebody like Srinivas, wishing to change the world, or at least his little part of it, back in 1949.

*The Financial Expert* is a more tightly constructed novel than the other two in this volume. Margayya, the usurer, is a thoroughly unattractive character – a man for whom money is an end in itself and whose life is dedicated to its acquisition. At the beginning of the book we see him as a small-time facilitator of loans, sitting under a tree with his notebook and inks and the precious loan application forms winkled out of the bank across the road. It is a perfect picture of the financial parasite: the peasants who come to him for advice are manipulated and encouraged into indebtedness, and although they are his bread and butter Margayya treats them with contempt. Indeed all the money-lender's relationships take second place to his business concerns, and this leads inevitably to the gradual widening of the gulf between him and his family. Balu, his son, who is something of a failure, eventually runs away from home, and is falsely reported to be dead. That at least arouses some emotion in Margayya, but even in his grief he is suspicious of the sympathy extended by his brother, from whom he is also alienated: the offer which his brother makes to accompany him to the city to find out what happened is interpreted as an attempt to wangle a free trip to town.

Narayan gives us in *The Financial Expert* a striking account of the conversion of a mean-spirited person to the single-minded worship of money. In Margayya's case, the seeds of obsessive greed are encouraged to grow into full-scale money worship after a remarkable meeting with a priest who explains to him the workings of Lakshmi, the Goddess of Wealth. The goddess can be invited to smile upon a supplicant, but, as the priest explains, this requires single-minded devotion to her – as well as a series of elaborate, self-denying rituals. All of this works for Margayya, who becomes immensely wealthy by enmeshing his clients in ruinous debt agreements and then proceeding to seize their assets. Thus he acquires property – land and houses – and of course the rupees that he regards with mystical awe. His business dealings are, of course, exploitative and rotten, no more so than when he converts to his own ends *Bed Life*, the manuscript of the sexual visionary, Dr Pal. Armed with the proceeds of this questionable product, he develops his money-lending business and becomes a respected and influential citizen. Greed, though, triumphs, and his spectacular bankruptcy is achieved when the same Dr Pal triggers a run on his bank. Margayya, of course, has learned no real lessons, and returns to his place under the tree to start afresh.

*The Financial Expert* is a satisfying novel at many different levels. It is, in the first place, a fine study of a selfish, shrivelled personality – a man who is prepared to do anything for money and who can lie with complete equanimity. These lies are sometimes comic, as in the scene where he is discussing the publication of *Bed Life* with the printer and pretends to know much more about books and printing than he actually does (which is nothing). And we are similarly both amused and appalled when Margayya brazens his way through a blatant refusal on his part to pay an optician for his glasses. It is the optician who is made to feel guilty for raising the issue of the unpaid bill: 'Haven't you the elementary courtesy to know the time and place for such reminders?' Margayya says to his creditor. The transferring of blame to others supports the diagnosis that we might be tempted to make: Margayya is a classic psychopath (or sociopath). This view is confirmed in the scene in which he summons an astrologer to cast a horosope for Balu, who wishes to marry. The fact that the stars are inauspicious does not deter him. If the planets are initially unwilling to give their blessing to the proposed union, then they shall be made to do so. And so a new astrologer is summoned – one who can be bribed sufficiently to make the planets conduct themselves as Margayya wishes. Money itself is not the problem here: it is the complete self-centredness and coldness of the psychopathic personality that strikes and appals us.

Narayan is not a 'preachy' writer. We see a wide variety of human types in his novels, and we also witness a great deal of bad behaviour. His descriptions of human failings are very matter-of-fact and in some cases almost dry, and yet this does not mean that there is no authorial viewpoint. There is such a viewpoint, but it is a discreet one and it is delicately advanced. Unlike many modern writers who leave us in no doubt about their personal position and objectives, Narayan is a very unobtrusive writer. He does have a world view, but it is one which is as much anchored in a shared culture as in personal conviction; it is a world view that is linked with a profound understanding of Hindu myths and legends. These novels can all be seen as reflections of various themes explored in that body of belief, and this lends them a universal significance. In the context of such elemental and ancient legends, it is not surprising that the novelist himself should seem modest and somewhat in the background. And that, in a sense, is the real nature of this great novelist's achievement: the portrayal of the world and its great themes through the depiction of the minutiae of life. Narayan does not start with a generalization, with a theory; he lets his characters demonstrate to us, through their very ordinary thoughts and actions, what it is to be human. And to do this he stands in the crowded streets, in the houses, in the workplaces, listening to the things that people say, the small things, the poignant things, the laughable things; listening and taking notes.

Alexander McCall Smith

# SELECT BIBLIOGRAPHY

R. K. NARAYAN, *My Days: A Memoir*, Viking, New York, 1974, Chatto & Windus, London, 1975.

SUSAN RAM and N. RAM, *R. K. Narayan: The Early Years*, 1906–1945, Viking, New Delhi, 1996.

RANGA RAO, *R. K. Narayan* ('Makers of Indian Literature' series), Sahitya Akademi, New Delhi, 2004.

WILLIAM WALSH, *R. K. Narayan: A Critical Appreciation*, William Heinemann Ltd., London, 1982, University of Chicago Press, Chicago, 1982.

# CHRONOLOGY

| DATE | AUTHOR'S LIFE | LITERARY CONTEXT |
|------|---------------|------------------|
| 1906 | Rasipuram Krishnaswami Narayanaswami is born in Madras on 10 October at 1 Vellala Street in the Purasawalkam, district. He is one of several children in a middle-class family. His mother is frail and his father, a headmaster in the government educational service, moves frequently, so the boy is brought up by his grandmother. | Kipling: *Puck of Pook's Hill.* Galsworthy: *The Man of Property* (vol. 1 of *The Forsyte Saga*). |
| 1907 | | Conrad: *The Secret Agent.* Kipling first English Nobel laureate for literature. |
| 1909 | | Wells: *Ann Veronica*; *Tono-Bungay.* |
| 1910 | | Forster: *Howards End.* Wells: *The History of Mr Polly.* |
| 1911 | | Conrad: *Under Western Eyes.* Bennett: *Clayhanger.* Chesterton: *The Innocence of Father Brown.* |
| 1912 | Attends a severe Lutheran missionary school where, as the only Brahmin boy in the class, he is often mocked by the teachers. Begins to learn English (his native language is Tamil). Dissatisfied with his schooling, his grandmother coaches him every evening. | Mann: *Death in Venice.* Tagore: *Gitanjali: Song Offerings.* |
| 1913 | | Tagore: *The Crescent Moon.* Tagore awarded Nobel Prize for Literature. |
| 1914 | | Tagore: *The King of the Dark Chamber*; *The Post Office.* Joyce: *Dubliners.* W. W. Jacobs: *Night Watches.* |

Foundation of Muslim League, first Muslim political party in India. Simla deputation to British Viceroy, Lord Minto, asking for separate electorates for Muslim community.

Asiatic Registration Act becomes law in the province of Transvaal, South Africa.

Minto-Morley Reforms: Indians given more power in legislative affairs; creation of separate Muslim electorates. Blériot flies across the English Channel.
Dalai Lama flees from the Chinese and takes refuge in India.

George V recognized as King-Emperor in Delhi (during a hunting trip in Nepal the King bags 21 tigers, 8 rhinos, and a bear). Transfer of capital to Delhi announced.

Sinking of *Titanic*.

Gandhi arrested as he leads a march of Indian miners in South Africa.

Beginning of World War I (to 1918); large numbers of Indians, Hindu and Muslim, rally to the British cause. General Smuts begins negotiations with Gandhi to eradicate many of the racist laws imposed on South African Indians.

| DATE | AUTHOR'S LIFE | LITERARY CONTEXT |
|---|---|---|
| 1915 | | Buchan: *The Thirty-nine Steps*. Lawrence: *The Rainbow*. Maugham: *Of Human Bondage*. |
| 1916 | | Tagore: *Fruit Gathering*. Joyce: *A Portrait of the Artist as a Young Man*. |
| 1917 | | Kipling: *A Diversity of Creatures*. |
| 1918 | Joins Besant Scouts of India, vowing to serve 'God, Freedom, and India'. | |
| 1919 | | Woolf: *Night and Day*. Wodehouse: *My Man Jeeves*. Saki: *The Toys of Peace*. |
| 1920 | Begins attending CRC High School, 'a school with no particular quality of good or evil about it'. | Mansfield: *Bliss*. Wharton: *The Age of Innocence*. |
| 1921 | | Maugham: *The Trembling of a Leaf*. |
| 1922 | Admitted to Christian College High School. | Eliot: *The Waste Land*. Joyce: *Ulysses*. Mansfield: *The Garden Party*. |
| 1924 | Sent to Mysore, where his father has been appointed headmaster of Maharaja's Collegiate High School; begins studies at this school. | Ford: *Parade's End*. Forster: *A Passage to India*. |
| 1925 | Fails university entrance exams; is left free for a year to read what he pleases. Starts to write, 'in the style of any writer who was uppermost in my mind at the time', and begins sending off manuscripts. | Tagore: *Red Oleanders*; *Broken Ties and Other Stories*. Hemingway: *In Our Time*. Eliot: *Poems 1909–25*. Fitzgerald: *The Great Gatsby*. Kafka: *The Trial*. |
| 1926 | Enters Maharaja's College, Mysore, studying for a BA. | Ghose: *Songs of Love and Death*. Kafka: *The Castle*. |
| 1927 | | Gandhi: *My Experiments with Truth*. Proust: *A la recherche du temps perdu*. Woolf: *To the Lighthouse*. |
| 1929 | | Tagore: *Farewell, My Friend*. Faulkner: *The Sound and the Fury*. Hemingway: *A Farewell to Arms*. Graves: *Goodbye to All That*. |

# CHRONOLOGY

| DATE | AUTHOR'S LIFE | LITERARY CONTEXT |
|------|---------------|------------------|
| 1930 | Graduates from Maharaja's College. Begins work on *Swami and Friends* while staying with his grandmother in Bangalore. After abortive attempts to become a railway officer and bank official he takes up teaching at a government school in Chennapatna. | Faulkner: *As I Lay Dying*. Pritchett: *The Spanish Virgin and Other Stories*. |
| 1931 | Gives up teaching and resolves to become a full-time writer, which he is able to do with the support of his family. Stays in Madras where he pursues editors of newspapers and magazines; one book review and an article published. His friend Kittu Purna leaves for Oxford, promising to find a publisher for *Swami and Friends*. | Premchand: 'Deliverance'. Woolf: *The Waves*. Walpole: *Judith Paris*. Hammett: *The Glass Key*. |
| 1932 | Receives 18 rupees for the publication of a short story in *The Hindu*. | Tagore: *Sheaves, Poems and Songs*. Premchand: *Arena of Action*. Huxley: *Brave New World*. Waugh: *Black Mischief*. |
| 1933 | Publication of a children's story brings in 30 rupees. A short piece, 'How to Write an Indian Novel', lampooning Western writers, is accepted by *Punch*. In July, while staying with his sister in Coimbatore, sees a young girl drawing water from a street-tap and falls in love with her. Befriends her father, a headmaster, and asks for her hand in marriage. After some difficulties, the wedding takes place a few months later, and Rajam joins her husband's household. Takes a job as Mysore correspondent for *The Justice*, a Madras newspaper. | Maugham: *Ah King*. Wodehouse: *Mulliner Nights*; *Heavy Weather*. Hemingway: *Winner Take Nothing*. |
| 1934 | His father becomes bed-ridden after a severe stroke. Purna approaches Graham Greene, who is living in Oxford, and gives him the manuscript of *Swami and Friends*. | Fitzgerald: *Tender is the Night*. Waugh: *A Handful of Dust*; *Ninety-two Days*. |

# CHRONOLOGY

Mahatma Gandhi sets off on famous salt march, sparking off a wave of anti-British demonstrations and boycotts. Chandrasekhara Raman wins Nobel Prize for Physics.

Inauguration of New Delhi as India's capital. Series of Round Table Conferences in London to discuss the future of India (to 1933).

Clampdown on demonstrators in India; 60,000 Congress activists are imprisoned. Gandhi's hunger strike against the treatment of untouchables. Election of Roosevelt in US.

Gandhi's hunger strike to protest against British oppression in India. Hitler becomes German Chancellor. Roosevelt announces 'New Deal'.

Gandhi resigns from Congress Party.

| DATE | AUTHOR'S LIFE | LITERARY CONTEXT |
|------|---------------|------------------|
| 1935 | Shortens his name to R. K. Narayan on Graham Greene's suggestion. With the help of Greene, his first novel *Swami and Friends*, set in the fictional town of Malgudi, is published in the UK by Hamish Hamilton. The book receives enthusiastic reviews though sales are disappointing. Gives up his job on *The Justice*. | Anand: *Untouchable*. Isherwood: *Mr Norris Changes Trains*. |
| 1936 | Birth of his daughter, Hemavati. | Anand: *Coolie*. Premchand: *The Gift of a Cow*. Orwell: *Keep the Aspidistra Flying* |
| 1937 | *The Bachelor of Arts* is published by Nelson, thanks again to Graham Greene's recommendation. Death of his father. Money is short and Narayan works as a hack journalist to make ends meet. | Anand: *Two Leaves and a Bud*. Kumar: *Tyagapatra* (The Resignation). Steinbeck: *Of Mice and Men*. |
| 1938 | *The Dark Room* is published by Macmillan and receives enthusiastic reviews. | Rao: *Kanthapura*. Greene: *Brighton Rock*. Bowen: *The Death of the Heart*. |
| 1939 | Narayan's wife, Rajam, dies of typhoid. He elects to bring up his daughter himself. Endures a period of depression, during which time he attempts to contact his wife through spiritual mediums. Publishes *Mysore*, a travel book. Begins a regular Sunday column for *The Hindu*. | Anand: *The Village*. Joyce: *Finnegans Wake*. Steinbeck: *The Grapes of Wrath*. |
| 1940 | | Anand: *Across the Black Waters*. Greene: *The Power and the Glory*. Hemingway: *For Whom the Bell Tolls*. |
| 1941 | Begins publishing his own quarterly journal, *Indian Thought*. Abandons it after three issues due to disappointing sales. | |
| 1942 | | Anand: *The Sword and the Sickle*. Camus: *The Stranger*. Eliot: *Four Quartets*. |

# CHRONOLOGY

Government of India Act creates a central legislature; provincial government handed over to elected Indian representatives. Burma separated from India. In Germany Nuremberg laws deprive Jews of citizenship and rights.

Outbreak of Spanish Civil War (to 1939). Hitler and Mussolini form Rome–Berlin Axis. Stalin's 'Great Purge' of the Communist Party (to 1938).

Japanese invasion of China.

Germany annexes Austria; Munich crisis.

Hitler invades Poland; outbreak of World War II. Gandhi calls on the world to disarm. The Indian subcontinent contributes the largest volunteer army in history (some 2.5 million servicemen and women) to the Allied cause.

Italy enters war as German ally. Fall of France. Battle of Britain. Muslim League adopt the Pakistan Resolution, which demands an independent state for Muslims.

Japanese attack Pearl Harbor; US enters war. Japanese invasion of Burma begins. Hitler invades USSR. India's population is 389 million.

Sir Stafford Cripps visits India with British government's offer of complete self-government after the war: described by Gandhi as 'a post-dated cheque on a failing bank', it is rejected by Hindus and Muslims alike. Gandhi calls on British to 'Quit India' but the movement to eject the British is quickly suppressed. Japanese troops capture Rangoon and consolidate their position in Burma.

| DATE | AUTHOR'S LIFE | LITERARY CONTEXT |
|------|---------------|------------------|
| 1943 | *Malgudi Days* published by Indian Thought Publications, which also publishes *Dodu and Other Stories* the same year. | |
| 1944 | | |
| 1945 | *The English Teacher* published by Eyre & Spottiswoode, where Greene is a director. *Cyclone and Other Stories* published by Indian Thought Publications, Mysore, and Rock House & Sons, Madras. | Borges: *Fictions*. Orwell: *Animal Farm*. Waugh: *Brideshead Revisited*. |
| 1946 | | |
| 1947 | *An Astrologer's Day and Other Stories*. | Rao: *The Cow of the Barricades*. Maugham: *Creatures of Circumstance*. C. P. Snow: *The Light and the Dark*. |
| 1948 | Begins building his own house on a plot of land outside Mysore. | Desani: *All About H. Hatterr*. Greene: *The Heart of the Matter*. |
| 1949 | *Mr Sampath*. | Orwell: *Nineteen Eighty-Four*. Bowen: *The Heat of the Day*. |
| 1950 | | Powell: *A Question of Upbringing* (vol. 1 of *A Dance to the Music of Time*). |
| 1951 | | Ruskin Bond: *The Room on the Roof*. Chaudhuri: *Autobiography of an Unknown Indian*. Salinger: *The Catcher in the Rye*. |
| 1952 | *The Financial Expert* published in the UK by Methuen. The following year it becomes the first of Narayan's works to be published in the US (by Michigan State College Press). | Beckett: *Waiting for Godot*. Waugh: *Men at Arms* (vol. 1 of *The Sword of Honour Trilogy*). Ezekiel: *A Time to Change* (poems). |

# CHRONOLOGY

Major famine in Bengal leaves three million people dead. Allied invasion of Italy. Fall of Mussolini.

D-Day: Normandy landings. Japanese troops driven out of Burma.
Fall of Berlin and suicide of Hitler. Unconditional surrender of Germany. Atomic bombs dropped on Hiroshima and Nagasaki. End of World War II. Foundation of the United Nations. Truman US President. Labour Party comes to power in Britain, with Attlee as Prime Minister.

Cabinet Mission: three British ministers led by Lord Pethwick-Lawrence visit India to negotiate terms for Indian independence. They refuse to accept Muslim claims for partition and their proposals are rejected by both Congress and the Muslim League. Riots between Hindus and Muslims; 5,000 lose their lives in Calcutta. USSR extends influence in Eastern Europe. Beginning of Cold War.
In February, British government resolves to hand over power in June 1948 regardless of whether or not a new Indian constitution is in place. Newly appointed viceroy Lord Mountbatten, persuaded that partition is the only way forward, puts pressure on the Congress leaders to agree. Indian Independence Act is hurried through and on 15 August India is partitioned into two Dominions; India (Hindu) and Pakistan (Muslim). Jawaharal Nehru Prime Minister of India.
Assassination of Mahatma Gandhi. Campaign of violence by Communists in India crushed by new government. The last British troops leave India. Jewish state of Israel comes into existence. Soviet blockade of West Berlin. Apartheid introduced in South Africa.
Chinese Revolution. North Atlantic Treaty signed.

Beginning of Korean War. Mother Teresa founds the Missionaries of Charity in Calcutta.

India declares itself a Republic within the British Commonwealth; first national general election confirms India's status as world's largest democracy; Congress Party is dominant. First Five-Year Plan in India sets in motion huge number of irrigation projects.

Eisenhower elected US President. Accession of Elizabeth II in UK.

| DATE | AUTHOR'S LIFE | LITERARY CONTEXT |
|------|---------------|------------------|
| 1953 | *The English Teacher* published in the US by Michigan State College Press under the title *Grateful to Life and Death.* Narayan's new house at Yadavagiri being finally ready for occupation, he uses it as a retreat for writing, continuing to live with his extended family at their home in the Laxmipuram district. | Anand: *Private Life of an Indian Prince.*<br>Hartley: *The Go-Between.* |
| 1954 | | Markandaya: *Nectar in the Sieve.*<br>Masters: *Bhowani Junction.*<br>K. Amis: *Lucky Jim.* |
| 1955 | *Waiting for the Mahatma.* | Ezekiel: *Sixty Poems.*<br>Nabokov: *Lolita.* |
| 1956 | Marriage of Hema with her cousin Chandru. Although their home is 120 miles from Mysore, Narayan visits them frequently over the years and plays an important role in the life of his two grandchildren. *Lawley Road and Other Stories* and *Next Sunday: Sketches and Essays.* Leaves for the United States. | Pillai: *Chemmeen* ('Shrimps').<br>Mishima: *The Temple of the Golden Pavilion.*<br>Mahfouz: *The Cairo Trilogy* (to 1957). |
| 1957 | | Dom Moraes: *A Beginning* (poems).<br>Kerouac: *On the Road.*<br>Pasternak: *Doctor Zhivago.* |
| 1958 | *The Guide* (written while travelling in America), the first of Narayan's novels to be published by Viking in the US. | Jhabvala: *Esmond in India.*<br>Achebe: *Things Fall Apart.*<br>Lampedusa: *The Leopard.* |
| 1959 | | Chaudhuri: *A Passage to England.*<br>Bellow: *Henderson the Rain King.*<br>Burroughs: *Naked Lunch.*<br>Grass: *The Tin Drum.* |
| 1960 | Narayan wins the Sahitya Akademi (India's National Academy of Letters) Award for *The Guide.* | Malgonkar: *Distant Drum.*<br>Moraes: *Poems.*<br>Rao: *The Serpent and the Rope.*<br>Updike: *Rabbit, Run* (vol. 1 of *Rabbit* tetralogy). |

HISTORICAL EVENTS

Death of Stalin. European Court of Human Rights set up in Strasbourg. Korean War ends.

Indo-Chinese Treaty. Vietnam War begins.

India establishes a policy that bars foreign print media from publishing within the country. India's parliament accepts Hindu divorce. Second Five Year Plan in India aims to increase national income by 25 per cent. Soviets invade Hungary. Suez crisis.

European Economic Community founded.

India begins designing and buying equipment for a plutonium reprocessing plant at Trombay.

Castro seizes power in Cuba.

Union of Kashmir with India. Bombay state split into Gujarat and Maharashtra states.

| DATE | AUTHOR'S LIFE | LITERARY CONTEXT |
|---|---|---|
| 1961 | *The Man-Eater of Malgudi.* | Markandaya: *A Silence of Desire.* Naipaul: *A House for Mr Biswas.* Heller: *Catch-22.* Spark: *The Prime of Miss Jean Brodie.* |
| 1962 | | Malgonkar: *Combat of Shadows.* Nabokov: *Pale Fire.* Solzhenitsyn: *One Day in the Life of Ivan Denisovich.* |
| 1963 | | Malgonkar: *The Princes.* Markandaya: *Possession.* |
| 1964 | *My Dateless Diary: An American Journey* (travel book). *Gods, Demons and Others* (retelling of stories from the Sanskrit religious epics). Meets Graham Greene briefly while visiting London. | Malgonkar: *A Bend in the Ganges.* Naipaul: *An Area of Darkness.* Bellow: *Herzog.* |
| 1965 | Opening of *Survival,* the film based on *The Guide.* | Jnanpith Award, Indian literary prize, established. Das: *Summer in Calcutta* (poems). Moraes: *John Nobody* (poems). Rao: *Cat and Shakespeare.* Scott: *Raj Quartet* (to 1975). Tagore: *The Housewarming.* |
| 1966 | | Markandaya: *A Handful of Rice.* Bulgakov: *The Master and Margarita.* |
| 1967 | *The Vendor of Sweets.* | Das: *The Descendants.* Márquez: *One Hundred Years of Solitude.* |
| 1968 | Play version of *The Guide,* by Patricia Rinehart and Harvey Breit, opens on Broadway on 6 March and closes within a week. | Solzhenitsyn: *Cancer Ward.* |
| 1969 | | Markandaya: *The Coffer Dams.* |
| 1970 | *A Horse and Two Goats* (short stories). | |
| 1971 | | Tagore: *The Broken Nest.* |
| 1972 | *The Ramayana* (shortened modern prose version of the Indian epic). | Malgonkar: *The Devil's Wind.* |

# CHRONOLOGY

HISTORICAL EVENTS

Third Five Year Plan in India propels the country into the ranks of the ten most industrialized nations; India's population rises to 434 million. Goa liberated from Portuguese rule. John F. Kennedy elected US President. Erection of Berlin Wall. Yuri Gagarin becomes first man in space.

Sino-Indian border clashes lead to threats of Chinese invasion. Cuban missile crisis.

Assassination of John F. Kennedy.

Death of Nehru; succeeded by Shastri. Khrushchev deposed and replaced by Brezhnev.

Indo-Pakistan War. Tamil riots against Hindi language; English confirmed as official language of India.

Mrs Indira Gandhi, daughter of Nehru, becomes Prime Minister of India.

Arab–Israeli Six-Day War. Population of India reaches 500 million.

Student unrest in US and throughout Europe. Soviet-led invasion of Czechoslovakia. Assassination of Martin Luther King. Nixon US President. India refuses to sign Nuclear Non-Proliferation Treaty. The *Beatles* arrive in India for transcendental meditation with the Maharishi Mahesh Yogi.

Americans land first man on the moon.
The shooting of tigers is banned in India.

Revolt in East Pakistan, state of emergency, formation of Bangladesh. Indira Gandhi strips Indian princes of their titles and abolishes privy purses. Pakistan leaves the Commonwealth. President Amin expels Ugandan Asians.

| DATE | AUTHOR'S LIFE | LITERARY CONTEXT |
| --- | --- | --- |
| 1973 | | Das: *The Old Playhouse and Other Poems.* Markandaya: *Two Virgins.* Jhabvala: *A New Dominion.* Pynchon: *Gravity's Rainbow.* Solzhenitsyn: *The Gulag Archipelago* (to 1975). |
| 1974 | *My Days: A Memoir. Reluctant Guru* (essays). | Das: *My Story* (autobiography). Bellow: *Humboldt's Gift.* |
| 1975 | | Das: *Manas* (novel). Jhabvala: *Heat and Dust.* Singh: *Train to Pakistan.* Rushdie: *Grimus.* Levi: *The Periodic Table.* |
| 1976 | *The Painter of Signs.* | Das: *Alphabet of Lust* (novel). Rao: *Comrade Kirillov.* |
| 1977 | *The Emerald Route* (travel book). | Desai: *Fire on the Mountain.* Morrison: *Song of Solomon.* |
| 1978 | *The Mahabharata* (shortened modern prose version). | Pillai: *Kayar* (The Rope). Greene: *The Human Factor.* P. Fitzgerald: *The Bookshop.* |
| 1979 | | Desai: *Games at Twilight.* Naipaul: *A Bend in the River; India: A Wounded Civilization.* Calvino: *If on a winter's night a traveler.* |
| 1980 | Made an Honorary Member of the American Academy and Institute of Arts and Letters. Awarded the A. C. Benson award by the Royal Society of Literature. | Desai: *Clear Light of Day.* |
| 1981 | | Naipaul: *Among the Believers: an Islamic Journey.* Rushdie: *Midnight's Children.* |
| 1982 | *Malgudi Days* (short stories). | Levi: *If not Now, When?* |
| 1983 | *A Tiger for Malgudi.* | Rushdie: *Shame.* |
| 1984 | | Brookner: *Hotel du Lac.* Barnes: *Flaubert's Parrot.* |
| 1985 | *Under the Banyan Tree and Other Stories.* | Márquez: *Love in the Time of Cholera.* |

# CHRONOLOGY

Arab–Israeli War. Rising prices and downturn in Indian economy. India establishes a network of tiger reserves.

Resignation of Nixon following Watergate scandal. Strikes and demonstrations against Indira Gandhi. India explodes its first nuclear device.
State of emergency declared in India because of growing strikes and unrest (to 1977). First Indian satellite launched into space, on a Soviet rocket. End of Vietnam War. Civil war between Christians and Moslems in Lebanon.

Death of Mao Tse-Tung. Soweto massacre in South Africa.

First defeat of Congress Party in India since Independence. Morarji Desai becomes Prime Minister. Zulfiqar Ali Bhutto, Prime Minister of Pakistan since 1971, overthrown by the military, and later hanged (1979). Carter US President.
P. W. Botha comes to power in South Africa.

Margaret Thatcher first woman Prime Minister in UK. Carter and Brezhnev sign SALT-2 arms limitation treaty. Soviet occupation of Afghanistan. Mother Teresa is awarded the Nobel Peace Prize.

Indira Gandhi wins election and returns to power. Sanjay Gandhi killed in plane crash. Lech Walesa leads strikes in Gdansk, Poland. Iran–Iraq War (to 1988).

Ronald Reagan becomes US President.

Falklands War.
Emergency rule invoked in Punjab to suppress Sikh terrorism.
Indira Gandhi assassinated by Sikh bodyguard; her son, Rajiv, becomes Prime Minister (to 1989). Bhopal gas leak kills 2,000. Indian troops storm the Sikh Golden Temple in Amritsar. Famine in Ethiopia.
Heavy fighting in Kashmir. India files suit against Union Carbide over Bhopal disaster. Riots in South Africa. Gorbachev General Secretary in USSR.

| DATE | AUTHOR'S LIFE | LITERARY CONTEXT |
|---|---|---|
| 1986 | *Talkative Man.* | Seth: *The Golden Gate.* |
| 1987 | | Rushdie: *The Jaguar Smile: A Nicaraguan Journey.* Morrison: *Beloved.* |
| 1988 | *A Writer's Nightmare: Selected Essays 1958–1988.* | Chatterjee: *An English August.* Desai: *Baumgartner's Bombay.* Ghosh: *The Shadow Lines.* Rao: *The Chessmaster and His Moves.* Rushdie: *The Satanic Verses.* |
| 1989 | Made a member of the Rajya Sabha (the non-elective House of Parliament in India). His inaugural speech is on the plight of Indian children. Visiting professor for the fall semester at the University of Texas at Austin. *A Story-Teller's World* (essays). | Ezekiel: *Collected Poems.* Tharoor: *The Great Indian Novel.* |
| 1990 | *The World of Nagaraj.* | Naipaul: *India: A Million Mutinies Now.* Rushdie: *Haroun and the Sea of Stories.* P. Fitzgerald: *The Gate of Angels.* Trevor: *Two Lives.* |
| 1991 | | Mistry: *Such a Long Journey.* Kanga: *Heaven on Walls.* Okri: *Songs of Enchantment.* |
| 1992 | *Malgudi Landscapes: The Best of R. K. Narayan.* Leaves his home in Yadavagiri, Mysore, and settles down in Madras, closer to his grandchildren. | Das: *Padmavati the Harlot and Other Stories.* Ghosh: *In an Antique Land.* Ondaatje: *The English Patient.* |
| 1993 | *The Grandmother's Tale* (three novellas: 'The Grandmother's Tale', 'Guru' and 'Salt and Sawdust') published by Heinemann in the UK. *Salt and Sawdust: Stories and Tabletalk* published by Penguin in India. | Seth: *A Suitable Boy.* |
| 1994 | *The Grandmother's Tale and Selected Stories* published by Viking in the US. Narayan's daughter, Hema, dies of cancer. Narayan is looked after by Hema's husband Chandru for the remainder of his life. | Gunesekera: *Reef.* |

# CHRONOLOGY

Benazir Bhutto returns to Pakistan. Gorbachev–Reagan summit. Nuclear explosion at Chernobyl.
Seventy-two people killed by Sikh extremists.

Benazir Bhutto Prime Minister of Pakistan. George Bush elected US President. Gorbachev announces big troop reductions suggesting end of Cold War.

Pakistan rejoins the Commonwealth. V. P. Rao becomes Prime Minister of India. De Klerk becomes South African President. USSR loses control of Eastern Europe; fall of Berlin Wall.

V. P. Singh forms coalition government.

First Gulf War. Yeltsin President of Russia. USSR disbanded. Rajiv Gandhi assassinated during Indian election campaign by Tamil suicide bomber; Narashima Rao becomes Prime Minister in tenth general election. Destruction of the Mosque of Babur at Ayodhya by Hindus leads to Hindu–Muslim rioting in several Indian cities. Bill Clinton elected US President. Civil war in former Yugoslavia.

Israel hands over West Bank and Jericho to the Palestinians.

Mandela and ANC swept to victory in South African elections. Rwandan massacres. Russian military action against the Chechen republic.

| DATE | AUTHOR'S LIFE | LITERARY CONTEXT |
|------|---------------|------------------|
| 1995 | | Desai: *Journey to Ithaca*. Kesavan: *Looking Through Glass*. Rushdie: *The Moor's Last Sigh*. |
| 1996 | *Tales from Malgudi*. | Mistry: *A Fine Balance*. |
| 1997 | | |
| 1998 | | Arundhati Roy becomes first Indian-based writer to win Booker Prize for her novel *The God of Small Things*. Rao: *Great Indian Way: A Life of Mahatma Gandhi*. |
| 1999 | | Seth: *An Equal Music*. Desai: *Feasting, Fasting*. |
| 2000 | | Desai: *Diamond Dust*. |
| 2001 | Narayan dies aged 94 in a private hospital in Chennai (formerly Madras) on 13 May. | |

# CHRONOLOGY

Bharatha Janata Party (BJP) government collapses after a matter of days.
Bombay becomes Mumbai, Madras becomes Chennai.
Fiftieth anniversary of Indian Independence. Death of Mother Teresa.
India declares itself a nuclear weapons state. BJP form coalition
government. Amartya Sen wins the Nobel Prize for Economics.

Pakistani troops cross India-Kashmir border leading to fierce fighting in
Kargil–Drass region. Thirteenth general election; BJP government.
India's population reaches 1 billion. Sonia Gandhi becomes President of
Congress Party. Vishvanath Anand wins World Chess Championship.
Twin towers of World Trade Center in New York collapse after terrorist
attack. Earthquake in northern Gujarat leaves 20,000 dead and an
estimated 100,000 trapped in the debris. Terrorist attack on Indian
parliament.

# ABOUT THE INTRODUCER

---

ALEXANDER MCCALL SMITH is a professor of medical law at Edinburgh University. He was born in what is now known as Zimbabwe and taught law at the University of Botswana. He is the author of over fifty books on a wide range of subjects, including the internationally bestselling novels of the No. 1 Ladies Detective Agency series and the Sunday Philosophy Club series. He lives in Scotland.

# MR SAMPATH –
# THE PRINTER
# OF MALGUDI

# CHAPTER ONE

Unless you had an expert knowledge of the locality you would not reach the offices of *The Banner*. The Market Road was the life-line of Malgudi, but it had a tendency to take abrupt turns and disrupt itself into side-streets, which wove a network of crazy lanes behind the façade of buildings on the main road.

Kabir Lane was one such; if you took an inadvertent turn off the Market Road you entered it, though you might not if you intended to reach it. And then it split itself further into a first lane, a second lane, and so on; if you kept turning left and right you were suddenly assailed by the groans of the treadle in the Truth Printing Works; and from its top floor a stove-enamelled blue board shot out over the street bearing the sign 'The Banner'.

It was the home of truth and vision, though you might take time to accept the claim. You climbed a flight of wooden stairs (more a ladder), and its last rung was the threshold of *The Banner*. It was a good deal better than most garrets: you wouldn't knock your head on roof-tiles unless you hoisted yourself on a table; you could still see something of the sky through the northern window and hear the far-off rustle of the river, although the other three windows opened on the courtyards of tenement houses below. The owners of the tenements had obtained a permanent legal injunction that the three windows should not be opened in order that the dwellers below might have their privacy. There was a reference to this in the very first issue of *The Banner*. The editor said: 'We don't think that the persons concerned need have gone to the trouble of going to a court for it, since no one would open these windows and volunteer to behold the spectacle below.'

This stimulated a regular feature entitled 'Open Window', which stood for the abolition of slums and congestion. It described the tenements, the pigsties constructed for human dwellings in the four corners of the town by rapacious landlords. It became an enemy of landlords. In fact, it constituted itself an enemy of a great many institutions and conditions. Within twelve pages of foolscap it attempted to set the world right.

From the garret of *The Banner* the world did not appear to be a common place. There always seemed to be something drastic to be done about it. It had all the appearance of a structure, half raised – and the other half might either go up or not at all. 'Some day,' *The Banner* felt, 'it must either go down or go up. It can't be left standing as it is indefinitely.' There was a considerable amount of demolition to be done, and a new way to be indicated. The possibilities of perfection seemed infinite, though mysterious, and yet there was a terrible kind of pig-headedness in people that prevented their going the right way. *The Banner* thus had twin work to do: on the one hand, attacking ruthlessly pig-headedness wherever found, and on the other prodding humanity into pursuing an ever-receding perfection. It was an immense task for anyone, with every conceivable equipment and support. It would be a tall order to give an editor. But in this case it worked because the editor had to take orders from only himself. And he felt that, after all, he had not made such a fool of himself as his well-wishers had feared, although the enterprise meant almost nothing to him financially.

In 1938, when the papers were full of anticipation of a world war, he wrote: '*The Banner* has nothing special to note about any war, past or future. It is only concerned with the war that is always going on – between man's inside and outside. Till the forces are equalized the struggle will always go on.'

Reading it over a couple of weeks later, Srinivas smiled to himself. There was a touch of comicality in that bombast. It struck him as an odd mixture of the sublime and the ridiculous. 'There is a curse hanging over an editorial table, vitiating everything a man wishes to say. I can't say "I want a cup of coffee" without appearing to be a slightly pompous donkey,' he told himself. 'I wish I could write all that stuff here,' he reflected, lying on his mat at home. Going to an office, sitting up in a chair at the table – there was something wrong with the entire procedure. 'I wish I could do all my writing here,' he said to himself again and looked forlornly about him. The house was very quiet now because it was eleven at night and all the nerve-racked neighbours and their children were asleep.

There were four other families living in the same house. The owner of the house himself lived in a small room in Anderson Lane – an old widower who tried to earn the maximum money and spend less than ten rupees a month on himself. He had several sons and daughters, all of them in various prosperous activities all over the country, from the Himalayas down to the South. He had a daughter in Malgudi, with whom he was not on speaking terms. He had led a happy family life in this house till the death of his wife, when the family scattered and disrupted. Thereafter the old man, with the help of a carpenter, partitioned off the entire house, so that half a dozen families might be lodged in it, the screens and partitions creating an illusion that each unit was living in a home with privacy for food, sleep and washing.

It was said that he bathed at the street-tap and fed himself on cooked rice, which was distributed as charity in a nearby temple. He was known to have declared to everyone concerned: 'The true *Sanyasi* has no need to live on anything more than the leavings of God.' He made himself out to be an ascetic. He collected the rent on the second of each month, took away the entire amount and placed it in Sarayu Street post-office bank. It was said that he never paid any rent for his room in Anderson Lane. The story was that he had advanced a small loan to the owner of the house, which multiplied with interest and became an unrecognizable figure to the borrower in due course. When his wife died the old man moved in to occupy the room in his debtor's house at such a low rent that he could stay there for over twenty years working off the loan.

The very first time Srinivas met him he saw the old man bathing at a street-tap, while a circle of urchins and citizens of Anderson Lane stood around watching the scene. They were all waiting for the tap to be free. But the old man had usurped it and held his place. Srinivas felt attracted to him when he saw him spraying water on the crowd as an answer to their comments. The crowd jeered: he abused it back; when they drew nearer he sprayed the water on them and kept them off, all the while going through his ablutions calmly. Srinivas asked someone in the crowd: 'What is the matter?' 'Look at him, sir, this is the same story every day. So many of us wait here to fill our vessels, and he spends hours bathing there, performing all his prayers. Why should he come to the tap built for us poor people? We can't even touch it till he has done with it.'

'Perhaps he has no other place.'

'No place!' a woman exclaimed. 'He is a rich man with many houses and relations!' At the mention of houses, Srinivas pricked up his ears. He was desperately searching for a house: all his waking hours were spent on this task.

The old man came out of his bath dripping, clad only in a loin-cloth. He told the crowd: 'Now go and drain off all the water you like. I don't care.' Srinivas felt it might be useful to ingratiate himself in his favour and asked: 'Do you do this every day?' The old man looked at him and asked: 'Who are you?'

'It is a profound question. What mortal can answer it?'

'You are joking with me, are you?' the old man said, briskly moving off. Srinivas watched the wet old man going away angrily. It seemed to him, watching his back, that the chance of a lifetime was receding from him. An irresistible piece of jocu-larity was perhaps going to place a gulf between him and this man, who might have provided a solution to his housing prob-lem. 'Half a moment, please,' he cried and ran after him. 'I have an answer for you. At the moment I am a frantic house-hunter.' The other halted; his face was changed. 'Why didn't you say so? I will give you a house if you are prepared to abide by all the rules I mention. Make up your mind. I don't want to meet indeter-minate souls.'

'What is your rent?' asked Srinivas.

'Tell me what you will pay. I have one for seventy-five, one for thirty, fifty, ten, five, one. What is it you want?'

'I will tell you presently. But perhaps you might first like to go home and dry yourself.'

'Home! Home!' he laughed. 'I have no home. Didn't I tell you that I am a *Sanyasi*, though I don't wear ochre robes? Come,

6

come with me. I live in a small room which a friend has given me.' He went through the lane, pulled out a thin key knotted to his sacred thread, turned it in the lock and opened the door of a small room. It was roofed with old cobweb-covered tiles, with a window, one foot square, opening at the top of the wall; there was another window opening on the road. He stooped in through the narrow doorway. Srinivas followed him.

'Sit down,' said the old man. 'You have to sit on the floor. I have not even a mat.' Srinivas sat down, leaning against the wall. A few children from the main house came and stood by the doorway, looking in. The old man was spreading out his wet clothes on a cord tied across the wall. He opened a small wooden box and took out a dry *dhoti* and towel, a box containing ingredients for marking his forehead, and a rosary. He proceeded to decorate his forehead with a symbol, looking into a hand-mirror. The children stood in the doorway, blocking it. The old man turned from the mirror with a hiss. 'Get away. What are you doing here? Do you think a fair is going on?' The children turned and ran away, shouting mischievously, 'Grandfather is angry.' Srinivas felt hurt by the old man's conduct. 'Why are you hard upon those children?'

'Because I don't want them. Children are a bane. I must tell this fellow not to let them loose on me.'

'They called you grandfather,' Srinivas said.

'They will call you uncle presently. How do you like it? I am only a tenant here. I hate all children. I have had enough trouble from my own children; I don't want any more from strangers. Are you in the habit of praying?'

Srinivas fumbled for a reply. 'Not exactly – '

'Well, I am. I am going to pray for about fifteen minutes. You will have to wait.' Srinivas settled down. The other took out his beads, shut his eyes, his lips muttering. Srinivas watched him for a moment and felt bored. He sat looking out. Someone was passing in and out of the main house. Children were dashing to and fro. The old man said, without opening his eyes: 'If you are a lover of children you have plenty to watch. All the children of the town seem to be concentrated in this street.' After this he continued his silent prayers.

Srinivas reflected: 'Who will know I am here, cooped up in a cell with a monstrous old man? If I ceased to breathe at this moment, no one would know what had happend to me. My wife and son and brother – ' His thought went back to the home he had left behind. His elder brother could never understand what he was up to. 'He has every right to think I am a fool,' he reflected. 'Man has no significance except as a wage-earner, as an economic unit, as a receptacle of responsibilities. But what can I do? I have a different notion of human beings. I have given their notions a fair trial.' He thought of all those years when he had tried to fit in with one thing or another as others did, married like the rest, tried to balance the family budget and build up a bank balance. Agriculture, apprenticeship in a bank, teaching, law – he gave everything a trial once, but with every passing month he felt the excruciating pain of losing time. The passage of time depressed him. The ruthlessness with which it flowed on – a swift and continuous movement; his own feeling of letting it go helplessly, of engaging all his hours in a trivial round of actions, at home and outside. Every New Year's Day he felt depressed and unhappy. All around he felt there were signs that a vast inundation was moving onward, carrying the individual before it, and before knowing where one was, one would find oneself senile or in the grave, with so little understood or realized. He felt depressed at the sight of his son: it seemed as though it was an hour ago that he was born, but already he was in Second Form, mugging history and geography and dreaming of cricket scores.

'What exactly is it that you want to do?' his brother asked him one day.

'The answer is late in coming, but you will get it,' Srinivas replied, feeling rather awkward. The question of a career seemed to him as embarrassing as a physiological detail. His brother was the head of the family, an advocate with a middling practice – a life of constant struggle with rustic clients and magistrates in that small town Talapur, where he had slipped into his position after his father's death. His father had been an advocate in his time and had had a grand practice, acquired extensive property in the surrounding villages, and had become a very respectable citizen. The family tradition was that they should graduate at Malgudi in the Albert

Mission College, spend two years in Madras for higher studies in the law, and then return each to his own room in their ancient sprawling house.

This suited Srinivas up to a point. But he always felt suffocated in the atmosphere of that small town. His wife had to put up with endless misery at home through his ways, and his little son looked ragged. They put up with his ways for a considerable time before shooting the question at him. He remembered the day clearly even now. He had settled down in his room with a copy of an Upanishad in his hand. As he grew absorbed in it he forgot his surroundings. He wouldn't demand anything more of life for a fortnight more, and then he observed his elder brother standing over him. He lowered the book, muttering 'I didn't hear you come in. Finished your court?' And his brother asked: 'What exactly is it that you wish to do in life?' Srinivas flushed for a moment, but regained his composure and answered: 'Don't you see? There are ten principal Upanishads. I should like to complete the series. This is the third.'

'You are past thirty-seven with a family of your own. Don't imagine I am not willing to look after them, but they will be far happier if you think of doing something for their sake. They must not feel they are unwanted by you. Don't think I wish to relieve myself of the responsibility.' It was a fact: his elder brother looked after the entire family without making any distinction. 'Such a question should not be fired at me again,' he said to himself after his brother had left the room. He tried to get reabsorbed in the Upanishad he was reading. His mind echoed with the interview: perhaps something had been happening in the house. His mind wandered from one speculation to another; but he gathered it back to its task:

'Knowing the self as without body among the embodied, the abiding among the transitory, great and all-pervading – '

said the text before him. On reading it, all his domestic worries and all these questions of prestige seemed ridiculously petty. '*My* children, *my* family, *my* responsibility – must guard *my* prestige and do *my* duties to *my* family – Who am I? This is a far more serious problem than any I have known before. It is a big problem and I have to face it. Till I know who I am, how can

I know what I should do? However, some sort of answer should be ready before my brother questions me again – '

The solution appeared to him in a flash. He knew what he ought to do with himself. Within twenty-four hours he sat in the train for Malgudi, after sending away his wife and son to her parents' house in the village.

The old man came out of his prayer and said: 'Would it be any use asking who you are?'

'I'm from Talapur and I am starting a paper here – '

'What for?' asked the man suspiciously.

'Just to make money,' Srinivas replied with a deliberate cynicism which was lost on the old man. He looked pleased and relieved. 'How much will it bring you?'

'Say about two thousand a month,' Srinivas said and muttered under his breath: 'Is this the only thing you understand?'

'Eh, what?'

'Come along, show me a house – '

They started out. The old man elaborately locked up his cell, and took him through a sub-lane to the back of Anderson Lane. As he came before a house he cried to someone who was driving a nail in the wall: 'You! You! ... Do you want to ruin my wall? I will give you notice to quit if you damage my house – '

Srinivas received a very confused impression of the whole house. It had a wet central courtyard with a water-pipe, and a lot of people were standing around it – four children, waiting to wash their hands, three women to draw water, and three men, who had eaten their food, were waiting also to wash their hands. In addition to these there was a little boy with a miserable puppy tied to a string, waiting to bathe his pet. On seeing the old man, one woman turned on him and asked: 'Ah, here you are! Can't you do something about this dog? Should it be washed in the same pipe as the one we use for our drinking water?' The young boy tugged his dog nearer the tap. Somebody tried to drag it away, and the boy said: 'Bite them – ' At which the dog set up a bark and wriggled at the end of its tether, and people grew restless and shouted at each other. The old man tried to pass on, without paying attention to what they were saying. One of the men dashed up, held him by the elbow and demanded: 'Are you going to give us another water-tap or are you not?'

'No – you can quit the house – '

'It is not how you should talk to a tenant,' said the other, falling back.

The old man explained to Srinivas: 'I tell you, people have no gratitude. In these days of housing difficulties I give them a house – only to be shouted at in this manner – '

'It must be heart-breaking,' agreed Srinivas. The old man looked pleased and stopped before a doorway in a dark passage and said: 'This is going to be your portion. It is an independent house by itself.' He turned the key, flung the door open; darkness seemed to flow out of the room. 'It only requires a little airing ... Nobody to help me in any of these things. I have to go round and do everything myself ...' He hurried forward and threw open a couple of window shutters.

'Come in, come in,' the old man invited Srinivas, who was still hesitating in the passage. Srinivas stepped in. The walls were of mud, lime-covered, with an uneven and globular surface; bamboo splinters showed in some places – the skeleton on which the mud had been laid. The lime had turned brown and black with time. The old man ran his hand proudly over the wall and said: 'Old style, but strong as iron. Even dynamite couldn't break it – '

'That's obvious,' Srinivas replied. 'They must have built it in the days of Mohenjodaro – the same building skill – '

'What is that?'

'Oh, very rare specimens of building thousands of years ago. They have spent lakhs of rupees to bring them to light ...'

'Walls like these?'

'Exactly.' The old man looked gratified. 'How wise of them! It is only the Europeans who can understand the value of some of these things. We have many things to learn from our ancients. Can our modern cement stand comparison with this?' He waited for an answer, and Srinivas replied: 'Cement walls crumble like rice-flour when dynamite is applied.'

'You see, that is why I look after my houses so carefully. I don't allow any nail to be driven into a wall – The moment I see a tenant driving a nail into the wall ... I lose myself in anger. I hope you have no pictures – '

'Oh, no. I have no faith in pictures.'

'Quite right,' said the old man, finding another point of agreement. 'I don't understand the common craze for covering walls with pictures.'

'Most of them representation of Gods by Ravi Varma.'

'His pictures of Gods are wonderful. He must have seen them in visions, that gifted man – ' remarked the old man.

'And yet some people who know about pictures say that they aren't very good or high-class – '

'Oh, they say it, do they?' the old man exclaimed. 'Then why do people waste their money on the pictures and disfigure their walls? I have not seen a single house in our country without a picture of Krishna, Lakshmi and Saraswathi on it – '

'Lakshmi, the goddess of wealth, must patronize every home, Saraswathi, the goddess of intelligence and learning, must also be there. Well, don't you talk so lightly of these; you would get no rent or not have the wit to collect it, if it were not for the two goddesses. So be careful – '

'That is a very clever interpretation,' the old man said, and added a Sanskrit epigram to support the same idea.

Srinivas found that his house consisted of a small hall, with two little rooms to serve for kitchen and store ....

'This is my best flat. I have refused it to a score of people. Such a clamour for it! Quite spacious, isn't it?' the old man asked, looking about. 'How big is your family?'

'We are three.'

'Oh, you will be very comfortable, I'm sure. There was once a person who lived here with his eleven children.'

He pointed out of the window. 'You have a very fine view from here. See the plant outside?' A half-withered citrus plant drooped in a yard-wide strip of garden outside. 'You must see it when it is in bloom,' he added, seeing that the plant didn't make much of an impression on his prospective tenant. 'You have a glorious view of the temple tower,' he said, pointing far off, where the grey spire of Iswara temple rose above the huddling tenements, with its gold crest shining in the sun.

'But – but,' Srinivas fumbled. 'What about water – a single tap?'

'Oh, it is quite easy. Only a little adjustment. If you get up a little earlier than the rest – . All a matter of adjustment. Those others are savages – '

On the very first day that he moved in with his trunk and roll of bedding a fellow tenant dropped in for a chat. He was a clerk in a bank, maintaining a family consisting of his father, mother and numerous little brothers and sisters, on a monthly income of about forty rupees. He paid a rent of two rupees for one room in which his entire family was cooped up. The children spent most of their time on the pyol of a house at the end of the street. Now, ever since Srinivas had come this man looked happy, as though Srinivas had settled there solely to provide him with a much-needed sitting-room. He spent most of his time sitting on Srinivas's mat and watching him. He had been the very first tenant to befriend Srinivas. He said: 'Do you know why the old devil agreed to give this to you for fifteen rupees?'

'No.'

'Because nobody would come here. It's been unoccupied for two years now. A tenant who was here hanged himself in that room, a lonely bachelor. Nobody knows much about him. But one morning we found him swinging from the roof – '

Srinivas felt disquieted by this information. 'Why did he do that?'

'Some trouble or other, I suppose; a moody fellow, rather lonely. Every day the only question he used to ask was whether there were any letters for him. He died, the police took away his body, and we heard nothing further about it. One or two tenants who came after him cleared out rather abruptly, saying that his ghost was still here.' Srinivas remained thoughtful. The other asked: 'Why, are you afraid?'

'Not afraid. I shall probably see it depart. And even if it stays on, I won't mind. I don't see much difference between a ghost and a living person. All of us are skin-covered ghosts, for that matter.' Since his boyhood he had listened to dozens of ghost stories that their cook at home used to tell them. The cook dared

Srinivas, once, to go and sleep under the tamarind tree in the school compound. He went there one evening, stayed till eight with a slightly palpitating heart, softly calling out to the ghost an appeal not to bother him in any way. 'I think I shall be able to manage this ghost quite well,' he said.

'I think good people become good ghosts and bad fellows – I dread to contemplate what kind of ghost he will turn out to be when our general manager dies.'

'Who is he?'

'Edward Shilling – a huge fellow, made of beef and whisky. He keeps a bottle even in his office room. I am his personal clerk. God! What terror it strikes in me when the buzzer sounds. I fear some day he is going to strike me dead. He explodes "Damn", "Damn" every few minutes. If there is the slightest mistake in taking dictation, he bangs the table, my heart flutters like a – ' He went on talking thus, and Srinivas learnt to leave him alone and go through his business uninterrupted. At first he sat listening sympathetically; but later found that this was unpractical. Though the man had numerous dependants, he had less to say about them than about his beefy master. His master seemed to possess his soul completely, so that the young man was incapable of thinking of anything else, night or day. He seemed to have grown emaciated and dazed through this spiritual oppression. Srinivas had learnt all that was to be learnt about him within the first two or three days of his talk with him. So, though he felt much sympathy for him, he felt it unnecessary to interrupt his normal occupation for the sake of hearing a variation of a single theme.

He was setting up a new home and he had numerous things to do. He took the landlord's advice and got up at five o'clock and bathed at the tap before the other tenants were up. He went out for a cup of coffee after that, while the town was still asleep. He discovered that in Market Road a hotel opened at that hour – a very tiny restaurant off the market fountain. It meant half a mile's walk. He returned directly to his room after coffee. He prayed for a moment before a small image of Nataraja which his grandmother had given him when he was a boy. This was one of the possessions he had valued most for years. It seemed to be a refuge from the oppression of time. It was of sandalwood, which had deepened a darker shade with years, just four inches high. The carving represented Nataraja with one foot raised and one foot pressing down a demon, his four arms outstretched, with his hair flying, the eyes rapt in contemplation, an exquisitely poised figure. His grandmother had given it to him on his eighth birthday. She had got it from her father, who discovered it in a packet of saffron they had brought from the shop on a certain day. It had never left Srinivas since that birthday. It was on his own table at home, or in the hostel, wherever he might be. It had become a part of him, this little image. He often sat before it, contemplated its proportions, and addressed it thus: 'Oh, God, you are trampling a demon under your foot, and you show us a rhythm, though you appear to be still. I grasp the symbol but vaguely. You hold a flare in your hand. May a ray of that light illumine my mind!' He silently addressed it thus. It had been his first duty for decades now. He never started his day without spending a few minutes before this image.

After this he took out his papers. He was about to usher his *Banner* into the world, and he had an immense amount of preparatory work to do. He had a thin exercise book and a copying pencil. He covered the pages of the exercise book with minute jottings connected with the journal. The problems connected with its birth seemed to be innumerable. He did not want to overlook even the slightest problem. He put down each problem with a number, and on an interleaf against it put down a possible solution. For instance, problem No. 20 in his notebook was: 'Should the page be made up as three column with 8-point type or double column with 10-point? The latter will provide easier reading for the eye, but the former would be more true to its purpose, in that it will give more reading matter. Must consult the printer about it.' He made the entry: 'Problem 20: The answer has been unexpectedly simplified. The printer says he favours neither two columns nor three columns; in fact, he has no arrangement whatever for printing in columns. Nor has he anything but 12-point in English — a type that looks like the headings in a Government of India gazette. He insists upon saying that it is the best type in the whole country: no other press in the world has it. I fear that with this type and without the columns my paper is going to look like an auctioneer's list. But that can't be helped at this stage.' On the day his printer delivered the first dummy copy, which had to go up before a magistrate, his heart sank. It was nowhere near what he had imagined. He had hoped that it would look like an auctioneer's list, but now he found that it looked like a handbill of a wrestling tournament. One came across this kind of thing at week-ends, the thin transparent paper with the portraits of two muscular men on it, the print soaking through. It had always seemed to him the worst specimen of printing; but then the promoters of wrestling bouts could not be fastidious. But *The Banner*? He said timidly to his printer: 'Don't you think we ought to – '

The printer said with a smile: 'No,' even before he completed his sentence. 'This is very good, you cannot get this finish in the whole of South India.' He spoke so very persuasively that Srinivas himself began to feel that his own view might not be quite correct. The printer was a vociferous, effusive man. When he took a sheet from the press he handled it with such delicacy, carrying it on his palms, as if it were a new-born infant, saying: 'See the finish?' in such a tone that his customers were half hypnotized into agreeing with him. He never let anyone look through the curtain behind him. 'I don't like my staff to watch me talking to my customers,' he often explained. He spoke of his staff with great pride and firmness, although Srinivas never got a precise idea of how many it included, nor what exactly lay beyond that printed curtain, on which was represented a purple lion attacking a spotted deer. Srinivas could only vaguely conjecture how many might be working there. All that he could hear was the sound of the treadle. Of even this he could not always be certain. Some days the printer appeared in khaki shorts, with grease spots on his hands, and explained: 'The best dress for my type of work. I'm going on the machine today. You see, I solve the labour problem by not being a slave to my workmen. When it comes to a pinch, I can do every bit of work myself, including gumming and pasting – '

His help was invaluable to Srinivas. He felt he was being more and more bound to him by ties of gratitude. The printer declared: 'When a customer enters our premises he is, in our view, a guest of the Truth Printing Works. Well, you think, *The Banner* is yours. It isn't. I view it as my own.'

He acted up to this principle. In the weeks preceding the launching of *The Banner* he abandoned all his normal work: he set aside a co-operative society balance-sheet, four wedding invitations, and a small volume of verse, all of which were urgent, according to those who had ordered them. He dealt with all his customers amiably, but to no purpose. 'You will get the proofs positively this evening, and tomorrow you may come for the finished copies. Sorry for the delay. My staff is somewhat overworked at the moment. They've instructions to give you the maximum co-operation.' With all this suaveness he was not to be found in his place at the appointed hour. He threw a scarf around his throat, donned a fur cap, and was out on one or the other duties connected with *The Banner*. He arranged for the supply of paper, and he went round with Srinivas canvassing subscribers. The very first thing he did was to print a thousand handbills, setting forth the purpose and nature of *The Banner*. He had spent four nights and days devising the layout for it. Finally he decided upon a green paper and red lettering; when Srinivas saw it his heart sank within him. But the printer explained: 'This is the best possible layout for it; it must catch people's eye. I won't bill you for it except some nominal charge for paper.' He also printed a dozen tiny receipt books. He scattered the green-and-red notices widely all over the town, into every possible home; and then followed it up with a visit with the receipt book in hand. He worked out the annual subscription at about ten rupees, and managed to collect a thousand rupees even before the legal dummy was ready.

Srinivas was convinced that he could never have got through the legal formalities but for his printer. He had always disliked courts and magistrates; and he was really fearful as to how he would get through it all. The dummy to be placed before the magistrate was ready. Srinivas implored him: 'Please make another copy. Is this the paper we are going to use?'

'Oh, you don't like this paper! Norway bond – I've refused it to some of our oldest customers, you know – it is the strongest parchment in the market.'

'But the ink comes through.'

'Oh, we will check that. I have put a little extra ink on this because magistrates usually like the title to be very dark. They like to carry some printers' ink on their thumbs, I suppose,' he said. 'You had better leave this magistrate business to me.'

He walked into the hall of the court at Race-Course Road nonchalantly, adjusted his cap, stood before the court clerk, and handed up his application.

'Can you swear that all your statements in this are true?'

'Yes, I swear.'

'You declare yourself the printer of *The Banner*?'

'Yes, I'm the printer.' The clerk scrutinized the paper once more. As he was standing there, the printer took out of his pocket a pod of fried groundnut, cracked its shell, and put the nut into his mouth. Srinivas was shocked. He feared he might be charged with contempt of court. The printer's eye shone with satisfaction; he put his fingers into his pocket, took out another bit, and held it out for Srinivas under the table. Srinivas looked away, at which the printer cracked it gently and ate that also. All around there were people: lawyers sitting at a horseshoe table, poring over books and papers or wool-gathering; policemen in the doorway; prisoners waiting for a hearing at the dock. Srinivas felt that they were going to be thrown out – with that printer of his cracking nut-shells. They were standing immediately below the magistrate's table. But the printer was deft and calm with his nuts, and it passed off unnoticed. The clerk fixed his gaze on Srinivas and asked: 'Your name? You declare yourself the editor and publisher of *The Banner*?'

'Yes.'

'Are you speaking the whole truth?'

'Absolutely.' The clerk picked up the papers and handed them up to the magistrate, who seemed to be looking at nothing in particular. The magistrate's lips moved, and the clerk asked: 'Will you promise to avoid all sedition and libel?'

The printer quickly answered: 'On behalf of both of us, we promise.' The magistrate's lips moved again; the clerk asked: 'Are you going to deal in politics?'

Once again the printer answered swiftly: 'No, it is a literary magazine.' The magistrate slightly nodded his head and then the clerk pressed a couple of rubber stamps on the papers, and the magistrate signed on the dots indicated by him. It was over. The permission was secured.

Before they crossed the court compound Srinivas protested: 'Why did you say it was going to be literary? Far from it. I shall certainly not avoid politics; while I don't set out to deal only in politics, I can't bind myself – '

'You go on with politics or revolution or whatever you like, but you can't say so in a court; if you do, they may ask for deposits, and you will have all kinds of troubles and worries. You know, I have achieved an ambition in life: I've always wanted to crack nuts and eat them in a court – something to foil the terrible gloom of the place. I have done it today.'

His brother's letter reached him, addressed to the office. He had not written home ever since he came to Malgudi. His brother wrote:

'I am very pleased to know your whereabouts through your paper, the first issue of which you have been good enough to send me. I have read the explanations you have given in your first editorial, but don't you think that you have set yourself an all too ambitious task? Don't you have to give some more reading for the four annas you are demand-ing? As it is, the magazine is over too quickly and we have to wait for a whole week again. And then, will you allow me this criticism? You are showing yourself to be a pugnacious fellow. Almost every line of your paper is an attack on something. You give a page for politics – and it is all abuse; you don't seem to approve of any party or any leader. You give another page for local affairs, and it is nothing but abuse again. And then a column for cinema and arts – and even here you deal hard knocks. Current publications, the same thing – what is the matter with you? Though different articles are appearing under different initials and pen-names, all of them seem to be written remarkably alike! However, be careful; that is all I wish to say. It wouldn't at all do to get into libel suits with your very first effort.'

Srinivas pondered over this letter, sitting in his office. He admired his brother for detecting the similarity in all the contributions: all of them were written by himself. Heaven knew what difficulties he went through, on one side, churning up the matter for the twelve pages, and on the other keeping in check the printer, who threatened to overflow on to the editorial side. Not content with appointing himself the dictator in matters of format and business, he was trying to take a hand in the editorials also, but Srinivas dealt with him tactfully and nicely. He could not pass a copy downstairs without feeling like a schoolboy presenting a composition to his master. He waited with suspense as the printer scrutinized it before passing it on: 'You wouldn't like me to advise you here, I suppose?'

'No,' Srinivas said, meaning it but trying to make it sound humorous.

'Well, all right. But you see, sir, that film was not produced at Bombay, but at a Calcutta studio.'

'Oh! In that case – ' Srinivas hastily snatched it back and scrutinized it again. 'Sorry for the blunder – '

'It is quite all right – natural,' replied the printer expansively, forgivingly, as if to suggest that anyone who was forced to write about so many things himself was bound to commit such foolish mistakes. Srinivas did not very much like the situation, but he had to accept it with resignation. It was true: he was putting his hand to too many departments. But there was no way of helping it. He could not afford to engage anyone to assist him. And his programme was more or less as follows: Monday, first page; Tuesday, second page; Wednesday, cinema and arts; Thursday, correspondence and main editorial; Friday, gleanings, comments and miscellaneous. This virtuous calendar was constantly getting upset, and all the items jammed into each other, and he found himself doing everything every day, and all things on Friday, the printer shouting from the bottom of the staircase for copy every five minutes. He flung the matter down the stairs as each page got ready, and the printer picked it up and ran in with it. Or if he had a doubt he shouted again from the bottom of the staircase. At four o'clock the last forme went down and then the major worries were over. The treadle was silenced at six, and peace descended suddenly on the community at Kabir Lane.

The intellectual portion of the work was now over, signified by the passing of the editor down the stairs; after which he stepped into the press to attend to the dispatch of copies. The printer lent him a hand in this task. Five hundred copies of *The Banner* were all over the floor of the printer's office. They squatted down and gummed, labelled and stamped the copies with feverish speed, and loaded them on the back of a very young printer's devil, who ran with his burden to the post office at the railway station, where it could always be posted without late fee till 8 p.m.

This brought him up against the R.M.S. It took him time to understand what R.M.S. meant. But he had to grow familiar with it. He received a letter in his mail-bag one day saying: 'You are requested to see the undersigned during the working hours on any day convenient to you.' He was writing his editorial on the new housing policy for Malgudi. Plenty of labour from other districts had been brought in because the district board and the municipality had launched a feverish scheme of road develop-ment and tank building, and three or four cotton mills had suddenly sprung into existence. Overnight, as it were, Malgudi passed from a semi-agricultural town to a semi-industrial town, with a sudden influx of population of all sorts. The labour gangs, brought in from other districts, spread themselves out in the open spaces. Babies sleeping in hammocks made of odd pieces of cloth, looped over tree branches, women cooking food on the road-side, men sleeping on pavements – these became a common sight in all parts of Malgudi. The place was beginning to look more and more like a gipsy camp.

Srinivas made it his mission to attack the conditions in the town in every issue. The municipality feared that they were being made the laughing-stock of the whole country, and decided to take note of the editorials appearing in *The Banner*. And they revived an old plan, which they had shelved years ago, of subsidizing the development of a new town on the eastern outskirts. It was gratifying to the editor of *The Banner* to see the effect of his words! He felt that after all something he was saying had got home. He had the pleasure of reflecting on these lines when he received a note from the municipality: 'The president would like to meet the editor at any time convenient to him on any working day.' He opened the next and read that the R.M.S. would like to meet him. 'God! How many people must I go and meet? When have I the time?' On working days and other days he had to sit in the garret and manufacture 'copy'; if there was the slightest delay the smoothness of life was affected. That life went on smoothly was indicated by the purring of the treadle below. All went well as long as that sound lasted. The moment it paused he knew he would hear the printer's voice calling from the bottom of the staircase: 'Editor! Matter!' He worked under a continuous nightmare of not being able to meet his printer's demand. That meant continuous work, night and day, all through the week, and even on a Sunday. He seldom approved of what he wrote and would rewrite and tear up and rewrite, but it was always the printer's call that decided the final shape.

'When I'm so hard-pressed for time I can't be bothered in this way,' he remarked to himself, and tossed away the two letters to a farther corner of his table, where they lost their individualities in a great wilderness of paper. He had learnt to deal with the bulk of his correspondence in this way. 'Till I can afford to have a secretary and an assistant editor and a personal representative, an accountant, office boy, and above all, a typewriter – all correspondence must wait,' he said to his papers. Every post brought him a great many letters. He flung away unopened everything that came to him in long envelopes. He shoved it away, out of sight, under the table. He knew what the long envelope contained: unsolicited contributions, poems, essays, sketches. It was surprising how many people volunteered to write, without any other incentive than just seeing themselves in print. And then an equal number of letters demanding to be told what had happened to their contributions; and why there was no reply, even though postage was enclosed. 'It is not enough, my friend,' Srinivas said to them mentally, 'I must have a fair compensation for looking at your handiwork; that is why I don't open the envelope. Any time you are free you can come and collect it from under my table.'

And then there were letters from readers, marriage invitations from unknown people, sample packets of ink powder and other things for favour of an opinion, and copies of Government and municipal notifications on thin manifold paper. The last provided him with a miscellany of unwanted information: 'Note that from the 13th to 15th the railway level-crossing will be closed from 6 a.m. to 6 p.m.,' said one note.

'Well, I note it for what it is worth; what next?' Srinivas asked. The municipality sent him statements of average rainfall and maximum and minimum temperatures; somebody sent him calendars, someone else the information that a grandchild was born to him. 'Why do they think all this concerns me?' he at first asked, rather terrified. But gradually he grew hardened and learnt to put them away. Most of his correspondence was snuffed out in this manner; but not the R.M.S. and the municipal chairman.

Very soon he had another letter from the R.M.S. 'Your kind attention is drawn to our previous letter, dated ... and an early reply is solicited.'

'Don't imagine I'm a member of your red-tape clan,' he said, putting away the letter once again. The municipal chairman also wrote again, but he had changed his subject matter. 'I have pleasure in enclosing copy of our Malgudi extension scheme, for favour of your perusal ... You will doubtless see that the question engaged our attention even as far back as 1930. The question had to be shelved owing to practical difficulties ...' And so the letter continued.

He glanced through the scheme. It visualized a garden city at the eastern end of the town, with its own market, business premises, cinema, schools and perfect houses. Somebody had evidently been dreaming about the town. He went through it feeling happy that *The Banner* had roused the municipal conscience to the extent of making it pull something off a shelf. He studied the pamphlet carefully, and it provided him matter for an article under the heading: 'Visions on the Shelf'.

The R.M.S. turned out to be more aggressive in their subsequent correspondence. 'Our repeated efforts to contact you have borne no fruit. Please take note that by posting your journal in a mass at the last clearing time you are causing great dislocation and blocking the R.M.S. work. It would facilitate R.M.S. work if the dispatch were distributed throughout the day, if possible throughout the week.' Reading this, Srinivas was aghast at their ignorance. Did they imagine that the bundles were ready all through the week?

He could not resist writing an immediate reply: 'Sir, Friday 8 o'clock is our posting time at present. If we acted up to your suggestion it would result in something like the following: at 12 midday we should be posting the fourth page, at 1 p.m. the sixth page, at 5 p.m. ninth and tenth, 7 p.m. eleventh and at 8 p.m. twelfth page. Since our readers would doubtless have a great objection to receiving the journal piecemeal we are forced to post the journal in its entirety at 8 p.m. Posting the journal on the other days is not practicable, since no part of it is ready on those days.' To which he received the reply: 'It would be considered a favour if you will kindly meet the undersigned on any day during working hours.' This brought the question back to the starting-point, and he did what he did with the first letter – obliterated it, and the R.M.S. continued to suffer.

# CHAPTER TWO

He hurt his thumb while pinning up a set of proofs. He put away the paper to suck the drop of blood that appeared on his thumb, and sat back. He cracked his fingers: they felt cramped, the tips of his fingers were discoloured with the printers' ink transferred from rugged proof sheets. His joints ached. He realized that he had been sitting hunched up for several hours correcting proofs. He rose to his feet, picking up the proofs, folded them and heaved them downstairs with the shout: 'Proofs' directed towards the printer. He paused for a moment at the northern window, looking at a patch of blue sky, and turned away. He paced up and down. He was searching for the right word. He had been writing a series: 'Life's Background'. The entire middle page had been occupied with it for some numbers. He had tried to summarize, in terms of modern living, some of the messages he had imbibed from the Upanishads on the conduct of life, a restatement of subjective value in relation to a social outlook. This statement was very necessary for his questioning mind; for while he thundered against municipal or social shortcomings a voice went on asking: 'Life and the world and all this is passing – why bother about anything? The perfect and the imperfect are all the same. Why really bother?' He had to find an answer to the question. And that he did in this series. He felt that this was a rather heavy theme for a weekly reading public, and he was doing his best to word it in an easy manner, in terms of actual experience. It was no easy task. And that entire Thursday he spent in thinking of it, pacing up and down, pricking himself with the pin through absent-mindedness; he roamed his little attic, round and round like a sleep-walker, paused at the farthest window to listen to the rumble of Sarayu. It seemed ages since he had gone to the river. He resolved to remedy this lapse very soon. When he came to the window he could hear the uproar emanating from the tenements below – he always spent a few minutes listening to the medley of voices. He wished he could open the window and take a look at the strife below, just to see what exactly was troubling them, but the owners of the tenements had their legal injunction against it. His mind dwelt for a brief moment on landlords.

Awaiting the right sentence for his philosophy, he had spent several hours already; he must complete the article by the evening if he was to avoid serious dislocation in the press. Tomorrow there were other things to do. He suddenly flung out his arm and cried: 'I have got it, just the right – ' and turned towards his table in a rush. He picked up his pen; the sentence was shaping so very delicately; he felt he had to wait upon it carefully, tenderly, lest it should elude him once again: it was something like the very first moment when a face emerges on the printing paper in the developing tray – something tender and fluid, one had to be very careful if one were not to lose it for ever ... He poised his pen as if he were listening to some faint voice and taking dictation. He held his breath, for fear that he might lose the thread, and concentrated all his being on the sentence, when he heard a terrific clatter up the stairs. He gnashed his teeth. 'The demons are always waiting around to create a disturbance; they are terrified of any mental concentration.' The printer appeared in the doorway, his face beaming. He came in, extending his hand:

'Congratulations! I bring you jolly news. Your wife and son are waiting downstairs.'

Srinivas pushed back his chair and rose. 'What! What!' He became incoherent. He ran out on the landing and looked down: there he saw his wife and son standing below, with their trunks and luggage piled up on the ground.

'Oh!' he cried. 'Oh!' he repeated louder. 'Come up! Come up!' He felt foolish and guilty.

His wife was struggling hard to keep a cheerful face. She came in and stood uncertainly near the only chair in the room, with his son behind her. She looked weary with the journey; her face was begrimed with railway smoke. With considerable difficulty she essayed a smile. The printer said effusively: 'Take a seat, madam. You should not keep standing.' It was evident that she was very tired, and she immediately acted on this advice. She sat down at the table and viewed it with bewilderment.

'Why? Why have you all come so suddenly? Why didn't you write to me?'

'I wrote four letters and my father wrote two,' she said quietly. He looked helplessly at the printer. He knew what it meant. He must have put them in the company of unopened letters. The boy said: 'Grandfather wrote to this address – ' 'Because we didn't know any other address,' his mother finished the sentence. There was a certain strain and artificiality in the air, and the printer turned without a word and went downstairs muttering: 'I will send the boy to fetch some coffee and tiffin.'

Now his wife burst into a sob as she asked: 'What is the matter with you? Why do you neglect us in this way? You have not written for months; what have I done that I should be treated like this?' Her voice was cracked with sorrow. Srinivas was baffled.

'No, no, look here, you should not have worried. I was very busy these months. Being single-handed and having to do every-thing myself – '

'But just one postcard. You could at least have told us your address. You treated me as if I were dead and made me the laughing-stock of our entire village. I have had to write to you four times to ask if I may come – '

The boy said: 'Grandfather got your address from a copy of the paper.' The boy spoke as if they had been doing a piece of detective work.

'Oh, I see. But such a lot of letters come here. Sometimes it happens – ' he meandered.

His wife stopped crying, surveyed the room, and asked: 'Is this where you live?'

'Oh, no. I have a house. Let us go there.'

His eye fell on the sheet of paper on the table. He couldn't afford to leave it now. He asked: 'How did you find your way here? It must have been difficult.'

'We arrived here at the station at two o'clock, and for over three hours we went about searching for you, and then a student brought us here.' Her voice shook, and she was on the point of crying once again. She gulped down a sob and said: 'This little fellow, Ramu, he was like an elder. I never knew he could take charge of me so well.' She looked proudly at her son. Srinivas cast him a smile and patted his back. He scrutinized his son: he seemed to have grown an inch or two since he saw him last. The coat he wore was too small for him, appearing to stop at his waist, his sleeves stopped four inches beyond the wrist, the collar was frayed: he had neglected his family. He cast a look at his wife: she wore a very inferior discoloured cotton *sari*, patched here and there. 'Am I guilty of the charges of neglect?' he asked himself. 'Family duties come before any other duty. Is it an absolute law? What if I don't accept the position? I am sure, if I stick to my deeper conviction, other things like this will adjust themselves.'

There was a moment's silence as he ruminated over this question. His wife had already risen, ready to start out. He muttered: 'Just a minute,' gripped his pen, dipped it in ink and wrote: 'Notes for article for third week. Family life: Did the philosopher mean family life's all-absorbing nature when he cried for relief from its nightmare? Family preoccupation is no better than occupying oneself solely with one's body and keeping it in a flourishing condition. Man is condemned to be charged with neglect either here or in the heavens. Let him choose where he would rather face the calumny.'

He had completed the sentence when the printer came in again, blowing out the remark: 'I say, Srinivas, you are trying them too much, I fear, keeping them waiting!' Srinivas put away his pen, explaining apologetically: 'I had to note down something at once; otherwise I'm in danger of losing it for ever.' Now a boy entered, bearing plates and cups on a tray. The printer said: 'Take your seat, madam, have some coffee.'

'No, no,' she protested. 'I'm not in need – ' She was shy and inarticulate in the presence of the printer. Ramu watched the scene with dislike and boredom. He kept throwing at the tray hungry side-glances, hoping that his mother's refusal would not lead to the removal of the tray. Noticing it, the printer said: 'Come on, young man,' and handed him a plate; he then rose, saying to Srinivas: 'Please persuade your wife to take something. She has had a tiring journey.' He went down the steps. Srinivas held a plate to his wife. 'Come on – '

'Hotel food! I can't,' she said. She was brought up in a very orthodox manner in her little village. 'And I can't eat any food without a bathe first. It'd be unthinkable.' The boy tried to say through his full mouth: 'Mother has been fasting since yesterday – wouldn't take anything on the way.'

'Why?' asked Srinivas.

'Should you ask?' she replied.

'What foolish nonsense is this?' Srinivas cried. He stood looking at her for a moment as if she were an embodiment of knotty problems. He knew what it was: rigorous upbringing, fear of pollution of touch by another caste, orthodox idiocies – all the rigorous compartmenting of human beings. He looked at her with despair. 'Look here, I don't like all this. You eat that stuff. What does it matter who has prepared it, as long as it is clean and agreeable? It is from a Brahmin hotel. Even if it isn't, you have got to eat it, provided it is clean and the sort of thing you eat. We have all been eating it, and I assure you we have neither felt poisoned in this life nor lost a claim for a place in heaven. You could share the same fate with us, I think.' He pressed a plate into her hand and compelled her to accept it. The boy added: 'It is quite good, Mother, eat it.'

Having been used to the spacious courtyards and halls of their village home, his wife stood speechless when she beheld her home at the back of Anderson Lane. The very first question she asked was: 'How can we live here?'

'Oh, you will get used to it,' Srinivas replied.

'But what small rooms and partitions!'

'Oh, yes, yes. He is a rapacious rascal, our landlord. You are welcome to tackle him whenever you like.'

'But what a locality! Couldn't you get – ?'

'Yes, it is a horrible locality. But a lot of men, women, and children are living here; we are one of them.'

Meanwhile they found Ramu missing. Looking about, Srinivas saw him engaged in a deep conversation with a boy of his own age, living in an adjoining block of rooms. They saw Ramu open his friend's wooden box and dive into it and bring out something. 'He seems to know already where everything is kept in that house,' Srinivas said. 'Ramu, come here,' he called. His son came up with his friend behind him. 'This is our house,' Srinivas told him. Ramu seemed very pleased to hear it. 'Do you like it?' Ramu looked about, looked at his friend, and they both giggled. 'What is your friend's name?'

Ramu said: 'I don't know. Can I go to the same school as he, Father?'

'Certainly; yes, yes,' Srinivas said.

It seemed to have excited the entire community that Srinivas's wife had arrived. Everybody seemed relieved to see Srinivas's home-life return to a normal shape. They said: 'Your husband was paying a rent here unnecessarily. Your part of the house was always locked up all day long. He doesn't seem to have cared for anything except his work.' Even the old landlord turned up to see her. He said: 'I'm an elder, listen to my advice. I have experience of life enough for four of you. You should never leave your husband's side, whatever happens. Make yourself comfortable. Don't drive nails into the wall; I don't like it.'

Srinivas found domestic duties an extra burden. What a round of demands. He could clearly see that his wife was being driven to despair by his habits. This was the first time that he was in sole charge of his wife and son, and he found that it gave him a peculiar view of them. All along in the joint family home they had been looked after by others, and he had no occasion to view his wife as a sole dependant. But now he found that it was so with a vengeance. At every turn he found he was violating some principle or other of domestic duty. 'This is going to leave me no time for attending to the paper,' he often reflected. He secretly admired those hundreds and hundreds of people who did so much in the world, in spite of a domestic life, even with many more to make demands upon them. 'There is perhaps some technique of existence which I have not understood,' he told himself. 'If I get at it I shall perhaps be able to manage things better. Am I such an idiot that I cannot manage these things better?' he often reflected. 'Here I am seeking harmony in life, and yet with such a discord at the start of the day itself.' His troubles began then. Somehow his wife didn't seem to like the idea of his waking up so early and going out for coffee. 'When you have a house, why should you go out for coffee? What will people say if they find the master of the house going out for coffee?'

'You are the master of the house,' he replied jokingly, 'so it doesn't matter if I go out.'

'Don't joke about it,' she said, annoyed with him. 'Don't you see, people will think it odd?' It seemed to him an appalling state of affairs to have no better guiding lamp in life than other people's approval – which they so rarely gave. He felt, with an extravagant seriousness, that a whole civilization had come to an abrupt stalemate because its men had no better basis of living than public opinion. He raved against their upbringing. His wife as a child must have pleased her grandmother by her behaviour, and been rewarded for it. A child's life was reduced to a mere approved behaviour in the midst of father, mother, grandmother and uncles; and later in life parents-in-law, husband, and so on and on endlessly till one had no opportunity to think of one's own views on any matter, till it grew into a mania as in his wife. She didn't want him to get up and go out early in the day, lest it should upset the neighbours; she didn't want to raise her own voice in her own house, lest the neighbours should think of her as a termagant; she wouldn't send the little fellow out to play with some children in the neighbourhood because they were too ragged, and there were still others who might think her plebeian. He himself wondered that he had observed so little of her in their years of married life. He suffered silently, since he kept his opinions to himself and ruminated upon these questions in the garrets of *The Banner*.

The moment he stepped past the threshold of his home he had to face an annoyed inquiry: 'Do you forget that you have a home?'

'What is the matter?' he asked, going on to his coat-stand, removing his coat or upper-cloth, and putting it on the hook. He found his son already asleep on a mat in the front room while his wife sat in a corner reading some obscure novel. It was unnecessary for him to ask 'What is the matter?' He knew that it must be the same set of causes over and over again: first and foremost his late-coming; secondly, his lack of interest in home-management; thirdly, his apparent neglect of his child; fourthly, insufficient money; and so on and so on – stretching on to infinity. He didn't receive a reply, and he preferred not to press his question further, for he saw outlined against the opposite window the bank clerk's mother, doubtless waiting to follow the progress of the exchanges between them. He passed on to the dining-room, where a couple of leaves were spread out ready. 'Why can't you sit down and eat when you are hungry,' he said, 'instead of sitting up like this for me?'

'I certainly can't do that,' she retorted, put away her novel, and rose without a smile, carrying the lamp in her hand. The leaf spread under the window was for him. He sat down before it; his fingers were ink-stained and cramped.

'Please wash your fingers,' she implored, 'that ink may be poison.'

'I've tried. I should have to scrub off my skin. That stain won't go. I seem to be born with it,' he said, feeling pleased with the idiom. The lamp was placed in the middle doorway so that there should be light both in the front room, where the child was sleeping, and in the kitchen. She served him rice, remarking apologetically: 'Don't blame me if you find the dinner bare. I couldn't get even the simplest vegetable.'

'That's all right,' he said. 'You know I don't bother about these things.'

'But it does no good to be swallowing bare rice morning and night. I don't know what has happened to all the vegetable-sellers. I can't find anyone to go up to the street-end and get it. I tried to persuade Ramu to go and buy three pies' worth of coriander leaves, but he came back without them.'

'He is such a child,' Srinivas said, throwing a look at the sleeping form in the shadowy hall. His wife was argumentative about it: 'But who else is there to go, if he can't?'

'Why don't you go out and do the shopping yourself? It will give you such a nice outing, too!' Srinivas said.

She looked up at him, puzzled whether to take his remark literally or as a joke. And finally she said: 'I don't know – but if someone escorts me I could go and do the shopping; it would be the best thing to do.'

# CHAPTER THREE

Srinivas had just cleared his table of a bundle of proofs. He had finished writing his editorial and some of the miscellaneous contributions and letters to the editor. He cracked his aching fingers, leaned back in his chair, got up and paced a few steps up and down, and then stood in the doorway, looking at the lane. He was surprised to see his neighbour, the bank clerk, walking down the lane. He called out his name: 'Ravi! Ravi!' The other looked up and hesitated. Srinivas said: 'Come up and see *The Banner*.' The other came up, looking timidly around. He asked: 'Am I not disturbing you?'

'Not now,' Srinivas replied. 'I'm fairly free. What brought you here? Have you no office?' The other seemed reluctant to notice so many questions. He merely pursed his lips, drew up the pincushion, and started pulling out the pins and rearranging them. Srinivas observed him for a while and asked: 'How is your boss?'

'Bad as ever,' he replied. 'Today I wanted an hour off, and how he shouted when he heard it. My ear-drums are still trembling.'

'He let you off?'

'Oh, yes. He exhausted himself so much that he banged the table and said "Damn it. You are persistent. But don't do it again", and so I'm here.' He laughed. 'It is his usual way of blessing any idea that I conceive. I've grown used to it.'

'Rarely do people come up this way,' Srinivas said testingly.

Ravi pushed away the pin-cushion, picked up a paperweight, and tried to make it stand on its top before answering: 'You doubtless wish to know why I'm here. I came to look for someone I lost sight of ages ago, as it seems.' Srinivas smiled and didn't wish to press the question further. He scented some complexity. Meanwhile Ravi picked up a pencil, snatched a piece of paper, and after plying the pencil for a few minutes, pushed the paper across. 'Well, this is the person,' he said. It was a perfect pencil sketch of a girl of about nineteen: the pencil outline was thin and firm, etched finely like an image in the mind. A couple of flowers in her hair, a light caught by a gem on her ear-ring, and a spot of light caught by the pupil of her eye. Srinivas became breathless at the sight of it. 'I say – this is – ' He sought and fumbled for a correct expression, but could get nothing more than: 'This is wonderful. I never knew you could draw so well.'

'Drawing's not required in a bank,' Ravi replied. He picked up the picture, gazed at it, tore off an edge and rolled it away.

'Don't tear it,' Srinivas cried, snatching it back. He gazed at it. 'I almost feel like returning the smile on her lips!' he exclaimed.

'That's her expression,' Ravi said enthusiastically. 'She always smiled very slightly, but you know – what a power it had!'

'Who is she?'

'Why go into all that now?' Ravi said with a sigh. 'It was some years ago. I saw her one evening coming out of Iswara's temple –'

'What were you doing there?'

'I was very religious then. For months I went there without noticing anything, but that day I saw her, suddenly, as in a vision; she stood framed on the threshold of the temple; there were just six stars in the sky, and the grey tower rose among them. She had a flower in her hair, and a silver tray balanced ever so elegantly on her palm – so tall and slender. I don't know how to describe – I saw her just as I was about to go into the temple – I stood arrested on the spot.'

The boy brought in coffee. Srinivas pushed a cup across to the other. They sipped their coffee in silence, while the treadle groaned below and a hawker's voice rang along the street. Ravi asked: 'Would you like me to continue my story?'

'Yes, yes, certainly.'

'I used to meet her regularly after that at the temple. I started to make an oil portrait of her at home at the end of each day. It is an unfinished picture now, because I suddenly lost sight of her.'

'Oh, you didn't know where she lived?'

'Yes, I knew. They were in Car Street.'

'Did you visit them?'

'Oh, no; they would have thrown me out. Her father was a severe-looking man. I used to hurry off whenever I saw him standing at his gate; but I passed that way several times every day.'

'What was her name?'

He shook his head sadly. 'I don't know, I couldn't ask.'

'You were friends?'

'I don't know. We were friends in the sense that she was used to seeing me at the temple, and once she gave me a piece of coconut offered to the gods. Oh! How I treasured it! But how long can a piece of coconut keep?'

'Was she married?'

'I don't know. I didn't ask. Oh, what excitement it was for me, following her back home every day at a distance of about ten yards. Not a word passed between us, but I was there every day at the temple, and she looked for me, I think. And at her gate she just turned her head slightly and passed in; and I ran straight off to my house and worked on the picture, though it was so difficult without sufficient light.'

'I never knew you were an artist,' Srinivas declared.

'I'm not. I'm only a bank clerk. In those days it was different. I was a student in college. My father was in good health and was a flourishing lawyer. Nobody bothered about what I did in those days – all the family responsibility came on me rather suddenly, you know, when my father was stricken with paralysis.'

'What happened to the picture you were working on?'

'Nothing. I had to drop it. She disappeared one day; and with that the picture ended, and I put away my paint-box for ever. The picture is still there at the bottom of a lumber box.'

'What happened to the girl?'

'I missed her one evening at the temple, and then I waited there till late in the evening; I still remember what a fool I must have looked to passers-by. I waited there till about eight p.m. and went up to Car Street. Their house was dark. I later learnt that they had left the town. I lost all trace of them for years. Just today as I sat at my table I saw through the window someone looking like her father going by in a car and at once I left the office to find out if they were back here. I have been all over the town this afternoon, looking here and there. You know this is the first sketch I've done after that day.' He added, half humorously: 'Now that you have that sketch you will keep it with you and keep your eyes open. If ever you see her you must – '

'Oh, yes, certainly, I will tell you.'

Ravi's eye lit up with joy at the mention of this possibility. He leaned over the table and gripped my arm and said: 'You will tell me, won't you? You will save me. I promise I will draw hundreds of sketches; only tell me that she is here – that you have seen her – '

After that Ravi began to drop in at the office now and then, just to ask for news. It was Srinivas's greatest dread lest anyone should disturb him on a Friday – the day on which the journal emerged in its final shape. Srinivas was in a state of acute tension on that day, and he dreaded hearing any footsteps on the creaking wooden staircase. But Ravi seemed to choose just those days. Directly his office closed he came there, crossed the threshold, grinning a little nervously. Srinivas looked up with a very brief lifeless smile and returned to the papers on his table, as Ravi seated himself on a stool at the other end of the room. He felt annoyed at this interruption, and he wanted to say aloud: 'Why do you pester me, of all days, today?' But, as a matter of self-discipline, he tried to smother even the thought. Some corner of his mind said: 'Don't be such an uncivilized brute. He is suffering silently. It is your duty, as a fellow being, to give him asylum.' And he looked up at him and murmured: 'Office over?' 'Yes,' the other said, and he timidly added: 'How is the sketch?' Srinivas put away the pen and looked at him with a smile and then took out of a drawer a cardboard file, in which he carefully preserved the sketch. He brought it out and gazed at it, and that transformed the entire situation. The light emanating from the eyes of the portrait touched with an exaltation the artist sitting before him and gave him a new stature. He was no longer a petty, hag-ridden bank clerk, or an unwelcome, thoughtless visitor, but a personality, a creative artist, fit to take rank among the celestials.

Srinivas knew what silent suffering was going on within that shabby frame. He knew that an inspiration had gone out of his life. He had no doubt a home, mother, and brothers and sisters, but all that signified nothing. His heart was not there, any more than it was in the bank. Srinivas felt pity for him and murmured as if apologizing to him: 'You see, this is a day of pressure and so – ' And the other replied: 'Yes, yes, I shall be very quiet. Don't disturb yourself; I just came to know how you were faring,' which was false, since Srinivas very well knew that he came there only in the hope of news about his lost love; and Srinivas knew that that was the meaning of the question: 'How is the sketch?' though he pretended to treat it at its face value, and handed the other the sketch and returned to his duties. For a long hour or more Ravi sat there, gazing at the pencil sketch in the fading evening light, as Srinivas grew more and more sunk in his papers and work.

When the final proof had gone Srinivas got up, saying: 'I'm going down to the press.' Ravi handed him back the sketch. Srinivas locked it up in his drawer again, and they went downstairs. The printer looked at him with an irrepressible curiosity. Srinivas explained: 'A friend of mine, my neighbour.' And the printer ostentatiously said: 'Come in, please, come in, you are welcome.' There on the floor were heaped copies of *The Banner* waiting to be folded and posted. The editor sat down, along with the printer and his urchin, to accomplish this task. The treadle continued to grind away more copies, the printer shouting from where he was: 'Boys, go on slowly – watch the ink.'

And this made Srinivas wonder, as he again and again wondered, how many people might be slaving at the task of turning out *The Banner* beyond that purple screen. For he never could pluck up enough courage to peer into that sanctum, since he always heard the printer declare with considerable emphasis: 'That is the one point on which I'm always very strict – the best of my friends and relations have not seen inside there. For instance, you have never seen my machine-room, sir, and how much I appreciate your respecting my principles: I've pointed out your example to hundreds of my customers.' A statement which made Srinivas keep away from that room more than ever. He remembered that at Chidambaram temple there was a grand secret, beyond the semi-dark holy of holies, beyond the twinkling lights of the inner shrine. He had always wondered what it might be; but those who attempted to probe it too deliberately lost their sight, if not their lives. There was a symbolism in it: it seemed to be expressive of existence itself; and Srinivas saw no reason why he should grudge the printer his mysterious existences and mazes beyond the purple curtain.

Ravi sat in a chair scanning the page of a copy of *The Banner*, while the others were busily packing and gumming. The printer threw him a look once or twice, and then held up a folded paper to him: 'Mister – I have not the pleasure of knowing your name – '

'Ravi.'

'What a fine name. Mr Ravi, will you please apply this gum lightly here, and press it?' Ravi did as he was told. And the next stage for him was to share the task with the others, and he received no small encouragement from the printer. 'That's right. We must all pull together. Why do I do this when my business should be over with the printing of the copies? It is because I treat it as a national duty; it is neither the editor's nor anybody else's; it is the country's, and every man who calls himself a true son of the country should do his bit for it.' Srinivas felt that this was a flamboyant sentiment. 'No, no, nothing so grand about it, I assure you. It is just a small weekly paper, that is all. It is not right to call everything a national service.' The printer brushed him aside with: 'Modesty has done no good to anyone in this world, as I told a customer only this morning. He started raving over some slight delay in the matter of a visiting card. I told him, "You can offer me a lakh of rupees, but that will not tempt me to do anything other than *Banner* work on *Banner* press day".'

Srinivas wended his way home through the dark, ill-lit lanes. Ravi followed him silently. 'Isn't it very late for you?' Srinivas asked. 'It is all the same,' the other remarked. 'I really enjoyed being in your office. In fact, I love this whole place.' He pointed at the soft stabs of feeble, flickering light emanating from door chinks and the windows of humble homes, the only light available here, since the municipal lighting stopped at Market Road. 'I like this lighting. I feel like doing an entire picture with half-lights and shadows some day; I don't know when.'

His aged mother waited at the door anxiously. 'Ravi!' she exclaimed anxiously. 'Why are you so late?' His youngest brother and sister clung to his arms as he turned into his portion of the house without a word.

With a copy of the latest *Banner* rolled in his hand Srinivas entered his home. His wife sat by the lamplight reading her novel. He held his latest copy to her with the remark: 'I hope you will find something to interest you at least this week.' She hastily opened it, ran her eyes through and put it away with: 'I will read it later,' and she went in to get his dinner ready. She had accommodated herself to his habits fairly well now, and accepted his hours without much grumbling. But she was an uncompromising critic of his journal. She always glanced through the copy he brought in and said: 'Why don't you put in something to interest us?'

'If you keep on reading it, you will find it interesting,' he said, and loathed himself for appearing to be so superior. He felt that in all the welter of economic, municipal, social and eternal questions he was threshing out he was making the journal somewhat heavy and that he was putting himself one remove from his public. This was a pathological mood that seized him now and then, whenever he thought of his journal. He was never very happy on the day his journal came out. He ate his dinner silently ruminating over it. His wife stooped over his leaf to serve him. She had fried potato chips in ghee for him and some cucumber soaked in curd; she had spent the day in the excitement of preparing these and was now disappointed to see him take so little notice of them. She watched him for a moment as he mechanically picked up the bits and stuffed them into his mouth. He was thinking: 'There is some deficiency in *The Banner*. I wish I knew what it was. Something makes it not quite acceptable to the people for whom it is intended. There is a lot of truth in my wife's complaint.' She watched him for a moment and asked: 'Do you remember what you have just been eating?' He came to himself with a start and smiled uncomfortably. She could not be put off with that. She insisted: 'Tell me what you have eaten off that corner.' He looked at the corner of the leaf helplessly and answered: 'Some fried stuff.' 'Yes – what vegetable?' He puckered his brow in an effort to recollect. He knew how much it would hurt his wife. He felt rather pained. 'I'm sorry, I was thinking of something else. Was it raw plantain?'

She lightly patted her brow with her hand and said: 'Raw plantain! What an irony! Here I have spent the whole evening ransacking my money-box and procuring you potato for frying, and you see no difference between it and raw plantain. Why should we take all this trouble if it makes so little difference?' He looked up at her. By the dim light he saw that her face was slightly flushed. Clearly she was annoyed at his indifference. He felt angry with himself. 'I don't know the art of family life. There is something lacking in me as in the journal, which leaves a feeling of dissatisfaction in people's minds.' He saw that unless he was careful he might irritate her. He merely said: 'Don't make much of all this,' and cut her short. He went through his meal silently, washed his hands, sat down on his mat with *The Banner* held close to a lamp; he glanced through it again, line by line, in order to decide what changes he should adopt for the next issue. A corner of his brain was noticing the noise in the kitchen: his wife scrubbing the floor, the clanking of vessels being restored to their places, and the blowing out of the kitchen lamp and finally the shutting of the kitchen door. She paused before him for a moment and then went to her bed and lay down beside their sleeping son. Srinivas noted it and felt pity for her. He viewed her life as it was: a lonely, bare life. He had not the slightest notion how she was spending her days: she probably spent them awaiting his return from the office. She was justified if she felt her grievances were there. 'I have neglected her lately. It seems ages since I touched her, for when all is said and done a husband–wife relationship is peculiar to itself, being the most tactile of all human relationships. Perhaps she is wilting away without the caress and the silly idiom softly whispered in the ear.' He hesitated for a moment, undecided whether to follow up this realization. But he put away the question for the moment to finish the work on hand, and reached out for a tablet on which to note down his points.

Srinivas decided to spend the next day completely at home. The day after the issue of the journal must be a holiday. 'I must remember I'm a family man,' he told himself. Next morning he surprised his wife by lying on in bed. His wife woke him up at seven-thirty. 'Don't you have to get up?'

'No, my dear sir!' he said. 'It is a holiday. I won't go near the office today.' She let out a quiet little cry of happiness. 'Will you be at home all day?'

'Absolutely.' She called: 'Ramu, Ramu,' and their little son came in from somewhere. 'What is it, Mother?'

'Your father is not going to his office today.'

'Why, Father?' he asked, looking at him dubiously. Srinivas had no ready answer to give. He was really very pleased to see the effect of his decision. 'Well, now run off; I will sleep for half an hour more and then you will know.'

The boy picked up his top and string and ran out again. Srinivas shut his eyes and let himself drown in the luxury of inactivity. Mixed sounds reached him – his wife in the kitchen, his son's voice far off, arguing with a friend, the clamour of assertions and appeals at the water-tap, a pedlar woman crying 'Brinjals and greens' in the street – all these sounds mingled and wove into each other. Following each one to its root and source, one could trace it to a human aspiration and outlook. 'The vegetable-seller is crying because in her background is her home and children whose welfare is moulded by the amount of brinjals she is able to scatter into society, and there now some-body is calling her and haggling with her. Some old man very fond of them, some schoolboy making a wry face over the brinjal, diversity of tastes, the housewife striking the greatest measure of agreement, and managing thus – seeing in the crier a welcome solution to her problems of house-keeping, and now trying to give away as little of her money as possible in exchange – therein lies her greatest satisfaction. What great human forces meet and come to grips with each other between every sunrise and sunset!' Srinivas was filled with great wonder at the multi-tudinousness and vastness of the whole picture of life that this presented; tracing each noise to its source and to its conclusion back and forth, one got a picture, which was too huge even to contemplate. The vastness and infiniteness of it stirred Srinivas deeply. 'That's clearly too big, even for contemplation,' he remarked to himself, 'because it is in that total picture we perceive God. Nothing else in creation can ever assume such proportions and diversity. This indeed ought to be religion. Alas, how I wish I could convey a particle of this experience to my readers. There are certain thoughts which are strangled by expression. If only people could realize what immense schemes they are components of!' At this moment he heard over everything else a woman's voice saying: 'I will kill that dirty dog if he comes near the tap again.'

'If you speak about my son's dog I will break your pot,' another voice cried. 'Get away both – I've been here for half an hour for a glass of water.' Now they formed to him a very different picture. A man's voice ordered: 'I will remove this tap if you are all going to –' It was the voice of the old landlord and quietened the people. One heard only the noise of water falling in a pot. Next moment the old man appeared in the doorway, peeped in and called: 'Mister Srinivas. Oh, still sleeping? Not keeping well?' He walked up to Srinivas lying in bed and stood over him: 'I thought you would be getting ready to go out.' He sat down on the floor, beside his bed, and said: 'I tell you, I sometimes feel I ought to lock up all my houses and send away all those people. They seem to be so unworthy of any consideration.'

'What consideration do you show them?'

'I've given them a water-tap which they have not learnt to use without tearing each other. I sometimes feel so sick of seeing all these crudities that I blame God for keeping me in this world so long.'

'If it makes you so sick, why don't you put up a couple of taps more?'

'Give them twenty more taps, they would still behave in the same manner,' he said irrelevantly. 'I have known days when people managed without any tap at all; there used to be only a single well for a whole village. It doesn't depend upon that, but people have lost all neighbourliness in these days, that is all.' He went on with further generalizations. Srinivas felt that it would be useless to remain in bed any longer; he got up, rolled up his bed, and picked his green-handled toothbrush and paste from a little wall-shelf and unscrewed the toothpaste top. The old man remarked: 'What is the world coming to? Everybody has taken a fancy to these toothbrushes; they are made of pig's tail, I'm told. Why should we orthodox, pure Aryans go in for these things?

Have you ever tried Margosa or Banyan twigs? They are the best and they were not fools who wrote about them in the *shastras*. They knew more science than any of us today – you see my teeth.' He bared his teeth. 'How do you like them?'

'Most of them are missing,' Srinivas said.

'Never mind the missing ones, but they stayed long enough when they did. And do you know what I've used?' Srinivas didn't wait for him to finish his sentence, but made his way towards the bathroom.

He stayed in the bathroom just a little longer, hoping that the old man would have left by then. But he found him still there when he returned, sitting just as he had left him. He came rubbing a towel over his face, and the old man asked: 'What are these towels, looking like some hairy insect? Must be very costly.'

'H'm, yes, if you are still thinking of your own days,' said Srinivas.

'You are right. Do you know, I used to buy twenty towels to a rupee, the Malayalam variety? I'm still using some of them I bought in those days.'

'It was due to bargains like yours that no industry ever found it possible to raise its head in our country.'

'You are right,' said the old man without comprehending the other's statement. 'They should not try to rob us of all we have with their prices.' Srinivas moved to the window-sill, on which was fixed a small looking glass; there was a small wooden comb beside it. He ran it through his greying hair mechanically as by immemorial custom, wondering what comment this was going to provoke in the old man. It was not long in coming. He said with a cynical leer: 'Fancy men parting and combing their hair like women! How beautiful and manly it was in those days when at your age you had only a very small tuft and shaved off the head. That's why people in those days were so clear-headed.'

'Yes, but we don't get the same amount of co-operation from our barbers these days. That is the worst of it,' said Srinivas. 'And so we are compelled to go from stupidity to stupidity.'

The old man laughed at the joke and said: 'You have not yet asked my purpose in visiting you today.' 'Just a minute,' Srinivas said and went into their small kitchen. His wife was at the little oven, frying a rice-cake. Her eyes seemed swollen with smoke. But she seemed to be in great spirits. She was sitting with her back to him, humming a tune to herself as she turned the cake. The place was fragrant with the smell of burning ghee. Srinivas stood in the doorway for a moment and listened. 'That is a nice bit of singing,' he said. She turned to him with a smile. 'I'm making these cakes for you. Don't drink up your coffee yet.' He had never been given tiffin in the morning except today, and he understood that she was celebrating his holiday. He was disturbed for a moment by the thought that his holiday pleased her so much more than his working – when all his pride and seriousness were bestowed on the latter. 'Your meal will be late today,' she explained. 'I'm going to give you *Aviyal* for your dinner; Ramu has gone out to the market to buy the vegetables for it.' A stew of over a dozen vegetables; Srinivas was very fond of it: his mother used to feed him with it whenever he came home during vacation in those days: how the girl remembered his particular taste in all these things and with what care she tended him now. He was touched for a moment. 'But all this puts an additional burden on one in life,' he told himself. He asked: 'I've a guest; can you manage some coffee for him?'

'Yes, who is he?' He held the door slightly open for her to see through. 'Oh, that man!' she exclaimed. 'Why has he come? Have you not paid the rent?' She added: 'Not enough coffee for two.' Srinivas said: 'Hush! Don't be so cantankerous. Poor fellow! Put out the sitting-planks.'

The old man was overjoyed when he heard the invitation. He became nearly incoherent with joy. He was torn between the attraction of the offer and shyness. For the first time Srinivas observed that the man could be moved by shyness. 'No, no, I never eat anywhere. Oh, don't trouble yourself about it ... No, no ...' he said, but all the same got up and followed Srinivas into the kitchen. He grinned affably at Srinivas's wife and commented flatteringly: 'I have always told a lot of people to come and observe this lady for a model. How well she looks after the house. I wish modern girls were all like her.' Srinivas gently propelled him to a plank, on which he sat down. He observed from his wife's face that she was pleased with the compliment, and Srinivas felt that the old man's coffee was now assured him. His wife came out with a tumbler of water and two leaves and set them in front of them. She then served a couple of cakes on each leaf, and the old man rubbed his hands with the joy of anticipation. At a signal from Srinivas he fell to; and Srinivas wondered how long it was since the other had had any food. 'What do you eat at nights?' he asked testily. The old man tore off a piece of cake and stuffed it in his mouth and swallowed it before he answered, shaking his head: 'I'm not a youth. Time was when I used to take three meals a day — three full meals a day in addition to tiffin twice a day. Do you know — '

'That's remarkable,' agreed Srinivas admiringly. 'But now what do you do?'

'I'm a *Sanyasi*, my dear young man — and no true *Sanyasi* should eat more than once a day,' he said pompously. He ate the cakes with great relish. When a tumbler of coffee was placed beside him he looked lovingly at it and said: 'As a *Sanyasi* I have given up coffee completely, but it is a sin not to accept something offered,' he said.

'You are right,' Srinivas replied, and added: 'So drink it up now.' The old man raised the tumbler, tilted back his head, and poured the fluid down his throat; he put down the tumbler and wiped his mouth with the back of his hand. He shook his head appreciatively and murmured: 'If somebody is going to make coffee as good as this, it will prove very difficult for people like me to who wish give it up.' Srinivas's wife acknowledged the compliment with a smile and asked, half peeping out of the doorway: 'When are you going to give us another tap?'

'Oh!' cried the old man. 'How many people ask me this question every morning!'

'I have to fill up every vessel at three in the morning, and even then people try to be there earlier,' she said. The old man made a noise of sympathy, clicking his tongue, got to his feet and passed on to the washing-room without a word. After cleaning his hands and face he went on to the front room and sat down on the mat. Srinivas still sat on the plank, saying something to his wife, and the old man's voice reached him from the hall. 'Just one small piece of areca-nut, please; cannot do without it after eating anything – one bad habit which I'm not able to conquer ...'

Srinivas asked his wife: 'Have you a piece of areca-nut anywhere?' His wife muttered: 'The old man is making himself a thorough guest today, although he is so indifferent about the water-tap.' She went over to a cupboard, took out a small wicker-basket and gave Srinivas a pinch of spiced areca-nut. Srinivas transferred it immediately to his mouth. 'Fine stuff,' he said.

'It's not for you!' she cried. She handed him another pinch and said: 'Let him demand them immediately if he wants betel leaves also.'

Srinivas felt himself in a leisurely mood – the sort of relaxation he had never experienced for months now. 'Even an oven is given its moments of rest to cool,' he told himself. 'It's senseless to go on working and forgoing this delicious feeling of doing nothing,' he muttered to himself, as he carried the pinch of areca-nut to his guest. The old man sprinkled it on his tongue and shut his eyes in an ecstasy of relish. 'You don't want betel leaves and lime or tobacco?' 'Oh, no,' the old man replied with a shudder. 'Do you want to see me make a fool of myself, with my lips reddened with betel juice at my age!' He seemed to view it as a deadly sin, and Srinivas left it at that and began to wonder what he should do next. The old man now said, looking up at him, moving away a little on the mat: 'Won't you sit down for a moment?' Srinivas remained silent, wondering if he could conjure up some excuse which might be both truthful and tactful and free him of the other's company. But the old man followed up: 'You have not yet asked me what business brought me here so early in the day. I have come here on a definite business.' Srinivas sat down beside him, leaned on the wall and stretched his legs, saying: 'Do you mind my stretching before an elder?' 'Not at all. It is your house as long as you pay the rent regularly,' he replied. He bent over and said: 'Do you know, I have a granddaughter of marriageable age?'

'I heard only recently that you had a daughter. How is it none of them come this way?'

'Oh – ' he wriggled in despair. 'Don't go into all that now. I have a granddaughter, that is all I wish to say. I would forget my daughter, if possible. That is an ungrateful brood,' he said.

'How many sons and daughters have you?' Srinivas persisted relentlessly. The old man glared at him angrily for a moment and asked: 'Won't you leave that subject alone?'

'No,' Srinivas replied, 'I have got to know. I'm not prepared to hear about your granddaughter unless you tell me first about your daughters and sons.'

'Oh, if that is so I will tell you. I have three sons and two daughters; one daughter is in this town — the other daughter is in Karachi: I'm not concerned with her, because her husband is a customs officer, and she thinks it is not in keeping with her status to think of her father and the rest of us. It is over twelve years since she wrote. She pretends that she is of Persian royal descent, I suppose, and not an ordinary South Indian.' He laughed at his own joke and continued: 'Why should I care? I don't. It saves me postage to forget her. Sometimes her mother used to fret about her, and for her sake I used to waste a postcard now and then. But since the old lady's death I have forgotten that daughter ... I'm not talking about my second daughter.'

'You have not told me anything about your two sons.'

'Oh, won't you leave them alone? Why do you trouble a *Sanyasi* like me with such reminders?'

'Where are they?' Srinivas asked.

'In heaven or hell, what do I care?' the old man replied. 'I refuse to talk about them: they are all an ungrateful, rapacious brood; why talk of them?'

'Has this second daughter of yours a daughter?' At the mention of the granddaughter his eyes glittered with joy. 'You are absolutely right. Oh, what an angel she is! Whenever I want to see her I go to the Methodist girls' school, where she reads, talk to her during the recess, and come away.' His tone fell to cringing: 'I wish to see her married. I have set apart five thousand rupees for her marriage. Let them produce a good husband for her, and the amount will go to her; and they must manage the wedding celebrations as well as the dowry within that amount.'

'What is your son-in-law?'

'He is a teacher in the same school.'

'So you are bound to see him also when you go there?'

'H'm, I never go in. I call her up from outside, see her for a moment, and go away. I don't talk to that fellow nor to that wife of his.'

'What did they do?'

'They neglected their mother and wouldn't spend even an anna when she was ill. I had to pay the doctor's bill – one hundred and seventy-five rupees – all myself. Not an anna was contributed by any of them. Do you know how much the old woman doted on them? I was always telling her that she was spoiling them. But she wouldn't listen. After her death I cut off the entire brood completely. I have no use for ungrateful wretches of that type. Do you agree with me or not?' Srinivas slurred over the question. The old man said: 'For this granddaughter of mine, why don't you find a bridegroom? I may die any moment. I'm very old, and as they say in *Gita* – ' He quoted a Sanskrit verse from *Bhagavad Gita* regarding mortality. He shrank his eyes to small slits and begged: 'I want to see this girl married.'

Srinivas said: 'I don't know what I can do.'

'My tenant in that portion – Ravi, isn't he your friend? I have often seen him going with you. I observe all things. Why don't you persuade him to give me his horoscope? I think he will be a good match for this girl.'

Srinivas could hardly believe his ears. At the sound of Ravi the entire picture of his complicated life flashed across his mind and he didn't know what to say. 'Why have you pitched on Ravi?'

'Because I have observed him, and he is in a respectable job.'

'But he has a very large number of dependants.'

'Yes, that's a fact. But I shall probably reduce his rent and give him another room. What can we do about his people? We will see about it all later. But will you kindly speak to him about my granddaughter and get me his horoscope? Ever since I saw him I have been thinking what a perfect match he would be for the girl. Tell him that the girl is beautiful and reads in sixth form.' Srinivas promised to do his best, without much conviction.

The printer sat down on the stool before Srinivas's table and said: 'I rather liked the friend you brought in the other evening – who is he?' Srinivas told him about him. He took out the sketch and passed it on to the other for his scrutiny, saying: 'Do you know, there are very few in India who can do that with a pencil?'

'Fine girl,' the printer agreed, shaking his head, as if appreciating a piece of music or a landscape. 'Who is she?'

'God knows. They were in Car Street, and they are no longer there. That's all he knows. He lost sight of her, and will not draw till he finds her again. He drew this because he thought they were back here.' The printer pondered over it deeply. 'What a fool to be running after an unknown girl – a man must shut his eyes tight if it proves useless to look any longer. That's my principle in life.' This was the first time Srinivas had heard the other talk in this strain. He had known very little of his family life, except that sometimes he referred to his home, away there by a cross-road in the new extension, containing a wife and five children. Srinivas opened his lips to ask something and hesitated; the printer seemed to read his mind, and said with a smile: 'I'm not such a bad husband, sir, as you may think!' He tossed the picture across the table and said: 'I thought there was something funny about that young man – these artists are futile: they can neither get along with their jobs properly nor forget a face.'

'But,' Srinivas said, 'I wish he could get that girl back, if it is only to make him go on with his drawing.'

'You think it is so important!' asked the printer. 'Why, I can get a score of fellows to do this sort of thing.' He scrutinized it again, making an honest effort to see what there might be in it. 'Well, anyway, it is not his profession; what is there to sorrow about?' Srinivas stared at him for a moment and rapped the table with his palm as if to get the other's fullest attention. 'Don't you see what a great artist we are losing? He is an artist; don't you see that?'

'Oh!' the other exclaimed, as if the truth were dawning upon him for the first time. 'Oh!' He added: 'Yes – you are right.' He looked at the sketch intently as if comprehending it better now. 'You just leave him to me; I will tackle him; you will see him drawing these pictures one after another till you cry "Enough. No more"!'

* * *

A few days later, going down to the press one evening, he saw Ravi sitting in a chair opposite the printer. Srinivas was rather surprised. Ravi, who would usually come up and occupy his stool, had now been short-circuited by the printer. By the look on the artist's face Srinivas understood that they had been in conclave for a long while. The moment Srinivas appeared the artist rose, gripped his arm and cried, pointing at the other: 'Oh, he knows, he knows!' His voice trembled with joy and his hands shook. The printer said, with his eyes twinkling: 'He has promised to come and draw a picture of my little son tomorrow evening. Would you like to have any done for you?'

When he went home the artist accompanied him. The printer saw them off at the door, effusively as ever. His parting word to the artist as they stepped into the street was: 'The baby will be ready to receive you at seven o'clock sharp. Fourth cross-road, new extension. I will wait at the gate.'

The artist chatted happily all the way. 'Tomorrow I must leave home pretty early – a couple of hours at the printer's house and from there on to the office direct. I shall be just there in time; I hope that child is sketchable. What sort of child is he; have you seen?'

'No,' replied Srinivas. 'And what else did he tell you?'

'Oh, my friend. I never knew I was so near help. All that I want is just another look at that girl, and that will transform my entire life. I never knew that our printer was a man who could be so helpful. What a fine man he is!' Srinivas didn't like to pursue the matter further and remained silent. He somehow felt disinclined to speak about the printer. When they passed the last crossing in Market Road and turned down Anderson Lane he ventured to ask: 'What would be your reaction if someone seriously proposed his daughter to you?' 'I would kick him,' the other replied promptly and recklessly. Srinivas left it at that, feeling that he had discharged the duty laid upon him by the old man.

The old man appeared just as he was hurrying to his office. He turned the corner of the street, and the old man hailed him from under the street-tap where he had been bathing. 'Mister Editor! Oh! Mister Editor,' he called from the tap, and his cry rang past a ring of spectators waiting for the tap to be free. Srinivas turned and wished he could clear the entire street at a jump. But it was not possible. The old man came up to him, dripping with water. He shook his head disapprovingly. 'No, no, you must not be so very inconsiderate to an old man.' Srinivas tarried and said: 'I'm in a hurry.'

'Who is not?' asked the old man promptly. 'Every creature is in a hurry, every ant is in a hurry, every bird is in a hurry, every fellow I meet is in a hurry, the sun is in a hurry, the moon is in a hurry – all except this slave of God, I suppose.' Srinivas was too much engrossed in his own thoughts to say anything in reply. He said: 'Now I will be off. I will see you this evening.' And he tried to cover the rest of the street at one stride. But the old man would not let him go. He almost cantered behind him and caught up with him. He was panting with the effort. His chest heaved. Srinivas felt that if the old man dropped down dead on the spot, the responsibility would be his, and made a quick decision to change his route from that day. The old man panted: 'Have you forgotten that I have such a thing as a granddaughter?'

'I haven't,' said Srinivas. 'I remember your request. But the time is not yet.'

'Are you going to tell me that you have not seen the boy?' Srinivas paused to consider if he might make such an evasion. But the old man went on: 'Don't say that, because some evenings ago I saw you both going home. Didn't you turn the street together? I may be old, but not too old to see by street light when there is something to see.' Srinivas felt exasperated. 'Why is this man plaguing me like this?' He had left home a few minutes earlier in order to clear up some heavy work in the office. He looked hard at the old man and said: 'The boy doesn't seem to be in a mood to marry anyone, that is all.'

The old man gripped his arm and said: 'Do you think I believe a word of what you say?' He gazed on Srinivas's face with his eyes half covered with water drops and attempted to express a merry twinkling at the same time: 'Young fellows are always shy about marriage. They will not say so. In fact, do you know, when they came and proposed I should marry, I tried to hide myself in the paddy barn on the wedding day. I was just twelve – '

'But he is twenty-eight – '

'Bah! What an age!' the other commented. 'What can a fellow decide at twenty-eight? And why have they left him unmarried for so long? All this is due to the idiotic things they say about child marriage. I was eleven when I married and my wife nine, and yet what was wrong with our marriage?'

Srinivas said: 'I will positively come and see you tonight in your room. I promise. I'm in a hurry now.'

'All right, go; I like people who attend to their duties properly. Don't forget that I have a granddaughter!' Srinivas almost broke into a run for fear he might be stopped again.

The artist dropped in one afternoon, went straight to his stool, drew it near the window, turned his back on Srinivas and sat looking out. Srinivas was, as usual, submerged in his papers; his mind noted the steps on the creaking staircase, but he did not like to interrupt himself or allow his mind to speculate about the visitor. He went on writing and correcting without lifting his head. He laid his pen aside, rolled up a manuscript, and flung it downstairs. He returned to his seat, leaned back and asked: 'Ravi, are you asleep or awake?'

'Neither. I'm dead,' the other replied and came nearer, dragging the stool. He planted the stool right in front of the table and cleared his throat as a prelude to a harangue. Srinivas knew he would have to listen to a great deal now. He kept himself receptive. He felt it was his duty to give every possible encouragement to the other, now that he had shown an inclination to go on with his drawings. As a sort of lead he asked: 'Well, how far are you progressing with your sketch?' Ravi leaned over and asked: 'Of that child?' indicating his fingers down the staircase. 'Don't you see that I have avoided him and come up direct?'

'Not finished it yet?'

'It will never be finished,' he replied in a hushed voice. 'But I dare not tell him.'

'Why? What is wrong?'

'It is an awful subject. I won't go on with it.'

'But I hear that you go there every day.'

'Yes, yes, every day I go and sit before the child, study it for about an hour in the hope of discovering even the faintest thing to hold on to. But I definitely give it up. Nothing is right about it: all its lines are wrong; its expression is awfully dull and lifeless. It is a pity!'

'But the poor fellow is hoping every day that you are going to do it!'

'That is why I'm trying to avoid him, though I've got to see him. How am I to manage it? I can't tell him about his child, can I?'

'No, no, that'd hurt any parent.'

'I wish I could get the view of a parent. You haven't seen the child?' Srinivas didn't answer: his mind went off on another line. He wondered if he should tell the printer. 'No,' he told himself. 'There's no sense in interfering in other people's lives ...' His mind perceived a balance of power in human relationships. He marvelled at the invisible forces of the universe which maintained this subtle balance in all matters: it was so perfect that it seemed to be unnecessary for anybody to do anything. For a moment it seemed to him a futile and presumptuous occupation to analyse, criticize and attempt to set things right anywhere.

As an example: here was the printer telling Ravi imaginary stories about his ability to find the other's sweetheart. Ravi's head was in the clouds on account of those stories; and here was the artist helping the printer also to keep his head in the same cloudland with promises of sketching his child: these two seemed to balance each other so nicely that Srinivas felt astounded at the arrangement made by the gods. If only one could get a comprehensive view of all humanity, one would get a correct view of the world: things being neither particularly wrong nor right, but just balancing themselves. Just the required number of wrongdoers as there are people who deserved wrong deeds, just as many policemen to bring them to their senses, if possible, and just as many wrongdoers again to keep the police employed, and so on and on in an infinite concentric circle. He seized his pen and jotted down a few lines under the heading 'Balance of Power'. He was occupied for fully fifteen minutes. He said: 'Don't mistake me, Ravi, I had to jot down some ideas just as they came, otherwise I'd lose them for ever.' He felt thrilled by the thought that he stood on the threshold of some revolutionary discoveries in the realm of human existence – solutions to many of the problems that had been teasing his mind for years. He merely said: 'You see, I'm getting some new ideas which may entirely change our *Banner*.'

# CHAPTER FOUR

The expected revolution in *The Banner* came in another way. On a Friday, when the editor flung down the manuscript with: 'Matter' – the shout came back from the bottom of the staircase: 'Editor, you have to spare me a few minutes today,' and the printer came upstairs. His face didn't have the usual radiance; he leaned over the table and said: 'Your formes are not going in.'

'What's the matter?'

'My men have gone on a strike today.'

Srinivas was aghast. He jumped to his feet, crying: 'We can't let down our subscribers.'

'Yes, I know,' said the printer. 'We've got to do something – I don't know: labour trouble – we are helpless against labour everywhere.'

'How many?' Srinivas asked, hoping that at least now he'd know how many worked behind that purple curtain.

'All of them are on strike,' replied the printer, and shattered his hope. 'All of them: the entire lot. They gave no signs of it and went on a lightning strike at midday; even the first forme for the day had gone on the machine. They walked out in a body.' Srinivas's mind once again wondered how many workers could form a strike, and his speculations lashed vainly against that purple-dotted curtain.

He looked helplessly down the stairway and ruminated over the hollow silence that reigned in the treadle-room. The printer pushed away a few papers and seated himself on the edge of the table. Srinivas's head was buzzing with alternative suggestions. His mind ran over all the available presses in the town: the Crown Electric, the City Power, Acharya Printing, Sharpe Printing Works, and so on and so forth. He had gone the round once before, when starting the journal, and recollected what a hopeless task it had proved to get any press to undertake the printing of his journal. There was a press law which terrified most printers: they understood very little of it, but always seemed to feel it safer not to go near a periodical publication: they had not enough confidence to read the articles and judge whether they would land themselves in trouble or not (the printer being a willy-nilly partner, by virtue of the Government's order, in all that an editor or publisher might do). They avoided trouble by confining themselves to visiting cards, catalogues and wedding invitations. Everywhere Srinivas got the same reply: 'Journal? Weekly. Oh! Sorry, we are not sure we should be able to print the issues in time. Oh, sorry we cannot undertake – ' It was only this printer who had said at once: 'Leave it to me. I will manage somehow.' Going round the town in search of a printer Srinivas had wasted nearly a week, and was weary of the stock reply. He had gone up and down, and accidentally met this man at the Bombay Anand Bhavan in Market Road, where he had gone in for a cup of coffee. Srinivas had by now almost decided to give up all ideas of printing his work in Malgudi, as he sat gloomily in the noisy hall of the Bombay Anand Bhavan, sipping his coffee. He was attracted to his future printer by his voice, a rich baritone, which hovered above the babble of the hall, like a drone. Srinivas understood little of what he had been saying, since he spoke in Hindi and could be easily mistaken for a North Indian, with his fur cap and the scarf flung around his neck. He sat in a chair next to the proprietor at the counter and seemed to be receiving special attention, by the way waiters were carrying him plates and cups and pressing all sorts of things on him. Apparently he said something amusing to everyone who went near him, since everyone came away from him grinning. He seemed to be keeping the whole establishment in excellent humour, including the fat proprietor. Srinivas was so much struck by his personality that he asked the boy at his table: 'Who is that man?'

'He is our proprietor's friend. He prints all our bill-books and invoices.'

'What!'

'Prints – '

'Has he a press? Where?'

Next moment he had left his half-finished cup of coffee on the table and gone over to the counter. He looked at the printer and asked: 'I wish to talk to you.'

'To me? Well, I'm all attention.'

'Will you kindly come with me for a minute? Let us sit over there.'

'Oh, yes.' He descended from the counter with great dignity. He appeared to take charge of Srinivas immediately, although he had come at the latter's invitation. It was as if he were arranging a grand reception. He cried something to the proprietor in northern Indian accents and then called someone and sent him running upstairs. He sent someone else running in another direction. He kept the whole place spinning around. His voice commanded people hither and thither and held itself monarch above the din. People turned their heads and stared at them. Presently he said, with an elaborate note of invitation in his voice, pointing at the staircase: 'This way, please.' Srinivas felt embarrassed and uttered a mild protest, which the other brushed aside gently and said: 'You will be more comfortable there; we can talk quietly.' Srinivas began to be troubled by an uneasy feeling that he had perhaps given a totally false and grand impression of himself. Perhaps the other was completely mistaken. He proceeded to say at once, stopping half-way up the step: 'You see, it is nothing so − ' The other would not allow him to proceed. He categorically said: 'I know all that. Please go up.'

They came to a cosily furnished room upstairs − a very special room as a board hung outside it said: 'For ladies and families only'. Srinivas halted before it, finding another excuse: 'We are neither ladies nor families. How can we go in?'

'These rules are not for me,' the other said. He unhooked the board and handed it to a passing server and said: 'Take it to the Saitji and tell him not to send up any ladies or families or anyone into that room while I'm there, and come back.' The servant hesitated, at which the other went over to the landing and cried down: 'Sait Sab,' and was eloquent in some northern language. After that he led Srinivas into the special room, drew up a cushioned chair for him and seated him on it. He then proceeded to give elaborate orders to a server who was waiting at the door. The table was presently littered with plates and cups, and he would not allow Srinivas to speak a word till they had had their repast. After that he called a servant to clear the table. He ordered *pans* and cigarettes. He lit a cigarette, blew out the smoke, leaned back in his chair, and said: 'Well, sir, I'm at your service – what can I do for you?' Srinivas was stunned by all this hospitality. He said: 'You are extremely kind to me.' The other asked: 'Do you think so?' with such earnestness that Srinivas felt constrained to explain: 'I'm, after all, a stranger.'

'There are no strangers for Sampath.'

'Who is Sampath?' asked Srinivas, rather puzzled.

'Speaking,' the other said, as if into a telephone. Srinivas looked up at him for a moment and cried: 'Oh!' and burst into a laugh. The other joined unreservedly. He said: 'I tell you, sir, I'm an optimist in life. I believe in keeping people happy. I have not the pleasure of knowing your name.' 'My name is – ' The other cut him short. 'It is immaterial to me. I don't want it – what am I going to do with your name?'

'Shall I at least state my business?'

'If it pleases you.'

'I'm the editor of an unborn journal. Can you print it?'

'Do you want me to print it?'

'Yes.'

'Well, in that case I've nothing to say. Customers are God's messengers, in my humble opinion. If I serve them aright I make some money in this world and also acquire merit for the next.'

'All the printers in this town seemed to be afraid of taking up my journal.'

'The worst lot of printers in any part of the world is to be found in this town,' Sampath said.

'They seem to be always afraid of breaking the law.'

The other said: 'By the look of you I don't think you would wish to see me in gaol, but if ever you, as the editor, get into trouble it will be my business to share your trouble. When a person becomes my customer he becomes a sort of blood relation of mine; do you understand? But, first of all, let us go to the press.'

* * *

That was Srinivas's first entrance into Kabir Lane: it was within a few minutes' walk of the hotel. After twisting their way through some lanes Sampath went a little ahead, stepped on his threshold, and said: 'You are welcome to the Truth Printing Works, Mr Editor.' The treadle was grinding away out of sight. The printer pointed out a seat to Srinivas and then cried: 'John! John!' There was no response. The machine was whirring away inside, but there was no sign of John.

'Boy! Boy!' he cried.

'Yes, sir,' answered a thin, youngish voice, and the machine ceased.

The curtain behind the printer parted and a head peeped out — of a very young fellow. He waited for a moment, watching the back of his employer, and then withdrew his head and disappeared softly. Presently the rattle of the machine began again. 'Well, sir, I thought I could introduce my staff to you, but they seem to be – '

'Oh, don't disturb them; let them go on with their work. How many have you there?'

The printer turned and took a brief look at the curtain behind him and said with an air of confidence, jerking his thumb in the direction of the other room: 'I tell you, labour is not what it used to be. We have to go very cautiously with them. Otherwise we invite trouble. Well, sir, I'm at your service. Here is a sample of my work.' He opened a cupboard and threw down on the table a few handbills, notices, pamphlets and letter-heads. He held up each one of them delicately with a comment. 'I don't like this, sir,' he said, holding up a letter-paper. 'I don't approve of this style, but the customer wanted it. Printing is one of the finest arts in the world, sir, but how few understand it!'

At this moment there appeared at the door a middle-aged man wearing a close coat and turban. His face was rigid, and with a finger he was flicking his moustache. At the sight of him the printer jumped out of his seat and dashed towards him with a lusty cry of welcome: 'What an honour this is today for Truth Printing!'

'I'm tired of sending my clerk and getting your evasive answers. That is why I have come myself.'

'What a blessing! What a blessing!' cried the printer and took him by the hand and pulled him to a chair. 'I don't want all this,' the other said curtly. 'Are you going to give me your printed forme today or not? I must know that immediately.'

'Of course you are getting it,' said the printer, turning and going back to his seat. 'Meet our editor. He is going to print his weekly here.' The other looked at Srinivas condescendingly, his second finger still on his moustache, his face still rigid, and asked: 'What sort of weekly – humorous or – ' Srinivas turned away, looked at the printer, and asked with cold, calculated indifference: 'Who is he? You have not told me.'

'Haven't I?' cried the printer, almost in a panic. 'He is our District Board President, Mr Soma Sundaram. I'm one of the few privileged to call him Mr Somu.' Mr Somu's face slightly relaxed and a suspicion of a smile appeared somewhere near his ears. He said rather grimly: 'You promised me the printed speech ten days ago, and I don't think you have started it at all; the function is coming off on Wednesday.'

Sampath explained to Srinivas: 'He is opening a bridge, five miles from here, across the Saraya – a grand function. Do you know that it is going to transform our entire Malgudi district? This is going to be the busiest district in South India. Do you know what odds he had to face, with the Government on one side and the public on the other?' Mr Somu added: 'Mr Editor, public life is a thankless business. If you knew how much they opposed the scheme!'

'It is a history by itself,' Sampath continued. 'It is all in his speech. It is going to create a sensation.'

The other pleaded: 'But please let me have it in time.'

Sampath said: 'My dear sir, I don't know what you think of me, but I treat this bridge-opening as my own business. When a customer steps over this threshold all his business becomes mine: if you have trust in Sampath you will be free from many unnecessary worries.' The other was completely softened by now. He wailed: 'I have come to you, of all printers in this town, doesn't it show you how I value your service?' Sampath bowed ceremoniously, acknowledging the sentiment. 'With the function only five days ahead, you have not yet given me the proof,' began the other.

'Don't I know it? There is a very special reason why I have not given you the proof yet. You will not get it till a day before the function – that's settled.'

'Why? Why?' Sampath took no notice of the question. He rummaged among the papers in a tray and brought out a manuscript. He opened the manuscript and said: 'Now listen. Ladies and gentlemen,' as if addressing a gathering. It was a masterly declamation, giving a history of the Sarayu bridge and all its politics. The idea of putting up a bridge over the Sarayu was as old as humanity. Sarayu was one of the loveliest rivers in India, coming down from the heights of Mempi Hills and winding its way through the northern sector of Malgudi, an ornament as well as a means of irrigating tens of thousands of acres. The preamble consisted of a long dissertation on the river Sarayu, followed by a history of the whole idea of bridging it, starting with a short note by a Collector, Mr Frederick Lawley (later Sir Frederick), in a District Gazeteer nearly a century old and culminating in Mr Somu's own enthusiasms and struggles. It was a hotch-potch of history, mythology, politics and opinion. It was clear that several hands had written that speech for Mr Somu.

The district board president's face was beaming by this time. He listened appreciatively to his own speech, nodding his head in great approbation. He constantly looked up at Srinivas in order to punctuate the reading with an explanation. 'You see, it refers to the Government note issued at that time. Oh! Public life is a thankless business. Do you know what they tried to do when the voting was demanded? Sometimes people stoop to the lowest means to gain their ends ...' It was quite half an hour before Sampath put down the speech and leant back in his chair. He let out a slight cough before saying: 'Mr Somu, do you now see why I can't give you the proof until a day before the show?' The president scratched his head and tried to make out what the reason could be. He turned to Srinivas and said: 'Don't you think that the speech is very good?' Srinivas simpered non-committally, and the district board president looked greatly pleased. He begged: 'Sampath, if you will kindly give it me in time, I can go through it and make any additions.'

'That's one of the reasons why I'm holding up your proof. I don't want you to touch up the speech, which is very good as it is. And then, do you note that your reference in the third paragraph to your predecessor in office cannot yet be printed?'

'Why so?'

'In my view you may have to put everything into the past tense, and I don't want to waste paper and stationery. Don't you know that he has had a heart attack and is seriously ill?'

'I didn't know he was so bad,' said the president, pausing.

'I can't take risks, sir. You would have got the two thousand printed copies delivered to you twelve days ago. I even set up a page, but then I heard that Mr So-and-so was ill. I at once put it away and sent my boy running to ascertain how he was.'

'It is very considerate of you.'

'Thank you, sir. I've a great responsibility as a printer, sir. If there is any blunder in the speech it is the printer who will be laughed at, sir.'

'True, true,' the other agreed, completely carried off his feet.

'I never delay unnecessarily, without sufficient reason. You may rest assured of it,' Sampath said in a tone full of resentment. The president said: 'I'm so sorry, Mr Sampath. I didn't mean to – '

'Pray don't mention it,' Sampath said. 'You are perfectly within your rights in hustling me. It is your duty. Your speech will be in your hands in time, sir,' he said formally. The other was too pleased to say anything. He showed signs of making his exit, and Sampath clinched it for him by saying: 'I will go with you a little way.'

When he was gone Srinivas found himself all alone and surveyed the room – a small table and chair blocking the doorway, which was curtained off, beyond which lay a great mystery. The sound of a machine could be heard. He felt tempted to part the curtain and peep in. But he dared not. He turned over in his mind the recent scene he had watched between the printer and his customer, and he felt greatly puzzled about his future printer. He speculated: 'Suppose he does the same thing with the weekly when it is out?' He felt a little uneasy, but told himself presently: 'I have no right to disbelieve what I have heard and seen. He may have genuine feelings for the president's predecessor. All the same, I must take care that some such thing doesn't happen to the weekly on the due date. If I don't accept his services, where is the alternative? Anyway, God alone must save me — ' Just at this moment the printer returned, apologizing profusely for his absence, and said: 'Sir, let us get on with your journal.'

It went smoothly on until today — until this moment when Sampath came to announce the strike which had taken place among his men. For Srinivas the world seemed to be coming to a sudden end. He was facing the most disgraceful situation in his life. What explanation was he to give to those hundreds of subscribers? He looked at his table littered with proofs and manuscripts; only the editorial and one or two other features remained to be set up today. His editorial entitled 'To all whom it may concern', dealing with a profound subject — the relation between God and the State — was almost finished: he had only another paragraph to add, after ascertaining how much space was available on the page. Now he pushed across the manuscript and asked: 'Will this fill up the first page or can I add another paragraph?' The printer scrutinized it, measured the lines. 'Make your paragraph short, and we can squeeze it in. If you have something important to say, how can we omit it?'

'Thank you; wait a moment,' said Srinivas. He seized his pen and dashed off the concluding paragraph: 'If you are going to reserve a seat for various representatives of minorities, you could as well reserve a seat for the greatest minority in the world — namely, God. A seat must be reserved for Him in every council and assembly and cabinet: then we shall perhaps see things going right in the world.' The printer read it and said: 'Well, sir, I am beaten now. I can't make out a line of what you have written. However, it is none of my business. But how are we going to print it?'

'I will help you. Do it somehow.'

'How is it possible, sir?' He remained brooding for a while and then said, with a great deal of determination in his voice: 'Well, sir, I will do my best, if it costs me my life. I can't be defeated by my men, the ingrates, I gave them a bonus last year. But I don't think we can catch tonight's train: we shall probably have the bundles ready for tomorrow morning.'

'But that will mean a day's delay,' wailed Srinivas.

'Don't you think, Mr Editor, that your readers would prefer it to not getting the journal at all?' He looked at his watch and said: 'We've only three hours for the night train. Impossible, even if we employ supernatural powers. Now, sir, give me the stuff, and I will start.'

Srinivas was very happy to see Sampath in his usual spirits again. 'Come on, I will help you in the pressroom.'

'No, sir, I have never heard of any printer using an editor to assist him. No, sir, I should make myself the laughing-stock of the entire printing community. Please stay where you are.' He hastily got up and went out. Srinivas picked up the pages of his manuscript and followed him without a word.

Downstairs the printer flung off his coat, and took out a blue overall which had lain folded up in a cupboard. With elaborate care he put it on and tied up the strings, rolled up his sleeves, smiled, and without a word parted the purple-dotted curtain and passed in. Srinivas hesitated for a while, wondering what he should do. He wondered how far he could make bold to push that curtain aside and follow. Sampath's oft-repeated compliment that he had told many people the editor had never seen beyond the curtain rang in his ears. But he told himself: 'I'm not going to be beaten by a compliment.' This seemed a golden chance to enter the great mystery. He felt on the verge of an unknown discovery, and let his impulse carry him on. He pushed through the curtain, a corner of his mind still troubled whether he would find himself thrown out next moment.

He found himself in a small room with no window whatever, in which stood a treadle, a cutting machine, a stitching machine, and a couple of type-boards. The printer was standing before one of them with a composing stick in his hand. He looked at Srinivas very casually and said: 'Would you like to try your hand at type-setting?'

'With pleasure,' said Srinivas, and the other took him to a type-board, put a stick in his hand and spread out a manuscript on the board. 'You just go on putting these letters here – all capitals here, and the lower-cases you will find here. If you can get used to seeing objects upside down or right to left, you will be an adept in no time.'

The printer's page was set up, corrected and printed off at midnight. Srinivas for his share produced an uproarious proof-sheet. The printer corrected it. 'I think it will be immensely enjoyed by your readers if you print a page of your own as it is,' he remarked, laughing heartily at all the inverted letters and the unpronounceable words that had filled the page.

It was 4 a.m. when the printing of the issue was completed. A cock crew in a neighbouring house when the treadle ceased, and Srinivas went on to learn the intricacies of the stitching and folding apparatus. His fingers felt stiff and unwieldy when he knelt on the floor and wrote the addresses on labels and wrapped them round the copies drying on the floor. His eyes smarted, his temples throbbed, and the sound of the treadle remained in his ears, as the copies were gathered into bundles. The trains were passing Malgudi in an hour's time. The printer had become less loquacious and even a little morose through lack of sleep. His voice was thick and tired as he said: 'Even that boy has joined the strikers! Fancy! I'm afraid we shall have to help ourselves.' He heaved a bundle on to his shoulder. Srinivas followed his example and took up the second bundle. They put out the lights, locked the front door and started out. There was already a faint light in the eastern sky, more cocks were crowing in the neigh-bourhood; cows and their milkmen were on the move, and the town was stirring. As they were about to turn into Market Road a figure halted before them. It was Srinivas's wife accompanied by her very sleepy youngster. 'What are you doing here at this hour?' Srinivas asked. She was visibly taken aback by the sight of her husband, carrying a load on his shoulders. 'What are you doing at this hour? One might mistake you for a robber!' she cried, as her son hung on to her arms, almost asleep. 'I was so worried all night.' 'Well, go home now. I'm quite well. I'll come home and tell you all about it.'

At the railway station Sampath woke up the station-master and left the bundles in his charge to be sent up with the guards of the two trains. The station-master protested, but Sampath said: 'It is no pleasure for us to come here at this hour, but, sir, circum-stances have forced us. Have pity on us and don't add to our troubles. You are at perfect liberty to throw these out. But please don't. You will be making hundreds of people suffer; just tell the guard to put these down at the stations marked and they will be taken charge of.'

There was still a quarter of an hour for the first train to arrive, and they decided to trust the station-master and go home. The thought of bed seemed sweet to Srinivas at this moment. At the big square in Market Road, Sampath paused to say 'Good-night or good-morning or whatever it is, sir. This is my road to New Extension and bed.'

'To say that I'm grateful to you – ' began Srinivas. 'All that tomorrow,' said the other, moving away. He cried: 'Just a moment,' and came back. 'Oh, I forgot to show you this, Editor; I printed and put this slip into the middle page of every copy.' And he handed him a green slip. Srinivas strained his aching eyes and read by the morning light: 'Owing to some machine breakdown and general overhauling, *The Banner* will not be issued for some time. We beg the forgiveness of our readers till it is resumed.'

'You have done this without telling me – '

'Yes, I set it up while you were busy and I didn't like to bother you with it.'

'But, but – '

'There is no other way, Editor. We can't repeat our last night's performance next week or the week after that. The readers have got to know the position; isn't that so? Good-night or good-morning, sir.' He turned and went away, and Srinivas dully watched him go, his brain too tired to think. He heaved a sigh and set his face homeward.

The following days proved dreary. Srinivas left for his office punctually as usual every day. He took his seat, went through the mail, and sat till the evening making notes regarding the future of *The Banner*. Sampath was hardly to be seen. The room below was locked up and there was no sign of him. Srinivas hardly had the heart to open his letters. He could anticipate what they would contain. He did not have a very large circle of readers; but the few that read the paper were very enthusiastic. They complained: 'Dear Editor: It's a pity that you should be suspending the journal. Our weekend has become so blank without it.' He felt flattered and unhappy. His brother wrote from Talapur: 'I was quite taken aback to see your slip. Why've you suspended your journal indefinitely? Have you found it financially impossible? Is that likely to be the secret?' Srinivas felt indignant. Why did these people assume that a journal was bound to land itself in financial difficulties – as if that alone were the chief item? He wrote back indignantly a letter saying that financially it was all right, quite sound, and nobody need concern himself with it. He folded the letter and put it in an envelope. He put it away for posting, and went on to answer another letter and to say that *The Banner* would resume publication in a very short time; he wrote the same message to another and another. They piled up on one side of his untidy table. It was midday when he finished writing the letters. He looked at them again, one by one, as if revising, and told himself: 'What eyewash and falsehood! I'm not going to post these.' He tore up the letters and flung them into the wastepaper basket. His letter to his brother alone remained on the table. He went through it and was now assailed by doubts. He put it away and took out his accounts ledger. This was an aspect of the work to which he had paid the least attention. He now examined it page by page, and great uneasiness seized him. He picked up a sheet of paper and wrote on it: 'Mr Editor,' addressing himself, 'why are you deluding yourself? An account-book cannot lie unless you are a big business man and want to write it up for the benefit of the income-tax department. *The Banner* ledgers have no such grandeur about them. They are very plain and truthful. You have neglected the accounts completely. Your printer alone must be thanked for keeping you free from all worries regarding it. He was somehow providing the paper and printing off the sheets and dispatching copies. You received the money orders and disposed of the receipts in every eccentric way – sometimes paying the legitimate bills, more often paying off your rent and domestic bills. The printer has been too decent to demand his money, and so let it accumulate, taking it only when he was paid. I've a great suspicion that all his trouble with his staff was due to *The Banner*, it being almost the major work he did, and without getting any returns for it. If it is so, Mr Editor, your responsibility is very great in this affair. You have got to do something about it. I remain, yours truthfully, Srinivas.'

He folded it and put it in an envelope, pasted the flap, and wrote on it: 'To Mr Sampath, for favour of perusal.' He put the letter in his pocket and got up. He took his upper-cloth from the nail on the wall, flung it over his shoulders and set out. He locked the room and went downstairs, his heart missing a beat at the sight of the bright brass lock on the front door of the press. He crossed Kabir Lane and entered the Market Road. It was midday and the sun was beating down fiercely. A few cars and buses drove along the road, stirring up the hot afternoon dust. The languor of the afternoon lay upon the place. Some of the shops in the market were closed, the owners having gone home for a nap. The fountain of the market square sparkled in the sun, rising in weak spurts; a few mongrels lay curled up at the market gate, a couple of women sat there with their baskets, a workman was sitting under a tree munching a handful of groundnuts he had bought from the women. Srinivas felt suddenly drowsy, catching the spirit of the hour himself. It was as if he were breathing in the free air of the town for the first time, for the first time opening his eyes to its atmosphere. He suddenly realized what a lot he had missed in life and for so long, cooped up in that room. 'The death of a journal has compensations,' he reflected. 'For instance, how little did I know of life at this hour!' He toyed with the idea of going to the river for a plunge. 'I had nearly forgotten the existence of the river.' He hesitated, as he came before the National Stores. He would have to turn to his right here and cross into Ellaman Street if he were going to the river, but that would take him away from his destination, which was Sampath's house at New Extension. He had two miles to go along the South Road. He felt suddenly very tired and his head throbbed faintly through the glare from the bleached roads; a couple of cars and lorries passed, stirring up a vast amount of dust, which hung like mist in the air. He saw a *jutka* coming in his direction, the horse limping along under the weight of the carriage. He called: 'Here, *jutka*, will you take me to Lawley Extension?' The *jutka*-man, who had a red *dhoti* around his waist and a towel tied round his head, with nothing over his brown body, was almost asleep with the bamboo whip tucked under his arm. He started up at the call of '*Jutka!*' and pulled the reins.

'Will you take me to Lawley Extension?' Srinivas repeated. He looked at Srinivas doubtfully. 'Oh, yes, master. What will you give me?'

'Eight annas,' Srinivas said without conviction. Without a word the *jutka*-man flicked the whip on the horse's haunch, and it moved forward. Srinivas watched it for a moment, and started walking down the South Road. The *jutka* driver halted his carriage, looked back and shouted: 'Will you give me fourteen annas?' Srinivas stared at him for a second, scorned to give him a reply and passed on. 'I would rather get burnt in the sun than have any transaction with these fellows,' he muttered to himself. A little later he heard once again the voice of the *jutka*-man hailing him: 'Sir, will you give me at least twelve annas? Do you know how horse-gram is selling now?' Srinivas shouted back: 'I don't want to get into your *jutka*, even if you are going to carry me free,' and walked resolutely on. He felt indignant. 'The fellow would not even stop and haggle, but goes away and talks to me on second thoughts!' He felt surprised at his own indignation. 'There must be a touch of the sun in my head, I suppose. The poor fellow wants an anna or two more and I'm behaving like a – ' His thoughts were interrupted by the rattling of carriage wheels behind him; he turned and saw the *jutka* pulling up close at his heels. The *jutka* driver, an unshaven ruffian, salaamed with one hand and said, rather hurt: 'You uttered a very big word, master.' Srinivas was taken aback. 'I say, won't you leave me alone?' 'No, master. I'm fifty years old and I have sat at the driver's seat ever since I can remember. You could give me the worst horse, and I could manage it.'

'That's all very well, but what has that to do with me?' Srinivas asked unhappily, and tried to proceed on his way. The *jutka* driver would not let him go. He cried ill-temperedly: 'What do you mean, sir, by going away?' Srinivas hesitated, not knowing what to do. 'Why is this man pestering me?' he reflected. 'The picture will be complete if my landlord also joins in the fray with petitions about his granddaughter.' The *jutka* driver insisted: 'What have you to say, master? I've never been spoken to by a single fare in all my life – ' And he patted his heart dramatically. 'And this will never know sleep or rest till it gets a good word from you again. You have said very harsh things about me, sir.' Srinivas wondered for a moment what he should do. It was getting late for him; this man would not let him go nor take him into his vehicle. The sun was relentless. He told the *jutka* driver: 'I'm a man of few words, and whatever I say once is final ....'

'Sir, sir, please have pity on a poor man. The price of grass and horse-gram have gone up inhumanly.'

'I will give you ten annas.'

'Master's will,' said the *jutka*-man, dusting the seat of the carriage. Srinivas heaved himself up and climbed in, the horse trotted along, and the wheels, iron bound, clattered on the granite. The carriage had its good old fragrance – of green grass, which was spread out on the floor, covered with a gunny-sack for passengers to sit upon. The smell of the grass and the *jutka* brought back to his mind his boyhood at Talapur. His father occasionally let him ride with him in the *jutka* when he went to the district court. He sat beside their driver, who let him hold the reins or flourish the whip if there were no elders about, when the carriage returned home after dropping his father at the court. Some day it was going to be made quite a stylish affair with shining brass fittings and leather seats, but it remained, as far as he could remember, grass-spread, gunny-sack covered. The driver of that carriage used to be an equally rough-looking man called Muni, very much like the man who was driving now. Srinivas wondered whether it could be the same person. It seemed so long ago – centuries ago – yet it was as if here once again was the same person, his age arrested at a particular stage. Somehow the sight of the hirsute, rough-looking driver gave him a feeling of permanence and stability in life – the sort of sensation engendered by the sight of an old banyan tree or a rock. The smell of the grass filled him with a sudden homesickness for Talapur. He decided to make use of the present lull in activities to visit his ancient home. The driver went on repeating: 'The price of gram is – Master must have mercy on a poor man like me.'

At Lawley Extension the driver stopped his horse and grumbled at the prospect of having to go half a mile farther to New Extension. 'I clearly heard you say Lawley Extension, master.' Srinivas edged towards the foothold. 'All right, then, I will get down and walk the rest of the distance.' The driver became panicky. He almost dragged him back to his seat, pleading: 'Master has a quick temper. Don't discredit me,' and whipped the horse forward. He went on to say: 'If only grass sold as it used to I would carry a person of your eminence for four annas ... as it is, I heard you distinctly say Lawley Extension. You had better tell me, sir, would anyone quote fourteen annas for New Extension? Please tell me, sir; you are a learned person, sir; please tell me yourself, sir ... Horse-gram – '

Sampath's house was at the third cross-road; he was standing at the gate of a small villa. Sampath let out a cry of welcome on seeing Srinivas and ran forward to meet him. Srinivas halted the *jutka*, paid him off briskly, and jumped out of the carriage. 'I was not certain of your door number, though I knew the road.' Broad roads and cross-roads, fields of corn stretching away towards the west, and the trunk road bounding the east, with the bungalows of Lawley Extension beyond; one seemed able to see the blue sky for the first time here. 'What a lovely area!' Srinivas exclaimed.

'Yes, it looks all right, but if your business is in the town it is hell, I tell you. All your time is taken up in going to and fro.'

'What a fine bungalow!' Srinivas exclaimed.

'Yes, but I live in the backyard in an outhouse. The owner lives in this.'

He led him along a sidewalk to the backyard. On the edge of the compound there was an outhouse with a gabled front, a veranda screened with bamboo-trellis, and two rooms. It was the printer's house. Srinivas felt rather disappointed at seeing him in his setting now, having always imagined that he lived in great style. The printer hurriedly cleared the veranda for his visitor; he rolled up a mat in great haste, kicked a roll of bedding out of sight, told some children playing there: 'Get in! Get in!' and dragged a chair hither and thither for Srinivas and a stool for himself. Srinivas noted a small table at the further end littered with children's books and slates; a large portrait hung on the wall of a man with side whiskers, wearing a tattered felt hat, with a long pipe sticking out of a corner of his mouth. His face seemed familiar, and Srinivas was wondering where he might have met him. The printer followed his eyes and said: 'Do you recognize the portrait? Look at me closely.' Srinivas observed his face. 'Is that your picture?'

'Yes. You don't know perhaps that side of me. But I have not always been a printer. In fact, my heart has always been in make-up, costumes, and the stage – that was in those days. Lately I have not had much time for it. But even now no amateur drama is ever put on without me in it, and what a worry it is for me to squeeze in a little hour at the rehearsal, after shutting the printing office for the day.' He became reflective and morose at this thought, then abruptly sprang up and dashed inside and returned in a few minutes.

Srinivas guessed his mission indoors and said: 'I'm not in need of coffee now. Why do you worry your people at home?' The printer said: 'Oh! Is that so?' and addressed loudly someone inside the house: 'Here! Our editor doesn't want you to be troubled for coffee; so don't bother.' He turned to Srinivas and said: 'Well, sir, I've conveyed your request. I hope you are satisfied.' Presently Srinivas heard footsteps in the hall; someone was trying to draw the attention of the printer from behind the door. The printer looked round with a grin and said: 'Eh? What do you say? I can't follow you if you are going to talk to me in those signals. Why don't you come out of hiding? Are you a *Ghosha* woman?' He giggled at the discomfiture of the other person at the door, and then got up and went over. A whispered conversation went on for a while and then the printer stepped out and said: 'Well, sir, my wife is not agreeable to your proposition. She insists upon your taking coffee as well as tiffin now. She has asked me how I can disgrace our family tradition by repeating what you said about coffee.' He looked at the door merrily and said: 'Kamala, meet our editor.' The person thus addressed took a long time in coming, and the printer urged: 'What is the matter with you, behaving like an orthodox old crone of seventy-five, dodging behind doors and going into *Purdha*. Come on, come here, there

72

is no harm in showing yourself.' Srinivas murmured: 'Oh, why do you trouble her?' and stepped forward in order to save the lady the trouble of coming out. 'This is my wife,' the printer said, and Srinivas brought his hands together and saluted her. She returned it awkwardly, blushing and fidgety. She was a frail person of about thirty-five, neither good-looking nor bad-looking, very short, and wearing a *sari* of faded red, full of smoke and kitchen grime. She was nervously wiping her hands with the end of her *sari*, and Srinivas stood before her, not knowing what to say; an awkward silence reigned. The printer said: 'Very well, good woman, you may go now,' and his wife turned to go in with great relief, while Srinivas resumed his seat.

In a short while a tender voice called: '*Appa, Appa,*' and the printer looked at the door and said: 'Come here, darling, what do you want?' A child, a girl of about four, came through, climbed on to his knee, approached his right ear and whispered into it. 'All right, bring the stuff down. Let us see how you are all going to serve this uncle,' pointing at Srinivas. The child went in with a smile, and came back with a tumbler of water and set it on the stool; it was followed by another child bringing another tumbler. The second child was slightly older. She complained: 'Look at Radhu; she will not let me carry anything.' The printer patted their backs and said: 'Hush! You must not fight. All of you try and bring one each.' He turned to Srinivas and said: 'Would you like to wash your hands?' Srinivas picked up the tumbler, went to the veranda steps and washed his hands, drying them on his handkerchief.

Now he found a sort of procession entering – a procession formed by four children, all daughters, ranging from nine to three, each carrying a plate or tumbler of something and setting it on a table and vying with each other in service. The small table was littered with plates. The printer dragged it into position before Srinivas and said: 'Well, honour me, sir – '

'What a worry for your wife, doing all this,' Srinivas said apologetically.

'She has got to do it in any case, sir. We've five children at home, and they constantly nag her – so this is no extra bother. Please don't worry yourself on that score.'

After the tiffin and coffee the printer cleared the table himself and came out bearing on his arm a small child under two years, who had not till then appeared. Srinivas, by a look at the child, understood that it must be the one the artist would not draw. 'Is this your last child?' he asked. 'Yes, I hope it is,' the printer said, and added: 'I'm very fond of this fellow, being my first son. I wanted that artist to draw a picture of him. I don't know, he is somehow delaying and won't show me anything – '

'Artists are difficult to deal with. They can't do a thing unless the right time comes for it.'

'I thought it would be so nice to hang up a sketch of this boy on the wall ...' Srinivas wondered for a brief second if he could tell him the truth, but dismissed the idea. 'Well, we will have some entertainment now,' he said. He called: 'Radhu!' and the young child came up. He said: 'Come on, darling, this uncle wants to see you dance. Call your sisters.' She looked happy at the prospect of a demonstration and called immediately: 'Sister! Chelli – ' and a number of other names till all the four gathered. She said: 'Father wants us to dance.' The eldest looked shy and grumbled, at which their father said: 'Come on, come on, don't be shy – fetch that harmonium.' A harmonium was presently placed on his lap. He pressed its bellow and the keys. The children assembled on a mat and asked: 'What shall we do, Father?' darting eager glances at their visitor. He thought it over and said: 'Well, anything you like, that thing about Krishna – ' He pressed a couple of keys to indicate the tune. The eldest said with a wry face: 'Oh, that! We will do something else, Father.'

'All right, as you please. Sing that – ' He suggested another song. Another child said, 'Oh, Father, we will do the Krishna one, Father.'

'All right.' And the printer pressed the keys of the harmonium accordingly. There were protests and counter-protests, and they stood arguing till the printer lost his temper and cried arbitrarily: 'Will you do that Krishna song or not?' And that settled it. His fingers ran over the harmonium keys. Presently his voice accompanied the tune with a song – a song of God Krishna and the cowherds: all of them at their boyish pranks, all of them the incarnation of a celestial group, engaging themselves in a divine game. The children sang and went round each other, and the words and the tune created a pasture land with cows grazing under a bright sun, the cowherds watching from a tree branch and Krishna conjuring up a new vision for them with his magic flute. It seemed to Srinivas a profound enchantment provided by the father and the daughters. And their mother watched it unobtrusively from behind the door with great pride.

Srinivas was somehow a little saddened by the performance; there was something pathetic in the attempt to do anything in this drab, ill-fitting background. He felt tears very nearly coming to his eyes. Two more song and dance acts followed in the same strain. Srinivas felt an oppression in his chest, and began to wish that the performance would stop; the printer pumping the harmonium on his lap, the bundles of unwashed clothes pushed into a corner, and the children themselves clad uniformly in some cheap grey skirt and shirts and looking none too bright – it all seemed too sad for words. There was another song, describing the divine dance of Shiva: the printer's voice was at its loudest, and the thin voice of the children joined in a chorus. Just at this moment someone appeared in the doorway and said: 'Master says he can't sleep. Wants you to stop the music.' An immediate silence fell upon the gathering. The printer looked confused for a moment and then said: 'H'm – seal up your master's doors and windows if he wants to sleep – don't come here for it. I'm not selling sleep here.' The servant turned and went away. Srinivas felt uncomfortable, wondering whether he were witnessing a very embarrassing scene. The printer turned to Srinivas: 'My landlord! Because he has given me this house he thinks he can order us about!' He laughed as if to cover the situation. He told the children: 'All right, you finish this dance, darlings.' He resumed his harmonium and singing, and the children followed it once again as if nothing had happened. It went on for another fifteen minutes, and then he put away the harmonium. 'Well, children, now go. Don't go and drink water now, immediately.' Srinivas felt some compliment was due to them and said: 'Who taught them all this?'

'Myself – I don't believe in leaving the children to professional hands.'

Srinivas addressed the children generally: 'You all do it wonderfully well. You must all do it again for me another day.' The children giggled and ran away, out of sight, and the printer's wife withdrew from behind the door. The printer put away the harmonium and sat back a little, sunk in thought. The children's voices could be heard nearly at the end of the street: they had all run out to play. The wife returned to the kitchen, and the evening sun threw a shaft of light through the bamboo-trellis, chequering the opposite wall. A deep silence fell upon the company. Srinivas took the envelope out of his pocket and gave it to the printer, who glanced through it and said: 'It's my duty to see that *The Banner* is out again. Please wait. I will see that the journal is set up on a lino machine and printed off a rotary and dispatched in truck-loads every week. For this we need a lot of money. Don't you doubt it for a moment. I am going to make a lot of money, if it is only to move on to the main building and get that man down here to live as *my* tenant. And if ever I catch him playing the harmonium here, I will – I will – ' He revelled in visions of revenge for a moment, and then said: 'A friend of mine is starting a film company and I'm joining him. Don't look so stunned: we shall be well on our way to the rotary when my first film is completed.'

'Film? Film?' Srinivas gasped. 'I never knew that you were connected with any film – '

'I've always been interested in films. Isn't it the fifth largest industry in our country? How can I or anyone be indifferent to it? Come along, let us go, and see the studio.'

'Which studio? Where is it?'

'Beyond the river. They have taken five acres on lease.'

His fur cap and scarf and a coat hanging on a peg were in a moment transferred on to his person. They started out. Sampath stopped a bus on the trunk road. The bus conductor appeared very deferential at the sight of him and found places for him and Srinivas. As the bus moved, Sampath asked the conductor: 'What sort of collection have you had today?'

'Very good, sir,' he said, leaning forward.

'Tell your master that I travelled in his bus today.'

'Yes, sir.' Sampath turned to Srinivas and said: 'This is almost our own service, you know.'

'You have printed for them?' Srinivas asked.

'Tons of stuff – every form in their office.'

'What will they do now?'

'They will wait till my rotary is ready.'

'Why, sir?' the conductor asked, 'Is your press not working now?'

'Old machines: they are worn out,' he said easily.

The bus stopped at the stand beyond Market Square. They got down. Sampath waved his arm. An old Chevrolet came up, with its engine roaring above the road traffic and its exhaust throwing off a smoke-screen. They took their seats. The driver asked: 'Studio, sir?' The car turned down Ellaman Street, ground along uneven sandy roads, and then forded the river at Nallapa's mango grove. People were relaxing on the sands, children played about, the evening sun threw slanting rays on the water. A few bullock-wagons and villagers were crowding at the crossing; the bulb-horn of the taxi rasped out angrily, the driver swore at the pedestrians till they scattered, and then the wheels of the taxi splashed up the water and drenched them. Srinivas peeped out and wished that his friend would put him down there and go forward. He was seized with a longing to sit down on the edge of the river, dip his feet in it, and listen to its rumble in the fading evening light. But the Chevrolet carried him relentlessly on till, half a mile off, it reached a gateway made of two coconut tree-trunks, across which hung the sign 'Sunrise Pictures'. They got out of the car. Sampath swept his arms in a circle and said: 'All this is ours.' He indicated a vast expanse of space enclosed with a fencing of brambles. Groups of people were working here and there; sheets of corrugated iron lay on a pile; some hammering was going on.

They moved through the lot and reached a brick hutment with a thatched roof. A man emerged from it. He let out a cry of joy on seeing Sampath: 'I was not sure if you were coming at all.' The orange rays of the setting sun from beyond the bramble fencing touched him and transfigured for a second even that rotund, elderly man, in whose ears sparkled two big diamonds, and whose cheeks came down in slight folds. He was bald and practically without eyebrows, and his spectacle frames gleamed on his brow.

'This is our editor,' began Sampath, and Srinivas added: 'I've met him before at your press. Is he not Mr Somu – the district board president?'

'Yes; I relinquished my office six months ago. It is too hard a life for a conscientious man.'

'How is that bridge over Sarayu?' asked Srinivas.

'Oh, that!' The other shook his head gloomily. 'Somehow the function never came off.' Srinivas looked at the printer questioningly. The printer read his thought at once and hastened to correct it: 'Not due to me. I printed his speech and delivered the copies in time.'

'Oh, what a waste the whole thing proved to be! I must somehow clear off all that printed stuff; gathering too much dust in a corner of the house,' said Mr Somu and added: 'Why keep standing here? Come in, come in.' He took them in. They sat round a table on iron chairs. Sampath said by way of an opening: 'The editor wanted to see the studio.'

'I never knew that there was a studio here,' added Srinivas.

'There is no encouragement for the arts in our country, Mr Editor. Everything is an uphill task in our land. Do you know with what difficulty I acquired these five acres? It was possible only because I was on the district board. I've always wanted to serve Art and provide our people with healthy and wholesome entertainment.' And Srinivas felt that Mr Somu could really still keep his bridge speech, which might serve, with very slight modifications, for the opening of the studio. 'I'm sparing no pains to erect a first-class studio on these grounds.'

'He has an expert on the task, who is charging about a thousand rupees a month.'

'Come on, let us go round and see – '

They rambled over the ground, and Mr Somu pointed out various places which were still embryonic, the make-up department, stage one and two, processing and editing, projection room and so forth.

'When do you expect to have it ready?'

'Very soon. The moment our equipment is landed at Bombay. Well, I am entirely depending upon our friend Sampath to help me through all this business, sir. I want to serve people in my own humble way.'

# CHAPTER FIVE

In Kabir Lane the old stove-enamelled blue board had been taken down. In its place hung the inscription 'Sunrise Pictures (Registered Offices)'. Over Sampath's door shone the brass inscription 'Director of Productions'. The director was usually to be found upstairs in Srinivas's garret. Somu was also to be found there several hours a day. Sampath had planted a few more chairs in Srinivas's office, because, as he said, it was virtually the conference room of Sunrise Pictures.

A young man in shirt-sleeves, clad in white drill trousers, of unknown province or even nationality, whose visiting card bore the inscription 'De Mello of Hollywood' was the brain behind the studio organization. He called himself C.E. (chief executive), and labelled all the others a variety of executives. He was paid a salary of one thousand rupees a month, and Somu had so much regard for him that he constantly chuckled to himself that he had got him cheap. Sampath, too, felt overawed by the other's technical knowledge, and left him alone, as he roamed over the five acres, from morning to night, supervising and ordering people about, clutching in one hand a green cigarette tin. In addition to raising the studio structure and creating its departments, De Mello established a new phraseology for the benefit of this community. 'Conference' was one such. No two persons met, nowadays, except in a conference. No talk was possible unless it were a discussion. There were story conferences and treatment discussions, and there were costume conferences and allied discussions. Lesser persons would probably call them by simpler names, but it seemed clear that in the world of films an esoteric idiom of its own was indispensable for its dignity and development. Kabir Lane now resounded with the new jargon. They sat around Srinivas's table, and long stretches of silence ensued, as they remained stock still with their faces in their palms, gazing sadly at paperweights and pin-cushions. One might have thought that they were enveloped in an inescapable gloom, but if one took the trouble to clarify the situation by going three miles across the river and asking De Mello he would have explained: 'The bosses are in a story conference.'

And what story emerged from it? None for several days. The talk went round and round in circles and yet there was no story. A few heavy books appeared on the table from time to time. Srinivas suddenly found himself up to his ears in the affair. Sampath piloted him into it so deftly that before he knew where he was he found himself involved in its problems, and what is more, began to feel it his duty to tackle them. It took him time to realize his place in the scheme. When he did realize it his imagination caught fire. He felt that he was acquiring a novel medium of expression. Ideas were to march straight on from him in all their pristine strength, without the intervention of language: ideas, walking, talking and passing into people's minds as images like a drug entering the system through the hypodermic needle. He realized that he need not regret the absence of *The Banner*. He felt so excited by this discovery that he found himself unable to go on with the conference one afternoon. He suddenly rose in his seat, declaring: 'I've got to do some calm thinking. I will go home now.' He went straight home, through the blazing afternoon. At Anderson Lane he saw his wife sitting in front of Ravi's block, along with his mother and sister. A cry of surprise escaped her at the sight of him. She left their company abruptly.

'What is the matter?' she asked eagerly, following him into their house and closing the main door. He turned on her with amusement and said: 'What should be the matter when a man returns to his own house?' She muttered: 'Shall I make coffee for you? I have just finished mine.'

'Oh, don't bother about all that; I've had coffee. Get me a pillow and mat. I'm going to rest.'

'Why! Are you ill?' she asked apprehensively, and she pulled a pillow out of the rolls of bedding piled in a corner. The beds fell out of their order and unrolled on the floor untidily. She felt abashed, muttered 'careless fool', and engaged herself in rolling them up and rearranging them, while Srinivas took off his upper-cloth and shirt and banyan and went to the bathroom. In the little bathroom a shaft of light fell through a glass tile on the copper tub under the tap and sent out a multi-coloured reflection from its surface. He paused to admire it for a moment, plunged his hands into the tub, splashed cold water all over his face and shoulders. As he came out of the bathroom he hoped that his wife would have spread out the mat for him. But he found her still rolling up the beds.

'Where is my mat?' he cried. 'I have no time to lose, dearest. I must sleep immediately.'

'Why have you splashed all that water on yourself like an elephant at the river-edge?'

'I found my head boiling – that's why I have to do a lot of fresh thinking now.' He paused before the mirror to wipe his head with a towel and comb back his hair. After that he turned hopefully, but still found her busy with the beds. He cried impatiently: 'Oh, leave that alone and give me a mat.' She shot him a swift look and said: 'The mat is there. If you can't wait till I put all this back ... I hate the sight of untidy beds.' She went on with her work. Srinivas picked up a mat and spread it in a corner, snatched a pillow and lay down reflecting: 'How near a catastrophe I have been.' He looked on his wife's face, which was slightly flushed with anger. He felt he had come perilously near ruining the day. He knew her nature. She could put up with a great deal, except imperiousness or an authoritarian tone in others. When she was young a music master, who once tried to be severe with her for some reason, found that he had lost a pupil for ever. She just flung away her music notebook, sprang out of the room and bade farewell to music. Everybody at her house respected her sensitiveness, and even Srinivas's mother was very cautious in talking to her. Srinivas had, on the whole, a fairly even life with her, without much friction, but the one or two minor occasions when he had seemed to give her orders turned out to be memorable occasions. His domestic life seemed to have nearly come to an end each time, and it needed a lot of readjustment on his part later. He respected her sensitiveness. He told himself now: 'Well, I shot the shaft which has hurt her and brought all that blood to her face.' He rebuked himself for the slightly authoritative tone he had adopted in demanding the mat. 'It's the original violence which has started a cycle — violence which goes on in undying waves once started, either in retaliation or as an original starting-ground — the despair of Gandhi — ' He suddenly saw Gandhi's plea for non-violence with a new significance, as one of the paths of attaining harmony in life: non-violence in all matters, little or big, personal or national, it seemed to produce an unagitated, undisturbed calm, both in a personality and in society. His wife was still at the beds. He felt it his duty to make it up with her. He asked: 'When does Ramu return from school?'

'At four-thirty,' she replied curtly.

'Come and sit down here,' he said, moving away a little to make space for her. She looked at him briefly and obeyed. Her anger left her. Her face relaxed. She sat beside him; he took her hand in his. She was transformed. She sat leaning on him. He put his arm around her and pressed his face against her black *sari*. A faint aroma of kitchen smoke and damp was about her. He told her softly: 'I'm taking up a new work today.' He explained to her and concluded: 'Do you realize how much we can do now? I can write about our country's past and present. A story about Gandhiji's non-violence, our politics, all kinds of things.' He chattered away about his plans.

'This seems so much better than that paper!' she exclaimed happily. 'I'm sure more people will like this — that *Banner* was so dull! You will not revive it?'

'Can't say. When Sampath gets a new machine with the money he is going to make — '

'Why should you bother about it?' she asked. 'Will this bring you a lot of money?'

'I don't know,' he said.

'We must have a lot more money to spend,' she said. 'We must go and live in a better house,' she pleaded.

'I don't know, I don't know,' he said, looking about helplessly. 'I don't know if I would care to live elsewhere. I like this place.' And he smiled weakly, realizing at once what a hopeless confusion his whole outlook was. He could not define what he wanted. They went on talking till the boy knocked on the door and cried at the top of his voice: 'Mother! Mother! Why have you bolted the door?' 'Oh, he has come,' she cried, and ran up and opened the door. The boy burst in with a dozen inquiries. He flung his cap and books away and let out a shout of joy on seeing his father, and threw himself on him. His mother attempted to take him in and give him his milk and tiffin, but he resisted it and announced: 'In our school there was a snake today – '

'Oh, really!'

'But it didn't bite the masters,' he added.

'Then what else did it do?'

'I don't know,' he said. 'I didn't see it. A friend of mine told me about it.' His mother took him by his hand and dragged him into the kitchen. Srinivas shut his eyes tight with almost a sense of duty. But his wife presently came out of the kitchen and said: 'Take me out this evening. Let us go to the market.'

'Oh, but – ' Srinivas began. The boy became irrepressible. 'Oh, don't say but, Father, let us go, let us go, ask him, Mother. Don't let him say "but", Mother. Let us go to a cinema.' His mother said: 'Yes, why not? I will finish the cooking in a moment and be ready.'

'All right,' Srinivas said, unable to refuse this duty.

All night his head seethed with ideas and would not let him snatch even a wink. Half a dozen times he interrupted a possible coming sleep to get up, switch on the light, and jot down notes. He got up late next day and rushed to his office. He knew no peace till he was back at his untidy table. He seized his rose-coloured penholder, dipped it in the inkpot, and kept dipping it there, as if excavating something out of its bed. The sheets before him filled up, and he became unconscious of the passing of time, till he heard a car stop and the shout from below: 'Editor!' He concluded a sentence he had begun, and put away his pen as footsteps approached.

Somu and Sampath sat in their chairs. 'We have just come from the studio – took a few test shots with the camera.' Sampath pointed at Somu and said: 'They have taken five hundred feet of our friend entering the studio. He makes such a fine screen personality, you know.' Somu tried to blush and remarked: 'It's a good camera, sir, it has cost us forty thousand.'

'Forty thousand!' Srinivas exclaimed. The scales of value in this world amazed him. All calculations were in terms of thousands. 'Where do they find all this money?' he wondered.

'Everything is ready,' Sampath said. 'Camera at forty thousand; De Mello costing a thousand rupees a month, and other executives spending ten thousand in all – all waiting; but where is the story?' Srinivas felt that he was somehow responsible for keeping the great engines of production waiting. Sampath added: 'If we have a story ready – '

'We can go into production next month.' Somu confessed: 'I have tried to jot down a few ideas for a story. I don't know if it will look all right.' He fumbled in his pocket, but Sampath, stretching out his arm, prevented the other from bringing out his paper, saying at the same time: 'Well, Editor, we rely upon you to give us something today.'

Srinivas cleared his throat and said: 'Here is an outline. See if you can use it.' He read on. The others listened in stony silence. The hero of the story was one Ram Gopal, who had devoted his life to the abolition of the caste system and other evils of society. His ultimate ambition in life was to see his motherland freed from foreign domination. He was a disciple of Gandhi's philosophy, practising *ahimsa* (non-violence) in thought, word and deed, and his philosophy was constantly being put to the test till in the end a dilemma occurred when through circumstances a single knife lay between him and a would-be assailant; it was within the reach of both; it was a question of killing or getting killed ...

Srinivas had not decided how to end his story. The other two listened in grim silence. Somu looked visibly distressed. He looked at Sampath as if for help in expressing an opinion. 'It is a beautiful story, Editor. I wish I had the press so that we might print and broadcast it.'

'You see,' Srinivas explained. 'This is the greatest message we can convey, the message of Gandhiji in terms of an experience. Don't you agree?'

'Yes,' Sampath replied a little uncomfortably. Somu fidgeted in his seat. There was an uncomfortable pause, and Sampath said: 'But we need something different for films.'

'Do you mean to say that this cannot be done in a film?' Srinivas asked as calmly as he could. He felt slightly irritated by this cold reception, but told himself: 'Take care not to be violent in discussing a story of non-violence. They are entitled to their view.' Somu cleared his voice and ventured to mutter within his throat: 'You see, we must have romance in the story.'

'Romance!' Srinivas gasped. 'What sort of romance?'

'You see, we are bound to engage a leading lady who will cost us at least two thousand a month, and we have got to give her a suitable role.'

Sampath said: 'Of course, the type of subject you think of needs much skill and experience in making. Only Russians or Americans would be able to tackle it. I have just been glancing through a book by Pudovkin. De Mello lent me his copy. There is a great deal in it for us to learn, but it will take time. You see, our public – '

'Don't abuse the public, please,' said Srinivas.

'We have got to be practical in this business ...'

Srinivas was amazed at the speed with which they seemed to imbibe ready-made notions (including Pudovkin, whom everyone in the studio mentioned at least once a day: it was a sort of trade-mark).

'I would like to see that book myself,' Srinivas said. 'Yes, I will bring it down tomorrow,' Sampath said. 'You will see what our difficulties are. After all, we are making a start. After we have made three or four films we shall perhaps gain confidence enough to take up a subject like yours, but now we have to move on safe ground.' Somu kept up an accompanying murmur, stamping his approval on all that Sampath was saying. Srinivas saw their point, their limitations and their exigencies. He merely said: 'Well, I was viewing it differently. Let us consider the question afresh.' Somu sat up, his face beamed with relief. He quickly plunged his hand into his pocket and brought out a roll of paper and his spectacle case. He put his glasses on and read too quickly for Sampath to check him: '*Krishna Leela* – the boyhood of Krishna and his friends, up to his killing of the demon *Kamsa* – ' He looked up to add: 'I was talking to my grand-aunt, you know how our people are a treasure-house of stories, and she mentioned these stories one by one. You see, we can do wonderful camera tricks, and Krishna will always be popular with our audience. Or if you don't like it' – he went on to the next – 'the burning of Lankha by the Monkey-god Hanuman; the disrobing of Draupadi by the villainous gambler Duryodhana; the battle of Kurukshetra, and teaching of Bhagavad Gita; the pricking of the vanity of Garuda – the Divine Eagle, who served as God's couch ...' And so he continued for over twenty subjects, all from the epics and mythology. The grand-aunt, like all grand-aunts, was really a treasure-house, and Somu did not hesitate to draw on it to its fullest capacity.

Sampath briefly dismissed each one of them with: 'This subject is not new. Already been done by others; this story has been produced three times over ...'

'What if it has? We shall do it again,' said Mr Somu.

'The public will run away on hearing the name of the story.'

'Oh, what about this then? Has this been done by anyone before? The Burning to Ashes of Kama – God of Love.'

Sampath said: 'No one has attempted this subject, I'm sure of it. Let us hear the story.' Mr Somu narrated the story, humming and hawing and clearing his throat. 'You see, sir,' he began, and looked about in a terrified way, like a man who cannot swim when he gets into water.

'Go on, go on,' said Sampath encouragingly.

'You see, you know Shiva – '

'Which Shiva? The God?' said Sampath, unable to resist a piece of impishness. 'Yes, we all happen to know him fairly well.'

Mr Somu was saying: 'You see ... !' He was still fumbling with 'You sees!' and Srinivas felt that the time had come to succour him. He said in a quiet way: 'I happen to know the story. Shiva is in a rigorous meditation, when his future bride, Parvathi, is ministering to his needs as a devotee and an absolute stranger. One day, opening his eyes, he realizes that passion is stirring within him, and looking about for the cause he sees Kama, the Lord of Love, aiming his shaft at him. At this, enraged, he opens his third eye in the forehead and reduces Kama to ashes ...' Srinivas's imagination was stirred as he narrated the story. He saw every part of it clearly: the God of Love with his five arrows (five senses); his bow was made of sugar cane, his bowstring was of murmuring honey-bees, and his chariot was the light summer breeze. When he attempted to try his strength on the rigorous Shiva himself, he was condemned to an invisible existence.

Srinivas read a symbolic meaning in this representation of the power of love, its equipment, its limitation, and saw in the burning of Kama an act of sublimation.

'You are perfectly right, Somu!' he cried, almost reaching out his hand across the table and patting Somu on the shoulders. Somu's face beamed with satisfaction; he looked like a child rewarded with a peppermint for a piece of good behaviour.

Sampath declared with great relief: 'I'm glad, Editor, you like the subject. Now you will have to go on with the treatment. We will fix up other things.'

'The advantage in this is,' Somu put in, 'there is any amount of love in the story, and people will like it. Personally, also, I never like to read any story if it has no love in it.'

Three days later the front page of most papers announced: 'Sunrise Pictures invite applications from attractive young men and women for acting in their forthcoming production, "The Burning of Kama". Apply with photographs.'

Day after day Srinivas sat working on his script. He now seemed to be camping in Kailas, the ice-capped home of Lord Shiva and his followers. Srinivas could almost feel the coolness of the place and its iridescent surroundings. He saw, as in a vision, before his eyes Shiva, that mendicant-looking god, his frame ash-smeared, his loin girt with tiger hide, his trident in his hand; he was an austere god; he was the god of destruction. His dance was in the burial-ground, his swaying footsteps produced a deluge. As Srinivas described it, his mind often went back to the little image of Nataraja that he had in a niche at home, before which his wife lit a small oil-lamp every day.

He was sketching out the scenes, and felt it a peculiar good fortune to have been allowed to do this work. He never bothered about anything else. His wife understood his mood and listened attentively to all that he said about it at home. She, too, knew the story, and the talk at home was all about Kama and his fate. Srinivas constantly explained the subtle underlying sense of the whole episode. His son, too, listened with great interest and boasted before his friends that his father knew all about Shiva's burning of the Love God.

At his office, sheet after sheet filled up. Srinivas read and re-read the dialogues and descriptions he had written. His mind had become a veritable stage for divine beings to move and act, and he had little interest in anything else. Coffee came to him from time to time, sent up by Sampath. He now left Srinivas alone for a great part of the day so as to enable him to produce the story with the least delay, while he tackled the vast volume of corres-pondence that resulted from their advertisements in the papers.

Into this delicately arranged world Ravi walked one day. Srinivas's mind noted the creaking on the staircase. Srinivas put away his pen and paper and received him warmly. 'Seems years since you visited us. Any progress with any picture?' he asked. Ravi shook his head. 'What has happened that I should draw now?' Srinivas took out of his table-drawer the little sketch Ravi had drawn. Ravi looked at it and said: 'I can make a full-length portrait in oils, the like of which no one else will have done in India. Give me another glimpse of my subject, and the picture is yours.'

Srinivas said: 'Like Shiva, open your third eye and burn up Love, so that all its grossness and contrary elements are cleared away and only its essence remains: that is the way to attain peace, my boy. I don't know how long you are going to suffer in this manner; you have to pull yourself together.'

'Oh, shut up ... You don't know what you are talking about. All that I'm asking is another glimpse of my subject, that is all, and nothing more, and you go on talking as if I were asking someone to go to bed with me. Before I am able to open my third eye and burn up love I am myself likely to be reduced to ashes; that is the position, sir; and you want me to draw my pictures with a firm hand!' He laughed grimly and leaned back in his chair. Srinivas looked at him in despair. 'Something is ser-iously wrong with him,' he reflected. 'He won't be sane unless he paints and he can't paint unless he is sane; he can't be sane unless he finds that girl; and he cannot find that girl unless he can – Heaven alone knows how many more "cans" and "ifs" are going to play havoc with his life.' He looked at him despairingly. Ravi remained silent for a moment and suddenly said with tears in his voice: 'I have lost my job today.'

'Lost it? What do you mean?' Srinivas cried.

'It is all so hopeless,' Ravi said. 'It is all over ... I don't know ... I don't know,' he sighed, thinking of all his dependants. 'I think it is finished. I have three months' arrears of rent to pay and the school fees of the children, and then and then – '

'Don't worry about all that now,' Srinivas said. 'Don't lose heart. We will do something. Tell me, what has happened?'

'The clerical staff of our office decided to present a memorial to our general manager, asking for promotions. We were all drafting it in our office when the manager called me in urgently. You know him – that compound of beef and whisky. He had found fault in the spelling of some word in a letter he had previously dictated; some mistake in a proper name; those wonderful names of English people. "Chumley", it seems, must be spelt "Cholmondeley". Who can understand all this devilry of their language! And he thundered and banged the table and flung the letter at me and asked me to take the dictation again. At this moment the others were coming towards our room to present the memorial. They were nearly thirty, and we could hear them coming. "What the hell is that noise?" he remarked, and went on with his dictation. Very soon we could hear them outside the door: a scurrying of feet and restless movement outside. I hoped that they would open the door and walk in in a body. We could see their feet below the half-door. We could see them moving up and down and shifting but not coming in. On the other hand, we presently saw them pressing their noses against the frosted glass pane of a window, trying to look in and see if the boss was in a good mood. It was of frosted glass, and though they could not see us we could see them on the other side.

'"What is all this tomfoolery? What are they up to? Go and find out. Is this a peep-show?" I went out and told them: "Why do you shuffle and hesitate? Come in and speak to him boldly." They looked at each other nervously, and before they could decide, the boss sounded the buzzer again and called me in. "What is it?"

'"They have come with a representation, sir."

'"How many?"

'"The entire staff, sir."

'"Damn!" he exclaimed under his breath. "I can't see the whole gang here. Ask them to choose someone who can talk for them." I went out and told them that. They looked at each other and would not choose anyone. They could not come to a decision about it. They were all for edging away and putting the responsibility on someone else. Even the man who held the memorial paper seemed ready to drop it and run away. I picked it up and went in.

'"They want to come in a body, sir," I said.

'"No," he cried. "This is not a bloody assembly hall, is it?"

'"This is the memorial they want to present, sir," I said, and put it before him. He looked at it without touching it. "All right, now leave me for a time, and go back to your seats." He didn't call me again. This note came to me at the end of the day, when I was starting to go home.' He took it out of his pocket and held it up. It was a brief typewritten message: 'Your services are terminated with effect from tomorrow. One month's salary in lieu of notice will be paid to you in due course.'

Srinivas went over next day to Ravi's office to see what he could do. It was a very unprepossessing building in a side-street beyond the market square, with a faded board hanging over a narrow doorway: 'Engladia Banking Corporation'. A peon in a sort of white skirt (a relic of the East India Co. costume at Fort St George) and a red band across his shoulder sat on a stool at the entrance. On the ground floor sat a number of typists and clerks, nosing into fat ledgers; uniformed attendants were moving about, carrying trays and file-boards. A bell kept ringing.

'Where is the manager?' asked Srinivas.

The servant pointed up the staircase. Srinivas came before a brass plate on the landing, and tapped on the half-door.

'Come in,' said a heavy voice.

Srinivas saw before him a red-faced man, sitting in a revolving chair, with a shining bald front and a mop of brown hair covering the back of his head. He nodded amiably and said: 'Good-morning,' and pointed to a chair. Srinivas announced himself, and the other said: 'I'm very pleased to see you, Mr Srinivas. What can I do for you?'

'You can take back my friend Ravi into your service. It is not fair – '

'You are friends, are you?' the other cut in. He paused, took out his cigarette-case, and held it out. 'I don't smoke, thanks,' said Srinivas. The other pulled out a cigarette, stuck it in a corner of his mouth, looked reflective and said: 'Yes, it is a pity he had to go, but we are retrenching our staff; those are the instructions from our controlling office at Bombay.'

'He is the only one to suffer,' said Srinivas. 'Yes, at the moment,' the other said with a grim smile.

Srinivas burst out: 'You are very unfair, Mr Shilling. You cannot sack people at short notice – '

'I'm afraid I agree with you. But the controlling office at Bombay – '

'This is all mere humbug. You know why you have dismissed my friend. Because you think he is an agitator.'

'I don't know that I would care to discuss all that now. Other things apart, Mr Srinivas, there is such a thing as being fit for a job. What can I do with a stenographer who cannot understand spelling?'

'Why the devil do you spell Chumley with a lot of idiotic letters? You cannot penalize us for that.'

'You are certainly warming up,' the other said, quite unruffled. 'I quite agree with you. English spelling needs reforming. But till it is done, stenographers had better stay conventional. You see my point?' He raised himself in his seat slightly, held out his thick hand, saying: 'If there is nothing else I can do – '

Srinivas pushed his chair back and rose, and said: 'This is not the India of East India Company days, remember, when you were looked upon as a sahib, when probably your grand-uncle had an escort of five elephants whenever he stirred out. Nowadays you have to give and take at ordinary human levels, do you understand? Forget for ever that God created Indians in order to provide clerks for the East India Company or their successors.'

'Well, you are saying a lot – ' The other left his seat and came over to him. 'Mr Srinivas, you are not helping your friend by making a scene here. I don't understand what you are driving at.'

'Don't you see how you are treating the man? Can't you see the lack of elementary justice? He has a family dependent upon him, and you are nearly driving him to starvation.'

'Now you must really go away, Mr Srinivas,' he said, holding open the door. 'Good-morning.'

His self-possession was a disappointment to Srinivas. He muttered weakly: 'Good-morning,' and passed out. He ran downstairs, past the man in skirt-like dress, out into the Market Road. He paused for a moment at the turning of Market Road to collect his thoughts. A few cyclists rang their bells at him impatiently. The sun was warm – though it was October it still looked like June. Edward Shilling was red as blotting-paper and suffocated with the heat, and yet he sat there in his shirt-sleeves, worked for his controlling office, and kept his self-possession. Turning over what he had said, Srinivas felt he had spoken wildly and aimlessly. 'What is it that I've tried to say?' he asked himself. He felt that his ideas arranged themselves properly and attained perspective only when he was writing in *The Banner*. He wished he could sit down and spin out a page under the heading: 'Black and White' or 'East India Company' and trace Shilling's history from the foundation-stone laying of Fort St George.

At the Kabir Lane office downstairs, Sampath was in conference with an odd assortment of people – actors, musicians and so on, who had besieged him after the advertisements in the papers. Srinivas stood in the doorway unnoticed, wondering how he was going to have a word with the other. 'Will you come out for a minute?' he cried. Sampath got up and elbowed his way out. They stood at the foot of the staircase. 'Ravi is done with at his office. We shall have to do something for him now.' Sampath was a man of many worries now. This was just one more. He rubbed his forehead and said: 'I'm interviewing some of these artists. I will come up in a moment.'

Srinivas turned and went upstairs, feeling very confused and unhappy. He felt he would never be able to finish that third scene today. His mind was in a whirl of cross-currents. 'I don't know how the poor fellow is going to manage things on the first of next month.'

He found Ravi dozing off in a corner, with his head resting on the arm of a chair. He was snoring loudly. Srinivas looked at him for a moment, and went to his table on tiptoe. He had left a sentence unfinished. He mechanically picked up his pen and tried to continue. But his mind wouldn't move. He found that it was impossible to pursue the scenes of Kailas at a moment like this. 'I had better put it away and spend my evening in some other way,' he told himself. He lifted a fat dictionary (which served as paperweight), and laid the sheets of paper under it.

Ravi opened his eyes, sat up, and yawned. 'Did you meet the bully?'

'Yes,' Srinivas said. 'He didn't seem to be much of one, though. He didn't say "damn" or bang the table even once.'

'Oh, yes, that is a privilege he has reserved for his staff, not for his visitors. He won't take me back, I suppose?'

Srinivas shook his head. 'Not a chance. But don't bother; we will do something for you. It has all happened for the best,' he said, not feeling very convinced of it. And Ravi at once added: 'A benefit which will become known after all my people have perished and I am in the streets; the old devil will drive me out if I don't pay the rent next month.'

'God has gifted you with art and he will not let you starve, if you are true to yourself.' At the mention of art, Ravi's eyes blazed with anger and he almost let out a hiss. 'What is the matter with you, calling me artist and all that bunkum? Go and tell it to those who are likely to feel flattered by it.' He subsided into a sort of unintelligible whimper. Srinivas said nothing in reply, but merely held up the old sketch. Ravi looked at it and became somewhat quietened. He gazed at it fixedly and said: 'If you think I am an artist on the strength of that – ' He added: 'She is the real artist and not I. A picture is produced only when she appears. A flash of her eyes can make a picture. I think she could do that even to you. If you saw her you would produce a master-piece, I'm sure – a grand canvas. But where is she? Everybody deceives me.' He pointed downstairs. 'I've even given up asking him about it. I've grown tired.'

'But have you done his son's picture for him?'

'Oh, that!' He became reflective. 'How can I? When I tell you I cannot draw?'

Presently Sampath came up and went to a chair. He looked tired. 'I have interviewed nearly fifty persons today. Not one fit to be seen even in a crowd scene. I don't know why they keep coming like this.'

Srinivas scribbled on a piece of paper: 'Have you thought of anything for Ravi? If you have, don't speak it out yet.' He passed it unobtrusively to Sampath. Sampath looked at it, looked at Ravi, crumpled the paper and threw it away. Srinivas suddenly got up and started to go downstairs. Sampath followed him. On seeing them rise, Ravi, too, got up. 'I will be going – '

'Where?'

'I don't know,' he said, and moved on to the door.

Srinivas said: 'Don't go away yet; I will be back in a moment.' Ravi obeyed him mutely and resumed his seat.

At the foot of the stairs Sampath told Srinivas: 'I can speak to Somu and take him in the art department. He can become an art director in due course.'

'Will he get enough to support him?'

'Yes, about a hundred now – '

'Oh, that's ample; twenty-five rupees more than what he got in the bank – '

'Will he accept it?' asked Sampath. 'He doesn't talk to me much nowadays.'

'I will make him accept it,' said Srinivas. 'But don't tell him that it is anything connected with the arts.'

'But he will have to take his brush and start work almost immediately, otherwise it will create difficulties for me with Somu,' Sampath said.

'You just take him in somewhere, and we will settle about his future later. For the present take him into your office section. Just for our sakes, please – '

'Yes, I will see what I can do. But it is going to be rather difficult with Somu – '

Srinivas went upstairs and took his seat. He felt there was no use leaving the choice in any matter to Ravi. He assumed a peremptory tone and said: 'I've a job at a hundred rupees for you.'

'Where? Where?'

'You are good at accounts, aren't you? All you will have to do is to keep the debits and credits in good shape, and they will give you a hundred rupees – '

'Yes, gladly, provided you don't expect me to draw any pictures.'

'Not at all. How can we? You have told us of your limitations.' Ravi's face shone with relief. He said: 'I won't even mind if there is a bully there who will worry me to death.'

Sampath dropped in at Srinivas's house one morning. Srinivas cried from bed: 'What a rare visit! So early in the day!'

'Just left home early, and I thought I might as well drop in – '

Srinivas hurriedly rolled up his bed. He spread out a mat for Sampath and said: 'I will be back in a minute.' Before going he called to his son, who was still sleeping. Ramu opened his eyes and stared at Sampath, at his fur cap and the scarf. 'Who are you?'

Sampath grinned and answered: 'Uncle Sampath. Have you forgotten me?'

He took off his cap and scarf and lifted the little fellow out of his bed and said: 'Now, do you see?' The child rubbed his eyes wide and said: 'Oh, you! Oh, you print father's paper.'

'Oh, that was in another age,' Sampath said, looking wistfully at him. 'Won't you give me one type?' Ramu pleaded.

'Why one? You can have the entire lot, when I can get at them myself. Anyway, why do you want types?'

'I want to print my name very urgently on my books.'

'Oh! What a pity!' Sampath burst into a laugh. 'I am never able to face my customers with a straight reply. It's the same story for everyone!' He laughed heartily. Ramu was puzzled. 'Why do you laugh?' he asked.

'Yes, you will get your name-slip from a Lino – '

'When?' asked the boy. Sampath scratched his chin thoughtfully, and said: 'As soon as possible. Ask your father. It all depends upon him. As soon as we have Shiva and Kama set up before the camera.'

'Why before a camera?' the boy asked, rather puzzled.

'We are making a cinema-picture, don't you know?' Srinivas asked.

'Yes, will you take me there?'

'Certainly; I will bring a car and take you there some day, provided you read your lessons well. How do you do in your class-work?'

'There is a boy in our class called Sambu who always stands first in all subjects. He is my friend.' He added reflectively: 'Do you know there was a snake in our school one day, but it did not bite any of the masters?'

'Did it bite any of the boys?' asked Sampath.

'Oh, no,' he replied, shaking his head and smiling indulgently. 'Boys are not allowed to go near it.'

'Oh, that's the rule in your school, is it?' asked Sampath.

'Yes,' Ramu replied.

Srinivas returned, bearing a plate of tiffin and a tumbler of coffee, and set them down before Sampath.

'You have put yourself to a lot of trouble,' muttered Sampath.

'Oh, stop all that formal courtesy,' Srinivas said.

'All right, sir, I'm hungry and the stuff seems to be of rare quality.' Ramu watched him for a moment, uttered some comment, and tried to resume his sleep. His father said: 'Now, little man, don't try to sleep again. Get up and get ready for your school. It's seven-thirty.' At the mention of seven-thirty Ramu sprang up with a cry of 'Oh! My teacher will skin me if I am late,' and ran out.

When they were left alone Sampath said: 'I came here in order to talk to you undisturbed.'

'Wait a minute then,' Srinivas said, picked up the empty tumbler and plates and carried them away, and returned, closing the middle door.

'Oh, so much precaution is not necessary. It is only about our Somu. I wanted to say something. I don't like to be under any obligation to him. I can't go on at the present rate – '

'What has happened?'

'Nothing definitely, but the trouble is always there. He is the proprietor of the studio, and he is prepared to give us the best service the studio can give.'

'Well, it is all right for everybody concerned, isn't it?'

'Please wait till I finish my sentence. Provided he is taken as a studio partner and nothing more; that is, not as the producer and investor. He has been grumbling about it for some days now.'

'Why, he seemed quite enthusiastic about it ...'

'That he is still, but it seems to me that he wants me also to invest. His partnership will take the form of studio service; that is all; for the rest we will have to find the money ourselves.'

'Why is he backing out now?'

'It is not backing out – '

'If he is not backing out, what else is he doing, and why are you worried about it?'

Srinivas found this entire financial transaction mystifying; he was trying hard to follow the threads of the problem. Sampath talked for over an hour, and Srinivas gathered from his speech that he needed money for putting the picture into production. 'But you must already be spending a great deal.'

'But that's all studio account,' said Sampath, and once again Srinivas found his understanding floundering. It seemed to him somewhat like relativity – giving brief flashes of clarity which prove only illusory. Now he definitely gave up any attempt at understanding the problem. Srinivas asked point-blank: 'So, what? What's to be done now?'

'I must find fifty thousand rupees if I have to produce the picture. This will enable me to go through the picture with a free and independent mind, and when it is done, or rather, even when we are half-way through it, we can realize the entire amount and more by selling the territorial rights for distributors.'

Srinivas was pleased to hear this note of hope. Sampath continued: 'I've found one or two people who are prepared to join me. I just want another person who will give ten thousand, and that will complete the sum.'

'Oh, you know my position,' Srinivas said apprehensively.

'Oh, no,' Sampath said. 'I wouldn't dream of bothering you about it. I'm told that your landlord has a lot of money. Can't you speak to him and persuade him to invest?'

'My landlord! Oh!' Srinivas burst out laughing. He checked himself presently, and quietly said: 'He is a great miser. He won't spend even ten rupees on himself.'

'That's true. But he will get about $12\frac{1}{2}$ per cent assured.'

'I don't know if anybody has succeeded in getting any money out of him. He won't spend anything on another water-pipe for us.'

'Can't you try?'

'Oh, I have never spoken to him about money. He always calls himself very poor. All the mention he has made of money with me is some five thousand which he's reserved for his grand-daughter's marriage; and that, too, he mentioned to me, because he wanted me to recommend her to Ravi.' He explained the old man's persistent pursuit of Ravi.

'You won't mind if I meet the old man and talk to him?' asked Sampath.

'Not at all – why should I? But don't say that I sent you there.'

When Srinivas passed that way Ravi's aged father, who was blind, somehow sensed him and called to him. It was a most painful experience for Srinivas to go into their house. The single room, crowded with Ravi's younger brothers and sisters, the smoke from the kitchen hanging over the whole place like December mist, the impossible heaping of boxes and bedding and clothes ... The old man stretched out his hand to feel the hand of Srinivas, fumbled and asked almost in a cry: 'What, what did my son do at that office?'

'Nothing; they merely retrenched,' replied Srinivas.

'Are you sure? If he has done anything to merit punishment he is not my son.' He drew himself up proudly. 'Our family has gone on without a blemish on its members for seven generations, do you know?' he asked. 'Whatever happens to us we want to preserve a good name in society.' The old man went on talking; the ragged children stood around and gaped. Ravi's mother came in and said: 'Can't you do something for the boy? He goes out somewhere and returns late every day.'

'You get in,' thundered the old man. 'Get in and mind your business. I don't want you to trouble this gentleman with all your idiotic words.'

'It is no trouble,' said Srinivas. The lady said: 'Oh, you are standing.' She told one of the boys: 'He is standing, give him a mat.'

'I won't bring the mat,' said the boy suddenly, and pointed to another and said: 'Let him do it. Why should I alone do every-thing?' The other fellow pounced upon him for making this suggestion. This quarrel came to a stop when the old man thundered at his wife: 'Why can't you leave the children alone – always nagging and worrying them?' The lady quietly spread out a mat on the floor and said: 'Be seated, please.'

'Yes, yes, pray don't keep standing,' added the old man. And then: 'Yes – I was saying something, what was it?'

'Family honour,' Srinivas felt like saying, but suppressed the impulse and said: 'Don't you worry about your son. I will see him fixed up satisfactorily in a new place.' He felt consolation was due to the old man.

'What office?' the old man asked.

'Connected with film production – '

'What film production?'

'They have recently started a studio – ' and he went on to explain its nature and scope. The old man said emphatically: 'That will never do. I wouldn't like my son to work in a place like that, among play-boys and dancing girls. I won't have him go there.'

'He is not acting,' said Srinivas.

'If he is not, what business has he there?' asked the old man. The lady fidgeted about nervously, fearing what the old man might say at any moment. Srinivas said: 'He is not acting – he is going to do quite a respectable piece of work.'

'What is that?'

'He is going to be given a start of a hundred rupees, and he may rise very fast.'

'I don't care if he is going to earn ten thousand; it is of no consequence to me; tell me what he will have to do to earn his salary.' And then Srinivas had to blurt out: 'He is an artist – probably will prove to be the greatest artist of the century some day.'

'Art! Art!' the old man mimicked offensively. 'What does he know of art?'

'Please don't be offended with him,' begged the lady. 'He doesn't mean to offend you.'

'You go in and do your cooking and don't come and interfere with us here,' the old man ordered. The lady quietly went in, sighing a little as she went. The children trooped behind her with war cries. Srinivas felt like counting their numbers, but refrained from doing so, since he felt that it might fill him with infinite rage against the old man. The old man said: 'Do you know what difficulty I had in finding him a job in the bank? I went from door to door, and how lightly he has thrown it up! And now he wants to pursue art, is that it? What does he know of art? Where has he studied it?'

'He is born with it,' Srinivas said.

'Don't put notions into his head, please,' the old man said. 'I would like him to keep up the family honour and not do anything that may bring it discredit in any way. We have lived without dishonour for seven generations and now this fellow wants to associate with dancing girls and that sort of gang. He will be spoilt. He can't go there, that is certain. Let him beg and cringe and get back to his old office – '

'I saw the manager. It's no use,' said Srinivas.

The old man shook his head. 'Then he had better try and do something else. For a man with his wits about him, there must be dozens of ways of making a living without becoming a performing monkey.'

Srinivas rose to go. He was afraid to open his lips and say anything. Everything connected with Ravi seemed to get into such complications that he wondered how he was going to survive at all.

'Can't you stay a few minutes more?' implored the old man. 'I have nothing to offer you in this bare house. There was a time when in our old house we had fifty guests, and all of them were treated royally. It was a mistake to have left our old house in the village, and it was not my mistake exactly, but my father's. He always – All right, why should I think of all that now? I was saying – what was I saying before?'

Srinivas was in no mood to help him out of the constant difficulty into which he seemed to be getting. He merely said: 'I have got to be going now.' He did not wait for further permission from the old man.

When he had gone a few yards from the house, a little girl came up behind and stopped him. She was one of Ravi's numerous sisters. 'Mother wants to know if you can give us a loan of ten rupees for buying rice.'

'Your mother?'

'Yes, she didn't want to ask before Father, and so sent me on to see you. We have had no rice for two days and we have been trying to eat something else.' Srinivas opened his purse and put ten rupees into her hands. 'Give it to your mother and tell her not to bother about returning it yet ... and tell her that Ravi will soon be earning enough to keep you all free from worry.'

At his office he found Ravi, sitting up as usual in a semi-doze. Srinivas hung his upper-cloth on the nail, came to his seat, and said: 'Ravi, I had an interesting talk with your father; this is the first time I've met him, you know; an interesting man.'

'What did he say?' Ravi asked anxiously. 'Did he speak about me?'

'Of course; he is bound to talk about you. Well, I assured him that things will be all right. All that doesn't arise now, since you are well on your way to a new job ...' It seemed to be a delicate negotiation, steering him into a job. He had to be put in without much ado, without his own knowledge, so to speak.

'You can go and start duties tomorrow at the office of Sunrise Pictures down below.' He added for the sake of safety: 'They need someone with experience in accounts. Sampath will help you to pick up the work.' Ravi seemed to hear the news without showing any enthusiasm. On the first day when it was mentioned he had seemed so enthusiastic. Today, somehow, his mood had changed. He looked dully at Srinivas and asked: 'Why should I work and earn? For whom? For whose benefit? Why can I not be allowed to perish as I am?' Srinivas found that a little peremptoriness always helped him with Ravi. He said: 'We can decide all that later. You are free today; probably from tomorrow you will be very busy. Why don't you hear me read out the story to you?' Ravi sat up attentively. Srinivas picked up his manuscript sheets and started reading from the first scene.

\* \* \*

Evidence of Sampath's handiwork came to light. The old landlord dropped in quite early one morning and said: 'Tell your wife
not to trouble to give me coffee or anything every time I come.
I have come now on business. I can't catch you unless I come so
early.' Srinivas called up his wife to bring a tumbler of coffee for
the old man. When the coffee arrived the old man's eyes shone
with joy. 'You are going to force it on me?'

'Yes,' said Srinivas, 'why not?'

'You forget, sir, that I am a very old man and a *Sanyasi*, at that;
I should never indulge in all this, though I'm inclined that way. It
is not good for my soul.'

'This is not alcohol, after all – only coffee,' said Srinivas.

The old man said: 'What if it were alcohol? Does a man's
salvation depend upon what he drinks? No, no – it depends
upon ...' He became reflective and paused as if wondering what
it really depended on. Srinivas could not resist asking: 'On what
does it really depend?'

The old man looked very puzzled and said, with his fingers
fondly curling round the coffee tumbler: 'Shall I drink this off
before it gets cold?' He lifted the tumbler, tilted back his head
and gulped it off. Srinivas asked: 'You would like a piece of
areca-nut, I am sure, after this?'

'Areca-nut? Areca-nut, at my age? Oh! But how good of you
to think of my needs. Who can ever forget the lovely scented
nuts that your wife provides her guests?' He revelled in visions of
this supreme luxury. Srinivas got up and put a little bottle containing them in his hands. He looked at it fondly and put it away
with a sigh. 'A man should not succumb to more than one
temptation.' He raised his voice in a song and quoted an *Upanishad* which said: 'Food is *Brahman* ...' A few children came up
from Ravi's house and stood in the doorway and watched him
with interest. He glared at them and said: 'That is what I hate
about children – their habit of hanging about and staring at
people. After this I'm not going to give my house to anyone who
has children. They are a nuisance.'

'We have all been children,' Srinivas said.

'Yes, yes,' the old man agreed. 'But what of it? We don't
remain children. Leave that vexed question aside. I want to tell

you a happy piece of news.' He lowered his voice and said: 'It seems that that boy is going to get a hundred rupees a month. I always knew that he would rise.'

'Who told you?' asked Srinivas.

'Ah, nobody can conceal such things from me. I know everything that goes on in the town,' said the old man rather boastfully. Srinivas thought of Ravi with pity once again. This was another unwanted element in his already complicated life. The fates seemed to have chosen him for their greatest experiment in messing things up. Srinivas asked the old man: 'Has Sampath seen you?'

'He is a good man,' the old man said. 'I had not the pleasure of seeing him before. But he came to my humble room and sat there one day. I liked him at first sight. It is always my habit. Nobody can deceive me. I know when I meet a good fellow, and I know when I meet a bad one. Association is an important thing. Otherwise, why should I ever come in search of you and talk to you, though I have not spoken to anyone in all my life, especially if they are my tenants?'

'What did Sampath say?' asked Srinivas.

'Nothing. He showed a desire to learn a few things in *Bhagavad Gita* and *Upanishads*. Somebody seems to have told him that I have perused these things, and he wanted to clear some doubts.'

'Oh!' exclaimed Srinivas, picturing Sampath, racked with metaphysical doubts.

'Why do you cry out in such surprise? There are some young men like him even in these days who have spiritual interests. How can we say "No" to them? He said he would come to me two or three days in a week, whenever he found time. Do you know, he asked what fee he should pay me? I grew very angry with him and told him "I'm not here to sell my knowledge as a market commodity". But he said: "Very well, master. But any piece of learning accepted becomes worthless, ineffectual, unless a man has given a *Guru Dakshina* [master's fee]." What a reasonable argument! Yes, there is that verse.' The old man quoted another scripture to prove that learning which has not been properly paid for is like water held in a vessel without a bottom.

Srinivas reflected that here was Sampath unfolding yet another surprise. The old man lowered his voice and said: 'Do you know, he has agreed to fix up the marriage of my granddaughter with your friend, though you forgot this old man's appeal?'

'I have not forgotten,' replied Srinivas. 'But – '

'It seems Ravi is working under him and will listen to what he says. I knew that that girl was fortunate and would not get any husband less than one getting a hundred rupees a month. You will keep all this to yourself?' begged the old man, starting to go. 'I came here expressly to give you this piece of good news. You are my only well-wisher. Who else is there to feel happy about the good things that happen to me? You make me think less and less of those blighted sons and daughters of mine, those vultures.' Ravi was very rarely to be seen nowadays. He sat making entries in ledgers in the office below. Sampath had managed to put him into the accounts section, transferring his accountant to the art section of the studio. 'That's how I have been able to manage this affair with Somu,' he confessed to Srinivas.

'But the other man, what can he do in the art department?' asked Srinivas in genuine doubt.

'He will have to do something, otherwise he will lose his job. Do you know, under such a pressure, anybody will turn his hand to anything; that's how I find that most of our actors, musicians, and technicians are produced. You watch; in a short time that fellow will refuse to come back to accounts, because he will have bloomed into an artist, just when Ravi is prepared to do art work. And then I will be faced with a further complication with Somu. Do you know, I'm facing peculiar difficulties with Somu nowadays?'

At this moment Somu himself arrived in a big car. As soon as he entered, he said: 'It's so difficult to approach this place, Sampath. We must very soon look out for a good building on the main road itself.

'How is the story progressing, sir?' he asked, turning to Srinivas. Srinivas tried to recapitulate to himself Sampath's account of Somu's partnership complications, and wondered in what way his present question was connected with that report. He found himself getting into a maze once again, and gave up the attempt. He merely replied: 'All the scenes will be ready very soon.'

'Ah! Ah! That's very good news. We must fix up an auspicious day for cranking. I want to invite our district judge to switch on.' Seeing that Srinivas received the suggestion without enthusiasm, he hastened to add: 'Of course, you must allow us business people to do things in our own way.'

'What's the point in asking the judge to do it?'

Somu turned to Sampath, and said with a very significant wink: 'Tell him some time.' Sampath rose to the occasion and said: 'You will know soon. All this has its own value.'

Srinivas turned to go upstairs, back to his work. He had been spending a considerable amount of time at the foot of the staircase with Sampath. They had to do all the talking here because inside Sampath's office, in an ante-chamber, Ravi worked, and they had to talk of certain matters without his knowledge. Srinivas now felt that the time had come for him to beat a retreat, since the foot of the staircase was threatening to become a conference room. Somu stopped him and said: 'We must have another story conference shortly to see how far we have progressed.'

'You can go ahead with your other plans. I will tell you when it is all ready.'

'One thing, mister, I want you to remember. You must not fail to introduce a comic interlude.' A slight frown came on Srinivas's face. 'I don't see how any comic interlude can be put into this.'

'Please try. It would make the picture very popular. People would come again and again to laugh. Personally, do you know, I always like something that makes me laugh.'

The old landlord waited for Srinivas at the road-bend, explaining: 'I could have come to your house and caught you, but didn't. You are sure to press on me your hospitality, and what will people say? "This old fellow goes there to snatch a free cup of coffee." No, sir, I don't want that reputation. I have always had honourable dealings with all my tenants.'

'Except in the matter of water-taps.'

'Oh! You always have a word about that. All right. I will add a new tap – not one, several – one for each block. Are you satisfied?'

'When?'

'When? Oh! You cross-examine me like a lawyer, sir; that's why people always say "Beware of people who write!" '

'You have not answered my question,' Srinivas said.

'You are very difficult to satisfy,' he replied, as if paying a compliment. 'If it were any other landlord he would have become distracted – well, I'm not here to talk about all that now. I've an important matter on which to consult you. You are going to your office. Shall I walk along with you?'

'Oh, you will feel bored and tired, coming back all alone,' said Srinivas, trying to put him off.

'That shows you don't know me,' said the old man. 'There is no loneliness for a *Sanyasi* like me. If I keep repeating "Om", I have the best companion on a lonely way. Don't you know this *sloka:* "Wherever my mind, there be your form; wherever my head, there be your feet"?'

Srinivas slowed down his pace, and the old man followed him. After several more questions he said: 'What do you think of Sampath's film company? What are they doing?'

Srinivas explained as well as he could its various aspects and purposes. 'Do you really think it is a very profitable concern?' Srinivas could not easily answer the question. 'I'm sorry, I don't know much about that.' The old man stopped for a moment to hold him by the arm and say: 'Ah, how careful! You don't want to give away trade secrets, is that it?' He gave the other a knowing wink. Srinivas tried not to look portentous, and said: 'I will find out, if you like, from Sampath all about it.' 'No, no, no,' the old man cried, alarmed. 'Not that way. I don't want you to speak to Sampath about it. I don't want him to think I've been talking about it. He trusted me with a confidence .... No, no. I was just thinking that if I invested five thousand at twelve and a half per cent – '

'Why not ten thousand?'

'Why not fifty thousand?' asked the old man. 'You seem to imagine I've a lot of cash!' He looked horror-stricken at the thought of someone thinking him rich. 'I've only a few coppers kept for the marriage of that child. If it can be multiplied without any trouble it will mean a little more happiness for the child. Sampath is taking an interest in her, and so I thought ...' He meandered on, and then feeling that he had spoken too much of his finances, shut up suddenly. 'Well, I will get back. I thought you might be able to give me some information.' He turned abruptly round, leaving Srinivas to go forward alone. Srinivas went to his office, trying to divine what exact technique Sampath was employing with the old man. An indication of it was not long in coming.

Sampath followed him upstairs to his room. 'Well, Mr Editor, I think after all I can make up the capital.' Srinivas did not feel it necessary to put any question, since he was listening to something he already knew. He hooked up his upper-cloth and went to his chair. Sampath looked at his wrist-watch. Recently a watch had appeared on his wrist, and he constantly looked at it. 'I can manage to stay with you for a quarter of an hour more. I've asked some people from the music department to come and meet me.'

Apparently he intended to become reflective for those fifteen minutes. 'I'm really puzzled, nowadays, Mr Editor. I shall be obliged if you will enlighten me. What am I in this scheme of things? On one side I interview actors, artists and musicians; I run about for Somu, doing various errands for the studio, and I have the task of our picture, its direction and so on.' He swelled with importance. 'Now what am I?' He looked so puzzled that Srinivas felt obliged to answer: 'Who can answer that question? If you understood it, you would understand everything.' He thought that perhaps Sampath's formal studies with the old man had wakened him to new problems. This idea was soon dispelled by Sampath: 'Am I the producer of this picture or am I not? It was just to decide this question that I wanted capital. I think I can make up the amount; at any rate your landlord is showing an interest in the proposition.' 'And also clearing a lot of your philosophical doubts, I suppose?' Srinivas added. Sampath laughed heartily, 'Well, sir, believe me, I do wish to know something about Self and the universe. What greater privilege can one have than studying at the feet of a great master?' He shut his eyes reverently and pressed his palms in a salute at the memory of his *Guru*. And Srinivas asked: 'And how are you going to fulfil your promise to see his granddaughter married?'

'Oh, that! Well, that is really a problem; I hope' – he lowered his voice – 'that our friend downstairs will help us.'

'But you have already promised to find him his sweetheart,' Srinivas reminded him.

'Oh, yes, yes.' He looked agonized at the number of the undertakings that weighed him down. An idea flashed into his mind and he looked relieved. 'Probably it was this granddaughter that he used to see at the temple. Who knows? Let us have a look at that sketch, Editor.' Srinivas took out the sketch. At the sight of it, with its ray of light reflected off the diamond on the ear-lobe, Srinivas was thrilled and cried out: 'Oh, the boy ought to be drawing and painting and flooding the world with his pictures. This is a poorer world without them.' He sighed.

'Yes, sir, I agree. Even today if he were prepared to get on to the art department, I would make a place for him there.' He scrutinized the picture and shook his head despondently. 'No, the landlord's granddaughter is different.'

'Have you seen her?'

'Oh, yes, daily. I am coaching her in the arts. Smart girl. I wish Ravi would see sense. But' – he became reflective – 'I don't know what we can do if he has set his heart on this type, though a girl in the flesh ought to be worth a dozen on paper. Can't you put some sense into him? I think he will listen to you, and it will please the old man.' Srinivas said nothing in reply. Sampath remained gazing at the picture absent-mindedly, and suddenly cried: 'This face looks familiar – wait a minute.' He got up and ran downstairs and returned bearing an album under his arm. He opened its leaves, placed it on the table and pointed at a snapshot of a girl pasted in it. Under it was written: 'Appln. No. 345, Madras – Name Shanti.' Srinivas looked at the face and then compared it with that in the sketch. 'Well, it looks very much like it. Have you got her address?'

'Of course; we can call her up. Her face struck me as the most feasible type for Parvati.' Sampath scrutinized her face very carefully now. 'I will send off a telegram!' he cried. 'We must give her a mike and camera test at once, and if that is O.K. I am sure she will do very well. We can make a star of her.' Srinivas felt happy. 'So this means Ravi's worst troubles are over. He will be so glad. Let us tell him.' Sampath was hesitant. 'Oh, please wait. She may be someone else or she may have some other problems; I think we'd better wait.'

'Well, there doesn't seem to be any harm. All that he wants is to take a look at her; that'll ease his mind so much that we can get him to work.' Sampath was very lukewarm about that proposition. He shut the album, put it under his arm and started to go. He paused in the doorway to say: 'No, Mr Editor. Please do not tell him anything yet. It's studio business; it's better that such things should not get complicated. You see, we have to move cautiously. As you know, Somu is a funny sort of man, and he may misconstrue the whole thing.' He wandered on, Srinivas not comprehending much. When Somu's name cropped up, there were always hints of vast complications, and Srinivas left it all alone.

A story conference met on the day Srinivas mentioned that his writing was completed. Somu was beside himself with joy, and Sampath was stung into fresh activity. De Mello said: 'Well, sir, the studio only starts its real work now.' He rolled up his sleeves and lit a cigarette and gave an affectionate pat to his green cigarette tin. They sat around Srinivas's table as he began the reading. 'Scene one, Kailas – mountain peaks in the background, rolling peaks, with ice gleaming in multicolour – ' De Mello interrupted to say: 'Oh, don't bother about all that detail; it is the business of the art department. You can just indicate the location.'

'Go ahead, Mr Srinivas,' implored Somu, who looked docile and pleased. He seemed quite ready to do Srinivas's bidding at this moment; he was so awestruck by his ability to fill up a hundred-odd foolscap sheets with the story. But he was not prepared to confess his admiration in full. He said: 'Writing requires a lot of patience; you must sit down and fill up page after page – a thing which we business men cannot afford to do. That is why we have to depend upon intellectuals like you, sir.' He spoke as if he were presenting a casket and reading out the address printed on silk. Sampath cut him short with: 'Shan't we go on with the story?' De

Mello put down a cigarette stub and pressed his shoe on it. Tobacco smoke hung in the air. Srinivas read on. 'Second scene, Parvathi − a young woman of great beauty, with her maids.' De Mello interrupted: 'How can we be sure till we fix up the actress?' Somu looked despondent. He looked pathetically at Sampath and asked: 'Yes. What do you say to that?'

'In Hollywood we never approach the story till we have fixed up the chief artists.'

'This is not Hollywood,' Srinivas said. 'So let us try to find the people who will do the part ....'

'But that doesn't pay, Mr Srinivas. In films the real saleable commodity is the star-value. All other things are secondary.' Sampath tried to smooth matters out with: 'We will make stars, if the ready-made ones are not available.' Somehow this seemed to please the other members of the conference, and Somu and De Mello said almost simultaneously: 'That is a very good point, Sampath. We've got to make stars.' To Srinivas it seemed as if they were going to cling to this phrase now and for ever. He shuddered to think that they might be going to repeat it like a litany: 'Star! Star! We must make a star!' But he realized that the matter was proceeding on correct conference lines. It was the essence of a conference that somebody should say something, and somebody else should say something else, and a third person should throw out a catch phrase for all to pick up and wear proudly like a buttonhole. This was the approved method of a conference, and he could not object to it. And so, although he was being constantly interrupted, he curbed his own annoyance and continued his reading. He felt he was emulating a street preacher he had encountered in his younger days in his town, a man who came to propagate Christianity and lectured to a crowd, unmindful of the heckling, booing, and general discouragement. Srinivas had even seen a grass-seller throwing her burden at the preacher's head, but he went on explaining the gospels. Such a faith in one's mission was needed at this moment. Srinivas persisted: scene after scene with the description, action and dialogue followed; and this continuous drone lulled them into silence. As darkness gathered around his room and voices rose from the tenements below he became lost in his own narration; his listeners seemed to him just shadows. Even De Mello's tobacco fog rose to the cobweb-covered ceiling and paused there. Srinivas read on, inspired by his own vision, though he could not decide whether they were lost in enjoyment of his reading or were asleep. He read with difficulty in the gathering darkness, afraid to get up and switch on the light, lest that should break the spell and set them talking.

# CHAPTER SIX

The next important event was the opening ceremony. A special bus ran from the city to the studio on the other bank of the river. The bus was painted 'Sunrise Pictures' along its whole body, and placards were hung out on its sides: 'The Burning of Kama — Switching-on Ceremony'. It slowly perambulated along the Market Road, and anyone who carried an invitation to the function could stop it and get in.

The invitation was printed on gold-sprinkled cartridge sheets, on which was stamped a map of India, represented as a mother with a bashful maiden kneeling at her feet, offering a spring of flowers, entitled 'Burning of Kama'. The maiden was presumably 'Sunrise Pictures'.

'Is this your idea?' Srinivas asked Sampath, who worked without food and sleep for the sake of the function. Sampath was cautious in answering: 'Why, is it not good?' Srinivas hesitated for a moment whether he should be candid or just not answer the question. He decided against expressing an opinion and asked: 'What do others say?'

'Everybody says it is so good. Somu was in raptures when he saw it. Our boys did it, you know – something patriotic: we offer our very best to the country, or something like that.'

'Your idea?' Srinivas asked. Sampath was rather reluctant to be cross-questioned, and turned the subject to the task of printing: 'What a trouble it was getting this through in time! They couldn't fool me. I sat tight and got it through.' Srinivas quietly gloated over this vision of Sampath harassed by printers. 'I've not been home at all for three nights; I sat up at the Brown press and handled the machine myself. How I wish I'd my own press now!' He sighed a little. 'No need to worry; we are on the way to getting our big press.' He seemed distressed at the memory of printing, and Srinivas obligingly changed the subject. 'How many are you inviting?'

'Over a thousand!' Sampath said, brightening. 'It is going to be the biggest function our city has seen.'

As the bus turned into Nallapa's Grove, far off one saw the bunting flying in the air, made up of flags of all nations, including China, Scandinavia and the Netherlands. One could pick them out by referring to Pears' Encyclopaedia. The bunting was an odd treasure belonging to the municipal council; no one could say how they had come to gather all this medley of ensigns; but they were very obliging and lent them for all functions, private and public, unstintingly. And no gathering was complete unless it was held under the arcade of these multi-coloured banners: there were even a few ships' signals included among them.

The vast gathering was herded into studio number one, in which hundreds of wooden folding chairs were arrayed. The switching-on was fixed for 4.20, since at 4.30 an inauspicious period of the day was beginning. The district judge, who was to preside, was not to be seen. They fidgeted and waited for him and ran a dozen times to the gate. Sampath calmed Somu by pulling him along to the microphone and announcing: 'Ladies and gentlemen, the president is held up by some unexpected work, but he will be here very soon. Meanwhile, in order not to lose the auspicious hour, the switch will be put on.' He himself passed on to the camera on the tripod, and asked: 'Ready?' and pressed the switch. The lights were directed on to a board fixed on an easel on which the art department had chalked up: 'Sunrise Pictures proudly present their maiden effort, "The Burning of Kama" ', and they shot a hundred feet of it. De Mello cried 'Cut'. He had come in a dark suit, his moustache oiled and tipped. Thus they caught the auspicious moment, although the big wicker-chair meant for the president was still vacant.

A committee of astrologers had studied the conjunction of planets and fixed the day for the inauguration ceremony. There had been a regular conference for fixing the correct moment, for as Somu explained to the others: 'We cannot take risks in these matters. The planets must be beneficial to us.' And he gave three rupees and a coconut, each on a plate, for the Brahmins who had given him the date. The Brahmins officiated at the ceremony now, after deciding what the ritual should be. A couple of framed portraits of Shiva and a saint, who was Somu's family protector, were leant against the wall, smothered under flowers. The holy men sat before them with their foreheads stamped with ash and vermilion and their backs covered with hand-spun long wraps. They each wore a rosary around the throat, and they sat reading some sacred texts. In front of them were kept trays loaded with coconut, camphor and offerings for the gods. A few minutes before the appointed moment they rose, lit the camphor, and circled the flame before the gods, sounding a bell. Then they went to the camera and stuck a string of jasmine and a dot of sandal paste on it. De Mello trembled when he saw this. They seemed to be so reckless in dealing with the camera. He felt like crying out: 'It's a Mitchel, so – please ... It costs Rs 40,000,' but he checked himself as he confessed later: 'In this country, sir, one doesn't know when a religious susceptibility is likely to be hurt. A mere sneeze will take you to the stake sometimes – better be on the safe side.' The priests finished with the camera and then offered him a flower, which he did not know what to do with, but vaguely pressed it to his nose and eyes, and then they gave him a pinch of vermilion and ash, which also worried him, till he saw what others did, and followed their example and rubbed it on his brow. He looked intimidated by these religious observances. It was an odd sight: De Mello in a dark suit, probably of Hollywood cut, and his forehead coloured with the religious marking. 'It's just as well,' Srinivas remarked to himself. 'They are initiating a new religion, and that camera decked with flowers is their new god, who must be propitiated.' To him it seemed no different from the propitiation of the harvest god in the field. To Somu and all these people, God, at the present moment, was a being who might give them profits or ruin them with a loss; with all their immense commitments they felt they ought to be particularly careful not to displease Him. As he was a champion of this religious sect, there was nothing odd in De Mello's submissiveness before it. Srinivas wished he had his *Banner*. What an article he could write under the heading: 'The God in the Lens'.

And these rituals were being witnessed by an audience of over five hundred with open-mouthed wonder. There was suddenly a bustle: 'The president has arrived,' and Somu ran out in great excitement to receive him. There was a stir in the audience, and people craned their necks to look at the president. Though they saw him every day, they never failed to see him as the president with renewed interest, and in this setting he was peculiarly interesting. In strode a strong dark man, wearing coloured glasses and grinning at the assembly. 'I'm sorry,' he said loudly. 'I was held up by court work. Is it all over?' They propelled him to his wicker-chair; he pulled the invitation out of his pocket, to study the items of the programme. He looked at the flower-decked camera and the Brahmins and asked: 'Is this the first scene you are going to shoot?' Sampath explained to the president and apologized, garlanded him, and gave him a bouquet. 'Why are they centring all their affection on him? Have they met here today to fuss about him or to get their film started?' Srinivas wondered. He was struck with the rather pointless manner in which things seemed to be moving. 'Subtle irrelevancies,' he told himself as he sat, unobserved on an upturned box in a corner of the studio. They presently brought the president to the microphone. He said, with the rose garland around his neck: 'Ladies and gentlemen, I know nothing about films, and court work held me up and delayed the pleasure of being here earlier. I don't usually see films – except probably once a year when my little daughter or son drag me there.' And he smiled in appreciation of this human touch. He rambled on thus for about an hour; and people looked as though they were subsiding in their seats. He went on to advise them how to make films. 'I see all around too many mythological and ancient subjects. We must throw all of them overboard. Films must educate. You must appeal to the villager and tell him how to live, how to keep his surroundings clean; why he should not fall into moneylenders' hands, and so on. The film must not only tell a story but must also convey a message to the ignorant masses. There are problems of cultivation and soil – all these you can tackle: there is nothing that you cannot include, if only you have the mind to be of service to your fellow men. They say that the film is the quickest medium of instruction; we all like to see films;

let us see ones that tell us something. You have been too long concerned with demons and gods and their prowesses. I think we had better take a vow to boycott Indian films till they take up modern themes.' At this point he was gently interrupted. They had all along wished they could gag him, but it was not an easy thing to choke off a district judge, particularly when he was the president of the occasion. So Sampath and Somu popped up on either side of the judge and carried on a prolonged conversation with him in an undertone. After they withdrew, the judge said: 'I'm sorry I forgot to notice' – he fumbled in his pocket and pulled out the invitation – 'what story they are starting. Now my friend Somu tells me it is an epic subject. Our epics undoubtedly are a veritable storehouse of wisdom and spirituality. They contain messages which are of eternal value and applicable to all times and climes, irrespective of age, race, or sex and so on. The thing is that they must be well done. India has a lesson to teach the rest of the world. Let us show the world a sample of our ancient culture and wisdom and civilization. Blessed as this district is by a river and jungles and mountains, with these energetic captains at the helm, I've no doubt that Malgudi will soon be the envy of the rest of India and will be called the Hollywood of India.' De Mello's voice could be heard corroborating the sentiment with a timely 'Hear! Hear!' and resounding applause rang out. The president went to his seat, but came back to the microphone to say: 'I'm sorry I forgot again. I'm asked to announce the happy news that there is going to be a dance entertainment by some talented young artists.' To the accompaniment of the studio orchestra some new recruits to the studio threw their limbs about and gave a dance programme with the studio lights focused on them. Afterwards with the president beside the camera, and Somu and Sampath touching the switch, still photos were taken from four different angles. This was followed by a few baskets being brought in, out of which were taken paper bags stuffed with coconuts and sweets, which were distributed to all those present. Sampath went to the microphone and thanked the audience and the president for the visit.

When they were moving out, Srinivas noticed a familiar head stirring in the third row. It was his old landlord, transformed by a faded turban, a pair of glasses over his nose, and a black alpaca coat, almost green with years. Srinivas ran up to him and accosted him. He felt so surprised that he could not contain himself. 'Oh, you are here!' The old man gave him his toothless smile. 'First time for thirty years I have come out so far – Sampath wouldn't leave me alone. He sent me a car. Where is your artist friend? I thought he would be here.'

'Ravi! He must be in the office. He doesn't usually fancy these occasions.' The old man looked about for Sampath and called to him loudly. Srinivas slipped away, somehow not wishing to be present at their meeting, feeling vaguely perhaps that Sampath might try and get a cheque out of the old man at this opportunity.

Srinivas was busy putting the finishing touches to his script. He worked continuously, not budging from his seat from nine in the morning till nine in the evening. Even Ravi, who came in when he had a little leisure, hesitated at the door and turned back without uttering a word. Srinivas worked in a frenzy. He was very eager to complete his part of the work, though he had at the back of his mind a constant misgiving about the final treatment they might hatch out of it, but he ruthlessly pushed away this doubt, saying to himself: 'It is not my concern what they do with my work.'

Sampath was not to be seen for nearly a week, and then he turned up one evening, bubbling with enthusiasm. A look at him, and Srinivas decided that it would be useless to try to get on with his work. He put away his papers. Sampath began: 'She has come!'

'When?'

'Five days ago, and we have been putting her through the tests. De Mello says she is the right type for the screen. She is a fine girl.'

'Is she the same as – ?' asked Srinivas, indicating the old sketch. Sampath smiled at this suggestion. He scrutinized the sketch, remarking under his breath: 'Extraordinary how two entirely unconnected people can resemble each other.' He laughed heartily, as if it were the biggest joke he had heard in his life. He seemed extraordinarily tickled by it. 'Yes, she is somewhat like this picture, but there is a lot of difference, you know. In fact, this is her first visit to this town. She has never been here before. She was born and bred in Madras.'

'Where is she at the moment?' asked Srinivas.

'I've found her a room in Modern Lodge. I could've put her up at my house if it was necessary; after all, I find that she is related to me, a sort of cousin of mine, though we never suspected it. Anyway, our problem is solved about Parvathi. She is going to do it wonderfully well. I foresee a very great future for her. We are finalizing the rest of the cast tomorrow; after that we must go into rehearsals.'

Srinivas was present at the rehearsal hall in the studio. It was a small room on the first floor, furnished with a few lounges covered with orange and black cretonne, a coir mattress spread on the floor and a large portrait of Somu decorating the wall. On the opposite wall was a chart, showing the life history of a film – starting with the story-idea and ending with the spectator in the theatre. The rehearsal was announced for eleven, and Srinivas caught an early bus and was the first to arrive. He sat there all alone, looking at the portrait of Somu and at the chart. A medley of studio sounds – voices of people, hammerings, and the tuning of musical instruments – kept coming up. Through the window he could see far off Sarayu winding its way, glimmering in the sun, the leaves of trees on its bank throwing off tiny reflections of the sun, and a blue sky beyond, and further away the tower of the municipal office, which reminded him of his *Banner*. Its whole career seemed to have been dedicated to attacking the Malgudi municipality and its unvarying incompetence. He felt a nostalgia for the whirring of the wheels of a press and the cool dampness of a galley proof. 'When am I going to see it back in print?' he asked himself. His whole work now seemed to him to have a meaning because, beyond all this, there was the promise of reviving *The Banner*. He had not yet spoken to Sampath about what he was to be paid for his work. He felt he could never speak about it. He found on his table on the second of every month a cheque for one hundred and fifty rupees, and that saw him through the month, and he was quite satisfied. How long it was to continue and how long he could expect it, or how much more, he never bothered.

His wife occasionally, waiting on him for his mood, asked him, and all that he replied was: 'You get what you need for the month?'

'Yes. But – '

'Then why do you bother about anything? You may always rest assured that we will get what we need without any difficulty. You will be happy as long as you don't expect more.'

'But, but – '

'There are no further points in this scheme of life,' he cut her short. And that was the basis on which his career and daily life progressed. 'Of course, if *The Banner* could be revived,' he reflected, 'I could breathe more freely. Now I don't know what I'm doing, whether I'm helping Sampath or Sampath is helping me – the whole position is vague and obscure. The clear-cut lines of life are visible only when I'm at my table and turning out *The Banner*.' He had now a lot of time to reflect on *The Banner*. For one thing, he decided to rescue Ravi and get him to work for *The Banner*. '*The Banner* can justify its existence only if it saves a man like Ravi and shows the world something of his creative powers ...' He made a mental note of all the changes he was going to make in *The Banner*. He would print thirty-six pages of every issue; a quarter for international affairs, half for Indian politics, and a quarter for art and culture and philosophy. This was going to help him in his search for an unknown stabilizing factor in life, for an unchanging value, a knowledge of the self, a piece of knowledge which would support as on a rock the faith of Man and his peace; a knowledge of his true identity, which would bring no depression at the coming of age, nor puzzle the mind with conundrums and antitheses. 'I must have a permanent page for it,' he told himself. 'This single page will be the keystone of the whole paper – all its varied activities brought in and examined: it will give a perspective and provide an answer for many questions – a sort of crucible, in which the basic gold can be discovered. What shall I call the feature? The Crucible? Too obvious ...'

It was so peaceful here and the outlook so enchanting with the heat-haze quivering over the river-sand that he lost all sense of time passing, leaning back in the cane chair, which he had dragged to the window. He presently began to wish that the others would not turn up but leave him alone to think out his plans. But it seemed to him that perverse fates were always waiting around, just to spite such a wish. He heard footsteps on the stairs and presently Sampath and the new girl made their entry.

'Meet my cousin Shanti, who is going to act Parvathi,' Sampath said expansively. Srinivas rose in his seat, nodded an acknowledgement, and sat down. He saw before him a very pretty girl, of a height which you wouldn't notice either as too much or too little, a perfect figure, rosy complexion, and arched eyebrows and almond-shaped eyes – everything that should send a man, especially an artist, into hysterics. Srinivas, as he saw her, felt her enchantment growing upon him. Her feet were encased in velvet sandals, over her ankles fell the folds of her azure translucent *sari*, edged with gold; at her throat sparkled a tiny diamond star. She seemed to have donned her personality, part by part, with infinite care. Srinivas said to himself: 'It's all non-sense to say that she does all this only to attract men. That is a self-compliment Man concocts for himself. She spends her day doing all this to herself because she can't help it, any more than the full moon can help being round and lustrous.' He caught himself growing poetic, caught himself trying to look at a piece of her fair skin which showed below her close-fitting sheeny jacket. He pulled himself up. It seemed a familiar situation; he recollected that in the story Shiva himself was in a similar plight, before he discovered the god of the sugar-cane bow taking aim. He seemed to realize the significance of this mythological piece more than ever now. And he prayed: 'Oh, God, open your third eye and do some burning up here also.' 'Mankind has not yet learned to react to beauty properly,' he said to himself. Shanti, who had by now seated herself on a sofa with Sampath beside her, muttered something to Sampath. And Sampath said: 'My cousin says you look thoughtful.' She at once puckered her brow and blushed and threw up her hands in semi-anger, and almost beat him as she said in an undertone: 'Why do you misrepresent me? I never said any such a thing.' She shot scared glances at Srinivas, who found his composure shaken. He said: 'Don't bother. I don't mind, even if you have said it,' and at once all her confusion and indignation left her. She said with perfect calm: 'I only said that we seemed to have disturbed you while you were thinking out something, and he says – ' She threw a look at Sampath. Srinivas wanted to cut short this conversation and said rather brusquely: 'I have waited here for two hours now. You said that rehearsals were at ten.'

'Apologies, Editor,' replied Sampath. 'Shall I speak the truth? The real culprit is – ' He merely looked at his cousin, and she at once said apologetically: 'Am I responsible? I didn't know.'

'Well, you have taken a little over three hours dressing up, you know,' Sampath said. Srinivas noted that they seemed to have taken to each other very well. He said to the girl: 'You are his cousin, I hear?'

'I didn't know that when I applied,' she said.

'Have you a lot of film experience?' he asked and felt that he was uttering fatuous rubbish. Before she could answer he turned to Sampath and asked: 'Have you told her the story?' And he realized that it was none of his business and that he was once again uttering a fatuity. But that fact didn't deter Sampath from building up an elaborate reply of how he had been talking to her night and day of the part she was to play, of how he was constantly impressing upon her the inner significance of the episode, and he added with warmth: 'My association with you is not in vain, Editor.' He constantly shot side-glances to observe the effect of his speech on the lady, and Srinivas listened to him without saying a word in reply, as he told himself: 'I don't seem to be able to open my mouth without uttering nonsense.'

Presently more footsteps on the staircase, and half a dozen persons entered, followed by Somu. Somu, who came in breezily, became a little awkward at seeing the beauty, and shuffled his steps, stroked his moustache, and in various ways became confused. 'He will also find it difficult to speak anything but nonsense,' Srinivas said to himself. The visitors spread themselves around, and Somu said, pointing at a strong paunchy man: 'This is Shiva.' The paunchy man nodded agreeably as if godhead were conferred on him that instant. He had a gruff voice as he said: 'I have played the part of Shiva in over a hundred dramas and twenty films for the last twenty years. I act no other part because I'm a devotee of Shiva.'

'You must have heard of him,' Sampath added. 'V.L.G. – ' Srinivas cast his mind back and made an honest attempt to recollect his name. It suddenly flashed upon him. He used to notice it on the wall of the magistrate's court at Talapur, years and years ago – 'V.L.G. in ...' some Shiva story or other. He almost cried out as he said: 'Yes, yes, I remember it: rainbow-coloured posters' – that colour scheme used to make his flesh creep in those days; and at the recollection of it he once again shuddered. 'Yes, it was in *Daksha Yagna*,' Shiva said, much pleased with his own reputation. 'I always do Shiva, no other part, I'm a devotee of Shiva.'

'He gets into the spirit of his role,' Sampath said. Shiva acknowledged it with a nod and repeated for the third time: 'I do no other role. I'm a devotee of Shiva. Both in work and in leisure I want to contemplate Shiva.' True to his faith his forehead was smeared with sacred ash and a line of sandal paste. Srinivas viewed him critically, remarking to himself: 'His eyes are all right, but the rest, as I visualized Shiva, is not here. He certainly was without a paunch – the sort of austerity which is the main characteristic of Shiva in the story is missing. And he should not have such loose, hanging lips, all the inconvenient, ungodly paddings of middle age are here – what a pity! Some tens and thousands of persons have probably formed their notions of a god from him for a quarter of a century.' As if in continuation of his reflections Sampath said: 'When his name is on the poster as Shiva, the public of our country simply smash the box-office.' Shiva accepted the compliment without undue modesty. He added in a gruff tone: 'So many people were troubling me, and I refused them because I wanted some rest. But when I heard about the starting of this studio I said I must do a picture here,' and Somu beamed on him gratefully. Srinivas felt inclined to ask more questions, so that he might clear the doubt at the back of his mind as to what special reason the actor had for conferring this favour on this particular studio; but he left the matter alone, one of the many doubts in life which could never be cleared. V.L.G. took out of his pocket a small casket, out of it he fished a piece of tobacco and put it in his mouth, and then proceeded to smear a bit of lime on the back of a betel leaf and stuffed it also into his mouth. He chewed with an air of satisfaction; and from his experience of tobacco chewers, Srinivas understood that V.L.G. was not going to talk any more, but would be grateful to be left alone to enjoy his tobacco. He seemed to settle down to it quietly and definitely. Others, too, seemed to understand the position, and they left Shiva alone and turned their attention to the man next him – a puny youth, with a big head and sunken cheeks and long hair combed back on his head. 'He is going to be Kama,' said Sampath. 'He has been doing such roles in various films.' Srinivas looked at him. He wondered if he might get up and make a scene. 'I'm not going to allow the story to be done by this horrible pair.' But presently another inner voice said: 'If it is not this horrible pair, some other horrible pair will do it, so why bother?' And his further reflections were cut short by the lady remarking as she looked at her tiny wrist-watch: 'It's four o'clock. When do we start the rehearsal?'

'As soon as we finish coffee, which is coming now,' said Sampath. It was six-thirty when they finished their coffee, and then they unanimously decided to postpone the rehearsals, and got up to go away with relief and satisfaction.

Srinivas was touching up the conversation between the disembodied Kama and his wife. Kama said: 'Here I am. Don't you see?' And his wife answered: 'Seen or unseen, you are my lord. You are in my thought. I will beg of Shiva to make me also invisible.' Srinivas pondered over the sentence: it seemed too cloying for him. 'Can't I make it sound a little more natural?' But another part of his mind argued: 'You are not dealing with a natural situation. The agony of a wife whose husband is made invisible can be understood only by another in a similar position. What would my wife say if she suddenly found I'd been made invisible? I must find out from her.' As he was contemplating this scene, without being able to come to a decision, Sampath came in jubilantly, crying: 'I've achieved a miracle.' Srinivas said: 'I will listen to your miracle presently. But first sit down and answer my question. Suppose you were made suddenly invisible, what would be your feelings?' Sampath thought it over and answered: 'I should probably think that the clothes I wear are unnecessary.' He laughed and added: 'I think it would be a gain, on the whole.'

'What do you think your wife would say?' Srinivas asked.

'If she were in her normal mood she would probably break down, but if she were in her ten a.m. mood she might say: "This is another worry. How I am to manage with an unseen husband God alone knows. But please tell me where you are; don't surprise me from corners." '

'What is that ten a.m. mood?' asked Srinivas curiously.

'Every day at ten a.m. she is in a terrible temper; just about the time when the children have to be fed and sent to school and shopping has to be done and some lapse or other on my part comes to light, and all sorts of things put her into a horrible temper at that hour, and she will be continuously grumbling and finding fault with everyone. She is always on the brink, and if I don't have my wits about me we might explode at each other damagingly.'

'You must try to reduce all her irritations, poor lady!' Srinivas said, much moved by the memory of how she stood behind the door on the day he visited Sampath. He suspected that Sampath hardly went home nowadays, spending all his time in the studio and running about, completely lost in his new interests. So he pleaded with him with special fervour: 'You must forgive me if I appear to be presumptuous.' He lectured him on family ties and responsibilities, a corner of his mind wondering at the same time what his wife might have to say about his own habits of work; he wondered if Sampath would retaliate. But he was too good to do it. He became rather sombre at the end of the lecture.

'Has anyone been complaining about me?' asked Sampath.

'Well, not yet,' replied Srinivas.

Srinivas felt that he had encroached too much into personal matters and checked himself. He said: 'Now tell me how this dialogue sounds.' He read what he had written. Sampath listened to it intently and said: 'It's very elevating. Let us try to add a song there.' He then passed on to the business that had brought him. 'Do you know, your landlord has, after all, agreed to finance our scheme!'

'That's the miracle, is it?' asked Srinivas.

'Isn't it?' Sampath said.

Srinivas declared warmly: 'You are a great fellow. People must bow before you for your capacity.' 'Well, wait, wait,' Sampath said grinning. 'You can compliment me after I show you the first instalment of cash. He is going to give it in five instalments. And he wants separate notes for each. He will give me each instalment, deducting his twelve and a half per cent interest in advance, but writing up the note for the full amount.'

'Oh, God! You have not agreed to it?'

'I have no choice.'

'And you are going to deal with his granddaughter's marriage, too?'

'Of course.' Sampath lowered his voice and pointed downstairs. 'I don't know why that old man has set his heart on him. He has never even spoken to him. I must get at him some time and do something.' He looked worried at the thought of Ravi. 'Why will he not listen to reason? That girl is bringing five thousand plus twelve and a half per cent interest. I think artists should be trained up in more practical ways of thinking. Tomorrow morning we are going to a lawyer's office to write the first note and then he will hand me the money. I'm also mortgaging with him some gold and silver knick-knacks we have at home.'

'Your wife's?'

'We have accumulated a variety of silver things during our marriage, you know!' he said with affected lightness. He remained moody for a moment. 'That'll help me face Somu's conditions. After that I shall really be able to make a substantial deal. Our rotary is not so far out of reach, sir. I'm really grateful to you for introducing me to the old man; under him I have made tremendous progress in Sanskrit studies. Though it is so difficult to make him talk of his passbook, he readily opens his mind and soul to every spiritual inquiry. It is a pleasure to sit with him and hear him talk.' He raised his voice and recited in fluent Sanskrit: 'The boy is immersed in play; the youth, in the youthful damsel; the old, in anxiety; (but) none in the Supreme Being!'

'Do you know, he gives six different interpretations for the same stanza?'

\* \* \*

It was getting on towards evening, and Srinivas left his table to go home. There was a car waiting for Sampath downstairs. 'I will drop you at home,' Sampath said.

'I prefer to walk home.'

Sampath got into his seat. 'Boy!' he cried, sitting in his car, and a servant came up, brightly buttoned, wearing a cap. 'This is our old office boy – he has come back.' The boy smiled affably, and Srinivas recognized the young printer's devil of *Banner* days, transformed by an inch more of height and a white-and-green uniform. 'White and green is our studio colour,' Sampath said. 'I've ordered even our paperweights to be made in this colour.' The boy stood waiting. 'Boy, is Master Ravi there? Ask him if he is coming home with me.' The boy ran in and returned in a moment to say: 'He is not coming now, sir. He says he has work.' Sampath said gloomily: 'That boy Ravi, somehow he is very reserved nowadays. He is aloof and overworks. I thought I might take him out with me and speak to him on the way and do something about that old man's pet. Well, another occasion, I suppose. You see how smart that little devil is! I knew he would come back. This is only the beginning. I know that all the rest of my staff will also come back: I shall know how to deal with them. Well, good-night, sir; I will go home and take the wife and children for a drive. Your advice is very potent, you know.' He drove away.

In Anderson Lane, Srinivas noticed an unusual liveliness. Groups of people were passing to and fro. They stood in knots and seemed deeply concerned. But Srinivas was absorbed in his own thoughts. He didn't bother about it. The citizens of Anderson Lane had a tendency to get excited over nothing in particular almost any evening; but what struck him now was the number of persons from other streets who were moving about, and it made him pause and wonder. He found the crowd very thick in one place, in front of the house where his landlord had his room. Young boys chatted excitedly, old men, women, students and adults stood staring at the house. 'What is the matter?' he asked a young fellow. Three or four young men and an adult gathered round and started talking at once. The young fellow said: 'We were playing cricket in this road. Every day we play here, our team is known as Regal, and we had a match today with Champion Eleven ...' His voice was a high-pitched shriek. But a higher-pitched shriek of another was superimposed on it: 'But we couldn't complete the match. We could play only half the match today. We won't take it as a draw.' Yet another member of the team was eager to add, even before the previous sentence was finished: 'The ball went through that window.' And they looked at each other guiltily, twirling their little bats in their hands, and said: 'The old man is dead.' 'Which old man?' They pointed sadly at the landlord's room. Srinivas ran in that direction. A constable was there on duty. He would let no one pass. Srinivas pushed his way through the crowd. The crowd watched him with interest. 'He is his son,' he heard someone remark. 'No, can't be; he has no son,' remarked another. 'They won't let you go there,' said another. Srinivas ignored them all and went on. The constable barred his way. The crowd watched the scene with interest. 'Go back,' the constable said. His face was lined with gloom and boredom. Srinivas did not know what to do. He said: 'Look here, constable, I have got to go and see him.'

'Our inspector has ordered that no one should be allowed to go near the body.'

'Just let me. I won't take even five minutes. I wish to have a last look at him. Wouldn't you want to do the same thing in my place?' There was such earnestness in his request that the constable asked: 'Are you related to him?' Srinivas thought for a minute and said: 'Yes, I'm his only nephew. I live in his house. He is my uncle.' And at the same time he prayed to God to forgive him the falsehood. 'I can't help it at this horrible moment,' he explained to God. The policeman said, his face relaxing: 'In that case it is different. I always allow blood relations to go and see, whatever may happen. The inspector reprimanded me once or twice for it, but I told him "Even a policeman is a human being, after all. Relations are relations ..." '

Srinivas did not hear the rest of the statement. He went past him and stood in the doorway. The policeman came up, and the crowd pressed forward. The policeman said: 'You should not go into that room, sir. You can stand in the doorway and watch. Don't take a long time; the inspector will be back any moment.'

Srinivas stood and looked in. The old man seemed to sit there in meditation, his fingers clutching the rosary. His little wicker box containing forehead-marking was open, and his familiar trunk was in its corner. Dusk had gathered and his face was not clear. The boys' ball lay there at his feet. Srinivas felt an impulse to snatch it up and return it to the boys, but he overcame it. He felt a silly question bobbing up again and again in his head: 'Are you sure he is dead?' he wanted to ask everybody. He felt he had stared at the body long enough. It seemed to him hours, but the constable said: 'Hardly a minute; you could have stayed there a little longer. But what can you do? People must die, old people especially.' Srinivas passed out of the crowd. They looked on him as a hero. They asked eagerly, thronging behind him: 'What, sir, what?' He didn't reply, but went straight home, went straight to the single tap, which was fortunately free, took off his shirt, and sat under it and then went into his house. 'A great final wash-off to honour his memory,' he told his wife. She told him the rest of the story. 'It seems they saw him bathe at the street-tap as usual and saw him go in at about eleven in the morning. But no one saw him again.' His son, who had just come in from Ravi's house, added: 'We were playing against Champion Eleven, and some rascal of that team shot the ball in; they got up to the window to ask for it and called him to throw up the ball, but – ' he shook his head. 'I came running home when I heard he was dead. I was the first to tell Mother.'

'Your ball didn't hit and kill him, I hope?' said Srinivas with serious misgivings.

'How could it, Father? We were playing the match with a tennis ball. It hits us so many times. Are we all dead?' He added ruefully: 'It was their batting, and they are claiming a boundary for it. Is that right, Father?'

The greater part of the next day Srinivas had to spend at the inquest. The *Panchayatdars* (a board of five) sat around a room, examining the post-mortem report. They summoned Srinivas because he had called himself his nephew. They took a statement from him as to when he had seen the old man last, and about his outlook and antipathies and phobias. They summoned Sampath because he was often seen going there. He looked panicky, as if they were going to haul him up for murder. A statement from him was recorded as to why he visited the old man so often. He explained that he was his student and was learning Sanskrit from him. And then they set out a number of exhibits – a savings bank passbook, a piece of paper on which were scrawled $12\frac{1}{2}$ per cent, 5,000, and the name Sampath. He was asked if he had seen the passbook before. Sampath said 'No'. He was asked to explain what he knew about the piece of paper containing his name and the $12\frac{1}{2}$ per cent calculation. He said that he was consulted by the old man regarding some investment calculations, and possibly he had tried to work it out. The *Panchayatdars* pried further and wanted to know what the investment was. Sampath, who had by now recovered something of his composure, answered: 'How should I know? Occasionally my master would talk of investments generally, and work out hypothetically some figures. I don't know what he had in mind.' Two more witnesses had been summoned, the owner of the house where the old man had his room, and his son-in-law. They were questioned very briefly, and then the board adjourned for a moment into another room, and came out to say: 'We are satisfied that ... died seven hours before he was seen, as the doctors think. Death is due to natural causes, old age and debility.'

# CHAPTER SEVEN

The sound of a car moving off reached Srinivas's ears, and at the same moment he heard the cry on the stairs: 'Editor! Editor! Editor!' It was such an excited cry that he ran out to the landing. He saw Ravi at the foot of the staircase. 'Editor! Editor!' he cried. 'Did you see?'

'What?' asked Srinivas.

'Are you free? Shall I come up?' Ravi asked. He climbed up in three bounds. Srinivas moved back to his chair and pointed the other to his usual seat. Ravi wouldn't sit down. He was too excited. He could speak neither in whispers nor in a loud voice and struggled to find a *via media* and made spluttering sounds. He came over to Srinivas's chair, gripped its arms and said: 'She – she – ' He couldn't finish his sentence. His face was flushed. Srinivas had never seen him so excited. He gently pushed him to a chair and said: 'Calm yourself first.' But Ravi was not one to be calmed. It didn't seem necessary at the moment. He said: 'Give me that sketch.' He held out his hand. Srinivas took it out and passed it to him. It seemed to act as a sedative, and Ravi became calmer. 'I can do it now; on a big canvas, in oils, if you like.' Srinivas felt, amidst the various misgivings in his mind, that this was the moment he had been waiting for all his life.

Ravi was lost in the contemplation of the sketch he had in his hand. He was going into a sort of loud reverie. 'Nobody told me she was here. I didn't know she had come to the studio. How providential! Don't you see the hand of God in it?' Srinivas asked: 'Did you speak to her?'

'Yes, yes. I was in the office attending to those damned accounts. I heard footsteps and went on with my work, thinking it was just another of those damned visitors dropping in all through the day. I heard little sandals pit-patting: that itself seemed music to my ears, but as a rule I never look up. But the

131

footsteps approached and stopped at my table. "Accountant," the voice called, and I looked up, and there she was. Oh, Editor, it was a stunning moment. I don't remember what she asked and what I said: I fell into a stupor, and she turned round and vanished. I thought it was an apparition, but the office boy was also there, and he says that she asked for Sampath and went away.' He was rubbing his hands in sheer joy and pacing up and down. Srinivas watched him uneasily. He felt he should tell him the truth and check him a little. 'Ravi, are you sure she is the same?' 'What doubt is there? She gets a high light on her right cheek bone. That is the surest mark. Even if other things are a mistake, nobody can go wrong in this. I challenge – '

'But she says this is her first visit to this town.'

'She says that, does she? But I have seen her; I know her, that high light no one else can have.'

'Did she recognize you?' Srinivas asked.

'How could she? She never knew me before. I used to see her every day and she might or might not have seen me. How can I be sure?'

'But you have spoken a word or two to her and you used to say she gave you a piece of coconut and so on; isn't that so?'

Ravi suddenly thrust out his chest and said, defying the whole world: 'I said so, did I? I don't care. What do I care what she or anyone says or thinks? It is enough for me. She is there. Let her not notice me at all. It is enough if I have a glimpse of her now and then. Mr Editor, you must help me. I will not do these accounts any more. I can't. I hate those ledgers. I want to work in the studio now – in the art department. Please speak to Sampath. Otherwise, I don't want this job at all. I will throw up everything and sit at the studio gate. That will be enough for me.' He sat down, fatigued by his peroration. He added: 'If you are not going to speak to Sampath, I will.' He held the sketch in his hand. Srinivas gently tried to take it back. But the other would not let it go; he gazed on it solemnly, pointed at a spot and said: 'You know how long ago I drew this? But you see that high light where I have put it. Go and look at her in the studio; that is her peculiarity. A human face is not a matter of mere planes and lines. It is a thing of light and shade, and that is where an individual appears. Otherwise, do you think one personality is different from another through the mere shape of nose and eyes? An individual personality is – ' He was struggling to express his theories as clearly as he felt in his mind. He concluded with: 'It is all no joke. High lights and shadows have more to do with us than anything else.'

Srinivas undertook a trip to the studio in order to meet Sampath, who seemed to be too busy nowadays to visit his office downstairs regularly. 'Mr Sampath comes only at three,' they told him. Srinivas sat down in a chair in the reception hall and waited. Girls clad in faded *saris*, with flowers in their hair, trying to look bright, accompanied by elderly chaperons; men, wearing hair down their napes and trying to look artistic; artists with samples of their work; story-writers with manuscripts; clerks, waiting for a chance; coolies, who hoped to be absorbed in the works section, all sorts of people seemed to be attracted to this place. De Mello had framed strict rules for admission which were so rigorous that the studio joke was that the reception hall ought to be renamed rejection hall. But hope in the human breast is not so easily quenched. And so people hung about here, without minding the weariness, trying to ingratiate themselves with the clerk and vaguely thinking that they might somehow catch the eye of the big bosses as they passed that way in their cars. The reception hall marked the boundary between two classes – aspirants and experts. But from what he had seen of those inside, Srinivas felt that there was essentially no difference between the two: the only difference was that those on the right side of the reception hall had got in a little earlier, that was all, and now they tried to make a community of themselves, and those here were the untouchables!

The afternoon wore on. The reception clerk scrutinized a leather-bound ledger, entreated a few people who went in to sign their names clearly and fully, threw a word of greeting at a passing technician, and after all this task was over, opened a crime novel and read it, lifting his eye every tenth line to see if there was anyone at the iron gate at the end of the drive.

The hooting of a car was heard, and he put away his book and said: 'That's Mr Sampath.' And now there swung into the gate the old Chevrolet with Sampath at the wheel and his cousin by his side. The clerk looked very gratified and said: 'Didn't I say he would be here at three o'clock? Shall I stop and tell him?' 'No, let him go in, I will follow.' The car went up the drive and disappeared round a bend. Srinivas got up, and the others looked at him with envy and admiration. They reminded him of the alms-takers huddled at a temple entrance, a painting he had seen years ago, or was it a European painting of mendicants at the entrance to a cathedral? He could not recollect it. He went on.

He went to the rehearsal hall. Sampath said on seeing him: 'Ah, the very person I wished to meet now. I'm putting my cousin through line rehearsals and she has difficulty in following some of the interpretations.' She was dazzling today, clad in a fluffy *sari* of rainbow colours, with flowers in her hair to match. Srinivas thought: 'Surely God does not create a person like this in order to drive people mad.' She smiled at him, and he felt pleased. 'Oh, God, don't spare the use of your third eye,' he mentally prayed. She had a fine voice as she asked: 'How do you want Parvathi to say these lines?' She quoted from a scene where Parvathi is talking to her maids and confesses her love for Shiva. She says: 'How shall I get at him?' and Shanti now wanted to know: 'How do you want me to say it? Shall I ask it like a question or a cry of despair?' It seemed a nice point, and Srinivas felt pleased that she was paying so much attention to her rôle. She spoke naturally and easily, without a trace of flirting or striving for effect. Srinivas said: 'It is more or less a desperate cry, and that dialogue line has to lead to that song in *Kapi Raga*. Do you follow?' She turned to Sampath triumphantly and said: 'Now, what do you say? We've got it straight from the author!' She said: 'All day Sampath has been trying to rehearse me in these lines, saying that they are to be asked like a question. I have been protesting against it, and we did not progress beyond ten lines today. And he wagered ten rupees, you know!' Sampath took out his purse and laid a ten-rupee note in her hand. 'Here you are, sweet lady. Now that this question is settled, let us go ahead. Don't make it an excuse for stopping.' She picked up the ten-rupee note, folded it and put it in her handbag made of a cobra hood. Srinivas observed on it the spectacle-like mark; a shiver ran through his frame unconsciously. He felt it incongruous that she should be carrying on her arm so grim an object. He asked: 'Where did you get that? Is it a real cobra hood?'

'Isn't it?' she asked. 'I had gone to a jungle in Malabar once on a holiday, and this thing ...' She struggled to hide something and ended abruptly: 'Yes, it was a king cobra. It was shot at once, and then a bag was made of it.' She trailed off, and Srinivas did not like to pursue the matter.

Later, when she went away for some costume rehearsals, Sampath said: 'My cousin married a forest officer, and they had to separate, you know, and all kinds of things, and then she became a widow. She feels somewhat uncomfortable when she thinks of all that, you know.'

'Well, I didn't intend to hurt her or anything. But I was struck by her bag because it seemed such a symbolic appendage for a beautiful woman and for us men to see and learn.'

'Yes, yes, quite right,' Sampath said. He was more keen on continuing his narrative. 'They were in a forest camp. The cobra cornered her in her room, as she lay in a camp cot in their forest lodge and it came over the doorway, hissing and swaying its hood. She thought that her last hour had arrived, but her husband shot it through a window.' Srinivas decided to turn the topic from the cobra. People might come in, and he might lose all chance of talking to Sampath alone for the rest of the day. So he at once said: 'I came here to talk to you about Ravi.'

'Oh! Yes, I wanted to speak to you, too. It seems he has not been coming to the office for three or four days now. What is he doing?'

Srinivas said: 'He is prepared to work in the art section. Why don't you take him in? We ought to do everything in our power to give him the chance, if it will make him draw pictures. It is our responsibility.'

In his habitual deference to Srinivas's opinions, Sampath did not contradict him. 'If I were free as I was before, I would do it before you finished the sentence. But there are difficulties. I'm now in a place which has become an institution.'

'Look here. Are you going to take him in or not? That's what I want to know.'

'I will ask Somu. I don't wish to appear to be doing things over his head. After all, he is very important.'

Of late, after the old landlord's death, Srinivas noted a new tone of hushed respect in Sampath's voice whenever he referred to Somu.

'All right, talk to him and tell me. I will wait.'

'Now? Oh, no, Mr Editor! Please give me a little time. I don't know what he is doing now.' Srinivas looked resolute. 'Don't tell me that you can't see him when you like. Surely you shouldn't tell me that.' There was in his tone a note of authority which Sampath could not disobey.

'Well, my editor's wishes before anything else – that's the sign of a faithful printer, isn't it?' he said and went downstairs. When he was gone his cousin came up. 'I've finished the costume business,' she said. 'Where is he?'

'I've sent him down on some business.' This seemed to Srinivas a golden chance to get her to talk. But he dismissed the thought instantly as unworthy. He wanted at best to ask her: 'I heard you were at the office yesterday,' but he suppressed that idea also. He knew it would not be a very sincere question. He would ask it only with a view to getting her to talk about Ravi. But even that seemed to him utterly unworthy. He hated the idea of being diplomatic with so beautiful a creature. So he merely asked: 'Do you like the part you are going to play?'

'Really?' she said. 'I have got to do what is given to me, and I wish to do my best. That's why I get into such a lot of trouble with Sampath over the interpretations. I like to give the most correct one. But we've so little voice in these matters: we shall have to do blindly what the director orders.' During her costume trials she seemed to have disarranged her hair and *sari* ever so slightly and that gave her a touch of mellowness. 'What a pleasure to watch her features!' Srinivas thought. 'No wonder it has played such havoc with Ravi's life.' She didn't pursue the conversation further, but went to a corner and sat there quietly, looking at the sky through the window.

Sampath returned. He looked fixedly at his cousin for a second. She remained looking out of the window. He beckoned to Srinivas to go out with him for a moment and told him, when they were on the terrace: 'I've managed it.'

'Thanks very much,' said Srinivas. 'You will see what wonderful pictures he will draw now ...'

'Well, I hope so, sir. But I hope he will not create complexities here,' he said, glancing in the direction of his cousin.

Ravi's new chief was the director of art and publicity, a large man in a green sporting shirt and shorts, who went about the studio with a pencil stuck behind his ear. He had an ostentatious establishment, a half-glass door, a servant in uniform, and a clerk at the other end of the room. He sat at a glass-topped table on which were focused blinding lights; huge albums and trial-sheets were all over the place. He wore rimless glasses with a dark tassel hanging down. He called this the control room; it was in the heart of the arts and publicity block, and all around him spread a number of rooms in which artists worked, some at their tables and some with their canvases and sheets of paper spread out on the floor.

Sampath walked in two days later, almost leading Ravi by the hand into the hall. 'Well, Director of art and publicity, here I've brought you the best possible artist to help you.' The director looked him benignly up and down and asked: 'Where were you trained?' Ravi was struggling to find an answer when Sampath intervened and said: 'Wouldn't you like to make a guess? See his work and then tell me.'

'Very well,' said the director and rang the bell. His servant appeared. 'Three cups of coffee,' he called out. Ravi muttered an apology. 'No, it's my custom to drink a cup with my assistants at least on the first day,' said the director. After coffee he ceremoniously held out his large palm and said: 'Your room is over there, I will send you instructions.' He pressed a bell again. A boy entered. 'Show him room four.' Ravi followed him out without a word. His docility pleased Sampath. He said: 'Director, he is a good boy .... If I may give you a little advice ...'

'Yes?' began the director, all attention. Sampath wondered for a moment how he could finish the sentence, and then rose to go. 'Oh, nothing, you know how best to handle your boys.' He went out and completed the sentence at Srinivas's office in Kabir

Lane: 'If you don't think it strange of me, I'd like to suggest that you give some advice to Ravi – '

'Yes, what about?' Srinivas asked, looking up.

'Well – ' Sampath drawled, and Srinivas saw that he was awkward and could not say what he had in his mind. This was probably a very rare sight – Sampath unable to speak freely. 'I mean, Editor, I have transferred Ravi as you desired: I want you to do me a little favour in return, that is – well, I suppose, I must say it out. You know Shanti is there. I wish he would keep out of her way as far as possible.'

'He may have to see her in the course of his work.'

'Oh, that doesn't matter at all. That is a different situation. I'm not referring to that, but don't let him – '

'Pursue her or talk to her, isn't that what you wish to say?' asked Srinivas with a twinkle in his eye. Sampath merely smiled, and Srinivas said: 'Well, I don't think he will do anything of the kind, but I will caution him, all the same. Let us hope for the best. In any case, she is a different person. Isn't that so?'

Sampath made a gesture of despair. 'Well, who can say how an artist looks at things? I've always been rather bewildered by Ravi's ways.'

Srinivas waited for Ravi to come home that night. Srinivas heard him arrive in the studio van and then went over and called softly: 'Ravi!' Ravi came out. 'If you are not too tired, let us go out for a short stroll.' 'Very well,' he said. A little sister clung to his arm and tried to go out with him. But he gently sent her back with a promise: 'I will buy you chocolates tomorrow; go in and sleep, darling – ' As they went through the silent Anderson Lane with people sleeping on pyols, talking or snoring, Srinivas wondered how he was to convey the message from Sampath. But he viewed it as a duty. He simply let Ravi follow him in silence for a while. 'How do you like your work?' he asked.

'It is quite good,' Ravi said. 'They leave me alone, and I leave the others alone. I just do what I'm instructed to do. At ten o'clock the van is ready to take me back home, and I come back here. I'm doing a portrait. Come and see it some time, when you are in the studio.'

'I'm very happy to hear it,' said Srinivas. 'What is the subject?'

'My only subject,' Ravi said. 'I've only one subject on this earth, and I'm quite satisfied if I have to do it ...'

'You are not asking for a sitting, are you?' Srinivas asked. In the darkness Srinivas could see Ravi shaking with laughter. 'Sitting? Who wants a sitting? It's all here,' he said, pointing at his forehead, 'and that is enough. I'm doing a large portrait, all in oils – that's a work I'm not paid for, but I'm snatching at it whenever I'm able to find a little time. I'm experimenting with some vegetable colours also, some new colouring matter. My subject must have a tint of the early dawn for her cheeks, the light of the stars for her eyes, the tint of the summer rain-cloud for her tresses, the colour of ivory for her forehead, and so on and on. I find that the usual synthetic stuff available in tubes is too heavy for my job ...'

Srinivas was somewhat taken aback by this frenzy. At the same time he was happy that a picture was coming. He could hardly imagine what it would turn out to be. He felt it would probably convulse the world as a masterpiece, the greatest portrait of the century – to thrill human eyes all over the world. At this moment he felt that any risk they were taking in keeping Ravi there was well worth it. Any sacrifice should be faced now for the sake of this masterpiece. It struck him as a very silly, futile procedure to caution Ravi. A man who followed his instincts so much could not be given a detailed agenda of behaviour. He decided at the moment not to convey to him Sampath's warning. They had now reached Market Road. It was deserted, with a few late shops throwing their lights on the road, and municipal road lights flickering here and there. The sky was full of stars, a cool breeze was blowing. And it appeared to Srinivas a very lovely night indeed. He felt a tremendous gratitude to Ravi for what he was doing or going to do.

Srinivas bade him good-night without saying a word of what Sampath had commissioned him to say. But he decided to take the first opportunity to tell Sampath, since he hated the idea of keeping him under any misapprehension about it. The chance occurred four days later, when Sampath came to his room, ostensibly to discuss some point in the story, but really to ask about

Ravi. His discussion of the story did not last even five minutes. He mentioned a few vague objections about the conclusion of some sequence, and ended by agreeing with every word Srinivas said. He then passed direct to the subject of Ravi. 'You will not mind my coming back to the subject, Editor,' he said. 'Which subject?' asked Srinivas, bristling up. 'I'm very sorry to worry you so much about it,' Sampath said pleadingly. And at once Srinivas's heart melted. He felt a pity for Sampath and his clumsy fears. He looked at him. He had parted his hair in the middle and seemed to be taking a lot of care of his personal appearance. There were a few creases under his eyes. Clearly he was going through a period of anxiety at home, in the studio, about Ravi and about all kinds of things. His personality seemed to be gradually losing its lustre. Srinivas wished that Sampath would once again come to him, not in the silk shirt and muslin *dhoti* and lace-edged upper-cloth which he was flaunting now, but in a faded tweed coat with the scarf flung around his neck, and his fingers stained with the treadle grease. He looked at the other's fingers now. The nails were neatly pared and pointed, his fingers were like a surgeon's, and one or two nails seemed to be touched with the garish horrible red of a nail polish. Srinivas was alarmed to note it and asked: 'What's that red on your finger?' Sampath looked at his finger with a rather scared expression and, trying to cover it up, said in an awkward jumble of words: 'Oh, that cousin of mine; she must have played some joke on me when I was not noticing. She has all kinds of stuff on her table,' he tried to add in a careless way. He flushed and looked so uncomfortable that Srinivas dropped the subject, and went on to talk of what was most in the other's mind: 'I know you want to tell me about Ravi – well, go on.'

'Have you spoken to him about what I said?' Sampath asked.

'I'm not going to,' replied Srinivas, with as little emphasis as possible. 'Things will be all right; don't worry.'

'Listen to my difficulties, please. He is a little conspicuous nowadays. I see him almost every day at the gate; he hangs about the costume section at odd hours.'

'Does it mean that he is not doing his work properly?'

'Oh, no, it wouldn't be fair to say such a thing, but he is a little noticeable here and there.'

'What is wrong with that?' asked Srinivas.

Sampath took time to answer, because there seemed to be an element of challenge in this question. He said: 'There is a studio rule that people should not be seen unnecessarily moving about except where they have business.'

'I guarantee you that he won't go where he has no business,' Srinivas said, and his reply seemed to overwhelm the other for a moment. He remained silent for a little before he said: 'You see, there is this trouble. Even my cousin has noticed it. She said she is oppressed with a feeling of being shadowed all the time. She even remarked: "Who is that boy? I find him staring at me wherever I go. The way he looks at me, I feel as if my nose were on my cheek or something like that." '

'Let her not worry, but just look into a mirror and satisfy herself.'

'But you see it affects her work if she feels that she is being stared at all the time.'

'Sampath, she cannot know she is being stared at unless she also does it – the cure is in her hands. I find her a good girl; tell her not to get ideas into her head, and don't put any there yourself.'

When he next paid a visit to the studio Srinivas went over to meet Ravi. He was not in his seat in room number four. He found him coming out of the works department with an abstracted air. He didn't seem to notice anything around him now. 'I've been to see you,' Srinivas said. He seemed to come back to himself with a start. 'Oh, Editor, I'm sorry I didn't notice you here.'

'I thought I might see your new picture.'

'Oh, that!' He seemed hesitant. 'Let me get on with it a little more. I don't like anyone to see it now.' They were in the little park. 'I am free for about half an hour. Care to sit down for a moment?' he asked. Srinivas followed him. They sat under a bower. De Mello had engaged a garden supervisor who was filling up the place with arcades and bowers and lawns wherever he could grow anything. Ravi sat down and said: 'Something must be done about this gardening department. It is getting on my nerves. This horrible convolvulus creeper everywhere. That garden supervisor is an idiot; he has trained convolvulus up every drainpipe. His gardening sense is that of a forest tribesman.'

'It looks quite pretty,' Srinivas said, looking about him.

'But don't you see how inartistic the whole thing is? There is no arrangement, there is no scheme, no economy. What can we achieve without these?' He looked so deeply moved that Srinivas accepted his statement and theories without a murmur. And Ravi went on: 'Our art director is the departmental head of this gardening section, and he ought to sack the supervisor. But how can we blame him? He is not an artist. You must see the frightful composition he has devised for Parvathi – both her ornaments and settings. He probably wants her to look like a – like a – like a – ' He could not find anything to compare her with, and he abandoned the sentence. He said: 'He is an awful idiot. But I take my orders from him, and obey him implicitly. Let him give me the worst, the most hideous composition, and I execute it gladly without a murmur: I'm paid for that. But let them stop there!' He raised his voice as if warning the whole world. He waggled his fingers as he said: 'Let them stop there. Let them not come near my own portrait: that's my own. I do it in the way I want to do it. No one shall dictate to me what I should do. If I didn't have that compensation I would go mad.' Srinivas found that his mood of calm contentment of a few nights ago during the walk had altered; some dark, irresponsible mood seemed to be coming over him. But Srinivas didn't bother about it. 'It's all in the artist's make-up,' he told himself. Srinivas felt that it was none of his business to pass any comment at the moment. He listened in silence. Ravi said: 'My portrait is come to a blind end, do you know? I'm not able to go on with it: that's why I don't wish to show you anything of it now. I'll tell you what has happened. My director called me up a couple of days ago and told me not to go about the studio unless I'd any definite business anywhere. I felt like hitting him with my fist and asking "Why not?" But I bowed my head and said "Yes, sir", and I have tried to keep myself in confinement. What's the result? I see so little of her now. I can't get even a glimpse of her. How can I work? Even at the gate, while she comes in, the car has side curtains put up. Do you know where I'm coming from now? From the works department, where I have no business at the moment. But there, if I stand on a block of wood – a gilded throne pedestal of some setting really – I can see the courtyard of the costume section which she crosses. That's helped me to clear a point or two, and I shall be able to add something to her portrait today.' A clock struck four, and he sprang up, saying: 'I must leave you now, Editor, there is a publicity conference in the directors' room.' And he sped away.

On the first of the following month Srinivas was wondering to whom he should pay the rent. He had not long to wonder, for a stranger turned up at 6.30 a.m. and woke him. Srinivas opened the front door and saw a middle-aged man, wearing a close alpaca coat and a turban. He remembered seeing the same turban and coat somewhere else and then suddenly saw as in a flash that he had seen his old landlord wear it on the day he was present at the inauguration of their film. Srinivas concluded there was some connexion between this visitor and the old man. He had a pinched face and sharp nose and wore a pair of glasses. 'I'm Raghuram, the eldest son-in-law of your landlord. I've come for the rent.' Srinivas took him in and seated him on a mat, though he was still sleepy. He wondered for a moment if he might send the man away, asking him to return later, while snatching a further instalment of sleep. But his nature would not perpetrate such a piece of rudeness. He sat the man on a mat, and in about fifteen minutes returned to him ready for the meeting.

The stranger said: 'My name is ... and I'm the eldest son-in-law of your late landlord. My father-in-law has assigned this property to my wife, and I shall be glad to have the rent.'

'How is it I have never seen you before?' asked Srinivas.

'You see, my father-in-law was a peculiar man, and we thought it best to leave him alone: he must always go his own way. We'd asked him to come and stop with us, but he did what he pleased.'

'He used to tell me about you all, but he said he had a daughter in Karachi.'

'That is the next sister to my wife. I came early because I didn't know when else to find you.' He looked about uncertainly, eagerly awaiting the coming of the cash. Srinivas did not know how to decide. He went in and consulted his wife as she was scrubbing a brass vessel in the backyard. 'The old man's son-in-law is here; he will be our landlord now. He has come for rent. Shall I give it him?'

'Certainly,' she said, not liking to be interrupted in this job she liked so much. She would give her consent to anything at such a moment. 'Ask him when he is going to give us an independent tap.' Srinivas returned, opened an *almirah*, took out a tiny wooden box, and out of it six five-rupee notes. He put it into his hand. 'Do you want a receipt?' he asked. He pulled out a receipt book, filled it up and gave it to Srinivas. Srinivas said: 'You have to give us an independent water-tap.' 'Haven't you got one? Surely, surely – of course I must give you one, and' – he surveyed the walls and the ceiling – 'yes, we must do everything that's convenient for our tenants.'

During the day, as he sat working in the office, another visitor came – a younger person of about thirty-five. 'You are Mr Srinivas?' he asked timidly, panting with the effort to climb the staircase. He was a man of slight build, wearing a *khadar jiba*, and his neck stood out like a giraffe's. Srinivas directed him to a chair. He sat twisting his button and said: 'I'm a teacher in the corporation high school. I'm your late landlord's son-in-law. My wife has become the owner of this property. I've come for the rent.'

Srinivas showed him the receipt. The visitor was greatly confused on seeing it. 'What does he mean by coming and snatching away the rent in this way?' He got up abruptly and said: 'I can't understand these tricks! My daughter was his favourite, and he set apart all his property for her, if it was going to be for anyone.'

'Your daughter is the one studying in the school?'

He was greatly pleased to hear it. 'Oh, you know about it, then!' He went back to the chair. He lowered his voice to a conspiratorial pitch and asked: 'I say, you will help me, won't you?'

'In what way?'

He rolled his eyes significantly and reduced his speech to a whisper as he said: 'My daughter was his one favourite in life. He mentioned an amount he had set apart for her marriage. Has he

ever mentioned it to you?' He waited with bated breath for
Srinivas's reply, who was debating within himself whether to
speak to him about it or not. Srinivas said finally: 'Yes, he
mentioned it once or twice,' unable to practise any duplicity in
the matter. The visitor became jumpy on hearing it. His eyes
bulged with eager anticipation.

'Where did he keep this amount?' he asked.

'That I can't say,' replied Srinivas. 'I don't know anything
about it.'

The other became desperate and pleaded: 'Don't let me down,
sir, please help me.'

Srinivas looked sympathetic. 'How can I say anything about it?
He mentioned the matter once or twice – I really don't know
anything more.'

'I hear that he has all his money in the Post Office Savings
Bank. Is it true?' Srinivas had once again to shake his head. He
could not help adding: 'It is difficult to get any money, even of
living people, out of the Post Office Savings Bank!'

'Oh, what shall I do about my daughter's marriage?' the visitor
asked sullenly. He looked so concerned and unhappy that Srinivas felt obliged to say: 'If he had lived a little longer, I am sure he
would have done everything for your daughter. He was so fond
of her.'

'Just my luck,' the other said, and beat his brow. 'Why should
he have held up his arrangements?' He complained against sudden death, as if it were a part of the old man's cunning, and
looked completely disgusted with the old man's act of dying. He
got up and said: 'I will look into it. Till then, please don't pay the
rent to anyone else.' He took a step or two, then returned and
said: 'He used to confide in Mr Sampath. Do you think he will
be any use and tell us something?'

'Well, you can try him. He will probably be downstairs. You
can see him as you go.'

Towards evening yet another person came: a tall man, who
introduced himself as the eldest son of the old man.

'I know my father wrote a will. Do you know anything
about it?'

'Sorry, no ...'

The man looked pleased. 'That's right. He wrote only one will and that is with me. If anyone else starts any stunt about any codicils I shall know how to deal with them. It's a pity you have paid the rent for this month. After this don't pay it to anyone else till you hear from me.' Yet another called on him next morning, demanding the rent and a hidden will, and Srinivas began to wonder if he would ever be able to do anything else than answer these people for the rest of his life. 'I hear,' said this latest visitor, 'that he has put everything in the Car Street Post Office Savings Bank. How are we to get at it? He has left no instructions about it.' All this seemed to Srinivas a futile involvement in life. 'Where were all these people before this? Where have they sprung from?' he wondered.

He decided to get clear of their company and its problems, and started looking for a house. But Malgudi being what it was, he could not get another. He forgot that if such a thing were possible he would not have become a tenant of the old man at all, and so he wasted a complete week in searching for a house. His wife had meanwhile become so enthusiastic about it and looked forward to a change with such eagerness that every evening when he came home her first question at the door was: 'What about the house?'

'Doesn't seem to be much use; tomorrow I must try Grove Street and Vinayak Street. And after that – ' She became crest-fallen. Mentally she had accommodated herself in a better house already, and now it seemed to her impossible to live in this house any more. She found everything intolerable: the walls were dirty and not straight, plaster was crumbling and threatening to fall into all the cooked food; the rafters were sooty and dark, the floor was full of cracks and harboured vermin and deadly insects, and, above all, there was a single tap to draw water from. Srinivas listened to her troubles and felt helpless. His son added to the trouble by cataloguing some of his own experiences: 'Do you know, when I was bathing, a tile fell off the roof on my head? There is a pit in the backyard into which I saw a scorpion go,' and so on. They had both made up their minds to quit. The relations of the old man also drove him to the same decision. But no house was available. What could anyone do? He confided his trouble to Sampath. 'We shall manage it easily,' Sampath said, very happy to be set any new task.

The final version of the will which the old man was supposed to have made proved to be a blessing for the moment. When one of the relatives came next, Sampath neither accepted nor denied knowledge of the matter, and very soon had all of them running after him. 'We shall have to convene a lost-will conference,' he said. He was nearly in his old form, and Srinivas was delighted to notice it. Through his finery and tidiness an old light came back to his eyes.

He got the half-dozen relatives sitting around Srinivas's table on a Saturday afternoon. They threw poisoned looks at each other; not one of them seemed to be on speaking terms with the others. Sampath said unexpectedly in a voice full of solemnity: 'We are all gathered today to honour the memory of a noble master.' They could not easily dispute the statement. 'I have had the special honour of being in his confidence. I've had the privilege of learning the secrets of truth. Even in mundane matters, I think, I was one of the few to whom he opened his heart...' Here they looked at each other darkly. 'I must acknowledge my indebtedness to our Srinivas, our editor, for introducing me to the old gentleman.' They once again looked at each other darkly. He added vaguely: 'Let us now pull together – his relations and sons and friends – and do something to cherish the memory of this great soul; that we can do by treating each other liberally and charitably.' Srinivas was amazed at Sampath's eloquence. Presently he came down to practical facts. 'He has left us his houses, his money in the post office, and all the rest that may be his. No doubt, if he had had the slightest inkling of what was coming, he might have made some arrangements for the distribution of his worldly goods. But this I doubt, for after all, for such a saintly man, worldly goods were only an impediment in life and nothing more. He used to quote an old verse:

' "When I become a handful of ash what do I care who takes
      my purse,
Who counts my coins and who locks the door of my safe,
When my bones lie bleaching, what matter if the door of my
      house is left unlocked?"

'However, this is a digression. Now it is up to us to decide what we should do. Here is Srinivas and my other friend Ravi in a portion of the house in Anderson Lane, among the tenants I have most in mind. Now the position is that our editor does not know to whom he should pay the rent.' A babble arose. Sampath silenced them with a gesture and said: 'It's certainly going to someone or everyone; that I don't dispute. It will certainly be decided very soon, but till then, where is he to pay the monthly rent, since he is a man who does not like to keep back a just due?'

'That question is settled,' said several voices. Sampath made an impatient gesture and then said without any apparent meaning: 'Yes, as far as everyone of us is concerned. But where is a tenant to pay in his rent till the question is established beyond a shadow of doubt? My proposal is that till this is established my friends will pay their monthly rents into a Savings Bank account to be specially opened.' There were fierce murmurs on hearing this, and Sampath declared: 'This is the reason why my friend wants to move to another house. He says "How can I live in a house over which people fight?" ' And he paused to watch the effect of this threat on the gathering. They looked bewildered. They need not have been. But somehow, since the remark was delivered as a threat, they were half frightened by it. 'You cannot afford to lose an old, valued tenant,' Sampath added, driving the threat home.

'No, no, we do not want to disturb him,' they all said and looked at each other sourly. 'What we want to know is, where is the will?' asked a voice. 'I thought we had come here about that. Do you know anything about it?' Now all eyes were fixed on Sampath. He replied simply: 'In a delicate matter like this, how can I say anything? I have heard him mention so many things.'

'You need not tell us anything of other things. But, surely, you could tell us about the will,' they cried. Sampath said decisively: 'No. I will not speak of it for two months. By that time whatever there is to be known will be known. Of that I'm certain.'

'Here is the copy of the will, registered by my father. Please examine this, Mr Sampath,' said the eldest son. The others became feverish. Sampath bent over and read out its contents ceremoniously: 'I do hereby bequeath ... and I hold that there is no further will.'

'What about my daughter?' 'What about my share?' 'You certainly were not his dearest one ...' 'Have you forgotten ...' A babble broke out. 'It must be tested in a court and not here,' Sampath said. 'We do not care to be involved in all this. After all, blood relations may quarrel today and unite the day after. It is none of a stranger's business to get involved in such a matter. We will pay the rent to whoever is justly entitled to it ... Meanwhile, whoever thinks that he is entitled to the house, ought to complete all the unfinished business of the old gentleman; he will have to undertake some responsibility; that'll establish his claim.'

'What responsibility?' they asked.

Sampath said: 'There is a car below; please follow me.' He got up. They trooped behind him. They seemed very happy to have the chance of a car ride. They sat crushing each other. Sampath went straight to Srinivas's house. It was like an investigation committee examining the spot. The first thing he said was: 'This is the only source of water for four families – imagine!' And then the various families, including Srinivas's, gathered round and mentioned a list of all their requirements.

The result was: in a few days the block of houses in Anderson Lane became transformed: it only meant a little dislocation for Srinivas – having to shift with his family to his office. When he returned he found the walls scraped and lime-washed, tiles changed, floor smoothed with cement, and an independent water-tap planted in his own backyard; some of the partitions behind Ravi's house were knocked down, and now only three families lived where there had been four or five before. It would not have been easy to investigate and say who was mainly responsible for these changes. All the relations seemed to have vied among themselves to give their tenants amenities. Srinivas's wife was delighted. Sampath said: 'So that settles your problem, Mr Editor. You will have to send your rent to the Savings Bank on the first. They've agreed to it. Meanwhile, the entire gang is going to the court for succession rights. But it's none of our business at the moment.'

One of the most important sequences. Shiva is in a trance. He opens his eyes and keeps looking at Parvathi. Vague desires stir in him. He looks into his own mind for the reason. Till today he was able to receive her ministrations with absolute detachment, but today he finds himself interested in her. He feels that there is some mischief afoot and looks for the reason, and he espies in a corner the God of Love aiming his shaft at him, and burns him up immediately; then he resumes his meditation.

This was filmed and projected on the screen. They lounged in their comfortable cushion chairs, lit their cigarettes and watched in silence. Somu, Sampath, Sohan Lal, who was buying the picture, De Mello, and a number of technicians in the back row. The operator in his cabin was tired of mechanically throwing the same reel on the screen over and over again. Somu was the first to break the gloomy silence. He asked Mr Lal: 'Well, what do you say, Mr Lal?'

Lal said: 'It's no good. I shall be obliged if you will retake it. It is lacking in something.'

'It's lacking in pep, if I may put it in a word,' added De Mello. 'There is a lot of scope for working up this sequence on the right lines. I agree with Mr Sohan Lal.'

'Well, if everyone thinks the scene must be retaken, we've got to do it, that is all. The script will have to be rewritten.' They all looked at Srinivas. 'Do you think that the scene can be rewritten?'

'How?' asked Srinivas, trying to look as calm and considerate as possible. He felt pity for them, for the hunted look they wore. They were dealing with things beyond them, and the only pressure was commerce. He tried to sympathize with them and suppress the indignation that was rising within him. His question remained unanswered. They looked at each other in a frightened way and whimpered uncomfortably. It was De Mello who plucked up enough strength to say: 'Perhaps a dance act will serve the purpose: that will appeal to the public.'

'Yes,' agreed Sohan Lal. 'A dance act would be excellent. This picture needs some entertainment.'

'The comedy is there,' said Somu, for he was particularly proud of this contribution. Srinivas tried not to hear, for his blood boiled whenever he thought of those comic scenes. He had detached himself from them early; and Sampath and Somu had hatched them between themselves, shot them separately, and cut them up and scattered them like spice all along the story. He found that some of the most sublime moments he had conceived faded into the horseplay of Gopu and Mali and their suggestive by-play. They were the highest-paid comedians on the films, and they propped up any picture by this means. The public always flocked to see them and hear their gags. Somu was highly gratified with his own efforts. To his remark Sohan Lal replied: 'Well, that's only comedy. We must have an entertainment item like a dance sequence.' And they decided to convert this scene into a dance act, and they at once called up a number of people from various parts of the studio. Srinivas accepted the position with resignation. He only exerted himself to the extent of refusing to write the scene any further. This was one of his favourite scenes. By externalizing emotion, by superimposing feeling in the shape of images, he hoped to express very clearly the substance of this episode: of love and its purification, of austerity and peace. But now they wanted to introduce a dance sequence. Srinivas found himself helpless in this world. He tried not to take a too tragic view of the situation. He wanted to avoid further tortures to his mind, and so leaned over and whispered to Sampath: 'I'm going. I don't have to explain why?'

'Yes, yes,' said Sampath, and Srinivas went out. He walked along the open drive of the studio. So many people, so busily engaged, and going from place to place with a serious preoccupied air for at least ten hours in the day. 'With this manner of theirs, why can't they do something worth while?' he reflected and went on. He came to the art and publicity block.

In his room Ravi was busily working on a publicity poster. He was sitting on the ground with a huge board leaning against the wall. He was clutching a brush in his hand. A huge outline of Shanti was pencilled, and he was colouring it. It seemed to be an enlargement of the little pencil sketch he had done long ago. Its eyelashes were so full of life, its eyes shone so much with light, and a ray of light reflected off a diamond in the ear; it was coloured so elegantly that it seemed a masterpiece worthy to hang in any art gallery. Srinivas stood admiring it.

'How do you like it?' Ravi asked.

'Is this the portrait you mentioned?'

'Oh, no, this is only a poster for a theatre gate. The other's in oils and is my own.'

'Where is it?'

'There, turned to the wall.' Srinivas saw the back of a wooden board in a far-off corner. He made a motion towards it, asking: 'May I see it?'

'Oh, no, it'll probably be years before I can let anyone see it ...' He put away the brush, sat down in a chair and said: 'It gives me a feeling of being near her when I do this. I want nothing else in life when I'm doing her picture, even if it is only a poster. Do you think he is quite truthful in saying that she is different?'

'Don't you worry about all that,' Srinivas implored.

'I am not worrying. I see her going home every day, sitting close to Sampath and touching him; they are always together. He doesn't allow me to approach her at all. Does he take me for a fool?' he laughed bitterly. 'I'm not going to talk to her, even if she comes and speaks to me. She is pretending she is someone else.'

'Don't keep brooding over all that, Ravi; you do your work and forget the rest.'

'Practically what I'm doing now. What else should I do? As long as I'm doing a portrait like this, even if it is only a poster, I'm at peace. Let that fellow keep her to himself, I don't care; I've got something better out of her.'

All round the room there were preliminary advertisement layouts. One of them said: 'Golden opportunity to see God himself.' Ravi pointed at the caption and said: 'How do you like the lettering? This is the advertisement slogan I'm asked to write out.'

'God has never had a worse handling anywhere.'

Ravi merely shrugged his shoulders. 'What do I care? I just do what I'm asked. If they want me to write "I'm an unmatched fool", I will provide the required lettering for it. What do I care? I tell you, we have an art director who is fit only to be a clock-winder in the studio. He cannot even draw a straight line or a curve, but yet he is our boss, and we get our salary only if he approves of our work.' He laughed uncontrollably. The veins on his forehead stood out like pipes, and he spoke loudly. He was very careless in his talk and seemed to want to challenge every-body with his remarks. He did not bother either to subdue his voice or speak discreetly. He seemed to have become very garrulous, too. This Srinivas suddenly noticed in him; and he also saw that his complexion was turning yellow and waxen. 'I say, you must take care of your health. Why are you neglecting yourself in this way?' Ravi made a wry face at the thought of looking after himself. He got up, looked at himself in a looking glass on the wall with distaste. 'This is the best that can be done about you, my dear chap,' he said, addressing himself. 'Don't demand further concessions. You are being treated better than you really deserve.' And he once again broke into a laugh. He interrupted it to explain: 'You see, my director wants a dozen different advertisement posters to be ready, and then we have the actual work on the sets. I go on working here all night nowadays. I have not been home.' A shiver ran through him at the thought of his home. 'I prefer this place. My father has completely given up talking to me. He becomes so rigid when he hears my voice at home that I fear he will have a seizure some day. Of course, he keeps hectoring my poor mother, and that is the worst of it. But for those young fellows and my mother,' he said reflectively, 'I should have blasted my so-called home ages ago.'

'You aren't free to come out for a moment, I suppose?'

'Where to?' asked Ravi.

'Come to my house. I will give you good coffee and some-thing to eat. You can rest there and return to the studio when-ever you want.' Ravi revolved the offer in his mind and rejected it. 'I have to finish three different styles of this god notice before tonight.' And he settled down resolutely.

At home Srinivas's wife said: 'Do you know, Sampath's wife was here this afternoon?'

'How did she come all this way? You have not seen her before?'

'No, she managed to come in a car. What a lot of daughters she has.'

'Why, do you envy her?' Srinivas asked, and she replied: 'What is there to joke about in all this! She came on a very serious business. She wants me to speak to you about her husband.'

'What about him?'

'It seems that their household has become impossible. There is that woman who is playing Parvathi. He is always with her.'

'He is her cousin.'

'It seems they are not cousins. They are of different castes.'

'What if they are?' Srinivas asked, thinking what an evil system caste was. She flared up. 'Let her be any caste she pleases, but what business has she to come and ruin that family? They were so happy before. Now he doesn't care for the house at all. He is always with her. And it seems now that he is threatening to marry her and set up another household. The poor girl has been crying for days now. You have got to do something about her.' She was so much worked up and became so vehement that Srinivas felt that he ought to speak to Sampath.

Srinivas waited for an opportunity to meet Sampath alone at the studio. He was always with Shanti, except when she went in to dress or into the women's make-up room, when he hung about Sohan Lal, who had still to pay him a lakh and a half. The mastery of the studio was now gradually passing into the hands of Sohan Lal, and Sohan Lal was completely absorbed in arranging the dance act. Sampath was told: 'Give me the dance act completed, and I will pay the first half of the agreed amount.' And if he received that lakh and a half, Sampath was going to buy up the interests of Somu also and become virtually the owner of the picture; then he would put on hand another picture almost at once. So it was in his interest to complete the dance act as quickly as possible, and night and day he was being dragged hither and thither to complete it. Sohan Lal was dogging his steps, and he dogged the steps of Sohan Lal, and Somu went round and round these two, hoping for the completion of the dance act, when he, too, hoped to get various payments made to him. It was, on the whole, a very intricate mechanism of human relationships. In this maze Srinivas walked about unscathed, because he had trained himself to view it all as a mere spectator. This capacity saved him all the later shocks. He saw, without much flutter, the mangling that was going on with his story. The very process by which they mangled his theme attracted him, and he moved from room to room, studio to studio, through floor-space and setting, labora-tory and sound processing and moviola, into the projection room, watching, and he very soon accommodated himself to the notion that they were doing a picture of their own entirely unconnected with the theme he had written.

It was difficult to get at Sampath alone. All the same, when they were passing from their discussion chamber to the second studio to see a test arrangement for the dance act, he managed to ask him: 'Please spare me fifteen minutes.'

Sampath looked at him in pained surprise. He was wearing a silk shirt with gold studs, and on his wrist gleamed a platinum watch, bound with a gold strap. He wore a pair of spectacles nowadays. 'Every sign of prosperity is there,' Srinivas remarked to himself. 'All except your old personality, which is fast vanish-ing.' He went everywhere now by car, and that habit had given him a new rotundity. Srinivas felt like saying: 'I do hope you will not acquire the appearance of Mr Somu in due course. Pull yourself together in time.'

'Anything urgent?'

'Absolutely,' Srinivas said.

'I will free myself after seeing the dance test. It won't take ten minutes. Come along, have a look at it.' Srinivas excused himself and stayed behind in the garden. Presently Sampath came down. 'This dance idea is very good, you know. It is going to make the picture top-class, the most artistic production in India. We may even send it abroad. Of course, you are not annoyed about these changes, are you?'

'Not at all; why should I worry about it?'

'We are only taking liberties with the details, you know, but we are keeping to your original in the main treatment.'

'Oh, yes, yes,' Srinivas said, feeling that this was the familiar eyewash every film-maker applied to every writer. 'It's not about that that I wish to trouble you now. It's about another matter.' He mentioned it gently, apologetically. At first Sampath pooh-poohed the entire story. But later said, with his old mischievous look coming back to his eyes: 'Some people say that every sane man needs two wives – a perfect one for the house and a perfect one outside for social life ... I have the one. Why not the other? I have confidence that I will keep both of them happy and if necessary in separate houses. Is a man's heart so narrow that it cannot accommodate more than one? I have married according to Vedic rites: let me have one according to the civil marriage law ....'

'Is it no use discussing it?'

'I'm afraid not, Mr Editor .... You will forgive me. I love her, though you may not believe it.'

'How can you ever forget that you are a father of five?'

'As I have told you, man's heart is not a narrow corner.'

'Think of your wife.'

'Oh, these women will make a scene. She will be all right. She must get used to it.' He remained for a moment brooding, but soon set himself right, saying airily: 'It's her nature to fuss about things sometimes. But she always changes for the better. I've been meaning to tell you about it, Mr Editor, but somehow – '

'I can't say that I'm very happy to hear this news, Sampath. I do hope you will think it over deeply,' said Srinivas, feeling a little uncomfortable at having to sound so pontifical. He got up. 'You have to take into consideration the future of all your five children.'

'Oh.' Sampath remained brooding. 'Well, I'm going to have different establishments. I'm doing nothing illegal, to feel apologetic. After all, our religion permits us to marry many wives.'

'Yes, no law forbids you to have more than one head, so why not try and grow as many as you can?' asked Srinivas. 'Let me be frank: I'm convinced that you are merely succumbing to a little piece of georgette, powder and curves. You have no right to cause any unhappiness to your wife and children.'

'Well, sir,' Sampath said with mock humility. 'Here goes my solemn declaration that my wife and children shall lack nothing in life, either in affection or comfort. Will this satisfy you? If I buy Shanti a car my wife shall have another; if I give her a house I will give the other also a house; it will really be a little expensive duplicating everything this way, but I won't mind it. Later on, when they see how much it is costing me, I'm sure they will bury the hatchet and become friends again ...'

It was the great day of shooting the dance act. They were determined to complete the act in about twelve hours of continuous shooting, starting at six in the evening. The studio was stirring into tremendous activity.

On the floor of Stage A a gorgeous Kailas was standing – the background of ice peaks was painted by the art department. All the previous night and throughout the day Ravi had sat up there and painted it; foliage, cut and propped up, stood around. Shiva, with his matted hair and a cobra around his neck, sat there in the shade of a tree in meditation. De Mello, script in hand, was roving about giving instructions. The sound-van outside was all ready to record. Assistants stood around, fingering switches and pushing up screens and running to and fro. The make-up assistant constantly ran forward and patted the cheeks of the artists. De Mello stepped on the trolley, put his eye to the camera and cried: 'Light – four – seven – baby – seventeen.' As Shiva sat there in the full glare of several lights, Parvathi came up to him from a side wing. Sampath grew excited at the sight of her. Sohan Lal, Somu and Sampath sat up in their canvas chairs and viewed her critically. Sampath cried: 'Shanti, move on a little more gradually,' and she adjusted her steps. He ordered a make-up assistant: 'Push away that lock of hair on her forehead, so that it doesn't dangle right in the centre.' He tilted his head to one side and surveyed her as the assistant went up to carry out the instruction. Somu murmured: 'Yes, you are right. If the hair is too artificially made up it spoils the effect.' Sampath went to the camera and applied his eye to the view-finder. He stood there, looking for a long time at Shanti, and murmured: 'I think you had better remove the foliage behind her.' He took his eye from the finder so as to enable De Mello to view her. He stood there for a long time and said: 'It's O.K. now', making some adjustment with the camera. He went up the stage to readjust the branch of a tree. 'Yes, we shall have a final rehearsal now,' said Sampath, 'Ready!' he cried. Lights were wheeled about. He looked at them with bored indifference. As they were getting into position he went over and spoke a few words to Shanti, while she remained standing at her post. 'Do you want a chair?' he asked her, and carried a chair for her. 'How long am I to keep like this?' she asked complainingly, and he said: 'This is the final rehearsal. We will take it; just one more rehearsal.' She made a wry face and sat down. Beads of perspiration stood on her pink painted face. Sampath beckoned to an assistant and had her face dabbed as she sat motionless like a piece of lumber.

'Can I have an iced drink?'

'Oh, no!' He threw up his arms in alarm. 'No ice for you till this is over – not for the entire season.'

She looked agonized on hearing it and made a wry face again and grumbled: 'You never give me anything I want – never.' Into their banter came the voice of Lord Shiva, who had been asked to sit rigid in a corner and who had been left neglected by everyone. 'I want to go out for a moment,' he said. His face was streaming with perspiration; his matted locks and beard were fierce, no doubt, but his eyes were bloodshot with fatigue. He tried to move in his seat. 'Don't move,' Sampath commanded him. 'You have another rehearsal; it's going to be difficult to focus your place again.'

'My legs are cramped, and I can't sit any more.'

'Don't talk back,' commanded Sampath. All the others looked at each other in consternation. 'I'm not only talking back, but I'm going out – out of this.' Shiva got up. Somu felt that he must smooth out the situation, and so said: 'Don't get excited, please; let no one get excited. We must all pull together.' Shiva's eyes (real ones, and not the third one on the forehead) blazed with anger as he said: 'I've borne this with patience: five or six days of continuous rehearsals. Do you want to kill us with rehearsals? And yet you are not satisfied.'

'Be calm, my dear fellow,' said Somu, patting his back, and De Mello on the other side tried to pacify him.

'Leave me alone!' cried Shiva in rage. 'All this sequence has already been shot, and yet you want to retake it – why?'

'We're not prepared to explain,' said Sampath. 'You had better read again your contract, particularly with reference to retakes and rehearsals. Our agreement is clear on that point. If you talk any further about it, it will go against you, remember.'

Shiva was not to be cowed so easily. He said, almost grinding his teeth: 'Yes, but an ordinary retake is different: now you have included two songs and a full-scale dance act. It's not in our agreement.'

Sohan Lal tried to pacify the fighters now in his own way. 'We must not quarrel over such small matters. Of course, you take a lot of trouble, we all appreciate it. Every film is a co-operative effort.' Shiva, who tried to follow this conversation in order to find any useful suggestion, was more enraged when he found on analysis that there was nothing in it. He lost his head completely. He came towards the camera and said: 'If you pay me another five thousand rupees I'm prepared to go through this act, rehearsals and all, otherwise no.'

'Why should you ask for extra pay, mister? You must not,' said Sohan Lal.

'Why not? I'm labouring for it!' cried Shiva passionately. 'And I am entitled to it.'

'It is unthinkable!' cried Sampath and Somu in one voice.

'Not unthinkable in her case, I suppose?' Shiva cried, pointing at Parvathi, sitting on her chair and fanning herself. 'Aren't you giving her five thousand extra? Do you think I don't know all that?' He came towards the producers menacingly. Somu shrank back a little; Sampath stepped forward, rolling up his sleeve. 'What are you up to?' The other checked himself. Sampath asked in a tone of finality: 'Are you going through this or not?'

'I have said my say. Are you going to revise my contract?'

'I don't want conditions. We may give you more or we may not. Leave all that to our discretion. At the moment I won't have you talk of any such things on the set. Are you going to your place or not?'

'I'm not.'

'Very well, get out of here,' he thundered.

'Give me my salary; I will go,' said Shiva, descending from Kailas defiantly.

'That'll be settled in a court of law. You have violated a contract, and you will have to face the consequences.'

'What injustice is this!' cried Shiva, completely losing his head.

Sampath told De Mello: 'De Mello, take him out of the studio. I don't want any further indiscipline in this studio,' and De Mello assigned a couple of assistants to lead Shiva out. Sampath subsided in his chair, exhausted by the effort. There remained a strained silence as everybody waited, and top-light boys looked down from their platforms, and assistants stood hushed at their posts. Somu was the first to break the uncomfortable silence. He said timidly: 'Well, Mr Sampath, what shall we do now?'

'Leave that to me,' Sampath said grandly. 'We need not be at the mercy of these mercenaries. I will do Shiva myself. I've been an actor once.'

He looked up at the make-up artist and asked: 'You can make me up for Shiva?' The artist looked at him critically and said: 'Yes, sir.'

'But the dance, sir?' Somu said.

'We've bothered our heads with it for four days. I always felt that we might do it ourselves, save all trouble instead of trying to teach it to these fools. What do you say, Dance Master?'

'Yes, sir, they do not easily learn.'

Sohan Lal said: 'We must always be ready to do many things.' And then he spoke for a long while with Sampath in his western Indian dialect, and Sampath smiled and said something in reply. Sohan Lal was perhaps recounting a reminiscence of a similar nature. Sampath went over to Shanti and said: 'So sorry. Further delay. Forgive us, dear. I'll be ready in a moment. You can relax for half an hour in your room, while they make me up.'

Some time later when Srinivas came into the studio he was surprised at being greeted by the familiar voice: 'Hallo, Editor, don't be shocked!' But it came from within a heavy beard and matted locks. 'Sampath! What is the matter?' He wore a tiger's skin at his loins.

'Well, people do not realize that no one is indispensable in this world,' he said and explained the position. Sampath's versatility took his breath away.

'We are determined to finish this scene today, even if it is going to mean twenty-four hours of continuous shooting.'

'You have to wear a cobra around your neck.'

'Yes, yes, I know; we've got that tame one, I tried it: it is not bad, though it feels unearthly cold at the first touch.'

'Play back! Play back!' Sampath shouted presently. 'Sound!' He went over and gave instructions to De Mello, who stood at the camera, and then went to Shiva's seat on Kailas. A song blared forth from the loud-speaker – a song with a sentimental lilt, and drums producing a kind of hot-air rhythm. The music department fully realizing the need of the hour had produced a brand-new tune by adapting a couple of tunes born in Hollywood from a South American theme. Srinivas despaired on hearing it. It produced anything but the holy-of-holies feeling that he had hoped would be the essence of the scene. As he saw Somu and Lal tapping their feet instinctively to the music he was filled with a desperation which he could not easily place or classify. Other feet picked up the rhythm, and presently he saw Sampath slowly stirring in his meditation. He rose to his feet. He twisted and wriggled his body and assumed the pose of a dance-carving one saw on temple walls. He moved step by step and approached the chair, which marked Parvathi's place.

'Cut!' rang out De Mello's voice. 'This will be the first cut,' he explained. Shiva relaxed his rigid pose. 'Call Parvathi!' he ordered.

People went out and returned, followed by Parvathi, with her anklets jingling and very modern ear-drops swinging on her ear-lobes and a crown scintillating on her brow. She stood there in her place. Once again the cry 'Music!' and 'All lights' and 'Final rehearsals'; and lights shot up all around, and Srinivas noted how cunningly they had managed to make her clothes unnecessary by the No. 10 light, which shot up a beam of illumination from behind her at ground level. 'What ingenuity!' he commented to himself. Her body stood out as if X-rayed, her necklace and diadem glittered and shone and seemed to be the only apparel she wore. Everyone, the principals in canvas chairs, went over to the camera to look through the view-finder and shake their heads with academic approval. There was suddenly a small discussion on the same academic level.

'Will the censors pass this?'

'Censors! What have they to object to? It's only artistic. At that rate they should stop all dances and Bharata Natya; while professors and ministers are clamouring everywhere that we should revive our classical art – ' another said.

'Lights off!' rang the voice, and switches pit-patted.

'We will have a final rehearsal and take the first shot afterwards.'

'Music!'

Music – the South American tune – started once again. Shiva got up from his trance and executed his slow rhythmic steps, but Parvathi stood still, and when they questioned her about it pleaded: 'No rehearsals are necessary for me. Don't tire me, please.' Shiva opened his eyes for a moment to say: 'Yes, don't tire her out.'

'Yes, yes, it is better that you don't tire her out,' repeated three more voices, catching the contagion. Everybody seemed to be saying the same thing and feeling the same way. And then they sounded a buzzer and stopped the music. Shiva returned to his place and sat under the tree once again in meditation. He said: 'De Mello, get ready to shoot. Call in the extras, Parvathi's companions. Fetch the cobra.'

Lights were once again wheeled about, with their little wheels creaking, porters moved hither and thither, assistants took out their long entry-books and made notes, make-up assistants dashed backward and forward: the cameraman and his assistants disposed themselves around the camera like sentries on duty. Someone went up with a tape and measured, someone else held up an exposure guide over Parvathi's nose – elaborate rites of a very curious tribe, with their own high priests and medicine men. 'This is really an anthropological specimen,' Srinivas thought. His reflections were interrupted by the entry of Ravi at this stage. He came in bearing a portfolio in his hand and was waiting for an opportunity to catch the eye of the art director, who was busy on the set, making some final readjustment to the heavenly background. Seeing Srinivas, Ravi edged up to him and whispered: 'I have to get his approval for a design and send it up for block-making immediately.'

'He seems reluctant to get down from yonder heaven,' whispered Srinivas, but found no response. Ravi's eye was caught by the figure of Parvathi, and he looked hypnotized. Srinivas wanted to jerk him back to his normal state and asked: 'What is that thing in your file?' Ravi answered absently: 'Design and lettering.'

'Is it urgent?'

'Yes – yes,' replied Ravi, without looking at him, with his eye still on Parvathi, who was now fanning herself. He stood transfixed. 'That is Sampath,' he whispered. 'See the cobra around his neck!' A live cobra was coiled about his throat, where he formerly wore his scarf, and it was making imperceptible gliding movements. Srinivas felt that he must say something to draw away Ravi's attention, searched about for a remark, and could only say: 'What a dangerous thing!'

'It has no fang, unfortunately!' remarked Ravi. Srinivas felt that he had made a blunder, and hastened to repair it with some other remark, but all to no purpose. Ravi stood as if transfixed, with his eyes on Parvathi and answering in monosyllables. Srinivas: 'Shall we go to the canteen for something? I feel rather parched.'

'No. I've got to get that fellow's approval.'

'Ready!' went up a cry. A whistle rang out. The extras lined up behind Parvathi and Shiva. 'Silence!' rang out another cry. 'Lights! All lights.' The lights flashed out, X-raying the dancer once again. 'Music!' Music started. 'Start! Silence.' The camera was switched on. Each man was at his post. The music squeezed all sense out of people and only made them want to gyrate with arms around one another. Shiva went forward, step by step; Parvathi advanced, step by step: he was still in a trance with his eyes shut, but his arms were open to receive her. Shanti's brassière could be seen straining under her thin clothes. She bent back to fit herself into the other's arms. The Mexican melody worked up a terrific tempo. All lights poured down their brilliance. Scores of people stood outside the scene, watching it with open-mouthed wonder.

It was going to be the most expert shot taken. The light-boys looked down from their platforms as if privileged to witness the

amours of gods. If the camera ran on for another minute the shot
would be over. They wanted to cut this shot first where Shiva's
arms went round the diaphanous lady's hips. But it was cut even a
few seconds earlier in an unexpected manner. A piercing cry,
indistinguishable, unworded, like an animal's, was suddenly
heard, and before they could see where it originated, Ravi was
seen whizzing past the others like a bullet, knocking down the
people in his way. He was next seen on the set, rushing between
Shiva's extended arms and Parvathi, and knocking Shiva aside
with such violence that he fell amidst his foliage in Kailas in a
most ungodly manner. Next minute they saw Parvathi struggling
in the arms of Ravi, who was trying to kiss her on her lips and
carry her off ....

They soon realized that this scene was not in the script. Cries
rang out: 'Cut.' 'Power.' 'Shut down.' 'Stop.' And several people
tried to rush into the scene. Ravi attempted to carry off his prize,
though she was scratching his face and biting his hands. In the
mess someone tripped upon the cables and all the lights went out.
Ravi seemed to be seized with a superhuman power. Nobody
could get at him. In the confusion someone cried: 'Oh! Camera,
take care!' 'Lights, lights, fools!' Somebody screamed: 'The cobra
is free; the cobra is creeping here, oh!' People ran helter-skelter
in the dark. While they were all searching and running into each
other they could hear Ravi's voice lustily ringing out in another
part of the studio. And all ran in his direction.

He was presently heard saying: 'She has slipped away again.
Bring her, do you hear me?' His voice rose and filled the whole
place in the dark. 'I'm not to be cheated again. She is – ' He
uttered aloud a piece of ribaldry. 'And if anyone goes near her
I will murder him.' And he let out a whoop of joy and cried: 'Ah,
here she is.' And somebody else cried: 'Oh, he has got me,'
amidst other noises. There was the noise of a struggle in the
dark. 'Leave me, leave me – oh, save me,' some 'extra' girl
screamed. And the crowd rushed in her direction. In the mean-
time one or two candles were brought in, and by their flickering
light, people moved about in the direction of Ravi's voice. But
the moment they came there, Ravi's voice was heard in another
part of the building challenging them. In this pale light Srinivas

could be seen trying to follow Ravi and persuade him – persuade him to do what? Srinivas wondered in the middle of it all. He was blindly running along with the rest of them, catching the mood of the mob. It was evident that for most people now this was an exciting diversion, though the two who looked maddened and panicky were Sampath and Somu. Sampath had still Shiva's matted locks on his crown, and the tiger's skin girt his loins, but he looked despondent; even in that feeble light of a single candle his eyes looked care-worn and anxious as he paused to say: 'Editor, what is this! What devil has seized him! We are ruined. Do something. Stop him – ' Ravi like a shadow was seen racing up a flight of steps. 'Oh, he is going into the storage. Stop him, stop him.' Somu's portly figure was hurrying towards the stairs. He was seen going up a few steps, when Ravi turned swiftly on his heel with a war cry and tried to fling himself on him; and Somu, startled beyond description, stood arrested for the fraction of a second, and turned and ran down again at full speed. This was the first time anyone had seen Somu running; and people forgot their main pursuit for a moment in watching this spectacle. Sohan Lal came up from somewhere, moving along with the general stream of the crowd and cried into Srinivas's face: 'I should not have given that advance on the picture. Now what is to happen to my money?' Somu was crying: 'Sampath! Sampath!' pointlessly in the dark. Srinivas felt so dumbfounded by everything that he merely stopped where he was, leaning for rest on one of the creeper-covered shed walls. 'Can't you get some more candles?' someone shouted. 'They are all required near the fuse-box.'

'Which fool is responsible for this?' Sampath cried somewhere. 'Carrying open lamps!' He ordered all the candles to be put out. And utter darkness enveloped them again.

De Mello was the only person who seemed to plan the campaign with any intelligence. He conducted himself as though such things were a part of the ordinary Hollywood training. 'There is no need to lose our heads over this,' he was heard saying again and again. 'It is only a mishap.' With a handful of picked men from the works section, armed with sticks, he surrounded the block and led the procession up the staircase.

He proceeded stealthily, flashing his torch. 'Not enough torches to go round. That is our chief handicap.' He tiptoed into the top room, as if going into a tiger cage when the tiger was not looking. There was for a moment no sound after he went in. People down below held their breaths and waited with anxious faces. Presently the door opened and De Mello appeared on the landing and declared: 'He is not here.'

'Not there! What do you mean, not there, Mr De Mello?'

De Mello shouted something back and added: 'God knows, vanished probably through the window. He has made a frightful mess. Come up, please.'

They hesitated, trying to pluck up courage to go. Sampath moved a step or two, when a man came down. 'Shanti has swooned. She has a cut on her forehead – bleeding.' Sampath exclaimed: 'Ah! Ah! Get a doctor,' and vanished from the spot. Meanwhile Somu gripped Srinivas's hand and cried: 'Please come up and see, sir.'

'Yes, yes, it is better you come up and see also,' added Sohan Lal, taking his other arm. Srinivas allowed himself to be steered. There was no need to question the relevancy of any action. This was not the moment for it.

This block contained the laboratory, storage, editing and allied departments, full of shelves, tables, wheels, troughs – all kinds of apparatus resembling an alchemist's workshop.

The torch flashed and went out as they examined their surroundings. Somu cried in despair: 'Can't someone get a torch which doesn't go out?' The floor was strewn with broken bottles, chemicals and salt and trailing lengths of film. 'Be careful! Broken glass,' De Mello warned. Somu snatched a flashlight, stooped to the floor, picked up a film and held it up. They saw a close-up of Shanti, and farther along Shiva on Kailas, with dirt and scratches on both of them. 'Who left the negatives about so carelessly?' Somu thundered, glaring from his kneeling position on the floor. No one answered. All questions at this moment were destined to die without an answer.

'Well, sir, no one is particularly responsible for this; it's usual to keep the cut negatives in these racks. Nothing unusual,' said De Mello. Somu grunted and said: 'Our loss must be heavy.' He felt like saying a few other things, but somehow feared that he might hurt De Mello. He was too cautious even now. He suppressed many pungent remarks that rose to his lips, and merely said: 'Won't someone get a light?' In answer to this they heard a thundering command go forth. 'Here! Get Shanti and all her lights!'

Somu looked about panic-stricken and cried: 'He is here, get the light quick!'

'Get Shanti lights!' echoed the command. De Mello flashed his torch and saw Ravi crouching under a table, his eyes sparkling in the torch light. De Mello acted quickly, too quickly even for Ravi. He just stooped, thrust his hand in and pulled Ravi out. Somu shivered and tried to run. He became hysterical and chattered incoherently. Ravi struggled in De Mello's grip and mumbled: 'You are hurting. Love me, darling. Love me, darling,' he said in a sing-song. 'Darling, love me. Love is lust. Lust is portrait in oils, Editor. And all his colour of rain. What colour is lust?' In reply to all this, De Mello's left fist shot out, hit him under the chin, and knocked him down flat.

The lights were ablaze once again at 5 a.m. The police arrived in a van soon after.

The major part of the next four days Srinivas spent in running between the Market Road Police Station and his home.

Ravi's household was in a turmoil. His father was mad with rage, his mother wrung her hands helplessly, and even the little brothers and sisters looked stunned.

After his outburst Ravi became docile and uncommunicative. He didn't seem to recognize anyone. When Srinivas addressed him through the bars, Ravi would not even turn in his direction. His look had no fixed point. He kept muttering something to himself under his breath. No one could follow the sense of it. It sounded like the language of another planet.

Srinivas became familiar with the comings and goings of the police station. He saw a policeman pushing in a *jutka* driver for some traffic offence; he saw an urchin brought in and sent away with a couple of slaps on his face; he saw a terrified villager brought in for questioning and pushed away somewhere out of sight. All the while a sergeant sat at a table, implacably writing

on brown forms, except when a bulky inspector came in swinging a short cane, when he stood up respectfully and saluted.
Ravi sat hunched up in a corner seeing nothing, hearing nothing,
but occupied with his own repetitions. Srinivas carried him food
every day in a brass vessel. He had the lock-up opened, went in,
sat beside Ravi and persuaded him to eat the food. Ravi seemed
to have forgotten the art of eating. Srinivas attempted to feed
him with a spoon, but even that was difficult. He kept a morsel
on his tongue and swallowed only when he was persistently told
to do so. It was an odd spectacle — Srinivas sitting there in
that dark corner beyond the bars, coaxing Ravi to eat, as the
Market Road babble continued outside. Sampath came on
the evening of the fourth day and stood watching the scene
through the bars. He had a few scratches on his face and he limped
slightly: otherwise there was no sign of the recent events. He still
wore his smart silk shirt and gold studs. He stood watching silently
till Srinivas finished the feeding and came out. Sampath said with a
sigh: 'It was an evil hour that brought me and Ravi together.
I never knew that a fellow could go so mad. Won't you come out?
Let us sit in the car and talk.' Srinivas followed him to the car
outside. Sampath opened the door and sat down in the driver's
seat with Srinivas beside him. It was five in the evening, and
traffic rolled past them. The babble of the market place kept a
continuous background to their talk as Sampath said: 'I couldn't
see you for three or four days, Mr Editor. There has been so
much to do, mainly checking up the damage! Why should a
thing like this happen to us?' Srinivas remained silent, feeling
that an answer was beyond him. Sampath said with the air of a
martyr: 'I've only been trying to do him a good turn and yet ...
You know our losses?'

'Must be heavy,' Srinivas said casually, determined to discour-
age martyrdom at all costs.

'Damage to the settings, chemicals, lights, films exposed, and so
on; we shall have to retake several shots. It is amazing how much
havoc one man could do within an hour. It will be days before we
set the studio right again. More than all this — Shanti. She is so
much shaken that she will be unfit for work for many weeks. She
swore she would never come near the studio again. I couldn't

mention the word "studio" without her getting hysterical. This would have been our greatest blow, but thank God, since yesterday she has grown calmer! I know I can manage her. She needs complete rest before she can return to work. But I'm sure she will be all right, and we will complete the film yet. Not a hundred Ravis can stop us from doing our work. Well, you will see us all up and doing once again. I'm sorry, though, to see that boy there, but I always felt he was not quite sound.'

'I wanted to see you about him, too. Will you withdraw your complaint? He should be in a hospital, not in prison,' pleaded Srinivas.

'But – but – ' Sampath hesitated.

'He will not come near you or the studio. I will guarantee you that.'

'Somu has lost his head completely. He is dead set on pursuing the matter.'

'You had better explain to him how silly it will be and that he will gain nothing by it. Please withdraw your complaint. You will not be troubled by him. I will see to it. You can do it on behalf of the studio. I promise I will ask nothing else of you in life.' He pleaded so earnestly that Sampath got down without a word, approached the sergeant, spoke to him and left with him a letter for the inspector. 'It is done, sir,' he said, getting back into his seat in the car. 'I only came to say goodbye. We are going to Mempi hills tomorrow.'

'Why Mempi hills, of all places?'

'It has a fine rest-house and it is a quiet place. I'm sure a couple of weeks' stay there will immensely benefit Shanti.' His car moved off. Srinivas watched him go. A vast sigh of despair escaped his lips – at the irrepressible inevitable success that seemed to loom ahead of Sampath. 'God alone can rescue him,' he muttered to himself as he saw the car turn into Ellaman Street.

The inspector came down an hour later. He said: 'Well, you can take your friend home. I am glad they have withdrawn the complaint. What can we do with mentally defective people? It is like dealing with drunkards. We keep them in custody for three or four days and then send them off. If kept longer they prove a bother to themselves and to us.'

Srinivas walked into the cell and persuaded Ravi to leave with him. The inspector followed them to the door. He said: 'I used to read your *Banner* with great interest. What has happened to it?' This was a piece of encouragement from a most unexpected quarter. Srinivas stood arrested like a man recovering a lost memory. Traffic was passing, policemen were walking in and out with their boot-nails clanking on the hard stone floor. 'Why, what's the matter?' asked the inspector, turning the little stick in his hand. 'No, nothing,' Srinivas replied. All the jumble of his recent months came in a torrent: Sampath, the press, film, rotary, Linotype – each struggling to be expressed and jostling the other out. Srinivas stood looking at the point of light in the inspector's belt-buckle, which caught a ray of light from the shop opposite. Ravi, his hair ruffled, his dress dirty and loose, stood beside him mutely. Srinivas felt that he himself had stood mute too long, and some answer from him was overdue. But he found himself tongue-tied. He felt he had been involved in a chaos of human relationships and activities. He kept saying to himself: 'I am searching for something, trying to make a meaning out of things.' The inspector kept looking at him, half amused and half puzzled. The groan of a man in custody was feebly heard ... The implications of *The Banner* and all that it stood for flashed across Srinivas's mind for a brief second. He said desperately, imploringly: 'If I had a press I could start it tomorrow.'

The inspector said: 'What has happened to the press you were doing it in?' Once again he felt it impossible to speak; he struggled for expression. He overcame the struggle with a deliberate effort and said: 'Sampath, Sampath – you know he is no longer a printer.'

'No, he is no longer a printer; I know.'

'I can't get anyone else to print my work,' said Srinivas, and felt like a baby talking complainingly. It sounded to him silly and childish to be talking thus at the police-station gate.

'If you will come here any time tomorrow evening I will take you to the Empire Press, who will print for you. He is a good printer and will oblige me. We must revive your weekly. It used to be interesting,' said the inspector.

Srinivas gripped his hand in an access of inexpressible gratitude. 'Please ...' he implored. 'I'll be here tomorrow at eleven positively.'

He drew his arm through Ravi's and led him along through the crowded Market Road; a bus hooted, country carts tumbled by, villagers passed along with loads on their heads. But Srinivas felt that he had got back his enchantment in life. He chattered happily as he walked along: 'Ravi, something to keep me sane – absolutely – without *The Banner*... Well, you will be well enough again, and then you can draw dozens of pictures for our paper. It will be your own paper,' he said and looked at the dull, uncomprehending eyes of Ravi, who walked beside him like a lamb, his lips muttering some unknown chant under his breath. They walked on a few paces thus, silently, on the edge of the road, avoiding and pushing their way through the groups of people going in the opposite direction. Srinivas slackened his pace and whispered: 'Don't you worry any more about Sampath or anyone else... They all belong to a previous life.' He looked up at the other as he said it. A feeble ray of understanding seemed to glow in Ravi's eyes: that was enough for Srinivas. His heart was filled with joy and he forgot all else in the relish of this moment.

# CHAPTER TEN

Srinivas had nowadays little time to bother about the outside world, being fully engaged on the revived *Banner*. It now emerged from an office in Market Road itself – coming off the Empire Press, which, though small in itself, seemed to Srinivas a vast organization; it had at least half a dozen type-boards, a twin cylinder machine turned off the formes, and one did not have to wait for four pages to be printed to get the types ready for the next four. In contrast with the Truth Printing Works, this appeared to be a revolutionary step forward. A small room was partitioned off with a red movable screen, and that separated the printer from the editor. The printer was a taciturn, dull man, who took no interest in the matter he printed, who would show no accommodation in financial matters, but who was thoroughly punctual and precise in doing his work.

Srinivas found himself facing, for the first time, financial problems as a reality. He couldn't restart *The Banner* without paying an advance and buying the paper for it. There was no longer Sampath between him and financial shocks. He spent long worrying hours speculating how he should manage it. He solved the problem by writing a letter to his brother, asking for the amount out of his share in the ancestral property. He hated himself for writing thus, but it was the only way out. He avoided deliberately any highfalutin references to his work, any abstract principles involved in it, but tried to appear sordid. He wrote: 'You know the old fable of a man who mounted a tiger – I'm in the same position. *The Banner* has to be kept fluttering in the air if I'm to survive. I may tell you that it has built itself up nicely, and there is not much groundwork to be done for it now. I've still all the old subscribers' rolls, and I'm also taking in a few pages of advertisements; and so don't you worry at all about its finances. But I require some temporary accommodation. If you can lend me a couple of thousands or, if it is impossible, give me two thousand out of my share in our property, I shall be grateful for the timely help.' His brother accepted it as a legitimate demand and sent him the amount with only the admonition: 'Please be a little more practical-minded in the management of your affairs. I would strongly advise you to have an accountant to look after your accounts and tell you from time to time how you stand. Don't grudge this expense.' He added a note of warning: 'You will understand that ancestral property is after all a sacred trust, and not loose money meant for the fanciful expenditure of the individual; it really belongs to our children and their children.' 'Children and their children'; it produced a lovely picture on the mind like the vista of an endless colonnade. But the first part of the sentence made him indignant. 'He blesses with his hand, and kicks with his feet,' he moaned. 'Shall I send back this amount?'

His wife advised him: 'He has merely said that you must be careful with the money. Why should that make you angry?'

Srinivas cooled down and said: 'All right then, I will take it now, but return it at the earliest possible moment.' He wrote to his brother to this effect, while acknowledging the amount, and it had the unexpected result of bringing from him a warm letter appreciating the resolution and repeating the advice to provide himself with an accountant. He accepted the reasonableness of this suggestion and acted upon it immediately. The Empire Press man lent him his own accountant for a couple of hours each day, for a small consideration.

Srinivas turned his back on Kabir Lane without a sigh. He rummaged his garret, filled a couple of baskets with all the papers there, and descended the steps for the last time. The building was now held on lease by Sunrise Pictures, and no life stirred there. The door of the registered offices and of the director of productions remained locked up. He felt he could no longer stand a meeting with Somu, Sohan Lal or De Mello. They seemed to him figures out of a nightmare. He merely sent the key to the studio with a messenger. Out of all the welter of paper he was carrying away he took care not to miss the little sketch of Ravi's in the cardboard file.

* * *

'Nonsense — an adult occupation' was one of the outstanding editorials he wrote after *The Banner*'s rebirth. He analysed and wrote down much of his studio experience in it. Adulthood was just a mask that people wore, the mask made up of a thick jowl and double chin and diamond ear-rings, or a green sporting shirt, but within it a man kept up the nonsense of his infancy, worse now for being without the innocence and the pure joy. Only the values of commerce gave this state a gloss of importance and urgency.

This brought Somu into his office one day. His fingers sparkled with diamonds as he clutched his cane. Srinivas sent up a silent prayer at the sight of him. 'Oh, God, save me from these people and give me the strength to face them now.' Somu's incapacity to speak out was once again evident. He sat clearing his throat and trying to smile. Srinivas forbore to ask him about the studio or their picture. 'Oh, God, don't involve me again with these people,' he prayed. Somu asked: 'How is it, you don't come near the studio?'

Srinivas felt it was unnecessary to give any answer. Somu persisted, and Srinivas merely said: 'I have no business there.'

'Ah! Ah! How can you say so? How can we run a studio without the help of story-writers like you, sir?'

Srinivas had no answer to give. He felt a deep hurt within him; seeing those fat cheeks and diamonds and the memory of Ravi in the cell, mumbling incoherently, he felt like crying out: 'You are all people who try to murder souls.'

Somu said: 'Your journal, your journal. We see you have said something about us.' This seemed to be interesting. Srinivas asked: 'What exactly have I said?'

Somu tapped the table nervously and said: 'I didn't read it fully.'

'How much of it really did you read then?'

'H'm ... In fact, I meant to read it later, but De Mello took it away and told me about it. He said that there was something about the studio,' said Somu.

'In that case you may read it now,' said Srinivas, taking out a copy of the issue and handing it to him. Somu looked at it for a few moments, turned its pages curiously, and rolled it up. 'Why are you folding it up?' asked Srinivas.

'I will read it at home,' replied Somu apologetically.

'No. I want you to read it at once,' said Srinivas. A look of panic came into Somu's eyes. 'All of it?' he asked, looking at the rolled-up copy in his hand.

'Yes, it is only twelve pages.'

'Oh, sir, please excuse me,' begged Somu. Srinivas became adamant. He enjoyed very much bullying Somu. It seemed to him that he was getting a bit of his own back after all. He wanted to cry 'Ah, how should I have felt when you fellows worried me to death and had everything your own way?' He enjoyed Somu's discomfiture, and again and again insisted upon his going through the journal on the spot. He wondered why Somu did not brush him aside and ask him to mind his business. But he didn't. He meekly said: 'I came only to spend a few minutes with you and find out about the article.'

'Yes, but how can you talk about it unless you read it? Go on, at least read the article you wish to discuss.' Somu looked at him appealingly for a moment, took out his glasses and poised them over his nose, spread out the issue and tilted it towards the window light. Looking at him thus, Srinivas felt that this must be counted as a major conquest in his career. He attended to the papers on his table, and a clearing of the throat from the other drew his attention: he looked up and saw Somu anxiously looking at him, wondering if he would be permitted to put down the paper now. He started taking off his glasses when Srinivas looked at him fixedly and said: 'Yes?'

'I've finished reading it.'

Srinivas wondered for a moment whether he could command him to go through the next article, but he refrained: it might prove to be the last straw: Somu might, after all, assert his independence and refuse. Srinivas felt, seeing the agonized face of the other as he was put through this trial, that all his wrongs of recent months were sufficiently avenged, and he felt his humanity returning. He became almost tender as he asked: 'Well, sir, what about it now?'

'De Mello said there was something about our production in it,' said Somu. 'That's why I came here.'

'Now you find nothing in it?' asked Srinivas.

'Nothing about our production. I don't know what made De Mello say so.' He appeared indignant at the trick played upon him.

Srinivas said quietly: 'De Mello is right. If you take the copy home and read it carefully, you will understand, and then you can come and talk it over with me.'

He looked puzzled. 'Why should you attack our film, sir?' he asked angrily. 'After all, you wrote the story. It is not right, sir, that you should be unkind to us.' He clutched his walking-stick and got up to go.

Srinivas said: 'You must read the paper regularly if you are to understand my point of view. It is not unkindness. Why don't you take out a subscription for a year? It is only ten rupees.'

'I have no time to read, sir, that is the trouble.'

'Just as you find the time to eat and sleep you must find the time to read a paper like *The Banner*. It's meant for people like you.' Somu took out ten rupees and placed it on the table. Srinivas wrote out a receipt and gave it him. Somu folded it and put it in his purse and started to go, but said, stopping half-way: 'After all, we spend lakhs of rupees on our pictures, and you must be careful not to prejudice the public against us and damage us.'

Srinivas kept Ravi in his own home. He had more or less the task of running both the households on his own means. Ravi's little sister came in several times a day with a petition for a rupee or two, and Srinivas ungrudgingly parted with them and advised his wife to do so in his absence. Ravi's father had given up talking not only to Ravi but also to Srinivas. He let out a sort of growl whenever he sensed Srinivas passing in front of his house. He was reported (by Srinivas's wife) to be continually saying: 'He ruined my son by putting notions into his head. Now he wants to ruin the rest of the family.' This naturally roused her indignation, and she asked: 'Why should we ever bother about these people when they are so ungrateful!' Srinivas merely told her: 'Don't waste your energy listening to what he or anybody says. Just give them any help you can.'

'For how long?' she asked.

Srinivas scratched his head. There seemed to be really no means of saying how long.

'And what are you going to do about him?' she asked, indicating the corner of the hall where Ravi sat mumbling his chant. Srinivas kept him with him because he had a feeling that Ravi's own home might hinder rather than help a possible recovery. He fed him, looked after his personal needs and kept him there. 'He must be protected from his family,' he explained. All this discussion had to be carried on in subdued voices in the kitchen while dining, since the front half of their house was occupied by one or the other of Ravi's relations. His little brothers and sisters came round and sat there in front of him. Sometimes they laughed at him and sometimes they ran away in fear. Unremittingly he kept repeating his sentences, though no one could follow anything that he was saying. Often his mother came up and sat in front of him, coaxed him to eat this or that, some special preparation that she made at home with her meagre resources. Srinivas's wife, after her initial protests, was often moved by this spectacle and sat down with her and tried to comfort her.

The old lady was beginning to think that the matter with Ravi was that he was possessed. She recounted a dozen instances similar to his, where exorcizing restored a man to his normal state.

So one evening, returning home from his office, Srinivas found strange activities going on. Ravi had become the centre of the picture. In front of him were set out trays of saffron and flowers, huge twigs of margosa leaves, and a camphor flare. A wild-looking man with huge beads around his neck, clad in red silk, his forehead dabbed with vermilion, officiated at the ceremony. He looked very much like Shiva in make-up. The air choked with incense burning in a holder. He had a couple of assistants sitting behind him, one bearing a cymbal and the other a little rattling drum which produced a peculiarly shrill noise. The chief man had a thin cane of a whip-like thinness at his feet, and he had smeared it with saffron and vermilion. Ravi's mother sat near this group with a reverent look in her eyes, and Srinivas saw his own wife running about, ministering to their wants ungrudgingly. Little Ramu and the other youngsters of the neighbouring house stood peeping in at the doorway. They looked slightly scared and thought it safer to keep their distance so. Srinivas stood at the threshold, arrested by this scene. Ramu had wanted to bound towards him and tell him in advance, but he was unwilling to forfeit his place in the doorway, and so kept calling in a suppressed voice: 'Father, Father.' But before he could say anything more Srinivas had come upon the scene. An exclamation of surprise escaped his lips. His wife came to him in great haste and drew him away into the kitchen. She closed the middle door and cautioned him: 'Don't say any inauspicious word now.'

'Whose idea is this?' he asked sourly.

'That lady has been wanting to do it. You must not say anything against it. Where can she go, poor lady? Her husband might not allow it or he might swear at them all the time.'

'Ah! You know now why I wanted Ravi to be kept here, do you understand?' he said with mild glee. She accepted his triumph without a protest. 'Yes, yes, with that old man there, how can they?' And this pacified Srinivas. He realized at once that he had become mildly vengeful: the other day it was Somu on whom he had tried to take it out, and today his wife. 'At this rate I fear I may do a lot of people to death in due course,' he told himself. He looked at his wife. He found her eyes dancing with interest. She was fully part of the affair and seemed to feel specially gratified at being the hostess of this exotic function. He muttered under his breath: 'The whole thing is too silly for words.' He recollected the tribal worship done before the camera at the studio on the inauguration day. 'This is no worse. At least this is more innocent and uncommercial,' he reflected. His wife said: 'It is also a good thing, you know. He knows all about the ghost that haunts this house that people talk about. He says it has got into Ravi. He will drive it out, and we can live here with a free mind afterwards.' Seeing that she had not made much of an impression, she asked: 'Isn't it wonderful?' He replied: 'He probably got the story out of some gossip-monger.'

'I don't know why you are so cynical,' she said and left him and went away to the front room. He followed her, feeling that he might as well watch the scene. Ravi's mother looked up at him from time to time with grateful eyes. The magician was reciting something monotonously in a stentorian voice, and his pauses were punctuated rhythmically by the cymbals and the rattle-drum. Her eyes were shut, and Ravi sat oblivious of his surroundings: a few margosa leaves were scattered on him. The chants and rhythmic beats went on and on and produced a kind of hypnosis in everyone assembled there, and Srinivas saw Ravi gradually shaking his head and swaying. He found the atmosphere oppressive and unbearable – the gong and the drum-beat, the pungent, piercing smell of the incense, its smoke hanging in the air, and the camphor-flare illumination. Srinivas suddenly said to himself: 'I might be in the twentieth century B.C. for all it matters, or 4000 B.C.' In that half-dim hall a sweep of history passed in front of his eyes. His scenario-writing habit suddenly asserted itself. His little home, the hall and all the folk there, Anderson Lane and, in fact, Malgudi itself dimmed and dissolved on the screen. There was a blankness for a while, and then there faded in an uninhabited country; the Mempi jungle extended everywhere. The present Market Road was an avenue of wild trees, a narrow footpath winding its way through the long grass. Presently appeared on this path Sri Rama, the hero of Ramayana. He was a perfect man, this incarnation of Vishnu. Over his shoulder was slung his famous bow which none could even lift. He was followed by his devoted brother Laxman and Hanuman, the monkey-god. Rama was on his way to Lanka (Ceylon) to battle with evil there, in the shape of Ravana who abducted Sita. The enemy was a perfection of evil with all its apparent strength and invincibility. Rama had to redeem righteousness. He was on his way to a holy war, which would wipe out wrong and establish on earth truth, beauty and goodness. He rested on a sandy stretch in a grove, and looked about for a little water for making a paste for his forehead-marking. There was no water. He pulled an arrow from his quiver and scratched a line on the sand, and water instantly appeared. Thus was born the river Sarayu.

The river flowed on. On its banks sprang up the thatched roofs of a hamlet – a pastoral community who grazed their cattle in the jungles and brought them back home before nightfall and securely shut themselves and their animals in from prowling tigers and jackals. The jungle, with its sky-touching trees, gradually receded further and further, and cornfields appeared in its place. The waving tufts of rice, standing to a man's height, swayed in the air and stretched away as far as the eye could see.

When the Buddha came this way, preaching his gospel of compassion, centuries later, he passed along the main street of a prosperous village. Men, women and children gathered around him. He saw a woman weeping. She had recently lost her child and seemed disconsolate. He told her he would give her consolation if she could bring him a handful of mustard from any house where death was unknown. She went from door to door and turned away from every one of them. Amongst all those hundreds of houses she could not find one where death was a stranger. She understood the lesson ... A little crumbling masonry and a couple of stone pillars, beyond Lawley Extension, now marked the spot where the Buddha had held his congregation ...

The great Shankara appeared during the next millennium. He saw on the river-bank a cobra spreading its hood and shielding a spawning frog from the rigour of the midday sun. He remarked: 'Here the extremes meet. The cobra, which is the natural enemy of the frog, gives it succour. This is where I must build my temple.' He installed the goddess there and preached his gospel of *Vedanta*: the identity and oneness of God and his creatures.

And then the Christian missionary with his Bible. In his wake the merchant and the soldier – people who paved the way for Edward Shilling and his Engladia Bank.

Dynasties rose and fell. Palaces and mansions appeared and disappeared. The entire country went down under the fire and sword of the invader, and was washed clean when Sarayu overflowed its bounds. But it always had its rebirth and growth. And throughout the centuries, Srinivas felt, this group was always there: Ravi with his madness, his well-wishers with their panaceas and their apparatus of cure. Half the madness was his own doing, his lack of self-knowledge, his treachery to his own instincts as an artist, which had made him a battle-ground.

Sooner or later he shook off his madness and realized his true identity – though not in one birth, at least in a series of them. 'What did it amount to?' Srinivas asked himself as the historical picture faded out. 'Who am I to bother about Ravi's madness or sanity? What madness to think I am his keeper?' This notion seemed to him so ridiculous that he let out a laugh.

The others in the small room looked at him startled. His wife came near him and peered into his face anxiously and asked: 'Why did you laugh?''

'Did I?' he asked. 'I recollected some joke, that's all. Don't bother about me.'

Now they had stopped their recitations and drum-beats. Ravi, with half-shut eyes, was swaying. The exorcist picked up his cane and thwacked it sharply over Ravi's back and asked at the same time: 'Now will you go or not?' Ravi smarted a little under the blow, and rolled his eyes, and the thwacking was renewed with vigour. The question was addressed to the evil spirit possessing him. Ravi winced under the repeated blows. Srinivas felt an impulse to cry out: 'Stop it! It is absurd and cruel.' But he found himself incapable of any effort. The recent vision had given him a view in which it seemed to him all the same whether they thwacked Ravi with a cane or whether they left him alone, whether he was mad or sane – all that seemed unimportant and not worth bothering about. The whole of eternity stretched ahead of one; there was plenty of time to shake off all follies. Madness or sanity, suffering or happiness seemed all the same ... It didn't make the slightest difference in the long run – in the rush of eternity nothing mattered. It was no more important or remembered than an attack of malaria in the lifetime of a cen-tenarian. Whether one was mad or sane or right or wrong didn't make the slightest difference: it was like bothering about a leaf floating on a rushing torrent – whether it was floating on its right side or wrong side.

He got up abruptly and left the room. He went into the street and stood there uncertainly, looking up and down. There was a momentary haziness in his mind as to what period he was existing in – existence seeming so persistent and inescapable. Later Ravi's mother came out to say: 'Shall I take Ravi to the temple at

Sailam? It is a day's journey from here. The exorcist says that if Ravi is kept there at its portals for a week, he will be quite well. There are hundreds of people living there.'

'By all means,' said Srinivas, and added with conviction: 'He is bound to get well again. Even madness passes. Only existence asserts itself.'

'Your wife has promised to look after Ravi's father's needs.' It was with difficulty that he could repress the remark: 'It's all the same whether he is looked after or not. What if he perishes?'

'What can we do? We have to trouble you. He is so unreasonable and difficult to manage. We are sorry to put the burden on you, but for the sake of that boy – '

'We don't mind the trouble in the least. We will look after the old gentleman.'

Later Srinivas's wife told him: 'I've given them twenty rupees of house-keeping money. You must replace the amount. Poor folk!'

'Of course, of course. I will replace it and more. Go ahead and do what you like.' His wife felt baffled by his elated manner.

Srinivas engaged a carriage to take Ravi and his mother to the railway station next evening. The old lady had rolled up a couple of carpets and pillows and tied them with a hemp rope. She had stuffed a few items of clothing into a tin trunk. She had a basket in which she carried a pot of water and a few plantains. The old gentleman was in an utter mental confusion. If he could have got up and moved about he would have prevented the trip. He kept on shouting at them, 'Why should she go? With whose permission is she leaving the town and travelling? What brazenness has come over our women!' The old lady finished an early dinner. The numerous children gathered around and pestered her for this and that, and all of them set up a howl, demanding to be taken along to the railway. She carried with them the two youngest; she had oiled and parted their hair, washed their faces, and thrust them into new clothes. They were bubbling over with joy. The other children threw murderous looks at them and shouted imprecations. The old man shouted above it all: 'Why should she go, leaving these children to cry? Is there no one to whom she will listen?' He cried: 'Mr Editor, oh, Mr Editor!' He had spurned Srinivas all these days, but turned to him now out of desperation. He called so insistently that Srinivas could not help responding. He went up to the doorway and stood there and asked: 'What is it, sir?'

'Oh, you are there! Come nearer! Come and sit down here. Take a seat; you are a learned man ...'

'I'm quite comfortable here, what is it?' Srinivas asked.

'Please tell her to stop. She is going away. She is disobeying me.'

'She will be back in ten or fifteen days, don't worry.'

'You need not tell me that. She must not go.'

'She is not going for her pleasure. She is going – '

'Yes, I know. For that brigand's sake. Why should she go? He is not our son. No man who has been in prison can be our son. Why should she trouble about him? If she is my wife let her give him up. What has she to do with him?'

'Don't lose your head, sir. Be calm.'

'Who are you to tell me about my head? You have ruined that rascal son of mine by dragging him into your associations, and you are ruining my wife and family. You are out to blight our family.'

'Don't mind what he says,' said the lady, wringing her hands in despair. But her face was bright with the anticipation of a journey.

'Not at all,' Srinivas said. 'He will get his food all right.'

'Food! I will fling it out, if anyone brings the food cooked in another's house,' raved the old man. Srinivas looked at the lined face of Ravi's aged mother. 'How much must she have stood from him for forty years,' he reflected and admired her fortitude.

The *jutka* arrived at the door. The lady picked up her baggage and the two children and went to her husband to bid him good-bye. The old man averted his face, put out his arms without a word, and touched the two children. Tears rolled down his cheeks. Srinivas went over to Ravi's corner in his house and told him: 'Come along, let us go to the station.' Ravi looked up at him. That was some improvement. After the thwacking he was showing responses to stimuli. Srinivas helped him up and led him to the *jutka* and assisted him in. His mother and the children followed. She took an elaborate farewell of Srinivas's wife, who followed her down the street and, for inexplicable reasons, started crying when the *jutka* began to move. 'Any farewell or parting will bring tears, I suppose,' Srinivas reflected as he sat beside the driver and urged him to run fast enough to catch the 8.20 train towards Trichy.

# CHAPTER ELEVEN

It was late in the evening. Srinivas sat in his office jotting down details of the vision he had had at the exorcist's performance in his house, and attempted to communicate it to his readers. He jotted down the heading 'The Leaf on the Torrent'. He didn't like it. He noted down an alternative title 'The Cosmic Stage: the willy-nilly actor on the Cosmic Stage'. He thought it over. It didn't satisfy either. He didn't like to use the word 'Cosmic' if he could help it. The intensity of the experience seemed to be gradually disintegrating now in commonplace expression. He sat brooding, when the printer's office boy came up and said: 'There is a gentleman to see you, sir; asks if you can see him.' Srinivas looked sadly for a moment at the scribbling on his pad and its incomplete characters, wondering how he was going to finalize it for the press next day. The office boy stood before him, awaiting his reply, and suggested: 'Shall I ask him to go away, sir?'

'Bring him in,' said Srinivas, picking up his pen and desperately hoping to jot down something in the short interval that lay before him.

The door opened and there stood Sampath before him. 'Sampath!' Srinivas cried. 'Sampath! Why couldn't you come straight in?'

'Oh, I didn't like to disturb you. This is Thursday, and I know what you should do today.' He came over and sat in the chair. There was a subdued quality about him. He still wore his silk shirt; but he had an intimidated look in his eyes. 'Well, how are you?' asked Srinivas.

Sampath leaned over and whispered: 'I'm still a monogamist. Don't worry.'

'Ah, that's very good.'

'Things have happened as you wished.'

'How did you like the Mempi hills?'

'Oh, full of tigers and all sorts of beasts, howling all night, and I had a most harrowing time keeping Shanti quiet. She was hysterical throughout and wanted to get away from there the moment we reached the place. Have you been there?'

'No; some time I hope to.'

'I hope you will have a better companion and a more reasonable companion to go with; otherwise it is not worth the labour. Do you know how one goes? The train puts you down at Koppal – that's the last railway link. From there you go twenty miles in a bus and then up in bullock-carts; and then you allow yourself to be carried by porters in a sort of basket slung on bamboo poles; and then you reach the place, practically on foot. And when you have arrived there, what do you expect to see?'

'Someone to welcome you?' asked Srinivas.

'Not a chance, sir... A bleak forest bungalow full of horrible, wide verandas, sir. God knows what fellow ever thought of putting up a building there, and how he managed to gather the materials and men to build, for, do you know, we could not get a single person to bring up a glass of milk or a banana for us. We had carried a hamper and that saved us from starvation. The jungle life comes on you when there is still light, say, at about five o'clock. The birds make a tremendous uproar, the huge trees seem to close in on you, and the jackals start their wails. Ah, those jackals: every time they cried, this lady let out a shriek and trembled all over. She tried to shut herself in, but there was only one room, and that was full of glass shutters, evidently built by someone who wished to watch the arrivals and departures in the jungle at night. She gave me hell that night. I have never been so much bothered by anyone before. We could see in the dark jungle eyes shining. She was a miserable sight, I tell you. She became roaring mad. If you had seen her you would have thought Ravi was sanity itself!'

Srinivas tried to receive this narrative as casually as possible. He felt that there was no need for him to put any question. So much was coming out spontaneously.

'Every time a tiger roared she had fits, she was sick; it became disgusting to stay with her in the same room. So I went over and stayed in the veranda, not minding the risk. I preferred it to her company.'

Srinivas could not help remarking: 'I cannot imagine how she could've become suddenly so unacceptable.'

'Well, I didn't much mind her physical condition. It was her temperament that disgusted me. She was quarrelsome, nagging. In all my years of married life I have never been nagged so much before. She demanded to be taken back to the town that very night and wouldn't leave me in peace! Imagine! It was at that moment that I decided to stick to your advice. Next afternoon I arranged for her descent. At Koppal I put her into the train and bade her goodbye. She went towards Madras, and I came away here, and I thank God for the relief.' He smiled weakly and looked at Srinivas. Srinivas sat biting a corner of his lips, his eyes were on the caption on his pad. 'Cosmic ...' A corner of his mind seized it and struggled with it. 'Cosmic! Cosmic what ...What other title, I must find it before tomorrow, this time ...' He looked up. Sampath watched his face to study his reaction to the story. Srinivas observed that Sampath's face did not register the satisfaction and relief that his words expressed. He looked downcast. He knew that Sampath was only waiting for a remark from him. He revolved the whole episode in his mind and declared: 'Sampath, what you say seems too good to be true.'

Sampath covered his eyes with his palm and shook with laughter. He muttered: 'My editor knows me too well; nothing short of absolute truth will pass with him.'

'Won't you tell me exactly what happened?' Srinivas asked. He added: 'Don't, if you don't like to talk about it.'

'I wouldn't be here if I didn't want to talk about it, sir, the only thing left for me now.' He paused, looked about; the press was running inside. 'The press seems to be working; I can tell from its sound it is a good one. Is it Simkins' double cylinder?'

'Perhaps it is. How do you know?'

'By mere sound. I am a printer, when all is said and done. Do you agree?'

'Undoubtedly.'

'This is purely a temporary arrangement, I hope. When my plant is ready I cannot allow The Banner to come from any other press. It's my responsibility, sir.' Srinivas muttered something non-committally and asked: 'How near are you to your rotary?'

Sampath stretched himself out across the table and whispered: 'Come out, let us sit down somewhere and talk. I don't like to speak about anything in a fellow printer's establishment.' Srinivas threw a desperate look at the paper on his table. He put it away resolutely. He got up. When they came out Srinivas hesitated on the last step, looked up and down and asked: 'Where is the car you used to ride in?'

'I suppose carburettor trouble, like me,' Sampath said, tapping his heart.

'Shall we walk?' Srinivas asked.

'It's good exercise, isn't it?' Sampath said.

They walked along in silence down the Market Road. Traffic flowed past them. Dusk was about them. A few lights twinkled here and there. They walked on in silence.

Srinivas said: 'When did you come? You have not told me that.'

'There is a great deal more I haven't told you,' he said. Conversation once again became difficult; Srinivas allowed the silence to envelop them completely. He felt mystified by Sampath's talk and actions. When they had gone a couple of furlongs he asked Sampath: 'Where shall we go?'

'Anywhere you like; where we can talk quietly.'

'Shall we go to Anand Bhavan restaurant, to that special room upstairs?' asked Srinivas, recollecting their first meeting-place. Sampath said: 'Yes, a good idea,' paused for a second and then said: 'No, sir, not now. I wouldn't like to go there now; say somewhere else; why not to the river?' Srinivas gasped with surprise. 'I didn't know you cared for the river,' he said. 'One has got to like all sorts of things now,' Sampath said, and ran across to a wayside shop to buy a packet of cigarettes.

At the river he stood on the sand and looked about as if searching for a seat in a theatre hall. Clumps of people were sitting on the sands. 'I don't like to be seen by anyone,' he said. Beyond the other bank, half a mile off, they saw the glare of the studio lights. He blinked at them for a moment and said: 'They seem to be very busy there.' Srinivas led him along, and they sat down in a quiet nook, where there was no one. Darkness had gathered about them. The river flowed on into the night. Sampath remained silent for a moment, drawing circles on the sand. Srinivas left him alone and listened to the murmur of the river and the distant, muffled roar of the town. Sampath said: 'I told you a lie, and you found it out. How I wish it had happened as I said! Then it would have left me without regrets. Could you guess what percentage of it was true?'

'Yes, up to your reaching the bungalow on the hill-top,' said Srinivas.

'Well, sir, you can grant me even a little more. That bungalow was as I said, and her terror was real as she saw the flashing eyes of panthers on the other side of the glass at night; but oh, how sweet she was! I could see her trembling with fright, but she said not a word. She sat up all night trying to brave it. Few women there are in the world who could have helped screaming, under those conditions. You know she was not in the best condition of nerves, but all the same, what self-possession she showed! She sat speaking of some books she had read in her younger days.' He paused to take out a cigarette and lit it. He blew the smoke into the dark sky. 'She stood it for three or four days, and then suggested that we might return. I was also glad to get back. As you might know, we should have gone up to a registrar before leaving for Mempi, but she always made some excuse or other and put it off. Finally we decided that we were to go through the formality on coming back here. That was our understanding. We got down from the hills, and we were to catch our train at Koppal at five a.m. next day. It is the most unearthly station you can imagine, with jungles on all sides and a disused railway compartment serving as the station-master's office. We stayed cooped up in that little office all night. The station-master allowed us to stay up there. We sat on a couple of stools and tried to talk through the night. The bus had put us down at Koppal at six in the evening and we had nearly twelve hours before us for the train. We ate our food and then sat up, intending to talk all night till the arrival of the train. But really there was so little to talk about. Having done nothing but that for five days continuously, I think both of us had exhausted all available subjects. And a passing thought occurred to me that we might have to spend the rest of our lives in silence after we were married. This problem was unexpectedly simplified for me. I must have fallen asleep on my stool. When the train arrived and I woke up, her chair was empty.

The train halts there only for four minutes or so, and we had to hurry up.

'The station-master said: "She left by the eleven down. I gave her a ticket for Madras."

'"When?"

'"At twenty-three hours."

'I gnashed my teeth. "What time is that in earthly language?"

'"Eleven at night."

'"What nonsense!" I raved at him.

'"But the lady gave me to understand that you were going to different places," he said.

'I shook my fists in his face and said: "Don't you see that a husband and wife have got to go together?"

'"Not always, not necessarily," he said, and went on to attend to his business. The train halted there for only four minutes.

'One had to hurry up. "Can I go to Madras?" I asked.

'"No train towards Madras till ..."

'I was appalled at the prospect of spending half a day more there. I felt like knocking down the station-master. "You should not have allowed her to go."

'"We cannot refuse tickets to bona-fide passengers." He quoted a railway Act.

'"Oh! Great one, what shall I do now?" I asked. I must have looked ridiculous.

'"Only a minute more, sir, please make up your mind. I cannot delay the train for anybody's sake."

'I discovered meanwhile a note she had left. It was scrawled on a brown railway sheet. "I am sick of this kind of life and marriage frightens me. I want to go and look after my son, who is growing up with strangers. Please leave me alone, and don't look for me. I want to change my ways of living. You will not find me. If I find you pursuing me, I will shave off my hair and fling away my jewellery and wear a white *sari*. You and people like you will run away at the sight of me. I am, after all, a widow and can shave my head and disfigure myself, if I like. If it is the only way out I will do it. I had different ideas of a film life." Well, sir, that was her letter ...'

Sampath pulled out his kerchief and dabbed his eyes and blew his nose. 'I went to Madras, Trichy, Coimbatore, Mangalore,

Bombay and a dozen other places, and tired myself out searching for her ... It has all turned out to be a great mess.'

'What is to happen to the film?' Srinivas asked.

'It must be dropped. We've been abandoned by both Shiva and Parvathi. And only Kama, the God of Love, is left in the studio.'

'And he, too, will have to remain invisible for the rest of the story,' Srinivas added.

'I shall have to become invisible, too. Otherwise, Sohan Lal and Somu have enough reason to put me in prison,' Sampath said. He remained in thought for a moment and added, almost with a sigh: 'Well, I may probably try and save myself if I can interest them in a new story.' Now Srinivas suddenly saw that this might prove to be the nucleus of a whole series of fresh troubles. He roused himself and said: 'I think it is time to get up. Tomorrow is press day.'

They walked back in silence. At Market Square, Srinivas realized that they must part. He wanted to ask where Sampath's family was, what he had done with them, what he was going to do with himself, and so on. But he checked himself. It seemed to him a great, unnecessary strain, sifting grain from chaff in all that he might say. He might probably have his family about him. He might have abandoned them; he might, after all, still have Shanti with him and be planning further adventures, or he might disappear or still dangle a new carrot for Somu and Co. to pursue. But whatever it was, he felt that he was once again in danger of getting involved with him if he asked him too many questions. He saw Sampath hesitating in the square. Bare humanity made him say: 'Will you come home with me and dine?'

'Thanks. I'm going to the railway station. I'll manage there.' Srinivas forbore to ask 'Why railway station?' He told himself: 'He may meet someone, or go away somewhere or have a dozen other reasons, but I've nothing to do with any of them.' So he merely said: 'All right then. Goodbye,' and passed on resolutely. While turning down Anderson Lane he looked back for a second and saw far off the glow of a cigarette end in the square where he had left Sampath; it was like a ruby set in the night. He raised his hand, flourished a final farewell, and set his face homeward.

# THE FINANCIAL EXPERT

## PART ONE

From time immemorial people seemed to have been calling him 'Margayya'. No one knew, except his father and mother, who were only dimly recollected by a few cronies in his ancestral village, that he had been named after the enchanting god Krishna. Everyone called him Margayya and thought that he had been called so at his naming ceremony. He himself must have forgotten his original name: he had gradually got into the habit of signing his name 'Margayya' even in legal documents. And what did it mean? It was purely derivative: 'Marga' meant 'The Way' and 'Ayya' was an honorific suffix: taken together it denoted one who showed the way. He showed the way out to those in financial trouble. And in all those villages that lay within a hundred-mile radius of Malgudi, was there anyone who could honestly declare that he was not in financial difficulties? The emergence of Margayya was an unexpected and incalculable offshoot of a co-operator's zeal. This statement will be better understood if we watch him in his setting a little more closely.

One of the proudest buildings in Malgudi was the Central Co-operative Land Mortgage Bank, which was built in the year 1914 and named after a famous Registrar of Co-operative Societies, Sir — —, who had been knighted for his devotion to Co-operation after he had, in fact, lost his voice explaining co-opera-tive principles to peasants in the village at one end and to the officials in charge of the files at the Secretariat end. It was said that he died while serving on a Rural Indebtedness Sub-committee. After his death it was discovered that he had left all his savings for the construction of the bank. He now watched, from within a teak frame suspended on the central landing, all the comings and goings, and he was said to be responsible for occasional poltergeist phenomena, the rattling of paperweights, flying ledgers, and sounds like the brisk opening of folios, the banging of fists on a table, and so on – evidenced by successive night watchmen. This could be easily understood, for the ghost of the Registrar had many reasons to feel sad and frustrated. All the principles of co-operation for which he had sacrificed his life were dissolving under his eyes, if he could look beyond the portals of the bank itself, right across the little stretch of lawn under the banyan tree, in whose shade Margayya sat and transacted his business. There was always a semi-circle of peasants sitting round him, and by their attitude and expression one might easily guess that they were suppliants. Margayya, though very much their junior (he was just forty-two), commanded the respect of those who sat before him. He was to them a wizard who enabled them to draw unlimited loans from the co-operative bank. If the purpose of the co-operative movement was the promotion of thrift and the elimination of middlemen, those two were just the objects that were defeated here under the banyan tree: Margayya didn't believe in advocating thrift: his living depended upon helping people to take loans from the bank opposite and from each other.

His tin box, a grey, discoloured, knobby affair, which was small enough to be carried under his arm, contained practically his entire equipment: a bottle of ink, a pen and a blotter, a small register whose pages carried an assortment of names and figures, and above all – the most important item – loan application forms of the co-operative bank. These last named were his greatest asset in life, and half his time was occupied in acquiring them. He had his own agency at work to provide him with these forms. When a customer came, the very first question Margayya asked was, 'Have you secured the application form?'

'No.'

'Then go into that building and bring one – try and get one or two spare forms as well.' It was not always possible to secure more than one form, for the clerks there were very strict and perverse. They had no special reason to decline to give as many forms as were required except the impulse to refuse anything that is persistently asked for. All the same, Margayya managed to gather quite a lot of forms and kept them handy. They were taken out for use on special occasions. Sometimes a villager arrived who did not have a form and who could not succeed in acquiring one by asking for it in the bank. On such occasions Margayya charged a fee for the blank form itself, and then another for filling in the relevant details.

The clerks of the bank had their own methods of worrying the villagers. A villager who wanted to know his account had to ask for it at the counter and invariably the accounts clerk snapped back, 'Where is your passbook?' A passbook was a thing the villager could never keep his hand on. If it was not out of sight it was certain to be out of date. This placed the villager fully at the mercy of the clerk, who would say: 'You will have to wait till I get through all the work I have now on hand. I'm not being paid to look after only your business here.' And then the peasant would have to hang about for a day or two before getting an answer to his question, which would only be after placating the clerk with an offering in cash or kind.

It was under such circumstances that Margayya's help proved invaluable. He kept more or less parallel accounts of at least fifty of the members of the bank. What its red-tape obstructed, he cleared up by his own contrivance. He carried most of the figures in his head. He had only to sight a customer (for instance Mallanna of Koppal, as it now happened to be) to say at once: 'Oh! you have come back for a new loan, I suppose. If you pay seventy-five rupees more, you can again take three hundred rupees within a week! The bye-law allows a new loan when fifty per cent is paid up.'

'How can I burden myself with a further loan of three hundred, Margayya? It's unthinkable.'

Now would begin all the persuasiveness that was Margayya's stock-in-trade. He asked point blank, 'What difference is it going to make? Are you not already paying a monthly instalment of seventeen rupees eight annas? Are you or are you not?'

'Yes ... I'm paying. God knows how much I have to – '

'I don't want all that,' Margayya said, cutting him short. 'I am not concerned with all that – how you pay or what you do. You may perhaps pledge your life or your wife's *saris*. It is none of my concern: all that I want to know is whether you are paying an instalment now or not.'

'Yes, master, I do pay.'

'You will continue to pay the same thing, that is all. Call me a dog if they ask you for even one anna more. You fool, don't you see the difference? You pay seventeen rupees eight annas now for nothing, but under my present plan you will pay the same seventeen rupees eight annas but with another three hundred rupees in your purse. Don't you see the difference?'

'But what's the use of three hundred rupees, master?'

'Oh! I see, you don't see a use for it. All right, don't come to me again. I have no use for nincompoops like you. You are the sort of fellow who won't – ' He elaborated a bawdy joke about him and his capacity, which made the atmosphere under the tree genial all round. The other villagers sitting around laughed. But Margayya assumed a stern look, and pretended to pass on to the next question in hand. He sat poring over some papers, with his spectacles uneasily poised over his nose. Those spectacles were a recent acquisition, the first indication that he was on the wrong side of forty. He resisted them as long as he could – he hated the idea of growing old, but 'long-sight' does not wait for approval or welcome. You cannot hoodwink yourself or anyone else too long about it – the strain of holding a piece of paper at arm's length while reading stretches the nerves of the forearm and invites comments from others. Margayya's wife laughed aloud one day and asked: 'Why don't you buy a pair of glasses like other young men of your age? Otherwise you will sprain your hand.' He acted upon this advice and obtained a pair of glasses mounted in silver from the V.N. Stores in the Market. He and the proprietor of the shop had been playmates once, and Margayya took the glasses on trial, and forgot to go that way again. He was accosted about it on the road occasionally by the rotund optician, who was snubbed by Margayya: 'Haven't you the elementary courtesy to know the time and place for such reminders?'

'Sorry, sorry,' the other hastened to apologize, 'I didn't intend to hurt or insult you.'

'What greater insult can a man face than this sort of thing? What will an onlooker think? I am busy from morning to night – no time even for a cup of coffee in the afternoon! All right, it doesn't matter. Will you send someone to my house? I'm not able to use those glasses either. I wanted to come and exchange them if possible, but – ' it trailed off into indefiniteness, and the optician went away once again and soon ceased to bother about it. It was one of his many bad debts, and very soon he changed his commodity; gradually his show-case began to display powder-puffs, scents, chocolate bars – and the silver-rimmed glasses sat securely on Margayya's nose.

He now took off his spectacles and folded the sides as if disposing once and for all of the problem of Mallanna. He looked away at a man on his right and remarked: 'You may have to wait for a week more before I can take up your affair.'

'Brother, this is urgent, my daughter's marriage is coming off next month.'

'Your daughter's marriage! I have to find you the money for it, but the moment my service is done, you will forget me. You will not need your Margayya any more?' The other made several deprecating noises, as a protestation of his loyalty. He was a villager called Kanda who had come walking from his village fifteen miles away. He owned about twenty acres of land and a house and cattle, but all of it was tied up in mortgages – most through Margayya's advice and assistance. He was a gambler and drank heavily, and he always asked for money on the pretext of having to marry his daughters, of whom he had a good number. Margayya preferred not to know what happened to all the money, but helped him to borrow as much as he wanted. 'The only course now left is for you to take a joint-loan, but the difficulty will be to find someone as a partner.' He looked round at the gathering before him and asked, 'All of you are members of the Co-operative Society. Can't someone help a fellow creature?' Most of them shook their heads. One of them remarked, 'How can you ask for our joint-signature? It's risky to do it even for one's own brother.'

'It's most risky between brothers,' added Margayya. 'But I'm not suggesting it for brothers now. I am only suggesting it between human beings.' They all laughed and understood that he was referring to an elder brother of his with whom he was known to be on throat-cutting terms. He prepared to deliver a speech: 'Here is a great man, a big man, you cannot find a more important man round about Somanur. He has lands, cattle, yes, he's a big man in every way. No doubt, he has certain habits: no use shutting our eyes to it: but I guarantee he will get over them. He must have a joint-loan because he needs at least five hundred rupees immediately to see him through his daughter's marriage. You know how it is with the dowry system – ' Everybody made a sympathetic noise and shook their heads. 'Very bad, very bad. Why should we criticize what our ancestors have brought into existence?' someone asked.

'Why not?' another protested.

'Some people are ruined by the dowry.'

'Why do you say some people?' Margayya asked. 'Why am I here? Three daughters were born to my father. Five cart-loads of paddy came to us every half year, from the fields. We just heaped them up on the floor of the hall, we had five halls to our house; but where has it all gone? To the three daughters. By the time my father found husbands for them there was nothing left for us to eat at home!'

'But is it not said that a man who begets a son is blessed in three lives, because he gives away the greatest treasure on earth?' said someone.

'And how much more blessed is he that gives away three daughters? He is blessed no doubt, but he also becomes a bankrupt,' Margayya said.

The talk thus went on and on, round and round, always touching practical politics again at some point or other. Margayya put his spectacles on, looked fixedly at Mallanna, and said: 'Come and sit near me.' The villager moved up. Margayya told the gathering, 'We have to talk privately.' And they all looked away and pretended not to hear although all their attention was concentrated on the whispering that now started between the two. Margayya said: 'It's going to be impossible for Kanda to get a joint-loan, but he ought to be ready to accept whatever is available. I know you can help him and help yourself – you will lose nothing. In fact, you will gain a little interest. You will clear half your present loan by paying seventy-five rupees and apply for a fresh one. Since you don't want it, give it to Kanda. He will pay you seven and a half per cent. You give the four and a half per cent to that father-in-law' (Margayya always referred to the Co-operative Bank with a fresh sobriquet) 'and take the three per cent yourself. He will pay back the instalments to you. I will collect and give them to you.' Mallanna took time to grasp all the intricacies of this proposition, and then asked: 'Suppose he doesn't?' Margayya looked horrified at this doubt. 'What is there to be afraid of when I am here?' At this one of the men who were supposed to be out of earshot remarked: 'Ah, what is possible in this world without mutual trust?' Margayya added, 'Listen to him. He knows the world.'

The result of all this talk was that Mallanna agreed to the proposal. Margayya grew busy filling up a loan application form with all the details of Mallanna's heritage, etc. He read it out aloud, seized hold of Mallanna's left thumb, pressed it on a small ink pad he carried in his box and pressed it again on the application form and endorsed it. He took out of the box seventy-five rupees in cash, and handed them to Mallanna with: 'Why should I trust you with this without a scrap of paper? Now credit this to your account and halve your loan; and then present that application.'

'If they refuse to take it?'

'Why should they refuse? They have got to accept it. You are a shareholder, and they have got to accept your application. It's not their grandfather's money that they are giving you but your own. Bye-law – ' He quoted the bye-law, and encouraged by it, the other got up and moved on.

It is impossible to describe more clearly than this Margayya's activity under the tree. He advanced a little loan (for interest) so that the little loan might wedge out another loan from the Co-operative Bank; which in its turn was passed on to someone in need for a higher interest. Margayya kept himself as the centre of all the complex transaction, and made all the parties concerned pay him for his services, the bank opposite him being involved in it willy-nilly. It was as strenuous a job as any other in the town and he felt that he deserved the difficult income he ground out of a couple of hundred rupees in his box, sitting there morning till evening. When the evening sun hit him on the nape of the neck he pulled down the lid of his box and locked it up, and his gathering understood that the financial wizard was closing his office for the day.

Margayya deposited the box under a bench in the front room of his house. His little son immediately came running out from the kitchen with a shout: '*Appa!* – ' and gripped his hand, asking: 'What have you brought today?' Margayya hoisted him up on his shoulder: 'Well, tomorrow, I will buy you a new engine, a small engine.' The child was pleased to hear it. He asked, 'How small will the engine be? Will it be so tiny?' He indicated with his thumb and first finger a minute size. 'All right,' said Margayya and put him down. This was almost a daily ritual. The boy revelled in visions of miniature articles – a tiny engine, tiny cows, tiny table, tiny everything, of the maximum size of a mustard seed. Margayya put him down and briskly removed his upper-cloth and shirt, picked up a towel that was hanging from a nail on the wall, and moved to the backyard. Beyond a small clump of banana trees, which waved their huge fan-like leaves in the darkness, there was a single well of crumbling masonry, with a pulley over its cross-bar. Margayya paused for a moment to admire the starry sky. Down below at his feet the earth was damp and marshy. All the drain-water of two houses flowed into the banana beds. It was a common backyard for his house and the one next door, which was his brother's. It was really a single house, but a partition wall divided it into two from the street to the backyard.

No. 14 D, Vinayak Street had been a famous land-mark, for it was the earliest house to be built in that area. Margayya's father was considered a hero for settling there in a lonely place where there was supposed to be no security for life or property. More-over it was built on the fringe of a cremation ground, and often the glow of a burning pyre lit up its walls. After the death of the old man the brothers fell out, their wives fell out, and their children fell out. They could not tolerate the idea of even breathing the same air or being enclosed by the same walls. They got involved in litigation and partitioned everything that their father had left. Everything that could be cut in two with an axe or scissors or a knife was divided between them, and the other things were catalogued, numbered and then shared out. But one thing that could neither be numbered nor cut up was the backyard of the house with its single well. They could do nothing about it. It fell to Margayya's share, and he would willingly have seen his brother's family perish without water by closing it to them, but public opinion prevented the exercise of his right. People insisted that the well should remain common property, and so the dividing wall came up to it, and stopped there, the well acting as a blockade between the two brothers, but accessible from either side.

Now Margayya looked about for the small brass pot. He could not see it anywhere.

'Hey, little man!' he called out, 'where is the well-pot?' He liked to call his son out constantly. When he came home, he could not bear to be kept away from him even for a moment. He felt uneasy and irritated when the child did not answer his call. He saw the youngster stooping over the lamp, trying to thrust a piece of paper into the chimney. He watched him from the doorway. He suppressed the inclination to call him away and warn him. The child thrust a piece of paper into the lamp, and when it burned brightly he recoiled at the sudden spurt of fire. But when it blackened and burnt out he drew near the lamp again, gingerly putting his finger near the metal plate on the top. Before Margayya could stop him, he had touched it. He let out a shriek. Margayya was beside him in a moment. His shriek brought in Margayya's wife, who had gone to a neighbouring shop. She came rushing into the house with cries of 'What is it? What is it? What has happened?' Margayya felt embarrassed, like a man caught shirking a duty. He told his wife curtly, 'Why do you shout so much, as if a great calamity had befallen this household – so that your sister-in-law in the neighbourhood may think how active we are, I suppose!'

'Sister-in-law – how proud you are of your relatives!' Her further remarks could not be continued because of the howling set up by the child, whose burnt finger still remained unattended. At this the mother snatched him up from her husband's arms, and hugged him close to her, hurting him more, whereupon he shouted in a new key. Margayya tried to tear him out of his wife's arms, crying: 'Quick, get that ointment. Where is it? You can keep nothing in its place.'

'You need not shout!' the wife answered, running about and rummaging in the cupboard. She grumbled: 'You can't look after him even for a second without letting him hurt himself.'

'You need not get hysterical about it, gentle lady, I had gone for a moment to the well.'

'Everyone gets tap-water in this town. We alone – ' she began, attacking on a new front.

'All right, all right,' he said, curbing her, and turning his attention to the finger. 'You must never, never go near fire again, do you understand?'

'Will you buy me a little elephant tomorrow?' the child asked, his cheeks still wet with tears. By now they had discovered a little wooden crucible containing some black ointment in the cupboard, hidden behind a small basket containing loose cotton (which Margayya's wife twisted into wicks for the lamp in God's niche). She applied the ointment to the injured finger, and set the child roaring in a higher key. This time he said, 'I want a big peppermint.'

At night when the lights were put out and the sounds of Vinayak Street had quietened, Margayya said to his wife, lying on the other side of their sleeping child: 'Do you know – poor boy! I could have prevented Balu from hurting himself. I just stood there and watched. I wanted to see what he would do alone by himself.' His wife made a noise of deprecation: 'It is as I suspected. You were at the bottom of the whole trouble. I don't know ... I don't know ... that boy is terribly mischievous ... and you are ... you are ...' She could not find the right word for it. Her instinct was full of foreboding, and she left the sentence unfinished. After a long pause she added: 'It's impossible to manage him during the afternoons. He constantly runs out of the house into the street. I don't have a moment's peace or rest.'

'Don't get cantankerous about such a small child,' said Margayya, who disliked all these adverse remarks about his son. It seemed to him such a pity that that small bundle of man curled beside him like a tiny pillow should be so talked about. His wife retorted: 'Yes, I wish you could stay at home and look after him instead of coming in the evening and dandling him for a moment after he has exhausted all his tricks.'

'Yes, gladly, provided you agree to go out and arrange loans for all those village idiots.'

The child levied an exacting penalty on his parents the next day for the little patch of burn on his finger. He held his finger upright and would not let anyone come near him. He refused to be put into a new shirt, refused food, refused to walk, and insisted on being carried about by his mother or father. Margayya examined the hurt finger and said: 'It looks all right, there seems to be nothing wrong there.'

'Don't say so,' screamed the boy in his own childish slang. 'I'm hurt. I want a peppermint.' Margayya was engaged all the morning in nursing his finger and plying him with peppermints. His wife remarked: 'He'll be ill with peppermints before you are done with him.'

'Why don't you look after him, then?' he asked.

'I won't go to mother,' screamed the boy. 'I will be with you.'

Margayya had some odd jobs to do while at home in the mornings. He went to the nearby Urban Stores and bought sugar or butter, he cut up the firewood into smaller sizes if his wife complained about it, or he opened his tin box and refreshed his memory by poring over the pages of his red-bound account-book. But today the boy would not let him do anything except fuss over him.

The child kept Margayya at home for over an hour beyond his usual time. He could leave for the Co-operative Bank only at midday, stealing out when, oblivious of his surroundings, the little fellow's attention was engaged in splashing about a bucket of water in the backyard. When the water was exhausted he looked all round and let out such an angry shout for his father that the people on the other side of the wall remarked to each other: 'This is the worst of begetting sons late in life! They pet them and spoil them and make them little monsters.' The lady on the other side of the wall could well say this because she was the mother of ten.

* * *

Margayya looked up as a shadow fell on his notebook. He saw a uniformed servant standing before him. It was Arul Doss, the head peon of the Co-operative Bank, an old Christian who had grown up with the institution. He had wrinkles round his eyes, and a white moustache and mild eyes. Margayya looked up at him and wondered what to do – whether to treat him as a hostile visitor or as a friend. Instinctively he recoiled from anyone coming out of that building, where he knew he was being viewed as a public enemy. He hesitated for a moment, then looked up silently at the figure before him. 'Sit down, won't you, Arul Doss?' Arul Doss shot a glance over his shoulder at the office.

'He will not like it if he sees me dallying here. He, I mean the Secretary, asks you to come – ' said Arul.

'Me!' Margayya could hardly believe his ears. 'The Secretary! What have I to do with your Secretary?'

'I don't know at all, but he said, "Go and tell Margayya to come here for a moment." '

On hearing this, Margayya became indignant. 'Go and tell them I am not their paid – paid – ' He was about to say 'servant', but he remembered in time, even in his mental stress, that the man standing before him was literally both paid and a servant, and thought it would be injudicious to say so now. So he left off the sentence abruptly and asked: 'Do they pay me to appear before them when they want me?'

'I don't know,' said this very loyal Co-operative man. 'He told me to tell you. The Secretary is no ordinary person, you know,' he added. 'He receives a salary of over five hundred rupees a month, an amount which you and I will probably not see even after a hundred years of service.' Now Margayya's blood was stirred. Many angry memories welled up in him of all the indignities that he had suffered at the hands of his brother, who cut him off with half a house, while he himself passed for a man of means, a respectable citizen. Margayya felt that the world treated him with contempt because he had no money. People thought they could order him about. He said to Arul Doss: 'Arul Doss, I don't know about you; you can speak for yourself. But you need not speak for me. You may not see a hundred rupees even after a hundred years of service, but I think I shall do so very soon – and who knows, if your Secretary seeks any improvement of his position, he can come to me.'

Arul Doss took a few moments to understand, then swayed with laughter. Tears rolled down his cheeks. 'Well, I have been a servant in this department for twenty-nine years, but I've never heard a crazier proposal. All right, all right.' He was convulsed with laughter as he turned to go. Margayya looked at his back helplessly. He cast his eyes down and surveyed himself: perhaps he cut a ridiculous figure, with his *dhoti* going brown for lack of laundering and with his shirt collar frayed, and those awful silver spectacles. 'I hate these spectacles. I wish I could do without them.' But age, age – who could help long-sight? 'If I wore gold spectacles, perhaps they would take me seriously and not order me about. Who is this Secretary to call me through the peon? I won't be ridiculed. I'm at least as good as they.' He called out: 'Look here, Arul Doss.' With a beaming face, Arul Doss turned round. 'Tell your Secretary that if he is a Secretary, I'm really the proprietor of a bank, and that he can come here and meet me if he has any business – '

'Shall I repeat those very words?' Arul Doss asked, ready to burst out laughing again.

'Absolutely,' Margayya said. 'And another thing, if you find yourself thrown out of there, you can come to me for a job. I like you, you seem to be a hard-working, loyal fellow.' Further parleys were cut off because a couple of villagers came round for consultation, and started forming a semi-circle in front of Margayya. Though Arul Doss still lingered for a further joke, Margayya turned away abruptly, remarking: 'All right, you may go now.'

'Please,' said a peasant, 'be careful, sir. That Arul Doss is a bad fellow.'

'I'm also a bad fellow,' snapped Margayya.

'It's not that. They say that the Secretary just does what this fellow says. If we go in to get just one single form, he charges us two annas each time. Is that also a Government rule?' asked the peasant.

'Go away, you fools,' Margayya said. 'You are people who have no self-respect. As long as you are shareholders, you are masters of that bank. They are your paid servants.'

'Ah, is that so?' asked the peasant. And the group looked up at each other with amazement. Another man, who had a long blanket wrapped round his shoulder, a big cloth turban crowning his head, and wore shorts and was barefoot, said: 'We may be masters as you say, but who is going to obey us? If we go in, we have to do as they say. Otherwise, they won't give us money.'

'Whose money are they giving away?' asked Margayya. 'It is your own.'

'Margayya, we don't want all that. Why should we talk of other people?'

'True, true,' said one or two others approvingly.

Encouraged by this, the peasant said: 'We should not talk about others unnecessarily.' He lowered his voice and said: 'If they hear it they may – '

Margayya's blood rushed to his head: 'You get away from here,' he thundered. 'I don't want to have anything to do with people without self-respect, who don't know their importance and strength. What better words can we expect from someone like you who wraps himself in that coarse blanket at this time of the day? What better stuff can we expect from a head weighed down by so many folds of a dirty turban?' The peasant was somewhat cowed by Margayya's manner. He mumbled: 'I didn't mean to offend you, sir. If I did would I be here?'

'That's all right. No further unnecessary talk. If you have any business, tell me. Otherwise get out of here. Before dusk I have to attend to so many people. You are not the only one who has business with me.'

'I want a small loan, sir,' began the peasant. 'I want to know how much more I have to pay to clear the balance loan.'

'Why don't you go in there and ask your Arul Doss?'

'Oh, they are all very bad, unhelpful people, sir; that's why I never like to go there, but come to you first. Why do we come to you, sir, of all persons in this big city? It's because you know our joys and sorrows and our troubles, our difficulties and – '

'All right, all right,' Margayya said, cutting him short, yet greatly mollified by his manner. 'I know what you are trying to say. Don't I?' He looked round at his clients. And they shook their heads approvingly, making appropriate sounds with their tongues, in order to please him.

After all these bouts he settled down to business. He had a busy day: filling up forms, writing applications, writing even petitions unconnected with money business for one or two clients, talking, arguing, and calculating. He was nearly hoarse by the time the sun's rays touched him on the nape of his neck, and the shadows of the banyan tree fell on the drive leading to the Co-operative Bank. He started to close his office. He put back his writing-pad, neatly folded up some pieces of paper on which he had noted figures, scrutinized again the little register, counted some cash, and checked some receipts. He arranged all these back in the small tin box, laid a few sheets of loan application forms flat on top of them so as to prevent their creasing, restored to its corner the ink-bottle, and laid beside it the red wooden pen. Everything in its place. He hated, more than anything else, having to fumble for his papers or stationery; and a disordered box was as hateful to him as the thought of Arul Doss. His mind was oppressed with thoughts of Arul Doss. He felt insulted and sore. What right had he or anyone to insult or browbeat him? What had he done that they themselves did not do? He would teach this Arul Doss a lesson – no matter at what cost ...

At this moment he heard a step approaching, and looking up saw a man, wearing a brown suit, standing before him. His hands were in his pockets, and behind him at a respectable distance stood Arul Doss. The man looked very smart, with a hat on his head; a very tidy young man who looked 'as if he had just come from Europe', Margayya reflected. Looking at him, he felt himself to be such a contrast with his brown *dhoti*, torn shirt, and the absurd little tuft under the black cap. 'No wonder they treat me as they do,' he said to himself. 'Perhaps I should have exercised greater care in my speech. God knows what that Arul Doss has reported ... I should not have spoken. This fellow looks as if he could do anything.' Margayya looked at Arul Doss, and shuddered, noting the wicked gleam in his eye. He soon recovered his self-possession: 'I am not a baby to worry about these things. What can anybody do to me?' He resolutely fixed his gaze on the hard knobs on his box, gave its contents a final pat, and was about to draw down the lid when the other man suddenly stooped, thrust his hand inside and picked out a handful of papers, demanding: 'How did you come by these? These are our application forms!'

Margayya checked the indignation that was rising within him: 'Put them back, will you? What right have you to put your hand into my box? You look like an educated man. Don't you know that ordinary simple law?' In his indignation he lost for a moment all fear. Arul Doss came forward and said, 'Take care how you speak. He is our Secretary. He will hand you over to the police.'

'Stop your nonsense, you earth-worm! Things have come to this, have they, when every earth-worm pretends that it is a cobra and tries to sway its hood ... I will nip off your head as well as your tail, if you start any of your tricks with me. Take care. Get out of my way.'

Arul Doss was cowed. He withdrew a little, but he was not to be dismissed so easily. He began: 'He is our Secretary – '

'That's all right. It's written all over him,' yelled Margayya. 'What else can he be? He can speak for himself, can't he? You keep away, you miserable ten-rupee earner. I want none of your impertinence here. If you want an old piece of cloth, torn or used, come to me.' The Secretary seemed to watch all this with detachment. Arul Doss fretted inwardly, tried to be officious, but had to withdraw because the Secretary himself ordered him away. 'You go over there,' he said, indicating a spot far off. Arul Doss moved reluctantly away. Margayya felt triumphant, and turned his attention to the man before him. 'Secretary, you will put back that paper or I will call the police now.'

'Yes, I want to call the police myself. You are in possession of something that belongs to our office.'

'No, it belongs to the shareholders.'

'Are you a shareholder?'

'Yes, more than that – '

'Nonsense. Don't make false statements. You'll get into trouble. Reports have come to me of your activities. Here is my warning. If you are seen here again, you will find yourself in prison. Go – ' He nodded to Arul Doss to come nearer, and held out to him the loan application forms. Arul Doss avidly seized them and carried them off like a trophy. The Secretary abruptly turned round and walked back to the porch of the building, where his car was waiting.

Presently Margayya bundled up his belongings and started homeward. With his box under his arm and his head bowed in thought he wandered down the Market Road. He paused for a moment at the entrance of the Regal Hair-Cutting Saloon, in whose doorway a huge looking glass was kept. He saw to his dismay that he was still wearing his spectacles. He pulled them off quickly, folded up their sides and put them into his pocket. He didn't feel flattered at the sight of his own reflection. 'I look like a wayside barber with this little miserable box under my arm. People probably expect me to open the lid and take out soap and a brush. No wonder the Secretary feels he can treat me as he likes. If I looked like him, would he have dared to snatch the papers from my box? I can't look like him. I am destined to look like a wayside barber, and that is my fate. I'm only fit for the company of those blanket-wrapped rustics.' He was thoroughly vexed with himself and his lot.

He moved to the side of the road, as cyclists rang their bells and dodged him; *jutka*-men shouted at him, and pedestrians collided against him. His mind was occupied with thoughts of his own miserableness. He felt himself shrinking. Two students emerged laughing and talking from the Bombay Anand Bhavan, their lips red with betel leaves. They stared at Margayya. 'They are laughing at me,' he thought. 'Perhaps they want to ask me to go with them to their rooms and give them a hair-cut!' He kept glancing over his shoulder at them, and caught them turning and glancing at him too, with a grin on their faces. Somebody driving by in a car of the latest model seemed to look at him for a fleeting second and Margayya fancied that he caught a glimpse of contempt in his eyes .... Now at the western end of Market Road he saw the V.N. Stores, with its owner standing at the door. 'He may put his hand into my pocket and snatch the glasses or compel me to give him a shave.' He side-stepped into Kabir

Lane, and, feeling ashamed of the little box that he carried under his arm, wished he could fling it away, but his sense of possession would not let him. As he passed through the narrow Kabir Lane, with small houses abutting the road, people seemed to stare at him as if to say: 'Barber, come early tomorrow morning: you must be ready here before I go for my bath.' He hurried off. He reached Vinayak Street, raced up the steps of his house and flung the box unceremoniously under the bench. His wife was washing the child on the back veranda. At the sound of his arrival the little fellow let out a yell of joy, through the towel.

'What's happened to make you come back so early?' asked Margayya's wife.

'Early! Why, can't I come home when I please? I am nobody's slave.' She had tried to tidy herself up in the evening after the day's work. 'She looks ...' He noticed how plebeian she looked, with her faded jacket, her patched, discoloured *sari* and her anaemic eyes. 'How can anyone treat me respectfully when my wife is so indifferent-looking?' His son came up and clung to his hand: 'Father, what have you brought me today?' He picked him up on his arm. 'Can't you put him into a cleaner shirt?' he asked.

'He has only four,' his wife answered. 'And he has already soiled three today. I have been telling you to buy some clothes.'

'Don't start all that now. I am in no mood for lectures.' His wife bit her lips and made a wry face. The child let out a howl for no reason whatever. She felt annoyed and said: 'He is always like this. He is all right till you come home. But the moment you step in, he won't even finish washing his face.'

'Where should I go if you don't want me to return home?'

'Nobody said such a thing,' she replied sullenly. The little boy shouted, put his hand into his father's coat-pocket and pulled out his reading glasses, and insisted upon putting them over his own nose. His mother cried: 'Give those glasses back or I'll ...' She raised her arm, at which he started yelling so much that they could not hear each other's remarks. Margayya carried him off to a shop and bought him sweets, leaving his wife behind, fretting with rage.

In the quiet of midnight, Margayya spoke to his wife seriously: 'Do you know why we get on each other's nerves and quarrel?'

'Yes,' she said at last. 'Now let me sleep.' And turned over. Margayya stretched out his hand and shook her by the shoulder. 'Wake up. I have much to tell you.'

'Can't you wait till the morning?' she asked.

'No.' He spoke to her of the day's events. She sat up in bed. 'Who is that secretary? What right has he to threaten you?'

'He has every right because he has more money, authority, dress, looks – above all, more money. It's money which gives people all this. Money alone is important in this world. Everything else will come to us naturally if we have money in our purse.'

She said: 'You shouldn't have been so rude to Arul Doss. You should not have said that you'd employ the secretary. That's not the way to speak to people earning five hundred rupees a month.'

'Let him get five thousand, what do I care? I can also earn a thousand or five thousand, and then these fellows will have to look out.' Much of his self-assurance was returning in the presence of his wife. All the despair and inferiority that he had been feeling was gradually leaving him. He felt more self-confident and aggressive. He felt he could hold out his hand and grab as much of the good things of life as he wanted. He felt himself being puffed up with hope and plans and self-assurance. He said, 'Even you will learn to behave with me when I have money. Your rudeness now is understandable. For isn't there a famous saying: "He that hath not is spurned even by his wife; even the mother that bore him spurns him." It was a very wise man who said it. Well, you will see. I'll not carry about that barber's box any more, and I'll not be seen in this torn *dhoti*. I will become respectable like anyone else. That secretary will have to call me "Mister" and stand up when I enter. No more torn mats and dirty, greasy *saris* for you. Our boy will have a cycle, he will have a suit and go to a convent in a car. And those people' (he indicated the next house) 'will have to wonder and burst their hearts with envy. He will have to come to me on his knees and wait for advice. I have finished with those villagers.'

He became like one possessed. He was agitated, as if he had made a startling discovery. He couldn't yet afford to keep away from the place where he worked. He went there as usual, but he had taken care to tidy himself up as much as possible. He wore a lace-edged *dhoti* which he normally kept folded in his box. It was of fine texture, but much yellowed now. He had always kept it in his box with a piece of camphor, and he now smelt like an incense-holder as he emerged from his small room, clad in this gorgeous *dhoti*. It had been given to him, as it now seemed a century and a half ago, on the day of his wedding when he was sitting beside his wife on a flower-decked swing, surrounded by a lot of women-folk joking and singing and teasing the newly-weds, after the feast at night. He sighed at the thought of those days. How they had fussed about him and tried to satisfy his smallest request and keep him pleased in every way. How eminent he had felt then! People seemed to feel honoured when he spoke to them. He had only to turn his head even slightly for someone or other to come rushing up and inquire what his wishes were. He had thought that that would continue for ever. What a totally false view of life one acquired on one's wedding day! It reminded him of his brother. How he bargained with the bride's people over the dowry! He used to be so fond of him. His brother's face stood out prominently from among the wedding group in Margayya's memory, as he sat in the corner, beyond the sacrificial smoke, in their village home. Margayya sighed at the memory of it; they had got on quite nicely, but their wives couldn't. 'If women got on smoothly ...' Half the trouble in this world is due to women who cannot tolerate each other.

His wife was amused to see him so gaudily dressed. 'What's the matter?' she asked. 'Are you going to a wedding party?' 'This is the only good one I have. They will never see me in that again,' he said, indicating his discarded *dhoti*. 'Keep it and give it to Arul Doss. He may come for it.' He was pleased with his own venom aimed at the distant Arul Doss. This quiet pleasure pricked his veins and thrilled his body. He put on a new shirt which he had stitched two years ago but had not had the heart to wear – always reserving it for some future occasion. The child too seemed to be quite pleased to see his father in a new dress. He clapped his hands in joy and left him in peace, concentrating his attention on a piece of elephant made of lacquer-painted wood. Margayya had elaborately tied up his *dhoti*, with folds going up, in the dignified Poona style, instead of the Southern fashion, looked down upon by people of other provinces. He explained to his wife: 'You see, if we are treated with contempt by people it is our fault. Our style of tying *dhoti* and our style of dressing – it is all so silly! No wonder.' He talked like a man who had just arrived from a far-off land, he spoke with such detachment and superiority. His wife was somewhat taken aback. She treated him with the utmost consideration when she served him his frugal meal. Usually he would have to ask, 'Food ready? Food ready?' several times and then pick up his plate and sit down and wait indefinitely as she kept blowing the fire. If he said: 'Hurry up, please,' she would retort: 'With my breath gone, blowing on this wet firewood, have you the heart ...' etc. But today she said: 'Your plate is there, food is ready.' She served him quietly, with a sort of docile agreeableness. 'I got this brinjal from the back garden,' she said. 'You didn't know I had a garden.' 'No. Nice stuff,' he murmured agreeably. Even the little fellow ate his food quietly, only once letting out a shout when he thought his mother wouldn't serve him his *ghee*. On that occasion he threw a handful of rice in his mother's face. She just ignored it, instead of flying at him, and the episode ended there. At the end of the meal Margayya picked up his plate as usual to wash and restore it to its corner in the kitchen. But she at once said: 'Oh, don't, I will attend to it.' He got up grandly and washed his hands, wiping them on a towel readily brought to his side by his wife. She gave him a few scented nuts and a betel leaf and saw him off at the door as he went down the street. He had opened his little box and picked up a few papers, which he carried in his hand. It looked better. He walked with the feeling that a new existence was opening before him.

His clients were somewhat surprised to see him in his new dress. He didn't squat under the tree, but remained standing.

'Why are you standing, Margayya?'

'Because I am not sitting,' Margayya replied.

'Why not?'

'Because I like to stand – that's all,' he replied.

He handed a filled-up application to someone and said: 'Give it in there, and come away.' He told another: 'Well, you will get your money today. Give me back my advance.' He carried on his business without sitting down. One of the men looked up and down and asked: 'Going to a marriage party?'

'Yes,' replied Margayya. 'Every day is a day of marriage for me. Do you think I like a change of wife each day?' He cracked his usual jokes. He placed his paper on the ledge of a wall and wrote. He had brought with him, hidden in his pocket, the little ink-bottle wrapped in paper, and his pen. As he bowed his head and wrote he muttered: 'I just want to help people to get over their money troubles. I do it as a sort of service, but let no one imagine I have no better business.'

'What else do you do, sir?' asked a very innocent man.

'Well, I have to do the same service for myself too, you see. I have to do something to earn money.'

'You get interest on all the amounts you give us.'

'Yes, yes, but that's hardly enough to pay for my snuff,' he said grandly, taking out a small box and inhaling a pinch. It sent a stinging sensation up his nostrils into his brain, and he felt his forehead throbbing with excitement. It made him feel so energetic that he felt like thumping a table and arguing. He said aggressively: 'I want to do so much for you fellows, do you know why?' They shook their heads bewildered. 'Not because of the petty interest you give me – that's nothing for me. It is because I want you all to get over your money worries and improve your lives. You must all adopt civilized ways. That's why I am trying to help you to get money from that bastard office.' He pointed at the Co-operative Bank. They all turned and looked at it. Arul Doss was seen approaching. 'He is coming,' they all said in one voice. Arul Doss approached them somewhat diffidently. His gait was halting and slow. He stopped quite far away, and pretended to look for a carriage or something on the road. Margayya thrust himself forward and watched him aggressively. Arul Doss stole a glance now and then at Margayya. Margayya felt annoyed. The sting of the snuff was still fresh. He cried out: 'Arul Doss, what are you looking for? If it is for me, come along, because I am here.' Arul Doss seemed happy to seize this opportunity to approach. Margayya said: 'Mark my words, this is god-given shade under the tree; if you or your secretary is up to any mischief, I will make you feel sorry for your – ' The villagers were overawed by Margayya's manner of handling Arul Doss. Arul Doss had no doubt come spying but now he felt uncomfortable at Margayya's sallies. If Margayya had been squatting under the tree with his box, he might have had a tale to bear, but now he saw nothing wrong. He had only one worry – that of being called an earth-worm again before so many people. He tried to turn and go, saying, 'I just came to see if the Secretary's car had come.'

'Has your secretary a car?' Margayya asked patronizingly.

'Haven't you noticed that big red one?'

Margayya snapped his fingers and said: 'As if I had no better things to observe. Tell your secretary – ' He checked himself, not being sure what his tongue might utter. 'Arul Doss, if you are in need of an old *dhoti* or shirt, go and ask my wife. She will give it to you.' Arul Doss's face beamed with happiness.

'Oh, surely, surely,' he said. He approached nearer to Margayya and whispered. Margayya raised his hand to his face and put his head back. The other's breath smelt of onion. Margayya asked: 'Do you nibble raw onion in the morning?' Arul Doss ignored the question and whispered: 'You must not think that I myself tried to bother you yesterday. It's all that fellow's orders.' He pointed towards his office. 'He is a vicious creature! You won't think that I ... You can carry on here as you like, sir. Don't worry about anything.' He turned and abruptly walked back. Margayya looked after him and commented to his circle: 'That's the worst blackguard under the sun – both of them are. This fellow carries tales to him and then he comes and behaves like a great governor here. What do I care? If a man thinks that he is governor let him show off at home, not here, for I don't care for governors.'

As he went through the town that day he was obsessed with thoughts of money. His mind rang with the words he had said to the villagers: 'I'm only trying to help you to get out of your money worries.' He began to believe it himself. He viewed himself as a saviour of mankind. 'If I hadn't secured three hundred rupees for — — —, he would be rotting in the street at this moment. So and so married off his daughter, educated his son, retained his house.'

His mind began to catalogue all the good things money had done as far as he could remember. He shuddered to think how people could ever do without it. If money was absent men came near being beasts. He saw at the Market Fountain a white sheet covering some object stretched on the pavement. It was about six in the evening, and the street was lit up with a blaze of sunlight from the west. Pedestrians, donkeys and *jutkas* were transformed with the gold of the setting sun. Margayya stood dazzled by the sight. A ragged fellow with matted hair thrust before him a mud tray and said, pointing at the sheet-covered object on the ground, 'An orphan's body, sir. Have pity, help us to bury him.' Margayya threw a look at the covered body, shuddered and parted with a copper, as so many others had done. There was a good collection on the tray. Margayya averted his face and tried to pass quickly. Farther on yet another man came up with a mud tray whining: 'Orphan body – '

'Get off, already given,' said Margayya sternly, and passed on. There was money on this tray too. Margayya was filled with disgust. He knew what it meant. A group of people seized upon an unclaimed dead body, undertook to give it a burial and collected a lot of money for it. He knew that they celebrated it as a festive occasion. When they saw a destitute dying on the roadside they cried to themselves: 'Aha! A fine day ahead.' They left their occupations, seized the body, carried it to a public place, put it down on the pavement, placed a few flowers on it, bought a few mud trays from the potter, and assailed the passers-by. They collected enough money at the end of the day to give a gorgeous funeral to the body. They even haggled with the grave-digger and were left with so much money at the end of it all that they drank and made merry for three or four days and gave up temporarily their normal jobs, such as scavenging, load-carrying, and stone-quarrying. It made Margayya reflective. People did anything for money. Money was men's greatest need, like air or food. People went to horrifying lengths for its sake, like collecting rent on a dead body: yet this didn't strike Margayya in his present mood as so horrible as something to be marvelled at.

It left him admiring the power and dynamism of money, its capacity to make people do strange deeds. He saw a toddy tapper going a hundred feet up a coconut tree and he reflected: 'Morning to night he wears a loin-cloth and goes up tree after tree for fifty years or more just for the eight annas he gets per tree.' He saw offices and shops opened and people sweating and fatiguing themselves, all for money. Margayya concluded that they wanted money because they wanted fellows like the Secretary of the Cooperative Bank to bow to them, or to have a fellow like Arul Doss speak to them with courtesy, or so that they might wear unpatched *dhotis* and be treated seriously. Margayya sat down for a moment on a park bench. The Municipality had made a very tiny park at the angle where the Market Road branched off to Lawley Extension. They had put up a cement bench and grown a clump of strong ferns, fencing them off with a railing. He passed through the stile and sat down on the bench. Cars were being driven towards Lawley Extension. Huge cars. He watched them greedily. 'Must have a car as soon as possible,' he said to himself. 'Nothing is impossible in this world.' A cool breeze was blowing. The sun had set. Lights were lit up here and there. 'If I have money, I need not dodge that spectacle dealer. I need not cringe before that stores man. I could give those medicines to my wife. The doctor would look at her with more interest, and she might look like other women. That son of mine, that Balu – I could give him everything.' His mind gloated over visions of his son. He would grow into an aristocrat. He would study, not in a Corporation School, but in the convent, and hobnob with the sons of the District Collector or the Superintendent of Police or Mangal Seth, the biggest mill-owner in the town. He would promise him a car all for himself when he came to the College. He could go to America and obtain degrees, and then marry perhaps a judge's daughter. His own wife might demand all the dowry she wanted. He would not interfere, leaving it for the women to manage as they liked. He would buy another bungalow in Lawley Road for his son, and then his vision went on to the next generation of aristocrats.

At this moment he saw a man coming from Lawley Extension: a cadaverous man, burnt by the sun, wrapped in a long piece of white cloth, his forehead painted with red marks and his head clean shaved, with a tuft of hair on top. A tall, gaunt man, he was the priest of the temple in their street. An idea struck Margayya at the sight of him. He was a wise man, well versed in ancient studies, and he might be able to give advice. Margayya clapped his hands till the gaunt man turned and advanced towards him.

'Ah! Margayya! What are you doing here?'

'Just came for a little fresh air. The air is so cool here, unlike our Vinayak Street.'

'Oh, these are all aristocratic parts, with gardens, and fresh air. Our Vinayak Mudali Street! It's like an oven in summer.'

'And what a lot of mosquitoes!' Margayya added.

'I couldn't sleep the whole night,' the priest said.

'Why should they make such a row in our ears? Let them suck the blood if they want, but it's their humming that is so unwelcome,' said Margayya.

They spoke of weather and mosquitoes and fresh air and the diseases prevalent in the town for about half an hour. The priest lived in a sort of timelessness and seemed to be in no hurry. The stars were shining in the sky. Margayya asked: 'How was it you were coming this way?'

'I had gone to perform a *Pooja* in a house in Lawley Extension. You know that Municipal Chairman's house: they are very particular that I alone should perform these things. They won't tolerate anyone else. So every evening I do it there and then rush back to our temple, where the devotees will be waiting. A man can't be in two places at the same time.'

'Truly said. I will walk back with you to the temple, if you are going there.'

'I have to go to another place on the way and then on to the temple. Just a minute's delay there, that's all. Do come with me. There's nothing so good as company on the road. I've to walk miles and miles from morning to night.'

They walked back towards the Market Road. The priest led him into some unnamed lanes behind the Market. He stopped in front of a house and said: 'If you will wait here, I will be back in a moment.' He went in. Margayya sat up on the pyol. There was a gutter below him. 'This is worse than our Vinayak Street,' Margayya reflected. The place was occupied by a class of hand-loom weavers. All along the lane they had set up weaving frames with yarns dyed in blue and hung out to dry on frames. Somebody came out of the house and said to Margayya: 'Won't you come in?' Margayya felt pleased at this attention and followed him in. There was a very small front hall in the house piled up with weaving frames, stacks of woven *saris* in different colours, and several rolls of bedding belonging to the members of the household. At one corner they had put up a small wooden pedestal on which a couple of figures of Gods and one or two framed pictures were hanging. An incense stick was burning. His friend the priest sat up before the pedestal, with his eyes shut, muttering something. The master of the house with his wife and children stood devoutly at a distance. There were four children. One or the other of them was being constantly told: 'Don't bite your nails before God.' And they were so much overwhelmed by the general atmosphere that they constantly put their finger tips to their lips and withdrew them quickly as if they had touched a frying-pan. Margayya was very much impressed with their seriousness, and wondered at the same time what his Balu would have done under these circum-stances. 'He'd have insisted upon doing what he pleased – and not only bitten his own nails but other people's as well. He would have upset all this holy water and camphor flame,' Margayya reflected, with gratification. It seemed to him a most enchanting self-assertiveness on the part of his child. It gave him a touch of superiority to all these children, who wouldn't bite their nails when ordered not to. He felt a desire to go home and spoil his son. 'I left so early in the day,' he reflected. He suddenly asked himself, 'Why am I knocking around with this priest instead of going home?' An old lady, probably the grandmother of the house, sat before the God with a small child on her lap. Only the child's eyes were visible, gleaming in the sacred lamps. It was entirely wrapped in a blanket. Margayya guessed that it must be very sick. They were all fussing over it. 'How old is that child?' Margayya wondered, unable to get a full glimpse of it. Somehow this worried him. 'If Balu were in his position would he have consented to be chained up like this? Some children are too dull – '

It was nearly nine o'clock when they came out. Margayya followed the priest mutely through the streets. The town had almost gone to sleep. The streets were silent.

'It's so late!' he murmured.

'What is late?' asked the priest.

'We are so late.'

'Late for what?'

Margayya fumbled for a reply. He said clumsily: 'You said you'd be kept there only for a short time. I thought you would be kept only a short time – that's why – '

'In holy business can we be glancing at a wrist-watch all the time? That child has been crippled with a dreadful disease from childhood. It is now much better. It is some wasting disease – '

'Do you perform *Poojas* for his sake?'

'Yes, every Friday. It is the *Pooja* that enabled young Markandeya to win over *Yama*, the God of Death.'

'Oh!' Margayya exclaimed, interested but not willing to show his ignorance.

'Every child knows that story.'

'Yes, of course, of course,' Margayya said non-committally. He felt he ought to say something more and added: 'Those people,' indicating over his shoulder a vast throng of wise ancestors, 'those people knew what was good for us.'

'Not the people you mean, but those who were there even before them,' corrected the priest in a debating spirit.

'All right,' Margayya agreed meekly.

The priest asked him further on: 'What do you gather from the story of Markandeya?'

Margayya blinked, and felt like a schoolboy. He said ceremoniously: 'How can I say? It's for a learned person like you to enlighten us on these matters.'

'All right. What was Markandeya?' asked the man persistently.

Margayya began to feel desperate. He feared that the other might not rest till he had exposed his ignorance. He felt he ought to put a stop to it at once, and said: 'It's a long time since I heard that story. My grandmother used to tell it. I should like to hear it again.'

'Ask then. If you don't know a thing, there is no shame in asking and learning about it,' moralized the priest. He then narrated the story of Markandeya, the boy devotee of God Shiva, destined to die the moment he completed his sixteenth year. When the moment came, the emissaries of *Yama* (the God of Death) arrived in order to bind and carry off his life, but he was performing the *Pooja* – and the dark emissaries could not approach him at all! Markandeya remained sixteen to all eternity, and thus defeated death. 'That particular *Pooja* had that efficacy – and it's that very *Pooja* I am performing on behalf of the child, who is much better for it.'

'Will the child live?' asked Margayya, his interest completely roused.

'How can I say? It's our duty to perform a *Pooja*; the result cannot be our concern. It's *Karma*.'

'Yes, yes,' agreed Margayya, somewhat baffled.

They now reached the little temple at the end of Vinayak Mudali Street. There under a cracked dome was an inner shrine containing an image of Hanuman, the God of Power, the son of Wind. According to tradition this God had pressed one foot on the very spot where the shrine now stood, sprang across space and ocean and landed in Lanka (Ceylon), there to destroy Ravana, a king with ten heads and twenty hands, who was oppressing mankind and had abducted Rama's wife Sita.

The priest was part and parcel of the temple. There was a small wooden shack within its narrow corridors, where he ate his food and slept. He looked after the shrine, polished and oiled the tall bronze lamps and worshipped here.

Margayya hesitated at the entrance. It seemed already very late. 'I'll go now,' he said.

'Why don't you come in and see the God, having come so far?' asked the priest. Margayya hesitated. He was afraid to ignore the priest's suggestion. He feared that that might displease God. As he hesitated, the priest drove home the point: 'You stopped me there at the park to say something. You have been with me ever since and you have not spoken anything about it.' Margayya felt caught. He found himself behaving more and more like a schoolboy. He remembered his old teacher, back there in his village, an old man with a white rim around his black pupils that gave him the look of a cat peering in the dark, whose hands shook when he gripped the cane, but who nevertheless put it to sound use, especially on Margayya's back, particularly when he behaved as he behaved now, blinking when he ought to be opening his lips and letting the words out. Later in life Margayya remedied it by not allowing any pause in his speech, but the disease recurred now and then. This was such a moment. He wanted to talk to the priest and seek his advice, but he felt reluctant to utter the first word. As he stood there at the portals of the temple he feared for a second the old whacking from a cane. But the priest only said: 'Come in.'

'Isn't it late?'

'For what?'

Margayya once again blinked. He mutely followed the priest into the shrine. The main portion of the image went up into the shadows, partly illuminated by a flickering oil-lamp. The priest briskly swept into a basket some broken coconut, plantains, and coins, left on the doorstep by devotees. He held up a plantain and a piece of coconut for Margayya. 'Probably you are hungry. Eat these. I will give you a tumbler of milk.' He went into his shack and came out bearing a tumbler of milk.

Margayya squatted on the floor, leaning against the high rugged wall of the corridor. The town had fallen asleep. Vinayak Mudali Street was at the very end of the town, and no one moved about at this hour. Even the street dogs, which created such a furore every night, seemed to have fallen asleep. A couple of coconut trees waved against the stars in the sky. The only noise in the world now seemed to be the crunching of coconut between Margayya's jaws. It was like the sound of wooden wheels running over a sandy bed. Margayya felt abashed, and tried to eat noiselessly. At this a bit of coconut went the wrong way, and he was seized with a fit of coughing, which racked his whole frame. He panted and gasped as he tried to explain: 'It ... It ... It ...' The priest seemed to watch with amusement, and he felt indignant. 'What right has this man to keep me here at this hour and amuse himself at my expense?'

The priest said: 'Drink that milk, it will make you all right.'

'He asks me to drink milk as if I were a baby. Next, I think, he will force it between my lips.' He suddenly grew very assertive and said resolutely: 'I don't like milk ... I have never liked it.' He pushed away the tumbler resolutely.

The priest said: 'Don't push away a tumbler of milk with the back of your hand.' Margayya was no longer going to be treated and lectured like a schoolboy. He said: 'I know. But who doesn't?'

'And yet,' said the priest with amused contempt, 'you push away milk with the back of your hand as if it were a tumbler of ditch water.'

'No, no,' said Margayya semi-apologetically. 'I didn't push it with the back of my hand. I just tried to put away the tumbler so that you might take it.'

Ignoring this explanation and looking away, far away, the priest said: 'Milk is one of the forms of Goddess Lakshmi, the Goddess of Wealth. When you reject it or treat it indifferently, it means you reject her. She is a Goddess who always stays on the tip of her toes all the time, ever ready to turn and run away. There are ways of wooing and keeping her. When she graces a house with her presence, the master of the house becomes distinguished, famous and wealthy.' Margayya reverently touched the tumbler and very respectfully drank the milk, taking care not to spill even a drop.

'That is better,' said the old man. 'There was once upon a time – ' He narrated from Mahabharata the story of Kubera, the wealthiest man in creation, who undertook a long arduous penance as atonement for spilling a drop of milk on the floor of his palace. When the story ended and a pause ensued, Margayya felt he could no longer keep back his request. He felt somewhat shy as he said: 'I want to acquire wealth. Can you show me a way? I will do anything you suggest.'

'Anything?' asked the first emphatically. Margayya suddenly grew nervous and discreet. 'Of course, anything reasonable.' Perhaps the man would tell him to walk upside down or some such thing. 'You know what I mean,' Margayya added pathetically.

'No, I don't know what you mean,' said the old man point blank. 'Wealth does not come the way of people who adopt half-hearted measures. It comes only to those who pray for it single-mindedly with no other thought.'

Margayya began to tremble slightly at this statement. 'Perhaps he is a sorcerer, or a black magician or an alchemist.' He threw a frightened look at him and then at the shack in which he usually dwelt. 'Perhaps he has hidden human bodies in that shack, and extracts from the corpses some black ointment, with which he acquires extraordinary powers.'

Margayya wanted to get up and run away. In the starlight the man looked eerie; his hollow voice reverberating through the silent night. Margayya's mind was seized with fears. 'Perhaps he will ask me to cut off my son's head.' He imagined Balu being drugged and taken into the shack. 'It's midnight or probably dawn. Let me go home.'

He got up abruptly. The old man did not stop him. He merely said: 'Yes, go home. It is very late. Probably your wife will be anxious.' Margayya felt tremendously relieved that after all he was permitted to leave. He got up, prostrated before the God's image, scrambled to his feet hurriedly, lest the other, sitting immobile where he had left him, should call him back. He hurried off through the silent street. Far off a night constable's whistle was heard. 'I hope he will not take me for a thief.' He was wearing his wedding *dhoti*, carrying his account papers under his arm; the whole thing struck him at this hour as being extremely ridiculous.

He stood before his door unable to make up his mind to knock. It might rouse his wife or his son. But unless his wife was roused ... And how could he explain his late coming? 'Something has happened to me – everything seems to be going wrong. That Arul Doss has perhaps cast a spell: can't be sure what everybody is up to – ' The world seemed to be a very risky place to live in, peopled by creatures with dark powers. As he stood there un-decided, his wife threw back the bolt and let him in. She hadn't put out the kerosene lamp. She looked at him sourly and asked: 'What have you been doing so late?' Once inside his home all his old assertiveness returned. He was the master in his house, with nobody to question him. He ignored her and quickly went into the smaller room to undress and change. He washed himself briskly at the well. His son was sleeping near the doorway of the smaller room on a rush mat. He threw a loving look at him, with a feeling that but for a quick decision on his part the little fellow might be in that shack put to no end of tortures. His wife was very sleepy as she waited for him in the kitchen. He found that she had spread out two leaves. 'What? You have not had your dinner yet!' he said, feeling pleased that she had waited for him.

'How could I without knowing what had happened? Here-after, if you are going to be late – '

'I must ask your permission, I suppose,' he said arrogantly.

They consumed their midnight dinner in silence. They went to bed in silence. He lay on the mat beside his son. She went down into her room, and lay on a carpet on which she had already snatched a few hours of sleep before he arrived. Margayya lay in bed unable to shut his eyes. He lay looking at the ceiling, which was dark with smoke; cobwebs dangled from the tiles like tapestry. 'She ought to clean it and not expect me to have to see such things,' he said to himself angrily. He got up and blew out the kerosene lamp and lay down. He slept badly, constantly harassed by nightmares composed of the priest, the secretary, and Arul Doss. One recurring dream was of his son stepping into the shack in the temple, with the priest standing behind the door, and all his efforts to keep him back proved futile. The young fellow was constantly tiptoeing away towards the shack. It bothered Margayya so much that he let out a cry: 'Aiyo! Aiyo!' which woke up the child, who jumped out of bed with a piercing scream; which in turn roused his mother sleeping in the other room, and she sprang up howling: 'Oh, what has happened! What has happened!' It was about half an hour before the dawn. All this commotion awakened Margayya himself. He cried: 'Who is there? Who is there?' 'Someone was moving about.' 'Someone made a noise.' The uproar increased. 'Where are the matches?' Margayya demanded suddenly and cursed in the dark. 'Who asked you to blow out the light?' his wife said. He sprang up and ran towards the backyard thinking that the intruder must have run in that direction. The little boy cried, 'Oh, father, father, don't go ... Don't go ...' His mother clutched him to her bosom. He struggled and wildly kicked for no reason whatever. The people of the next house woke up and muttered: 'Something always goes wrong in that house. Even at midnight one has no peace, if they are in the neighbourhood.'

Margayya was sitting before his small box, examining the accounts written in his red book. His son came up to sit on his lap. Margayya said: 'Go and play, don't disturb me now,' and tried to keep him off. 'This is my play, I won't go,' said the child, pushing towards him again resolutely and climbing on his lap. Margayya had to peep over his head in order to look at the register before him; Balu's hair constantly tickled his nostrils and he felt irritated. He cried: 'Balu, won't you leave me alone. I will buy you a nice – '

'What?' asked the child.

'A nice little elephant.'

'All right, buy it now, come on.'

'No, no, not now ... I'm working now,' he said, pointing at the small register. Balu shot out his little leg and kicked away the register petulantly, and in the process the ink-well upset beside it and emptied on the page. Then the child stamped his heel on the ink and it splashed over Margayya's face and spoiled the entire book. Margayya felt maddened at the sight of it. He simply gripped the boy by his shoulder, lifted him as he would lift an unwanted cat, and almost flung him into a corner. Needless to say it made the child cry so loudly that his mother came running out of the kitchen, her eyes streaming with tears owing to the smoke there. 'What has happened? What has happened?' she cried, rushing towards the child, who, undaunted, was again making a dash for his father as he stooped over the wreckage trying to retrieve his damaged account-book. 'Look what he has done,' he cried excitedly. 'This monkey!'

'*You* are a monkey!' cried the boy, hugging his father's knee as he was blotting the spilled ink.

'If you don't leave me, I'll – I'll – ' He was too angry. 'I'll give you over to the temple priest ... He'll flay your skin.'

'He will give me plantains,' corrected the boy. He turned aside and suddenly pounced on the book, grabbed it and dashed off. His father ran after him with war cries. The boy dodged him here and there, going into this corner and darting into that. His tears had by now dried, he was enjoying the chase, and with hysterical laughter he was running hither and thither clutching the precious red notebook in his hand. It was a small space within which he ran, but somehow Margayya was unable to seize him. Margayya panted with the effort. He cried: 'If you don't stop, I'll flay you.'

'What is the matter with you? What has come over you?' asked the wife.

'I'm all right,' Margayya replied proudly. 'You'll see what I'll do to that little monkey, that devil you have begotten.' His wife gave some appropriate reply, and tried to help in the chase. She pretended to look away and suddenly darted across to seize the boy. He was too swift even for her calculations. She only collided against her husband, which irritated him more; and it allowed the child to dash into the street with his prize, with his father at his heels. He cried impatiently to his wife, 'Get out of the way – you – ' at which she turned and went back to the kitchen murmuring: 'What do I care? I only let the rice overboil watching this tomfoolery.' The boy dashed down the front steps, with his father following him. Margayya was blind to all his surroundings – all he could see was the little boy with his curly hair, and the small red-bound book which was in his hand. Some passers-by in Vinayak Mudali Street stopped to watch the scene. Margayya cried shamelessly: 'Hold him! Hold him!' At which they tried to encircle the boy. It was evident that by now he had become completely intoxicated with the chase. Presently he found that he was being outnumbered and cornered. As a circle of hunters hemmed in, he did an entirely unexpected thing – he turned back as if coming into his father's arms, and as he was just about to grasp him, darted sideways to the edge of the gutter and flung the red book into it. The gutter ran in front of the houses; roaring waters went down the drain God knew where. It was well known that any object that fell into it was lost for ever, it sank and went out of sight, sank deeper and deeper into a black mass, and was hopelessly gone. The gutter was wide as a channel. Once in a while, especially before the elections, the Municipal officials came down and walked along the edge peering into its dark current and saying something among themselves as to its being a problem and so on. But there they left it until the next election. It was a stock cynicism for people to say when they saw anyone inspecting the drains: 'They are only looking for the election votes there!' At other times the gutter continued its existence unhampered, providing the cloud of mosquitoes and the stench that characterized existence in Vinayak Mudali Street.

Presently a big crowd stood on the edge of the drain looking at its inky, swirling waters. People sympathized with Margayya. Wild, inaccurate reports of what had fallen into it were circulated. Margayya heard people tell each other: 'A box was dropped into it.' 'That child threw away a gold chain into it.' Everyone looked at Balu with interest. He seemed to have become a hero for the moment. He felt abashed at this prominence and hung his head. The sun was shining on them fiercely, though it was just nine-thirty in the morning. Margayya looked red with anger and exertion. His son's face was also flushed. The little boy crossed his arms behind him and stood on the edge of the gutter watching it with fascination. There was no trace of the book left anywhere. Margayya's blood boiled as he watched the unconcern of the boy, who, true to the type in that street, wore only a shirt which covered only the upper half of his body. Two pedlars carrying green vegetables, a cyclist who jumped off on seeing the crowd, a few school children, a curd-seller, and a few others formed the group which now watched the gutter with varying comments passing between them. A man was saying: 'Some people are so fond that they give their children everything they ask for.' On hearing this Margayya felt so enraged that he lifted the edge of the shirt the little boy was wearing and slapped him fiercely across his uncovered seat. The boy cried aloud: 'Oh!' and turned round on his father. It started a fresh scene. Someone dragged away the child crying: 'Save the child from this ruffian.' Another said: 'He would have pushed the child into the gutter.' A woman with a basket came forward to ask: 'Are you a heartless demon? How can you beat such a small child?' She flung down her basket and picked up the child on her arm. Balu copiously sobbed on her shoulder. Another woman tried to take him from her, commenting: 'Only those who bear the child for ten months in the womb know how precious it is. Men are always like this.' Someone objected to this statement; it turned out to be the man holding the cycle, who retorted with great warmth: 'Boys must be chastized; otherwise do you want them to grow up into devils?' Margayya looked at him gratefully. Here at last was a friend in this absolutely hostile world. He swept his arms to address all the women and the gathering: 'It's all very well for you to talk .... But he has thrown in there an important account-book. What am I to do without it?'

'How can a baby know anything about account-books and such things? God gives children to those who don't deserve them.'

'You should not have kept it within his reach. You must always be prepared for such things where there are children.'

A washerwoman, who had come forward, said: 'You were childless for twelve years, and prayed to all the Gods and went to Thirupathi: was it only for this?'

'What have I done?' Margayya asked pathetically. He was beginning to feel very foolish. Society was pressing in upon him from all sides – the latest in the shape of this woman who had on her back a bundle of unwashed linen. Vegetable-sellers, oilmongers, passers-by, cartmen, students – everyone seemed to have a right to talk to him as they pleased. Society seemed to overwhelm him on all sides. The lone cyclist was hardly an adequate support on which to lean. Margayya turned and looked for him. He too was gone. He saw his son clinging fast to the waist of the cucumber-seller, sobbing and sobbing, and gaining more sympathizers. Margayya knew that the little boy would not let his sympathizers go until they took him to the shop across the road and bought him peppermints.

The crowd turned away and was now following Balu, and Margayya felt relieved that they were leaving him alone. He broke a twig off an avenue tree, and vaguely poked it into the gutter and ran the stick from end to end. He only succeeded in raising a stench. A school-master who passed that way advised: 'Call a scavenger and ask him to look for it. He'll have the proper thing with him for poking here. Don't try to do everything yourself.' Margayya obediently dropped the stick into the drain, reflecting, 'No one will let me do what I like.' He turned to go back into his house. He climbed his steps with bowed head, because his brother's entire family was ranged along the wall on the other side. He quickly passed in. When he was gone they commented: 'Something is always agitating that household and creating a row.' Margayya went straight into the kitchen, where his wife was cooking, ignorant of all that had happened, and told her: 'The folk in the next house seem to have no better business than to hang about to see what is going on here ... Do they ever find the time to cook, eat or sleep?' This was a routine question needing no reply from his wife. She merely asked: 'Where is the child?' 'Probably rolling in the gutter,' he answered wearily. 'What has come over you?' she asked. 'You don't seem to be in your senses since last night.'

'I'm not. And if you try to imply that I have been drinking or spending the night in a brothel, I leave you free to think so – '

The loss of the little book produced endless complications for Margayya. He could hardly transact any business without it, he had to conceal the loss from his customers, who he feared might take advantage of it. He had to keep out of the tree shade, remain standing or moving about, and give out figures from his head – it was all most irksome. It was an important day; he had to collect money from three or four men to whom he had advanced cash.

'Where is the book, master?' asked Kali, one of his old customers. Margayya said: 'I'm rebinding it. You know it must look tidy. But it is really not necessary for me. I have everything I want here,' he added, tapping his forehead. Kali had not been here for some weeks now and so looked with suspicion at this man standing beyond the gate, without his box, without his book. 'Perhaps,' thought Margayya, 'Arul Doss has been speaking to him.' Kali was like a tiger which suddenly meets the ring-master, without the ring, or the whip in his hand.

'Why are you not in your place?' he asked.

'Oh! I'm tired of sitting and sitting – some sort of lumbago here,' Margayya said. He sat down on the short compound wall. A country cart passed along, and it threw up dust. Margayya sneezed. 'You see, you should not sit there,' moralized the other.

'I should not, that's why I'm looking for an office hereabouts with chairs and tables. When eminent people like you arrive, you will be seated in chairs,' he said. 'I must also look to your convenience, don't you see?'

'Of course,' said the other. 'But that banyan shade was quite good, sir. So much fresh air. I always like it.'

'I don't,' replied Margayya. 'It's all very well for a man like you, who comes out to lounge and have a nap in the afternoon. But for a business man it is not good. The uproar those birds make! I can hardly hear my own voice! And then their droppings! And those ants down below. I used to suffer agony when I was sitting there.'

'Where is your box, sir?' asked Kali, noticing its absence.

'Sent it for repainting: it's a lucky box, my dear fellow. I don't like to throw it away ... It's not looking quite tidy. I've sent it for painting. I have it more as a keepsake.'

'Yes, whatever article has grown up with us must be kept all our life ... In our village there was a fellow who had a hoe with a broken handle – '

'I know all that,' Margayya cut in, snubbing him just for the sake of effect. 'When he changed the handle, his harvest suffered, didn't it?'

'How do you know, sir?' asked Kali, overawed.

'I know everything that goes on in people's minds; otherwise, I should not have taken to this banking business ... Now I know what is going on in your mind. You have got in your purse, which you have tucked at the waist, money drawn from the bank.'

'No, no, sir,' he protested. 'Is it so easy to get money out of them?'

'Listen! Your loan application was considered and passed on Monday last. You must have in your purse now two hundred and seventy-nine rupees and four annas; that is, you have given eight annas to the clerk, and four annas as a tip to Arul Doss. Is it, or is it not a fact?' He cast a searching look at Kali, who had wrapped himself in a large sheet. There were a hundred corners over his person where he might tuck a whole treasure. Kali met his gaze, and turned to go. It was the dull hour of the afternoon when his other clients had gone into the bank or were dozing in the shade. They would all come a little later. Margayya was glad it was so, because he wanted to tackle this difficult man alone. Others would not be able to take a lesson from him. Kali was attempting to retreat. He looked up at the sky and said: 'Looks like three o'clock. They have asked me to call in at three again. You know how it is, if we go in even a minute late. They make it an excuse – ' Margayya looked at him. If he let him go out of sight, he would pass into the bank and then out of it by the back door.

He said firmly: 'You give me the fifty rupees I advanced, with interest.' The other looked puzzled.

'Fifty! With interest! What is it you are talking about, Margayya?' At other times, if anyone said such a thing, Margayya would open the pages of his red-bound book and flourish it. He thought of his son. Why did the boy do such a thing? He had left the book alone all these days! Kali stopped, looked at him haughtily and said: 'I never like to be called a liar! You may settle my account tomorrow, the first thing ... Let me see what it is, and I will settle it the first thing tomorrow, to the last pie.' He moved away. Margayya stood helplessly. He watched him with sorrow. He could not even throw after him any curse and threats (brilliant ones that occurred to him, as usual, a little too late). 'Margayya, you have been made a fool of. They have made a frightful fool of you.' 'They haven't ... I should have told him ... You son of a guttersnipe ... Don't I know what your father was! He went to gaol for snatching a chain from a child's neck! You come of a family which would steal a matchstick rather than ask for it ... I shouldn't have associated with you, but I'll get at you one day, don't worry. I can – ' But it was no use arguing with himself in this manner. The man was gone, while Margayya stood watching him dumbly. He recollected that he had helped him get loans four times – when his life and honour, as he said, were at stake. 'And this is what I get.' He was filled with self-pity. He thought of the account-book. Suppose he announced a reward to any scavenger who might salvage it? Even if it was salvaged what was the use? How was it to be touched again and read!

He had to wait at the gate, away from the line of vision of the secretary's room, sitting on the short parapet, and keep an eye on all his old customers who might go in and come out of the building. Without giving himself too much away, he was able to tackle a few of his old customers, and they didn't prove as tricky as Kali. He was able to salvage the bulk of his investments within the next fifteen days, which amounted to just two hundred rupees.

Margayya stepped into the temple, driven there by a vague sense of desperation. He told himself several times over that he was going to see the God and not the priest. But he did not believe it himself – nor did the priest let him view only the God and go away. As soon as he entered the portals of the temple the priest's voice came to him from an unknown, unobserved place, behind the image in the dark inner sanctum. 'Oh, Margayya, welcome to this God's home.' Margayya was startled as if a voice from Heaven had suddenly assailed him. He trembled. The last worshipper had prostrated before the image and was leaving. Margayya prostrated on the ground before the inner sanctuary. A couple of feeble oil-lamps were alight; a mixed smell of burning oil, flowers, and incense hung in the air. That was a combination of scent which always gave Margayya a feeling of elation. He shut his eyes. For a moment he felt that he was in a world free from all worrying problems. It was in many ways a noble world, where everything ran smoothly – no Arul Doss or Co-operative Society Secretary, no villagers with their complex finances, no son to snatch away an account-book and drop it in a gutter. Life was a terrible affair. The faint, acrid smell of oil seemed to detach him from all worries for a moment. He shut his eyes and let himself float in that luxurious sensation, with the tip of his nose pressed against the flag-stones of the corridor. It was still warm with the heat of the day's sun. Its smell of dust was overpowering – the dust carried by the feet of hundreds of devotees and worshippers or blown in by the wind from Vinayak Mudali Street. When Margayya withdrew from the feeling of ecstasy and lifted his head, he saw the feet of the priest near his face. He looked up. The priest said: 'Margayya's mind is deeply engrossed in God ... if a man's piety is to be measured by the length of time he lies prostrate before God. Get up Margayya. God

has seen your heart already.' Margayya got to his feet. He smiled at
him and felt some explanation was due. He began awkwardly:
'You see, you see ... I felt I should visit God at least once a week –'

'Yes, you were here only last evening, have you forgotten it
already?'

'Not at all, not at all,' Margayya replied. 'I wonder what the
time is.'

'In this house there is no need for us to look at a watch. If it is
dark, it is night. If it's sunny, it's day: that's all we know. This is
not a bank, you see.' At the word 'bank' Margayya gulped
suddenly. He thought it referred to him. He said: 'I don't have
a watch either.'

'But you ought to,' said the priest. 'A bank keeps a watch to
see how fast interest is accumulating.'

'My bank is finished. This is all I have,' said Margayya, taking
out of his pocket a small packet of currency notes – all that he was
able to salvage from his banking operations. 'Just two hundred
rupees – what is it worth?'

'Two hundred rupees,' replied the priest. 'Come in. I will give
you some milk and fruit!'

'What again!' asked Margayya.

'Yes, again, and again!' answered the priest. 'Is there anything
strange about it? Don't we have to eat every day, again and
again?' Margayya was cowed. He explained: 'It's not that. I was
wondering what the time might be.'

'It's not yet tomorrow, that's all I know,' replied the priest. 'If
it is really late for you, you can go.' He turned and moved down
the corridor and passed out of sight. Margayya stood still for a few
moments. He looked at the image of the God and threw it a
vague nod. His wife might once again start a lot of bother and
pull a long face and think he'd been visiting a brothel. 'Funny
creature, so jealous at this age!' he reflected. 'I can tell her I've
been out on important business. What makes her think I have
sweethearts!' Ever since he could remember she had always
shown a sort of uneasiness about Margayya. 'Who'd consent to
be a sweetheart to me!' he said. 'A fellow with the name "Margayya", which seems almost a branding with hot iron.' He
remembered how a year or so ago she raised quite a lot of bother

when he mentioned that a woman had come to him as a client under the tree. She looked sullen for two days until he convinced her that he had only been joking.

He found himself obeying the priest without a single thought of his own. At a look from this gaunt man, he peeled four plantains and swallowed them in quick succession, and he drank a huge vessel of milk, treating the matter with as much reverence as he could muster. When the priest said approvingly, 'That's very good indeed. That's an excellent performance,' he felt proud of the certificate. The priest added, 'You have been hungry without knowing it.'

'Yes, but when one's mind is full of worries, one does not notice,' he said, feeling that the time had come for him to say something. The stars were out. A cool breeze was blowing, and night seemed quiet; the nourishment he had taken filled him with a sense of harmony, and so when the priest said: 'Margayya! What is ailing you? You can speak out,' he felt that he could no longer hesitate and fumble; that all barriers between himself and the world had been swept away and that he stood alone; that he alone mattered. He had a right to demand the goods of life and get them, like an eminent guest in a wedding house – a guest who belongs to the bridegroom's party, with the bride dancing attendance, ever waiting for the slightest nod or sign to run to his side and do some pleasing act ... He swelled with his own importance ... When he inhaled the fresh night air it seemed to increase his stature so much that the earth and the sky were only just big enough to hold him ... He began to talk in a grand manner ... the priest with his eyes glinting in the starlight listened without speaking a word ... He looked like a sloth-cub in the darkness as he humped into a ball with his chin on his knees, his lank face thrust forward ... Margayya catalogued all his demands. He was like a Departmental Officer indenting for his stationery – a superior baize cover for his office table, a crystal paperweight, a shining mirror-like paper-knife, and so on. There was no reason why he should be given the inferior things. Let the department stores beware, he would throw it out of the window if they sent in the miserable stuff they put on their fourth clerk's tables. He would just throw it out, that's all ... He would be a man of consequence, let them beware: let the Gods beware – they that provided a man with a home, and cars, servants, the admiration of his fellow men, and good clothes. After letting him run on as long as he liked, the priest opened his mouth and said: 'That means you would propitiate Goddess Lakshmi, the Goddess of Wealth. When she throws a glance and it falls on someone, he becomes rich, he becomes prosperous, he is treated by the world as an eminent man, his words are treated as something of importance. All this you seem to want.'

'Yes,' said Margayya, authoritatively. 'Why not?' He took out of his pocket his little snuff-box and tapped its lid. He flicked it open and took a deep pinch. The priest said: 'Go on, go on, no harm in it. A devotee of Goddess Lakshmi need care for nothing, not even the fact that he is in a temple where a certain decorum is to be observed. It's only a question of self-assurance. He has so much authority in his face, looks, so much money in his purse, so many to do his bidding that he cares for nothing really in the world. It's only the protégé of Goddess Saraswathi* who has to mind such things. But when Saraswathi favours a man, the other Goddess withdraws her favours. There is always a rivalry between the two – between the patronage of the spouse of Vishnu and the spouse of Brahma. Some persons have the good fortune to be claimed by both, some on the contrary have the misfortune to be abandoned by both. Evidently you are one of those for whom both are fighting at the moment.' Margayya felt immensely powerful and important. He had never known that anybody cared for him ... and now to think that two Goddesses were fighting to confer their favours on him. He lifted his eyes, glanced at the brilliant stars in Heaven as if there, between the luminous walls, he would get a glimpse of the crowned Goddesses tearing at each other.

'Why should they care for me?' he asked innocently.

The priest replied: 'How can we question? How can we question the fancies of Gods? It's just there, that's all ... it's beyond our powers to understand.'

Intoxicated by this, Margayya said: 'A man with whom the Goddess of Wealth favours need not worry much. He can buy all

---

* Saraswathi is the deity presiding over knowledge and enlightenment.

the knowledge he requires. He can afford to buy all the gifts that Goddess Saraswathi holds in her palm.'

The priest let out a quiet chuckle at Margayya's very reckless statement. Margayya asked: 'Why do you laugh?' Already a note of authority was coming into his voice. The priest said: 'Yes, this is what every man who attains wealth thinks. You are moving along the right line. Let me see your horoscope. Bring it tomorrow.' Tomorrow! It seemed such along way off. 'Can't you say something today?' Margayya asked pathetically, feeling that he was being hurled back to the earth. The priest said: 'About the same time as today, meet me with your horoscope.'

'Yet another night out and all the trouble with my wife,' Margayya thought immediately.

The priest saw him off at the door and shut the temple gate.

The moment his wife opened the door Margayya demanded: 'Where is my horoscope?'

'Horoscope?' his wife said dreamily. 'What's happened that you want it so urgently at this hour?' She looked him up and down suspiciously and, feeling probably that it was not the right time to drag him into a talk, turned and went back to bed.

It was eight o'clock when Margayya got up. He would probably have slept on till eleven, but for the fact that Balu sat on his chest and hammered his head with his lacquered wooden elephant. When he opened his eyes, Balu let out a shout of joy, put his arms round his neck, and pretended to lift him out of bed. Margayya looked at him benignly. 'This boy must grow up like a prince. The Goddess willing, he'll certainly ...' He sprang up from bed. In a quarter of an hour he was ready, bathed, wearing a clean dress, and his forehead smeared with red vermilion and a splash of sacred ash. He seemed to be in such a great hurry that his wife, although she had resolved to ignore his recent eccentric ways, was constrained to ask, 'What is agitating you so much?'

'Is coffee ready?' he asked.

She laughed cynically. 'Coffee! The milk-vendor created a scene here last evening demanding his dues. It was such a disgrace with the people in the next house watching.'

'They seem to have nothing better to do,' he said irrelevantly, his mind going off at a tangent.

'Anybody will watch when there is something to watch,' she said.

'So, no coffee?' he asked with a touch of despair. It seemed terribly hard for him to start the day without a cup of coffee. It produced a sort of vacuum, a hollow sensation. He braved it out saying: 'That's right. Why should we want coffee? As if our ancestors – ' She added: 'There is no milk even for the child.' Margayya threw a sad look at Balu. Balu seemed happy to be missing his milk. He said: 'Let us drive away that milkman. It will be so nice.'

'Why, aren't you hungry?' Margayya asked.

'Yes, I'm hungry. Give me biscuits.'

Margayya said: 'Wait a little, young man. I'll fill a whole shelf with biscuits and chocolates and fruit.'

'All for me?' the boy asked eagerly.

'Yes, absolutely, provided you don't bother me, but leave me alone now,' Margayya said. He went into their little room and pulled out a wooden chest. It was filled with letters in their old envelopes of nearly thirty years ago: there you could find letters written by Margayya's father from a village; Margayya's father-in-law writing to his new son-in-law; a letter from an uncle saying that there was a nice girl to be married and proposing her for Margayya, enclosing horoscopes. There were several letters containing saffron-tipped horoscopes on old stiff paper. There were unknown names of girls – either proposed to Margayya or to his brother, with their horoscopes; and many acrimonious letters that passed between him and his brother before the partition. Every letter he picked up stirred a cloud of dust. Little Balu stole up and stood at his shoulder as he squatted on the ground. Margayya turned round and said: 'Balu, you must promise not to put your hand out.'

'Why?'

Margayya handed him over to his wife with: 'Take this fellow away. If you let him come near me again – '

She snatched him up as he protested and shouted and carried him away, muttering: 'This is only a trick to send me off. You don't like me to see what you are doing. I suppose. I don't know what you are up to! So mysterious!'

'Women can't hold their tongues, that's why,' Margayya replied. Little Balu made a good deal of noise in the other room and Margayya muttered: 'She has completely spoilt him, beyond remedy; I must take him out of her hands and put him to school. That's the only way; otherwise he will be a terrible scoundrel.' As he rummaged in the contents of the box his mind kept ringing with his wife's weak protests and grumblings: 'Seems to be bent upon worrying me – she's getting queer!' he said to himself. He took up every envelope, gazed on its postmark, examined the letters, became engrossed for a while in by-gone family politics, and finally came upon a couple of horoscopes tucked into an envelope addressed to his father. A short note by his father-in-law said: 'I'm returning to you the originals of the horoscopes of Sowbhagyavathi (ever-auspicious) Meenakshi, and your son Chiranjeevi (eternally-living) Krishna. Your daughter-in-law is keeping well. Any day you ask us to fix the nuptial ceremony I shall bring her over.' Margayya (he hadn't yet attained that name) felt a sudden tenderness for his wife. She seemed to become all at once a young bashful virgin bride.

'Meena!' he cried. 'Here are the horoscopes.' She came up, still bearing her son on her arm. Margayya flourished the horoscopes. 'I've found them.' He clung to them as if he had secured the plan of approach to a buried treasure. 'What is it?' she asked. He held up the letter and cried: 'This is a letter from your father about our nuptials.' She blushed slightly, and turned away: 'What has come over you that you are unearthing all this stuff?' Little Balu would not let her finish her sentence. He started wriggling in her arm, and showed an inclination to dash for his father's horoscope. 'Take him away,' cried Margayya. 'Otherwise we shall find all this in the gutter before our house – so much for this son of ours.'

Presently she came without their son to ask: 'What exactly are you planning?' Her face was full of perplexity. 'Don't worry,' he said, looking up at her. He still felt the tenderness that he had felt for her as a virginal bride. He told her: 'Don't worry. I've not been hunting out my horoscope in order to search for a bride.' He laughed. She found it difficult to enjoy the joke with him. It was too puzzling. She merely said: 'By all means, look for a bride. I shan't mind.' He was disappointed that she sounded so indifferent: he was proud to feel that she guarded him jealously. However, he bantered her about it without telling anything. He could not exactly say in all seriousness what he was trying to do. 'You will know all about it very soon.' When he started out that day, she asked rather nervously: 'Will you be late again today?'

'Yes,' he said. 'What if I am late? I'm only out on business, be assured.'

His son said: 'I will come with you too,' and ran down the steps and clung to him. Margayya could not shake him off easily. He carried him up to the end of the street and lectured him all the way on how he should behave in order to qualify for biscuits and chocolates. The lecture seemed to affect him since he became quite docile when Margayya put him back at his house and left.

That night, in his shack, the priest scrutinized the horoscope with the aid of an oil-lamp. He spread it out and pored over it for a long while in silence. He said: 'Saturn! Saturn! This God is moving on to that house. He may do you good if you propitiate him. Why don't you go and pray in that other temple where they've installed the Planetary Deities? Go there with an offering of honey.' 'Where can I get honey?' Margayya asked, looking worried. He suddenly realized that he had never bought honey in his life. It was just one of those things that one always had at home, when the household was managed by one's parents. Now he recollected that ever since he became an independent family head he had managed to get along without honey. Now the testing time seemed to have come. The priest burst into one of his frightening chuckles. He remarked: 'Margayya shows the whole world how to increase their cash – but honey! He stands defeated before honey, is that it?' 'I will manage it,' Margayya said haughtily. 'I was only saying – ' The priest arbitrarily cut short all further reference to the subject. 'On Saturday go to the temple and go round its corridor thrice. Do you know that Saturn is the most powerful entity in the world? And if he is gratified he can make you a ruler of this world or he can just drown you in an ocean of misery. Nobody can escape him. Better keep him in good humour.'

'All right; I will do as you say,' Margayya said, with quiet obedience in his voice. He felt as if Saturn were around him, and might give him a twist and lift him up for the plunge into the ocean of misery if he did not behave properly.

It was four o'clock when the priest had finished giving him instructions: a course of prayers and activities. He recited a short verse and commanded Margayya to copy it down in Sanskrit, and side by side take down its meaning in Tamil. He saw him off at the door and said: 'You need not see me again, unless you want to. Follow these rules.'

'Will they produce results?'

'Who can say?' the priest answered. 'Results are not in our hands.'

'Then why should we do all this?'

'Very well, don't; nobody compels you to.'

Margayya felt completely crushed under all this metaphysical explanation. He bowed his head in humility. The priest closed one door, held his hand on the other, and said: 'The *Shastras* lay down such and such rituals for such and such ends. Between a man who performs them and one who doesn't, the chances are greater for the former. That's all I can say. The results are ... you may have results or you may not ... or you may have results and wish that you had failed – '

'What is your experience with this *mantra*?'

'Me!' He chuckled once again. 'I'm a *Sanyasi*; I have no use for it ... Don't do it unless you wish to,' said the priest and shut the door. Margayya stood hesitating in the road with the stanza in his pocket, and all the spiritual prescription written down. He looked despairingly at the closed door of the temple and turned home-ward. He felt it was no use hesitating. He might go on putting questions; the other could answer, yet still the problem would remain unsolved. 'Problem? What's the problem?' he suddenly asked. It was a happy state of affairs not to remember what the problem was. The priest had been saying so much incomprehensible stuff that Margayya felt dizzy and fuddled. He stopped in the middle of the road and resolved: 'He has told me what to do. I shall do it honestly. Let me not bother about other things.'

Margayya's wife was overawed by his activities. He told her next day: 'Clear up that room for me,' indicating the single room in their house in which she slept with her child, and into which all the household trunks and odds and ends were also thrown.

'What are we to do with these things?'

'Throw them out. I want that place for the next forty days.'

'Where am I to sleep?'

'What silly questions you keep asking! Is this the time to think of such problems?'

She became docile at this attack and begged: 'Can't you tell me exactly what you want to do?'

He told her in a sort of way: he'd been advised not to talk of his method and aim even to his wife. The priest had said: 'Even to your wife – there are certain practices which become neutralized the moment they are clothed in words.'

She asked: 'Is this what people call alchemy, changing base metals?'

'No, it is not,' said Margayya, not liking the comparison.

'They say that it is like magic – black magic,' she wailed, looking very much frightened.

'Don't get silly notions in your head ... it is not that ... the priest is not a man who dabbles in black magic. Don't go talking about it to anyone – '

The little room was cleared and all the odds and ends – broken-down furniture, trunks and boxes, stacks of paper, spare bed-rolls, and pillows and mats were pulled out and heaped in a corner of their little central hall. Balu became ecstatic. He pulled down the things and mixed them up and generally enjoyed the confusion. Their neighbours heard the noise of shifting and thought: 'They are doing something in the next house; wonder what it is?' They tried to spy on them, but there was a blank wall between them. Margayya had the room washed clean, chased out the rats and cockroaches, and swept off the cobwebs that hung on the wall and corners. It was a very small room, less than eight feet broad, with a single narrow window opening on the street. If the shutter was closed the room became pitch dark. Margayya drew up several pots of water from the well and splashed the water about. He then commanded his wife to decorate the floor with white flour designs, a decoration necessary for all auspicious occasions. He had a string of mango leaves tied across the doorway. He took from a nail in the hall the picture of the Goddess Lakshmi, put up a short pedestal and placed the picture on it: the four-armed Goddess, who presides over wealth, distinction, bravery, enterprise, and all the good things in life. When he carried the picture in, his wife understood something of his plans: 'Oh, I see, I now understand.'

'That's all right. If you understand, so much the better – but keep it to yourself.'

He had two hundred rupees in his possession still, which he had to use up. He gave his wife a list of articles she should supply him with – such as jaggery, turmeric, coloured cooked rice, fruit, refined sugar, black-gram cake, sweetened sesamum, curd, spiced rice and various kinds of fruits and honey. He would require these in small quantities morning and evening for offering – and most of them were also to be his diet during the period of *Japa*. He gave his wife a hundred rupees and said: 'This is my last coin. You have to manage with it.'

'What about the provisions for the house – and the milkman?'

'Oh, do something ... manage the milkman and the rest for some time and then we will pull through. This is more urgent than anything else.'

A couple of days later, at the full moon, he began his rites. He sat before the image of Lakshmi. He shut the door, though his son banged on it from time to time. He kept only a slight opening of the window shutter, through which a small ray of light came in but not the curiosity of the neighbours. He wore a loincloth soaked in water. A variety of small articles were spread out before him in little pans. He inscribed a certain Sanskrit syllable on a piece of deer skin and tied it round his neck with a string. He had been in an agony till he found the deer skin. The priest had told him: 'You must carve out this on an antelope skin.'

'Antelope!' he gasped. Was he a hunter? Where did one go and find the antelope skin? 'You search in your house properly and you will find one. Our elders have always possessed them for sitting on and praying,' said the priest.

'Very well, I will look for one,' said Margayya.

'And then, have you seen any red lotus?'

'Yes, I have,' Margayya said apprehensively, wondering what was coming next.

'Where?' asked the priest. Margayya blinked and felt disgusted with himself: 'They usually sell them in the street for *Vara Lakshmi* festival.'

'Exactly!' said the priest. 'But now you will have to go where it is found. Formerly, you could pick up a lotus from any pond nearby – there were perhaps ten spots in a town where you could pick up a lotus in former days, but now ... our world is going to pieces because we have no more lotus about. It's a great flower – the influence it has on a human being is incalculable.' After a dissertation on lotus, the priest said: 'Beyond Sarayu, towards the North, there is a garden where there is a ruined temple with a pond. You will find red lotus there. Get one, burn its petals to a pitch black, and mix it with ghee.'

'Ghee! Oh, yes – ' Margayya said, feeling that here was at least one article which you could find in the kitchen. Even if the store-man was ill-disposed, one might still win him over in view of the impending change of circumstances.

'It must be ghee made of milk drawn from a smoke-coloured cow!' said the priest.

'Oh!' groaned Margayya, not being able to hide his feelings any more.

'You probably think all this is bluff ... some fantastic nonsense that I'm inventing.'

'Oh, no, I don't feel so for a moment, but only how hard ... what a lot of – '

'Yes, but that is the way it's done. It's so written in the *Shastras*. You have to do certain things for attaining certain ends. It is not necessary to question why. It'll be a mere waste of energy and you will get no answer .... Well, follow my words carefully. Take the blackened lotus petal, mix it with ghee, and put a dot of it on your forehead after the prayer, every day, exactly between your eyebrows.'

'Yes,' Margayya said weakly. He was feeling more and more in despair of how he was going to fulfil these various injunctions. 'Red lotus, grey-skinned cow, and antelope ... where am I? ...what a world this is – ' It seemed to him an impossible world. 'How am I to get all these?' He groaned within himself.

'Have trust in yourself and go ahead ... He will show you a way. Did you imagine that riches came to people when they sat back and hummed a tune?'

A whole day was spent by him in going after the red lotus. It took him through the northern part of the town, past Ellamman Street and the banks of the Sarayu. He forded the river at Nallappa's Mango Grove. A village cart was crossing the river. The man driving it recognized him and shouted: 'Oh, Margayya!' He jumped out of the cart, sending up a great splash of water, which struck Margayya in the eyes and face; it also cooled his brow after the exertion of the day. The villager was an old client of his. He said: 'What has come over you, sir, that we don't see you? Without you, we are finding it so difficult.'

'You can't expect me to be at your beck and call all the time. I have other things to do.'

'But you cannot just abandon us – '

'I have other business to look after, my dear fellow. Don't imagine this is my only task. I used to do it more as a sort of help to my fellow men.' They were both standing knee-deep in water. Margayya said: 'Let me ride with you up to the branch road.' The villager was only too eager to take him and asked his son, who was in the cart, to get down and walk so as to make room for Margayya.

He asked: 'So far out! May I know why you are going this way?'

Margayya said: 'You must never ask "Why" or "Where" when a person is starting out: that'll always have an adverse influence.' He felt he was beginning to talk like the temple priest.

'All right, sir,' the villager said obediently. 'We have to learn all these things from learned people. Otherwise how can we know?'

The wheels crunched, roared, and bumped along. Margayya wondered if he was expected to reach his lotus by walking and not by riding in a cart. Would that in any way affect the issues and would it violate the injunction laid by the priest? 'I don't think there is anything wrong in it. He'd have mentioned it. Anyway, better not raise the question. Perhaps this cart was sent here by God.'

He got off at the crossroads, and waited till the cart disappeared down the road. He turned to his left, and cut across a field. The sun was already tilting westward. He looked up and said: 'Heaven help me if it gets dark before I discover the lotus; I may not be able to know whether it is red or black or what – and then it'll be fine, having to start the whole business again tomorrow!' He cut across the field and walked half a mile, and came upon a garden, hedged off with brambles and thorn. His legs ached with this unaccustomed tramping, and his feet smarted with the touch of thorns. He passed through the thicket expecting any minute a cobra to dart across and nip at him: 'This place must be full of them – supply the entire district with cobras from here.' There was a small narrow gap in the hedge and he passed through it into a large wood, semi-dark with sky-topping trees – mango, margosa, and what not. The place looked wild and deserted and an evening breeze murmured grimly in the boughs above. Down below fallen leaves were ankle deep, and he passed through them with his feet sending out a resounding crick-crick. 'This is just where cobras live – under a blanket of dry leaves – ' Here flower gardens had gone wild – all kinds of creepers, jasmine bushes and nerium growing ten feet high, were intertwined and mixed up. 'Some fool has let all this go to waste,' he reflected. 'In fruit alone one might make ten thousand rupees out of this soil.'

He arrived at the pond. Its greenish water had a layer of moss, occasional ripples were thrown out by warts or some other darting water creature, and mosquito larvae agitated the surface here and there. Margayya felt very lonely. The steps of the pond were broken and slippery; half the bank on his side had fallen into the pond. On the other side there was a small *mantap*, its walls covered with cobweb and smoke. Three blackened stones in a corner indicated that some wayfarers had sojourned and lighted a fire here, it might be last year or a century ago. In the middle of the pond there were lotus flowers – red as the rising sun. They were half closing their petals. 'They know better than we do that it's nearing sunset,' Margayya reflected. He stood on the some-what slippery step thinking of how to reach the lotus. He'd have to wade through the greenish water. He stood ankle deep in it and wondered if he had better take off his clothes and go in. 'If this *dhoti* gets dirty, it will not merely be dirty but it'll acquire a permanent green dye, I suppose. And it'll be difficult to go back home wearing it. People might stare and laugh. Better take it off ... there's no one about.' He tucked up his *dhoti* and looked round in order to make sure. 'If a man lives here, he will not need a square inch of cloth,' he reflected. Far in a corner of the little *mantap* on the other bank he saw someone stirring. He felt a slight shiver of fear passing through him as he peered closer. 'Is it a ghost or a maniac?' He withdrew a couple of steps, and shouted: 'Hey, who are you?' vaguely remembering that if it were a ghost it would run away on hearing such a challenge. But the answer came back. 'I'm Dr Pal, journalist, correspondent and author.' Margayya espied a row of white teeth bared in a grin.

'And what are you doing in this lonely place?'

'Why not?' came back the voice. It was a hard resonant voice, and there was no doubt that it was of this earth.

'Why not what?' asked Margayya.

'Why not here as well as anywhere else?' asked the man, rising and coming out. He was a man of thirty or thereabouts, his face still youthful, with a three-day stubble on his chin; a lank, tall man, with sunken cheeks, and a crop of hair falling on his forehead and nape. He wore a pair of blue shorts and a banian. As he came down the steps Margayya pointed at the lotus and said: 'Get it for me. You are wearing only shorts.' The other nodded, waded through the water and came back with a lotus flower. He gave it to Margayya. Margayya felt over-whelmed with gratitude. 'You are a very good fellow,' he said patronizingly. 'What are you doing here, all alone in this place?'

'Working of course,' the other said.

'Single-handed?'

'Yes, it has to be a single-handed job.' Margayya looked at the wilderness round them and said: 'No wonder the place is as it is – too much for one man.' The other laughed and said: 'I have nothing to do with the garden. I'm here because I find it a very quiet place, and there seems to be no one to ask me to get out. Sit down; you will find it a really nice place – though it looks such a forest.'

Margayya feebly protested: 'I've got to go before it gets dark.' 'Why?'

'I have a long way to go ... there may be cobras – '

'Not one here. Sit down, sit down – ' Margayya sat down on the steps. The other sat beside him. A breeze stirred the leaves and sent a few ripplets rolling and striking against the stone steps. Casuarina trees which loomed over the little *mantap* murmured. Brilliant sun from the west made the entire garden glitter.

Margayya held the lotus delicately by the stalk and looked at it. 'Now and then people come here for lotus,' said the other. Margayya wondered if he was going to ask him to pay for it. He didn't like the idea. Before he should entertain any such notion, just to divert his mind, Margayya asked: 'What is your connection with this place?'

'The same as yours,' he replied promptly. 'As I said, I am here because it doesn't seem to bother anyone. I discovered this by a pure fluke. I'm given to cross-country hikes ... I have to in my profession – '

'What is your profession?'

'I'm a journalist. I'm a correspondent for all these districts of a paper called *Silver Way* published in Madras.'

'Tamil paper?'

'Yes, of course. It is the most widely circulated paper in Tamil, with an enormous circulation in F.M.S., Ceylon, and South Africa. I cover these districts for them, and in my spare time write my own books.'

'Oh, you write books?' Margayya asked, full of wonder.

'Yes, yes, during my spare time – so difficult to find the leisure for it as a correspondent. All day I must knock about courts and offices and meetings on my cycle in search of news. I don't get much time. That's why I stay here, where I can work without disturbance.' Margayya was greatly impressed. He had always thought very highly of newspaper people. 'How many books have you written?'

'Four,' came the reply; and he added: 'Three are here,' tapping his forehead. 'Only one has been got down on paper – '

'What is it? A story?'

'A story! Oh, no, something more serious than that.'

'Oh!' said Margayya, feeling that he had better not make inquiries in a region where he was a stranger. Books and writing were not for him: he was only a business man. Margayya rose to go.

'It's getting late,' he murmured.

'I will go with you up to the road,' said the other and followed him down to the edge of the pond. Margayya was fascinated by the sight of some more red lotus floating on water, with their petals already closing. He reflected: 'Even if there is a pound of paste to be made, we have enough lotus here – provided I can find the grey cow.' His mind started worrying about the next stage of the search. 'Where are grey cows to be seen?' Perhaps this author and journalist by his side might be able to help. They walked down the grassy path in silence for a while. Margayya surprised the other with the sudden inquiry: 'Have you seen a smoke-coloured cow?'

'Where?' the other asked, stopping suddenly.

'Anywhere ... I mean ... do you know where a smoke-coloured cow can be seen?'

'Why?'

Margayya felt embarrassed. He blinked again. 'I want its milk – for some special, medicinal purpose.'

'Are you an *Ayurvedic* doctor or an aphrodisiac-maker?' the other asked, looking at him. 'Trying to make some potent drugs with red lotus and so on. I have seen only *Ayurvedic* doctors coming here in a search of some herb or leaf or lotus and things like that.' Margayya felt that because he had no ready answer, and no name to give for his avocation in life, the other would give him no useful tip. He covered the entire topic with a loud, prolonged laugh, at the end of which he found the other completing his remark: 'I suppose the milk must always be white, whatever the colour of the cow.'

Margayya agreed with this remark, laughed afresh, and changed the subject immediately. 'What did you say your books were about?'

'Sociology,' said the other.

'Oh! I see,' said Margayya, trying to look clever, though completely bewildered by the term. He felt like asking: 'What is it?' but felt it might be an undignified inquiry. He just nodded his head and remained silent. The other asked: 'You know what sociology is, I suppose?' He was trapping him unnecessarily.

'Of course, in a manner, but you know I'm a business man; we business men have not much time for scholarly activities.'

Dr Pal understood the position and said: 'It's a subject that has been much neglected in our country – particularly in our own vernaculars, in our mother-tongue. They've everything in English, but in our mother-tongue – no. What should the thousands of persons who know only our language do to learn the subject?'

'Yes, yes, it is very difficult,' Margayya agreed. They had now reached a thatched hut. 'Come in for a moment and see my home and study,' said Dr Pal.

Margayya protested and said something about its being dark.

'I will escort you back safely,' said the other. 'Don't worry ... there are no cobras here.' He pushed the door open. A mat was spread on the ground with a greasy pillow on it, and away from it stood a small tin trunk with a bottle of ink and a stack of paper on it. A very small bedroom lamp was kept on the trunk. Dr Pal pushed away the pillow and said: 'Pray sit down, I have not much furniture to offer – this is all. But this is a nice place.'

Margayya sat down carefully holding the lotus so as to protect it from being crushed. The place smelt of straw, which was spread on the floor.

'I do all my writing here. I return here at the end of my day's roving in the town. I sit on this mat all night and write; at dusk I go out to that pond and sit contemplating in the *mantap* – it's a very inspiring place.' Margayya felt impressed and overawed, so he asked, as a piece of courtesy, 'I suppose that is your book. You send it afterwards for printing?'

'Yes, I hope to,' said the other. He picked up the manuscript and handed it to Margayya. Margayya received it with the utmost courtesy. The cover was of brown paper. He turned the last page and saw the number: 'Oh, a hundred and fifty pages?' he asked admiringly.

'Yes, I want it to be a short book, so that any person may buy and read it.' Margayya turned the pages and a chapter-heading caught his eye: 'Philosophy and the Practice of Kissing'.

'Oh! Kissing! You have written about kissing too!'

'Yes, of course, it is an important subject.'

'Who kisses? – children or – '

'Oh! Children's kisses are of no account here – ' Margayya felt interested, and turned to the title of another chapter: 'Basic Principles of Embracing'. He turned over the pages and started reading the first sentence of the opening chapter: 'Man embraces woman, and woman embraces man – ' He felt interested. Briskly turning over the leaves, he came upon the title sheet and read out aloud: 'Bed-Life or the Science of Marital Happiness'.

'What is this?' Margayya exclaimed. 'You said it was – '

'Sociology. Yes, this is a branch of sociology. I have spent many years studying this subject. A thousand years ago Vatsyayana wrote his Kama-Sutra or "Science of Love." I have based this whole work on it, plus research done by modern scientists like Havelock Ellis and so on. This subject must be understood by every man and woman. If people understood and practised this science there would be more happiness in the world.'

'But it seems to be all about ... about – ' Margayya could not find the right word. He felt too shy. He felt eager to read on, but put it away feeling that further inspection would seem indecorous.

'You can read it if you like,' said the other.

Margayya put it away as if avoiding a temptation.

'You will have everything you want in a nutshell there.' It seemed as if the other would not let him go. The author added: 'I want to have a few illustrations if I can find an artist.'

'What those ... illustrating those?' gasped Margayya.

'Yes, why not? I want to illustrate some of the parts. I want it to be of practical benefit ... I want it to serve as a guide book to married couples. My aim is to create happiness in the world.'

'Are you married?' Margayya asked, coming to the point.

'Yes ... otherwise how could I write all that?'

'But ... but ... you are alone – ' Margayya said, looking round.

'Yes ... I have to be – ' He seemed saddened by some domestic memory. Margayya's curiosity could no longer be kept in check: 'Where is she?' he asked bluntly.

'God knows,' said the other. 'I have had to leave her – '

'Why? Why?' Margayya said. 'How sad!' He sat brooding.

The other said: 'She was an impossible woman ... a terrible woman who was unfaithful, and tried to ogle every man who appeared before her. A woman with a polyandrous tendency.' Margayya was somewhat shocked at the free manner in which he spoke. The other laughed and said: 'How scared you look at my talk! Don't fear; I am not yet married. Probably you are already thinking how can this fellow write about the happiness of married life when he himself has been such a failure! Was it not the line of your thought?'

'How did you guess?' Margayya asked. Everyone seemed to guess correctly what went on in his mind – a most dangerous state of affairs it seemed to him. 'I never married,' the other assured him again. 'But I only gave you a sample of what is likely to happen when people are ill-matched.'

'True, true,' said Margayya.

'Reading this book will be a way of preventing such tragedies,' said Dr Pal.

The next few days Margayya was lost to the outside world. He sat in the small room repeating:

Oh Goddess, who affordest shelter to all the fugitive worlds! ... Thy feet, by themselves, are proficient in affording immunity from fear and bestowing boons.

He had to repeat it a thousand times each day, sitting before the image of the Goddess. He wore a red-silk *dhoti* and smeared his forehead and body with sacred ash. The cries of the pedlars in the street were submerged in the continuous hum that proceeded from his own throat: his son's continued shout of '*Appa! Appa!*' was heard by him as a distant muffled sound. A little light came through the small opening of the shutter. The room was filled with the scent of incense, camphor, sandal dust, and jasmine. All this mingled perfume uplifted the heart and thoughts of Margayya. He was filled with a feeling of holiness – engendered by the feel of the red silk at his waist. He was gratified at the thought of his wife's obedience. 'She is quite accommodating,' he reflected. She got up at five and prepared the jaggery-sweetened rice which had to be offered to the Goddess. As he sat down with his eyes shut, he said to himself: 'I have achieved difficult things, grey cow's milk butter, red lotus made into black paste ... This time last week I could not believe that I should be able to get together grey milk and red lotus. When the Goddess wants to help a man she sends him where all things are available; and who would have thought that there was a deserted garden – '

This brought to his mind Dr Pal and his works ... He felt an unholy thrill at the memory of Pal's book. It seemed as though his mind would not move from the subject. This man wanted to put in pictures – what a wicked fellow. It'd be most awkward ... Why was Dr Pal interested in the subject? Must be an awful rake ... if he could write all that and was unmarried .... Some of the chapter-headings came to his mind. He realized with a shock what line his thoughts were pursuing, and he pulled them back to the *verse*; the priest had told him to let his mind rest fully on its meaning while repeating it. He kept saying: 'Oh Goddess, who affordest ...' etc., and unknown to him his thoughts slipped out and romped about – chiefly about the fruits of the penance he was undertaking: forty days of this – afterwards? He visualized his future. How was wealth going to flow in? When he became rich, suppose he bought from his brother the next house too, tempting him with a handsome cash offer .... He realized that this was his major concern in life. He would be a victorious man if he could bring his brother to his knees and make him part with his portion of the house; and then he would knock down the partition wall .... Each day it took him eight hours of repetition to complete the thousand, and then he reverently put the black paste on his forehead, lit the camphor, called in his wife and child and sprinkled the holy water on them. His jaws ached, his tongue had become dry ... he felt faint with hunger, since he had to fast completely while praying.

He followed this course for forty days. When he emerged from the little room, he had a beard and moustache and hair on his nape. He had been told not to shave in the course of this penance. He looked venerable. His voice became weak; he could not utter any speech without automatically mixing it up with 'Oh, Goddess, who affordest shelter ...' He looked like an examination student who has emerged from the ordeal, sapped in every way but with his face glowing with triumph. Margayya had lost ten pounds in weight: much of the padding on his waist and jowl had gone.

# PART TWO

When he was again seen in the streets, shaven and clean, he looked like a young man. His chin sparkled with the long-delayed shave, and his moustache was trimmed to perfection. He looked so tidy when he went along the street again with his shirt and upper-cloth that people stopped and asked: 'Where have you been all this time, Margayya?' He had no answer. So he said: 'Here. All along. Where should I go?'

'I haven't seen you in your usual place or anywhere.'

'Usual place! Oh, there, you mean! That was only a side business for me, more for my own diversion. I'm busy with other plans,' he said grandly.

About the time he closed his business he had two hundred rupees in hand, out of which the previous month's household expenses took sixty rupees; the forty-day ritual cost him at least two rupees a day for fruit and flowers and special offerings; then he had to have a feast on the last day and feed four brahmins, and give them each a silver rupee on betel leaves after the meal. About a hundred rupees in all were gone. He found himself grudging this expense and explained to himself: 'How can I grudge it! Can't a man spend at least so much for earning the benevolence of a Goddess?' He had a magic syllable carved on leather and tied to his sacred thread. He wished he could know when the beneficial effect would start, when the skies would open and start raining down wealth. He wished he could get an answer to his question.

In his despair he tried to meet the priest. But somehow the priest had not encouraged him to call again. For a day Margayya was seized with the horrible thought that the man had played a practical joke on him. What if he had merely fooled him! Priests were capable of anything. Every word that the priest had uttered seemed to lend support to this suspicion. He had even taken the trouble to avoid him.

Days passed, and his misgivings increased. He seemed to have suddenly lost all plans in life. His purse was getting lighter each day. It was difficult to while away the time. From morning to night he had to think what he should do next. If he stayed at home, it invariably resulted in some clash with his wife, for his son misbehaved so much in his presence that either he or his wife felt impelled to chastize him, and each vehemently protested when the other did it. And then all kinds of controversies started between him and his wife. It was such a strain having always to talk in whispers – lest the people next door should overhear. He sat dejectedly facing Goddess Lakshmi and mentally saying to her: 'You have taken my last coin. What have you given me in return? Has the priest been fooling me?' He felt indignant at this thought. 'If he has fooled me! God help him, I'll have my fingers round his throat!'

As he lay across the hall on a towel spread on the floor, his mind was busy with these thoughts. In that small house, it was a bother to have the head of the house all the time lying across the floor. Margayya's wife had quite a number of visitors coming in each day. A brinjal-seller, who brought in her basket, walked across the hall and sat in the backyard veranda to transact her business; the servant-woman who came in to wash the vessels and scrub the backyard an hour a day; a fat lady, wife of a lawyer, who dropped in for a chat in the afternoons; and some school children who came running in during the afternoon recess for a drink of water. When Margayya lay across the hall of his house he obstructed their passage to the rear veranda and kitchen where the lady of the house received them. Every time a visitor arrived Margayya had to scramble to his feet and stand aside to let the visitor pass. They went on and asked Margayya's wife privately: 'Why is your husband not going out?' The lady felt confused and awkward and gave out some reply, but later questioned him: 'What has come over you that you don't go out at all – ?'

'Where should I go?'

'Like all the other men, why don't you try to do some work and earn some money?'

'Money is not a pebble in the street to be picked up by just going out.'

'Oh, is that so? I didn't know. I thought it was something to be had in the street.'

Thus their talk went on, entirely lacking in point. She had no clear idea of what she expected him to do and he had no clear idea of what he should do outside the house. He tried it for a few days. His steps naturally led him to the Co-operative Bank. But it was clear that he had lost his place. His previous clients only tried to avoid him, fearing that he might accost them for their old dues. He had no one to talk to. He went through the town like a lost soul, but although to begin with some people spoke to him, now nobody took any notice of him. He could not go down the Market Road for fear of being stopped by the optician ... So after a few days of aimless wandering, he took to staying at home. It delighted only his little son and no one else. Next door they remarked: 'What has come over that man? He is hardly to be seen outside. Is he hiding from creditors?' They had also wondered previously why so much scent of incense emanated from the next house. 'They must be up to some mischief; perhaps trying black magic on someone they don't like. We must be careful with such people.'

As the month came to an end and Margayya had to buy rice and salt for the pantry, he found himself short by ten rupees, and they had to manage without ghee. His wife declared: 'I have never been in this plight before.' Balu made matters worse by asking: 'Mother, I want ghee.'

'There is no ghee, my boy. You must eat your food as it is,' Margayya replied.

'I won't,' said Balu, throwing away the rice and getting up.

'You'll learn to be contented with what you get,' Margayya moralized foolishly.

'No. I won't. I want ghee,' said the boy rebelliously, kicking away his rice plate.

'If you kick away your rice, I will kick you,' Margayya said; at which the boy burst into tears and appealed to his mother. She burst into tears too because it reminded her of the story of Gora Kumbar, a potter, who was devoted to the God Vishnu and took no care of his family. At meal times his little son demanded ghee, without which, just like Balu, he would not eat. The lady went out to borrow ghee from the next house, leaving the child in the care of the father, who was stamping on wet clay all the time. When she was gone, he got into a mystic ecstasy and started dancing, and did not notice the child crawling under his feet ... and when the mother returned with ghee the child had been stamped into the wet mud. Margayya's wife burst into tears, remembering this story, which she had seen as a drama in her young days. Margayya, bewildered and pained by all the scene, ate his food in silence, but, without ghee and with all this misery, it tasted bitter.

He decided to search out the priest. 'I can't keep quiet any more. He will have to tell me what is what – otherwise, I will not let him off lightly.'

Margayya sought him out late that night. He pretended to go to the temple very late in the evening for worship, and hung about till the crowd cleared. He heard the priest's voice inside the sanctum. When the crowd dispersed he moved up to the thresh-old of the sanctum and peered in. There was a new man there.

Margayya asked: 'Where is he?'

'Who?'

'The other priest – '

'Why?'

Margayya felt annoyed. Why were these priests assuming such impudent and presumptuous manners? But the priest was in the proximity of God, and Margayya was afraid to speak sharply. He controlled his voice and temper and answered: 'I have some business with him.'

'What business?' asked the priest, tossing flowers on the image without turning in his direction. 'Does this man think he is God?' wondered Margayya. 'He is so indifferent!'

Probably, he thought, the other priest had told him: 'Margayya may be dropping in often, asking for me. If he comes, show him the utmost rudeness and keep him out.' It seemed quite possible to his sickly imagination. Margayya opened his lips to say some-thing, but in came some devotees with coconut and camphor, and the priest became busy attending to them. Margayya noted with pain the differential treatment that was being meted out. 'It's quite clear that he has been told to snub me ... see how warm and effusive he is to those people! It is because he hopes to get money out of them. Money is everything, dignity, self-respect .... This fellow is behaving towards me like the Co-operative Bank Secretary.' In his mind he saw arrayed against him the Secretary, Arul Doss, this man, and the washer-woman who abused him on the day his son destroyed the account-book. It seemed such a formidable and horrible world that he wondered how he had managed to exist at all.

The priest now came out bearing a plate with a camphor flame on it, which lit up his face. Margayya noted that he was a very young man. The others put money into the plate after touching the flame. The priest paused near Margayya, who just looked away. 'I have paid enough for these godly affairs,' thought Margayya. The priest threw a sour look at him and went in. The devotees left. The priest sat down before the image and started reciting some holy verse. Margayya stood on the threshold. The other paused during his recitation and asked: 'What are you waiting for?'

'I'm only waiting for your honour to come out and answer my question.'

'Am I an astrologer? What's your question?'

'This man is practising studied rudeness on me. He has been taught to ... this young fellow!' thought Margayya. His anger rose. He became reckless. 'Hey, young man, who taught you to speak so rudely?'

The young man looked surprised for a moment, and then raised his voice and resumed his recitation.

Margayya cried: 'Stop it and answer me! A very devout man, indeed!'

'You want to stop God's work. Who are you?'

'A youngster like you need not ask unnecessary questions. Learn to give correct answers before you think of putting questions ... At your age!'

The youth asked: 'What do you want?'

'What I want to know is, where is the old priest? And, if you can, answer without asking why.'

'He has gone on a pilgrimage.'

'When did he go?'

'About a month ago.'

'When will he come back?'

'I don't know.'

'Where has he gone?'

'To Benares – from there he is going on foot all along the course of the Ganges, to its very source in the Himalayas.'

'Why is he doing all this?'

'I don't know. How can I say?'

Margayya felt indignant. He walked out of the temple without another word. He felt he had been cheated. That old priest had played a trick on him, making him waste all his money in performing fantastic things. 'Benares, Ganges! Himalayas! How am I to get at him!' He wished he could go to the Himalayas and search him out. For a moment he speculated pleasantly on what might happen to the old man there. He might get drowned in the Ganges, or die of sunstroke on the way, or get frozen in the ice of the Himalayas.

Next day he wandered up and down, through the east and the west districts of the town, in search of an idea. He got up in the morning, hoping that some miracle would happen, some chance or fortune be picked up on the doorstep. He got up early and opened the door. There were the usual goings on of Vinayak Mudali Street, and nothing more – a curd-seller passing with the pot on her head, a couple of cyclists going to a mill, some children running out to play an early game, and so on. But he saw nothing that was likely to bring him the fruits of his penance. He felt acutely unhappy.

He wandered all over the town in search of an idea. He went up to the northern section and sat on the hot sands of the Sarayu thinking. He sat in the shade of a tree and watched the sky and river. His mind had become blank. He went down the Market Road, looking at every shop. He was searching for an idea. He watched every trade critically. Tailoring? Hair-cutting saloon? Why not? Any labour had dignity ... But all of them would be more troublesome than anything he had known. 'Nobody will give me money for nothing. I must give them something in exchange – ' He sat on the parapet of the Market Fountain and thought. What was it that people most needed? It must be something that every person could afford. The best business under the sun was either snuff or tooth powder or both. It had to be something for which every citizen would be compelled to pay a certain small sum each day. He was engrossed in profound economic theories. Snuff ... his mind gloated over the visions of snuff ... The initial outlay would be small, just enough to buy a bundle of tobacco .... He knew all about it, for there used to be a snuff-maker in front of his house. All his equipment was a few cinders of charcoal, a small iron grate, and a mud pot for frying the tobacco in. Fry and pound the tobacco, and a little lime, and leave the rest to the snuffers themselves. 'Margayya's snuff for flavour', this was worth trying. It was an investment of ten rupees. He must fry the leaves in a place far away from human habitation. Tobacco, while being fried, sent up a choking smoke which kept the neighbourhood coughing and complaining. He wondered how long it would take to realize the profits. A year or less or not at all. Suppose people never touched his snuff and it accumulated in tins up to the ceiling? What could he do with them? He might probably use the stock himself. But he himself had been addicted to the Golden Monkey Brand for years, and he dared not try any other. Or he might manufacture tooth powder. His mother used to make a sort of tooth powder with burnt almond shell and cinnamon bark and alum, and it was said to convert teeth into granite.

Margayya now thought of his mother with gratitude. There was always a big crowd of sufferers waiting for her at the hall of their old house. She was of a charitable disposition. She took the stock out of a large earthen jar, and distributed it liberally. His father used to declare: 'You will be reborn in a Heaven of Golden Teeth for this.' She did it as a form of charity, and their house was known as the Tooth Powder House. It seemed an ideal business to start now. The world was going to be transformed into one of shining teeth ... But a misgiving assailed him. How could he make people buy it rather than the dozen other tooth powders? He didn't know the art of selling tooth powder. He couldn't go about hawking it in the streets ... It would be a fine look out if the

Secretary of the Co-operative Society caught him at it. Arul Doss would call out 'Hey, tooth powder, come here, give me a packet. Here are three pies.' And he would have to gather the coppers like a beggar, with peals of laughter ringing out from the whole world. And the old priest might chuckle from the Himalayas for having reduced him to a picker of copper coins! 'No,' he told himself, 'I'm a business man. I can only do something on the lines of banking. It's no good thinking of all this.' He watched the fountain hissing and squirting, while the traffic flowed past, and sighed, as he had sighed so often before, at the thought of his banyan tree business. He sighed, reflecting: 'Here is an adult, sitting on the fountain like a vagrant when he ought to be earning.' He feared that if this state of affairs continued he might find himself looking for an orphan's corpse and dashing about with a mud tray in his hand.

'Hello, friend,' cried Dr Pal from the other side of the fountain. He was coming down the road on his cycle. 'I thought I should never see you again – you went away without telling me where you lived. You didn't come again for lotus!' It took time for Margayya to be shaken from his business reverie. 'Oh, you!' he cried, not exactly liking being disturbed by this man now. He felt shy of meeting him, associating him with smut. Dr Pal leaned his cycle on the parapet and came over and sat beside him.

'You didn't come again for lotus,' he said.

'Oh, lotus – one was enough for me,' said Margayya, putting into his tone all the despair he felt at the whole wasted activity.

'People always go for lotus in a series, never in singles – ' said the other obscurely. Margayya laughed, pretending that he read some inner meaning. 'Well, what makes you spend your time sitting here?' Pal asked.

Margayya thought: 'Why can't people leave me alone?' He didn't like to give the correct explanation. He said: 'Someone has promised to come up and meet me here.'

'Oh, a business meeting, I suppose.'

'Of course,' said Margayya. 'I have no time for just casual meetings. The time is – ' He looked around him.

'Four,' said the other, looking at his wrist-watch. 'You won't mind if I keep you company?'

'Oh, not at all,' replied Margayya mortified, but he overcame his mortification enough to add, 'I only fear it may hold you up unnecessarily. You may have other business.'

'I'm on duty even when I'm sitting here and talking to you. I'll make a story of it for my paper – that's all they want. They won't mind as long as I fulfil my duty.'

'Surely, you won't write about me!' Margayya said.

'Why not! I might say Mr — —. Oh, what's your name please? I've not enquired, although I've been around with you so much.'

'Why do you want my name?' Margayya asked defensively.

'Don't worry, I won't publish it. I just want to know as a friend, that's all. Suppose somebody asks me who is that friend with whom I have been talking and I say I don't know, it'd look grotesque. Isn't that so? What is your name?'

'People call me Margayya – '

'Excellent name; initials?'

'No initials – '

'Oh, no initials, that's excellent. Initials indicate town and parentage ... But that's for lesser folk who have to announce their antecedents.'

'It's not necessary for me. If you say Margayya, everyone will know. However, that's not my name.'

'Oh, I thought it was.'

'How?'

'How? How? The "how" of things is my trade secret. Otherwise I wouldn't be a writer. My business is to know things – not tell anyone how, you understand.'

'Extraordinary fellow,' Margayya said.

'Yes, I am,' said the other. 'I know it. Come along, let us go somewhere and gossip.'

'We are doing it here quite well,' said Margayya.

'Oh, no ... This place is too noisy. I want to talk to you privately. Come on, come on; don't say "no!" ' He was irresistible. Margayya remembered in time to protest: 'But I have told you I am waiting here for someone.'

'Oh, he will follow us there, don't worry.'

'Come along to my office. I must show you my office.'

They walked along, through the crowd. It seemed to be all the same for Margayya, what he did or where he went. He followed the other blindly. He took him through the eastern end of Market Road, turned into a lane, stopped before a house and knocked on the door. A little boy opened it. 'Who is inside?' Pal asked.

'No one,' the boy said.

'That's fine!' said Pal. 'As I expected. Open my office then, young fellow!'

The young man disappeared and opened a side door and put his head out. 'Hold the cycle,' commanded Pal. The young man came out with alacrity and took hold of the bicycle. Pal marched in, asking Margayya to follow. He followed him into a very small room stuffed with empty packing cases, piled up to the ceiling. There was a stool in the middle of it with a higher stool before it. On the wall hung a printed sheet: '*Silver Way* – Chief Representative's Office'. There were a few stacks of paper in a corner. 'Don't look shocked by the state of my office,' said Pal. 'This is only a temporary place. I'm moving into a big office and showroom as soon as it is ready.'

'Where?' Margayya asked.

'Wherever it may be available. That's all I can say. You know how it is with the present housing conditions!' Margayya did not feel disposed to agree with him. He said: 'You can get houses if you honestly try. After all, you want only a room – '

'But nobody will give it to me free, don't you see, and that is the only condition on which our chief office is prepared to accept any accommodation! You see my problem. They want a place in the town to be called their office, but they won't pay any rent for it. I got this because I also write accounts for these business men and they have allowed me to hang up my board.'

'What do they deal in? Tooth powder or something like that?' Margayya asked.

'They make cheap soap and export it to Malaya – make a lot of money – ' he said.

'Must be an easy job,' Margayya reflected aloud.

'Most messy, and a terrible gamble.'

'But I think there is a lot of money in it,' said Margayya. His mind at once went off. He had no clear idea how soap was made. He only remembered some piece of odd knowledge about coconut oil and caustic. Perhaps a hundred rupees invested might soon multiply, provided the soap became popular. Give it a lot of attractive colouring and sell it cheap and people would flock to buy it – Margayya's soap, Margayya's tooth powder, Margayya's snuff. The choice of his business now seemed to be between these three. He would have to make up his mind about it and start somewhere instead of idling away the day on the fountain parapet ... There was silence during these reflections. The other watched him, and then asked: 'Have you done with your deep reflections?'

'Some ideas connected with my business came to my mind suddenly – '

'Sit down there; it's not nice to remain standing,' said Pal.

Margayya sat down. Pal sat down on the higher stool.

'Margayya, listen to me very attentively,' he began. 'I am speaking to you on a very important matter now.'

'Go ahead, I am not deaf ... You can speak in whispers if you like, if it is such a great secret,' Margayya said.

'If you are thinking of making money or more money or just money, speak out,' said Pal almost in a whisper, coming close to his face. His eyes were so serious that Margayya said: 'How did you guess?'

'There are only two things that occupy men's minds. I'm a psychologist and I know.'

'What are they?' Margayya said.

'Money ... and Sex ... You need not look so shocked. It is the truth. Down with your sham and hypocritical self-deception. Tell me truthfully, is there any moment of the day when you don't think of one or the other?' Margayya did not know how to answer. It seemed a very embarrassing situation. Pal said: 'I'm an academician and I'm only interested in Truth and how human beings face it.'

'I think of plenty of other things too,' Margayya said defensively.

'What are they?'

'About my son and what he is doing.'

'What is it but sex?' asked the dialectician. 'You cannot think of your son without thinking of your wife.'

'Oh, that will do,' said Margayya indignantly. 'I don't like anyone to talk of my wife.'

'Why not?' persisted Pal. 'Have you considered why people make such a fuss about their wives? It is all based on primitive sexual jealousy.'

'No – you should not speak lightly about wives. You know nothing about them. If you are a bachelor, then I don't know what you are.'

'I am a sociologist, and I cannot sugarcoat my words. I have to speak scientifically.'

Margayya was overawed by the man's speech. He did not quite grasp what he was saying. All the same, he said: 'It is generally understood that you may talk of any subject freely – but you must not make free reference to another man's wife.'

'Nor to one's own wife,' added Pal. 'I don't think anyone can speak openly about his wife. If he could speak out openly what she means to him and what she thinks of him or he of her behind the screen of their house or behind the screen of their bed chamber, you will know.'

'Oh, stop, stop,' cried Margayya. 'I won't hear any more of it.' He felt ashamed. This 'sociologist' or whatever he called himself seemed to be preoccupied with only one set of ideas. Margayya said: 'I wish you would marry some strong girl and settle down. It will give you other things to think of.'

'I don't want to think of anything else. I feel I am made by God in order that I may enlighten people in these matters and guide their steps to happiness,' asserted Pal. 'And do you know it is the most paying, most profitable occupation in the present-day world?'

At this Margayya sat up. This was a sentiment which appealed to him. He said: 'What do you mean by that?'

'I'm going to start a sociology clinic, a sort of harmony home, a sort of hospital for creating domestic happiness, a sort of psychological clinic, where people's troubles are set right ... I can charge a small fee. Do you know how many people will come in and go out of it each day? I am certain to earn five hundred

rupees a day easily. My book "Bed Life" – you remember you
saw it? – '

'Yes.'

'That's only a first step in the scheme ... When that book is
published, I expect to have at least a lakh of copies sold.'

'At what price?' asked Margayya.

'Say at about a rupee per copy. You must not price it higher
than that. After all, our purpose is to reach the common man.'

'You mean to say that you are going to make a lakh of rupees
out of it?'

'Yes, what is strange about that? That's only for a start.'

One Lakh of Rupees! One Lakh of Rupees! In Margayya's eyes
this man began to assume grandeur. This lank fellow, cycling
about and gathering news, held within his palm the value of a
lakh of rupees. Margayya was filled with admiration. Tooth powder and snuff and all the rest seemed silly stuff beside this ...You
could never see a lakh of rupees with these commodities; it would
probably go back into the oven again and again, perhaps. But
here was a man who spoke of a lakh of rupees as if it were a five-
rupee note!

'That's only a starting point,' Pal added. 'There is no reason
why it should not go on earning a similar sum year after year. It's
a property which ought to bring in a regular rent. There is no
limit to your sales. The book will simply be – there will be such a
clamour from humanity for this stuff that ultimately every human
being will own a copy. The Tamil-speaking area in India gives us
a good start; add to it the tens and thousands of people in Siam,
Burma, South Africa and so on, and you get the number of
copies you should print. And then if it is translated into Hindi,
it should reach the whole of India – and the population of India is
three hundred and sixty millions according to the last census. If
every man parts with a rupee, see where you are.'

'Yes,' replied Margayya greatly impressed. 'I never thought
there was such a wide scope for selling books.'

'Not for all books. For instance, if I wrote a book of, say,
poems or philosophy, nobody would touch it – but a book like
"Bed Life" is a thing that everyone would like to read. Do
you know, people like to be told facts, people like to be

guided in such matters. Ultimately, as I told you, I shall open a clinic. I want to serve mankind with my knowledge. I don't want to keep it within my closed fists. We must all be helpful to each other. I have worked for years and years studying and writing, just in order that mankind may be helped.' He spoke without stopping for breath, and concluded: 'Do you know, if I just throw down a hint anywhere that there is such a book as this people will fall over each other to publish it.'

'Indeed!'

'Yes, there are offers of ten thousand rupees or more for it. But I won't part with it for ten times that amount.'

'Why not?' asked Margayya.

'Because I can do better than that if I keep it. If people come to make a business offer, they will find me very hard, let me assure you, because I know my mind.'

'So it will be impossible to get it out of you?' asked Margayya.

'Yes, generally, if anyone comes to me as a business man.'

'Oh!' Margayya said, remembering with despair that he came under that category.

The other added: 'But let a man come to me as a friend and hold out his hand, the book is his.'

'But you will lose your lakh – '

'I wouldn't care. Don't imagine I am so fond of money. I treat money as dirt.'

This was a shocking statement for Margayya. He cried: 'Oh, don't say such things. You must not.' He recollected how the Goddess Lakshmi was such a sensitive creature that if a man removed a tumbler of milk she fled from the place and withdrew her grace.

'I'm a man who cares for work, human relationships, and service to mankind,' said Dr Pal. 'Money comes last in my list.'

Margayya felt a desperate idea welling up in him. He could hold it back no longer. It almost burst through his lips, and he asked: 'Suppose I say "give me that for printing and selling", what would you do?'

In answer, the other went out and came back carrying the bag which had been hanging from his cycle handle. He thrust his hand into the bag, and brought out the manuscript. Without another look at it he dropped it on Margayya's lap as he sat on the stool.

'Are you playing?' asked Margayya, hardly able to believe his eyes. It was bound in a blue wrapper. He vaguely turned its leaves to assure himself that it was the right book. 'Principles of Embracing'.

'You take it. It's yours. Do whatever you like with it,' said Pal magnificently.

'No, no, no,' said Margayya. 'How can I?'

'It's no longer mine,' said the other. 'It is a bargain which is closed.' He looked resolute. He then held out his hand and said: 'Give me what you have in your pocket. I will take it in exchange. It's a bargain. You cannot back out of it.'

Margayya said: 'I haven't brought any money – '

'Then why have you brought that purse? I see its outline.'

Margayya looked down with a sigh. Yes, the damned stuff was showing. 'It's not a purse,' he tried to say. But the other said: 'Take it out, let me see what it is that looks like a purse, but isn't. Stick to your bargain.' Margayya put his hand in and brought out the little purse, which had a silver George V embossed on it. He opened it. Twenty-five rupees were all its contents. He took out a five-rupee note and placed it on the outstretched palm of Dr Pal. The other didn't close his fingers or withdraw his arm. He sternly said: 'Stick to your bargain. Empty it.'

'This is all I have,' pleaded Margayya.

'I'm giving you all that I have for my part.'

Margayya said: 'I have to buy rice. I have a wife and child.'

'Don't be theatrical. Stick to your bargain. Here is something I'm giving you worth at least a lakh of rupees. In return for it, give me your purse. I will take it whether it contains one rupee or one thousand or none. Isn't it a fair bargain?'

'I can't give you my purse. It's a lucky purse. I've had it for countless years now.'

'I don't want your purse. Give me only its contents.'

'I don't want your book. I don't know how to print or sell a book.'

'Go to a printer and he will print it. You tell the public the book is ready and they will come and buy it. There are no further complications. It's the easiest business under the sun. In fact you will hardly be able to meet the demand.'

'Then why have you not done it yourself?' asked Margayya.

'Well, I was about to. But just to show you what is a bargain, I've made my offer,' he drawled. 'If you are really keen on cancelling this bargain, I am ready for it. On second thoughts, I don't see why I should waste my breath on you.' He reached for the manuscript on Margayya's lap, saying: 'Every man must make his choice in life. This is a crossroads at which you are standing. Some day you will see another man going away in his Rolls, while you sit on the Market Fountain and brood over my words of this evening. I will give you five minutes to think it over. I'll have the entire contents of your purse or none at all.' He kept his arm outstretched to receive the manuscript back and fixedly gazed at his wrist-watch. His face was grim.

Margayya's face perspired with intense excitement. 'I'm losing twenty thousand each minute,' he told himself. 'Twenty, forty, sixty.' He wanted to say: 'Give me five minutes more,' but his throat had gone dry. No words came. By the time he could get his voice to produce a sound again another ten seconds were gone. Looking at this man, he prayed, 'God, why have you put me in the company of this terrible man amidst these wooden boxes?' A yellowish sunlight came in through a top ventilator, and fell on the opposite wall. 'He will probably choke me if I don't agree,' he ruminated. He wondered if he should scream for help. Somewhere a cycle bell sounded. Wasn't it auspicious, the sounding of a bell? 'Three seconds more,' said the other. The sound of the bell was the voice of God. God spoke through his own signs. Margayya's decision was made. He suddenly felt lighter and said jocularly: 'Three seconds! That's a great deal yet.' He added grandly: 'Tell me when there is still half a second to go,' and pushed away the other's out-stretched arm.

Margayya carried the manuscript home as if he was trying to secrete a small dead body. He was afraid lest somebody should stop him on the way and look at it. He had begged Pal at least to wrap it in paper. Pal snatched up an old issue of *Silver Way* and wrapped it up. Margayya told himself all along the road: 'I must see that the young fellow doesn't get at it.' His plan had been to tuck it within the folds of a stack of clothes in his box the moment he reached home. At the front door he saw his wife with his son on her lap, inducing him to swallow his food by diverting his attention to the stars in the sky and the street below. 'Father!' the little fellow cried joyfully, trying to jump out of his mother's arms. 'Wait, wait,' Margayya said, and passed in swiftly, trying to conceal the bundle under his arm.

'What is it that you are carrying?' his wife asked as he went by. 'Bread?'

He made no reply but walked straight in, opened his box and securely locked it up. He then went through his routine of changing and washing. His wife brought in the child and gave him into his care.

Balu said: 'A monkey came to our house.'

'That's very good,' Margayya said. 'What did it do?'

'It ate coconut and will come again tomorrow. Father, why don't you buy me a monkey?'

'Yes, when you are a good boy.'

'Balu is a good boy,' he replied, certifying to his own conduct.

Margayya sat in the corridor with his son on his lap. He felt light and buoyant, expansive, and full of hope that the good things of life were now within his reach. He hummed a tune to himself, and played with his son. All the time his wife was very curious to know what he had brought in the parcel. She knew by trying to look severe she would never get the truth out of him. She said something agreeable about the boy: 'Do you know what a change is coming over the little fellow? He is so quiet and obedient nowadays,' she said, coming and standing beside him.

Margayya replied: 'He is the finest youngster except when he is otherwise,' and laughed. The boy looked at him bewildered and said: 'Why do you laugh?'

'I don't know,' Margayya said, and all of them laughed heartily.

The boy, having heard a good report about himself, wanted to keep it up, and did nothing to exasperate his father. He ate a quiet dinner, lay down on his mat and ordered his father to tell him a story. Margayya strained his memory and began the story of the fox, the crow and the lion, till the boy interrupted him with: 'I don't like the fox story. Tell me a flower story.'

'I don't know any flower story,' Margayya pleaded. At this the boy threatened to kick his legs and cry. Margayya hastily began: 'Once upon a time there was a good flower – ' and fumbled and hemmed and hawed, wondering how people wrote hundreds of pages of stories; which brought to his mind Dr Pal and his book – how those people ever could sit down and write so many pages. He admired for a moment their patience, and subsequently corrected himself. He didn't like to admire anyone and so said to himself: 'These fellows have no better business; that's why they sit down and fill up sheets, whereas we business men have hardly any time left even to compose our letters.'

The boy insisted on knowing at this stage: 'What flower was it?'

'Lotus,' he felt like saying, but checked himself and said: 'Some flower – why do you want its name now?' and then blundered through a clumsy, impossible story, till the boy fell asleep out of sheer lack of interest.

After finishing all her work, his wife came up with an endearing smile and sat beside him on the mat. He put his arm round her and drew her nearer, recollecting the chapter on 'Principles of Embracing'. She nestled close to him. It was as if they had thrown off twenty years and were back in the bridal chamber. He said: 'Why don't you buy flowers regularly? I see that you don't care for them nowadays.'

'I am an old woman, flowers and such things – '

'But this old man likes to see some flowers in this old lady's hair,' he said. They laughed and felt very happy. And then she asked at the correct moment: 'What is that bundle you brought with you?'

'Oh, that! You wish to see it?'

'Yes, yes, of course,' she said, quite thrilled at the prospect.

He got up, opened his trunk and brought out the packet wrapped in *Silver Way*. He slowly opened the wrapping and took out the manuscript. At the sight of it her face shadowed with disappointment.

'What's this?' she asked.

'It's a book.'

'Oh! I thought you had brought me a *sari*, some surprise gift, I thought.' There was a note of disappointment in her voice. 'Book! Paper,' she said contemptuously. 'What book is this?'

'You see for yourself,' he said, and gave her the packet.

She turned the leaves and was horrified. 'What is it all about? It seems to be ...' But she could not say anything more. 'It seems to be so vulgar!'

'No, no, don't say such a thing,' he said. He didn't like to hear any disparaging reference to the book. 'It's a scientific book. It's going to bring in a lot of money.'

She made a wry face and said: 'How can anybody have written about all this? You men have no ...'

'What's wrong with it? It's something going on all over the world every moment. It's very important. People should possess correct scientific knowledge, and then all marriages will be happy. I'm going to educate Balu in all these matters the moment he is interested.'

'Oh, stop that,' she cried, and flung away the book.

He picked it up, bent close to the lamp and started reading it aloud. It was probably too scientific for ordinary mortals. She listened both horrified and fascinated.

A few days later, Margayya walked into the Gordon Printery in Market Road. It was a fairly big establishment in Malgudi – every form, letter-head, and bill-book in Malgudi was printed at Gordon's. Its proprietor was a man from Bombay who came and settled down here years ago – a hefty, rosy-cheeked man called Madan Lal. He sat at a table, right in the middle of a hall where a dozen people were creating the maximum amount of noise with various machines, which seemed to groan and hiss and splutter. In this general uproar he sat calmly poring over proofs, and opposite his table were ranged two iron chairs. Margayya stood at the entrance. He felt lonely and isolated and unhappy. They might sneer at him and tear up his manuscript. If the Secretary and Arul Doss came down at this moment to see some of their own printing ... He overcame this sinking feeling immediately. ' "Self-assurance" is the most important quality to cultivate,' he realized. He sounded quite assertive when he asked someone at the entrance: 'Where is your proprietor?'

'Sitting there,' the man replied.

'Oh, I didn't notice,' Margayya said, and went up. The man looked up from his papers and asked: 'What can I do for you?' He pointed at an iron chair. Margayya sat down, placed his manuscript before him and said with a lot of self-assurance: 'I wish to have this book printed. Can you take it on?'

'That I can say only after going through the manuscript.'

'Go on, read it.'

'I have no time now. You can leave it here.'

'Impossible,' said Margayya. 'I am not prepared to leave it with anyone. You can go through it here while I wait.'

'I've other business.'

'I've also other business. I have come to you for printing, not for any other business. If you are not prepared to take it on, say so,' and he put out his arms towards the manuscript.

'Oh, no, don't lose your patience,' the other pleaded. 'I was only – ' He picked up the manuscript and glanced at the title page: 'Ah!' he exclaimed. And then he passed on. Every chapter-heading and every page seemed to fascinate him. He kept exclaiming, 'Ah!' 'Ah!' and Margayya sat before him and watched with complete aloofness. He admired himself for it. 'This is the right attitude to cultivate in business. If we show the slightest hesitation or uneasiness others are only too ready to swallow us up.' Proof-bearers came up and waited around until Lal should look up. An accountant stood there with an open ledger in his hand, waiting to catch his attention. Lal kept exclaiming, 'Ah! Ah!' every few seconds. His staff stood around in a circle. 'Get out of the way everyone and give me light,' he suddenly shouted. The accountant alone came up and said un-daunted: 'This is urgent.' He placed the fat book on the manu-script; Lal snatched a minute to look into it, and pushed it away. When his accountant showed signs of looking over his shoulder, he said brusquely: 'Don't try to see what people are reading. Go away.' And the accountant went away. Lal looked for a moment at Margayya and said: 'The curiosity some people have! They have a lot of unhealthy curiosity about all sorts of things.'

Margayya said: 'Are you going to read through the entire manuscript?'

'Yes,' said the other. 'Otherwise, how can I know whether I can print it or not?'

'Have I to sit here all the time?' asked Margayya.

'Why not? That's what you said you would do. Otherwise you may go out and return.'

What was the man proposing? Margayya reflected. Perhaps he had some dark design. No, even if it took a whole day, he would sit up there. Never go out of sight of those papers. 'I will wait here,' said Margayya. 'Go through it fast.'

'Yes, yes,' the other cut in impatiently. 'Don't disturb me.'

Papers continued to come to him. Lal was indifferent. Proofs piled up on his table. Attenders waited around for approval of copy. The accountant came up again and again for his signature on a leather-bound book. Lal snapped at him and signed. And then he pushed the other papers unceremoniously off his table saying: 'No one is to come near me till I am through with this piece of work: this is very urgent and important. Don't you see this gentleman waiting?' The machine-room foreman came up presently. He hovered about, cleared his throat, and ventured to say: 'The School report, sir. The machine is idle.'

'Oh!' he replied, then rummaged amongst his papers, snatched a proof, and after the briefest glance at it, flung it at him. 'Go ahead.'

It was one o'clock in the afternoon when Lal looked up and said: 'I'm hungry, and yet I have not finished. Still thirty pages more. I have to go home. You wouldn't leave this with me, I suppose!'

'No,' said Margayya resolutely. 'How can I?'

'Then you come along with me for lunch.'

Margayya felt worried. This man from the North – God knew what he ate at home: perhaps beef and pork and strange spices. How could he go and sit with him? He said bluntly: 'I have already had my food.'

'That's excellent; come along with me.'

'No, I have to go home.'

'Why should you if you have had your dinner already?'

'I have got some other business.'

'Then what do you want me to do? Sit here with this, forgoing my meal, is that it?'

'As you please. You must have read enough of it to know what to tell me.'

'Be reasonable, Mister,' he appealed. 'If you give me a little more time, I will finish it and then I shall be in a position to discuss the matter with you.'

'Then go on,' Margayya said. 'I am not preventing your reading further.'

The other hammered on the call bell impatiently till an attendant came up and stood before him: 'Go home and tell them I'm not coming for my meal today. Send somebody and get something from the restaurant for two.'

Coffee and several plates arrived. Lal pushed away all the papers to make space for the plates and invited Margayya to eat. He kept the manuscript on his lap, his eyes running down the lines; his fingers strayed towards the plates on the table and carried the food to his mouth as if they had an independent life of their own. He looked up for a brief moment at Margayya and said: 'Go on, go on, make yourself comfortable.'

Margayya had some plates on his side of the table; he hesitated only for a moment, and then said to himself: 'Why not?' He was hungry. He had had a sparse meal hours ago. They had put before him many tempting coloured sweets and coffee. 'This is indeed lucky,' he reflected. 'This is good tiffin. It'd have cost me over a rupee.' He ate the *jilebis*, and wondered if it would be proper to carry a bit of it home for little Balu. He was racked with a feeling that he was stealing some delicacy which ought to have gone to his child.

'Make yourself comfortable,' Lal said hospitably from time to time without lifting his eyes from the manuscript.

Margayya noticed that the other was a voracious eater, and polished off all sorts of oddments in a lump, it didn't matter what. 'That's why he is so hefty,' Margayya reflected. 'He is not a half-fed, half-starving business man like me. That's why he is able to command so much business and income.'

When the plates were removed, Lal wiped his mouth with a handkerchief, looked at Margayya and announced: 'I have finished reading the book.'

'Well, what do you think you can do?'

'It's an interesting book, no doubt.'

'It's a book that must be read by everybody,' Margayya added.

'No, no, don't say that; it's not fit for everybody's reading. For instance, if a young unmarried person reads it – '

'He will know a lot of facts beforehand,' Margayya said; and this established a greater communion between the two.

Lal said: 'Mister, I must consult my lawyer first.'

'What has a lawyer to do with it?' Margayya asked. The mention of a lawyer was distasteful to him.

'The trouble is,' said the other, 'I must know if it comes under the obscenity law. There is such a law you know. They may put us both in prison.'

'It's not obscene. It's a work of sociology.'

'Oh, is it? Then there is no trouble. But I'd like to be told that by a lawyer. Will you please come again tomorrow at this time?'

'What for?'

'I will have discussed the matter with my lawyer, and then I shall be able to tell you something. If only you could leave the book with me!'

'That I can't do,' said Margayya, sensing another effort on the part of the printer to get at the manuscript. He added for emphasis: 'That I can't do, whatever may happen.'

'Won't you come with me to the lawyer?'

'When?' asked Margayya, with a profound air of having to consider his engagement diary.

'Sometime tomorrow.'

Margayya sat considering. It was no use going to a lawyer. The thought of a lawyer was distasteful to him. The Co-operative Society Secretary was a lawyer. All lawyers were trouble-makers. Moreover, why should he cheapen himself before this man? He said: 'Impossible. I have a busy day tomorrow. I can probably drop in just for a few minutes if you like, that is if you are going to tell me definitely yes or no.' He added: 'I came to you because yours is the biggest establishment. I knew you could do it, although a dozen other printers were ready to take on the job.'

'Ours is the best and biggest press,' Lal said haughtily. 'You will not be able to get this service anywhere else, so much I can assure you.'

'What will be your charge?'

'I can tell you all that only after we decide to take on the work.'

'Will you require a long time to print the book?' Margayya persisted.

'I will tell you tomorrow,' Lal said.

Margayya said: 'You are a very cautious man. You don't like to commit yourself to anything.'

'That's right,' the other said appreciatively, sensing a kindred soul. For among business men as among statesmen, the greatest dread was to be committed to anything. Being non-committal was the most widely recognized virtue among business men and it came to Margayya instinctively as his other qualities came to him. The musician hums the right note at birth, the writer goes to the precise phrase in the face of an experience, whereas for the business man the greatest gift is to be able to speak so many words which seem to signify something, but don't, which convey a general attitude but are free from commitment.

Next day Margayya tidied himself up more than ever and was at the press at the appointed time. He still carried his manuscript securely wrapped in a paper sheet. The moment he entered the press he had a feeling that all was going to go well. He went straight up to Lal and asked: 'Well, what does your lawyer say?'

'We can take it if you agree to a couple of small conditions.'

'You can speak your mind freely,' Margayya said, encouragingly. 'In business we either conclude a deal or we don't, but there is no room for mincing words. If you don't want it here, I can take it somewhere else,' he added.

'No, no, don't say such a thing, Mister,' the other said. 'I don't like negative statements to be made in this press.'

'I don't like negative statements myself unless I am forced to make them,' said Margayya, discovering instinctively yet another principle of business life: to have the last word. He concluded that he who spoke last gained most. He was burning with anxiety to know if the other would print the book, for he seemed to be a man who knew his job. Margayya looked about and asked in a business-like manner: 'What are the two conditions you mentioned just now?'

'I will take up the printing provided it's done on a basis of partnership.'

'What's the partnership for?'

'Well, that will make our work more interesting. Let us publish it together, and share whatever we get. I mean fifty-fifty in everything; expenses as well as returns. Do you agree?'

Margayya took a little time before answering: 'I won't say "Yes" or "No" before thinking over it deeply. What's your second condition?'

'You must indemnify me against any legal action that anyone may take at any time.'

'What do you mean?'

'You must bear the legal responsibility for bringing out this book.'

'I see!' said Margayya with deep suspicion. 'Why?'

'It's because you are bringing it out.'

'If I am bringing it out, you have nothing to do with it except to print it, isn't that so? Then why do you ask for profits? How are you concerned with profits?'

For a moment the other looked a little confused, but soon recovered enough composure to say: 'I mean to propose a non-liability partnership.'

Margayya was taken in by the high-sounding phrase. What did it mean? It meant evidently sharing his profits, not his troubles.

He said: 'I've done a variety of business. I'm experienced in different kinds of partnership.'

'What business were you doing before?' asked Lal.

'Chiefly banking,' Margayya said. 'You know when a man is a banker he is at once involved in a number of other things too,' picturing himself writing a letter here for a villager and arranging a joint-loan for another there.

Lal seemed to appreciate this. He said: 'We have a bank in Gujerat, but you know it also deals in oil-seeds in certain seasons.'

'It's inevitable,' Margayya said, with an air of profundity.

'It's impossible not to be interested in more than one business,' added Lal.

They went on talking far into the day. Once again lunch-time came. Once again they got their tiffin from a hotel and Margayya stuffed himself with sweets and coffee and began to feel quite at home in the press. They kept talking non-committally, warmly, discreetly and with many digressions, till late in the evening, but without concluding anything. Their talk, and counter-talk never ceased, and the manuscript lay between. At about six they dramatically stretched their arms over it, shook hands and concluded the pact, whereby Margayya had the satisfaction of seeing himself a fifty-fifty partner without any investment on his part. He covered the satisfaction he had in the deal with: 'I'm not keen on this, but you know you seem to have become such a friend to me that I find it difficult to refuse.' He pulled a long face and signed a partnership deed with the utmost resignation. He kept saying: 'You have won me over. You are a sharp business man,' a compliment which Lal accepted with the utmost cheerfulness.

'We can never be business men unless we give and take on a fifty-fifty basis,' Lal kept saying, a proposition heartily endorsed by Margayya, although its arithmetic was somewhat complex and beyond the understanding of ordinary men.

Margayya knocked on his door with great authority. Lal had offered to drive him home in his car. But Margayya declined it definitely. He didn't want him to see his house or street. He explained that after all the hours of sitting in a stuffy atmosphere he would prefer a walk, so as to be fit for work next day.

He knocked on his door with such authority that his wife came up hurriedly and opened it. She stood aside to let him pass in. She could not pluck up enough courage to put to him the usual irritating questions. She served him his food and then said in a forced light manner: 'This has almost become your usual hour?'

'Yes, it may have to be even later hereafter. I shall have to be very busy.'

'Oh!' she said. 'Is that book printed?'

'It's not so easy,' he replied. 'There are many complications.' And as she did not annoy him with further questions, he added: 'I have almost signed a partnership agreement with a big man.' He liked the sentence and the feeling of importance that it gave him. But he didn't like the word 'big' that he had used. Reflecting, he felt he might take the word out and knock it flat lest his wife should think he really meant anyone was bigger than he. He rectified his mistake by adding: '*Big* business-man! *Big!* A North Indian; he thinks he is very clever, but I was able to tweak his nose – '

'Oh!' said his wife gratified. He seemed to acquire a new stature and importance. He finished his dinner and when he got up she was ready with a bowl of water for his hands. And then she held a towel up to him.

He was pleased with all these ministrations, thinking, 'Yes, she is not a bad sort, except when she gets into a bad mood.' He said aloud: 'We can live differently hereafter, I think. A lot of money is coming in.'

The next day he had a very busy time discussing several technical matters, of which he was totally ignorant, with Lal. Lal seemed to assume that Margayya knew what he was talking about. Margayya true to his principles did not wish to show his ignorance.

Lal asked: 'Shall we print in demy or octavo?'

What was demy and what octavo? What strange terms were these; to what universe did they belong? Margayya frankly blinked, wondering: 'What was this man talking about?' He said grandly: 'Each has its own advantage, it's for you to decide; you are a technical man.'

Lal said: 'You see, demy will give us greater area.'

Margayya was hearing the word for the first time in his life. He could not understand to which part of a book or press or sales the word referred. He kept himself alert, deciding not to lose any hint that might fall in the course of the other's talk. He added: 'If it means extra area, what other consideration can you have?'

'It's not only that, octavo is more handy, and will look less like a gazetteer.'

At the mention of gazetteer Margayya made a wry face: 'Oh, no, we cannot afford to make it look like a gazetteer.'

'In that case we will print it on octavo.'

'All right,' he said, permitting it graciously. 'But as a matter of formality I shall be glad to know the difference in cost.'

'Not much, about an anna per pound,' Lal said.

Pound! Where did pound come in? He was about to blurt out the question, a survival of his boyhood days in the classroom where, whenever the word pound was mentioned, the immediate question was: 'Lb Pound or Shilling Pence Pound?' He almost opened his mouth to ask it, but pressed it back in time, remembering that it was a silly betraying question even in those days: the teacher caned all the boys who asked him that question, for it showed that they had not paid any attention to the sum they were doing. Margayya feared if he raised it the other might tear up their agreement or decide to swindle him with absolute impunity. What did they weigh in the book trade? He could understand nothing of it. He dropped it, hoping on some future occasion that he would know all about it. He had an unfailing hope that whatever there was to be known would be known by him one day. 'Only I must keep my eyes open, and in six months I shall be able to tell them what is wrong with them,' he thought, with much self-esteem.

Lal observed him for a moment and then said: 'Why are you silent? You are not saying anything.'

'It is because I have nothing to say,' said Margayya.

'So you accept my choice.'

'Yes, of course,' Margayya said, hoping this would once and for all save him from further embarrassment.

But Lal turned up with a new poser for him: 'Shall we use ordinary ten-point Roman or another series which I use only for special works? It's also ten-point but on an eleven-point body.'

Body? Points? Ten and Eleven? What was it all about? Margayya said: 'Ah, that is interesting ... I should like to see your eleven-point body.' He had grotesque visions of a torso being brought in by four men on a stretcher. When Lal reached out his arm and pulled out a book, he didn't think it had any relation to the question he had asked. He thought Lal was trying to read something. But Lal opened a page, thrust it before him and said: 'This is it. How do you like this type?' Margayya gazed at it for fully five minutes and said: 'It seems all right to me. What do you say?'

'It's one of our finest types,' said Lal. 'Do you wish to see our ordinary Roman?'

Now he roughly knew what this meant. 'If this is your best, there's not much reason why anything else should be seen,' he said with the air of a man who could employ those few minutes to better profit. He added, in order not to allow the other too easy a time, 'Only tell me if you have any special reasons from the point of view of costs.'

'A difference of a couple of rupees per forme, that's all.'

'That's all, is it?' Margayya said. 'How many formes will there be?'

Lal glanced through the script and said: 'Even if it's going to be page for page, it won't be more than ten formes.'

'I don't think we ought to worry about a bare difference of twenty rupees,' Margayya said, feeling happy that he could after all take part in the discussion.

'I agree with you,' said Lal. 'Now about the style of binding, etc.'

'Oh, these details!' Margayya exclaimed. 'They should not come as far as me. You ought to decide those things yourself.'

'But every item has to go into costs. I don't want you to feel at any time that I have incurred any expense without your knowledge.'

'That comes only at the end, doesn't it?' Margayya said.

'Of course, in the first quarter following publication.'

And Margayya felt relieved – he had a gnawing fear lest he should have to shell out cash immediately.

'And,' said Lal, 'my lawyer suggests that we had better call this book "Domestic Harmony" instead of "Bed Life". Have you any objection?'

'Oh, none whatever,' said Margayya. 'In these matters we must implicitly obey the lawyers.'

'Otherwise we shall get into trouble.'

'Yes, otherwise we shall get into trouble,' echoed Margayya, adding: 'We must do everything possible to avoid getting into trouble because a business man's time is so precious.'

'You are an uncanny fellow. You seem to understand everything,' Lal said admiringly.

When Balu was six years old Margayya had him admitted to the Town Elementary School. Margayya made a great performance of it. He took the young man in a decorated motor with pipes and drums through the Market Road: the traffic was held up for half an hour when Balu's procession passed. Balu sat with the top of his head shaved, with diamonds sparkling on his ear-lobes, and a rose garland round his neck, in a taxi with four of his picked friends by his side. Margayya walked in front of the car, and he had invited a few citizens of the road to go up with him as well. Strangest sight of all, his brother was also with him in the procession. They seemed to have made it up all of a sudden. On the eve of the Schooling Ceremony, Margayya stated: 'After all, he is his own uncle, his own blood, my brother. Unless he blesses the child, of what worth are all the other blessings he may get?' He grew sentimental at the thought of his elder brother. 'Don't you know that he brought me up?... But for his loving care ...' He rambled on thus. His wife caught the same mood and echoed: 'No one prevents them from being friendly with us.'

'There are times when we should set aside all our usual prejudices and notions – we must not let down ties of blood,' Margayya said pompously. As a result of this sentiment, at five a.m. they both knocked on the door of the next house and quietly walked past the astounded stare of his brother as he held the door open. Margayya's wife went straight into the kitchen to invite the sister-in-law, and Margayya stood before his brother in the hall and said: 'All of you are keeping well as usual, I suppose?' adding: 'Balu's Schooling Ceremony is tomorrow morning. Come and bless him – '

'Oh, yes, oh, yes,' his brother said, still somewhat dazed.

'Bring yourself and all the children for a meal,' Margayya said, and added, 'You must not light the oven in your own house. Come in for morning coffee. Where is my sister-in-law?'

His brother said: 'There.'

Margayya shouted: 'Sister-in-law!' familiarly, as he used to do in his boyhood days. It seemed to take him back decades when he was a student coming home during the afternoon recess for rice and buttermilk. He made a move towards the kitchen, when his wife came in the opposite direction, with bowed head, showing the respect due to the elder brother-in-law; she moved off fast, giving Margayya a swift glance, which he understood. He turned and followed his wife quietly into the street. Hardly had they gone up their veranda steps when she whispered: 'She will not come.'

'Why not?' Margayya asked.

'She bit her lips so and nodded – the vicious creature. She wouldn't speak a word to me.'

'Why not?'

'Why not? Why not? Don't keep saying that. She is that sort, that is all.'

'She used to be very kind to me in those days.' Margayya's sentimentality still lingered in him, as he remembered his school-days.

'No one prevents you from going and asking her again.'

'You invited her properly, I suppose,' Margayya said.

She flared up: 'I have abased myself sufficiently.'

'That's all right, that's all right,' Margayya said, scenting danger.

His brother and seven of his children came and presided over the function. He presented young Balu with a silver box, and at the sight of it Margayya felt very proud and moved. He asked his son to prostrate himself before his uncle ceremoniously and receive his blessings, after which the boy started out for his school in a procession.

Margayya's son had a special standing in the school, for Margayya was the school secretary. Teachers trembled before him, and the headmaster stood aside while he passed. They knew Margayya was a powerful man and also that he could be a pleasant and kindly man, who listened to their troubles when they met him at home to discuss small promotions or redress. He listened to them most attentively and promised to do his best, but hardly remembered anything of it next moment. This was purely a defensive mechanism. He simply could not keep in his head all the requests that people brought to him each day. The utmost he could do for them was to be pleasant to them. When they pestered him too much he merely said, 'See here, I took up this work as a sort of service for our people, but this is not my only occupation. As a matter of fact I did not want all this business, but it was thrust upon me and they wouldn't take my refusal.'

He spoke like the president of a political party after an election campaign, but his place on the school board did not come to him unsought nor was it thrust upon him. On the day he admitted Balu to the school he realized that his son would not have a chance of survival unless he admitted himself also to the school. Within fifteen days of the Schooling Ceremony he heard reports that Balu was being caned almost every day, was having his ears twisted by all and sundry, and that even the school peon pushed him about rudely. He loved his son and it seemed to him that the school was thoroughly in the wrong. He went there once or twice to rectify matters and was told by the headmaster that it was all false and perhaps the boy deserved all that and more. They treated him in an off-hand manner which angered him very much. They almost hinted that he might take his son away. At the end of the term Balu came home with his progress card marked zero. Margayya decided to take charge of the school.

He was a busy business man who could not afford the time for unprofitable honorary work, but he felt he ought to sacrifice himself for the sake of his son's educational progress. He wanted Balu to grow up into an educated man, graduating out of a college and probably going for higher studies to Europe or America. He had immense confidence in himself now. He could undertake any plan with ease; he could shape his son's future as if it were just so much clay in his hand. His son might become a great government official or something of the kind, or indeed anything in ten years, if this cursed school were not in his way ... He watched for the next election time. It was a strategy of extraordinary complexity and meant expense too; but he did not grudge it. He felt that no expense was too great for a child's future, and slipped into the place of a member whom he had persuaded to retire. After that one could notice a great improvement in Balu's career. He never lost his place in the class, and the teachers seemed to have adjusted themselves to his way of thinking. In addition Margayya picked up a home tutor for him. He made this selection with great astuteness. He kept an eye on all the teachers, and sounded his son himself as to whom he would like to have as teacher at home, to which Balu promptly replied, 'No one.'

Margayya said, 'You are not to say that. You must have a home teacher. Tell me whom you like most in your school.'

After a great deal of persuasion, the boy said 'Nathaniel.'

Margayya knew him to be a mild Christian gentleman whom all the children loved because he told them numerous stories, let them do what they pleased, never frowned at them even once, and taught them history and such innocuous subjects rather than mathematics. Margayya decided at once to eliminate this gentleman from his list as a home tutor. 'It is no good appointing a sheep to guard a tiger cub,' he told himself. He suddenly asked: 'Who is the teacher that beats the boys most?'

'The science attender,' replied the young innocent.

'I don't mean him,' Margayya said, 'I mean among the teachers.'

'But the science attender says he is also a teacher. Do you know, father, he beats any boy who doesn't call him "Sir"?'

'He does that, does he!' exclaimed Margayya angrily. 'You go and tell him that he is merely a miserable science peon and nothing more, and if he tries to show off I will cut off his tail.'

'Has he a tail, father?' asked Balu. 'Oh, I didn't notice.' He burst into a laugh, and laughed so loudly and rolled about so much that his father was forced to say, 'Stop that ... Don't make all that noise.' The vision of the science attender with a tail behind only made Balu roll about more and more. He made so much noise that his mother came out of the kitchen to ask, 'What is the matter?'

'Mother,' the boy screamed, 'father thinks that our science teacher has a tail, the science teacher has a tail ...' He danced about in sheer joy at this vision, and Margayya could not get anything more out of him. The boy was too wild. He left him alone for the moment but questioned him again later and found that the teacher he most detested was Mr Murti, the arithmetic and English teacher, an old man who always carried a cane in his hand, shaved his head and covered it with a white turban, and wore a long coat. To Margayya it seemed to be a very satisfactory picture of a teacher. None of your smart young men with bare heads and crop, with their entertaining stories and so forth. He immediately asked Murti to see him at his house and fixed him up at once as Balu's teacher at home and a sort of supervisor for him at school too. His own professional work was taking up more and more of his time each day; he wanted another agency to protect the interests of his son at school.

Murti was only too happy to accept this job since he earned only twenty-five rupees at school and the ten rupees that Margayya arbitrarily offered him was most welcome, as was the perpetual contact he would have with the Secretary of the School Board day in and day out. It enhanced his status at school among his colleagues and also with the headmaster, who, if he wanted to sound the secretary's state of mind over any important question at school, called aside Murti and spoke to him in whispers. All this Murti welcomed, but he also lost something in the bargain, and that was his power over his pupil, Balu. He knew that although Margayya had asked him to handle him as he would any other boy, the plan would not work. He had far too much experience with people who had an only child and a lot of money. They never meant what they said with regard to their children. No one lost his head so completely over a question of discipline as the parent of an only child. Murti did not want to offend the young boy and lose his favour so that one day he might tell his father, 'I won't be taught by that teacher.' On the other hand he did not want the father to feel that he was not able to handle Balu. So he walked warily. He tried to earn the goodwill and co-operation of the pupil himself so that his job might be easy. He gave him many gifts of sweets and pencils and rubbers if he did a sum well and forbore his mischief, and treated him generally as a friend. The scheme worked, although the boy was on the verge of blackmailing his teacher whenever he set him more sums than he cared to do. But on the whole the relationship was successful and Balu progressed steadily from class to class and reached the Fourth Form.

The teacher and the pupil were like old partners now, sea-soned partners who knew each other's strong points and weak points. Margayya stuck to his School Board election after election. He boasted to his friends and relations whenever he found a chance: 'Balu is just thirteen you know, and in two years ...' He gloated over a vision of his son passing into a college. He would give him a separate study in the new house he was planning to build in New Extension. He would buy table lamps with green shades; they said that a green shade was good for the eyes. He would send him to Albert Mission College, although it was at the other end of the town, far away from New Extension. He would buy him a car. People would look at him and say, 'Well, there goes Margayya's son. Lucky fellows, these sons of business men.'

Margayya had converted the small room into a study for Balu. Every morning Margayya carried out an inspection of this room in order to see that his son learnt civilized ways and kept his things in their proper places, but he always found the mat not spread out on the floor, but stood up against a corner half-rolled, his books scattered on the floor, and his little desk full of stones, feathers, cigarette foils and empty packets. These were all collected from a small shop made of dealwood planks near by which had recently been set up by a man from Malabar. Margayya felt unhappy when he saw the condition of this room. In his view a study had to be a very orderly place, with books arrayed on one side, and the clothes of the scholar folded and in their place on the wire stretched across the wall. Margayya had secured a small framed picture of the Goddess Saraswathi, the Goddess of Learning and Enlightenment, sitting beside her peacock and playing on the strings of a *veena*. He hung it in the study and enjoined his son ceremoniously to pray to the Goddess every morning as soon as he got up from bed. He inquired untiringly, 'Boy, have you made your prostrations before the Goddess?'

'Yes,' the boy answered, and ran in and performed them in a moment, then came back to the hall and just hung about staring at the sky or into the kitchen. Margayya felt angry. He told his son sharply: 'God is not like your drill class, to go and dawdle about half-heartedly. You must have your heart in it.'

'I prostrated all right, father.'

'Yes, but your mind was where?'

'I was thinking of ... of ...' He considered for a moment, and added, 'My lessons,' knowing it would please his father. But it did not seem to have that effect.

'When you prostrate, you must not prostrate so fast.'

'How long can I lie on the floor prostrate?' the boy asked sullenly. 'I can't be lying there all the time.'

'If you grumble so much about your duties to the Goddess, you will never become a learned man, that is all,' Margayya warned him.

'I don't care,' said the boy, very angry at the thought of an exacting Goddess.

'You will be called a useless donkey by the whole world, remember,' Margayya said, his temper rising. 'Learn to talk with more reverence about the gods ... Do you know where I was, how I started, how I earned the favour of the Goddess by prayer and petition? Do you know why I succeeded? It was because my mind was concentrated on the Goddess. The Goddess is the only one who can – '

The boy cut him short with, 'I know it is a different Goddess you worshipped. It is that Goddess Lakshmi. I know all that from mother.'

Margayya felt upset by this taunt. He called his wife and asked, 'Why have you been talking nonsense to this boy? He is saying all sorts of things.'

'What has he been saying?' asked the wife, wiping her wet hands on the end of her *sari*.

Margayya was at a loss to explain. There was really no basis for his charge. He merely said, 'That boy contradicts me.' He turned furiously on his son and said, 'It is all the same Goddess. There is no difference between Lakshmi and Saraswathi, do you understand?'

The boy was not to be cowed. He simply said, 'They are different, I know.' He said it with an air of finality. Margayya asked, 'How do you know? Who told you?'

'My master.'

'Who? Murti? I will speak to that fool. If he is putting obstinate ideas into your head, he is not fit to be your teacher.'

Then he added, 'Tell me as soon as he comes tomorrow or this evening.'

'But you won't be at home when he comes,' said the boy.

'Let him wait for me. Tell him he must see me,' said Margayya.

'All right,' said the boy.

Margayya then ordered him out, with, 'You can go and do your sums now. Don't waste the precious hours of the morning.' Balu ran off with great relief to his study and read a page out of his geography at the top of his voice so that all other sounds in the house were drowned.

He went to school trembling with the joyous anticipation of carrying a piece of unpleasant news to his teacher. The moment he sighted him he cried, 'Sir, sir, my father has asked you to wait for him this evening.'

The teacher's face turned pale. 'Why? Why?' he stammered nervously. There were some boys watching them, and he said, 'Go away, boys, attend to your work, why do you stand and gape,' as sternly as he could. He then took Balu aside and said: 'Tell me boy, why does your father want me to see him?' 'I don't know, sir,' Balu replied, enjoying the occasion completely. 'I don't know, sir.' He shook his head, but his eyes were lively with mischief and suppressed information. The teacher tried to frighten him: 'Should you not ask him why he wants to when somebody says he wants to meet somebody else? Must you be taught all these elementary things?'

'Oh, my father cannot be asked all that. He will be very angry if he is questioned like that. Why should I be beaten by him, sir? Do you want me to be beaten by him, sir?'

The teacher took him privately under the tamarind tree and begged: 'See here, what exactly happened today, won't you tell me, won't you tell your teacher?'

He sounded melodramatic, and Balu started bargaining, 'I couldn't do any sums this morning.' The teacher assured him that he would condone the lapse. And then Balu went on to the next bargaining point by which the teacher himself should do the sums and not bother Balu except to the extent of showing him what marks he had obtained for them. When it was granted, Balu demanded: 'You promised me *bharfi*; I must have it this afternoon, sir.'

'You will surely get a packet from me this afternoon,' said the teacher affably. After all this, Balu told him the reason why his father wanted to meet him. The teacher cried: 'I say, whatever made you speak thus? Have I ever mentioned to you anything about Lakshmi or anything of the kind?'

'My father asked who told me all that, and so I had to say it was you,' said Balu, with obscure logic.

The teacher waited for Margayya's arrival in the evening after finishing the lessons with Balu. Balu went in to demand his dinner. It was past eight when Margayya came home. As the pitpat of his sandals was heard outside the teacher felt acutely uneasy and stood up. Margayya carefully put away his sandals at the corridor and came in. He saw the teacher and asked, 'What is the matter, teaching so late?' The teacher went forward officiously, rubbed his hands and said, 'Oh, I finished the lessons long ago, and Balu has even gone to sleep. I only waited to see you, sir,' he added.

'Oh, now, impossible,' said Margayya. He proceeded to put away his upper-cloth and take off his shirt. 'I come home after a hard day's work and now you try to catch me for some idiotic school business, I suppose. Do you think I have no other business? Go, go, nothing doing now.'

'All right, sir,' the teacher said turning to go, greatly relieved.

'Is there anything else?' Margayya shouted as the other was going. The teacher thought for a moment and said: 'Nothing special, sir,' in a most humble tone, which satisfied Margayya. His self-importance was properly fed; and so he said, as a sort of favour to the teacher, 'I hope Balu is all right?'

'Oh, yes, sir; he is quite up to the mark although he needs constant watching ...'

'Well, as a teacher that is what you are expected to do, remember. And any time you see him getting out of hand, don't wait for me. Thrash him. Thrash him well.' As a sort of general philosophy, he added, 'No boy who has not been thrashed has come to any good. I am going to be extremely busy hereafter and won't have much time for anything. Don't take your eye off the boy.'

'Yes, sir, I will always do my best; as a teacher my interest is to see him rise in the world as a man of – '

Margayya turned and went away to the backyard without waiting for him to finish the sentence. His wife picked up a vessel of water and gave it to him. As he poured it over himself and she could be sure he was feeling cooler, she said, 'Why do you constantly say "Thrash" "Thrash" whenever you speak of the child? It is not good.'

Margayya replied, 'Oh, you believe it! It is just a formality with teachers, that is all. It keeps them in trim. After all, the fellow takes ten rupees a month and he must keep himself alert; but he dare not even touch our little darling. I would strike off that miserable teacher's head.'

It was all very bewildering to his wife. She asked, 'If you don't want him to do it why do you tell him to thrash him?'

'That is the way things have to be done in the world, my dear. If you see a policeman ask him to catch the thief, if you see a monkey ask him to go up a tree, and if you see a teacher ask him to thrash his pupil ... These are the things they do and it pleases them, they are appropriate. If you want to please me tell me to put up the interest, and I at once feel I am being spoken to by a friend and well-wisher!'

There was probably no other person in the whole country who had meditated so much on the question of interest. Margayya's mind was full of it. Night and day he sat and brooded over it. The more he thought of it the more it seemed to him the greatest wonder of creation. It combined in it the mystery of birth and multiplication. Otherwise how could you account for the fact that a hundred rupees in a savings bank became one hundred and twenty in course of time? It was something like the ripening of corn. Every rupee, Margayya felt, contained in it seed of another rupee and that seed in it another seed and so on and on to infinity. It was something like the firmament, endless stars and within each star an endless firmament and within each one further endless ... It bordered on mystic perception. It gave him the feeling of being part of an infinite existence. But Margayya was racked with the feeling that these sublime thoughts were

coming to him in a totally wrong setting. He disliked the atmosphere of the Gordon Printery. He detested his office and the
furniture. Sitting in a chair, dangling one's legs under a table,
seemed an extremely irksome process; it was as if you remained
half suspended in mid-air. He liked to keep his knees folded and
tucked – that alone gave him a feeling of being on solid ground.
And then his table and all its equipment seemed to him a most
senseless luxury. They were not necessary for the welfare and
progress of a business man; they were mere show stuff. And all
that calling-bell nonsense. The best way to call was to shout
'Boy,' and keep shouting till the boy's ear-drums split and he
came running. All this tinkling calling-bell stuff was a waste of
time. You were not a shepherd playing on a flute calling back
your flock! Margayya was so much tickled by this comparison
that he laughed aloud one day while he sat in his office, and was
supposed to be counting the orders for *Domestic Harmony*. The
boy came running in at the sound of this laughter, and Margayya
flung the call-bell at him and said: 'Don't let me see this on my
table. I don't want all this tomfoolery.' This was the starting-
point.

The business always seemed to him an alien one. The only
interesting thing about it seemed to be the money that was
coming in. 'But money is not everything,' he told himself one
day. It was a very strange statement to come from a person like
Margayya. But if he had been asked to explain or expand it
further he would have said: 'Money is very good no doubt, but
the whole thing seems to be in a wrong setting.' Money was not
in its right place here, amidst all the roar of printing machinery,
ugly streaming proof sheets, and the childish debits and credits
that arose from book sales with booksellers and book buyers,
who carried on endless correspondence over trivialities about six
and a quarter and twelve and a half per cent and a few annas of
postage and so forth. It was all very well if you spoke of those
percentages with a value of a hundred rupees at least; but here
you were dealing with two rupees per copy and involved yourself in all these hair-splitting percentages. It did not seem to
Margayya an adult business; there was really no stuff in it; there
was not sufficient adventure in it; there was nothing in it. 'Book

business is no business at all,' he told his wife one evening when he decided to part company with Lal. 'It is a business fit for youngsters of Balu's age.' The lady had no comment to offer since all business seemed to her equally complex and bewildering. She had to listen with patience as he expanded his theme: 'It is a rusty business, sitting there all the time and looking at those silly figures ... Well, to let you into a secret, there is not much of that either; the figures are falling off; sales are not as good as they used to be.' And then it hurt his dignity to be called the publisher of *Domestic Harmony*. He would prefer people to forget it if possible. When the profits dwindled he began to view the book in a peculiarly realistic light. 'Awful stuff,' he told his wife. 'Most vulgar and poisonous. It will do a lot of damage to young minds.'

'And also to old minds, I think. How can people write brazenly of all those matters?' she asked.

Margayya said, 'Did you ever notice how I have managed not to bring a single copy into this house? I don't want our Balu even to know that there is such a book.' His wife expressed deep appreciation of this precaution. Margayya felt further impelled to add, 'I don't want people to say that Balu enjoys all the money earned through *Domestic Harmony*. I would do anything to avoid it.' He felt very heroic when he said that. He seemed to swell with his goodness, nobility and importance, and the clean plans he was able to make for his son.

It was quite a fortnight before he spoke of it to Lal. Lal was thinking that Margayya was attending to his work as usual. Their quarterly statement system worked quite smoothly. There was no chance of any mistake or misunderstanding. Lal himself was a man who believed that in the long run honesty paid in any business. Margayya had complete charge of the sales, and the division of the spoils went on smoothly without a hitch. At tiffin time, Margayya called up his boy and told him: 'Go and ask Lal if he will come here for tiffin today. Tell him that there is something I have brought from home.' Lal came up. Margayya ceremoniously welcomed him and pointed to the chair opposite. 'My wife has sent something special today for my afternoon tiffin, and I thought you might like to taste it.'

'I have to go home for lunch,' said Lal. 'I have told them that I would be there.'

'I will send word to them. Boy!' Margayya cried. He took complete charge of the other. 'Call the master's servant, and send him up to inform the lady at the house that *Sab* is not coming there for his meal. And then run up and bring ...' He gave an elaborate list of tiffins to be purchased at the canteen next door. 'Ask him to make the best coffee.'

'I don't want coffee, mister. Let it be tea. I have taken coffee only for your sake once or twice. I don't want coffee.'

'All right, make it tea then; and coffee for me. Hurry up! Why are you still standing and blinking? Hurry up, young fellow.' There, consuming their repast, Margayya made his proposal. 'Lal, you have done a lot for me. I want to do a good turn to you.'

At the mention of this Lal sat up interested. 'Good turn,' he thought. That sounded suspicious. No one like Margayya would do a good turn except as a sort of investment. Lal wanted to know what the proposal was going to mean. He knew that it must be something connected with *Domestic Harmony*, but he felt he should have all his faculties alert. He said very casually, 'Well, mister, we must all be helpful to each other, isn't that so? Other-wise, what is life worth? What is existence worth? If we are always thinking of our profits, we shall not be able to do any good in this world. I am glad you think so much of my little service to you. But pray don't think too much of it. I have done the little I could, although financially it has really meant a loss. If I should put into my books all the time and energy, to say nothing of the materials, that have been put into our job, it would really turn out to be a loss. If I had engaged myself in something else ... But my mind will not run on these lines: I always like to think at the end of the day that I have done something without thought of profit, and only then do I feel able to go to sleep.'

Margayya felt it was time for him to interrupt this peroration. 'The same with me. I like to go a step further. Not only lack of profit: I like to feel that I have done something with a little sacrifice for another person's sake. It is not often one gets a chance to do such a thing, but when one does, one is able to sleep with the utmost peace that night.'

With their mouths stuffed with sweets and other edibles they spoke for about ten minutes more on sacrifices and the good life. When they came to the coffee there was a lull and Margayya said casually, 'Here is the proposal about *Domestic Harmony*. I don't like you to bear the burden any more since you say that you have had a loss. Why don't you let me take it over completely?'

'Why? How can that be? There is our partnership deed ... My lawyer ...'

'Oh, let your lawyer alone. We don't need lawyers. Why do you bring in a lawyer when we are discussing something as friends? Is this all the regard you have for our friendship? I am very much hurt, Lal. I wish you had not mentioned a lawyer.' He sat looking very sad and broken-hearted at this turn of events.

Lal remained quiet for a few moments. He took a cup of tea and gulped it down. He said: 'Why should you feel so much upset at the thought of lawyers? They are not demons. Somehow I don't like to do anything without telling my lawyer about it.'

'As for me,' said Margayya, 'you need not imagine that I have no use for lawyers. I consult not one but two or three at a time in business matters. I never take a step unless I have had a long and complete consultation with my lawyer ... But now there is nothing to warrant the calling of a lawyer or the police,' he added laughing.

The other could not view the matter with the same ease and still looked very serious.

Margayya said: 'I am not calling you here to give you trouble, Lal. I am only informally trying to talk over a matter with you, that is all, but if you are going to be so suspicious I had better not speak of it. You see, I am not a person who cares much for advantages; what seems to me the most important thing in human life is good relationships among all human beings.'

This maudlin statement had the desired effect and Lal softened a little, and asked, 'What is it that you are trying to say?'

'Merely that you should let me buy up the partnership for *Domestic Harmony*.'

'It is impossible,' he cried. 'I can prove that I have observed all the clauses faithfully. How can we cancel it, mister? What is it that you are suggesting?'

'It is only a suggestion,' Margayya said. 'Just to save you the bother, that's all; there's nothing more in it, especially since I thought you could employ your time and energies more profitably – '

'Impossible!' Lal cried. 'I will not listen to it.'

'Oh,' Margayya said, and remained thoughtful. Then he added, 'Well then, I will make a sporting offer.' He tapped his chest dramatically, 'Just to prove that all is well here I make this sporting offer to you. Take it if you can. You will then know that I am not trying to gain a mean advantage over you.'

'What are you saying, mister?'

'It is this ... I will speak if you promise you will not call your lawyer or the police after me!'

'Oh, you are a very sensitive man,' Lal said. 'I meant no offence.'

'You might not, but it is very depressing ... You are a business man and I am a business man. Let us talk like two business men. Either we agree or we don't agree ... Either give the *Domestic Harmony* solely – '

'Impossible,' cried Lal once again. 'There is our partnership deed.'

'What is the deed worth? Tear it up, I say, and take over the book yourself. I do not want any interest in it. I am prepared to give it to you this very moment, although in a couple of months the marriage season will be on and the demand for the book will go up. I am prepared to surrender it. Are you prepared to accept it?'

'No,' said Lal promptly. 'I do not like to take advantage of anyone's generosity.'

It needed, however, two more days of such talk, rambling, challenging, and bordering on the philosophical, before they could evolve an equitable give-and-take scheme; a scheme which each secretly thought gave him a seventy-five per cent advantage. By it Margayya abandoned for ever his interest in *Domestic Harmony* for a lump sum payment, and he tore up his document dramatically and put it into the wastepaper basket under Lal's table, at which Lal seemed to be much moved. He extended his hand and said: 'Among business men once a friend always a friend. Our friendship must always grow. If you have any printing of forms or anything remember us; we are always at your service. This is your press.'

He saw Margayya off at the door and Margayya walked down the Market Road with a satisfactory cheque in his pocket.

# PART THREE

Margayya went straight to the Town Bank. He refused to transact his business at the counter; he had to do it sitting in a chair in the Manager's room. But he found someone talking to the Manager and he had to wait outside for a moment. It was a crowded hour. Margayya never liked to do his transactions through the counter window. He despised the clerks. It was a sign of prestige for a business man to get things done in a bank without standing at the little window. That was for the little fellows who had no current account but only a savings bank book. He had the greatest contempt for savings bank operations: putting in money as if into a child's money box and withdrawing no more than fifty rupees a week or some miserable amount, not through cheques but by writing on those pitiful withdrawal forms ... Having a current account seemed to him a stamp of superiority, and a man who had two accounts, account number one and account number two, was a person of eminence. He saw waiting at the counters petty merchants, office messengers, and a couple of students of the Albert College attempting to cash cheques from their parents.

Hearing their inquiries, Margayya felt: 'Why do their parents send these boys cheques which they won't know how to cash?' He thought: 'What do these people know of cheques? What do they know of money? They are ignorant folk who do not know the worth of money, and think that it is just something to pass into a shop. Fools!' He pitied them. He felt that he must do something to enlighten their minds. He would not be a banker to them, but a helper, a sort of money doctor who would help people to use their money properly with the respect due to it. He would educate society anew in all these matters. He hoped he would be able to draw away all these people into his own establishment when the time came. The reason why people came here was that they were attracted by the burnished counters, the heavy ledgers, the clerks sitting on high stools and so on, and, of course, the calling bells and pin-cushions. Once again show, mere show. Showiness was becoming the real curse of all business these days, he thought. It was not necessary to have anything more than a box for carrying on any business soundly; not necessary to have too many persons or tables or leather-bound ledgers; all that was required was just one head and a small notebook in which to note down figures if they became too complicated, and above all a scheme. He knew that he had a scheme somewhere at the back of his mind, a scheme which would place him among the elect in society, which would make people flock to him and look to him for guidance, advice and management. He could not yet say what the scheme would be, but he sensed its presence, being a financial mystic. Whatever it was, it was going to revolutionize his life and the life of his fellow men. He felt he ought to wait on that inspiration with reverence and watchfulness.

A peon came up to say, 'The Manager is free.'

'All right, I'll be coming,' said Margayya. He liked to give an impression that he was in no hurry to run into the Manager's room at his call. He looked through some papers in his pocket, folded and put them back, and sauntered into the Manager's room.

The Manager was a very curt, business-like gentleman who had recently been transferred to this branch. 'Sit down, please, what can I do for you?' he asked. He was a man soured by constant contact with people who came to ask for overdrafts or loans on insufficient security. The moment he heard a footstep approaching, he first prepared himself to repel any demand. So, according to his custom, he put himself behind a forbidding exterior for a moment, and assumed a monosyllabic attitude.

'I wish to open an account,' said Margayya. The Manager could not take it in easily at first. He still had his suspicions. This man might be anybody; might have come to open an account or to open the safe ... This hostility affected Margayya too. He said at once, 'You don't seem to want a new client ... If that is so ...' He pretended to rise.

'Sit down please,' said the other. 'We have instructions not to admit too many new accounts, but I should like to know – '

'You would like to know whether I am a bankrupt or what. All right, I am not anxious to have an account here. I want it here because it is quite near to my own business place.'

'Where is it?'

'You will know it presently.'

'Really? What business?'

Margayya would not answer this question. The more the other pressed for an answer, the more he resisted. 'Let me tell you this: it is a very specialized business: my clients are chiefly peasants from the villages. I have a great deal to do with their harvests and advances and so forth.' To further inquiries by the Manager Margayya refused to give an answer: 'I cannot give any details of my business at the moment to you or to anyone. No one will be able to get these things out of me. But let me tell you: I have come here only to deposit my money and use it, not to take money out of you ... I can quite see what is at the back of your mind. Now tell me whether you would care to have my account here or not ...' Now he was taking out his trump, namely, the cheque given to him by Lal. 'If you don't want me here, give me cash for it; but if you think I am good enough for you, start an account with this.'

'Have you an account anywhere else?'

'I don't answer that question,' said Margayya out of sheer financial pugnacity; he could have told him that he had quite a sizeable account in Commerce Bank in Race Course Road.

The Bank Manager felt that here was a man who knew his mind and felt a regard for him. 'Of course I will open your account here,' he said with sudden warmth. 'What does a bank exist for unless to serve its clients?'

'Quite right,' Margayya said. 'I quite appreciate,' he said patronizingly, 'your precaution as a banker. Only a business man can appreciate it in another business man.'

He had a feeling that he had after all found the right place for himself in life – the right destination, the right destination being 10 Market Road. It was a block of four shops, each about twelve feet square, with a narrow corridor running in front which was thrown in as a sort of grace to the tenants. The other three were taken by a tailor whose single machine went on rattling all day and night over the din of clients who came to demand their overdue clothes, and next to it was a board announcing itself as the Tourist Bureau, having a number of small chairs and a few benches, and a fourth shop was a doctor's, who claimed to have practised under a great seer in the Himalayas and to be able to cure any disease with rare herbs. Margayya was pleased with this spot. It was a combination which seemed to him ideal. On the very first day he came there he felt that these were just the men with whom he could live: 'They are not people who are likely to interfere with my work. Moreover, it is likely that people who come to the tailor or the doctor or the tourist bureau are just the people who have some surplus cash and who are likely to be interested in my business too.'

It was Dr Pal who put him into this setting. Dr Pal sought him out one day at his house just as he was bullying his son over his lessons. He walked in saying, 'I didn't know your house exactly, but just took a chance and came over. I was just sauntering down the road wondering whom to ask when I heard your voice.'

Margayya had a slate in his hand and there was a frown on his face and tears in his son's eyes. He got over his confusion and affected a smile: 'Oh, Doctor, Doctor, what have you been doing with yourself?'

The doctor looked at Balu and said, 'You have evidently been trying to teach this young man. Don't you know that for parents to teach their off-spring is prohibited in all civilized countries?' He then said to the boy, as if taking charge of him immediately, 'Now run off, little man.' He turned ceremoniously to Margayya and added, 'Of course with your permission.' Balu did not wait for any further concession; he swept aside his books and ran out of sight as if a bear were behind him.

Margayya's mind had still not come to rest. He kept looking after his son and mumbled, 'You have no idea how indifferent and dull present-day boys are.'

'Oh, no, don't tell me that ... Remember correctly: do you think you gave an easy time to your father or the teachers? Just think over it honestly.'

305

It was not a line which Margayya was prepared to pursue. He brushed aside the topic, remembering suddenly that he had not been sufficiently hospitable. He burst into sudden activity, and began to fuss elaborately over his visitor. He jumped to his feet, clutched the other's hand, and said, 'Oh, oh, Doctor, what a pleasure to meet you after all these years! Where have you been all the time? What have you been doing with yourself? What is the meaning of cutting off old friends as you did?' He unrolled a new mat, and apologized, 'You know I have no sofa or chair to offer – '

'Well, I didn't come to be put on to a sofa.'

'That is right. I don't like furniture, the type of furniture which does not suit us; we are made to sit erect with our feet dangling – '

'I wonder,' said Dr Pal, 'if the prevalence of nervous disorders in the present day might be due to the furniture which has become popular. In ancient days our ancestors squatted on the floor, stretched themselves as much as they liked and lived to be wise old men.'

Margayya could not understand whether the man was joking with him or was in earnest. He called his wife and said, 'Get two cups of coffee ready immediately. My old friend has come.' While waiting for coffee he said, 'Now tell me what you have been doing with yourself, Doctor. Where have you been hiding all these days?'

The doctor said, 'I had gone for a little training in Tourism.'

Margayya was bewildered. This man was specializing in obscure and rare activities. 'What is Tourism?' he asked.

'It is a branch of social activity,' the doctor said. 'The basic idea is that all people on earth should be familiar with all parts of the earth.'

'Is it possible?'

'It is not, and that is why there must be a specialist in Tourism in every town and city.'

'What is Tourism?' Margayya asked innocently once again.

The doctor viewed him with pity and said, 'I will explain to you all about it by and by one day when we meet in my office ... Now tell me about yourself.'

'No, you tell me about yourself first,' Margayya said, with a vague desire to avoid the theme of himself for the moment. There was at the back of his mind a faint fear lest the doctor should ask him to render the accounts of *Domestic Harmony*. He wondered if the man had hunted him down for this and he wished to be on his guard. He had hardly made up his mind as to what he should say if he broached the subject, when, as if reading his thoughts, Pal said, 'I came here some time ago, but didn't like to meet you lest you should think I had come after my book.'

Margayya sniggered and said somewhat pointlessly, 'Oh, isn't it quite a long time since we met?'

'Yes, ages since. I have been away for a long time. You know I am no longer on that paper. I gave it up. It did not seem to me serious enough work. I always feel that we must do something that contributes to the sum and substance of human experience. Otherwise all our jobs seem to be just futile.'

'I also am about to start a new business.'

'Yes, I heard about it from the town bank manager,' said Pal.

The man seemed to know everything that was going on everywhere, thought Margayya with a certain amount of admiration. Margayya's wife brought two tumblers of coffee to the door of the kitchen and made some noise with the vessels in order to attract Margayya's attention. Margayya said from where he sat, 'You can come in, it is my friend Dr Pal. I have spoken to you about him.'

She was at once seized with fear whether the man was there in order to discuss another book on the same lines as the previous one. She withdrew a little, and Margayya went over and took the coffee from her hands and carried it to the front room.

The conversation languished while Dr Pal was relishing the coffee, and then he said, 'I heard from the bank manager that you are starting a new business. I just came to tell you that if you want a nice place on Market Road, there is one vacant in our block. There is some demand for it.'

They went to 10 Market Road. Margayya liked the building when he saw it. A man who made a lot of money selling blankets had bought up the vacant site next to the Municipal Dispensary and built these rooms. At the moment, the house was of one storey. Eventually he proposed to add a first floor and a second floor. The man himself had his own shop in one of the back lanes of the Market, a very small shop stacked with rough blankets. He was a strong dark man with a circular sandal paste mark on his forehead. He sat there all day chasing the flies. 'Flies come here, God knows why,' Margayya reflected when he went to meet him with Dr Pal. They had to stand outside the shop and talk to him as he peeped out of his blanket stacks. At the sight of Pal the other man brought his palms together and saluted. He had evidently great reverence for learned people.

'How are you, sir?' Dr Pal inquired genially. 'This is one of my greatest friends,' he told Margayya in an aside, and added, 'You cannot imagine how much he has helped me in my most difficult times.'

'Tut, tut,' said the other from the depth of his woollen stacks. 'This is not the place for you to start all that ... Don't. Now who is this person you have brought with you?'

'He is a friend of mine who wants to be your tenant. He is opening his business in a couple of days. Am I right?' he asked, turning to Margayya. With a sheet of paper Margayya fanned off the flies that were alighting on his nose. The man in the shop announced apologetically, 'Oh, too many flies here – '

'What have flies to do here?' Margayya asked, unable to restrain his question any more.

The other replied, 'They have nothing to interest them here, but behind this shop there is a jaggery godown. There is a gap in the roof through which flies pass up and down. It is a great nuisance, and I have written to the municipality to get the jaggery shop moved somewhere else ... but you know what our municipalities are!'

'He is himself a municipal councillor for this ward,' Dr Pal added, 'and yet he finds so much difficulty in getting anything done. He had such trouble to get that vacant plot for himself – '

'I applied for it like any other citizen. Being a municipal councillor doesn't mean that I should forgo the ordinary rights and privileges of a citizen.'

The conversation went on with the sun beating down on their heads, and a feeling of still greater warmth was given by the sight of the heavy dark blankets all round. Margayya felt somewhat irritated that he was being made to stand in the sun all the time. He suddenly told himself, 'I am a business man with all my time fully booked, why should I stand here in the sun and listen to this fellow's irrelevancies?' He told his friend somewhat sharply, 'Shall we get on with the business?'

Dr Pal looked at him surprised for a moment and asked the blanket merchant, 'Will you give the vacant shop to this gentleman?'

'Of course!' the other said. 'If you want it ... Give it to him if you choose.' Dr Pal turned to Margayya and said, 'Take it.' Margayya was unused to such brisk and straightforward transactions. He had always a notion that to get anything done one had to go in a round-about manner and arrive at the point without the knowledge of the other party. Margayya rose to the occasion and asked, 'What is the rent?'

'Seventy-five rupees,' said the other briefly.

'Seventy-five! Rather high isn't it?' Margayya asked, hoping against hope there would be a reduction from this stern and business-like man.

'Yes, if it were any other place ... but here the spot has market value. You can take it if you like. But if you are looking for a cheaper place – ' said the blanket man.

'I shouldn't be here,' said Margayya finishing his sentence for him. 'I am taking it definitely from tomorrow.' It pleased him very much to be able to speak up confidently in this manner. If it had been those horrible past days, he would have collapsed at the knees on hearing the amount of the rent.

Dr Pal said to the blanket-seller: 'This man is one of my oldest friends. I like him very much, you know.'

'Yes, I know, I know,' said the other. 'I could guess so, otherwise you would not have brought him here. Here is the key.' He held out a brass key for Dr Pal to take.

He asked Margayya, 'What may be your line of business?'

'Well ... sort of banking,' Margayya said without conviction, fearing at the word bank these people would at once visualize shining counters and all the gaudy ornamentation.

'It'd be more simple to call it moneylending,' said the other from within the blankets.

'It is not merely lending,' Margayya essayed to explain. 'It is not so cheap as that; I also try to help people about money whenever they are in difficulties.' Margayya started on his oration. 'Money is ...' He paused and turning to Dr Pal, asked, 'You have not told me your friend's name.' It was more to put the other in his place.

'Oh, we call him Guru Raj,' Dr Pal said.

Margayya began his sentence again. 'Guru Raj, money is the greatest factor in life and the most ill-used. People don't know how to tend it, how to manure it, how to water it, how to make it grow, and when to pluck its flowers and when to pluck its fruits. What most people now do is to try and eat the plant itself – '

The other roared with laughter. 'I say, you seem to be a very great thinker. How well you speak, how well you have understood all these matters! You are indeed a rare man. Where have you been carrying on your business all these days?'

'Mine is the sort of business that searches me out. I didn't have to move out of my house at all. But you see, it gives me no rest with so many people always coming in – '

'You must never allow your business transactions to invade your home, that will simply shatter the home-life,' said Guru Raj.

'I have a son studying in high school,' said Margayya. He liked the feel of the word. Studying in High School. He felt very proud of Balu for the moment, but at the same time he felt a tinge of pity at heart. He had been too severe with him during the day.

'Oh, if children are studying it will simply ruin their time to have visitors at all hours,' the other said.

After more such polite and agreeable talk, he said, 'All right, sir, I wish you all success. May God help you. You may please to go now. I cannot offer you a seat in this wretched shop. It is my fate to sit here amidst the flies, and why should I bother you with them too? And it is not proper to make you stand ... I will come and listen to your talk in your own shop, some day.'

It was midday and all the stalls in the market were dull and drowsy. Fruit-sellers were dozing before their heaps. Some loafers were desultorily hanging about. Stray calves were standing idly near a shop in which green plantain leaves were for sale. A seller of betel leaves held out a bundle saying, 'Finest betel leaves, sir, flavoured with camphor – ' applying the usual epithets that betel-sellers employ for recommending their wares. Pal took some, haggled for a moment, and paid the price. He stuffed the bundle of betel leaves into his pocket. He stopped for a minute at the next stall to buy a yard of strung jasmine. 'Excuse me,' he said. 'These are necessary to keep the peace at home, necessary adjuncts for domestic harmony, you know.'

'Oh!' Margayya exclaimed, and decided to ignore any special significance he might have put into the words *Domestic Harmony*.

'You are no longer alone?' Margayya asked.

'No.'

'Are you married?'

'No.'

'Are you going to be married?'

'Not yet.'

Margayya was mystified. 'Where is your house? Are you still in that garden?'

'No, no. I had to leave it long ago. Someone bought it, and has been farming on a large scale there. He cleared the place of all the weeds and undergrowth, which included me. But he appeared to be a nice man. I have been so far away and so busy. I have a house, I live in an outhouse in Lawley Extension ... Someone else is in the main building. You must come to my house some day.'

They reached 10 Market Road, and at once Margayya was enchanted. He had always visualized that he would get some such place. The Malgudi gutter ran below his shop with a mild rumble, and not so mild smell. But Margayya either did not notice or did not mind it, being used to it in his own home. Margayya's blood was completely the city man's and revelled in crowds, noise and bustle; the moment he looked out and saw the stream of people and traffic flowing up and down the road, he felt that he was in the right place. A poet would perhaps have felt exasperated by the continuous din, but to Margayya it was like a background music to his own thoughts. There was a row of offices and shops opposite, insurance agencies, local representatives of newspapers, hair-cutting saloons, some film distributors, a lawyer's chamber, and a hardware shop, into which hundreds of people were going every day. Margayya calculated that if he could at least filter twenty out of that number for his own purposes, he would be more than well off. In about a year he could pass on to the grade of people who were wealthy and not merely rich. He drew a lot of distinction between the two. A rich man, according to his view, was just one caste below the man of wealth. Riches any hard-working fool could attain by some watchfulness, while acquiring wealth was an extraordinary specialized job. It came to persons who had on them the grace of the Goddess fully and who could use their wits. He was a specialist in money and his mind always ran on lines of scientific inquiry whenever money came in question. He differentiated with great subtlety between money, riches, wealth, and fortune. It was most important people should not mistake one for the other.

Next to the subject of money, the greatest burden on his mind was his son. As he sat in his shop and spoke to his clients, he forgot for the time being the rest of the world, but the moment he was left alone he started thinking of his son: the boy had failed in his matriculation exam, and that embittered him very much. He wondered what he should do with him now. Whenever he thought of it, his heart sank within him. 'God has blessed me with everything under the sun; I need not bother about anything else in life, but ... but ...' He could not tell people, 'My son is only fifteen and he has already passed into college.' The son had passed that stage two years ago. Two attempts and yet no good. Margayya had engaged three home tutors, one for every two subjects, and it cost him quite a lot in salaries. He arranged to have him fed specially with nutritive food during his examination periods. He bought a lot of fruits, and compelled his wife to prepare special food, always saying, 'The poor boy is preparing for his examination. He must have enough stamina to stand the strain.' He forbade his wife to speak loudly at home. 'Have you no consideration for the young man who is studying?'

He was in agonies on examination days. He escorted him up to the examination hall in Albert College. Before parting from him at the sounding of the bell he always gave him advice: 'Don't get frightened; write calmly and fearlessly ... and don't come away before it is time,' but all this was worth nothing because the boy had nothing to write after the first half-hour, which he spent in scrawling fantastic designs on his answer book. He hated the excitement of an examination and was sullenly resentful of the fact that he was being put through a most unnecessary torment. He abruptly rose from his seat and went over to a restaurant near by. His father had left with him a lot of cash in view of the trying times he was going through. He ate all the available things in the restaurant, bought a packet of cigarettes, sought a secluded corner away from the prying eyes of his elders on the bank of the river behind the college, sat down and smoked the entire packet, dozed for a while, and returned home at five in the evening. The moment he was sighted his mother asked, 'Have you written your examination well?'

He made a wry face and said, 'Leave me alone.' He hated to be reminded of the examination. But they would not let him alone. His mother put before him milk, and fruits, and the special edibles she had made to sustain him in his ordeal. He made a wry face and said, 'Take it away, I cannot eat anything.' At this she made many sounds of sympathy and said that he must get over the strain by feeding himself properly.

It was at this moment that his father returned home, after closing his office early, and hastening away in a *jutka*. All day as he counted money, his and other people's, a corner of his mind was busy with the examination. 'Oh, God, please enlighten my son's mind so that he may answer and get good marks,' he secretly prayed. The moment he saw his son he said, 'I am sure you have done very well my boy. How have you done?' The boy sat in a corner of the house with a cheerless look on his face. Margayya put it down to extreme strain, and said soothingly, 'You stayed in the hall throughout?' That was for him an indication of his son's performance.

Whatever was the son's reply, he got the correct answer very soon, in less than eight weeks, when the results came out. At first Margayya raved, 'Balu has done very well, I know. Someone has been working off a grudge.' Then he felt like striking his son, but restrained himself for the son was four inches taller as he stood hanging his head with his back to the wall, and Margayya feared that he might retaliate. So he checked himself; and from a corner the mother watched, silently with resignation and fear, the crisis developing between father and son. She had understood long before that the boy was not interested in his studies and that he attached no value to them, but it was no use telling that to her husband. She pursued what seemed to her the best policy and allowed events to shape themselves. She knew that matters were coming to a conclusion now and she was a helpless witness to a terrific struggle between two positive-minded men, for she no longer had any doubt that the son was a grown-up man. She covered her mouth with her fingers, and with her chin on her palms stood there silently watching.

Margayya said, 'Every little idiot has passed his S.S.L.C. exam. Are you such a complete fool?'

'Don't abuse me, father,' said the boy, whose voice had recently become gruff. It had lost, as his mother noticed, much of the original softness. The more she saw him, the more she was reminded of her own father in his younger days; exactly the same features, the same gruffness, and the same severity. People had been afraid to speak to her father even when he was in the sweetest temper, for his face had a severity without any relation to his mood. She saw the same expression on the boy's face now. The boy's look was set and grim. His lips were black with cigarettes which she knew he smoked: he often smelt of them when he came home ... But she kept this secret knowledge to herself since she didn't like to set up her husband against him. She understood that the best way to attain some peace of mind in life was to maintain silence; ultimately, she found that things resolved themselves in the best manner possible or fizzled out. She found that it was only speech which made existence worse every time. Lately, after he had become affluent, she found that her husband showed excessive emphasis, rightly or wrongly, in all matters; she realized that he had come to believe that whatever he did was always right. She did her best not to contradict him: she felt that he strained himself too much in his profession, and that she ought not to add to his burden. So if he sometimes raved over the mismanagement of the household, she just did not try to tell him that it was otherwise. She served him his food silently, and he himself discovered later what was right and what was wrong and confessed it to her. Now more than in any other matter she practised this principle where their son was concerned. She knew it would be no use telling her husband not to bother the son over his studies, that it would be no use asking him to return home at seven-thirty each day to sit down to his books with his home teachers ... he simply would not return home before nine. It was no use shouting at him for it. It only made one's throat smart and provided a scene for the people next door to witness. She left it all to resolve itself. Once or twice she attempted to tell the son to be more mindful of his father's wishes and orders, but he told her to shut up. She left him alone. And she left her husband alone. She attained thereby great tranquillity in practical everyday life.

Now she watched the trouble brewing between the two as if it all happened behind a glass screen. The father asked in a tone full of wrath: 'How am I to hold up my head in public?' The boy looked up detached, as if it were a problem to be personally solved by the father, in which he was not involved. Margayya shouted again: 'How am I to hold up my head in public? What will they think of me? What will they say of my son?'

The boy spoke with a quiet firmness, as if expressing what immediately occurred to the mother herself. She felt at once a great admiration for him. He said in a gruff tone: 'How is it their concern?'

Margayya wrung his hands in despair and clenched his teeth. What the boy said seemed to be absolutely correct. 'You are no son of mine. I cannot tolerate a son who brings such disgrace on the family.'

The boy was pained beyond words. 'Don't talk nonsense, father,' he said.

Margayya was stupefied. He had no idea that the boy could speak so much. Talking till now was only a one-way business, and he had taken it for granted that the boy could say nothing for himself. He raved: 'You are talking back to me, are you mad?'

The boy burst into tears and wailed: 'If you don't like me send me out of the house.'

Margayya studied him with surprise. He had always thought of Balu as someone who was spoken to and never one who could speak with the same emphasis as himself. He was offended by the boy's aggressive manner. He was moved by the sight of the tears on his face. He was seized with a confusion of feelings. He found his eyes smarting with tears and felt ashamed of it before his son and before that stony-faced woman who stood at the doorway of the kitchen and relentlessly watched. Her eyes seemed to watch unwaveringly, with a fixed stare. So still was she that Margayya feared lest she should be in a cataleptic state. He now turned his wrath on her. 'It's all your doing. You have been too lenient. You have spoilt him beyond redemption. You with your – '

The boy checked his tears and interrupted him. 'Mother has not spoilt me, nor anyone else. Why should anyone spoil me?'

'There is too much talk in this house. That's what's wrong here,' Margayya declared, and closed the incident by going in to change and attend to his other activities. The boy slunk away, out of sight. In that small house it was impossible to escape from one another, and the boy slipped out of the front door. The mother knew he would return, after his father had slept, bringing into the home the smell of cigarette smoke.

Margayya stayed awake almost all night. When the boy sneaked back after his rounds and pushed the door open, it creaked slightly on its hinges and he at once demanded: 'Who is there? Who is there?'

Balu answered mildly: 'It's myself, father.'

Margayya was pleased with the softening that now seemed to be evident in his tone, but he wished at the same time that the boy had not disgraced him by failing. He said: 'You have been out so long?'

'Yes,' came the reply.

'Where?' he asked.

There was no further reply. Margayya felt that failing the Matric seemed to have conferred a new status on his son, and unloosened his tongue. He felt in all this medley a little pride at the fact that his son had acquired so much independence of thought and assertiveness. He somehow felt like keeping him in conversation and asked, with a slight trace of cajolery in his voice: 'Was the door left open without the bolt being drawn?'

'Yes,' replied the boy from somewhere in the darkness.

'That's very careless of your mother. Does she do it every day?'

There was once again a pause and silence. His wife seemed to have fallen asleep too, for there was no response from her. He somehow did not wish the conversation to lapse. He said as a stop-gap: 'What'll happen if a thief gets in?' There was no response from the son. After blinking in the dark for a few minutes, Margayya asked: 'Boy, are you asleep?' And the boy answered: 'Yes, I am.' And Margayya, feeling much more at peace with himself at heart for having spoken to him, fell asleep at once, forgetting for a few hours the Matriculation examination and his other worries.

They got into a sort of live and let live philosophy. He hoped that when the schools reopened he could put the boy back at school, prepare him intensively for his examination, and if necessary see some of the examiners and so on. Margayya had a feeling that he had of late neglected his duties in this direction. He had unqualified faith in contacting people and getting things done that way. He could get at anybody through Dr Pal. That man had brought into his business a lot of people known to him. Margayya's contacts were now improving socially. People were indebted to him nowadays, and would do anything to retain his favour. Margayya hoped that if he exerted himself even slightly in the coming year he would see his son pull through Matriculation without much difficulty. Of course the boy would have to keep up a show of at least studying the books and would have to write down his number correctly in the answer book and not merely scribble and look out of the door. It was extremely necessary that he should at least write one page of his answer and know what were the subjects he ought to study.

Margayya felt that if he could persuade Balu to make at least a minimum of effort for his own sake, his mind would be easier. He proposed it very gently to him about a fortnight later as they sat down to their dinner together. Margayya showed him extreme consideration nowadays; it was born out of fear and some amount of respect. The boy was always taciturn and grim. He recollected that it seemed ages since he had seen any relaxation in his face. He had a gravity beyond his years. That frightened Margayya. Except the one instance when he saw tears in his eyes on the day of the results, he had always found him sullen. He hoped to soften him by kindness, or, at least, outward kindness, for he still smarted inside at the results of the examination. He looked for a moment at the face of his son and said: 'Balu, you must make another attempt. I'll see that you get through the examination without the least difficulty.'

Balu stopped eating and asked: 'What do you mean, father?'

Margayya sensed danger, but he had started the subject. He could not stop it now under any circumstances. So he said: 'I mean about the Matriculation examination.'

'I will not read again,' said the boy definitely, defiantly. 'I have already spoken to mother about it.'

'H'm.' Margayya turned to his wife who was serving him and said: 'He has spoken to you, has he? What has he said?'

'Just what he has told you,' she answered promptly, and went back to the fireplace to fetch something.

'Why didn't you tell me about it?' Margayya asked, eagerly looking for some lapse on her part to justify him in letting off steam.

She merely replied: 'Because I knew he was going to tell you about it himself.'

Margayya burst out at her. 'What do you mean by discussing all sorts of things with the boy and not telling me anything? These are matters – '

His son interrupted him: 'Father, if you hate me and want to make me miserable, you will bother me with examinations and studies. I hate them.'

Margayya went on arguing with him all through the meal till the boy threatened to abandon his dinner and walk out of the dining-room. Margayya assumed a sullen silence, but the atmosphere ached with tension. Everyone was aware that the silence was going to be broken in a violent manner next moment, as soon as dinner was over. Father and son seemed to be in a race to finish eating first. Balu gobbled up his food and dashed to the backyard. He poured a little water on his hand, wiped it on a towel near by and moved towards the street door. Margayya jumped up from his seat, with his hand unwashed, dashed to the street door and shut and bolted it. Frustrated, the boy stood still. Margayya asked: 'Where are you going? I have still much to tell you. I have not finished speaking yet.' The boy withdrew a few steps in response.

Meanwhile his mother had brought in a vessel of water; Margayya snatched a moment to wash his hand at the little open yard. He said, 'Wait' to his son. He opened his office box and brought from it the boy's S.S.L.C. Register. He had secured it on the previous day from the headmaster of the school. The S.S.L.C. Register is a small calico-bound notebook with columns marked in it, containing a record of a high-school boy's marks, conduct, handwriting and physical fitness. Margayya had got the register from the headmaster and studied its pages keenly the whole of the previous day. Matters did not now appear to him so hopeless. The headmaster had marked 'Fair' both for his handwriting and drill attendance. Margayya had no idea that his son could shine in anything. So this was an entirely happy surprise ... His marks in almost all subjects were in single digits. The highest mark he had obtained was twelve out of a hundred in hygiene, and he had maintained his place as the last in the class without a variation.

One would have expected Margayya to be shocked by this, but the effect was unexpected. He was a fond and optimistic father, and he fastened on the twelve marks for hygiene. It seemed so high after all the diminutive marks the boy had obtained in other subjects. Margayya hoped that perhaps he was destined to be a doctor, and that was why his inclination was so marked for hygiene. What a wonderful opening seemed to be before him as a doctor! Doctor Balu – it would be very nice indeed. If only he could get through the wretched S.S.L.C. barrier, he'd achieve great things in life. Margayya would see to it that he did so; Margayya's money and contacts would be worth nothing if he could not see his son through ...

He had prepared himself to speak to Balu about all this gently and persuasively. He hoped to lead up to the subject with encouraging talk, starting with hygiene, and then to ask him if he wished to be a doctor. What a glorious life opened before a doctor! He would send him to England to study surgery. He could tell him all that and encourage him. Margayya had great faith in his own persuasiveness. He sometimes had before him a tough customer who insisted upon withdrawing all his deposits and winding up the account: a most truculent client. But Margayya remembered that if he had about an hour with him, he could always talk him out of it. The deposit would remain with him, plus any other money that the man possessed ... Now Margayya wanted to employ his capacity for a similar purpose with his son. That's why he had come armed with the S.S.L.C. Register. He could read out to him the headmaster's remarks 'Fair', etc., and prove to him how hopeful everything was if only he would agree to lend his name and spare time to go through the formality of an examination in the coming year.

At the sight of the notebook the boy asked: 'What is this? Why have you brought it from school?' as if it were the most repulsive article he had seen in the whole of his life. His face went a shade darker. It symbolized for him all the wrongs that he had suffered in his life: it was a chronicle of all the insults that had been heaped upon him by an ungracious world – a world of schools, studies and examinations. What did they mean by all this terrible torment invented for young men? It had been an agony for him every time the headmaster called him up and made him go through the entries and sign below. Such moments came near his conception of hell. Hell, in his view, was a place where a torturing God sat up with your scholastic record in his hand and lectured you on how to make good and told you what a disgrace you were to society. His bitterness overwhelmed him suddenly, as his father opened a page and started: 'Here is your hygiene – '

The boy made a dash for the book, snatched it from his father's hand before he knew what was happening, tore its entire bulk into four pieces (it had been made of thick ledger paper and only his fury gave him the necessary strength to tear it up at one effort), and ran out into the street and threw the pieces into the gutter. And Vinayak Mudali Street gutter closed on it and carried the bits out of sight. Margayya ran up and stood on the edge of the gutter woefully looking into its dark depth. His wife was behind him. He was too stunned to say anything. When he saw the last shred of it gone, he turned to his wife and said: 'They will not admit him in any school again, the last chance gone.' And then he turned to tackle his son – but the boy had gone.

* * *

The only sign of prosperity about him now was the bright handle of the umbrella which was hooked to his right forearm whenever he went out. He was a lover of umbrellas, and the moment he could buy anything that caught his fancy, he spent eight rupees and purchased this bright-handled umbrella with 'German ribs', in the parlance of the umbrella dealers. Hitherto he had carried for years an old bamboo one, a podgy thing with discoloured cloth which had been patched up over and over again. He protected it like his life for several years. He had his own technique of holding an umbrella which assured it a long lease of life and kept it free from fractures. He never twisted the handle when he held an umbrella over his head. He never lent it to anyone. Margayya, if he saw anyone going out in the rain in imminent danger of catching and perishing of pneumonia, would let him face his fate rather than offer him the protection of his umbrella. He felt furious when people thought that they could ask for an umbrella. 'They will be asking for my skin next,' he often commented when his wife found fault with him for his attitude. Another argument he advanced was, 'Do people ask for each other's wives? Don't they manage to have one for them-selves? Why shouldn't each person in the country buy his own umbrella?' 'An umbrella does not like to be handled by more than one person in its lifetime,' he often declared, and stuck to it. He had to put away his old umbrella in the loft, carefully rolled up, because its ribs had become too rickety and it could not maintain its shape any longer. It began to look like a shot-down crow with broken wings. Though for years he had not noticed it, suddenly one day when he was working under the tree in the Co-operative Bank compound, someone remarked that he was looking like a wayside umbrella repairer and that he had better throw it away; he felt piqued and threw it in the loft, but he could never bring himself to the point of buying a new one and had more or less resigned himself to basking in the sun until the time came when he could spend eight rupees without calculating whether he was a loser or a gainer in the bargain. That time had come, now that thousands of rupees were passing through his hands – thousands which belonged to others as well as to him.

Except for this umbrella, he gave no outward sign of his affluence. He hated any perceptible signs of improvement. He walked to his office every day. His coat was of spun silk, but he chose a shade that approximated to the one he had worn for years so that no one might notice the difference. He whitewashed the walls of his house inside only, and built a small room upstairs. He bought no furniture except a canvas deckchair at a second-hand shop. On this he lounged and looked at the sky from his courtyard. He told his wife to buy any clothes she liked, but she was more or less in mourning and made no use of the offer. She merely said, 'Tell me about Balu. That is what I need, not clothes.'

Margayya replied: 'Well, I can only offer you what is available. If you are crying for the moon, I can't help you much there.'

'I am asking for my son, not crying for the moon,' she said.

She was always on the verge of hysteria nowadays. She spoke very little and ate very little; and Margayya felt that at a time when he had a right to have a happy and bright home, he was being denied the privilege unnecessarily. He felt angry with his wife. He felt that it was her sulking which ruined the atmosphere of the home. They had so much accustomed themselves to the disappearance of their son that he ceased to think of it as a primary cause: the more immediate reasons became perceptible. He tried in his own clumsy manner to make her happy. He told her, 'Ask for any money you want.'

'What shall I do with money?' she said. 'I have no use for it.'

He disliked her for making such a statement. It was in the nature of a seditious speech. He merely frowned at her and went on with his business. What was that business? When at home he carried about him the day's financial position finely distilled into a statement, and was absorbed in studying the figures. When he wanted relaxation he bought a paper and went through its pages. Nowadays he did not borrow the paper from the newspaper dealer but subscribed for a copy himself. He read with avidity what was happening in the world: the speeches of statesmen, the ravings of radicals, the programme for this and that, war news, and above all the stocks and shares market. He glanced through all this because a certain amount of world information seemed to be an essential part of his equipment when he sat in his office. All kinds of people came in and it was necessary that he should be able to take part in their conversation. To impress his clients, he had to appear as a man of all-round wisdom.

He walked to his work every day soon after his morning meal. The house was in suspense till he was seen safely off. He did not believe in employing servants at home and so his wife had to do all the work. He often said, 'Why should we burden ourselves with servants when we are like a couple of newly-weds? Ours is not a very big family.' The lady accepted it meekly because she knew it would not be much use arguing it out with Margayya. She knew, as he himself did, that he did not employ a cook because he did not like to spend money on one. But he was sure to give some other reason if he was asked. He would in all probability say, 'Where is the need to show off?' She knew that he viewed money as something to accumulate and not to be spent on increasing one's luxuries in life. She knew all his idioms even before he uttered them. Sometimes when he saw her sitting at the fireplace, her eyes shrunken and swollen with the kitchen smoke, he felt uneasy and tried to help her with the kitchen work, keeping up the pretence of being newly-weds. He picked up a knife here and a green vegetable there, cut it up in a desultory manner, and vaguely asked, 'Is there anything I can do?' She hardly ever answered such a question. She merely said, 'Please come in half an hour, and I will serve your meal.' She had become very sullen and reserved nowadays.

She brooded over her son Balu night and day. She lost the taste for food. Margayya behaved wildly whenever he was reminded of their son. 'He is not my son,' he declared dramatically. 'A boy who has an utter disregard for his father's feelings is no son. He is a curse that the Gods have sent down for us. He is not my son.' It all sounded very theatrical, but the feeling was also very real. When he remembered the floating bits of calico in the street gutter, he felt sorry that his son was no longer there to be slapped. His fingers itched to strike him. He reflected: 'If he had at least disappeared after receiving the slap I aimed, I would not have minded much.' He discouraged his wife from mentioning their son again and had grandly ordered that the household must run on as if he had not been born. When he spoke in that tone his wife fully understood that he meant it. His affluence, his bank balance, buoyed him up and made him bear the loss of their son. He lived in a sort of radiance which made it possible for him to put up with anything. When he sat at his desk from early in the day till sunset, he had to talk, counsel, wheedle out, and collect money; in fact go through all the adventures of money-making. At the end of the day as he walked back home his mind was full of the final results, and so there was practically no time for him to brood over Balu.

Late at night when the voices of the city had died down and when the expected sleep came a little late, he speculated on Balu. Perhaps he had drowned himself. There was no news of him, although several days and weeks had passed. His wife accused him at first of being very callous and not doing anything about it. He did not know what was expected of him. He could not go and tell the police. He could not announce a reward for anyone who traced him. He could not ... He hated to make a scene about it, and solved the whole thing by confiding in Dr Pal. Dr Pal had promised to keep an eye on the matter and tell him if anything turned up. No one could do more than that. Margayya had generally given out that his son had gone on a holiday to Bombay or Madras, and lightly added: 'Young boys of his age must certainly go out by themselves and see a bit of the world: I think that's the best education.'

'But boys must have a minimum of S.S.L.C.,' someone remarked.

Margayya dismissed it as a foolish notion. 'What is there in Matriculation? People can learn nothing in schools. I have no faith in our education. Who wants all this nonsense about A squared plus B squared? If a boy does not learn these, so much the better. To be frank, I have got on without learning the A squared and B squared business, and what is wrong with me? Boys must learn things in the rough school of life.' Whatever he said sounded authoritative and mature nowadays, and people listened to him with respectful attention. These perorations he delivered as he sat in his office.

His office consisted of a medium-sized room with four mattresses spread out on the floor. At the other end of it there was a sloping desk where an accountant sat. He was a lean old man, with a fifteen-day-old silver beard encircling his face at any given time. He was a pensioner, a retired revenue clerk, who wore a close coat and a turban when he came to the office. He was expected to arrive before Margayya. It pleased Margayya very much to see him at his seat, bent over his ledgers. He was instructed not to look up and salute when Margayya came in since it was likely to disturb his calculations and waste his time. Margayya said: 'I do not want all this formality of a greeting. I see you every day. If you want to please me, do your work, and get on with it without wasting your time.' But when he felt he needed an audience for his perorations he addressed him, and any other clerks who might be there.

Margayya sat in one corner of the hall. He had a desk before him made of smooth polished wood which he had bought from the blanket merchant at a second-hand price. Margayya loved to gaze on its smooth, rippled grains – remnants of gorgeous designs that it had acquired as a tree-trunk – hieroglyphics containing the history of the tree. Whenever he gazed on it, he felt as if he were looking at a sea and a sky in some dream world. 'But what is the use of gazing on these and day-dreaming?' he told himself, sharply pulling his mind back. He lifted the lid and gazed inside, and there was the reality which he could touch and calculate and increase: a well-bound half-leather ledger, a bottle of red ink, a bottle of black ink, an oblong piece of blotting-paper, and a pen – the red holder of which his fingers had gripped for years now. And beside it was a small bag made of thick drill, into which went all the cash he collected. His clerk did not know what he collected each day. He did not look into the account-book which Margayya kept, nor did he count the cash. It was all done by Margayya himself. He did not believe that it was necessary for anyone to share his knowledge of his finances; it was nobody's business but his own. The work that he gave the accountant was copying down the mortgages that were left with him by the villagers who came round for financial assistance. He not only kept the deeds, but put the old man to the task of copying them down entirely in a big ledger. He alone could say why he wanted this done, but he would not open his mouth about it to anyone. The old man was being paid fifty rupees a month, and he was afraid of being thrown out if he questioned too much. He just did his duty. At about two o'clock Margayya locked his safe box and got up saying, 'I'm going out for tiffin – will be back in a minute. Look after the office, and keep anyone who may come here till I return.'

Margayya was always used to having a semi-circle of persons sitting before him as in the old days and never interrupted his studies or calculations to look at them or receive their greetings. He was a very busy man whose hours were valuable: as the day progressed it was a race with time, for he had to close his books before sunset.

The owner of the house, the blanket dealer, did not like to waste money on installing electric lights. He went on dodging his tenant's appeals day after day. His excuse was that materials were not available in quantities he needed or at prices he was prepared to pay. He went on saying that he had sent a direct order to the General Electric in America, that he had business associates of his blanket-contract days who would supply his wants direct, and that he was looking for a reply with every sailing; and thus he kept his tenants in hope. The plain fact seemed to be that he did not like to waste money. He confided to his friends: 'Why should anyone keep his shop or office open after six o'clock? Let him work and earn during the day: that is quite enough. I hear that they are going to introduce a law limiting working hours, when it will be a grave penalty to keep shops or offices open after sunset.' The result was that the shops remained without light, and since Margayya did not believe in spending his own money on an oil-lamp, he had to rush through his day's work and close the accounts before darkness fell. He worked without wasting a minute.

One or two of his clients, who had waited long enough to catch his attention, cleared their throats and made other small sounds. Margayya suddenly looked up from his desk and told one of them, 'Go there,' pointing at his accountant, sitting at the other end of the hall: 'He will give you the deed back.' The other showed no sign of moving, at which he said sharply, 'You heard me? If I have got to speak each sentence twice, I shall have to live for two hundred years and be satisfied with a quarter of my present earnings.'

'Why do you say such harsh things, master?' the other asked. 'Is it because I am asking for my deed back? Is it wrong?'

'It is not wrong. Why should anyone refuse to give a title deed that is yours by right?' He said it in such a tone that the other hesitated and said, 'You have been as a father to me in my difficulties and you have helped me as much as you could.'

'And yet you have not the grace to trust me with your title. Do you think I am going to make a broth of it and drink it off?'

The client rose and said, 'I will come again for it tomorrow, sir, just to show that I am in no hurry.' He rose and walked out.

Margayya said to the others, 'You see that fellow ... the ingratitude of some of these folk sometimes makes me want to throw up everything and ...' The others made sympathetic sounds just to please him. His accountant added from his corner his own comment in his hollow, hungry voice:

'He is afraid he may have further interest to pay if he leaves his papers here ... I know these people: they are docile and lamb-like as long as they hold our money, but the moment they return the principal and interest – '

Margayya did not like this: 'Don't disturb yourself, Sastri, go on with your work.' He hated the hungry, tired tone of his accountant.

'I was only giving you a piece of observation ... it is getting to be a nuisance, some of these fellows demanding their papers back at short notice,' Sastri persisted. At this Margayya realized that it would not be feasible to put his accountant down so easily, and cut him short with, 'True, true ... We must include a condition that they must give us at least three days for returning their papers.'

A visitor who felt that he had waited too long asked, 'Margayya, don't you recognize me?'

'No,' replied Margayya promptly.

'I am Kanda,' he said.

'Which?'

'Of Somanur – '

'No, you are not,' replied Margayya promptly.

The other laughed, leaned forward almost over the desk, and asked, 'Do you still say that I am not Kanda, master?'

Margayya scrutinized him closely and cried, 'You, old thief, it is you, yes! What has come over you? You look like a man a hundred years old ... Why those wrinkles round your nose? Why those folds at the chin and that silver filing all over your face? What is the matter with you and where are your teeth gone?' The other just raised his arms heavenward, lifted up his eyes as much as to say, 'Go and put that question to the heavens if you like.' Now Margayya wanted to clear his hall of all his visitors. He felt that here was the man he would like to talk to the whole day. He looked at the others, gave a paper back to someone, and said, 'I cannot advance you on this – '

'Sir, please ...' he began.

'Come tomorrow, we will see. Now leave me, I have many important things to talk over with old Kanda.'

He had lost sight of Kanda years ago. Margayya had been very fond of this man, who always said that he preferred fluid cash to stagnant land and that it was more profitable to grow money out of land than corn. Kanda had now come to ask Margayya's advice on how best to get money out of some new lands which had unexpectedly come to him through the death of a relative. These lands were in the regions of Mempi, whose slopes were covered with teak and other forests, and at whose feet stretched acres and acres of maize fields, with stalks standing over a man's height. Margayya was carried away by visions of this paradise of blue mountains, forest, and green fields. It was wealth at the very source and not second-hand after it had travelled up to town. The more he listened to Kanda's petition the more he felt that here was raw wealth inviting him to take a hand and help himself. Though it had grown nearly dark he sat and listened to Kanda as he narrated to him his financial ups and downs.

'I am glad you have come back to me, Kanda. I will pull you out of your difficulties,' he said as he rose to go.

Kanda explained, 'I cannot get any more loans from the Co-operative Bank; they have expelled me for default, although they auctioned the pledges ...'

'The crooks,' Margayya muttered. 'They are crooks, I tell you. I do not know why the government tolerates this institution. ...

They should put in gaol all the secretaries of co-operative societies.' The picture of the secretary and Arul came back to him with all the old force. Margayya warned him, 'Don't go near them again; they will see you ruined before they have done with you. I will look after you,' he added protectively, starting to lock up his door. He had sent away his accountant, and with a duplicate key he locked the door of his office. He generously indicated to Kanda the veranda. 'Sleep here, Kanda, no one will object. I will see you tomorrow morning and then we will go and inspect your property at Mempi. What time is your bus?'

'The first bus leaves the Market Square at six o'clock.'

'The next?'

'It is at eight-thirty ... Four buses pass Mempi village every day,' he said with a touch of pride.

'So that you may come oftener into town and borrow, I suppose!'

'There is also a railway station, about five or six stones off,' Kanda said. 'From here you can get the evening train and be down there at about twelve o'clock.'

'And get eaten by tigers, I suppose,' Margayya added, 'before reaching home.'

Kanda laughed at this piece of ignorance. 'Tigers are in the hills and generally do not come down.'

'Even then I prefer to come with you by the morning bus,' Margayya said. 'We will go by the second bus tomorrow. You can have your food in that hotel there.'

Margayya walked home. At his house he found a commotion. His wife's voice could be heard wailing, and a large crowd had gathered at his front door. He quickened his pace on seeing it.

'What is the matter?' he asked someone nearby. He hoped the people were not rushing in, in order to loot the house. He had kept a few important documents in the front room and a lot of cash. 'Must remove it elsewhere,' he thought as he pushed his way through the crowd on the front steps. 'Get out of the way,' he thundered. 'What are you all doing here?' Someone in the crowd said, 'Your lady is weeping – '

'I see that. Why?'

They hesitated to speak. He gripped one nearby by his shirt collar and demanded, 'What has happened? Can't you speak?' He shook him vigorously till he protested, 'Why do you trouble me, Margayya? I won't speak.' Margayya let him go and went in. He saw his wife rolling on the floor and wailing, in a voice he had never heard before. He never knew that she had such a high-pitched voice. There were a number of women sitting round her and holding her.

Margayya rushed towards them crying, 'What has happened to her? Meenakshi, what is the matter with you?' She sat up on hearing his voice. Her hair was untied. Her eyes were swollen. She wailed, 'Balu ... Balu ...' Her voice trailed off and she broke down again. She fell on the floor and rolled in anguish. Margayya felt helpless. He saw his brother and his wife also in the crowd. He knew something must be seriously the matter if these two were there, and their many children sucking their thumbs. His brother's wife was sitting beside Margayya's wife and trying to comfort her. Margayya rushed up and pleaded: 'Won't someone tell me what has happened?' His brother pushed his way through the crowd and handed him a card. Margayya's eyes were blurred with the mist of perspiration. His excitement had sent his heart racing. He rubbed his eyes and gazed on the card. He couldn't read it. He groaned, and fumbled for his glasses ... He could not pull them out of his pocket easily. He gave the card to the one nearest him and cried: 'Can't someone read it? Is it an illiterate gathering? What are you all watching for?' And then some person obliged him by reading out: 'Your son ... B ... Balu ... is no more – '

'What! What! ... Who says so?' Margayya cried, losing all control over himself. More perspiration streamed down his eye-lids and he wept aloud: 'My son! ... my son! Am I dreaming?' The assembly watched him in grim silence.

His wife was sobbing. She suddenly shot towards Margayya and cried: 'It's all your doing. You ruined him.'

Margayya was taken aback. There was a confused mixture of emotions now. He did not know what to say. One side of his mind went on piecing together his son's picture as he had last seen him.

'Did I treat him too harshly over the examination results? Or have I been too thoughtless over that cursed school record – ?'

He felt angry at the thought of examinations: they were a curse on the youth of the nation, the very greatest menace that the British had brought with them to India ... If he could see his son now he would tell him, 'Forget all about schools and books: you just do as you like, just be seen about the house – that's sufficient for us.' In this din, his wife's accusation reached him but faintly. He retorted: 'What are you saying, you poor creature! What are you trying to say?'

'You and your schools!' she arraigned him. 'But for your obsession and tyranny – '

'You keep quiet,' he said angrily. He turned round to someone and enquired: 'Do you know how it happened?'

Several voices chorused: 'He fell off a fourth floor of a building in Madras,' 'He must have been run over in that city,' 'Probably caught cholera,' 'We don't know – '

'Who was with him?' asked Margayya. He conducted a ruthless cross-examination.

'How can we know – the card is signed by a friend.'

'Friend! Friend!' Margayya cried. 'What sort of friend is it? Friend, useless blackguard.' He did not know what he was saying. Nor could he check the rush of his words. He babbled as if under the influence of a drug. He saw the whole house reeling in front of his eyes – the surroundings darkened and he sat down unable to bear the strain. He sat on the floor, with his head between his hands, quietly sobbing. His brother sidled up, put his arm round him, and said: 'You must bear it, brother; you must bear it.'

'What else can I do?' Margayya asked like a child. He still had on his coat and turban. Through all his grief a ridiculous question (addressed to his brother) kept coming to his mind: 'Are we friends now – no longer enemies? What about our feud?' A part of his mind kept wondering how they could live as friends, but the numerous problems connected with this seemed insoluble. 'We had got used to this kind of life. Now I suppose we shall have to visit each other and enquire and so on ...' All that seemed to be impossible to do. He wished to tell him then and there: 'Don't let this become an excuse to change our present relationship.'

Margayya did his best to suppress all these thoughts, but they kept bothering him till he could say nothing, till he was afraid to open his lips lest he should blurt them out. His brother whispered among other things: 'We will send you the night meal from our house.'

'No, we don't want any food tonight,' Margayya said. 'Please send all those people away.' He was indignant. Because Balu was dead, why should this crowd imagine that the house was theirs? 'Shut and bolt the door,' he thundered.

His brother left him, went up to the strangers about the house and appealed to them to leave. He said, with his palms pressed together in deference: 'Please leave us. This is the time when the family has to be together.'

'No,' Margayya thundered with deadly irony in his tone. 'How can they leave? How can they afford to ignore all this fun and go? If an entrance be charged – ' he began, then stopped, for in his condition he realized that he ought not to complete his sentence, which ran: 'We might earn lakhs – ' He did not think it was a good statement to make. So he merely said: 'Oh, friends and neighbours, the greatest service you could do us is to leave us alone.' The neighbours grumbled a little and started moving out. On the fringe of the crowd someone was muttering: 'When are they bringing the body?'

Margayya never knew till now that he had so many well-wishers in the city. The next day they proposed to bundle him off to Madras. He seemed to have no choice in the matter. All sorts of persons, including his brother, sat around and said: 'It's best that you go to Madras – at least once, and verify things for yourself.'

'What for?' asked Margayya. The others seemed to be horrified at this question, and looked at him as if to say: 'Fancy anyone asking such a silly question!'

'I can't go, I won't go, it is not necessary,' Margayya said offensively.

His wife had been transformed. She looked like a stranger, with her face swollen and disfigured with weeping. She glared at him and said: 'Have you no heart?'

'Yes, undoubtedly,' Margayya said in a mollifying manner. He felt that she had lost her wits completely and required to be handled with tact.

'If you have ordinary human feelings then go and do something ... at least ... at least – '

'Yes, I understand ... But it's all over.'

His brother said: 'Is this the time to argue about it all? You must go and do something.'

His sister-in-law added her own voice: 'It's your duty to go and find out more about it. Perhaps, there is still some chance of – '

'But,' wailed Margayya, 'where am I to go? Madras is a big world – where on earth am I to go there?' He despairingly turned the postcard between his fingers: 'There is no address here, nothing is said of where they have written from, nor who has written it.'

'Never mind,' they all said with one voice. Margayya felt now, more than ever, most unhappy to have been the father of Balu. The duties of a father seemed to be unshakable. He made yet another attempt to make others see reason: 'Look here, if I go to Madras, where am I to go as soon as I get down at the railway station?'

'Is this the time to go into all that?' they asked, looking on him as if he were a curious specimen. This encounter left him no time to brood over his own sorrow. There seemed to be so many demands upon him, following the catastrophe, that it was as much as he could do to keep himself parrying all the blows; it left him no time to think of anything else. When there was a pause and his eyes fell upon a little object, the lacquer-painted wooden elephant that Balu had played with as a child, it sent a sharp stab down his heart; it made him wince, he choked at the throat, and the tears came down in a rush, involuntarily – but he was spared more of that experience by the people around him. He almost regretted that his brother and his family were now back in the fold: they seemed to think up a new proposition for him every minute ... and his wife, who seemed to be already crazed, apparently fell in with every one of their proposals. One moment they kept saying that he must at once make arrangements to get through the ten-day obsequies for the peace of the departed soul and start right away the performance of those rites; the next, they immediately said that he must go to Madras and try and do what he could.

'You want me to buy a train ticket this moment, and in the same breath ask me to send for the *purohit* – '

At the mention of the word *purohit*, his wife clapped her hands over her ears and wailed afresh: 'I never hoped in my worst dreams to hear that word applied to my darling – '

'How can you be so callous as to utter that word so bluntly?' asked his sister-in-law, and another lady scowled at him.

He felt irritated, but practised gentle ways with a deliberate effort, fearing lest anything that he might say should once again bring a rupture between the families and continue it for another decade. He contented himself by saying under his breath: 'I don't seem to know what to say now – all the wrong things seem to come uppermost.' They did not encourage him to go on with even that reflection, but said, 'Do something; don't sit there and chat. This is no time for it.'

His brother added: 'If you are afraid to go to Madras alone, I will go with you. I know one or two people there.'

'Here is this man,' Margayya at once reflected, 'wangling a free journey to Madras.' And the prospect of his brother's constant company for so many days appalled him. Lest the women-folk and others should follow up the idea, he hastily said: 'Don't worry, I will go myself. I don't want anyone to think that I am reluctant to go.'

He suddenly saw it as a beautiful opportunity to escape. His grief was unbearable no doubt, but the atmosphere and the people about him made it worse. He saw himself being entangled with these folk for the rest of his life: that seemed to suit his wife, but he liked to be more independent. His house seemed to have lost all privacy. For the rest of their existence these people perhaps intended to sit around and wail over Balu. At the echo of the word 'Balu' in his mind he let a loud cry escape his lips and he beat his brow. It occurred almost involuntarily, and at once brought his brother and a cousin to his side: 'No, no, not that way. If you break down and lose all control, what is to happen to the others? You must be in a position to give them strength and – '

'How? How can I?' sobbed Margayya, moved by their sympathy. 'I prayed for him, and promised the Gods his weight in silver rupees if he should be born.'

'Did you fulfill that promise?' some asked, going off at a tangent. 'For that is a sacred pledge, you know.'

Margayya's wife answered: 'Yes, it was done within an hour of his birth.'

'Yes, these vows must be fulfilled within the shortest time possible. Otherwise the baby will acquire weight. How much did the child weigh?'

'About three hundred rupees weight at birth. We tramped to Tirupathi,' said Margayya, recollecting his pilgrimage with his young wife so many years ago.

She had worn a saffron-dyed *sari*, had carried the infant on her arms and walked behind him, as he went to ten houses and begged for alms. His pride would not let him beg, but it was once again his elder brother who bothered him by explaining: 'The God at Tirupathi does not like anyone to visit him as a holiday-maker, just for fun. He wants you to go there as a humble supplicant, in the attitude of a beggar.' He had put into it all the weight of scholarship that he had acquired. 'That's the symbol, that's why you are obliged to visit at least ten houses with a begging bowl, stand and cry at the door for alms, and then go on the pilgrimage, on foot, if possible. The God does not notice a person who goes to him in a holiday mood.'

And Margayya had clutched a brightly polished pot and, followed by his saffron-clad wife, had gone from door to door: 'Give me alms – ' People had come out of their houses and dropped a handful of rice into his copper pot.

He suddenly recollected now how amused he had felt when he saw his face in that burnished pot – its convex surface distorted his nose and cheeks; it was so grotesque that he could not help grinning at his reflection, which made it so much more funny that it became impossible for him to maintain the gravity needed for the occasion. He remembered that one or two people had felt scandalized by the way he grinned when they came out to give him alms. His wife had pulled him up, but he held the shining pot to her face and she too burst into a laugh. He remembered how at that time he wished he could also amuse the infant. He remembered how he carried the alms and the sovereigns equal to the weight of the child to the Tirupathi Hills and deposited them all in the treasure box in the shrine ... He felt he had done a good job, and it had been an enchanting pilgrimage. He sighed and groaned at the memory of his son. Through it all he remembered how he had not been a day too soon in weighing the youngster in gold as he showed a tendency to grow heavier each day.

'That vow was fulfilled all right. Nothing wrong there,' he said suddenly.

He sat in a third-class compartment in the train to Madras. He had become extremely unhappy when leaving home. He told his brother, 'Keep an eye on this house, will you?' He had told his wife, 'Don't ruin yourself with crying. I will go to Madras and do what I can.' It had sounded most futile – what could he do at Madras? Where could he go at Madras? It was all a very confused business. He felt unhappy that he was not even in a position to utter a promise. He bundled up a couple of shirts and *dhotis* into a small jute bag which had no clamp. It was to serve as a pillow for him at night. He had not travelled for years now, and he found it exciting. He wondered how he could leave his office. What was to happen to the business? Suppose somebody did something and killed his business? He wished he didn't have to leave at short notice. He wished he had had a little more time to arrange his affairs and then leave. But death gives no notice. They were bundling him about: and finally they thrust him and his bag into a *jutka* and sent him down to meet the six o'clock train to Madras coming from Trichy.

He asked at the ticket-window: 'Will you please give me a ticket?'

'What class?' he was asked.

'Class! I am not travelling in a saloon. If there is a fourth class – ' Margayya pushed in his money for a third-class ticket.

There was such a crowd that he had to push himself in through a window – not an easy task considering the paunch that he was developing as a prosperous man. The compartment was no more than normally crowded in a railway system which issued tickets 'till the fingers ached'. It was a compartment meant to seat twelve – a conception in an ideal world. Perhaps it technically satisfied the rule – because those who could technically be said to be seated were twelve. The rest kept themselves in it, in all manner of ways, with their bundles heaped about. People sat on each other's laps, hung by each other's necks, curled themselves on luggage racks overhead, spread their beds and stretched themselves comfortably in the space under the seats. One of them was explaining: 'This is the best way of travelling. I have always thought this better than even the first class. I always come two hours before and spread my bed.'

Margayya had extreme difficulty in hanging his legs down because quite a lot of people seemed to be sleeping there, and he could not cross his legs because he had managed to secure only half a seat, and had to dispose of the rest of himself somehow in mid-air. Seeing the manner in which the others had disposed themselves, he felt triumphant that he had at least got this seat – and he congratulated himself on his pluck. The moment he had shot in through the window, the impact of his arrival displaced someone who was already seated. Margayya just let himself down there before the other could recover. He was a villager.

When he did recover he cried: 'Get out of my seat.'

'Why don't you learn better manners?' Margayya said in his habitual masterful way with villagers.

'I have been sitting here from Trichinopoly,' the other began.

'Well, you must be tired of sitting – a change will do you good,' replied Margayya.

The others enjoyed the joke and laughed. Thick tobacco smoke hung in the air. Someone had opened even the lavatory door and forgotten to close it. Margayya cried: 'Why does not someone pull to that door?' Everyone agreed with him that it must be done, but no one was prepared to risk leaving his place to do it – and the man nearest the door did not care to put out his arm for the purpose. The train, clattering and jingling, went its way, stopping at every station, where more people tried to force their way in through windows and doors, but those inside formed themselves into a class and were unanimous in keeping them out. At about two o'clock the fever in the compartment seemed to subside: people slept and wriggled in the positions in which they found themselves, and snored. Margayya found a peculiar peace in these crazy circumstances. He had found a place for his neck, though not for the little bundle in his hand, which he closely hugged to his bosom. He was amused to see a seller of glass bangles, sitting right in the middle of the carriage with all his fragile merchandise tied up in a huge cloth bundle by his side, who kept warning everyone: 'Be careful, sirs, don't knock on this – ' And people were very considerate. There was a little girl who was looking wistfully at the bangles through her half-sleepy eyes. Margayya felt drawn to this man and found out that he was going to a fair at a wayside station on the following day. 'The day after tomorrow you will see me return this way without my bundle,' he said. 'But your purse fully loaded, I suppose,' said Margayya. He liked the man as a prospective bearer of money. He suddenly felt that he had kept away too long from the thought of money. It was like a tobacco chewer suddenly real-izing that he had been away too long from his pouch. Margayya took a pinch of snuff; at the sight of it a police officer sitting next him held out his fingers and Margayya passed him the box. The officer took a deep pinch, felt grateful and became communica-tive: 'Things are not quite good, yet, you know.'

'Yes, yes, of course,' replied Margayya, thinking it best to be agreeable with a policeman in plain clothes.

'All kinds of bothers,' he said. 'People will not leave us in peace – '

Margayya looked about cautiously and said: 'Can't you put them in their places?'

'Yes,' said the policeman. 'That's what keeps me on the move like this. My home is in Madras, but I don't get even a couple of hours a month to spend with my family. I have to be on the move constantly – well, they think I have a nose for ... for ... wrongdoers, political, criminal, or whatever – '

'Well, it's a dangerous job, I suppose,' Margayya said opening his eyes wide.

The policeman adjusted himself in his seat more comfortably and said: 'Well, it all depends how we view it. I have been in it for twenty years and have survived.'

'Well, one must do one's duty,' said Margayya, generalizing. 'As they say in Bhagavad-Gita, God helps those who do their duty.'

The other leaned forward and said: 'Do you know I had to carry a notice of arrest even to Mahatma Gandhi once? I would rather have prostrated before that man, but I had to arrest him. Such is life!' he philosophized vaguely, sleepily. Margayya noticed his sleepiness and said, 'But they ought to give you a second-class pass at least.'

This tickled the policeman considerably. 'I can travel first, if I like; nobody will question me. I am really an officer, you know. But what will be the use? I'm not travelling in order to sleep comfortably – that's why I travel third: my catches are almost all in a third-class carriage. Sometimes I have to follow political suspects, sometimes brigands, sometimes murderers – all kinds of things: they can assign me any job – but it is always necessary for me to keep wide awake and stay in a crowd.'

Most of the others in the compartment had gone to sleep. Only these two were awake. Margayya confided to him his troubles. 'I don't know where to go in Madras, or even what to do.'

'Have you got the card with you?' asked the policeman.

Margayya took it out of his pocket. The policeman examined it by the dim, insect-ridden light of the compartment. Looking carefully at the post-mark he said: 'It's from Park Town.'

Margayya asked: 'Where is that?'

The Inspector ignored his question, and asked, 'This hand-writing must also be analysed.' He turned the card and said: 'How long will you stay in Madras?'

'I don't know,' Margayya said pathetically, refraining from adding: 'They have pushed me out on this journey. I don't know where I'm going: I would not even know Madras when I arrived there.'

The police officer took charge of Margayya as soon as they arrived in Madras Egmore Station. He took him to the waiting-room and said: 'Make yourself at home. There is the platform restaurant. You can rest as much as you like. I will be back. Give me that postcard.' He spoke to a platform official about Margayya.

Margayya began to doubt how far he ought to trust the man. Perhaps he would throw him in gaol or perhaps he was a brigand himself. He was gradually changing his mind about wanting the man's help. In the cold, morning light of Madras, things seemed different and more reassuring; there was a certain hopelessness in the dim-lit compartment, which made him want to confide in someone and enlist his sympathy. But now it all seemed different. He reflected: 'Why not run away from here?' Suppose he opened the door on the off-side and cleared out. But the police officer gave him no chance. He said, taking him by the sleeve: 'Don't move out of here till I come back. I will see what I can do for you.'

'Oh, no, I wouldn't bother you,' said Margayya, trying to withdraw. The other paid no heed, but just turned round and went away. 'Why should anyone be so considerate to a stranger?' Margayya's devious mind kept ringing, 'particularly in this city, which is notoriously cold-blooded.'

After food, Margayya stretched himself on a bedstead in the waiting-room and slept soundly. He snored so loudly that the people moving about the platform stopped and looked in. Margayya dreamt that he had got down at Mempi, and someone whom he could not recognize pointed up to the sun-lit horizon, and said, 'All that is yours.' Margayya was struggling to work up the interest rate on this proposition and was involved in a terrible quantity of figures when the police officer came in again and woke him up. Margayya felt very apologetic for having fallen asleep. He said clumsily, 'You see ... I am sorry – '

'There is nothing to apologize about,' said the Inspector. 'Well, if you like to have a wash, let us go out.' Margayya got up and went round with him in search of a tap. The Madras heat seemed to prick him in a dozen places. He felt better after he emerged from under the tap. He went back to his room dripping, tidied himself up, and put on a long coat and turban. In the heat of Madras, it was like getting into steel armour and helmet.

The Inspector said: 'Well, I have good news for you.' He returned the postcard to Margayya and said: 'I have spent the whole day tracing the author of that postcard. It's a falsehood he has written.' Margayya's mind was still clouded with sleep and calculations of interest. He looked dull and uncomprehending. The Inspector held out his hand for a pinch of snuff. 'Give me your snuff. It's very good ... and I will tell you what you should do. You go back to your wife at once and tell her that your son is alive.'

'How do you know?' Margayya asked, still dazed.

'Because we've managed to trace it back to the author. He is a madman in Park Town who keeps writing messages like that to any address that he picks up.'

'How did he pick up my address?'

'Well, that's what we shall investigate, if you will stay for another day,' said the Inspector.

The Inspector took him along to a house in Park Town. It was a very big house in a lane, occupying the space of three or four blocks together. Its outside was painted green and red in alternating strips with oil distemper. Its front veranda was enclosed by iron rods painted yellow: the whole scheme made the house look like a crayon box with its lid open. Over it all was hung a board painted 'The House of Enlightenment'. It was a hot, dusty afternoon, and the taxi had run through several winding lanes. Seeing so much gaudy colour made Margayya's throat parched and thirsty; it also made him feel homesick. Before the car came to a halt the Inspector said: 'I was able to trace this man through the post office. Don't be surprised by anything you may see or hear, we are going out to meet a madman, remember. He is a very wealthy man, gone mad. He owns a theatre, and his relations are managing it.'

They got down. He knocked on the door. An attendant opened the door and showed the way. They went through several pillared halls. The pillars were of smooth granite, and the floors mosaic-covered. Potted ferns were kept here and there. Some parrots and miscellaneous birds were twittering in the cages hanging down from the ceiling. The house was so deep inside that the noises of the city came in from far off, completely muffled. The place was cool and shady. All along the walls of the corridors and passages and halls there were pictures of Gods in terrible shape and fury destroying the world. Margayya felt he was in an utterly strange world. The world of Vinayak Mudali Street, of his wife and brother, and Market Road, and banking, seemed to be distant and unreal ... The Inspector whispered to him: 'Don't you feel that you are in a zoo?'

'Yes, yes,' said Margayya, just to please him, although he did not know what it looked like inside a zoo. They were now in a large hall where a man sat on a divan, surrounded by cushions. He wore an ochre robe and had grown a beard. From two tall incense-holders smoke was curling. The man had about him a heap of postcards, a pen and a writing-pad. He was writing furiously when they entered. He had an attendant fanning him, although there was an electric fan above. There were two seating cushions along the wall. The man took no notice of the arrival of the visitors. The Inspector whispered to Margayya: 'Take your seat there.' They sat on the cushions and waited. The attendant bent over and whispered into the ear of the big man. He put away the pen, leaned back and looked at the Inspector. The Inspector salaamed. The other's face relaxed a little, and a smile hovered about it; but the next moment it became rigid again as he said: 'Who is that mortal next to you who does not seem to recognize us? Is it likely that we are invisible to his eyes?'

'Yes, that's so,' said the Inspector. 'That's the correct explanation.'

'Oh, it never occurred to me. I can make myself seen. We often forget that we divine creatures are transparent, and that we cannot be seen.'

'But it is easily remedied, if your holiness makes up his mind.' The other shook his head in approval, then waved his arm, looked at Margayya, and asked: 'Do you see me?'

The Inspector muttered: 'Salute him.'

'Yes,' replied Margayya with a reverential salaam.

'Now, what is your business, mortal?'

The Inspector said: 'He has come after his son Balu, about whom a card has emanated from here.' He held up the card and said, 'He wants to know in which world to look for him.'

The other shook his head and said: 'That I am not allowed to say. That only God can do. I am not God, but only God's agent. He ordered, "Go and prepare the world for my coming." That I am doing. I write every day to every King, Ruler, Viceroy, President and Minister in the world, that their boss is soon arriving, and let them get ready for it. Every day I write to President Roosevelt, Stalin, and Churchill, particularly.' He indicated a big file of letters waiting to be posted.

The Inspector said: 'That's fine – but we want to know the whereabouts of Balu. He is not a Maharaja or anything like that and it is enough for us to know in which world he is to be found. Will you please look up the necessary reference?'

'Is this his earthly father?'

'Yes,' said the Inspector.

'Does he believe in Death?'

'He does not,' replied the Inspector.

'I am very pleased about it. It's my mission in life to inform at least ten mortals about Death each day and educate them. People must learn to view Death calmly.'

'Of course, of course,' said the Inspector and added: 'Please look into your file.'

The other took out a ponderous file, turned over its leaves, muttering 'Balu ... Balu ... Son of ... Malgudi ...' Margayya could hardly believe his ears. He cried involuntarily: 'How did you get my address?' The Inspector suppressed him with a gesture and said: 'Where did you pick up this mortal's address?'

'How do I pick up George VI's address or Mahatma Gandhi's address?' he answered back. 'Whenever anyone comes to me for charity, I will not give them an anna unless they give me their true address. Whenever anyone comes to me for employment in any of my businesses, I won't take him in unless he gives me his true address.'

'How do you know it is his true address?'

'By writing a card to that address,' the other said triumphantly. 'You must not forget that there is God above me.'

'Did this boy come to you for employment?'

'Didn't he?'

'Or for charity?'

'I don't believe in charity. Whenever anyone comes to me for charity, I give them employment.'

'But when they come to you for employment – '

'I give them charity,' the other said.

'Where is this Balu?' persisted the Inspector.

'You may persist for a million years, but you will not get a reply unless God sanctions an answer.'

'Hasn't he sanctioned it?' asked the Inspector.

'No,' replied the madman.

'In that case we are going,' said the Inspector rising. The Inspector walked away unceremoniously. Margayya hesitated for a moment at the door, and then followed the Inspector out. 'What are we to make of it?' asked Margayya.

'Don't worry. Your son is living somewhere. We'll have to find that out. We will do it. Don't worry.'

'How do you know that my son still lives?'

'Because I know this man. Every day he writes ten death notices and sends them to the post. His servants usually do not post them, but your one card must have slipped through into the ordinary post.'

'My misfortune is that he should have got at my address!' Margayya wailed, suddenly realizing: 'It's three days since I went to my office. God knows what is happening to my business. Probably this is the beginning of the end – ' he reflected ruefully.

The Inspector took Margayya to the Central Talkies that evening. The Manager rose in his seat when the Inspector entered his room. The police were a troublesome lot and it was best to keep on good terms with them. The Manager became elaborately fussy and cried: 'What a pleasure! It's ages since you came here, Mr Inspector. Shall I order coffee? The film is on now. Would you like to see it?' He was as proud of the picture as if it were his own product. Margayya sat in a chair, idly gazing on the pictures of film stars hung on the walls in sepia print. A stale, surcharged tobacco smell pervaded the air and made Margayya more bilious than ever. The Manager said: 'We are showing — — — on the 26th. You must definitely send your children.'

The Inspector waved off the invitation with a gentle indifference and said: 'We saw your boss sometime ago – '

'Oh! How is he?'

'As usual, I suppose. How does he manage the business?'

'His son-in-law looks after everything. What he does is – he comes round occasionally, sits through a show, notes down the names of all the people he meets and goes – that he does once in a while.'

'Have you a new boy in your employment now?'

'Yes ... Yes ... We got one a few weeks ago. He seems to be an educated boy.'

'Is his name Balu?'

'Yes. That's it,' said the Manager. 'Why, anything wrong?'

'Is he about eighteen?' asked the Inspector, and gave a further description which the other accepted.

'What does he do?' asked Margayya interested.

'Well, miscellaneous things. Just now he is out with the sandwich boys. They will all come back before the evening show.'

They had to wait there till the crowd for the evening show began to arrive at the ticket-window. A kettle-drum was heard approaching over the noise of the crowd. It came nearer and stopped, and now through the gate streamed in street-arabs wearing sandwich boards, on which colourful posters were stuck announcing: '*Krishna Leela*.' The boys were ragged street-urchins with matted hair and sun-scorched complexions – covering their middles with loin-cloths and practically bearing on their bare bodies the sandwich frames. They put down their frames and gathered in front of the Manager's room along with the drummers and pipers. Presently Balu arrived, saying: 'Payment only for three, sir; the rest dozed off under the trees.' At which the rest started arguing furiously. 'What injustice to get work out of us and cheat us! Hey, you are no – '

Over all this Balu's voice rose: 'You won't be paid for just loafing.' His voice thrilled Margayya. But he checked himself. He feared that he might make a scene, or that his son might start to run away, out of sight once again, and then the Inspector and the others might blame him for spoiling the entire situation. So he edged away towards a corner of the room and turned his face towards the wall as Balu strode in. Balu came in saying: 'Manager, sir, we went through the People's Park, Rundall's Road, and Elephant Gate, and returned this way – except for the three boys, the rest skulked away for a nap in Moore Market. You must teach them a lesson, sir.'

Margayya could hold himself in check no more. He turned and observed that the boy wore a dirty *dhoti*, his cheeks were sunken, he was dark with wandering in the sun, and his hair was uncut. As he later explained to his relations, the moment he saw him he felt as if he had swallowed a live cinder. In this state he rushed forward with a loud cry, some indistinct words coming out in a rush in which the only clear words were: 'Is this spectacle my fate? Is it for this I prayed for your birth as my son? What has come over you?' His face was wet with tears. The boy was taken aback – so were the other two.

The Inspector had credited Margayya with greater self-possession. A crowd gathered at the door; the cinemagoers viewed this as a free show. The Inspector lost his temper at the sight of the crowd, and going up to the door, shouted: 'Get out of this place.' He stood at the doorway, and Balu felt that his retreat was cut off. He surrendered without a word.

The officer saw them off at the Egmore platform. Margayya gripped his arm and once again there were tears of gratitude in his eyes. He said: 'You have been like a God to me. Tell me, if there is any way in which I can repay you, write to me. You know my address.'

'Oh, yes. This is the first time I got at someone who was not a dacoit or a knave. I am glad to have done a good turn,' said the Inspector. He told Balu: 'Be a good son. Don't be a bother to your parents again. I have told the railway police to keep an eye on you.' It was this part that Balu did not like, and later commented after the Inspector went away.

'What can the railway police do? I'm not a thief. If I want to give them the slip there are a dozen ways.'

The Inspector had got them comfortable seats in an end compartment which was not too crowded. All night Margayya plied his son with questions and tried to know what he had been doing with himself ever since his disappearance after the results, but the boy sullenly declared: 'I won't speak of anything. Why couldn't you leave me alone? I was quite happy there.'

'But ... but ... have you no affection, don't you want to see your mother, your – ?'

'I don't want to see anybody.'

'But my dear boy, do you know what it will mean to them to see you back in the flesh? Your mother broke down completely – '

'Why couldn't you have given me up for dead? I was quite happy seeing pictures every day. I want to be in Madras. I like the place,' he said, already feeling dull at the prospect of living in Malgudi. 'What are you going to do with me? Make me read for exams I suppose?' he asked next.

'You need not go near books: you can do just as you please,' said Margayya indulgently. He was filled with love for his son. He felt an indescribable pity as he saw the dirty, greasy dress and the famished appearance the boy had acquired. He became absolutely blind to all the dozen persons packed into the compartment. He hugged his shoulders and whispered: 'You eat, rest, and grow fat – that is all you are expected to do, and take as much money as you like.'

The boy seemed to accept this advice with a hundred per cent literalness. As one supposed to be returned from the grave, he was treated with extraordinary consideration. His mother, he found, seemed to have become an entirely new person. She looked more youthful. A new flush appeared on her sallow cheeks. Her eyes had become very bright and sparkling. She became loquacious and puckish in her comments. She took the trouble to comb her hair with care and stuck jasmine strings in it. She seemed to feel that she was born anew into the world. She spoke light-heartedly and with a trembling joy in her voice. This was a revelation to Balu. He had never thought they attached so much importance to his person. He enjoyed it very much. His mother plied him with delicacies all the time. He had only to take a deep breath and look for his mother, and she at once asked: 'What do you want, my boy?' Balu found that he had returned to a new home. Everything now was different. His father left him alone according to his promise. It was a very agreeable situation for all concerned – except Margayya's brother and family.

The moment Balu was brought back home, their position as the helpers of the family disappeared. It was a relationship essentially thriving on a crisis. The moment that the crisis was over, the two families fell apart; and they were once again reduced to the position of speculating from the other side of the wall what might be happening next door. Margayya's wife ceased to bother about them: Balu never knew that there had been a momentary friendliness during his absence. On the day he arrived with his father, when he stepped in and saw his uncle and the family in their central hall, he was speechless.

His uncle demanded: 'What have you been doing with yourself? What is all this – ?'

And his aunt and the children of the next house surrounded him and gaped at him. He felt abashed. He simply moved into the little room at the side and shut the door on the entire gathering. That was the signal; when he reopened the door, the house was cleared and the front door bolted. Margayya briefly announced to him: 'They have all gone.'

'Where?' Balu asked with interest.

'To their own house,' Margayya said, and added: 'What is their business here, anyway?'

His wife chimed in: 'They probably wanted an excuse to plant themselves in here again!'

Margayya did not like to contradict her or say anything so utterly ungracious himself, although the moment he had secured his son, his first thought was to tell his brother's family, as diplomatically as his nature would permit, that they might go back to their house and resume their avocations! This he said very gently when the occasion came. As Balu shut himself into the small room, his brother wanted anxiously to know what had happened.

He said: 'Did I not tell you to go to Madras, and then it would turn out to be good for you?'

Here is this fellow, Margayya reflected, rubbing in his own wisdom and judgement as usual. He hated in his brother the 'Didn't I say so?' tone that he constantly adopted. It seemed to him a very irritating and petty habit of mind, and so he retorted sharply: 'That's all right, nobody doubts your wisdom.'

His brother ignored this sting and asked: 'Well, where did you find him? What was he doing? Who wrote that card?'

Margayya lowered his voice and said in a whisper: 'I will tell you all that later, when the boy is out of hearing. Now I had better attend to his wants.' He moved towards the street door.

His brother took the hint: he cast a glance at his wife, who got up, herded the children together and started out, telling Margayya's wife: 'I have so much to do at home – I think ... Anyway, let us thank God for this recovery,' and marched out. The moment the door shut on them, Margayya's brother's wife ground her teeth and said: 'Even if this house is on fire, let us not go near them again.' It was a sentiment which was not approved by the last but one toddling beside her: 'Why not, mother? It's so nice being in that house!'

'Now what has happened for you to make all this fuss?' her husband asked. There were tears in her eyes when she went up the steps of her own house. She said: 'I only want you to have self-respect, that's all. After all that we have done for them these three days, baking and cooking for them night and day – five seers of rice gone for those ingrates – '

'After all, she was the only person in their house. You have included the feeding of your own children,' her husband said; which enraged her so much that she stabbed his cheeks with her fingers screaming: 'Go and lick their feet for love of that wonderful brother of yours, you will do anything for him I am sure.'

Balu devoted himself to the art of cultivating leisure. He was never in any undue hurry to get out of bed. At about nine o'clock, his father came to his bedside and gently reminded him: 'Had you not better get up before the coffee gets too stale?' Balu drank his morning coffee, demanded some tiffin, dressed himself, and left the house. He returned home at about one o'clock and sat down to his lunch. His mother waited for him interminably. He came home any time after one. Sometimes he came home very late. Even then he found his mother waiting.

'What are you waiting for, mother?' he asked. She never answered the question but went on to serve him his dinner. After dinner, he went up to the shop opposite, bought betel leaves and areca-nut, chewed them with great satisfaction, and sat down on a dealwood box placed in front of the shop, watching the goings-on of the street for a while and smoking a cigarette, after making sure his mother was not watching. If he saw any elder of the house or of the next house coming out, he turned the cigarette into the hollow of his palm and gulped down the smoke. After this luxury, he suddenly got up, crossed the street, and went back to his house. He spread a towel on the granite floor, in the passage from the street, and, cooled by the afternoon breeze blowing in through the street door, was overcome with drowsiness and was soon asleep. He was left undisturbed. He woke from sleep only at five in the evening, and immediately demanded something to eat and drink, washed himself and combed his crop and went out. He returned home only after ten, when the whole town had gone to sleep. By this time, his father had already come home and was fretting, bothering his wife to tell him where Balu had gone. He had got into the habit of feeling panicky if Balu absented himself too long from home. But the moment the door opened and Balu came in, he became absolutely docile and agreeable.

He said: 'Oh, Balu has come!' with tremendous enthusiasm, and as he went in to change, asked with the utmost delicacy: 'Where have you been?' avoiding to the best of his ability any suggestion of intimidation or effrontery.

The boy just said: 'I've been here and there – what should I be doing at home?'

Six months of this life and the boy became unrecognizable: there were fat pads under his eyes; his chin was doubling, and his eyes seemed to shrink down to half their original size. Margayya wondered what to do with him. 'Must do something so that he is able to grow up like other normal boys of his age – otherwise he will rust.' He thought that the best solution would be to marry him. He sent out his emissaries, and very soon the results became evident. From far and wide horoscopes came in, and letters asking for his son's in return. Margayya carefully scrutinized the status of those who clamoured for his alliance. It was like the State Ministry scrutinizing the wedding proposals of a satellite Prince. The chief assistant in this business was his accountant Sastri. He had acquired a new status now as a matchmaker. As he sat in his corner copying in his ledger, Margayya said from his seat: 'Sastri, do you know anyone with a daughter?'

'Yes, sir,' Sastri said, pleased to have an opportunity to look up from his ledger. 'Yes, sir, quite a lot of inquiries have been coming my way, sir, for Balu – '

'Then why didn't you mention the matter to me?'

'You may be sure, sir, that when the right party comes they will be brought to you. Till then it does not seem to be very necessary to trouble you, sir.'

'Quite right,' said Margayya, pleased with his accountant and feeling his own eminence unquestioned and clearly placed. 'You are right, Sastri – I'm very keen that if there is to be an alliance it must be with a family who have a sense of – '

'I know, sir, they must at least be your equal in status, sir.'

'Status! Status!' Margayya laughed pleasantly. 'I don't believe in it, Sastri ... it's not right to talk of status and such things in these days. You know I'm a man who has had to work hard to make money and keep it. But I never for a moment feel that I am superior to anyone on earth. I feel that even the smallest child in the road is my equal in status.'

'Very few there are, sir,' said the other, 'who are so wealthy and are so free from vanity or showiness. I have known people with only a tenth of what you possess, sir, but the way they – '

'How do you know it is only a tenth of what I have?' Margayya asked, his suspicions slightly roused: for he let the other keep only one set of accounts: the other set which gave a fuller picture of his financial position was always in his possession. Had this fellow been peeping into his private registers? The man gave a reassuring reply: 'Any child in the town can say who it is if he is asked to name the richest man.' It was very flattering and true, but Margayya hoped that the income-tax people would not take the same view. Further development of this conversation was cut off because three clients from a far-off village came in asking: 'Is this Margayya's?' At once Margayya and his assistant fell silent and became absorbed in their work. When anybody entered with that question on his lips, it meant that he was a new client, he had been sent in by one of Margayya's agents, and he would want ready cash before departing for the evening.

Margayya said: 'Come in, come in, friends. May I ask who has sent you along?' They had come with the right recommendation. The three villagers came in timidly, tucking in their upper-cloth. Margayya became very officious and showed them their seats on the mat: it was as if he had reserved for them special seats on fresh carpets and divans. He then said: 'Will you have soda or coffee? Or would you care to chew betel leaves?' He turned to Sastri and said: 'Send the boy down to fetch something for them: they have come a long distance. You came by bus?'

'Yes, paying a fare of twelve annas; and we want to catch the evening bus, if possible.'

They went by the evening bus, but leaving their mortgage deed behind, and carrying in their pouches three hundred rupees, the first instalment of interest on what was already held at the source. The first instalment was the real wealth – whose possibilities of multiplication seemed to stretch to infinity. This was like the germinating point of a seed – capable of producing hundreds of such germinating points. Lend this margin again to

the next man, as a petty loan, withholding a further first instalment; and take that again and lend it with a further instalment held
up and so on ... it was like the reflections in two opposite mirrors.
You could really not see the end of it – it was a part of the mystic
feeling that money engendered in Margayya, its concrete form lay
about him in his iron safe in the shape of bonds, and gold bars, and
currency notes, and distant arable lands, of which he had become
the owner because the original loans could not be repaid, and also
in the shape of houses and blocks of various sizes and shapes, which
his way of buying interest had secured for him in the course of
his business – through the machinery of 'distraint'. Many were
those that had become crazed and unhappy when the courts
made their orders, but Margayya never bothered about them,
never saw them again. 'It's all in the business,' he said. 'It's up to
them to pay the dues and take back their houses. They forget that
they asked for my help.' People borrowed from him only under
stress and when they could get no accommodation elsewhere.
Margayya was the one man who easily lent. He made the least
fuss about the formalities, but he charged interest in so many subtle
ways and compounded it so deftly that the moment a man signed
his bonds, he was more or less finished. He could never hope to
regain his possessions – especially if he allowed a year or two to
elapse.

There were debt relief laws and such things. But Margayya
nullified their provisions because the men for whom the laws
were made were enthusiastic collaborators in his scheme, and
everything he did looked correct on paper. He acquired a lot of
assets. But he lost no time in selling them and realizing their cash
again, and stored it in an iron safe at home. 'What am I to do
with property?' he said. 'I want only money, not brick and lime
or mud,' he reflected when he reconverted his attached property
into cash. The only property he often dreamt of was the one at
the foot of the Mempi Hills, but somehow it was constantly
slipping away: that fellow, Kanda, came again and again, but
always managed to retain his ownership of his lands.

Sastri turned up with quite a score of offers for Margayya's
son. Margayya felt greatly flattered and puffed up with conceit.

This was evidence that he had attained social importance. He had never thought that anyone of consequence would care to ally with his family. There was a family secret about his caste which stirred uneasily at the back of his mind. Though he and the rest were supposed to be of good caste now, if matters were pried into deeply enough they would find that his father's grandfather and his brothers maintained themselves as corpse-bearers. They were four brothers. The moment anyone died in the village, they came down and took charge of the business from that moment up to dissolving the ashes in the tank next day. They were known as 'corpse brothers'. It took two or three generations for the family to mitigate this reputation; and thereafter, they were known as agriculturists, owning and cultivating small parcels of land. No one bothered about their origin, afterwards, except a grand-aunt who let off steam when she was roused by declaring: 'It's written on their faces – where can it go, even if you allow a hundred years to elapse.'

It was Margayya's constant fear that when the time came to marry his son, people might say: 'Oh, they are after all corpse-bearers, didn't you know?' But fortunately this fear was unfounded. At any rate, his financial reputation overshadowed anything else. Horoscopes and petitions poured in by every post. It produced a sense of well-being in Margayya, and a quiet feeling of greatness.

Sastri had done his part of the work efficiently. He had set aside all ledger work for the moment, and had written out scores of letters to men known to him within a radius of about two hundred miles. He was a compendium of likely parties with daughters to marry. He went out and saw in person quite a good many locally, as an ambassador. In all his correspondence and talk he described Margayya as the 'Lord of Uncounted Lakhs' or as one who was 'the richest in India'; and he spoke of Balu as inheritor of all this wealth and an apprentice in his father's own business and a young man whose education was deliberately suspended because his father, having his own idea of education, was more keen on training the young fellow in business than letting him acquire useless degrees. Margayya scrutinized quite a file of applications and horoscopes. He rejected most of the proposals. They were from quite unworthy aspirants. Margayya felt, 'Why should these people waste my time and their own? Are they blind? I have a certain position in life to keep up and I naturally want only alliances which can come up to that expectation.'

Finally he picked up the horoscope of a girl who seemed to him desirable from every point of view. Her name was Brinda. She was seventeen years old. Her father in his first letter described her as being 'extremely fair'. He was a man who owned a tea-estate in Mempi Hills. At once it biased Margayya's mind in his favour. It was not a very large estate but yielded an income of ten thousand rupees a year. Margayya sent Sastri out to fetch an astrologer. There was one practising in the lane behind the Market Road. A man presently entered with beads at his throat and sacred ash on his forehead, wrapped in a red silk toga and dressed every inch for his part. There were a few of Margayya's clients waiting for him, and he had to dispose of them before he could attend to the astrologer. He seated the astrologer and made him wait for a few moments. The astrologer fretted at having to wait. He sat shifting uneasily in his seat, cleared his throat, and coughed once or twice in order to attract attention. Margayya looked up and understood. He interrupted himself in his work to tell the astrologer: 'Hey, Pandit, can't you remain at peace with yourself for a moment?' The astrologer was taken aback, but curbed his restlessness. Margayya disposed of his clients, looked up and said: 'Come nearer, Pandit.' The astrologer edged his way nearer.

By his manner and words, Margayya had now completely cowed the man. It seemed necessary as a first step to dictate to the planets what they should do. Margayya had made up his mind that he was going to take no nonsense from the planets, and that he was going to tell them how to dispose their position in order to meet his requirement: his requirement was the daughter of a man who owned tea-estates in Mempi Hills, and he was consulting the astrologer purely as a formality. These were not days when he had to wait anxiously on a verdict of the stars: he could afford to ask for his own set of conditions and get them. He no longer believed that man was a victim of circumstances or fate – but that man was a creature who could make his own present and future, provided he worked hard and remained watchful. 'The gold bars in the safe at home and the cash bundles and the bank passbook are not sent down from heaven – they are a result of my own application. I need not have stayed at my desk for ten hours at a stretch and talked myself hoarse to all those clients of mine and taken all that risk on half-secured loans! ... I could just have sat back and lost myself in contemplation – '

His mind sometimes pursued such a line of thought. But he at once realized that it was not always quite safe to think so and added the rider: 'Of course Goddess Lakshmi or another will have to be propitiated from time to time. But we must also work and be able to keep correct accounts and pay for what we demand.' This was no doubt a somewhat confusing and mixed-up philosophy of life, but that was how it was – and its immediate manifestation was to say to the astrologer, as he pushed before him his son's horoscope and the tea-estate daughter's, 'Pandit, see if you can match these horoscopes.'

The Pandit put on his glasses and tilted the horoscopes towards the light at the door and studied them in silence.

Margayya watched his face and said: 'What is your fee for your services?'

'Let my fee alone,' the other said. 'Let me do my work properly first.'

Margayya said: 'Well, probably I shall be able to add a couple of rupees to your usual charges ... and if the alliance concludes successfully, well, of course, a lace *dhoti* and all honours for the Pandit – '

'Give me a pencil and paper,' the other said briefly.

The astrologer filled the sheet of paper with numbers and their derivatives, and worked up and down the page and on the back of it. He asked for another sheet of paper and worked up further figures. Margayya watched him anxiously. He said softly: 'I want this alliance to go through. I shall appreciate it very much if you will work towards that objective. I can show my appreciation concretely if – '

The astrologer shook his head and muttered: 'Impossible – you will have to find – '

'I don't want you to talk unnecessarily,' Margayya said.

'The seventh and ninth houses in your son's horoscope are ... are not quite sound. The girl's marriage possibilities are the purest. The two horoscopes cannot match – they are like soap and oil.'

'I have no faith in horoscopes personally – '

'Then you need not have gone to the extent of looking at these,' the astrologer said.

Margayya felt angry. He asked finally: 'Is there nothing that you can do?'

'Absolutely nothing. What can I do? Am I *Brahma*?'

Margayya could not trust himself to speak further. He called across the room: 'Sastri – '

'Yes, sir.'

'Give this Pandit a rupee and see him off.'

'Yes, sir,' Sastri proceeded to open a money bag.

The Pandit said: 'A rupee! Am I a street-astrologer! My fee is usually – '

'I am not interested. My fee for such service as you do is just one rupee maximum. You will not get even that if you mis-behave,' said Margayya, and he shot out his hand and snatched back the horoscopes and the sheet of calculations. He looked for a moment at it to see if he could read anything. It was a maze of obscure calculations and figures. He thought of tearing it up, but remembering that he had paid for it, folded it neatly and put it into his personal desk. The astrologer got up loftily and walked towards the accountant, received his rupee with an air of resig-nation, and strode out without relaxing his looks.

Dr Pal helped Margayya to find a different astrologer who rearranged the stars of Balu to suit the circumstances. Margayya did not meet the astrologer in person. Dr Pal took upon himself the task. He made several journeys between the astrologer and Margayya carrying the envelope containing the horoscopes, and finally came back one day with the astrologer's written report on a saffron-tipped paper; the report said that the two horoscopes perfectly matched, with reasons adduced. Considering the mightiness of the task the fee of seventy-five rupees which Dr Pal said the astrologer charged was purely nominal.

Events then moved briskly. Dr Pal's services became indispensable and constant. He saw Margayya through the preliminary negotiations, the wedding celebrations, and the culmination in a newspaper photo with Balu wearing tie and collar, his handsome bride at his side.

It was the third year of the war, and Margayya decided that the time was now ripe for starting a new line. He walked into Dr Pal's Tourist Home and asked: 'Doctor, how are you faring?'

'Not badly,' said the Doctor.

Margayya observed the dust-laden table, the penholder which had not been moved, and the unwritten sheets of paper before him – unmistakable signs of dull business. Margayya settled in the chair and began: 'Doctor, I think you ought to make more money.'

'Why?'

'Just for your own good. I will show you a way, if you like.'

'I'm quite contented with what I have.'

'You are not, sir,' said Margayya. 'You forget I'm also in the same building as you are. Don't tell me that there are many fellows coming into your office to seek your assistance in tourism or whatever it may be – '

Dr Pal became submissive: 'I have tried one thing after another in life. You know I am a qualified sociologist – one of the handful in this country – '

'Let us not talk of all that,' said Margayya, not liking the idea of going back to the *Domestic Harmony* days. It was something which had gone clean out of his mind, except one copy of the book which he retained as a memento of his earlier days and which he kept locked up in his iron safe at home for fear that Balu might get at it. Fortunately, he felt, his daughter-in-law's father did not seem to have heard anything about his association with it. Otherwise he might never have gone through with the alliance – it was as risky as the ancestry of his corpse-bearing grandfathers. And so now he cut short Dr Pal's reference to sociology and psychology as if it were dangerous talk, and said: 'I want to do you a good turn.'

'Why?' asked the Doctor.

'Because – ' began Margayya, and was about to say, 'you did me a good turn once by forcing on me your manuscript,' but checked these words, and said, 'Don't ask why. Because I have known you for a long while, and have seen you also – and I sincerely wish that you could make a little money and live comfortably – '

'Tourism,' said Dr Pal, 'is a very honourable and paying proposition in the West, but here nobody cares. There is not a single person anywhere here, who knows the history and archaeology of the country round about. Do you know that there are half a dozen different jungle-tribes to be found on the top of the Mempi Hills? All of them live, breed and die in the jungles – but there are so many differences between them. No inter-marriage? My tourism does not confine itself to telling people, "There is the river," "There is the valley," "Here is big game" – and pointing to a few ruined temples – that's not my idea of tourism; it's something different, something that's as good as education.'

'But it hasn't been a paying line,' said Margayya, growing impatient with his lecture. 'For the moment, if you want a good income, listen to me. If I throw out a word about it, I am sure there will be dozens ready to take it up, but I want to give you the first chance because – ' He once again narrowly avoided reference to *Domestic Harmony*, and said: 'Because, because, I've been seeing you for quite a long while, and I would like to see you prosper.'

There was another reason why Margayya wanted to help, which was also not mentioned. He found Dr Pal hanging too much about his son's establishment at Lawley Road. Margayya gave one of the houses he had acquired to his son for setting up a family independently, although Margayya's wife did not much like the idea of living separated from him. But Margayya told her: 'Think for a moment, my dear girl, Brinda comes from an up-to-date family, and already shows her superior training. Is she very comfortable in this house?'

His wife thought it over and agreed: 'I don't think so. Balu has been saying that the new room you have put up on the terrace is not good enough. In her father's house she has four rooms, all her own.' She added: 'The girl hardly comes out of her room all day.

I have to call her a dozen times before she will come downstairs for her meal. I hardly see anything of Balu either. He doesn't speak much. I'm probably not good enough for a modern girl like her.'

'Tut! Tut!' Margayya said to her. 'Don't get into the habits of a mother-in-law. I like the girl very much myself – if those two are happy, I think it's best they are left alone to manage their affairs in their own fashion. I have recently acquired a house in Lawley Extension. I think it best that they move off there.'

'So far!' exclaimed the mother horrified.

'It's not so far as you imagine ... just half an hour by a *jutka*.' He studied her face for a while and added: 'Don't make a fuss. The boy is eighteen years old and he ought to look after himself. The girl will manage the household for him.'

To Margayya's wife it seemed an unthinkable proposition. 'They hardly know how to boil water or even to light an oven.'

'They will learn everything,' Margayya said. 'And they can engage a cook if they want.' He was adamant: 'Sooner or later the boy will himself open the subject and ask for this and that. If he does that it will annoy me very much, and I will resist. I'd rather do things before he speaks – it'll look better. I will give him a house and a settlement. I want to see if that will make him think of doing something with his time.'

His wife did not like the note of irony in his voice and protested: 'You have already forgotten what happened. I dread to think you have already started again thinking you ought to improve him!'

Margayya's wife nearly broke down on the day Balu bundled up his clothes into a neat leather suit-case presented to him by his father-in-law, put them into a taxi and drove away with his young wife. Margayya's wife had spent a good part of an entire week in running up and down between Vinayak Mudali Street and Lawley Extension, arranging the bungalow at Lawley Extension for its new occupants. The girl prostrated at her mother-in-law's feet before taking leave of her.

Balu, a taciturn man, just said: 'I'm going,' got into the car, and sat down leaving space for his wife. Margayya's brother's family had crowded on the parapet of the next house.

Margayya himself was away, for it had been a busy day for him at his office.

The house for Margayya's wife seemed to have become dull and lonely without her son. It reminded her of the days when he had gone away without telling anybody, but Margayya noticed no difference because his mind was busy formulating a new plan which was going to rocket him to undreamt-of heights of financial success ...

Margayya observed that after Balu settled in his new house, Dr Pal became a constant visitor there. Whenever he went there, at the end of a day's work, he saw Dr Pal settled comfortably in the hall sofa. He played cards with Balu and his wife. He also suspected that Dr Pal constantly took cash from his son. Margayya did not like a man who could write *Domestic Harmony* to associate with young, impressionable minds; he would probably recite passages from it, talk over further projects with his son, and he couldn't say what Balu might or might not do under those circumstances. At any rate, it seemed imperative to wean his son away from Dr Pal – and it seemed best to do it by employing Dr Pal's hours usefully and so making it unnecessary for him to go to the youngster, at least for money.

Now Margayya told Dr Pal: 'You can make a thousand rupees a month easily if you will associate with me. After you have made some money it'll be much more feasible to try your tourism to your heart's content. Are you willing to try and do something?'

'Yes, definitely,' said Dr Pal. At which Margayya began a lecture on money conditions. The war had created a flood of inflated currency. All sorts of people were making money in all sorts of ways – some of it unaccounted or unaccountable.

'You know what the market has been!' said Margayya. 'This is the time when I wish to attract deposits rather than lend. People have money and are looking for a place to put it – and I look to you to get me a few contacts. I will make it worth while. You know all kinds of people as a journalist, and you are the man for me.'

'I will do my best,' declared Dr Pal enthusiastically, thinking: 'At least next month I can pay the stores, instead of dodging; I am tired of dodging.'

'I am tired of this tame business of lending to my rustic clients,' Margayya said. 'I want to do something better for a change. It does not mean I'm giving up my village clients. I shall continue to serve them as a sort of duty to them ... but – '

Margayya's instinct was right in choosing Dr Pal as his tout. He was a man who visited almost all the shopmen in the town every day. He knew the rice merchant in a certain back street who hoarded rice in a secret godown, whose frontage was stuffed with innocent-looking rag and old paper collected for the paper mills, who sold rice at about a rupee for half a *seer* to needy people, and made an enormous quantity of money each day. Dr Pal knew the man who supplied office glue to the army and hoarded enough cash by showing a joint stock firm with imaginary partners; another merchant who supplied screws in cartons only half-filled, the contractor who built huts and got enormous bills passed easily by bribing the Garrison Engineer. He was a rich man because his huts meant to stand for three years would stand only for a couple of months – till the bills were passed by the friendly Garrison Engineer! It was this margin that gave him real wealth. There were drug stockists who didn't show their stock, but bargained when it was a matter of life and death to a customer; there were military men with pensions, and go-betweens and busy-bodies who could secure contacts at New Delhi for a consideration, people who could manage export and import priority. All these people had a lot of money – the town was reeking with it. Only a part of it came out in income-tax returns, and the balance remained hidden in bundled-up currency notes in dark boxes – it was these that Margayya wanted to attract to his own stronghold. Besides these, people generally had a lot of cash these days. Margayya had decided that all the cash must go to him. He had a feeling that, though by ordinary standards he might be termed a man of wealth, yet the peak was still a long way off. He was like a fanatical mountaineer who sets his heart on reaching the summit of Everest. He might be standing on the highest peak. Yet he can never feel that he has really attained the highest ...

The blanket man was Dr Pal's first client. Dr Pal sat in his shop amidst piles of dark blankets and lectured him so long that he expressed a desire to meet Margayya. Dr Pal said: 'I will see him first and speak to him. He is very reluctant to accept deposits. But I think my recommendation will work – wait until I see you again tomorrow.'

The next day he came to the blanket shop and took the man along to meet Margayya at his office. Margayya effusively seated him on the mat, and went on with his work. He interrupted himself only for a moment to declare: 'Still no light! As our landlord, you should look to our convenience.'

'Certainly – I have ordered everything, it's coming,' he said in his routine manner. Dr Pal said: 'Our friend Guru Raj has some cash, and wants your advice as to what he should do – '

'He is himself an old business man. Why does he need my advice?' said Margayya.

The blanket man said: 'After all, you are an experienced banker. Your advice will be valuable.' As he hesitated, Margayya threw a look at Dr Pal and he got up and went away unobtrusively. Margayya drew nearer and in a confidential whisper asked: 'Are you really serious about depositing your cash with me? No doubt I can offer you an interest of twenty per cent on your deposit which you can draw monthly.' The blanket merchant gasped, 'Twenty per cent? Did I hear you all right?'

'Yes, I said twenty per cent,' said Margayya. 'I know what I am talking about.'

'The banks are offering only three per cent.'

'I'm not concerned with them. I'm not a bank, but I can guarantee you twenty per cent.'

'How do you manage it?'

'Well, that is my look out,' Margayya said. 'I have a business which yields me more; I have investments which give me probably twenty-five per cent. I keep five per cent and turn over the twenty per cent to the depositor; after all,' he said with a very virtuous look, 'I am using your money. Unlike the banks and co-operative societies, I believe you are entitled to the larger share as the owner of money. You see, I have made enough money,' he said with an air of sanctity. 'I don't want more. I only want to be of help to people, that is all,' he said vaguely.

At the end of his talk Guru Raj took out five thousand rupees in cash and placed them on the table. Margayya swept them into his desk and wrote out a receipt. 'This is the receipt. Any time you want your money back, just take it to my accountant and collect your five thousand. But as long as you don't cash it, you can collect the interest on every first. As long as you do not withdraw the principal, you can draw the interest.'

The blanket merchant went away with his head in the clouds. Twenty per cent! 'I have to dispose of a hundred blankets a day if I have to make that money. How does this man manage?' On the following month when he went to Margayya's, the accountant gave him the cash. When he got this interest as a reality, the man was aghast and cried: 'That man Margayya is a wizard. How does he manage it?'

Very soon the word 'Wizard' came to be bandied about freely whenever anyone referred to Margayya. His methods were too complex for anyone to understand. The banks were puzzled. The deposits in their possession were all going. People speculated how the wizard did it. No one had any clear idea. Nor could they get any enlightenment from Sastri or Dr Pal. Margayya assigned to them only portions of certain duties, and attended to all things personally, and they never had a full knowledge of what exactly he did. The whole town seemed to talk of nothing but this all day. People said that he underwrote shipments arriving at Madras Port or Bombay and made money; that he discounted bills of lading, that he paid interest on capital out of a sheer desire to impress. But the fact was there that he seemed to need new clients each day, and Dr Pal had proved invaluable in this task. He had now earned for himself a second-hand Baby Austin, and brought into Margayya's at least a dozen new clients each day. Margayya calculated: 'If I get twenty thousand rupees deposit each day and pay fifteen in interest, I have still five thousand a day left in my hands as my own – '

# PART FIVE

He might have been a movie celebrity. He could never take a few steps in the road without people gaping and pointing at him. It was now necessary for him to have a car, for it became a nuisance to walk in the roads. All sorts of people saluted him respectfully and stood aside while he passed. It made him feel very awkward. All sorts of people tried to make friends with him. All sorts of people tried to waylay him and explain their difficulties. One wanted help to get a daughter married, another to send his son to Madras for higher medical studies, a third applied for help to extricate his lands, or to buy rice for the next meal, and so on and so forth. In addition to this, public bodies seemed to have suddenly become aware of his existence – a Flood Relief Fund here, a Gandhi Fund there, Earthquake Relief for a far-off country, Prevention of Cruelty to Animals, Promotion of Child Welfare, Education, and the War Fund: the most constant demand was from the War Fund of the local district authorities. People called on him at all sorts of places and all sorts of hours – in the street, at home, or in his office. Quite a flood of visitors waited for him. All applications for charity instead of rousing pity only angered Margayya: 'What do they take me for? A Magic Pot? ... I work hard and wear myself out not in order to give gifts but to keep. Who came to my help in those days when I was in difficulties?'

He had to barricade himself at home and in his office. At his office he had to move out of his original place and take another room and shut himself in. He left the disposal of his visitors and applicants to Dr Pal, who just told people: 'This is only a bank not a charity home,' and sent away whoever came for cash. He was tactful where it was necessary, and diplomatic or downright rude where it was necessary. Sometimes he was visited by high Government officials who asked: 'Well, what is your contribution to the War Fund?'

Dr Pal said: 'Our boss is a convinced Congressman. We don't believe that this is our war ... unless the Congress High Command orders him to pay, he will never give a pie: he is a man of strict principles. Why should we contribute for a fund with which the British and U.S. fight their enemy – not our enemy; our enemy is Britain not Germany. When the Congress commands us to gather funds for fighting this enemy, you will see Margayya placing his entire wealth at the disposal of the country.' Or he said: 'Governor's War Fund! Nothing doing! Sir ... somebody or other they've sent from England as our Governor pockets half the war fund he collects, isn't it a fact? If he takes twenty thousand in cash for the war fund, he takes a similar sum in kind, in the shape of a casket or something, for domestic consumption. Can you disprove it? Till you can do that you cannot expect Mr Margayya to contribute anything. He is a man of strict principles.' Or if it was a highly placed police or income-tax official who was making the request, Dr Pal said: 'Margayya has been thinking over it. You may rest assured he will send in his contribution very soon.' And he advised Margayya to send off a cheque. 'It will not do at all to get into disfavour with these folk – after all they will be using the money for defeating the Nazis.' He also told Margayya: 'You must have a car. You simply should not be seen in the streets any more: you have passed that stage. If you like a walk, go along the river, but don't walk in the streets.' Margayya allowed the other to buy a car for him.

It was necessary for him to use a car also for another reason: at the end of a day, Margayya carried a huge bag of cash – notes of all denominations were in the old mail sack which he had picked up at an auction. 'Very good material,' said Margayya of the sack, which came near bursting when Margayya closed for the day. He now worked far into the night with the aid of kerosene lamps. The moment he reached home, he counted the notes again, bundled them up in tidy little batches, the lovely five-rupee and ten-rupee and the most handsome piece of paper – the green hundred-rupee note. He counted his cash over and over again, and locked it up in his safe and shut the door. It would be nearly midnight when he finished the counting and rose to have his dinner. His wife waited for him patiently and sat down for food after he had had his dinner. He hardly noticed that she waited for him: his mind was fully occupied with various calculations. He hardly spoke during the dinner. If she asked: 'Shall I serve?' he merely answered back without looking up: 'Don't bother me. Do what you please: only don't bother me.' He ate very little – just the quantity that a boy of ten would eat. It worried her secretly. She tried to improve it by putting more rice and stuff on his plate, but he just pushed it all aside, got up, and went back to work by the lamp, for further additions. She never knew when he went to bed, because even after she had finished all her work and gone to bed, she still saw him bent over his registers. She saw him with a drawn look and felt moved to say: 'Shouldn't you mind your health?'

'What's wrong with me? I'm all right. If you feel you need anything, go ahead and buy it and do what you like. Take any money you want. Only leave me alone.'

She felt it would be best to leave him alone. He seemed to have so little time left for rest that she concluded it would be better not to encroach upon it with her own comments. 'Balu has only taken after his father – his sullenness and silence,' she concluded. It became a household where perfect silence reigned. She was only secretly worried over his thin appearance and the dull weariness about his eyes. She often wanted to ask him: 'Why should you work so hard? Haven't we enough? And what are you aiming at?' But refrained from uttering it. She knew it would only annoy him. Perfect silence reigned in the house.

In the course of time, at the end of a day he brought home not one bag, but quite a number of them. It was no longer possible to count the currency notes individually. He could only count and check up the bundles – and even that took him beyond midnight. For now his fame had spread far and wide and it was not only the deposits of well-to-do people that arrived at his counter, but also those of smaller tradesmen and clerks and workers – who brought in their life's savings. 'If I have a hundred rupees, better hand it to Margayya, for he will give me twenty rupees per month for a lifetime. He is our saviour.' Margayya accepted any deposit that came to him, however small it might be. He explained: 'I like to make no difference between rich and poor in this business, which exists after all for serving society. We should not make distinctions.'

'I heard,' said Pal, 'they are thinking of conferring on you a title for your services.'

Margayya was really alarmed to hear it: 'What for?'

'For doing the greatest Public Service. If you only found the time to go round and see the number of people who are happy and secure through your help ... There is a talk in Government circles of giving you at least a Public Service medal.'

In his home the large safe was filled up, and its door had to be forced in, and then the cupboards, the benches and tables, the space under the cot, and the corners. His wife could hardly pass into the small room to pick up a *sari* or towel: there were currency bundles stacked up a foot high all over the floor. Presently Margayya ordered her to transfer trunks and effects to the room upstairs. She patiently obeyed him. Very soon this room had also to be requisitioned: more sacks emptied themselves into the house every day.

'They have carried in five sacks today,' said his brother in the next house.

'Do you really say all that is money?' asked his wife excitedly.

And then they heard Margayya going upstairs and a kerosene light burned far into the night. His brother's family would have given anything to know what Margayya was doing up there so late. His brother's wife strained her ears against a small crack in the wall and heard Margayya say to his wife; 'You will have to clear out of the upstairs room too.'

'Where shall I put my trunk?'

'Keep it in the store-room for the present.'

'Is it a safe place? I have some gold jewellery.'

'Oh, there are more valuable things for me to keep in the rooms. Don't make a fuss.'

'All right,' she said docilely.

'Only till I build a vault somewhere,' he said, feeling that he ought to be a little more mollifying. 'I must have a strong-room built somewhere: I wish I could find the time to attend to it.'

It was about seven in the evening. The lights had not been lit yet. Margayya's eyes pained him and he felt weak and weary. He had been skipping his morning food these days because he had lost the taste for it: he drank a cup of diluted buttermilk, kept himself on a few cups of coffee throughout the day and had his food only at night after closing his cash. 'With work ahead, I have no patience for food.' He went to his office almost as soon as he got up from bed: he washed and changed and rushed off, and returned home at indefinite hours. He said to his wife: 'Opening the office is in my hands, but the closing is in the hands of other people.' He had to cut out even his snuff – the one thing he liked and still enjoyed. Dr Subbu of the Reliance Medical Hall, one of his investors, advised Margayya to give up snuff. He consulted him with regard to a persistent pain at the back of his head, which kept him sleepless at night. The doctor examined him when he came over to collect his interest.

He said: 'Probably your snuff irritates the optic nerves. Why don't you stop snuff? Anyway, come over to my clinic for a thorough examination. We want to see you kept in the fittest condition possible, you know.' He laughed like many other doctors of his kind at his own joke.

Margayya gave up snuff with a resolute will, and felt better for it. It was not quite so easy to give it up, but he said to himself: 'If I do not sleep at night properly, I might mess up my calculations and then God knows what will happen.' He had mitigated his headache, but a sort of dizziness perpetually hung about his head.

Dr Subbu said when he visited him next: 'Why don't you take a holiday at Kodaikanal Hills? It'll do you good. Can't you afford a holiday?'

Margayya shook his head sadly: 'Not possible in this life. I'm tied up too much with various things – ' He figured himself as being in the centre of a tangled skein. 'If I move even slightly,' he began, but merely said: 'I cannot afford to move even slightly this way or that.'

His accountant, Sastri, was bundling up currency, stuffing it into mail sacks, and preparing statements. All his customers had left. Margayya felt ill. He sat in his room with his head resting on his arms. He called out: 'Sastri, hurry up with your stuff.'

'Yes, sir,' said Sastri from his corner. 'Your son is here to see you, sir.' The door opened and Balu entered and took his seat opposite to him.

'Balu, come in,' Margayya said, feeling happy at the sight of his son. 'It must be more than two weeks since I saw you. How is your family?'

'Baby has some stomach trouble and is crying.'

'Must be teething, I suppose. Take your mother there and show her the child. She will be able to do something: she understands these things better.'

'You never come to our house. I took Brinda to see mother today – '

'Oh! That's good ... otherwise ... I wish I could go over to your house ... Well, I suppose when the pressure here lessens, I suppose I shall ... I am virtually a prisoner here. Your cook is all right, I suppose.'

'Yes, but he is sometimes very impertinent. I want to send him away, but Brinda is too patient. She spoils him.'

'Don't quarrel with her. Leave these things to her. She is right.'

Now the common topics of conversation seemed to be over. There was a moment's silence. Balu sat moving a pebble on Margayya's desk as a paperweight.

'Why don't you buy a better paperweight and a good table and chair instead of squatting like this on the ground, father?' asked Balu.

He merely replied: 'I don't need all those luxuries.' He locked up his desk and made preparations to start out, calling: 'Sastri, is the statement ready?'

'Almost, sir,' replied Sastri, giving his customary reply.

'I want to talk to you seriously, father,' said Balu nervously.

Margayya looked at his face apprehensively before saying: 'I am not quite well today. Tomorrow I will come to your house.'

'No, I must speak to you now. You have got to listen to me,' said Balu authoritatively.

'Oh!' said Margayya. 'Wait a minute then.' He quickly passed out of the room, went over to Sastri and whispered: 'Don't bring in the cash bags yet,' returned to his seat, and settled down. He sat looking at his son fixedly, without saying anything.

The boy sat biting his nails for a moment. He did not know how to begin. His voice shook as he said: 'Father ... I ... I want more money.'

'Oh!' Margayya said, with a feeling of relief. 'I thought as much. Why do you hesitate? How much do you want?'

The boy felt encouraged by his kindness. He brightened up. Still he felt hesitant to answer the question. The father encouraged him: 'Come on, Balu, speak boldly. I always like a fellow who talks freely and openly and boldly. Have I refused you anything so far?'

The boy preferred to ignore this question: 'I ... I want to ask you something ... I want more money – '

'That is all right,' replied Margayya irritably. 'I've told you I'll give it you. How much do you want?'

'It depends. It depends on ... what you have ... I have no idea what you have. How can I say?'

'What do you mean? I do not understand you,' said Margayya, feeling puzzled. 'If you cannot talk clearly, you had better see me again some other time. I am not quite well,' he said sharply. He liked to have things clear cut as in interest calculations: vague indefinite talk annoyed him. He got up saying: 'I wish to go home and lie down. Come with me if you like.'

'No, can't talk to you there. Mother will be there. I don't like to talk before her.'

Margayya called out: 'Sastri, get the car ready,' and made a move towards the door. The boy sprang up and blocked the door, with arms spread out. 'You must let me talk to you and not go – '

Margayya did not like scenes in his office. He threw a look at Sastri, but he was engrossed in his accounts. Margayya went back to his seat calmly and sat down. He was completely bewildered. This was the first time he found his son so talkative – it was a revelation to him. The boy, though not docile, was always taciturn and quiet and never so aggressive. He asked for money, which was granted, and yet what happened? He had said, 'It depends on how much you have'! Margayya could hardly believe his ears. He sat in his seat and patiently waited. He felt weak and fatigued. He wanted so much to lie down.

Margayya struck a match and lit the dim kerosene lamp. He resigned himself to whatever might be coming. The boy said, 'I want to speak to you about something very serious.'

371

Margayya suppressed the annoyance that was coming over him. He felt afraid to be angry. Probably his son had taken to drinking: he sniffed the air to find if it was confirmed by his breath. He found himself clutching the ruler on his table – but relaxed his hold at the thought, 'After all it's Balu – ' It seemed to be an unworthy move to make. He let go his hold on the ruler and waited. The boy still would not open his lips. Margayya felt exasperated. He pulled out his watch and said: 'It's about seven o'clock. If you do not speak before the clock hand points to seven-five, I will go. I will knock you down and walk out if necessary.' He felt relieved after delivering this threat. He felt his authority re-established: 'The boy cannot have it all his own way,' he told himself. He placed the watch on his desk dramatically, turning it towards Balu.

Balu fidgeted for a moment with his eyes fixed on the clock and then said: 'I want a share of property – my share of property.'

'What property?' asked Margayya.

'Well, I mean, my share of property – our ancestral property.'

'H'm – I see. Why? Why do you want it?'

'Because I have attained my majority. You know it as well as I do. I am nineteen and entitled to my own share of property.'

'What property?' asked Margayya.

'Ancestral property,' the boy answered.

At this Margayya put his hand into his pocket, brought out a half-rupee coin, placed it on the table, pushed it over, and said: 'There it is, take it – that's exactly half of what your grandfather left in cash: take it and give me a receipt.'

The boy picked it up and looked at it: 'Is this all the movable and immovable property?'

'What movable and immovable property ... movable?' Margayya lost his temper on hearing it, lost his head completely: 'Movable! Immovable! You want me to give you a list, is that it? Here it is: this is, this is what it was, listen,' and he described in coarse terms the movable and immovable properties possessed by his worthy ancestors: he was filled with chagrin at the memory of the travails he had gone through with his brother before the partition of their single house, the trip to the courts, the hours of waiting on the old lawyer's bench, the Court Commission visiting their house and so on and so forth. He remembered how miserable he had felt, wondering where his wife was going to cook the next meal and where they were to put the youngster down to sleep, while the legal proceedings were going on and they hung on to his brother's house uncertainly. Those miseries could not be understood by the boy even if explained to him. He felt sorry. He said softly: 'Boy, let us go home now and discuss it. It's all right. This is not the right time to talk of all those things.'

'No,' said the boy. 'Don't try to dodge me.'

'Where did you pick up all this language?'

'I'm old enough to know the world,' retorted the boy. 'If you don't give me an immediate account, I will go to court.'

'Very well – go ahead, I have nothing more to say.' Margayya got up and tried to move out. The boy once again sprang up, spread out his arms and blocked the door. Margayya slapped his face, crying: 'Get out of the way, you swine.' The boy burst into tears, and sobbed. Margayya looked at his face and was moved. There were tears in his eyes too. He put his arm around the boy and said: 'You are being misled by someone, probably a lawyer, who wants an occupation. Don't listen to such people. Here I am, your father, ready to do anything for you: only ask what you want.'

'I want a share of your property – '

'Idiot! What obstinacy is this! What property is there?'

'I know how much you have made. I am entitled to half of it.'

'How do you make that out?'

'Because it is multiplied out of grandfather's property and I am entitled to half by right.'

'I have given you a house to live in, I give you three hundred rupees a month for your expenditure. Well, if you want, ask for some more, I will probably increase it to four hundred.'

The boy shook his head. 'I want nothing of it. I want my share.'

'And why?' asked Margayya.

'I want to buy – ' He stopped short, changed his mind and merely said: 'I want it for various things.'

Margayya said in a mollifying manner: 'All that I have is yours, my boy. Everything that I have will come to you: who else is there? To whom can I pass these on after my time?'

'After your time! When is that?'

'Are you asking when I am going to die?'

The boy looked abashed: 'I am not saying that, but I cannot wait. I want my share urgently.'

'Pray, what is the urgency, may I ask?' said Margayya cynically. 'Do you think that I ought to drink poison and clear the way for your enjoyment?' The boy did not know how to answer. Margayya could no longer keep standing. He pushed the boy aside and walked out. He told the accountant: 'Put the bags and the statement into the car.' He got into the car and drove off, leaving his son standing on the steps of the bank.

Margayya felt restless. After closing his accounts, putting away the cash, and bolting down his food, he told his wife: 'I am going out for a moment. Close the door.'

'At this hour!' she asked, but he had gone. She turned in with resignation.

His driver had locked the car and gone home. Outside, the stars were sparkling in the sky, and the streets were deserted and silent. Margayya had to walk the entire way – it was some months since he had walked – and he felt exhilarated by the exercise today. 'I have perhaps been too severe,' he told himself. 'I must investigate what his troubles are more sympathetically. Probably he is genuinely hard up. Perhaps I might take him into business and see that he has a better income and standing.' He wondered if the boy would be surprised to see him there at that hour. 'This is the only time I can spare,' he told himself. 'If the morning rush starts ... He must also be fairly annoyed that I have not been seeing the grandson. Young parents think the world exists in order to take an interest in a newborn child,' he reflected philosophically. 'When Balu was born, we cut off relations who didn't come and stand over the crib and say admiring things about him. All the same, he had no business to upset me – I have not been feeling well. He should have had more sense. Share of the property! The damned fool.' The recollection of this made him so angry that he stopped and almost turned to go back home. 'What right has that fool to make me walk to him at this hour? It is sheer nonsense, why should I go there?' he asked himself

374

suddenly. 'Share of the property! Accursed fool! What share – I gave him the right answer.' He chuckled at the memory of his vulgar repartee. 'Anyway, there is no other time when I can meet him and speak to him – might as well get through it and see what ails him. I will make him a proposition to join me in business. That is the thing to do. It is ages since I saw Brinda – nice girl – '

He came to Lawley Road. It was about one o'clock. He stood before number 17, at Fourth Cross Road, a small villa with a bluebell creeper over the gatepost and a mesh-covered veranda. He stood outside and admired the house: 'Got this practically for a song – less than two thousand rupees. If that fool of a fellow could not pay the interest even after two years, the fault is not mine if it falls in my lap – the fruit can only fall on the palm of him who holds up his hands for it.' As he opened the little wooden gate and entered, he saw no light in the house: 'Probably the boy has slept,' he reflected. He was hesitating whether to turn back and go. But the gate had creaked; a veranda light was now switched on and the bolt of the front door was being drawn back.

'Who is there?' asked Brinda's voice from inside.

Margayya called out, 'Brinda,' to disclose himself. Brinda had just risen from bed; she looked sleepy and rather tired. She was a very elegant girl. Looking at her Margayya thought, 'What a fortunate thing to have secured this daughter-in-law. If those fool astrologers had their way!' He climbed the steps.

'You have come walking at this hour,' his daughter-in-law asked; her voice was soft and musical.

Margayya said: 'I couldn't find any other time. How is the baby?' He walked in and stood looking at the little fellow sleeping on his mother's bed. He gently touched his cheek.

The girl demurely said: 'He wouldn't sleep and gets up at the slightest sound.'

'Why should you not let him stay awake?' asked Margayya.

'He gives us no peace. He wants to be carried about all the time,' she answered. She was showing him the utmost respect as an elder.

He admired her for it – her tone of courtesy, her soft movement and elegance. 'God bless her!' he told himself. 'Yes, Balu used to be troublesome too when he was a baby. Where is Balu?' he asked, noticing the vacant bed beside hers.

She hesitated ever so slightly before answering briefly: 'He has not yet come home.' Her face became serious when she said that.

'Where has he gone?' Margayya asked.

She still hesitated. She merely bit her lips. Margayya sensed something was wrong. He persisted, and she merely replied: 'He has gone to a cinema,' with an effort.

'A cinema! So late as this! How can he leave you and the child alone and go away like this?' There was so much genuine sympathy in his voice that the girl was affected by it and burst into tears. Margayya was totally at a loss to know what to do now. This was a new situation for him, and he did not know what to say. He said to her: 'Why don't you sit down? Why do you keep standing?'

She wouldn't sit down out of respect for her father-in-law. But he was able to persuade her. She rallied and said: 'I wanted to come and see you. Every day this happens: he comes home every day at two o'clock. If I ask him, he ... he ... I'm afraid of him.'

And then it came out bit by bit. Dr Pal was his constant companion. They gathered in a house and played cards – it was the house of a man who called himself a theatrical agent. She had learnt from their servant that there were a lot of girls also in the building. Pal had something or other to do with these people, and picked Balu up in his car. They sat there continuously playing cards till midnight. They chewed tobacco and betel leaves, some-times they drank also, and men and women were very free, and all of them dropped down wherever they sat and slept and became sick when they drank too much – it was a revolting description that she gave: all learnt from the servant who worked in the house, the uncle of the girl who looked after the baby. Brinda also said that Balu seemed to be thinking of becoming a partner in their business. In fact he always explained to his wife that it was business that kept him out late. 'If I speak ... he threatens to drive me out. It's that Pal ... Can't you do something to keep him away?'

'How long has this been going on?'

'For months – '

'Why didn't you tell us?'

'I was afraid. Even now, please don't tell him that I have said anything.'

Margayya brooded over it darkly. He now seemed to understand why his son was asking for a partition. 'Dr Pal! Dr Pal! What shall I do with him?' he reflected. He was torn between caution and an impossible rage. God knew where it would lead if he alienated Pal's sympathies: the fellow might do anything. He decided, within a fraction of a moment, that the thing to do was to separate his son from Pal without making a fuss about it, and then deal with his son separately. He would have to tempt Pal to go out of town – probably on the pretext of a contact outside; but if he went there and ... Margayya found he was in terror of him. The only element that kept people from being terrified of each other was trust – the moment it was lost, people became nightmares to each other; this seemed to be truly his problem, that he could neither keep the fellow in sight nor let him go out of sight. But anyway he had better move with the utmost caution. The daughter-in-law patiently sat in a chair and watched his face. He told her with a great deal of tenderness: 'You go in and sleep, my child. I will go home, and I will see about this tomorrow. Don't worry about anything. I will set your husband right. You lock the door now; look after the baby. Tell me if you need anything. Don't be afraid. I will send your mother-in-law to see you tomorrow morning.' He got up and left. The girl bolted the veranda door and put out the light.

As he was closing the wicket gate behind him, Dr Pal's Baby Austin drew up. The moment the rattling of its engine was heard the veranda light was switched on again and the bolt was drawn with a pat. At the same moment, Balu got down from the car. He leaned his elbow on the door and whispered something to Dr Pal, at which Dr Pal burst into a laugh and giggling sounds emanated from the back seat of the car. They did not notice Margayya's presence. Margayya could not restrain himself any longer. He was conscious of a desperation that impelled him on. All his caution and discretion was swept aside. He dashed to the other door of the car near the driving seat, thrust his arm in, got Pal by the scruff of his coat and dragged him out as Balu on the other side was saying: 'Good-night!' Nobody was prepared for it: and Dr Pal staggered out. The moment he was out of the car, Margayya took off one of his sandals and hit him with it; he kept hitting out with such tremendous power and frequency that Pal could hardly protect himself. He was blinded by pain, and blood oozed from the cuts on his face. The girls within the car screamed: Balu came over and demanded: 'What has come over you, father?'

Margayya turned on him, put his fingers around his neck and gave him a push towards the gate with: 'Get out of my way, you little idiot!' Balu staggered and hit his head on the gatepost.

His wife came down the veranda steps with the cry: 'Oh, are you hurt? What has happened?'

He rushed towards her asking: 'When did this father of mine come here?' Meanwhile the child had been awakened by the hubbub and started howling and Brinda turned and ran back into the house. Balu followed her blindly in.

Meanwhile, the two girls in the back seat of the car cried out: 'Help! Help!'

Margayya put his head in and ordered: 'Shut up, you whores!' He felt overpowered by the scent of powder filling the inside of the car. 'Who are you?' he demanded. They at once became silent, and his tone became more menacing: 'Who are you?' he thundered. His voice woke up a couple of street dogs and they started barking: which again woke up Balu's child so that it shouted more than ever.

The girls said: 'We belong to ... the theatre – '

'The theatre! Why don't you say what you really are! If you are seen again anywhere – '

The rest they could not hear, because Dr Pal wriggled himself free, and suddenly dashed into the car, started it, and was off. He looked back and remarked: 'You miserable miser, who cannot share your goods with your own son – all right – '

The red rear light of the car receded and vanished around a bend. Margayya hesitated on the road for a moment to decide whether he should follow his son into the house. But he saw his son bolt the veranda door, and put out the light. 'Good! Good! It is a good sign. He is a good son that trembles and runs away from his father,' he said to himself, and turned homeward.

Later in life Margayya often speculated what would have become of him if he had started back home after speaking to his daughter-in-law a little earlier and missed Dr Pal's Austin that night, or if he had remained in the shadows and had allowed Pal to go off after dropping Balu, whom he might probably have tackled with more circumspection and diplomacy: he might even have shared his property with him as he demanded: that would have saved him at least the rest of it – and prevented the doctor from doing what he did.

Dr Pal went straight to a police station and recorded an immediate complaint of assault. The two actresses and Balu were his witnesses. Next morning he went round with plaster on his face to his various customers and business men. His first visit was to the blanket merchant. He took Balu along with him in the car. The blanket merchant was the first to ask: 'What has happened to your face, Doctor?'

The doctor looked sad and said: 'I am an academic man, and I should not have associated with business men – '

'Can't you tell me what happened?' the blanket merchant persisted.

The doctor just shook his head and said: 'No, I can't – better leave things alone. It was my mistake to have associated with all sorts of folks, and I ought to blame only myself ... I'm paying for it.'

'Don't say so, sir. We have the greatest respect for you – '

'Business people have money, and they can help me to set up my Psychological Clinic – that was my chief interest: that would have been of the greatest benefit to them: nowadays psychological wear and tear has the highest incidence among business men: theirs is a life of the utmost strain. I thought I might be of some help to the business community more than to anyone else – and what is the result?'

'No, sir, you must not speak like that. We have the greatest regard for you. But business life is becoming difficult with so many controls and permit forms to be filled up for all sorts of things. You have no idea how many obstacles a business man has to face before he can get through anything in the Government – '

After this the doctor drew his attention again to the plaster over his cheeks. The merchant asked: 'You have not yet told me where you got it?'

Dr Pal lowered his voice to a whisper and said: 'You will not believe me! Margayya assaulted me last night near his son's house.'

'What! Why?'

'How can I say? He is somewhat queer these days. His son went up to him with some request and was slapped in the face. Later, I had to see him. Things are probably not going smoothly there.'

'Ah!' exclaimed the merchant.

He was the first to meet Margayya at his house that morning. 'I want to take back my deposit. There is a marriage proposal likely to shape out – ' He grinned awkwardly, nervously, and held out the receipt issued by Margayya.

'My accountant has all the figures,' began Margayya. The blanket merchant cringed: 'It's urgent. I've to find immediate cash.'

'You have already drawn interest on it?'

'Yes ... yes ... But I want the principal.'

'Oh, yes, certainly,' said Margayya, and went into the small room and came out with a bundle of currency.

'You are a clever rogue! You have earned so much interest and are now getting your capital! Very clever, very clever,' Margayya said light-heartedly, which pleased the blanket merchant tremendously as he counted the cash and went out. This was the starting-point. Margayya could not leave for his office. One after another they came with their receipts. Margayya returned their cash without a murmur. The street became congested with people converging on his house; people hung about his steps and windows. He bolted the front door and dealt with them through the window.

Margayya's wife looked panic-stricken: 'What has happened? Why so many people?'

'They are wanting their money back, that's all.'

'What are you going to do?'

'Well, give it back, that's all.'

'You have not eaten this whole day.'

'I have no taste for food.' He felt very weak and still could not stomach the thought of food. His eyes smarted with scrutinizing so many receipts. His wrist pained him with the counting of notes. He wished he could get his accountant by his side. He saw him through the window, struggling to approach the house in the midst of the crowd. But he could not come nearer. Some persons recognized the accountant, and turned upon him. Margayya saw them manhandling the old man.

'I knew nothing about it. I swear. I still know nothing about it,' he was crying.

'My life's savings gone! I am a beggar today!' one of them shouted into the ears of the old man.

They were pulling him here and there. His spectacles were broken and his turban torn. A policeman came into the crowd and took away the old man.

By about four o'clock all the cash in the house was gone. All the mail sacks lay about empty and slack; yet peeping through the window, Margayya saw seas and seas of human heads stretching to the horizon, human faces at their most terrifying. The babble of the crowd was deafening. Luckily for him the front door of the house was at least a century old and made of thick timber, and could stand the battering by a hundred hands. People jammed the passage and windows and shouted menacingly. There seemed to be only one theme for all the cries: 'My money! My money gone! All my savings gone – '

Margayya could sit up no longer. He just flung himself down on the floor beside the window. No air could come in. There were terrifying faces all around and the babble of voices; and over it all came the cry of an ice-cream pedlar: 'Ice cream! Ice cream for thirst!' as his bell tinkled.

Margayya's wife was scared by the siege and at the condition of her husband. She bent over him and asked: 'What shall I do? Oh, what shall I do?'

'Call my brother,' said Margayya.

She ran to the backyard. Very soon Margayya's elder brother climbed the lavatory wall and the parapet of the well, jumped into the backyard and was in a minute by his side.

'Brother, what is this? What has come over you?'

'I'm tired ... Please send for the police ... Hurry up, otherwise they will mob this house: they will kill us, they will set it on fire, they will – '

'Do you still owe all of them money?'

'To all of them and many more unseen; more will come tomorrow. More and more of them ... Get me the police to save us now and bring a lawyer. I am filing insolvency at once.'

'Insolvency! Think of your family reputation!'

'No other way out, none whatever.'

The brother, ever a man for a crisis, stood thinking. The hubbub outside was increasing every moment.

'The flood is outside,' Margayya said. 'It will wipe us out. Please, please run – ' He felt too weak with his effort and lay still with his eyes closed.

His brother ran to his sister-in-law standing at the door sobbing. 'Quick, give him something – '

'There is no milk in the house. The milkman could not come in. There is nothing in the house. We have been shut up here since the morning.'

'Oh, is that so?' He rushed away, and returned soon carrying a vessel full of coffee, and something to eat. He seemed to be enjoying the situation. He said excitedly: 'Now, try and give him something. I tried to see if there was a regular meal next door – but it was not available: your sister-in-law will send you food presently. She has just started cooking.' He bustled round spreading his utensils about. 'Give him something at once. I will go and get the police to guard us. I will also get a lawyer. I will do everything to exempt this house at least from the schedule. This is inalienable property. They cannot attach this.' His talk was full of technicalities. He rushed off to the backyard and then on to his task.

The tide rolled back in about three or four months. Days of attending courts, lawyers, inventories and so on and so forth. Margayya felt that he had lost all right to personal life.

He relaxed completely. He lay on a mat with his eyes closed, his wife in the kitchen. A *jutka* stopped outside, and in marched his son followed by his wife, carrying the infant on her arm. The *jutka*-man brought in a couple of trunks and beds and placed them in the hall. Margayya clutched the baby to his bosom. His daughter-in-law went into the kitchen. Balu stood about uncertainly.

Margayya did not speak to him for a long time. The boy stood in the passage undecided what he should do, his shirt unbuttoned at the throat. A feeling of pity overcame Margayya. The boy had lost some of the look of confidence that he wore before – the radiance that shone on his face when there was money in the background. Money was like a gem which radiated subdued light all round. The boy looked just dull and puzzled. Margayya kept looking at him so long that he felt he had to explain: so he just said: 'I have come away – they have attached the house.'

'With the furniture and all the other things?' Margayya asked. 'I was expecting it – '

'It was difficult to come out even with our clothes and Brinda's jewellery. They demanded a list.'

'I was expecting it. Come here, Balu.'

Balu approached him and sat beside him. Margayya put his arm round him: 'You see that box there. I have managed to get it out again.' He pointed to a corner where his old knobby trunk was kept. 'Its contents are intact as I left them years ago – a pen and an ink-bottle. You asked for my property. There it is, take it: have an early meal tomorrow and go to the banyan tree in front of the Co-operative Bank. I hope the tree is still there. Go there, that is all I can say: and anything may happen thereafter. Well, what do you say? I am showing you a way. Will you follow it?'

The boy stood ruminating. He was looking crushed: 'How can I go and sit there? What will people think?'

'Very well then, if you are not going, I am going on with it, as soon as I am able to leave this bed,' said Margayya. 'Now get the youngster here. I will play with him. Life has been too dull without him in this house.'

# WAITING FOR THE
# MAHATMA

# PART ONE

His mother, who died delivering him, and his father, who was killed in Mesopotamia, might have been figures in a legend as far as Sriram was concerned. He had, however, concrete evidence of his mother in a framed photograph which for years hung too high on the wall for him to see; when he grew tall enough to study the dim picture, he didn't feel pleased with her appearance; he wished she looked like that portrait of a European queen with apple cheeks and wavy coiffure hanging in the little shop opposite his house, where he often went to buy peppermints with the daily money given him by his granny. Of his father, at least, there were recurring reminders. On the first of every month the postman brought a brown, oblong envelope, addressed to his granny. Invariably Granny wept when it came to her hand, and his childish mind wondered what it could contain to sting the tears out of her eyes. Only years later he understood that his granny had been receiving a military pension meant for him. When the envelope came she invariably remarked: 'I don't have to spend your pension in order to maintain you. God has left us enough to live on.' Then she took it to the fourth house in their row, which was known as the 'Fund Office' (what the name meant, he never understood) and came back to say: 'There is nothing so fleeting as untethered cash. You can do what you like with it when you are old enough.'

That portrait in the opposite shop fascinated his adolescent mind. The shopman was known as Kanni, a parched, cantankerous, formidable man, who sat on his haunches all day briskly handing out goods to his customers. Until eleven at night, when he closed the shop, his hollow voice could be heard haranguing someone, or arguing, or cowing his credit-demanding clientele: 'What do you think I am! How dare you come again without cash? You think you can do me in? You are mistaken. I can swallow ten of you at the same time, remember.' The only softening influence in this shop of cigars, *beedis*, explosive aerated drinks, and hard words was the portrait of the lady with apple cheeks, curls falling down the brim of her coronet, and large, dark eyes. 'Those eyes look at me,' Sriram often thought. For the pleasure of returning the look, he went again and again, to buy something or other at the shop.

'Whose is that picture?' he asked once, pausing between sips of a coloured drink.

'How should I know?' Kanni said. 'It's probably some queen, probably Queen Victoria,' although he might with equal justification have claimed her to be Maria Theresa or Ann Boleyn.

'What did you pay for it?'

'Why do you want to know all that?' said Kanni, mildly irritated. If it had been anyone else, he would have shouted, 'If you have finished your business, be gone. Don't stand there and ask a dozen questions.'

But Sriram occupied a unique position. He was a good customer, paid down a lot of cash every day, and deserved respect for his bank balance. He asked, 'Where did you get the picture?'

Kanni was in a jovial mood and answered, 'You know that man, the Revenue Inspector in Pillaiah Street. He owed me a lot of money. I had waited long enough, so one day I walked in and brought away this picture hanging in his room. Something at least for my dues.'

'If there is any chance,' said Sriram with timid hesitation, 'of your giving it away, tell me its price.'

'Oh, oh!' said Kanni, laughing. He was in a fine mood. 'I know you can buy up the queen herself, master *zamindar*. But I won't part with it. It has brought me luck. Ever since I hung the picture there, my business has multiplied tenfold.'

One evening his grandmother asked: 'Do you know what star it will be tomorrow?'

'No. How should I?' he asked, comfortably reclining on the

cold cement window-sill, and watching the street. He had sat there, morning to night, ever since he could remember. When he was a year old his grandmother put him down there and showed him the traffic passing outside; bullock-carts, horse-carriages, and the first few motor-cars of the age, honking away and rattling down the road. He would not be fed unless he was allowed to watch what went on in the street. She held a spoonful of rice and curd to his lips and exclaimed: 'Oh, see that great motor-car. Shall our little Ram travel in it?' And when he blinked at the mention of his name and opened his mouth, she thrust in the rice. This window became such a habit with him that when he grew up he sought no other diversion except to sit there, sometimes with a book, and watch the street. His grand-mother often reproached him for it. She asked: 'Why don't you go and mix with others of your age?'

'I am quite happy where I am,' he answered briefly.

'If you left that seat, you would have many things to see and learn,' said the old lady sharply. 'Do you know at your age your father could read the almanac upside down, and could say at a moment's notice what star was reigning over which particular day?'

'He was probably a very wise man,' ventured Sriram.

'He *was* very wise. Don't say "probably",' corrected his grand-mother. 'And your grandfather, you know how clever he was! They say that the grandfather's reincarnation is in his grandson. You have the same shaped nose as he had and the same eye-brows. His fingers were also long just like yours. But there it stops. I very much wish you had not inherited any of it, but only his brain.'

'I wish you had kept a portrait of him for me to see, Granny,' Sriram said. 'Then I could have worshipped it and become just as clever as he.'

The old lady was pleased with this, and said: 'I'll teach you how you could improve yourself.' Dragging him by the hand to the little circle of light under the hall lamp, she took the brown paper-covered almanac from under a tile of their sloping roof. Then she sat down on the floor, clamoured for her glasses till they were fetched, and forced Sriram to open the almanac and go through it to a particular page. It was full of minute, bewildering symbols in intricate columns. She pushed his face close to the page.

'What is it you are trying to do?' he pleaded pathetically.

She put her finger on a letter and asked: 'What is this?'

'*Sa* ...' he read.

'It means *Sadhaya*. That's your star.' She drew her finger along the line and pointed at the morrow's date. 'Tomorrow is this date, which means it's your birth star. It's going to be your twentieth birthday, although you behave as if you are half that. I am going to celebrate it. Would you like to invite any of your friends?'

'No, never,' said Sriram positively.

So all alone next day he celebrated his twentieth birthday. His guest as well as hostess was his grandmother. No one outside could have guessed what an important occasion was being celebrated in that house in Kabir Street numbered '14'. The house was over two hundred years old and looked it. It was the last house in the street, or 'the first house' as his great-grandfather used to say at the time he built it. From here one saw the backs of market buildings and heard night and day the babble of the big crowd moving on the market road. Next door to Sriram's house was a small printing press which groaned away all day and next to it another two-hundred-year-old house in which six noisy families lived, and beyond that was the Fund Office, where Granny kept her grandson's money. A crooked street ran in front of these houses; their closeness to the market and to a Higher Elementary Town School, the Local Fund Dispensary, and above all to the half-dozen benches around the market fountain, was said to give these houses in Kabir Street a unique value.

The houses were all alike – a large single roof sloping down to the slender rosewood pillars with carvings and brass decorations on them, and a pyol, an open brick platform under the windows, on which the household slept in summer. The walls were two feet thick, the doors were made of century-old teak planks with bronze knobs, and the tiles were of burnt mud which had weathered the storms and rains of centuries. All these houses were alike; you could see end to end the slender pillars and tiles sloping down as if all of them belonged to a single house. Many changes had occurred since they were built two centuries ago. Many of them had changed hands, the original owners having been lost in the toils of litigation; some were rented out to tradesmen, such as the Sun Press, the Butter Factory, or the Fund Office, while their owners retired to villages or built themselves modern villas in Lawley Extension. But there were still one or two houses which maintained a continuity, a link with the past. Number 14 was such a one. There the family lineage began centuries ago and continued still, though reduced to just two members – Sriram and his grandmother.

Granny had somewhere secured a yard-long sugar cane for the celebration, although it was not the season. She said: 'No birthday is truly celebrated unless and until a sugar cane is seen in the house. It's auspicious.' She strung mango leaves across the doorway, and decorated the threshold with coloured rice-powder. A neighbour passing down the road stopped to ask: 'What's the celebration? Shall we blow out the oven fires in our houses and come for the feast in yours?'

'Yes, by all means. Most welcome,' said the old lady courteously, and added, as if to neutralize the invitation, 'You are always welcome.' She felt sorry at not being able to call in the neighbours, but that recluse grandson of hers had forbidden her to invite anyone. Left to herself she would have engaged pipes and drums and processions, for this particular birthday was a thing she had been planning all along, this twentieth birthday when she would hand over the savings passbook to her grandson and relinquish the trust.

It was an adventure accompanying Granny to the Fund Office, four doors off. She seemed to shrink under an open sky – she who dominated the landscape under the roof of Number 14 lost her stature completely in the open. Sriram couldn't help remarking, 'You look like a baby, Granny.' Granny half-closed her eyes in the glare and whispered, 'Hush! Don't talk aloud, others may hear.'

'Hear what?'

'Whatever it may be. What happens behind one's door must be known only to the folk concerned. Others had better shut up.'

As if confirming her worst suspicion, Kanni cried breezily from his shop: 'Oho, grandmother and her pet on an outing! A fine sight! The young gentleman is shooting up, madam!'

Sriram felt proud of this compliment; he was seized with a feeling of towering height, and he pursed his lips in a determined manner. He gripped in his right hand the brown calico-bound passbook presented to him with a somewhat dramatic gesture by his grandmother a moment ago.

'Oh, the young *subedhar* is going to the right school with the right book,' Kanni remarked. 'He must live to be as great as his father and grandfather put together.'

Granny muttered, quickening her steps, 'Don't stand and talk to that man; he will plague us with his remarks; that's why I never wanted your grandfather to sell that site opposite, but he was an obstinate man, such an obstinate man! He was also fond of this Kanni, who was then a young fellow.'

'Did Grandfather also buy plantains?'

'Not only plantains,' she muttered, with a shudder, recollecting his habit of buying cheroots in Kanni's shop. She had thought it degrading for any person to be seen smoking a cheroot. 'Like a baby sucking a candy stick!' she was wont to remark, disturbing the even tenor of their married life. She had always blamed Kanni for encouraging her husband to smoke and never got over a slight grudge on that account.

Before reaching the Fund Office they had interruptions from other neighbours who peeped out of their doorways and demanded to be told what extraordinary thing made the old lady go out in the company of her grandson. They could understand her going out all alone on the first of the month in the direction of the Fund Office – that was understandable. But what made the lady go out in the company of the young fellow, who was – an unusual sight – holding on to a bank book?

'What!' cried a lady who was a privileged friend of Granny's, 'does it mean that this urchin is going to have an independent account?'

'He is no longer an urchin,' cried the old woman. 'He's old enough to take charge of his own affairs. How long should I look after him! I'm not immortal. Each responsibility should be shaken off as and when occasion arises to push off each responsibility.' This was a somewhat involved sentiment expressed in a round-about manner, but her friend seemed to understand it at once, and cried, coming down the steps of her house, 'How wisely you speak! The girls of these days should learn from you how to conduct themselves,' which pleased Granny so much that she stopped to whisper in her ear: 'I was only a trustee of his money. From today he will take care of his own.'

'Wisely done, wisely done,' the other cried and asked, 'How much in all?'

'That you will never know,' said Granny and walked off. Sriram, who had gone ahead, asked: 'How is it, Granny, you stop and talk to everyone! What were you telling her?'

'Nothing,' she replied. 'You follow the same rule and you will be a happier man. Your grandfather ruined himself by talking. Anything that happened to him, good or bad, was bound to be known to everyone in the town within ten minutes; otherwise his soul felt restless.'

'Why should anything be concealed from anyone?' asked the boy.

'Because it's better so, that's all,' said the old lady.

All these interruptions on the way delayed her arrival at the bank. The clock struck four as she showed her face at the counter.

'Must you be on the last second, madam?' the manager asked. 'Is there any reason why you could not come a little earlier?'

'No, none,' she said, 'except that I'm not a young creature who can frisk along.' The manager, used to her ways, got down from his high seat, opened a side door, and without a word, let her in.

Sriram was being initiated into the mysteries of banking. The bank manager opened the last page of his passbook and said:

'What figure do you see here?' Sriram wondered for a moment if he was testing him in arithmetic, a terrible memory of his early schooldays. He became wary and ventured to say: 'Thirty-eight thousand, five hundred rupees, seven annas, and six pies.'

'Quite right!' cried Granny. She appeared surprised at the intelligence he exhibited.

Sriram asked petulantly, 'What did you take me for, Granny? Did you think I would not be good enough even for this?'

'Yes,' she said quietly. 'How should I think otherwise, considering how well you have fared in your studies!'

The manager, a suave and peace-loving man, steered them out of these dangerous zones by changing the subject: 'You see, this is your savings deposit. You may draw two hundred and fifty rupees a week, not more than that. Here is the withdrawal form. See that you don't lose it, and that nobody gets at it.'

'Why? Would it be possible for anyone else to get at my money with that form?'

'Probably not, but it's our duty to take all possible precautions in money matters,' said the manager.

Granny for some reason felt upset at Sriram's questions. 'Why do you ask so many things? If the manager says, "Do this," or "Do that," it's your duty to obey, that is all.'

'I always like to know what I am doing,' said Sriram, and added, 'There's nothing wrong in that.'

Granny turned to the manager and said with pride, 'You see the present generation! They are not like us. How many years have you been seeing me here? Have you ever heard me asking why or how and why not at any time?'

The manager made indistinct noises, not wishing to displease either his old customer or the new one. He placed a letter before the old lady, tapped the bottom of the page with his finger, and said, 'May I have your signature here? It's the new authorization, and you won't be bothered to come here often as before.'

'After twenty years, relief!' Granny cried. She had the triumphant expression of one who had run hard and reached the winning post. Sriram did not fully realize what it all meant, but took it quite casually. He simply said, 'If I had been you I wouldn't have taken all this trouble to accumulate the money.'

'You are not me, and that's just as well. Don't say such things before this man who has watched and guarded your property all these years!'

Sriram wanted to test how far the magic toy put into his hands would work. He seized the penholder, stabbed it into the ink-well, wrote off a withdrawal for two hundred and fifty rupees, tore off the page and pushed it before the manager with an air of challenge. 'Let us see if I am really the owner of this money!'

The manager was taken aback by the speed of his activity. He smiled and said: 'But my dear fellow, you know we close at four, and cash closes at two every day. If you want cash, you must be here before two on any working day. Change the date, and you can come and collect it the first thing tomorrow. Are you sure that you want all that sum urgently for the first draw?'

'Yes, I am positive,' said Sriram. 'I would have taken more if you had permitted more than two hundred and fifty at a time.'

'May I know why you need all this amount?' asked Granny.

'Is it or is it not my money?' asked Sriram.

'It is and it is not,' said Granny in a mystifying manner. 'Remember, I don't have to ask you what you do with your own funds. It's your own business. You are old enough to know what you do. I don't have to bother myself at all about it. It's purely your own business. But I want to ask you – just to know things, that is all – why you want two hundred and fifty rupees now. It's your business, I know, but remember one thing. One is always better off with money unspent. It's always safer to have one's bank balance undamaged.'

'Quite right, quite right,' echoed the bank manager. 'Great words of wisdom. I tell you, young man, come tomorrow morning,' he said, picking up the form.

Granny cried: 'Give it here,' and, snatching the paper from his hand, said, 'Correct it to fifty. You need only fifty rupees now and not two hundred and fifty. I'd have torn up this, but for the fact that it is your first withdrawal form and I don't want to commit any inauspicious act.'

'Ah! That's a good idea,' said the manager. 'It's better if you carry less cash about you nowadays with pick-pockets about.'

He dipped the pen in the ink and passed it to Sriram: 'Write your signature in full on all the corrections.'

Sriram obeyed, muttering, 'See! This is just what I suspected! I'm supposed to be the master of this money, but I cannot draw what I want! A nice situation!'

The manager took the form back and said: 'Come at ten-thirty tomorrow morning for your cash.'

'I hope you won't expect me to come again with my grand-mother!' Sriram said with heavy cynicism.

Next day Sriram stood at Kanni's shop and ordered coloured drinks and plantains. 'How much?' he asked after he was satisfied.

'Four annas,' said Kanni.

Sriram drew from his pocket several rolls of notes, and pulled one out for Kanni. It was a veritable display of wealth. Kanni was duly impressed. He immediately became deferential.

'Have you examined your pockets to see if there may not be some small change lying somewhere there?'

'If I had small change, would I be holding this out to you?' asked Sriram grandly.

'All right, all right.'

Kanni received the amount and transferred it immediately to his cash chest. Sriram waited for change. Kanni attended to other customers.

Sriram said, 'Where is my change?'

Kanni said: 'Please wait. I have something to tell you. You see – '

An itinerant tea-vendor just then came up with his stove and kettle to ask for a packet of cigarettes. And then there were four other customers. The place was crowded and Kanni's customers had to stand on the road below his platform and hold out their hands like supplicants. All the while Sriram stood gazing on the portrait of the rosy-cheeked queen who stared out at the world through the plantain bunches suspended from the ceiling. School children came in and clamoured for peppermints in bottles. Kanni served everyone like a machine.

When everybody had gone Sriram asked, 'How long do you want me to wait for my change?'

'Don't be angry, master,' Kanni said. He pulled out a long notebook, blew the dust off its cover, turned an ancient page, and pointed at a figure and asked, 'Do you see this?'

'Yes,' said Sriram, wondering why everybody was asking him to read figures these days. He read out: 'Nine rupees, twelve annas.'

'It's a debt from your grandfather which is several years old. I'm sure he'd have paid it if he had lived – but one doesn't know when death comes: I used to get him special cheroots from Singapore, you know.'

'Why didn't you ask Granny?'

'Granny! Not I. He wouldn't have liked it at all. I knew some day you would come and pay.'

'Oh,' Sriram said generously. 'Take it, by all means,' and turned to go.

'That's a worthy grandson,' muttered Kanni. 'Now the old man's soul will rest in peace.'

'But where will the soul be waiting? Don't you think he will have been reborn somewhere?' said Sriram.

Kanni did not wish to be involved in speculations on post-mortem existence, and turned his attention to the other customers.

Before going away Sriram said, 'I can buy that picture off you whenever you can sell it, remember.'

'Surely, surely. When I wind up this shop, I will remember to give it to you, not till then: it's a talisman for me.'

'If the lady's husband turns up and demands the picture, what will you do?' Sriram asked, which made Kanni pause and reflect for a moment what his line of action should be.

Sriram walked down the street, not having any definite aim. He felt like a man with a high-powered talisman in his pocket, something that would enable him to fly or go anywhere he pleased. He thrust his fingers into his *jiba* pocket and went on twirling the notes. He wished he had asked the manager to give him new ones: he had given him what appeared to be second-hand notes: probably the Fund-Office Manager reserved the good notes for big men. Who was a big man anyway? Anyone was a big man. Himself not excluded. He had money, but people still seemed to think he was a little boy tied to the apron strings of his grandmother. His grandmother was very good no doubt, but she ought to leave him alone. She did not treat him as a grown-up person. It was exasperating to be treated like a kid all the time. Why wouldn't she let him draw two hundred and fifty instead of fifty, if he wanted it? It would be his business in future, and she ought to allow him to do what he pleased. Anyway it was a good thing he had only fifty to display before Kanni. If he had shown two hundred he might have claimed half of it as his grandfather's debt. Sriram was for a moment seized with the problem of life on earth: was one born and tended and brought up to the twentieth year just in order to pay off a cheroot bill? This philosophical trend he immediately checked with the thought: 'I shall probably know all this philosophy when I grow a little older, not now ...' He dismissed his thought with: 'I am an adult with my own money, going home just when I please. Granny can't ask me what I have been doing ...'

He walked round and round the Market Road, gazing in shops, and wondering if there was anything he could buy. The money in his pocket clamoured to be spent. But yet there seemed to be nothing worth buying in the shops. He halted for a moment, reflecting how hard it was to relieve oneself of one's cash. A man who wore a cotton vest and a tucked-in *dhoti* held up to him a canvas folding chair,

'Going cheap, do you want it?'

Sriram examined it. This seemed to be something worth having in one's house. It had a red striped canvas seat and could be folded up. There was not a single piece of furniture at home.

'Ten rupees sir, best teakwood.'

Sriram examined it keenly, although he could not see the difference between rosewood and teak or any other wood.

'Is this real teak?' he asked.

'Guaranteed Mempi Hill teak, sir, that is why it costs ten rupees: if it were ordinary jungle wood, you could have got it for four.'

'I will give seven rupees,' said Sriram with an air of finality, looking away. He pretended to have no further interest in the transaction. The man came down to eight rupees. Sriram offered him an extra half rupee if he would carry it to his door.

Granny opened the door and asked in surprise, 'What is this?'

Sriram set up the canvas chair right in the middle of the hall and said, 'This is a present for you, Granny.'

'What! For me!' She examined the canvas and said, 'It's no use for me. This is some kind of leather, probably cow-hide, and I can't pollute myself by sitting on it. I wish you had told me before going out to buy.'

Sriram examined the seat keenly, dusted it, tapped it with his palm and said, 'This is not leather, Granny, it is only canvas.'

'What is canvas made of?' she asked.

Sriram said, 'I have no idea,' and she completed the answer with, 'Canvas is only another name for leather. I don't want it. You sleep on it if you like.'

He followed this advice to the letter. All day he lounged on this canvas seat and looked at the ceiling or read a tattered novel borrowed from the municipal library. When evening came he visited the Bombay Anand Bhavan and ordered a lot of sweets and delicacies, and washed them down with coffee. After that he picked up a *beeda* covered with coloured coconut gratings, chewed it with great contentment, and went for a stroll along the river or saw the latest Tamil film in the Regal Picture Palace.

It was an unruffled, quiet existence, which went on without a break for the next four years, the passing of time being hardly noticed in this scheme – except when one or the other of the festivals of the season turned up and his granny wanted him to bring something from the market. 'Another Dasara!' or 'Another *Deepavali*! It looks as though I lighted crackers only yesterday!' he would cry, surprised at the passage of time.

It was April. The summer sun shone like a ruthless arc lamp – and all the water in the well evaporated and the road-dust became bleached and weightless and flew about like flour spraying off the grinding wheels. Granny said as Sriram was starting out for the evening, 'Why don't you fetch some good jaggery for tomorrow, and some jasmine for the *pooja*?' He had planned to go towards Lawley Extension today and not to the market, and he felt reluctant to oblige her. But she was insistent. She said,

'Tomorrow is New Year's Day.'

'Already another New Year!' he cried. 'It seems as though we celebrated one yesterday.'

'Whether yesterday or the day before, it's a New Year's Day. I want certain things for its celebration. If you are not going, I'll go myself. It's not for me! It's only to make some sweet stuff for you.'

Grumbling a great deal, he got up, dressed himself, and started out. When he arrived at the market he was pleased that his granny had forced him to go there.

As he approached the Market Fountain a pretty girl came up and stopped him.

'Your contribution?' she asked, shaking a sealed tin collecting box.

Sriram's throat went dry and no sound came. He had never been spoken to by any girl before; she was slender and young, with eyes that sparkled with happiness. He wanted to ask, 'How old are you? What caste are you? Where is your horoscope? Are you free to marry me?' She looked so different from the beauty in Kanni's shop; his critical faculties were at once alert, and he realized how shallow was the other beauty, the European queen, and wondered that he had ever given her a thought. He wouldn't look at the picture again even if Kanni should give it to him free.

The girl rattled the money-box. The sound brought him back from his reverie, and he said, 'Yes, Yes'; he fumbled in his *jiba* side-pocket for loose change and brought out an eight-anna silver coin and dropped it into the slot. The girl smiled at him in return and went away, seeming to move with the lightest of steps like a dancer. Sriram had a wild hope that she would let him touch her hand, but she moved off and disappeared into the market crowd.

'What a dangerous thing for such a beauty to be about!' he thought. It was a busy hour with cycles, horse carriages and motor-cars passing down the road, and a jostling crowd was moving in and out of the arched gateway of the market. People were carrying vegetables, rolls of banana leaves and all kinds of New Year purchases. Young urchins were hanging about with baskets on their heads soliciting, 'Coolie, sir, Coolie?' She had disappeared into the market like a bird gliding on wings. He felt that he wanted to sing a song for her. But she was gone. He realized he hadn't even asked what the contribution was for. He wished he hadn't given just a nickel but thrust a ten-rupee note into her collection box (he could afford it), and that would have given her a better impression of him, and possibly have made her stand and talk to him. He should have asked her where she lived. What a fool not to have held her up. He ought to have emptied all his money into her money-box. She had vanished through the market arch.

He vaguely followed this trail, hoping that he would be able to catch another glimpse of her. If ever he saw her again he would take charge of the money-box and make the collection for her, whatever it might be for. He looked over the crowd for a glimpse again of the white *sari*, over the shoulders of the jostling crowd, around the vegetable stalls ... But it was a hopeless quest, not a chance of seeing her again. Who could she be and where did she come from? Could it be that she was the daughter of a judge or might she be an other-worldly creature who had come suddenly to meet him and whom he did not know how to treat? What a fool he was. He felt how sadly he lacked the necessary polish for such encounters. That was why it was urged on him to go to a college and pass his B.A. Those who went to colleges and passed their B.A. were certainly people who knew how to conduct themselves before girls.

He passed into the market arch in the direction she took. At the fly-ridden jaggery shop he said tentatively: 'A lot of people are about collecting money for all sorts of things.'

The jaggery merchant said sourly, 'Who will not collect money if there are people to give?'

'I saw a girl jingling a money-box. Even girls have taken to it,' Sriram said, holding his breath, hoping to hear something.

'Oh, that,' the other said, 'I too had to give some cash. We have to. We can't refuse.'

'Who is she?' Sriram asked, unable to carry on diplomatically any further.

The jaggery merchant threw a swift look at him which seemed slightly sneering, and said: 'She has something to do with Mahatma Gandhi and is collecting a fund. You know the Mahatma is coming.'

Sriram suddenly woke from an age-old somnolence to the fact that Malgudi was about to have the honour of receiving Mahatma Gandhi.

In that huge gathering sitting on the sands of Sarayu, awaiting the arrival of Mahatma Gandhi, Sriram was a tiny speck. There were a lot of volunteers clad in white *khadar* moving around the dais. The chromium stand of the microphone gleamed in the sun. Police stood about here and there. Busybodies were going round asking people to remain calm and silent. People obeyed them. Sriram envied these volunteers and busybodies their importance, and wondered if he could do anything to attain the same status. The sands were warm, the sun was severe. The crowd sat on the ground uncomplainingly.

The river flowed, the leaves of the huge banyan and *peepul* trees on the banks rustled; the waiting crowd kept up a steady babble, constantly punctuated by the pop of soda-water bottles; longitudinal cucumber slices, crescent-shaped, and brushed up with the peel of a lime dipped in salt, were disappearing from the wooden tray of a vendor who was announcing in a subdued tone (as a concession to the coming of a great man), 'Cucumber for thirst, the best for thirst.' He had wound a green Turkish towel around his head as a protection from the sun.

Sriram felt parched, and looked at the tray longingly. He wished he could go up and buy a crescent. The thought of biting into its cool succulence was tantalizing. He was at a distance and if he left his seat he'd have no chance of getting back to it. He watched a lot of others giving their cash and working their teeth into the crescent. 'Waiting for the Mahatma makes one very thirsty,' he thought.

Every ten minutes someone started a *canard* that the great man had arrived, and it created a stir in the crowd. It became a joke, something to relieve the tedium of waiting. Any person, a microphone-fitter or a volunteer, who dared to cross the dais was greeted with laughter and booing from a hundred thousand throats. A lot of familiar characters, such as an old teacher of his and the pawnbroker in Market Road, made themselves unrecognizable by wearing white *khadar* caps. They felt it was the right dress to wear on this occasion. 'That *khadar* store off the Market Fountain must have done a roaring business in white caps today,' Sriram thought. Far off, pulled obscurely to one side, was a police van with a number of men peering through the safety grill.

There was a sudden lull when Gandhi arrived on the platform and took his seat.

'That's Mahadev Desai,' someone whispered into Sriram's ears.

'Who is the man behind Gandhiji?'

'That's Mr Natesh, our Municipal Chairman.'

Someone sneered at the mention of his name. 'Some people conveniently adopt patriotism when Mahatmaji arrives.'

'Otherwise how can they have a ride in the big procession and a seat on the dais?'

Over the talk the amplifiers burst out 'Please, please be silent.'

Mahatma Gandhi stood on the dais, with his palms brought together in a salute. A mighty cry rang out, 'Mahatma Gandhi Ki Jai!' Then he raised his arm, and instantly a silence fell on the gathering. He clapped his hands rythmically and said: 'I want you all to keep this up, this beating for a while.' People were half-hearted. And the voice in the amplifier boomed, 'No good. Not enough. I like to see more vigour in your arms, more rhythm, more spirit. It must be like the drum-beats of the non-violent soldiers marching on to cut the chains that bind Mother India. I want to hear the great beat. I like to see all arms upraised, and clapping. There is nothing to be ashamed of in it. I want to see unity in it. I want you all to do it with a single mind.' And at once, every man, woman, and child, raised their arms and clapped over their heads.

Sriram wondered for a moment if it would be necessary for him to add his quota to this voluminous noise. He was hesitant.

'I see someone in that corner not quite willing to join us. Come on, you will be proud of this preparation.'

And Sriram felt he had been found out, and followed the lead.

Now a mighty choral chant began: *Raghupathi Raghava Raja Ram, Pathitha Pavana Seetha Ram,* to a simple tune, led by a girl at the microphone. It went on and on, and ceased when Mahatmaji began his speech. Natesh interpreted in Tamil what Gandhi said in Hindi. At the outset Mahatma Gandhi explained that he'd speak only in Hindi as a matter of principle. 'I will not address you in English. It's the language of our rulers. It has enslaved us. I very much wish I could speak to you in your own sweet language, Tamil; but alas, I am too hard-pressed for time to master it now, although I hope if God in His infinite mercy grants me the longevity due to me, that is one hundred and twenty-five years, I shall be able next time to speak to you in Tamil without troubling our friend Natesh.'

'Natesh has a knack of acquiring good certificates,' someone murmured in an aggrieved tone.

'Runs with the hare and hunts with the hounds,' said a school-master.

'He knows all of them inside out. Don't imagine the old gentleman does not know whom he is dealing with.'

'I notice two men there talking,' boomed Gandhiji's voice. 'It's not good to talk now, when perhaps the one next to you is anxious to listen. If you disturb his hearing, it is one form of *himsa.*' And at once the commentators lowered their heads and became silent. People were afraid to stir or speak.

Mahatma Gandhi said: 'I see before me a vast army. Every one of you has certain good points and certain defects, and you must all strive to discipline yourselves before we can hope to attain freedom for our country. An army is always in training and keeps itself in good shape by regular drill and discipline. We, the citizens of this country, are all soldiers of a non-violent army, but even such an army has to practise a few things daily in order to keep itself in proper condition: we do not have to bask in the sun and cry "Left" or "Right". But we have a system of our own to follow: that's *Ram Dhun*; spinning on the *charka* and the practice of absolute Truth and Non-violence.'

At the next evening's meeting Sriram secured a nearer seat. He now understood the technique of attending these gatherings. If he hesitated and looked timid, people pushed him back and down. But if he looked like someone who owned the place, everyone stood aside to let him pass. He wore a pair of large dark glasses which gave him, he felt, an authoritative look. He strode through the crowd. The place was cut up into sectors with stockades of bamboo, so that people were penned in groups. He assumed a tone of bluster which carried him through the various obstacles and brought him to the first row right below the dais. It took him farther away from the sellers of cucumber and aerated water who operated on the fringe of the vast crowd. But there was another advantage in this place: he found himself beside the enclosure where the women were assembled. Most of them were without ornaments, knowing Gandhiji's aversion to all show and luxury. Even then they were an attractive lot, in their *saris* of varied colours, and Sriram sat unashamedly staring at the gathering, for his favourite hobby at the moment was to speculate on what type he would prefer for a wife.

He fancied himself the centre of attraction if any women happened to look in his direction. 'Oh, she is impressed with my glasses – takes me to be a big fellow, I suppose.' He recollected Gandhiji's suggestion on the previous day: 'All women are your sisters and mothers. Never look at them with thoughts of lust. If you are troubled by such thoughts, this is the remedy: walk with your head down, looking at the ground during the day, and with your eyes up, looking at the stars at night.' He had said this in answering a question that someone from the audience had put to him. Sriram felt uncomfortable at the recollection: 'He will probably read my thoughts.' It seemed to be a risky business sitting so near the dais.

Gandhi seemed to be a man who spotted disturbers and cross-thinkers however far away they sat. He was sure to catch him the moment he arrived on the platform, and say, 'You there! Come up and make a clean breast of it. Tell this assembly what your thoughts were. Don't look in the direction of the girls at all if you cannot control your thoughts.' Sriram resolutely looked away in another direction, where men were seated. 'A most uninteresting and boring collection of human faces; wherever I turn I see only some shopkeeper or a school-master. What is the use of spending one's life looking at them?' Very soon, unconsciously, he turned again towards the women, telling himself, 'So many sisters and mothers. I wish they would let me speak to them. Of course I have no evil thoughts in my mind at the moment.'

Presently Mahatmaji ascended the platform and Sriram hastily took his eyes off the ladies and joined in the hand clapping with well-timed devotion and then in the singing of *Raghupathi Raghava Raja Ram*. After that Gandhi spoke on non-violence, and explained how it could be practised in daily life. 'It is a perfectly simple procedure provided you have faith in it. If you watch yourself you will avoid all actions, big or small, and all thoughts, however obscure, which may cause pain to another. If you are watchful, it will come to you naturally,' he said. 'When someone has wronged you or has done something which appears to you to be evil, just pray for the destruction of that evil. Cultivate an extra affection for the person and you will find that you are able to bring about a change in him. Two thousand years ago, Jesus Christ meant the same thing when he said, "Turn the other cheek."'

Thus he went on. Sometimes Sriram found it impossible to follow his words. He could not grasp what he was saying, but he looked rapt, he tried to concentrate and understand. This was the first time he felt the need to try and follow something, the first time that he found himself at a disadvantage. Until now he had had a conviction, especially after he began to operate his own bank account, that he understood everything in life. This was the first time he was assailed by doubts of his own prowess and understanding. When Mahatmaji spoke of untouchability and caste, Sriram reflected, 'There must be a great deal in what he says. We always think we are superior people. How Granny bullies that ragged scavenger who comes to our house every day to sweep the backyard!' Granny was so orthodox that she would not let the scavenger approach nearer than ten yards, and habitually adopted a bullying tone while addressing him. Sriram also took a devilish pleasure in joining the baiting and finding fault with the scavenger's work, although he never paid the slightest attention to their comments. He simply went about his business, driving his broom vigorously and interrupting himself only to ask, 'When will master give me an old shirt he promised so long ago?'

He suddenly noticed on the dais the girl who had jingled a money-box in his face a few days ago, at the market. She was clad in a *sari* of *khadar*, white homespun, and he noticed how well it suited her. Before, he had felt that the wearing of *khadar* was a fad, that it was apparel fit only for cranks, but now he realized how lovely it could be. He paused for a moment to consider whether it was the wearer who was enriching the cloth or whether the material was good in itself. But he had to postpone the whole problem. It was no time for abstract considerations. There she stood, like a vision beside the microphone, on the high dais, commanding the whole scene, a person who was worthy of standing beside Mahatmaji's microphone. How confidently she faced the crowd! He wished he could go about announcing, 'I know who that is beside the microphone into which Mahatmaji is speaking.' The only trouble was that if they turned and asked him, 'What is her name?' he would feel lost. It would be awkward to say, 'I don't know, she came jingling a collection box the other day in the market. I wish I could say where she lives. I should be grateful for any information.'

At this moment applause rang out, and he joined in it. Gandhiji held up his hand to say, 'It is not enough for you to clap your hands and show your appreciation of me. I am not prepared to accept it all so easily. I want you really to make sure of a change in your hearts before you ever think of asking the British to leave the shores of India. It's all very well for you to take up the cry and create an uproar. But that's not enough. I want you to clear your hearts and minds and make certain that only love resides there, and there is no residue of bitterness for past history. Only then can you say to the British, "Please leave this country to be managed or mismanaged by us, that's purely our own business, and come back any time you like as our friends and distinguished guests, not as our rulers," and you will find John Bull packing his suit-case. But be sure you have in your heart love and not bitterness.'

Sriram told himself, looking at the vision beside the microphone, 'Definitely it's not bitterness. I love her.'

'But,' Mahatmaji was saying, 'if I have the slightest suspicion that your heart is not pure or that there is bitterness there, I'd rather have the British stay on. It's the lesser of two evils.'

Sriram thought: 'Oh, revered Mahatmaji, have no doubt that my heart is pure and without bitterness. How can I have any bitterness in my heart for a creature who looks so divine?'

She was at a great height on the platform, and her features were not very clear in the afternoon sun which seemed to set her face ablaze. She might be quite dark and yet wear a temporarily fair face illumined by the sun or she might really be fair. If she were dark, without a doubt his grandmother would not approve of his marrying her. In any case it was unlikely that they would have her blessing, since she had other plans for his marriage: a brother's granddaughter brought up in Kumbum, a most horrible, countrified girl who would guard his cash. If Grandmother was so solicitous of his money she was welcome to take it all and hand it to the Kumbum girl. That would be the lesser of two evils, but he would not marry the Kumbum girl, an unsightly creature with a tight oily braid falling on her nape and dressed in a gaudy village *sari*, when the thing to do was to wear *khadar*. He would refuse to look at anyone who did not wear *khadi*, *khadi* alone was going to save the nation from ruin and get the English out of India, as that venerable saint Mahatmaji explained untiringly. He felt sad and depressed at the thought that in the twentieth century there were still people like the Kumbum girl, whom he had seen many many years ago when his uncle came down to engage a lawyer for a civil suit in the village.

Sriram wanted to go and assure the girl on the grandstand that he fully and without the slightest reservation approved of her outlook and habits. It was imperative that he should approach her and tell her that. He seized the chance at the end of the meeting. Mahatmaji started to descend from the platform. There was a general rush forward, and a number of volunteers began pushing back the crowd, imploring people not to choke the space around the platform. Mahatmaji himself seemed to be oblivious of all the turmoil going on around him. Sriram found a gap in the cordon made by the volunteers and slipped through. The heat of the sun hit him on the nape, the huge trees on the river's edge rustled above the din of the crowd, birds were creating a furore in the branches, being unaccustomed to so much noise below. The crowd was so great that Sriram for a moment forgot where he was, which part of the town he was in, and but for the noise of the birds would not have remembered he was on the banks of Sarayu. 'If that girl can be with Mahatmaji I can also be there,' he told himself indignantly as he threaded his way through the crowd. There was a plethora of white-capped young men, volunteers who cleared a way for Mahatmaji to move in. Sriram felt that it would have been much better if he had not made himself so conspicuously different with his half-arm shirt and *mull-dhoti*, probably products of the hated mills. He feared that any moment someone might discover him and put him out. If they challenged him and asked, 'Who are you?' he felt he wouldn't be able to answer coherently, or he might just retort, 'Who do you think you are talking to, that girl supporting the Mahatma is familiar to me. I am going to know her, but don't ask me her name. She came with a collection box one day in the market ...'

But no such occasion arose. No one questioned him and he was soon mixed up with a group of people walking behind Mahatmaji in the lane made by the volunteers, as crowds lined the sides. He decided to keep going till he was stopped. If someone stopped him he could always turn round and go home. They would not kill him for it anyway. Killing! He was amused at the word: no word could be more incongruous in the vicinity of one who could not hurt even the British. One could be confident he would not let a would-be follower be slaughtered by his volunteers.

Presently Sriram found himself in such a position of vantage that he lost all fear of being taken for an intruder and walked along with a jaunty and familiar air, so that people lining the route looked on him with interest. He heard his name called. 'Sriram!' An old man who used to be his teacher years before was calling him. Even in his present situation Sriram could not easily break away from the call of a teacher: it was almost a reflex: he hesitated for a moment wondering whether he would not do well to run away without appearing to notice the call, but almost as if reading his mind, his teacher called again, 'A moment! Sriram.' He stopped to have a word with his master, an old man who had wrapped himself in a coloured shawl and looked like an apostle with a slight beard growing on his chin. He gripped Sriram's elbow eagerly and asked, 'Have you joined them?'

'Whom?'

'Them – ' said the teacher, pointing.

Sriram hesitated for a moment, wondering what he should reply, and mumbled, 'I mean to ...'

'Very good, very good,' said the master. 'In spite of your marks I always knew that you would go far, smart fellow. You are not dull but only lazy. If you worked well you could always score first-class marks like anyone else, but you were always lazy; I remember how you stammered when asked which was the capital of England. Ho! Ho!' he laughed at the memory. Sriram became restive and wriggled in his grip.

The teacher said, 'I am proud to see you here, my boy. Join the Congress, work for the country, you will go far, God bless you ...'

'I am glad you think so, sir,' said Sriram and turned to dash away.

The teacher put his face close to his and asked in a whisper, 'What will Mahatmaji do now after going in there?'

'Where?' Sriram asked, not knowing where Gandhi was going, although he was following him.

'Into his hut,' replied the teacher.

'He will probably rest,' answered Sriram, resolutely preparing to dash off. If he allowed too great a distance to develop between himself and the group they might not admit him.

A little boy thrust himself forward and asked, 'Can you get me Mahatma's autograph?'

'Certainly not,' replied Sriram, gently struggling to release himself from his teacher's hold.

His teacher whispered in his ear, 'Whatever happens, don't let down our country.'

'No, sir, never, I promise,' replied Sriram, gently pushing away his old master and running after the group, who were fast disappearing from his view.

They were approaching a wicket gate made of thorns and bamboo. He saw the girl going ahead to open the gate. He sprinted forward as the crowd watched. He had an added assurance in his steps now he felt that he belonged to the Congress. The teacher had put a new idea into his head and he almost felt he was a veteran of the party. He soon joined the group and he had mustered enough pluck to step up beside the girl. It was a proud moment for him. He looked at her. She did not seem to notice his presence. He sweated all over with excitement and panted for breath, but could not make out the details of her personality, complexion or features. However, he noted with satisfaction that she was not very tall, himself being of medium height. Gandhi was saying something to her and she was nodding and smiling. He did not understand what they were saying, but he also smiled out of sympathetic respect. He wanted to look as much like them as possible, and cursed himself for the hundredth time that day for being dressed in mill cloth.

The Mahatma entered his hut. This was one of the dozen huts belonging to the city sweepers who lived on the banks of the river. It was probably the worst area in the town, and an exaggeration even to call them huts; they were just hovels, put together with rags, tin-sheets, and shreds of coconut matting, all crowded in anyhow, with scratchy fowls cackling about and children growing in the street dust. The municipal services were neither extended here nor missed, although the people living in the hovels were employed by the municipality for scavenging work in the town. They were paid ten rupees a month per head, and since they worked in families of four or five, each had a considerable income by Malgudi standards. They hardly ever lived in their huts, spending all their time around the municipal building or at the toddy shop run by the government nearby, which absorbed all their earnings. These men spent less than a tenth of their income on food or clothing, always depending upon mendicancy in their off hours for survival. Deep into the night their voices could be heard clamouring for alms, in all the semi-dark streets of Malgudi. Troublesome children were silenced at the sound of their approach. Their possessions were few; if a cow or a calf died in the city they were called in to carry off the carcass and then the colony at the river's edge brightened up, for they held a feast on the flesh of the dead animal and made money out of its hide. Reformers looked on with wrath and horror, but did little else, since as an untouchable class they lived outside the town limits, beyond Nallappa's Grove, where nobody went, and they used only a part of the river on its downward course.

This was the background to the life of the people in whose camp Gandhi had elected to stay during his visit to Malgudi. It had come as a thunderbolt on the Municipal Chairman, Mr Natesh, who had been for weeks preparing his palatial house, Neel Bagh in the aristocratic Lawley Extension, to receive Gandhi. His arguments as to why he alone should be Mahatmaji's host seemed unassailable: 'I have spent two lakhs on the building, my garden and lawns alone have cost me twenty-five thousand rupees so far. What do you think I have done it for? I am a simple man, sir, my needs are very simple. I don't need any luxury. I can live in a hut, but the reason I have built it on this scale is so that I should be able for at least once in my lifetime to receive a great soul like Mahatmaji. This is the only house in which he can stay comfortably when he comes to this town. Let me say without appearing to be boastful that it is the biggest and the best furnished house in Malgudi, and we as the people of Malgudi have a responsibility to give him our very best, so how can we house him in any lesser place?'

The Reception Committee applauded his speech. The District Collector, who was the head of the district, and the District Superintendent of Police, who was next to him in authority, attended the meeting as *ex officio* members.

A dissenting voice said, 'Why not give the Circuit House for Mahatmaji?'

The Circuit House on the edge of the town was an old East India Company building standing on an acre of land, on the Trunk Road. Robert Clive was supposed to have halted there while marching to relieve the seige of Trichinopoly. The citizens of Malgudi were very proud of this building and never missed an opportunity to show it off to anyone visiting the town and it always housed the distinguished visitors who came this way. It was a matter of prestige for Governors to be put up there. Even in this remote spot they had arranged to have all their conveniences undiminished, with resplendent sanitary fittings in the bathrooms. It was also known as the Glass House, by virtue of a glass-fronted bay room from which the distinguished guests could watch the wild animals that were supposed to stray near the building at night in those days.

The dissenting voice in the Reception Committee said, 'Is it the privilege of the ruling race alone to be given the Circuit House? Is our Mahatmaji unworthy of it?'

The Collector, who was the custodian of British prestige, rose to a point of order and administered a gentle reproof to the man who spoke: 'It is not good to go beyond the relevant facts at the moment: if we have considered the Circuit House as unsuitable it is because we have no time to rig it up for receiving Mr Gandhi.'

It was a point of professional honour for him to say *Mr* Gandhi and not *Mahatma*, and but for the fact that as the Collector he could close the entire meeting and put all the members behind bars under the Defence of India Act, many would have protested and walked out, but they held their peace and he drove home the point.

'Since Mr Gandhi's arrival has been a sudden decision, we are naturally unable to get the building ready for him; if I may say so, our Chairman's house seems to suit the purpose and we must be grateful to him for so kindly obliging us.'

'And I am arranging to move to the Glass House leaving my house for Mahatmaji's occupation.'

That seemed to decide it, and his partisans cheered loudly. It was resolved by ten votes to one that Mahatmaji should stay in Neel Bagh, and the Chairman left the meeting with a heavy, serious look. He wrote to Gandhiji's secretary, receiving a reply which he read at the next meeting: 'Mahatma Gandhi wishes that no particular trouble should be taken about his lodging, and that the matter may be conveniently left over till he is actually there.'

The council debated the meaning of the communication and finally concluded that it only meant that though the Mahatma was unwilling to be committed to anything he would not refuse to occupy Neel Bagh.

The dissenting voice said, 'How do you know that he does not mean something else?'

But he was soon overwhelmed by the gentle reprimand of the Collector. The communication was finally understood to mean, 'I know Mahatmaji's mind, he does not want to trouble anyone if it is a trouble.'

'He probably does not know that it is no trouble for us at all.'

'Quite so, quite so,' said another soothsayer. And they were all pleased at this interpretation.

A further flattering comparison was raised by someone who wanted to create a pleasant impression on the Chairman: 'Let us not forget that Mahatmaji takes up his residence at Birla House in Delhi and Calcutta; I am sure he will have no objection to staying in a palatial building like the one our Chairman has built.'

The dissenting voice said, 'Had we better not write and ask if we have understood him right, and get his confirmation?'

He was not allowed to complete his sentence but was hissed down, and the District Superintendent of Police added slowly, 'Even for security arrangements any other place would present difficulties.'

For this sentiment he received an appreciative nod from his superior, the District Collector.

When Gandhi arrived, he was ceremoniously received, all the big-wigs of Malgudi and the local gentry being introduced to him one by one by the Chairman of the municipality. The police attempted to control the crowd, which was constantly shouting, 'Mahatma Gandhi Ki Jai.' When the Chairman read his address of welcome at the elaborately constructed archway outside the railway station, he could hardly be heard, much to his chagrin. He had spent a whole week composing the text of the address with the help of a local journalist, adding whatever would show off either his patriotism or the eminent position Malgudi occupied in the country's life. The Collector had taken the trouble to go through the address before it was sent for printing in order to make sure that it contained no insult to the British Empire, that it did not hinder the war effort, and that it in no way betrayed military secrets. He had to censor it in several places: where the Chairman compared Malgudi to Switzerland (the Collector scored this out because he felt it might embarrass a neutral state); a reference to the hosiery trade (since the Censor felt this was a blatant advertisement for the Chairman's goods and in any case he did not want enemy planes to come looking for this institution thinking it was a camouflage for the manufacture of war material); and all those passages which hinted at the work done by Gandhiji in the political field. The picture of him as a social reformer was left intact and even enlarged; anyone who read the address would conclude that politics were the last thing that Mahatmaji was interested in. In any case, in view of the reception, the Collector might well have left the whole thing alone since cries of 'Mahatmaji Ki Jai' and 'Down with the Municipal Chairman' made the speech inaudible. The crowd was so noisy that Mahatmaji had to remonstrate once or twice. When he held up his hand the crowd subsided and waited to listen to him. He said quietly, 'This is sheer lack of order, which I cannot commend. Your Chairman is reading something and I am in courtesy bound to know what he is saying. You must all keep quiet. Let him proceed.'

'No,' cried the crowd. 'We want to hear Mahatmaji and not the Municipal Chairman.'

'Yes,' replied Mahatmaji. 'You will soon hear me, in about an hour on the banks of your Sarayu river. That is the programme as framed.'

'By whom?'

'Never mind by whom. It has my approval. That is how it stands. On the sands of Sarayu in about an hour. Your Chairman has agreed to let me off without a reply to his very kind address. You will have to listen to what he has to say because I very much wish to ...'

This quietened the mob somewhat and the Chairman continued his reading of the address, although he looked intimidated by the exchanges. The Collector looked displeased and fidgety, feeling he ought to have taken into custody the dissenting member, who had perhaps started all this trouble in the crowd. He leaned over and whispered to the Chairman, 'Don't bother, read on leisurely. You don't have to rush through,' but the Chairman only wished to come to the end of his reading; he was anxious to be done with the address before the crowd burst out again. He did not complete his message a second too soon, as presently the crowd broke into a tremendous uproar, which forced the Police Superintendent hastily to go and see what was the matter, an action which had to be taken with a lot of discretion since Gandhi disliked all police arrangements.

Through archways and ringing cries of 'Gandhi Ki Jai', Gandhi drove in the huge Bentley which the Chairman had left at his disposal. People sat on trees and house-tops all along the way and cheered Gandhiji as he passed. The police had cordoned off various side-streets that led off from the Market Road, so the passage was clear from the little Malgudi station to Lawley Extension. There were police everywhere, although the District Superintendent of Police felt that the security arrangements had not been satisfactory. All shops had been closed and all schools, and the whole town was celebrating. School children felt delighted at the thought of Gandhi. Office-goers were happy, and even banks were closed. They waited in the sun for hours, saw him pass in his Bentley, a white-clad figure, fair-skinned and radiant, with his palms pressed together in a salute.

When they entered Neel Bagh, whose massive gates were of cast iron patterned after the gates of Buckingham Palace, the Chairman, who was seated in the front seat, waited to be asked: 'Whose house is this?' But Gandhiji did not seem to notice anything. They passed through the drive with hedges trimmed, flower pots putting forth exotic blooms, and lawns stretching away on either side, and he kept his ears alert to catch any remark that Gandhiji might let fall, but still he said nothing. He was busy looking through some papers which his secretary had passed to him.

The thought that Gandhiji was actually within his gates sent a thrill of joy up and down the Chairman's spine. He had arranged everything nicely. All his own things for a few days had been sent off to the Circuit House (which the Collector had given him on condition that he lime wash its walls and repaint its wooden doors and shutters). He felt a thrill at the thought of his own sacrifice. Some years before he would never have thought of forsaking his own air-conditioned suite and choosing to reside at the Circuit House, for anybody's sake. The Chairman had now surrendered his whole house to Gandhiji. No doubt it was big enough to accommodate his own family without interfering with his venerable guest and his party (a miscellaneous gathering of men and women, dressed in white *khadar*, who attended on Mahatmaji in various capacities, who all looked alike and whose names he could never clearly grasp); but he did not like to stay on because it seemed impossible to live under the same roof with such a distinguished man and to take away a little from the sense of patriotic sacrifice that his action entailed. So he decided to transfer himself to the Circuit House.

He had effected a few alterations in his house, such as substituting *khadar* hangings for the gaudy chintz that had adorned his doorways and windows, and had taken down the pictures of hunting gentry, vague gods and kings. He had even the temerity to remove the picture of George V's wedding and substitute pictures of Maulana Azad, Jawaharlal Nehru, Sarojini Naidu, Motilal Nehru, C. Rajagopalachari and Annie Besant. He had ordered his works manager to secure within a given time 'all the available portraits of our national leaders', a wholesale order which was satisfactorily executed; and all the other pictures were taken down and sent off to the basement room. He had also discreetly managed to get a picture of Krishna discoursing to Arjuna on Bhagavad-Gita, knowing well Gandhi's bias towards Bhagavad-Gita. He had kept on the window-sill and in a few other places a few specimens of *charka* (spinning wheels).

No film decorator sought to create atmosphere with greater deliberation. He worked all the previous night to attain this effect, and had also secured for himself a *khadar jiba* and a white Gandhi cap, for his wife a white *khadar sari*, and for his son a complete outfit in *khadar*. His car drove nearly a hundred miles within the city in order to search for a white *khadar* cap to fit his six-year-old son's dolicho-cephalic head, and on his shirt front he had embroidered the tricolour and a spinning wheel.

Now he hoped as he approached the main building that his wife and son would emerge in their proper make-up to meet Gandhi: he hoped his wife would have had the good sense to take away the diamond studs not only in her ears but also in their son's. He had forgotten to caution them about it. The moment the car stopped in the decorated porch of the house, the Chairman jumped down, held the door open and helped Mahatmaji to alight.

'You are most welcome to this humble abode of mine, great sire,' he said in confusion, unable to talk coherently. Mahatmaji got down from the car and looked at the house.

'Is this your house?' he asked.

'Yes, sir, by the grace of God, I built it four years ago,' the Chairman said, his throat going dry.

He led Gandhi up the veranda steps. He had placed a divan in the veranda covered with *khadar* printed cloth. He seated Gandhi on it and asked his secretary in a whisper: 'May I give Mahatmaji a glassful of orange juice? The oranges are from my own estates in Mempi.' A number of visitors and a miscellaneous crowd of people were passing in and out. It seemed to the Chairman that Mahatmaji's presence had the effect of knocking down the walls of a house, and converting it into a public place – but that was the price one had to pay for having the great man there. People were squatting on the lawns and the Chairman saw helplessly that some were plucking flowers in his annual bed, which had been tended by his municipal overseers.

Gandhi turned in his direction and asked: 'What were you saying?' His secretary communicated the offer of oranges.

Gandhi said: 'Yes, most welcome. I shall be happy to look at the oranges grown in your own gardens.'

The Chairman ran excitedly about and returned bearing a large tray filled with uniform golden oranges. He was panting with the effort. He had gone so far in self-abnegation that he would not accept the services of his usual attendants. He placed the tray in front of Mahatmaji.

'My humble offering to a great man: these are from my own orchards on the Mempi hills,' he said. 'They were plucked this morning.'

Then he asked, 'May I have the honour of giving you a glass of orange juice? You must have had a tiring day.'

The Mahatma declined, explaining that it was not his hour for taking anything. He picked up one fruit and examined it with appreciative comments, turning it slowly between his fingers. The Chairman felt as happy as if he himself were being scrutinized and approved. On the edge of the crowd, standing below on the drive, Mahatmaji noticed a little boy and beckoned to him to come nearer. The boy hesitated. Mahatmaji said: '*Av, Av –* ' in Hindi. When it made no impression on the boy, he said in the little Tamil he had picked up for this part of the country, '*Inge Va.*' Others pushed the boy forward; he came haltingly. Gandhi offered him a seat on his divan, and gave him an orange. This acted as a signal. Presently the divan was swarming with children. When the tray was empty, the Mahatma asked the Chairman: 'Have you some more?' The Chairman went in and brought a further supply in a basket; and all the children threw off their reserve, became clamorous and soon the basket was empty. 'There are some flowers and garlands in the car,' Gandhi whispered to his secretary – these had been presented to him on his arrival and all along the way by various associations. The place was fragrant with roses and jasmine. These he distributed to all the little girls he saw in the gathering. The Chairman felt chagrined at the thought that the event was developing into a children's party. After the oranges and flowers he hoped that the children would leave, but he found them still there. 'They are probably waiting for apples, now, I suppose!' he reflected bitterly.

Gandhi had completely relaxed. His secretary was telling him: 'In fifteen minutes the deputation from — will be here, and after that — .' He was reading from an engagement pad.

The Chairman regretted that both the District Superintendent of Police and the Collector had turned away at his Buckingham Palace gate after escorting the procession that far as an act of official courtesy: if they had been here now, they would have managed the crowd. For a moment he wondered with real anxiety whether the crowd proposed to stay all night. But his problem was unexpectedly solved for him. Mahatmaji saw one child standing apart from the rest – a small dark fellow with a protruding belly and wearing nothing over his body except a cast-off knitted vest, adult size, full of holes, which reached down to his ankles. The boy stood aloof from the rest, on the very edge of the crowd. His face was covered with mud, his feet were dirty, he had stuck his fingers into his mouth and was watching the proceedings on the veranda keenly, his eyes bulging with wonder and desire. He had not dared to come up the steps, though attracted by the oranges. He was trying to edge his way through.

Mahatma's eyes travelled over the crowd and rested on this boy – following his gaze the Chairman was bewildered. He had a feeling of uneasiness. Mahatmaji beckoned to the young fellow. One of his men went and fetched him. The Chairman's blood boiled. Of course people must like poor people and so on, but why bring in such a dirty boy, an untouchable, up the steps and make him so important? For a moment he felt a little annoyance with Mahatmaji himself, but soon suppressed it as a sinful emotion. He felt the need to detach himself sufficiently from his surroundings to watch without perturbation the happenings around him. Mahatmaji had the young urchin hoisted beside him on the divan. 'Oh, Lord, all the world's gutters are on this boy, and he is going to leave a permanent stain on that Kashmir counterpane.' The boy was making himself comfortable on the divan, having accepted the hospitality offered him by the Mahatma. He nestled close to the Mahatma, who was smoothing out his matted hair with his fingers, and was engaged in an earnest conversation with him.

The Chairman was unable to catch the trend of their talk. He stepped nearer, trying to listen with all reverence. The reward he got for it was a smile from the Mahatma himself. The boy was saying: 'My father sweeps the streets.'

'With a long broom or a short broom?' the Mahatma asked.

The boy explained, 'He has both a long broom and a short broom.' He was spitting out the seeds of an orange.

The Mahatma turned to someone and explained: 'It means that he is both a municipal sweeper and that he has scavenging work to do in private houses also. The long broom ought to be the municipal emblem.'

'Where is your father at the moment?'

'He is working at the market. He will take me home when he has finished his work.'

'And how have you managed to come here?'

'I was sitting on the road waiting for my father and I came along with the crowd. No one stopped me when I entered the gates.'

'That's a very clever boy,' Mahatmaji said. 'I'm very happy to see you. But you must not spit those pips all over the place, in fact you must never spit at all. It's very unclean to do so, and may cause others a lot of trouble. When you eat an orange, others must not notice it at all. The place must be absolutely tidy even if you have polished off six at a time.'

He laughed happily at his own quip, and then taught the boy what to do with the pips, how to hide the skin, and what to do with all the superfluous bits packed within an orange. The boy laughed with joy. All the men around watched the proceedings with respectful attention. And then Gandhi asked:

'Where do you live?'

The boy threw up his arm to indicate a far distance: 'There at the end of the river ...'

'Will you let me come to your house?'

The boy hesitated and said, 'Not now – because, because it's so far away.'

'Don't bother about that. I've a motor-car here given to me, you see, by this very rich man. I can be there in a moment. I'll take you along in the motor-car too if you will show me your house.'

'It is not a house like this,' said the boy, 'but made of bamboo or something.'

'Is that so!' said the Mahatma. 'Then I'll like it all the more. I'll be very happy there.'

He had a brief session with a delegation which had come to see him by appointment; when it left, he dictated some notes, wrote something, and then, picking up his staff, said to the Chairman, 'Let us go to this young man's house. I'm sure you will also like it.'

'Now?' asked the Chairman in great consternation. He mumbled, 'Shall we not go there tomorrow?'

'No, I've offered to take this child home. I must not disappoint him. I'd like to see his father too, if he can be met anywhere on the way.'

421

Mahatmaji gave his forefinger to the young boy to clutch and allowed himself to be led down the veranda steps. The Chairman asked dolefully, 'Won't you come in and have a look round my humble home?'

'I know how it will be. It must be very grand. But would you not rather spare an old man like me the bother of walking through those vast spaces? I'm a tired old man. You are very hospitable. Anyway, come along with us to this little man's home. If I feel like it, you will let me stay there.'

The Chairman mumbled, 'I hoped –' But Gandhiji swept him aside with a smile:

'You will come along with me too. Let me invite you to come and stay with me in a hut.'

Unable to say anything more, the Chairman merely replied, 'All right, sir, I obey.'

The warmth of Mahatma's invitation made him forget his problems as a Chairman and his own responsibilities. Otherwise he would not have become oblivious of the fact that the sweepers' colony was anything but a show-piece. Not till the Collector later sought him out and arraigned him for his lapse did it occur to him what a blunder he had committed.

The Collector said, 'Have you so little sense, Chairman, that you could not have delayed Mr Gandhi's visit at least by two hours, time to give the people a chance to sweep and clean up that awful place? You know as well as I do, what it is like!' All of which the Chairman took in without a word.

He was gloating over the words spoken to him by Mahatmaji. Not till his wife later attacked him did he remember his omission in another direction. She said in a tone full of wrath, 'There I was waiting, dressed as you wanted, with the boy, and you simply went away without even calling us!'

'Why couldn't you have come out?' he asked idiotically.

'How could I, when you had said I must wait for your call?' She sobbed, 'With the great man at our house, I'd not the good fortune even to appear before him. And the child – what a disappointment for him!'

When they got over their initial surprise, the authorities did everything to transform the place. All the stench mysteriously

vanished; all the garbage and offal that lay about, and flesh and
hide put out to sun-dry on the roofs, disappeared. All that night
municipal and other employees kept working, with the aid of
petrol lamps: light there was such a rarity that the children kept
dancing all night around the lamps. Gandhiji noticed the hectic
activity, but out of a sense of charity refrained from commenting
on it. Only when it was all over did he say, 'Now one can believe
that the true cleansers of the city live here.' The men of the
colony tied round their heads their whitest turbans and the
women wore their best *saris*, dragged their children to the river
and scrubbed them till they yelled, and decorated their coiffures
with yellow chrysanthemum flowers. The men left off fighting,
did their best to keep away from the drink shops, and even the
few confirmed topers had their drinks on the sly, and suppressed
their impulse to beat their wives or break their household pots.
The whole place looked bright with lamps and green mango
leaves tied across lamp-posts and tree branches.

Gandhi occupied a hut which had a low entrance. He didn't
like to oust anyone from his hut, but chose one facing the river
sand, after making certain that it had been vacant, the occupant
of the hut having gone elsewhere. The Chairman brought in a
low divan and covered the floor with a coarse rush mat for
Gandhi's visitors to sit on. Sriram lowered himself unobtrusively
on the mat. Gandhi sat on his divan, and dictated to one of his
secretaries. They wrote voluminously. Mahatmaji performed a
number of things simultaneously. He spoke to visitors. He dictated. He wrote. He prayed. He had his sparse dinner of nuts and
milk, and presently he even laid himself down on the divan and
went off to sleep. It was then that someone turned off the lamp,
and people walked out of the hut.

Sriram now felt that he could not continue to sit there.
Although no one bothered to ask him what he was doing, he
could not stay any more. When he saw the girl was preparing to
leave the hut, he thought he had better get up and go; otherwise
someone might say something unpleasant to him.

The girl lifted Gandhi's spinning wheel, put it away noiselessly, and tip-toed out of the room. She passed without noticing
him at first, but the fixed stare with which he followed her

423

movements seemed to affect her. She went past him, but suddenly stopped and whispered: 'You will have to go now,' and Sriram sprang up and found himself outside the hut in one bound.

She said rather grimly: 'Don't you know that when Bapuji sleeps, we have to leave him?'

He felt like asking, 'Who is Bapuji?' but using his judgement for a second, he understood it must refer to the Mahatma, and not wanting to risk being chased out by the resolute girl said, 'Of course, I knew it. I was only waiting for you to come out.'

'Who are you? I don't think I have seen you before.'

This was the question he had been waiting to be asked all along, but now when it came he found himself tongue-tied. He felt so confused and muddled that she took pity on him and said, 'What is your name?'

He answered, 'Sriram.'

'What are you doing here?' she asked.

'Don't you remember me?' he said irrelevantly. 'I saw you when you came with a money-box in the market, the other day ...'

'Oh, I see,' she said out of politeness. 'But I might not remember you since quite a lot of people put money into my box that day. Anyway, I asked you what you are doing here now?'

'Perhaps I'm one of the volunteers,' Sriram said.

'Why "perhaps"?' she asked.

'Because I'm not yet one,' he replied.

'Anybody cannot be a volunteer,' she said. 'Don't you know that?' she asked.

'Don't I know that? I think I know that and more.'

'What more?' she asked.

'That I am not an anybody,' he replied and was amazed at his own foolhardiness in talking to the girl in that fashion; she could put him out of the camp in a moment.

'You are a somebody, I suppose?' the girl asked laughing.

'Well, you will help me to become somebody, I hope,' he said, feeling surprised at his own powers of rash and reckless speech.

She seemed a match for him, for presently she asked, with a little irritation, 'Are we going to stand here and talk the whole night?'

'Yes, unless you show me where we can go.'

'I know where I ought to go,' she said. 'You see that hut there,' she pointed to a small hut four doors off Gandhi's, 'that's where all the women of this camp are quartered.'

'How many of them are there?' Sriram asked just to keep up the conversation.

She answered sharply, 'More than you see before you now,' and added, 'Why are you interested?'

Sriram felt a little piqued. 'You seem to be a very ill-tempered and sharp-tongued girl. You can't answer a single question without a challenge.'

'Hush! You will wake up Bapuji standing and talking here,' she said.

'Well, if he is going to be awakened by anyone's talk, it will be yours, because no one else is doing the talking,' he replied.

'I have a right to ask you what you are doing here and report to our *Chalak* if I don't like you,' she said with a sudden tone of authority.

'Why should you not like me?' he asked.

'No one except close associates and people with appointments is allowed to enter Bapuji's presence.'

'I will tell them I am your friend and that you took me in,' he replied.

'Would you utter a falsehood?' she asked.

'Why not?'

'None except absolute truth-speakers are allowed to come into Mahatma's camp. People who come here must take an oath of absolute truth before going into Mahatma's presence.'

'I will take the vow when I become a member of the camp. Till then I will pass off something that looks like truth,' he said.

'When Mahatma hears about this he will be very pained and he will talk to you about it.'

Sriram was now genuinely scared and asked pathetically, 'What have I done that you should threaten and menace me?'

This softened her, and for the first time he noticed a little tenderness had crept into her tone.

'Do you mind moving off and waiting there? We should not be talking like this near Mahatmaji's hut. I will go to my hut and then join you there.'

She turned and disappeared; she had the lightning-like motion of a dancer, again the sort of pirouetting movement that she had adopted while carrying off other people's coins in a jingling box. She passed down the lane. He moved off slowly. He was tired of standing. He sat on a boulder at the edge of the river, kicking up the sand with his toes, and ruminating on his good fortune. He had never hoped for anything like it. It might have been a dream. This time yesterday he could not have thought he would talk on these terms to the money-box girl. He realized he had not yet asked her her name. He remembered that he had felt hungry and thirsty long ago. 'I wish they would give us all something to eat in Mahatmaji's camp.' He remembered that Mahatma ate only groundnuts and dates. He looked about hoping there would be vendors of these things. The Taluk Office gong sounded nine. He counted it deliberately, and wondered what his granny would make of his absence now. 'She will fret and report to the police, I suppose!' he reflected cynically. He wished he had asked his teacher to go and tell Granny not to expect him home till Gandhiji left the town. On second thoughts it struck him that it was just as well that he had not spoken to the teacher, who would probably have gone and spread the rumour that his interest in Gandhi was only a show and that he was really going after a girl. What was her name? Amazing how he had not yet asked her it, and the moment she came back he said, 'What is your name?'

'Bharati,' she answered. 'Why?'

'Just to know, that's all. Have I told you my name is Sriram?'

'Yes, you have told me that more than once,' she said. 'I have heard again and again that you are Sriram.'

'You are too sharp-tongued,' he replied. 'It is a wonder they tolerate you here, where peace and kindness must be practised.'

'I am practising kindness, otherwise I should not be speaking to you at all. If I didn't want to be kind to you I wouldn't have gone in and taken my *Chalak*'s permission and come right away here. We must have permission to talk to people at this hour.

426

There is such a thing as discipline in every camp. Don't imagine that because it is Mahatmaji's camp it is without any discipline. He would be the first to tell you about it if you raised the question with him.'

'You have the same style of talk as my grandmother. She is as sharp-tongued as you are,' Sriram said pathetically.

She ignored the comparison and asked, 'What about your mother?'

'I have never seen her, my grandmother has always been father and mother to me. Why don't you meet her? You will like her, both of you speak so much alike!'

'Yes, yes,' said the girl soothingly, 'some day I will come and meet her as soon as this is all over. You see how busy I am now.'

She became tender when she found that she was talking to someone without a mother, and Sriram noticing this felt it was worthwhile being motherless and grandmother-tended. She sat on the same step, with her legs dangling in the river, leaving a gap of a couple of feet between them. The river rumbled into the dark starlit night, the leaves of the huge tree over the ancient steps rustled and sighed. Far off bullock-carts and pedestrians were fording the river at Nallappa's Grove. Distant voices came through the night. Mahatmaji's camp was asleep. It was so quiet that Sriram felt like taking the girl in his arms, but he resisted the idea. He feared that if he touched her she might push him into the river. The girl was a termagant, she would surely develop into the same type as his grandmother with that sharp tongue of hers. Her proximity pricked his blood and set it coursing.

'There is no one about. What can she do?' he reflected. 'Let her try and push me into the river, and she will know with whom she is dealing,' and the next moment he blamed himself for his own crude thoughts. 'It is not safe with the Mahatma there. He may already have read my thoughts and be coming here.' He was a Mahatma because awake or asleep he was fully aware of what was going on all round him. God alone could say what the Mahatma would do to someone who did not possess absolute purity of thought where girls were concerned. It meant hardship, no doubt, but if one was to live in this camp one had to follow the orders that emanated from the great soul. He struggled against evil thoughts and said, 'Bharati!' She looked startled at being called so familiarly and he himself felt startled by the music of her name.

'What a nice name!' he remarked.

'I am glad you like it,' she said. 'The name was given by Bapuji himself.'

'Oh, how grand!' he cried.

She added, 'You know my father died during the 1920 movement. Just when I was born. When he learnt of it Bapuji, who had come down South, made himself my godfather and named me Bharati, which means – I hope you know what.'

'Yes, Bharati is India, and Bharati is the daughter of India, I suppose.'

'Right,' she said, and he was pleased at her commendation.

'After my mother died, I was practically adopted by the local Sevak Sangh, and I have not known any other home since,' she said.

'Do you mean to say you are all the time with these people?'

'What is wrong in it?' she asked. 'It has been my home.'

'Not that, I was only envying you. I too wish I could be with you all and do something instead of wasting my life.'

This appealed to her and she asked, 'What do you want to do?'

'The same as what you are doing. What are you doing?' he asked.

'I do whatever I am asked to do by the Sevak Sangh. Sometimes they ask me to go and teach people spinning and tell them about Mahatmaji's ideas. Sometimes they send me to villages and poor quarters. I meet them and talk to them and do a few things. I attend to Mahatmaji's needs.'

'Please let me also do something along with you,' he pleaded. 'Why don't you take me as your pupil? I want to do something good. I want to talk to poor people.'

'What will you tell them?' she asked ruthlessly.

He made some indistinct sounds. 'I will tell them whatever you ask me to tell them,' he said, and this homage to her superior intelligence pleased her.

'H'm! But why?' she asked.

He summoned all his courage and answered, 'Because I like you, and I like to be with you.'

She burst into a laugh and said, 'That won't be sufficient ... They ...' she indicated a vast army of hostile folk behind her back. 'They may chase you away if you speak like that.'

He became sullen and unhappy. He rallied and said presently, 'Well, I too would willingly do something.'

'What?' she taunted him again.

He looked at her face helplessly, desperately, and asked, 'Are you making fun of me?'

'No, but I wish to understand what you are saying.'

She relented a little, presently, and said, 'I will take you to Bapu, will you come?'

He was panic-stricken. 'No, no. I can't.'

'You have been there already.'

He could give no reasonable explanation and now he realized the enormity of his rashness. He said, 'No, no, I would be at a loss to know how to talk to him, how to reply to him and what to tell him.'

'But you sat there before him like someone always known to him!' she said, 'like his best friend.'

She laughed and enjoyed teasing him.

'Somehow I did it, but I won't do it again,' he declared. 'He may find me out if I go before him again.'

Suddenly she became very serious and said, 'You will have to face Bapuji if you want to work with us.'

Sriram became speechless. His heart palpitated with excitement. He wished he could get up and run away, flee once and for all the place, be done with it, and turn his back on the whole business for ever. This was too much. The gods seemed to be out to punish him for his hardihood and presumption.

He cried, 'Bharati, tell me if I can meet you anywhere else, otherwise please let me go.' He was in a cold sweat. 'What should I say when I speak to him? I would blabber like an idiot.'

'You are already doing it,' she said, unable to restrain her laughter.

He said pathetically, 'You seem to enjoy bothering me. I am sorry I ever came here.'

'Why are you so cowardly?' she asked.

Sriram said resolutely, 'I can't talk to Mahatmaji. I wouldn't know how to conduct myself before him.'

'Just be yourself. It will be all right.'

'I wouldn't be able to answer his questions properly.'

'He is not going to examine you like an inspector of schools. You don't have to talk to him unless you have something to say. You may keep your mouth shut and he won't mind. You may just be yourself, say anything you feel like saying. He will not mind anything at all, but you will have to speak the truth if you speak at all.'

'Truth! In everything!' He looked scared.

'Yes, in everything. You may speak as bluntly as you like, and he will not take it amiss, provided it is just truth.'

Sriram looked more crushed than ever. In this dark night he seemed to have a terrible problem ahead of him. After brooding over it for a while he said, 'Bharati, tell me if I may meet you anywhere else. Otherwise let me go.'

She replied with equal resolution, 'If you wish to meet me come to Bapuji, the only place where you may see me. Of course, if you don't want to see me any more, go away.'

This placed him in a dilemma. 'Where? How?' he asked.

'Come to the door of Bapu's hut and wait for me.'

'When? Where?'

'At three a.m. tomorrow morning. I'll take you to him.'

Saying this, she jumped to her feet and ran off towards her hut.

Granny had slept fitfully. She had gone up to Kanni's shop five times during the evening to enquire if anyone had seen Sriram, and sent a boy who had come to make a purchase there to look for Sriram everywhere. At last the school-master who lived up the street told her as he passed her house,

'Your pet is in Mahatma's camp. I saw him.'

'Ah! What was he doing there?' asked Granny alarmed. For her the Mahatma was one who preached dangerously, who tried to bring untouchables into the temples, and who involved people in difficulties with the police. She didn't like the idea. She wailed, 'Oh, master, why did you allow him to stay on there? You should have brought him away. It is so late and he has not come home. As his old teacher you should have weaned him away.'

'Don't worry, madam, he is perfectly safe. How many of us could have the privilege of being so near the Mahatma? You must be happy that he is doing so well! Our country needs more young men like him.'

Granny replied, 'It is teachers like you who have ruined our boys and this country,' and turned in, slamming the door.

When Sriram arrived and knocked she was half asleep and in the worst possible mood. She opened the door, let him in, bolted the door again, and went back to her bed saying, 'I have kept some rice in that bowl mixed with curd and the other one is without curd. Put out the lamp after you have eaten.' Lying in bed, she listened to the sound of Sriram putting away his plate and leaving the kitchen. And then she turned her face to the wall and pretended to be asleep. She hoped that her grandson would understand her mood, come over, and assure her that he would not get into bad ways: but the young man was otherwise engaged. He was in a state of semi-enchantment. Bharati's presence and talk still echoed in his mind, and he recollected the thrill of her touch. He liked to think that when he was not noticing she had touched his arm and patted his shoulder. He thought how he would prefer the rest of his life listening to her banter, but that meant – here was the conflict – he would have to go into the Presence. All else seemed to him insignificant beside this great worry. If it had been any other day he would have pulled his granny out of her sleep and narrated to her all the day's events. If she happened to be in a bad mood he would have pulled her out of it. He knew now that she was not in a proper temper; he could sense it the moment he stepped on the threshold, but he preferred to leave her alone; he felt he had a far greater problem to tackle than appeasing the mood of a mere granny.

He went to bed and slept in all less than an hour. Bharati wanted him there at three a.m., and he needed an hour to reach the place. He got up before one, washed and bathed and put on special clothes, bent over his granny's bed to whisper, 'I have to be going now, bolt the door.'

She tried to ask, 'What! At this hour, what has come over you?' but he was gone on soft footsteps, closing the door behind him.

He stood at the entrance to Mahatmaji's hut, holding his breath. It was very difficult to decide what he should do now. She had asked him to be present at the portals of the Great Presence, but perhaps she had been fooling him. He feared that any sound he made might rouse the Mahatma and bring the entire camp about his ears. He stood ruefully looking at the camp. Street dogs were barking somewhere. Occasionally the branches of trees over the river rustled and creaked. He stood looking ruefully towards the women's quarters. There a lantern was burning, people seemed to be awake and moving about. He thought, 'What if the lantern is burning? They may be sleeping with lights on. Women are cowardly anyway.' The stirring he heard might be them rolling in their beds, noisy creatures! Unaccountably he was feeling irritated at the thought of women, the species to which Bharati belonged. He saw a light in Mahatmaji's camp. The door was shut. He heard soft footsteps moving in there. Long ago the Taluk Office gong had struck some small hour. He could hardly believe he had actually sacrificed his sleep and was standing here in the cold wind, at an unearthly hour. Even the scavengers, the earliest to rise in the town, were still asleep. He felt suddenly afraid that he might be attacked by thieves or ghosts. Or if a policeman saw him and took him to be a prowler, how should he explain himself? He couldn't very well say, 'Bharati asked me to wait at Mahatmaji's hut at about three a.m.' He wanted to turn and go away: he could at least go home and make up to his grandmother instead of hanging around here and wondering what to do. He could tell her: 'I went to see the Mahatma, but changed my mind and came away. Why should I get to know him and then into all sorts of difficulties? Don't you think so, Granny?' And she was sure to revive and look happy again.

He gave one forlorn look at the women's quarters and turned away, his mind completely made up to earn the concrete goodwill of a granny rather than the doubtful and strange favours of big-wigs like the Mahatma and snobs like Bharati. Heaven knew who else would be there. But still the pull of Bharati was strong and he could not get away from the place so easily as he had imagined. He wanted to make just one more attempt to see her and bid her goodbye. Perhaps she was in a situation in which he could help her: people might have tied her up to her cot and gagged her mouth. Anything might happen to a beautiful girl like her. Otherwise there could be no explanation for her absence. Anyway, he felt it would be his duty to go and find out what was wrong and where. He'd have willingly gone near the women's quarters, but he lacked the necessary courage and did the next best thing: once again repeating a rash act he tip-toed towards Mahatmaji's hut: his idea was to peep in unobtrusively, and see if Bharati was there or anywhere else safe and sound and then move off. But in his befuddled state it did not occur to him that possibly he might be seen before he saw anyone. And it happened so. The door of Mahatmaji's hut was half open. Light streamed out through the gap. Sriram went towards it like a charmed moth. If he had paused to reflect he would not have believed himself to be capable of repeating a foolhardy act a second time. But through lack of sleep, and tension of nerves, a general recklessness had come over him, the same innocent charge that had taken him tumbling into the hut the previous evening took him there again now. He peeped in like a clown. The door was half open; he had over-estimated its width from a distance, for he could not peep in without thrusting his head through.

'Oh, there he is!' cried Bharati, with laughter in her voice. 'You may open the door if you wish to come in,' she said. Sriram felt again that the girl was making fun of him. Even in the great presence, she didn't seem to care. Here at least Sriram had hoped she would speak without the undertone of mischief. He felt so irritated at the thought that he replied with all the pungency he could muster in his tone: 'You have – I waited for you there – '

'Come in, come in,' said the Mahatma. 'Why should you be standing there? You could have come straight in.'

'But she asked me to wait outside,' said Sriram, stepping in gingerly. From the door to where the Mahatma sat the distance

433

was less than ten feet, but he felt he was taking hours to cover it. His legs felt weak and seemed to intertwine, he seemed to be walking like a drunkard, a particularly dangerous impression to create in the Mahatma, who was out to persuade even the scavengers to give up drinking. In a flash it occurred to him that he ought to have a sensible answer ready if the Mahatma should suddenly turn round and ask, 'Have you been drinking toddy or whisky?'

But his trial came to an end, when Gandhi said, 'Bharati has just been mentioning you.' He spoke while his hands were busy turning a spinning wheel, drawing out a fine thread. A man sitting in a corner, with a pad resting on his knee, was writing. Mahatmaji himself as always was doing several things at the same time. While his hands were spinning, his eyes perused a letter held before him by another, and he found it possible too to put in a word of welcome to Sriram. Through the back door of the hut many others were coming in and passing out. For each one of them Mahatmaji had something to say.

He looked up at Sriram and said: 'Sit down, young man. Come and sit as near me as you like.' There was so much unaffected graciousness in his tone that Sriram lost all fear and hesitation. He moved briskly up. He sat on the floor near Mahatmaji and watched with fascination the smooth turning of the spinning wheel. Bharati went to an inner part of the hut, threw a swift look at Sriram, which he understood to mean, 'Remember not to make a fool of yourself.'

The Mahatma said, 'Nowadays I generally get up an hour earlier in order to be able to do this: spinning a certain length is my most important work: even my prayer comes only after that. I'd very much like you to take a vow to wear only cloth made out of your own hands each day.'

'Yes, I will do so,' promised Sriram.

When the gong in the Taluk Office struck four, the Mahatma invited Sriram to go out with him for a walk. He seized his staff in one hand and with the other supported himself on the shoulder of Bharati, and strode out of the hut – a tall figure in white. He had tucked his watch at his waist into a fold of his white *dhoti*. He pulled it out and said: 'Half an hour I have to walk, come with me, Sriram. You can talk to me undisturbed.' A few others joined them. Sriram felt he was walking through some unreal dream world. The Mahatma was in between him and Bharati, and it was difficult to snatch a look at her as often as he wanted. He had to step back a quarter of an inch now and then, in order to catch a glimpse of her laughing face. They walked along the river-bank. The sky was rosy in the east. Gandhi turned and spoke some business to those behind him. He suddenly addressed himself to Sriram: 'Your town is very beautiful. Have you ever noticed it before?' Sriram felt unhappy and gasped for breath. The morning air blew on his face, birds were chirping, the city was quiet: it was all well known, but why did the Mahatma mention it especially now? Should he say 'Yes' or 'No'? If he said 'Yes' he would be lying, which would be detected at once; if he said 'No', God knew what the Mahatma would think of him. He looked about. A couple of scavengers of the colony who had joined the group were waiting eagerly to know what he would say: they were evidently enjoying his predicament, and he dared not look in the direction of Bharati. The Mahatma said: 'God is everywhere, and if you want to feel his presence you will see him in a place like this with a beautiful river flowing, the sunrise with all its colours, and the air so fresh. Feeling a beautiful hour or a beautiful scene or a beautiful object is itself a form of prayer.' Sriram listened in reverential silence, glad to be let off so lightly. When Gandhiji spoke of beauty, it sounded unreal as applied to the sun and the air, but the word acquired a practical significance when he thought of it in terms of Bharati. Gandhi said: 'By the time we meet again next, you must give me a very good account of yourself.'

He laughed in a kindly manner, and Sriram said, 'Yes, Bapuji, I will be a different man.'

'Why do you say "different"? You will be all right if you are fully yourself.'

'I don't think that is enough, Bapu,' said Bharati. 'He should change from being himself, if he is to come to any good. I think he is very lazy. He gets up at eight o'clock, and idles away the day.'

'How do you know?' Sriram asked indignantly.

'It's only a guess,' said the girl. Sriram felt angry with her for her irresponsible talk. Everyone laughed.

The Mahatma said: 'You must not say such things, Bharati, unless you mean to take charge of him and help him.'

During the last fifteen minutes of this walk the Mahatma said nothing; he walked in silence, looking at the ground before him. When the Mahatma was silent the others were even more so, the only movement they performed was putting one foot before another on the sand, keeping pace with him: some were panting hard and trying hard to suppress the sound. The Mahatma's silence was heavy and pervasive, and Sriram was afraid even to gulp or cough, although he very much wanted to clear his throat, cough, sneeze, swing his arms about. The only sound at the moment was the flowing of the river and the twitter of birds. Somewhere a cow was mooing. Even Bharati, the embodiment of frivolity, seemed to have become sombre. The Mahatma pulled out his watch, looked at it briefly and said, 'We will go back, that is all the walk I can afford today.' Sriram wanted to ask, 'Why?' but he held his tongue. The Mahatma turned to him as they were walking back, 'You have a grandmother, I hear, but no parents.'

'Yes. My grandmother is very old.'

'Yes, she must be, otherwise how can you call her a grand-mother?' People laughed, Sriram too joined in this laughter out of politeness.

'Does she not miss you very much when you are away from her so long?'

'Yes, very much. She gets very angry with me. I don't know what to do about it,' said Sriram courageously rushing ahead. He felt pleased at having said something of his own accord, but his only fear was that Bharati might step in and say something nasty and embarrassing, but he was happy to note that Bharati held her peace.

Mahatmaji said: 'You must look after your granny too, she must have devoted herself to bringing you up.'

'Yes, but when I am away like this she is very much upset.'

'Is it necessary for you to be away from her so much?'

'Yes, Bapu, otherwise how can I do anything in this world?'

'What exactly do you want to do?'

It was now that Sriram became incoherent. He was seized with a rush of ideas and with all the confusion that too many ideas create. He said something, and the Mahatma watched him patiently, the others too held their breath and watched, and after a few moments of struggle for self-expression, Sriram was able to form a cogent sentence. It was the unrelenting pressure of his subconscious desires that jerked the sentence out of his lips, and he said, 'I like to be where Bharati is.' The Mahatma said, 'Oh, is that so!' He patted Bharati's back and said, 'What a fine friend you have! You must be pleased to have such a devoted friend. How long have you known him?'

Bharati said like a shot, 'Since yesterday. I saw him for the first time sitting in your hut and I asked him who he was.'

Sriram interposed and added, 'But I knew her before, although I spoke to her only yesterday.'

The Mahatma passed into his hut, and went on to attend to other things. Many people were waiting for him. Bharati disappeared into the Mahatma's hut the moment they arrived. Sriram fell back and got mixed up with a crowd waiting outside. He felt jealous of Bharati's position. She sought him out later and said, 'You are probably unused to it, but in Bapu's presence we speak only the absolute truth and nothing less than that, and nothing more than that either.'

He took her to task: 'What will he think of me now when he knows that I have not known you long enough and yet – '

'Well, what?' she twitted him.

'And yet I wish to be with you and so on.'

'Why don't you go in and tell him you have been speaking nonsense and that you were blurting out things without forethought or self-control? Why couldn't you have told him that you want to serve the country, that you are a patriot, that you want to shed your blood in order to see that the British leave the country? That is what most people say when they come near the Mahatma. I have seen hundreds of people come to him, and say the same thing.'

'And he believes all that?' asked Sriram.

'Perhaps not, but he thinks it is not right to disbelieve anyone.'

'But you say we must only speak the truth in his presence.'

'If you can, of course, but if you can't, the best thing to do is to maintain silence.'

'Why are you so angry with me, is it not a part of your duty not to be angry with others?' asked Sriram pathetically.

'I don't care,' said Bharati, 'this is enough to irritate even the Mahatma. Now what will he think of me if he realizes I am encouraging a fellow like you to hang about the place, a fellow whom I have not known even for a full day yet!'

Sriram became reckless, and said breezily, 'What does it matter how long I have known you? Did you think I was going to lie to him if you had not spoken before I spoke?'

These bickerings were brought to an end by someone calling 'Bharati' from another hut. Bharati abandoned him and disappeared from the spot.

Bharati's words gave him an idea. He realized his own omission, and proposed to remedy it next time he walked with the Mahatma. Sriram's anxiety lest he fall asleep when the Mahatma was up kept him awake the whole night. He shared the space on the floor with one of the men in the camp. It was a strange feeling to lie down in a hut, and he felt he was becoming a citizen of an entirely new world. He missed the cosy room of his house in Kabir Lane, he missed the two pillows and the soft mattress and the carpet under it; even the street noises of Kabir Street added much to the domestic quality of life, and he missed it badly now. He had to adopt an entirely new mode of life. He had to live, of his own choice, in a narrow hut, with thatch above, with a dingy, sooty smell hanging about everything. The floor had been swept with cowdung and covered with a thin layer of sand. He had to snuggle his head on the crook of his arm for a pillow. He had to share this place with another volunteer in the camp, a cadaverous serious young man wearing *khadi* shorts, a *khadi* vest, and a white cap on his closely shaved head. He had a fiery look and an unsmiling face. He was from North India, he could only speak broken English and he was totally ignorant of Tamil words. This man had already stretched himself on the floor with a small bag stuffed with clothes under his head.

Bharati had told Sriram, 'You had better stick on here, around the camp, if you want to be with Mahatmaji. You won't have any comforts here, remember. We are all trained to live like this.'

Sriram sniffed and said, 'Oh, who wants any comforts? I don't care for them myself. You think I am a fellow who cares for luxuries in life?'

There was a class of society where luxuries gave one a status, and now here was the opposite. The more one asserted one cared for no luxury, the more one showed an inclination for hardship and discomfort, the greater was one's chance of being admitted into the fold. Sriram had understood it the moment he stepped into the camp. Here the currency was suffering and self-mortification. Everyone seemed to excel his neighbour in managing in uncomfortable situations, and Sriram caught the spirit, though it took him time to grasp the detail and get accustomed to it.

There had been a meeting in the evening and after that the Mahatma retired at his usual hour of seven-thirty, and it was a signal for the entire camp to retire. Bharati sought out Sriram and gave him a plateful of rice and buttermilk and an orange, and she also held out to him a small jasmine out of a bouquet which had earlier been presented to the Mahatma by some children's deputation. He received the flower gratefully, smelt it, and asked, 'How did you know I liked jasmine?'

'It is not so difficult a thing to know,' she said and dismissed the subject immediately.

She said, 'I have found a place for you to sleep, with a volunteer named Gorpad.'

Gorpad had been half asleep when Sriram entered his hut. Bharati peeped and said, '*Bhai* ...' and something in Hindi and turned and disappeared from the spot. The other lifted his head slightly and said, 'You can come in and sleep.'

'Only on the floor?' Sriram asked.

'Of course, of course,' said the other.

'Why?' asked Sriram.

'Why? Because Mahatmaji says so.'

'Oh,' said Sriram, feeling that he was treading on dangerous ground. 'I see that otherwise there is no reason why we should sleep on the floor.'

439

'What do you mean by otherwise?' said the other argumentatively.

Sriram settled himself beside Gorpad, and said, 'I didn't mean it.'

'Mean what?' said the other. He seemed to be a pugnacious fellow. Sriram felt afraid of him. What did the girl mean by putting him in with this fighter? Could it be that she disliked him, and wanted him to be beaten? If she disliked him, she would not have given him a jasmine flower. It was well known that jasmine was exchanged only between persons who liked each other, and yet the girl gave him a jasmine with one hand and with the other led him into the company of this terrible man. The other might sit on his chest while he slept and try to choke him.

Gorpad said, 'You are new, I suppose?'

'Yes,' said Sriram. 'I am new to this place. It is through Mahatmaji's kindness I am now here, otherwise I should have gone home and slept.'

'Yes,' Gorpad said seeming to understand the situation in a fresh light. 'You are welcome here. We are all persons who have to live like soldiers in a camp. We are indeed soldiers in our fight to eject the British from our land. We are all prepared to sacrifice our lives for the task. We sleep here on the bare floor because the major part of our lives we shall have to spend in gaol, where we won't be given such a comfortable bed unless we are A or B class prisoners. We are not important enough to be classified as A or B, and you had better get used to it all; and we are always prepared to be beaten by the police, *lathi*-charged, dragged to the gaol, or even shot: my father died ten years ago facing a policeman's gun.'

Sriram said, not to be outdone in the matter of political reminiscences, 'I know Bharati's father also died in the same way, when he was beaten by the police.'

'That was during the first non-co-operation days in 1920; her father led the first batch of *Satyagrahis* who were going to take down the Union Jack from the Secretariat at Madras. He was beaten with a police *lathi*, and a blow fell on his chest and he dropped dead, but my father was shot. Do you know he was actually shot by a policeman's rifle? I was also in the crowd watching him. He was picketing a shop where they were selling toddy and other alcoholic drinks, and a police company came and asked him to go away, but he refused. A crowd gathered, and there was a lot of mess and in the end the police shot him point blank.' He wiped away tears at the memory of it. 'I will not rest till the British are sent out of India,' his voice was thick with sorrow. 'My brother became a terrorist and shot dead many English officials, nobody knows his whereabouts. I should also have joined him and shot many more Englishmen, but our Mahatma will not let me be violent even in thought,' he said ruefully.

Sriram wishing to sound very sympathetic said, 'All Englishmen deserve to be shot. They have been very cruel.'

'You should not even think on those lines, if you are going to be a true *Satyagrahi*,' said the other.

'No, no, I am not really thinking on those lines,' Sriram amended immediately. 'I was only feeling so sorry. Of course we should not talk of shooting anyone, and where is the gun? We have no guns. My grandmother used to say that there was a gun in our house belonging to my father. Do you know that he died in Mesopotamia? He was also shot point blank.'

'He died in the war, the last war?'

'Yes,' said Sriram.

'Then he must have been a soldier in the British Army,' Gorpad said with a touch of contempt in his voice.

Sriram noted it, but accepted it with resignation. He added as a sort of compensation, 'They say he was a great soldier.'

'Possibly, possibly,' said the other with patronage in his voice. Sriram bore it as a trial.

That night he picked up a great deal of political knowledge. Gorpad went on speaking till two a.m. and afterwards both of them left for the river, performed their ablutions there, and by the time the camp was awake Sriram had returned fresh and tidy, so that Bharati said, 'You are coming through your first day with us quite well.' Through diligently listening to Gorpad he had picked up many political idioms, and felt himself equipped to walk with the Mahatma without embarrassment.

He told the Mahatma, 'It is my greatest desire in life to take a vow to oust the British from India.'

441

The Mahatma looked at him with a smile and asked, 'How do you propose to do it?'

Sriram could not find a ready answer; it was one of the many occasions when he felt that he had spoken unnecessarily. He caught a glimpse of Bharati on the other side, her mischievous face sparkled with delight at his confusion. He felt piqued by her look. He said haughtily, 'With your blessing, sir, I shall make myself good enough for the task. I shall be with you as long as possible, and if you will kindly guide me you can make me a soldier fit to take up the fight to make the British leave our country.'

The Mahatma took his resolve with every sign of pleasure. He remained silent for a while as their footsteps pit-patted on the sands, a sombre silence fell on the gathering. 'Well, young friend, if God wills it, you will do great things, trust in him and you will be all right.'

To Sriram this seemed a rather tame preparation for a soldierly existence. If it had been possible, he would have strutted before Bharati in khaki and a decorated chest, though the world was having a surfeit of decorations just then.

Presently the Mahatma himself spoke dispelling his notions: 'Before you aspire to drive the British from this country, you must drive every vestige of violence from your system. Remember that it is not going to be a fight with sticks and knives or guns but only with love. Until you are sure you have an overpowering love at heart for your enemy, don't think of driving him out. You must gradually forget the term "Enemy". You must think of him as a friend who must leave you. You must train yourself to become a hundred per cent *ahimsa* soldier. You must become so sensitive that it is not possible for you to wear sandals made of the hide of slaughtered animals; you should prefer to go barefoot rather than wear the hide of an animal killed for your sake, that is if you are unable to secure the skin of an animal that has died a natural death.'

Sriram said, 'Yes, I promise,' but while saying it his eyes were fixed on Mahatmaji's feet; he struggled to suppress the questions that were welling up in his mind.

The Mahatma read his thoughts and said, 'Yes, these are sandals made of just such leather. In our tannery at Wardha we specialize in it. No one in our Ashram wears anything else.'

Sriram wanted to ask, 'How do you know when an animal is dying, and how do you watch for it?' but ruthlessly suppressed the question as an unworthy one, which might betray him.

Sriram was told that he could accompany Mahatmaji in his tour of the villages on condition that he went home, and secured Granny's approval. Sriram tried to slur the matter over, he said it would not be necessary, he hinted he was an independent man used to such outings from home. The Mahatma's memory was better than that. He said with a smile, 'I remember you said that she didn't like to see you mixing with us.'

Sriram thought it over and said, 'Yes, master, but how can I for ever remain tied to her? It is not possible.'

'Are you quite sure that you want to change your style of life?' asked the Mahatma.

'I can think of nothing else,' Sriram said. 'How can I live as I have lived all these years?' He threw a quick glance at Bharati as she came in with some letters for the Mahatma. Her look prevented him from completing the sentence, which would have run, 'And I always wish to be with Bharati and not with my grandmother.'

The Mahatma said, 'I shall be happy to have you with us as long as you like, but you must first go home and tell your grandmother and receive her blessing. You must tell her frankly what you wish to do, but you must cause her no pain.'

Sriram hesitated. The prospect of facing Granny was unnerving. The thought of her was like the thought of an unreal troublesome world, one which he hoped he had left behind for ever: the real world for him now was the one of Bharati, Gorpad, unslaughtered naturally dying animals, the Mahatma, spinning wheels. He wanted to be here all the time: it seemed impossible for him to go back to Kabir Street, that pyol, and that shop, and those people there who treated him as if he were only eight years old. He stood before the Mahatma as if to appeal to him not to press him to go and face his grandmother, but the master was unrelenting. 'Go and speak to her. I don't think she is so unreasonable as to deny you your ambitions. Tell her that I like to have you with me. If you tour with me the next two weeks, you will observe and learn much that may be useful to you later in life.

Tell her she will feel glad that she let you go. Assure her that I will look after you safely.' Every word filled him with dread when he remembered the terms in which Granny referred to the Mahatma. He dared not even give the slightest indication as to how she would react. He felt a great pity for the Mahatma, so innocent that he could not dream of anyone talking ill of him. He felt angry at the thought of Granny, such an ill-informed, ignorant and bigoted personality! What business had she to complicate his existence in this way? If he could have had his will he would have ignored his grandmother, but he had to obey the Mahatma now.

He said, 'All right, sir. I will go and get my granny's blessing. I'll be back early tomorrow.'

Half a dozen times on the way he resolved to turn back and tell Mahatma Gandhi that he had seen Granny. How could he find out the truth, anyway? But he dismissed the thought as unpractical, though perhaps not so unworthy under the circumstances. Suppose Granny created a row, went into a faint or threatened to kill herself, and made enough noise to attract the neighbours who might come and lock him up in his house, refusing to let him out? Should he face this risk in order to tell Gandhiji that he had seen the obstinate old lady as ordered? Would it not be prudent like a sensible man to say that it had been done? Probably Granny would guess there was Bharati behind all this and disbelieve anything he might say about Mahatmaji. Or if she spoke insultingly about Mahatmaji, he couldn't trust himself to listen patiently. He might do something for which he might feel sorry afterwards. He visualized himself suppressing his granny's words with force and violence, but he remembered that it would not be right to act like that where the Mahatma was concerned. He would be upset to hear about it.

The thing to do was to turn the *jutka* back and tell the Mahatma that he had Granny's blessings. But then, being a Mahatma, he might read his thoughts and send him back to Granny or he might cancel all his programme until he was assured that Granny had been seen or begin a fast until it was done. What made the Mahatma attach so much importance to Granny when he had so many things to mind? When he had the all-important task of driving the British out he ought to leave simple matters like Granny to be handled by himself. His thoughts were in a welter of confusion while he was in the *jutka*, but soon the horse turned into Kabir Street. He paid the fare without haggling and sent away the *jutka* quietly. He didn't want his movements to become noticeable in the neighbourhood.

He found his granny in a semi-agreeable frame of mind. His prolonged absence seemed to have made her nervous, and she tried to be nice to him. She probably feared he would flounce out of the house if she attempted to talk to him in the manner of yesterday.

She merely said: 'What a long time you have been away, my boy,' attempting to keep out all trace of reproach from her tone. He pretended to settle down. He drew up the canvas chair he had bought for her and sat down under the hall lamp. His granny fussed about as if she had recovered someone long lost. She set before him a plateful of food fried in ghee, saying, 'They sent this down from the lawyer's house: the first birthday of his eighth son. They don't seem to miss anything for any child.'

Sriram put a piece into his mouth, munched it, nodded his approval and said: 'Yes, they have made it of pure ghee. Good people.' He crunched it noisily.

Granny said: 'I kept it for you, I knew you would like it. I was wondering how long I should keep it. You know I have no teeth. Who would want stuff like that when you are not here? Don't eat all of it, you will not be able to eat your dinner.'

'Oh, dinner! I've had my dinner, Granny.'

'So soon!'

'Yes, in the Ashram camp, we have to dine before seven usually. It's the rule.'

'What sort of a dinner can it be at seven!' she cried in disappointment. 'Come and eat again, you ought to be fit for a real dinner now.'

'No, Granny. It is all regulated very strictly. We can't do anything as we like. We have got to observe the rules in all matters. We get quite good food there.'

'Have you got to pay for it?' asked Granny.

'Of course not,' said Sriram. 'What do you think, do you think Mahatmaji is running a hotel?'

'Then why should they feed you?'

'It's because we belong there.'

'Do they provide a lot of public feeding?'

Sriram lost his temper at this. He was appalled at Granny's denseness. 'I said they feed all of us who belong there, don't you follow?'

'Why should they feed you?'

'It is because we are volunteers.'

'Nice volunteers!' cried Granny, threatening to return to her yesterday's mood any second. 'And what do they give you to eat?'

'*Chappatis*, curd, and buttermilk and vegetables.'

'I'm glad. I was afraid they might force you to eat egg and fowl.'

Sriram was horrified. 'What do you take the Mahatma for! Do you know, he won't even wear sandals made of the hide of slaughtered animals!'

Granny was seized with a fit of laughter. Tears rolled down her cheeks. 'Won't wear sandals!' she cried in uncontrollable laughter. 'Never heard of such a thing before! How do they manage it? By peeling off the skin of animals before they are slaughtered, is that it?'

'Shut up, Granny!' cried Sriram in a great rage. 'What an irresponsible gossip you are! I never thought you could be so bad!'

Granny for the first time noticed a fiery earnestness in her grandson, and gathered herself up. She said: 'Oh! He is your God, is he?'

'Yes, he is, and I won't hear anyone speak lightly of him.'

'What else can I know, a poor ignorant hag like me! Do I read the newspapers? Do I listen to lectures? Am I told what is what by anyone? How should I know anything about that man Gandhi!'

'He is not a man; he is a Mahatma!' cried Sriram.

'What do you know about a Mahatma, anyway?' asked Granny.

446

Sriram fidgeted and rocked himself in his chair in great anger. He had not come prepared to face a situation of this kind. He had been only prepared to face a granny who might show sullenness at his absence, create difficulties for him when he wanted to go away and exhibit more sorrow and rage than levity. But here she was absolutely reckless, frivolous, and without the slightest sense of responsibility or respect. This was a situation which he had not anticipated, and he had no technique to meet it. It was no use, he realized, showing righteous indignation: that would only tickle the old lady more and more, and when the time came for him to take her permission and go, she might become too intractable. She might call in the neighbours, and make fun of him. He decided that he must change his tactics. Suddenly springing up he asked: 'Granny, have you had your food? I am keeping you away from it, talking like this!'

'It doesn't matter,' she said, almost on the point of giggling. 'How many years is it since I had a mouthful of food at night – must be nearly twenty years. You couldn't have seen me in your lifetime eating at night.'

There was such a ring of pride in her voice that Sriram felt impelled to say: 'There is nothing extraordinary in it. Anybody might be without food.' He wanted to add, 'The Mahatma has fasted for so many days on end, and so often,' but suppressed it. The old lady however had no need of being told anything. She added at once, 'No! When Mahatma Gandhi fasts, everybody talks about it.'

'And when you fast at nights only, nobody notices it, and that is all the difference between you and Gandhiji?' She was struck by the sharp manner in which he spoke.

She asked: 'Do you want your dinner?'

'Yes, just to please you, that is all. I am not hungry, I told you that. And this stuff is good, made of good ghee. You may tell them so. I've eaten a great quantity of it and I'm not hungry.'

Granny came back to her original mood after all these unexpected transitions. She said: 'You must eat your dinner, my boy,' very earnestly. She bustled about again as if for a distinguished visitor. She pulled a dining leaf out of a bundle in the kitchen rack, spread it on the floor, sprinkled a little water on it, and drew the bronze rice pot nearer, and sat down in order to be able to serve him without getting up again. The little lamp wavered in its holder. He ate in silence, took a drink of water out of the good old brass tumbler that was by his side; he cast a glance at the old bronze vessel out of which rice had been served to him for years. He suddenly felt depressed at the sight of it all. He was oppressed with the thought that he was leaving these old associations, that this was really a farewell party. He was going into an unknown life right from here. God knew what was in store for him. He felt very gloomy at the thought of it all. He knew it would be no good ever talking to his granny about his plans, or the Mahatma or Bharati. All that was completely beyond her comprehension. She would understand only edibles and dinner and fasting at night in order to impress a neighbour with her austerity. No use talking to her about anything. Best to leave in the morning without any fuss. He had obeyed Mahatmaji's mandate to the extent of seeing her and speaking to her. The Mahatma should be satisfied and not expect him to be able to bring about a conversion in the old lady's outlook, enough to earn her blessing.

Granny was very old, probably eighty, ninety, or a hundred. He had never tried to ascertain her age correctly. And she would not understand new things. At dead of night, after assuring himself that Granny was fast asleep, he got up, scribbled a note to her by the night lamp, and placed it under the brass pot containing water on the window-sill, which she was bound to lift first thing in the morning. She could carry it to a neighbour and have it read to her if she had any difficulty in finding her glasses. Perhaps she might not like to have it read by the neighbours. She would always cry: 'Sriram, my glasses, where are the wretched glasses gone?' whenever anything came to her hand for reading, and it would be his duty to go to the cupboard, and fetch them. Now he performed the same duty in anticipation. He tip-toed to the *almirah*, took the glasses out of their case silently, and returned to the hall, leaving the spectacle case open, because it had a tendency to close with a loud clap. He placed the glasses beside his letter of farewell, silently opened the door, and stepped into the night.

## PART TWO

He was an accredited member of the group, and in many villages he was glad to find himself fussed over and treated with respect by the villagers. They looked on him with wonder. He formed a trio with Bharati and Gorpad; and whenever the villagers wanted to know anything about the Mahatma, they came and spoke to him reverentially, and that gave him an opportunity to work off all the knowledge he had gathered in his contacts with Gorpad and Bharati. It was a way of learning the job while being on it. Till then he had no notion of village life. He had been born and bred in the township of Malgudi, and even there his idea of the bounds of the universe were confined to Kabir Street, Market Road, one or two other spots. Whenever he heard the word 'villages', his mental picture was always one of green coconut groves, long and numerous steps leading down to the large tank, with elegant village women coming up bearing pitchers, and the temple spire showing beyond the tank bund, low roofed houses with broad pyols, and mat-covered waggons moving about dragged by bulls with tinkling bells around their necks, the cartmen singing all the time. He owed his idea to the various Tamil films, which he had frequently seen at the Regal. But he saw nothing of the kind here. The reality was different. Some villages were hardly more than a cluster of huts. For the first time he was seeing actual villages, and on the first day at a village ten miles from Malgudi, he felt so bewildered that he asked Bharati secretly: 'Where is the village?'

'Which village?'

'Why, any village,' he said.

'Doesn't this look like a village to you?' she asked.

'No,' he replied. They had found time for a chat, after the Mahatma had retired for the evening.

'What a pity,' she said, 'that it's so. But learn, young man, this is really a village. I'm not lying. There are seven hundred thousand other villages more or less like this in our country.'

'How do you know?' he asked to prolong the conversation.

'I learn from wise men,' she said.

'How wise?' he asked.

She ignored his frivolity and started talking of their mission. They were out to survey the villages which had recently been affected by famine. It was a mission of mercy; Mahatmaji had set out to study the famine conditions at first hand, and to put courage and hope into the sufferers. It was a grim, melancholy undertaking. The Mahatma attached so much value to this tour that he had set aside all his other engagements. A distant war being fought in Europe, and one probably about to start in the Far East, had their repercussions here. Though not bombed, they still suffered from the war; one did not see A.R.P. signs or even a war poster, but small wayside stations acted as a vital link, a feeding channel, to a vast war reservoir in Western Europe. The waggons at the sidings carried away night and day timber cut in the Mempi forests, the corn grown here, and the able-bodied men who might have been working on their land.

However grim the surroundings might be, Sriram and Bharati seemed to notice nothing. They had a delight in each other's company which mitigated the gloom of the surroundings. Gorpad alone looked oppressed with a sense of tragedy. He spoke less, retired early, mortified himself more and more. He said: 'See what the British have done to our country: this famine is their manoeuvring to keep us in enslavement. They are plundering the forests and fields to keep their war machinery going, and the actual sufferer is this child,' pointing at any village child who might chance to come that way, showing its ribs, naked and pot-bellied.

'There is no food left in these villages,' he cried passionately. 'There is no one to look after them; who cares for them? Who is there to help them out of their difficulties? Everyone is engaged in this war. The profiteer has hoarded all the grain beyond the reach of these growers. The war machine buys it at any price. It's too big a competitor for these poor folk.'

'Why does he say all that to me?' Sriram reflected while impatiently waiting to be left alone with Bharati. 'I'm not responsible for it.' Gorpad was an iron man and could be trusted to leave them alone because he had something else to do; and when his back was turned, their eyes met and they giggled at the memory of all the sad, bad matters they had just heard or noticed.

Sriram's idea of a village was nowhere to be seen. Hungry, parched men and women with skin stretched over their bones, bare earth, dry ponds, and miserable tattered thatched roofing over crumbling mud walls, streets full of pits and loose sand, unattractive dry fields – that was a village. Sriram could hardly believe he was within twenty miles of Malgudi and civilization. Here pigs and dogs lounged in dry gutters. Everything in these parts had the appearance of a dry gutter. Sriram wondered how people ever managed to go on living in such places. He wanted to stop and ask everyone: 'How long are you going to be here? Won't you return to Malgudi or somewhere else? Have you got to be here for ever?'

The Mahatma defeated the calculation of officials by refusing to give a programme of his tour, and by visiting unexpected places. The officials politely asked him to tell them where he wished to go. He merely replied: 'Everywhere if I can' or 'I wish I knew.'

'But we'd like to make proper arrangements.'

'For me? Don't trouble yourself. I can sleep in any hut. I can live where others are living. I don't think I shall demand many luxuries. Don't worry. We can look after ourselves. I'm not a guest here; I'm a host. Why don't you join us, as our guest?' He said this to the District Collector. 'We will promise to look after you, giving you all the comforts that you may want.'

Quite a band of officials followed him about on his tour. Mahatma Gandhi toured the villages mostly on foot. He halted wherever he liked. He stationed himself at the lowliest hut in the village if it was available, or in a temple corridor, or in the open air. For hours he walked silently, holding his staff and supporting his arm on one or other of his disciples. Often he stopped on the way to speak to a peasant cutting a tree or digging a field.

Sriram felt it unnecessary to know which village they were passing at a particular time. All were alike: it was the same

451

routine. Gandhiji's personal life went on as if he had been stationary in one place; the others adjusted themselves to it. He met the local village men and women, spoke to them about God, comforted the ailing, advised those who sought his guidance. He spoke to them about spinning, the war, Britain, and religion. He met them in their huts, spoke to them under the village banyan tree (no village was so bare yet that it was without its banyan tree). He trudged his way through ploughed fields, he climbed hard rocky places, through mud and slush, but always with the happiest look, and no place seemed too small for his attention.

Gandhiji's tour was drawing to an end. He was to board a train at Koppal, a tiny station at the foot of the Mempi Hills. The Mahatma wanted his arrival and departure to be kept a secret, and except a couple of officials deputed to see him off, there were no outsiders on the platform. The station-master, a small man with a Kaiser-like moustache, who wore a green lace-edged turban and *dhoti*, had, with the help of his porter, dragged a huge antique chair on to the platform. He had tidied up his children, six of them in a row, and made them stand quietly aside in the shade of a Gold Mohur tree in bloom. He had to act as Mahatmaji's host in between tapping various messages. He had begged Mahatmaji to occupy the chair on the platform. 'I can stand as well as anyone else,' said the Mahatma, looking around at his followers. Sriram noted the sadness in the other's face, and urged him, 'Please take your seat, Bapuji,' and the Mahatma sat down, his followers standing around. The little station-master was excited and agitated and beads of perspiration ran down his eyelids. Beyond the railway line there was a row of hills, standing against purple skies. The station-master panted for breath, and constantly nudged and instructed his children to behave themselves although they were all the time standing stiffly as if on a drill parade.

Mahatmaji said: 'Station Masterji, why don't you let them run about and play as they like? Why do you constrain them?'

'I'm not constraining them, master. It's their habit,' he said with the hope of impressing the visitor with the training of his children.

The Mahatma said: 'Friend, I fear you are trying to put them on good behaviour before me. I would love it better if they ran about and played normally, and picked up those flowers dropping on the ground, which they want to do. I'm very keen that children should be free and happy.'

True to his custom the Mahatma took out the garlands and fruits given to him on the way, called up the children, and distributed them. Their father fidgeted, his nerves on edge lest someone should suddenly misbehave. The sky was turning red beyond the railway line. A bell sounded inside his little office. He ran to it, and came back with more dew drops clouding his face: 'The seven down has left Periapur. It'll be here in fifteen minutes. At the stroke of eighteen forty-two.' He looked anxious in case the train might defeat his promise.

The Mahatma said: 'You may attend to your work in your cabin, don't bother about us.'

'May I?' he asked desperately. 'I've to write the fare records, sir, and prepare the line to receive the train.'

'Certainly, go on,' said the Mahatma.

For the first time during all these weeks Sriram felt depressed and unhappy. The thought of having to live a mundane existence without Mahatmaji appalled him. Not even the proximity of Bharati seemed to mitigate his misery. As the sound of the approaching train was heard, he looked so stunned that Mahatmaji said: 'Be happy. Bharati will look after you.' Sriram looked at Bharati hopefully. Mahatmaji added: 'Remember that she is your *Guru*, and think of her with reverence and respect, and you will be all right and she will be all right.' Sriram took time to digest this sentence. The train steamed in. Mahatmaji entered a third-class compartment.

Gorpad, a cold-headed stoic whom no parting moved, told Sriram: 'Now you know what your duties are, and how to do them. Sister, you will receive our instructions. *Namaste*,' and climbed into Gandhiji's compartment. His party followed him in.

The first bell rang, and then the second. The station-master came out, and said: 'The seven down generally halts here only two minutes, but today we have detained it for three and a half minutes, sir.' He looked despairingly at the crowd of passengers from other carriages gathered before Mahatmaji's window. The engine was humming. The engine driver from one end and the guard from the other had left their stations in order to see the Mahatma, who returned their greetings and asked: 'How can the train move sir, when its heart and soul are here?' The engine driver withdrew with a grin on his face. The Mahatma said to the other people, 'Now, you will all have to go back to your places.' The crowd dispersed and the station-master waved his flag.

Gandhiji told Sriram: 'Write to me often. I'll also promise you a fairly regular correspondence. In the future you know where lies your work. Become a master-spinner, soon. Don't be despondent.'

'Yes, master,' said Sriram; the parting affected him too much.

Bharati merely said in a clear voice: '*Namaste*, Bapu.'

Bapu smiled and put out his hand and patted her shoulder. 'You will of course keep up your programme and write to me often.'

'Yes, of course, Bapu.'

'Be prepared for any sacrifice.'

'Yes, Bapu,' she said earnestly.

'Let nothing worry you.'

'Yes, Bapu.'

The sky became redder and darker, and the seven down moved away, taking the Mahatma to Trichy, and then to Madras, Bombay, Delhi and out into the universe. Night fell on the small station, and the little station-master proceeded to light his gas-lamps and signals.

Though the Mahatma's physical presence was no longer with him, Sriram had a feeling that his movements were being guided. His home now was a deserted shrine on a slope of the Mempi Hill, overlooking the valley. Down below, the road zigzagged and joined the highway which ended a mile off at Koppal Station. He often saw the mail runner trudging up a curve, with a bag on his shoulder, a staff on one arm (the staff had little bells tied to its end, heralding his arrival even a mile away). Sriram expected no mail but he loved to watch the runner till he stepped on a rock, and took a diverging crosscut, leading him to various estates and villages on the higher reaches of the Mempi Hills.

This place seemed to have been destined for him, built thousands and thousands of years ago by someone who must have anticipated that Sriram would find a use for an abandoned building. The place was a ruin, a few sculptures showed along the wall, the masonry was crumbling here and there. There was an image of some god with four hands in an inner sanctum overgrown with weed. But it was the most comfortable ruin a man could possess. There were stately pillars in a central hall, with bricks showing; there were walls without a ceiling, but from which exotic creepers streamed down; one of the stubborn, undisturbed pieces of sculpture was a Bull-and-Peacock over the large portal, which had very large knobbed wooden doors that could not be moved at all on their immense hinges. This was no great disadvantage for Sriram since no one came this way, and even if they did, he did not have anything to lock up. If he wished to be out of sight, he had only to slip away beyond a curtain of weeds, into a cellar. He could hear the train arrive and depart far away. He could hear the voices of villagers as they moved up in groups from the villages down below to the estates above. His possessions were a spinning wheel, a blanket on which to sleep, and a couple of vessels, some foodstuff, and a box of matches. He lit the wick of a small lantern whenever he wanted to work at night. He had set duties to perform every day when he woke up with the cries of birds. 'Oh, God, it's much better in Kabir Street,' he used to think. 'The birds make so much uproar here that they won't allow a man to sleep in peace.' In spite of this he got up from bed. He was going through a process of self-tempering, a rather hard task, for he often found on checking his thoughts that they were still as undesirable as ever. He had thought that by practising all the austerities that he had picked up in Gorpad's company, he could become suddenly different. Mahatmaji had blessed his idea of self-development. He had said: 'Spin and read Bhagavad Gita, and utter *Ram Nam* continuously, and then you will know what to do in life.'

Sriram carried a change of dress and went downhill to a brook and bathed. He felt so invigorated after the cold bath that he sang aloud all alone in his wilderness. He went on repeating: '*Raghupathi Raghava Raja Ram, Pathitha Pavana Seetha Ram*' – Mahatmaji's litany. When he sang it, he had a feeling of being near him and doing something on his orders. He was overcome with such a sense of holiness that he nearly danced with joy when he went back to his retreat. He carried the two pieces of dress he had washed in the brook and put them out to dry on the green fence surrounding the shrine. He was very proud of wearing cloth made with his own hand. Bharati had taught him how to insert the cotton thread, how to turn the wheel, and how to spin. Gandhiji had presented him with a spinning wheel in one of the villages with the explanation: 'This is the key to your future.' Sriram had felt too respectful to ask what he meant. But he took the wheel with proper reverence and literally put it close to his heart, although it was a heavy cumbrous apparatus.

Bharati tried to teach him how to use it during their sojourn in one of the villages. He tried his hand at spinning and made countless blunders while learning. He never managed to produce more than a couple of inches of yarn at a time, without snapping – it looked more like bits of twisted cotton wool than yarn. Bharati could not restrain her laughter when she saw his handiwork. She remarked: 'You will waste all the cotton in India and Egypt before you make yourself a yard of yarn.' After this she held his fingers down at the correct pressure at the spinning point, but when she took away her hand, Sriram let go his fingers too, and the cotton fell down and became worthless for any purpose.

All through the tour he had worked at it, his lessons starting the moment they came to a halt for the day. Every day Mahatmaji enquired: 'Well, what is the progress?'

And before he could answer Bharati generally broke in and said: 'Two more inches Bapuji; in all he has produced six inches today, but the count must be specially measured. It must be a five count yarn, probably the same count as a lamp-wick!'

The Mahatma said: 'Well, there will be a time soon when he will give you a hundred count, don't be too proud, little daughter.'

'I'm not,' Bharati said. 'I'm merely mentioning the facts.'

'How proud she is! Do you know she won her prize in a *khadi* competition some years ago? Her yarn is kept in an exhibition.'

'She scores one over me in everything,' Sriram reflected. 'It's because of the excessive support she gets. She is being spoilt. That is what is wrong with her. She thinks no end of herself.'

'I'm sure Bharati will teach you how to excel her,' said the Mahatma, and Bharati lived up to this promise. She allowed Sriram no rest, night or day. Whenever there was the slightest respite from travel, she came up with, 'Now, what is the programme of the great pupil?' And Sriram dragged the wheel out, took the little packets of cotton, and started nervously. He dreaded making a mistake and provoking the girl's mirth. He hated her for her levity, and for making him feel like a fool so often. But he kept up a desperate effort. He slipped, he made her laugh, he struggled in the grips of unholy thoughts when she stooped over him, held his hand, and taught him the tricks. He concentrated until his mind was benumbed with the half whispering movement of the spinning wheel. His fingers ached with holding a vibrant ever-growing thread, and his eyes smarted.

Finally he did emerge a victor, nearly twelve weeks after Mahatmaji had left. Sriram had stationed himself for his novitiate at one of the spinning centres, about fifty miles from Malgudi. Bharati was perfectly at home there and proved herself to be a task-mistress of no mean order; she did not let go her grip on Sriram until he had spun enough yarn free from entanglement for a *dhoti* and a short shirt. It was a result of continuous work over weeks. But it was worth it. She became very excited at the success of his efforts. She tore off the blank edge of a newspaper and wrote on it in minute letters: 'This is to say that Sri Sriram is henceforth to be called a master-spinner, and he must be respected wherever he goes.' She helped him to bundle off the yarn to a central depot at Madras and secure in exchange woven cloth of the same count. Sriram suddenly felt that he was the inhabitant of a magic world where you created all the things you needed with your own hands. His regret was that he still could not make the hundred count, and that his yarn was somewhat rugged.

But Bharati said: 'The forty count is the real cloth that can be used: hundreds are merely for show and prizes, don't worry about it.'

On the day he got his *khadi* clothes, a simple *dhoti* and a *jiba* (cut and stitched on the spot by the village tailor), he took off the clothes he had been wearing (mill manufactured), heaped them in the middle of the street, poured half a bottle of kerosene over the lot, and applied a match; his old clothes caught fire and burned brightly. A few members of the spinning centre stood around the fire and watched. Some of the villagers looked on with interest.

Sriram explained to the gathering, fascinated by the leaping flames: 'I will never again wear clothes spun by machinery.' The *dhoti* and *jiba* were heavy, it was as if a piece of lead were interwoven with the texture. But he felt it was something to be proud of. He felt he had seen and reached a new plane of existence. He sat down and wrote to the Mahatma, 'Burnt my old clothes today. Spun forty count. Bharati satisfied.'

Mahatmaji immediately wrote back to him: 'Very pleased. Keep it up. God bless you.'

Bharati came uphill at dusk. Sriram became fussy: 'How can you walk barefoot in all these places?'

'Why not? We are not born with sandals on our feet. I have not yet got the leather from Wardha, and I shall have to manage with this until we get it. But – ' she said with a sigh, 'there is probably no one there who can attend to our wants. We don't even know how many of them are in prison. The government have stopped giving even that information.'

They were sitting on the cool mud floor, with a lamp between them. Sriram studied her face, so full of lines nowadays as if the burden of the country were on her back, with Mahatmaji in prison since the August of 1942. Bharati (along with Sriram) was a little cog in a vast complicated machinery working, in spite of the police hunting down politics everywhere, to eject the British from the land.

Sriram said again: 'You should not walk barefoot.'

'Why not? India's three hundred and sixty million walk barefoot.'

Her national statistics bored him. He said sharply: 'They may, but it doesn't mean you should also walk barefoot. There may be cobras about, this place is full of such things.'

'Bah, as if cobras would not bite if trodden upon with sandalled feet!'

'You are too argumentative.'

'I tell you I am not able to get the usual leather from Wardha,' she complained, and then added: 'I am not afraid of you, and I don't have to explain to you why I am like this or like that. I am not afraid of cobras either, or the lonely road. Otherwise I should not be here.'

'Of course, you need not be afraid of me,' said Sriram. 'Only you expect others to be afraid of you.'

'Yes, because I am your *Guru*.'

Sriram felt, 'The whole thing is extremely false. She ought to be my wife and come to my arms.' He wondered for a moment, 'What is it that prevents me from touching her? What can she do? She is all alone in this place. Even if she shouts nobody will hear her for ten miles around.' He revelled in this terrific possibility. But it was only a dream.

She explained her mission: 'I am leaving for Madras tomorrow, and you won't see me for some time.'

'When? Where are you going?'

'I have been summoned for instructions. The police are watchful, no doubt, but I can manage to go and return without any trouble.' She started to leave.

He wondered, 'Why has she come to tell me this? What is the matter? Can I interpret it as her love for me? No one would come two miles barefoot just to say there would be nothing to do for the next three days. She must have come with some other motive. Probably she likes me very much, waits for me to take her hand and tell her what I have in mind; and then she would yield to me.' Absurd to think that she was just his '*Guru*', *Guru* indeed! Absurd that a comely young woman should be set to educate a man! Educate him in what? He chuckled at the thought. She said: 'You have become suddenly very thoughtful. Why?' He touched her arm: the lonely atmosphere was very encouraging, but she pushed his hand down gently, remarking,

'You rest here till I am back with instructions,' and she turned and was off down the road saying, 'Don't show yourself too much outside.'

He said: 'I will escort you half-way.'

'It's not necessary,' she said and was off.

Sriram watched her go down hill. 'Some day, someone is going to abduct her; she doesn't seem to feel she is a woman,' he thought and turned in. He stood brooding over the ruins around him. Far away a train halted and proceeded on its journey, its shaded A.R.P. lights crawling along the landscape. He hoped that the girl would reach her village safely, without any mishap.

Three days later she turned up bringing instructions, and from that moment Sriram's activities took a new turn. Bharati came to him bearing a can of paint and a brush. She handed them over to him with the air of an ordnance chief distributing weapons from the armoury. She said: 'They have assigned to you all the plantations above. It means a lot of walking. You must not miss any of the dozen villages on the way. The villagers will help you everywhere. We shall be at work in Malgudi and the surroundings. Be careful, I will see you again sometime. With Mahatmaji in prison, we have to carry on the work in our own manner. We must spread his message everywhere.'

The Mahatma had in his famous resolution of August 1942 said: 'Britain must quit India,' and the phrase had the potency of a *mantra* or a magic formula. Throughout the length and breadth of the land, people cried 'Quit India.' The Home Secretary grew uneasy at the sound of it. It became a prohibited phrase in polite society. After the Mahatma uttered the phrase, he was put in prison; but the phrase took life and flourished, and did ultimately produce enough power to send the British away. There was not a blank wall in the whole country which did not carry the message. Wherever one turned one saw 'Quit India.'

On the following day Sriram trudged up the mountain path carrying his little tin can, brush and a rag, in a satchel slung over his shoulder. He stopped at the first village on the way, selected the most suitable wall, which happened to be the outer wall of a new house, on whose pyol the village children were learning the alphabet. Their lips had been reciting the letters of the alphabet in a chorus, which incidentally lulled their teacher into a slight doze, but their eyes were following the bullock-carts rattling down the road in a caravan, buses flying past and disappearing in a cloud of churned-up dust, and people passing to and fro. The day was bright and the glare on green trees and boughs and hedge creepers was enticing; their eyes wandered, their minds wandered. And so when Sriram came up to write on the wall they slipped out of their class with a feeling of profound relief. The elders of the village too suspended their normal occupations and stood around to watch.

Sriram dipped the brush in paint and fashioned carefully, 'Quit India' on the wall. He wished that he didn't have to write the letter 'Q', which consumed a lot of black paint. It was no use wasting all the available paint on a single letter. He wondered if, for economy's sake, he could manage without drawing its tail. They were launching on a war with a first-rate, war-equipped nation like England, all their armament being this brush and black paint and blank walls. They could not afford to squander their war resources in writing just a single letter. It also seemed to him possible that Britain had imported the letter 'Q' into India so that there might be a national drain on black paint. He was so much obsessed with this thought that he began to write a modified 'Q', expending the very minimum of paint on its tail so that it read, until one scrutinized it closely, 'Ouit India'. The villagers asked: 'How long ought this to be on our wall, sir?'

'Till it takes effect.'

'What does it say, sir?'

'It is "Quit" – meaning that the British must leave our country.'

'What will happen, sir, if they leave? Who will rule the country?'

'We will rule it ourselves.'

'Will Mahatmaji become our Emperor, sir?'

'Why not?' he said, shaping the letters, with his back turned to them. He taught the school children to cry, 'Quit India' in a chorus. They gleefully obeyed him. Their teacher came and expostulated: 'What is this you are doing, sir, you are spoiling them!'

'How?'

'By teaching them seditious behaviour. The police will be after us soon. Do you want us to end in gaol?'

'Yes, why not? When more important persons than you are already there.' The crowd jeered at the teacher. The boys were ever ready to seize an opportunity to jeer him. But the old man was more tough than he looked. He put on his spectacles and looked Sriram up and down.

The boys cried: 'Oh, the master is looking through his spectacles, oh! oh!' They laughed and cried: 'Quit India.'

The teacher pushed his way through and cried: 'Add if possible one "e" before "t"; what we need in this country is not a "Quit" programme, but a "Quiet India". Why don't you write that?'

Sriram finished his job of writing. He had borrowed a ladder from someone. He turned round and said to the teacher: 'Please do something more useful than standing there and talking, master. Please see that this ladder is returned to its owner, I forget his name, and you will have done your bit to free our country.'

The teacher relented a little. He came forward and said: 'It's not that I don't want to see our country freed. I am as much a patriot as you, but honestly do you think we are ready to rule ourselves? We aren't. Don't delude yourself. We are not ready yet for anything. Let this war be over, and you will find me the first to fight for *Swaraj*. Patriotism is not your monopoly.' The boys stood around and cried slogans.

Sriram said: 'Be careful, you will be beheaded when Britain leaves India. We have a list of everybody who has to be beheaded.'

The teacher lost his temper completely and said: 'How dare you say that! I don't want to see Britain go. I am not one of those who think that we'll be happier when Hitler comes, perhaps with the help of people like you. Let me tell you you will be the first to be shot then.'

Part of the crowd was appreciative of the teacher's point of view, and said: 'The master is right, why should we irritate the *sircar*?'

Sriram turned on them with rage and said: 'You should not only irritate, you must not recognize the government. You don't have to pay taxes to it at all. They are ten thousand miles away from us, why do you give them your tax?'

'Fellows like this should not be allowed to go about as they like: that's why I've always asked for a police outpost here. If there had been a policeman here, would he have dared to come and lecture like this?'

'How far away is the police station?' asked Sriram.

'The Circle Station is beyond ten stones,' replied someone.

'See that,' said Sriram, 'your *sircar* have not given you even a police station! Is it because it is unnecessary when there is a person like this master in your midst?'

The boys raised a shout of appreciation and cried, 'Quit India' in a sing-song manner. It was a vociferous, happy gathering. Their shouts and general riotous behaviour frightened a pair of bullocks drawing a load of hay down the road. The bullocks lowered their heads and pulled the cart into a ditch, and it created a general mêlée, people running hither and thither, and shouting directions to each other. The carter, while pulling the animals back to the road, swore at them and at the disturbance. 'These politicians, Gandhi folk, they won't leave anyone in peace. Why do you come and trouble us here?'

Sriram said: 'Hey, pull up your cart and listen. Don't talk like a baby. You are old enough to know what you are talking about. What's your age?'

The carter pulled up his reins and said over the jingle of the bells round the necks of his animals, 'I think I'm twenty!'

'Twenty! More likely you are fifty.'

'May be, sir, a little this way and that. I used to be twenty.'

'How many children have you?'

'Five sons, sir, and a grandson.'

'You are fifty, my dear fellow, and you look it. Don't talk irresponsibly. Do you know Mahatma Gandhi is in gaol?'

'Yes, master.'

'You know why he is there?' The man shook his head. 'So that you may be a free man in this country. You are not a free man in this country now.'

\* \* \*

463

Sriram's orbit of operations lay in the mountain villages scattered here and there, connected by more or less self-formed roads, which wound their way through thick wooded vegetation and forests. Their connection with the outside world was through a postal runner, who passed through some of the better villages once or twice a week, bringing in the mails dumped at the railway station at Koppal. There were a few police outposts scattered over the whole area, with a petty officer and a handful of men in each, who kept in touch with their headquarters through the telephone lines which passed overhead and often vanished into the vegetation on the mountain slope. One would hardly have associated this remote green wilderness with politics, but it was as good a front line in the fight with Britain as any other.

He went into a part of the jungle where elephants were haul-ing timber. Huge logs were being cut and herds of elephants picked them up on their trunks and rolled them and piled them on trucks waiting in the heart of the jungle. Sriram penetrated here with his own message. He watched them at work and remarked: 'You are cutting down green unripe timber. You know where it is going?' The mahouts on the elephants paused in their tasks, and looked down at him with amusement. Sriram explained, 'They are going into the making of ships and rifles and bridges and what not, all of which are to be used for the destruction of this world. They are going into a war which we are forced to fight because Britain chose to drag us into it. We shouldn't have to strip our forests for this task. It's going far away, to far-off countries, and the money you are getting is a puffed-up, illusory currency, which will lose its value soon. Don't supply these materials for the war, it will take centuries for us to grow all this timber again. Refuse to do this job; it's in your hands. Don't strengthen the hand that is oppressing you.'

The timber-contractor who was observing him came up and pleaded, 'Don't trouble us please, after all we are business men. If tomorrow you place an order with us for a fair quantity at a good price – '

'This is not the time for acquiring wealth. This is the time to join in the fight for independence.'

The contractor merely said, 'Please leave us alone. We don't wish to get into all this bother.' He whispered, 'Please don't disturb our labour, please.'

'I'm not out to create labour trouble. You must not send that timber out of the country for this hellish purpose. All wars are against Mahatmaji's creed of *Ahimsa*. Do you accept it or not?'

'Ah, Mahatmaji. I gave five thousand rupees to the Harijan Fund. I have a portrait of him in my house, the first face I see is his, as soon as I get up from bed.'

'Do you know what he means by non-violence?'

'Yes, yes, I never missed a day's lecture when he came to Malgudi.'

'You must also have attended an equal number of Loyalist Meetings, I suppose.'

The contractor bowed his head shyly. He muttered: 'After all, when the Collector comes and says, "Do this or that," we have to obey him. We cannot afford to displease government officials.'

'How much have you given to the War Fund?'

'Only five thousand. I'm very impartial; when the Governor himself comes and appeals how can we refuse? After all we are business men.'

The man had inveigled Sriram into entering his tent under a tree. It prevented the mahouts from wasting their time listening to their talk. The forest resounded with the sound of logs rolling down and mahouts goading the elephants, chaffing among themselves, and laughing. The air had a slight smell of eucalyptus and green leaf, and also of the tobacco that the mahouts had been smoking. The contractor seated Sriram on a chair, took out an aluminium kettle smoking on a stove and poured two cups of tea. Sriram felt depressed at the sight of him. He was a lank man with a clean-shaven head, wearing a knitted banian and a *dhoti*, and at his waist he had tucked in a leather purse and some rolls of paper. The man seemed prosperous, with a thin gold chain around his neck, and a wrist-watch on his left hand, but he looked haggard with overwork.

Sriram said: 'You are no doubt making a lot of money, but it is worth nothing unless you develop some spirit of – of – ' He fumbled for words. He wanted to say, 'National Service', or

'Patriotism', but he was tired of these expressions, they smacked of platform speeches. He said: 'If you have a photo of Mahatma Gandhi, pray that he may inspire you with reasonable thinking, that's all I can say.' He got up abruptly.

The man said: 'Drink your tea and go.'

Sriram said, 'I don't want it.' He walked out of the tent, slipped through a gap in the hedge, and was off.

He lost count of time. He went on doing things in a machine-like manner. He entered forests and villages and conveyed what he felt to be Mahatmaji's message. Wherever he went he wrote, 'Quit India'. And it was followed by loyalists amending it with: 'Don't' or an 'I' before 'Quit'. In one place a man asked Sriram: 'What is the use of your writing "Quit India" in all these places? Do you want us to quit?'

'It does not mean that.'

'Then write it where it can be seen by those for whom it is meant.'

'They are everywhere, sometimes seen and sometimes unseen. It is better to have it written everywhere.'

'Waste of time and paint,' said the man.

'I'm merely carrying out an order, and I cannot afford to stop and listen to too much wisdom.'

There was a plantation 4,000 feet above sea level, whither Sriram carried his pot of paint and his brush. It meant nearly half a day's job for him. He arrived at the estate late one afternoon. He saw a picturesque gatepost with the sign, 'Mathieson Estates', over it. There wasn't a single human being to be seen for miles around. Sriram wondered for a moment: 'Is it worth writing any message here?' He looked about and hesitated, but dismissed the doubt as unworthy. He briskly dusted a portion of the gatepost and wrote in a beautiful round handwriting: 'Quit India', and turned to go.

An estate labourer who was passing, stopped to look at the message and asked: 'Are you writing a board?'

Sriram explained at length the import of the message. The man listened for a while and said: 'Go away. That *Dorai* is a bad fellow. Always with a gun. He may shoot you.'

Sriram hesitated for a moment, wondering whether it would be more worth while to get shot or to go away peacefully. He suddenly felt he need not have come up so far if it were only to go back safely. He hadn't climbed 4,000 feet above sea level for nothing. The labourer with the pick-axe went away after uttering his warning. Sriram walked forward towards an ancient bungalow that he saw in front. 'Hope he doesn't have bull-dogs,' he reflected. He pictured the scene ahead in a somewhat gory way. He would approach the steps and the *Dorai* would level his double-barrelled gun, and Sriram would go up in smoke and blood. Probably that would fill Bharati with remorse. She would tell herself: 'I wish I had shown my love more definitely when he was alive.' Anyway why was he doing this? The High Command had not instructed him to go and bare his chest before a gunman.

A seven-foot figure with a red face and sandy hair accosted him by the porch. He was smoking a pipe, and had one hand comfortably tucked in his trouser pocket. For a second Sriram felt a little reluctant to go forward.

'Hullo! Who may you be?'

Sriram felt dwarfed by his side. He went up and said in a shrill voice: 'I have brought a message.'

'Oh, good. From where?'

'From Mahatmaji.'

The man took out his pipe and said: 'Oh! What?'

'From Mahatma Gandhi.'

'Well? What is it?'

'That you must quit India.'

The other looked abashed for a second. But he recovered his composure in a moment. He said: 'Why do you say that?'

'I'm not saying it. I'm merely giving you the message.'

'Oh! Come in and have a drink, won't you?'

'No. I never drink.'

'Oh, yes, yes. I didn't mean spirits, but you can have anything you want, sherbet, or coffee or tea.'

'I need nothing.'

'You look tired, come in, let us have a chat anyway. Boy!' he shouted and his bearer appeared. 'Two glasses of orange juice,' he ordered. 'Look sharp.'

'Yes, sir,' said the Boy, going away.

The servant wore a white uniform with a lot of buttons. Sriram reflected, 'This man wants even a particular kind of dress for Indians who act as his servants', and felt an inexplicable rage. The other watched his face for a while, then said, 'Come along, let us go on the veranda.' He conducted him up the steps to the veranda, which had been furnished with wicker chairs covered with a beautiful chintz: there were also a few decorative plants in large pots here and there. Sriram contrasted it with his own surroundings, a ruined building built thousands of years ago, full of snakes and scorpions and with only a mat to sleep on. He could not help asking, 'How do you manage to do all this? May I know?'

'Do what?' asked Mathieson.

'Manage so much decoration and luxury so far away?' said Sriram and pointed at all the things around.

Mathieson laughed gently and said, 'I wouldn't call this luxury, my friend.'

'And all this while millions of people here are going without food or shelter!' he said in a general way, the statistics he had picked up from Bharati deserting him for the moment.

'It is our prayer,' said Mathieson, 'that all of them may have not only enough to eat soon but also beautiful houses to live in, something, I hope, better than this, which is only a makeshift.'

Sriram put down this explanation to racial arrogance. 'It is his prosperity and the feeling of owning the country that makes him talk like this,' he reflected, and wanted to shout at the top of his voice, 'Quit, quit, we shall look after ourselves, we don't care for wicker furniture and gaudy coverings for them, we don't care even for food, what we care for – ' He was not clear how to end his sentence. He merely said aloud, 'What we most care for is to do what Mahatmaji tells us to do.'

'And what has he advised you to do?'

'We will spin the *charka*, wear *khadi*, live without luxury, and we shall have India ruled by Indians.'

'But you have rejected the opportunity to try it. Don't you think it is a pity you should have turned down Cripps's offer?'

Sriram did not reply for a while. It seemed to him a technical point with which he was not concerned. Such intricate academic

468

technicalities refused to enter his head, and so he merely said, 'Mahatmaji does not think so,' and there was an end to the discussion. He knew a jumble of phrases – Dominion Status, Reservation for Muslims, and this and that, but although he had gathered all these from the newspapers they seemed to him beside the point, the only thing that mattered was that Mahatmaji did not think the proposals had anything to do with the independence of India. 'It is just eyewash,' he said, remembering a newspaper comment. 'We don't want all that. We have no use for such proposals. We don't want charity.'

This last thought so worked him up that presently when the butler came bearing a tray with two glasses of orange juice he wanted to knock the tray down dramatically and say, 'I don't want it,' but it was a beautiful drink, yellow and fresh, in a long and almost invisible tumbler, and the climb and exertion had parched his throat. He hesitated.

Mathieson handed him a glass and, raising his own, said, 'Here's to your health and luck.'

Sriram could merely mumble, 'Thanks', and drained his glass. The passage of the juice down his throat was so pleasant that he felt he could not interrupt it under any circumstance. He shut his eyes in ecstasy. For a moment he forgot politics, Bharati, strife, and even Mahatmaji. Just for a second the bliss lasted.

He put down his glass and sighed. The other had taken an invisible infinitesimal layer off the top level in his glass and was saying, 'Care to have another?'

'No,' said Sriram and started to leave. The other walked with him half-way down the drive. Sriram said, 'Don't rub off the message I have painted on your doorway.'

'Oh, no, I shan't. It is a souvenir and I shall keep it proudly.'

'But won't you be leaving this country, quitting, I mean?' asked Sriram.

'I don't think so. Do you wish to quit this country?'

'Why should I? I was born here,' said Sriram indignantly.

'I was unfortunately not born here, but I have been here very much longer than you. How old are you?'

'Twenty-seven, or thirty. What does it matter?'

'Well, I was your age when I came here and I am sixty-two today. You see, it is just possible I am as much attached to this country as you are.'

'But I am an Indian,' Sriram persisted.

'So am I,' said the other, 'and perhaps I am of some use to the people of this country seeing that I employ five thousand field labourers and about two hundred factory hands and office workers.'

'You are doing it for your own profit. You think we can only be your servants and nothing else,' said Sriram, not being able to think of anything better, and then he asked, 'Aren't you afraid? You are all alone, if the Indians decide to throw you out, it may not be safe for you.'

Mathieson remained thoughtful for a moment and said, 'Well, I suppose I shall take my chance, that is all, but of one thing I feel pretty sure – I am not afraid of anything.'

'It is because Mahatmaji is your best friend. He wants this struggle to be conducted on perfectly non-violent lines.'

'Of course that is also a point. Well, it was nice meeting you,' he said, extending his hand. 'Goodbye.'

Sriram went down the pathway, overhung with coffee shrubs, hedge plants, bamboo clusters, and pepper vine winding over everything else, with very dark green grass covering the ditches at the side. He felt so tired that he wondered why he did not lay himself down on the velvet turf and sleep, but he had other things to do. He had unremitting duties to perform.

It was the village named Solur three miles away that was his next destination. The place consisted of about fifty houses on a hill slope. Valleys and meadows stretched away below it. It was seven o'clock when Sriram arrived. The village was astir with activity. Men, women and children were enthusiastically gathered under the banyan tree of the village, in bright chattering groups. A gas-light had been hung from the tree, and one or two people were arranging a couple of iron chairs brought in from one of the richer households in the village. The two iron chairs were meant for some distinguished men who were expected. Sriram went to the only shop in the village, purchased a couple of plantains, and washed them down with a bottle of soda-water.

He felt refreshed. He asked the shopman, 'What time does the meeting begin?'

'Very soon, they are bringing someone to entertain us. It is going to be a nice function. Can't you stay on for it?'

'Yes, I will.'

'Where are you coming from?'

'From far away,' said Sriram.

'Where are you going?' the other asked.

'Far away again,' said Sriram, attempting to be as evasive as possible. The other laughed, treating it as a nice joke. The man supported himself by clutching with one hand a rope dangling from the ceiling. It was a box-like little shop made entirely of old packing cases, with a seat cushioned with gunny-sacks for the proprietor to sit on. Bottles containing aerated water in rainbow colours adorned his top shelf, bunches of green bananas hung down by nails in front of his shop, almost hitting one in the face, and he had several little boxes and shallow tins filled with parched rice, fried gram, peppermints, sugar candy, and so forth. He enjoyed Sriram's joke so much that he asked, 'I have some nice biscuits, won't you try them?'

'Are they English biscuits?' Sriram asked.

'The best English biscuits.'

'How can you be sure?'

'I got them through a friend in the army. They are supplied only to the army now. Purely English biscuits which you cannot get for miles around. In these days, no one else can get them.'

'Have you no sense of shame?' Sriram asked.

'Why, why, what is the matter?' the other said, taken aback, and then said, 'Hey, give me the money for what you took and get out of here. You are a fellow in *khadi*, are you? Oh! Oh! I didn't notice. And so you think you can do what you like, talk as you like, and behave like a rowdy.'

'You may say anything about me, but don't talk ill of this dress. It is – it is – too sacred to be spoken about in that way.'

The shopman felt cowed by his manner and said, 'All right, sir, please leave us alone and go your way. I don't want you lecturing here. Your bill is two annas and six pies … two bananas one anna each, and soda six pies …'

471

'Here it is,' Sriram said, taking out of his tiny purse two small coins and a six-pie piece and passing them to him.

'You see,' the other said, softening, 'this is not the season for bananas and so they are not as cheap as they might be.'

'I am not questioning your price, but I want you to understand that you should not be selling foreign stuff. You should not sell English biscuits.'

'All right, sir, hereafter I will be careful, after I dispose of the present stock.'

'If you have any pride as an Indian you will throw the entire stock in the gutter and won't let even a crow peck at it. Do you understand?'

'Yes, sir,' said the shopman, not liking the little circle of watchful people who were gathering. At the end of the street the lecture platform was being set up with groups of people standing around watching. The villagers were very happy, some lively business was going on there as well starting here. The shopman saw an old enemy of his who liked to see him in trouble standing on the edge of the crowd with a grin on his face. As if to satisfy him, the gods had brought this man in *khadi* here, a born trouble-maker. He appealed to Sriram, 'Now sir, please go away a little. I must close the shop.'

'You may close the shop if you like but I want you to destroy those biscuits,' said Sriram firmly.

'What biscuits?' asked the shopman alarmed. 'Please leave me alone, sir.'

'You have English biscuits, you said.'

'I have no English biscuits, where should I get them? Even in the black market they are not available.'

'If they are not English biscuits, so much the better. My esteem for you goes up, but may I have a look at one of them?'

'I have no biscuits at all,' pleaded the shopman. The crowd guffawed. Somebody shouted to someone else, 'Hey, here is Ranga in the soup, come on.'

'You have got them in that box,' Sriram said, pointing to one of the tin boxes. The shopman immediately lifted its lid and displayed its contents, white flour, luckily for him.

'But did you not say that you had biscuits a moment ago?'

'Who? I? I was merely joking. I am a poor shopkeeper, how could I afford to pay black market rates for biscuits and keep them for sale?'

'He has got them inside, sir. Let him show us the inside of his shop,' said one of the wags.

'Shut up and go your way,' shouted the shopman.

The situation was getting more complicated every moment.

'I am very sorry to note that you are a liar, in addition to being a seller of foreign black market stuff. I am prepared to lay my life at your threshold, if it will only make you truthful and patriotic. I will not leave this place until I see you empty all your stock in that drain, and give me an undertaking that you will never utter a falsehood again in your life. I am going to stay here till I drop dead at your door.'

'You are picking an unnecessary fight with me,' wailed the man.

'I am only fighting the evil in you, it is a non-violent fight.'

A woman came to buy half an anna's worth of salt. Sriram interposed and said, 'Please don't buy anything here.' When the woman tried to get past him he threw himself before her on the muddy ground: 'You can walk over me if you like, but I will not allow you to buy anything in his shop.'

The shopman looked miserable. What an evil day! What evil face did he open his eyes on when he awoke that morning! He pleaded, 'Sir, I will do anything you say, please don't create trouble for me.'

Sriram said: 'You are completely mistaking me, my friend. It's not my intention to create trouble for you. I only wish to help you.'

The woman who came to buy salt said: 'The sauce on the oven will evaporate if I wait for your argument to finish,' and, looking at the figure lying prone on the ground, she pleaded: 'May I buy my salt at the other shop over there, sir?'

Sriram with his head down could not help laughing. He said: 'Why should you not buy your salt wherever you like?'

She didn't understand his point of view and explained: 'I buy salt once a month, sir. After all, we are poor people. We cannot afford luxuries in life. Salt used to cost – '

473

Sriram, still on his belly, raised his head and said, 'It's for people like you that Mahatma Gandhi has been fighting. Do you know that he will not rest till the Salt Tax is repealed?'

'Why, sir?' she asked innocently.

'For every pinch of salt you consume, you have to pay a tax to the English Government. That's why you have to pay so much for salt.'

Someone interposed to explain: 'And when the tax goes, you will get so much salt for an anna,' he indicated a large quantity with his hands.

The woman was properly impressed and said, opening her eyes wide: 'It used to be so cheap,' and added, throwing a hostile glance at the shopman standing on his toes, supporting himself by the dangling rope, with tears in his eyes, 'Our shopmen are putting up the prices of everything nowadays. They have become very avaricious,' a sentiment with which most people were in agreement. A general murmur of approval went round the gathering.

The shopman standing on his toes said, 'What can we do, we sell the salt at the price the government have fixed.'

'You might support those of us who are fighting the government on these questions,' said Sriram, 'if you cannot do anything else. Do you remember Mahatma's march to Dandi Beach in 1930? He walked three hundred miles across the country, in order to boil the salt-water on the beach of Dandi and help anyone to boil salt-water and make his own salt.'

The shopman was the very picture of misery. He said in an undertone, 'I'll do anything you want me to do, please get up and go away. Your clothes are getting so dirty lying in the dirt.'

'Don't bother about my clothes. I can look after them; I can wash them.'

'But this mud is clayey, sir, it is not easily removed,' said the shopman.

Someone in the crowd cried, 'What do you care? He will probably give it to a good *dhobi*.'

'If you can't find a *dhobi*, you can give it to our *dhobi* Shama, he will remove any stain. Even Europeans in those estates above call him for washing their clothes, sir.'

Someone else nudged him and murmured, 'Don't mention Europeans now; he doesn't like them.'

It seemed to Sriram that the people here liked to see him lying there on the ground, and were doing everything to keep him down. When this struck him, he raised himself on his hands and sat up. There was a smear of mud on his nose and forehead and sand on his hair. A little boy, wearing a short vest and a pair of trousers twice his size, came running, clutching tightly a six-pie coin in his hand. He shouted: 'Give me good snuff for my grandfather, three pies, and coconut *bharfi* for three.' He dashed past Sriram to the shop and held out his coin. The shopman snatched the coin from his hand in the twinkling of an eye. Sriram touched the feet of the young boy and importuned him: 'Don't buy anything in this shop.'

'Why not?'

Sriram started to explain, 'You see, our country – ' when two or three people in the crowd pulled the young boy by the scruff, saying, 'Why do you ask questions? Why don't you just do what you are asked to do?' They tried to pull him away, but he clung to a short wooden railing and cried: 'He has taken my money. My money, my money.'

People shouted angrily at the shopman, 'Give the boy his money.'

The shopman cried: 'How can I? This is a Friday, and would it not be inauspicious to give back a coin? I'll be ruined for the rest of my life. I am prepared to give him what he wants for the coin, even a little more if he wants; but no, I can't give back the cash. Have pity on me, friends. I am a man with seven children.'

The little boy cried: 'My grandfather will beat me if I don't take him the snuff. His box is empty. He is waiting for me.'

'Go and buy in that other shop,' someone said.

The boy answered, 'He'll throw it away if it is from any other shop.'

The shopman added with untimely pride, 'He has been my customer for the last ten years. He can't get this snuff from any other place. I challenge anyone.'

The boy clung to the railing and cried, 'I must have the snuff, otherwise – '

Someone from the crowd pounced upon him muttering imprecations and tore him away from the railing. The boy set up a howl. The crowd guffawed. The shopman wrung his hands in despair. Sriram sat in the dust like a statue, solemnly gazing at the ground before him. Someone pacified the boy, murmuring in his ears, 'Come and fetch your snuff after that fellow leaves.'

'When will he go?' whispered the boy.

'He will go away soon. He is not a man of this place,' another whispered.

'But my grandfather's snuff-box must be filled at once.'

'I'll come and speak to your grandfather, don't worry.'

Sriram sat listening to everything, but he said nothing, without moving.

The crowd by the shop gradually melted away as the gathering at the other end started to form. A second lantern was being taken up the tree. The crowd looked up and said, 'Ramu is climbing the tree with the lantern.' They pointed at a youth wearing a striped banian over his bare body and khaki shorts. His mother watching from below cried, 'Hey, Ramu, don't go up the tree, someone pull that boy down, he's always climbing trees.'

'Why do you bother, what if boys do climb trees?' asked someone. A quarrel started, the mother retorting, 'You wouldn't talk like that if you had a son always endangering himself.'

The boy shouted from the tree-top, 'If you are going to quarrel, I will jump down and make you all scream.' The crowd enjoyed the situation. For a moment the shopman lost sight of his own troubles, gazed at the tree-top, and remarked, 'That's a terrible boy, always worrying his mother with his desperate antics. She knows no peace with him about.'

'Well, he looks old enough to look after himself,' said Sriram.

'Yes, but he has been spoilt by his mother, he is always climbing trees, or swimming or teasing people, a rowdy,' said the shopman.

'You people trouble him too much. He will not bother anyone if he is left alone,' said Sriram. 'Everyone is advising and worrying him.'

Now came a shout from the tree-top: 'I have fixed the lantern. Who else could have done it?' The lantern swung in the air and threw moving shadows on the rocky hill slope behind. The crowd jeered and laughed at him. 'If anyone jeers at me, I'll cut the rope and throw the lamp on you all,' he challenged.

'Devil of a boy,' shouted his mother. It was pointless banter, it seemed to Sriram. He felt angry at the thought of all the aimless, light-hearted folk in this place. The shopman added, 'There is no peace in this village – those two are always bothering everyone in some way or other.'

'You are no better,' said Sriram angrily. The country was engaged in a struggle for survival; in a flash there passed before his mind Gandhi, his spinning wheel, the hours he spent in walking, thinking and mortifying himself in various ways, his imprisonment, and all this seemed suddenly pointless, seeing the kind of people for whom it was intended. He suddenly felt unhappy. All his own activity seemed to him meaningless. He might as well return to the cosy isolation of Kabir Street – that would at least make one old soul happy. What did it matter whether the shopman sold British biscuits or Scandinavian ones or Chinese crackers or French butter? It was only a matter of commerce between a conscienceless tradesman and a thick-skinned public. All this sitting in the mud and bothering and fighting was uncalled for. He felt suddenly weary. He asked the shopman, 'Can you give me a piece of paper and a pen and an envelope? I will pay for it.'

'No, sir,' said the shopman. 'There is no demand for paper and such things at this shop. People who come here are all simple folk, who want something to eat or drink.'

'And who ask only for English biscuits, I suppose?' said Sriram cynically.

'Forget it, sir. I'll never do it again,' assured the shopman, 'if you will only get up from that spot and forget me.'

Sriram felt pleased at the compliment and at the great import- ance his personality had acquired. It was very gratifying. 'You are not lying, I hope, about the paper and envelope?' he asked. 'Possibly you have only the costliest English paper and ink?'

'No, sir, I swear by the goddess in that temple. I have no stock, and I swear by all that is holy I will hereafter avoid all English goods. I will fling into the gutter any biscuit that I may ever see anywhere. I will kick anyone who asks for an English biscuit. At least in this village there will be no more English biscuits. Meanwhile, may I go to the school-master and fetch you a sheet of paper and a pen? He is the only one who ever writes anything in this place.' The shopman added, 'Please move up a little, I can't leave the shop open, there are too many thieves about.'

Sriram said, 'I'll look after your shop while you are away,' and then, in a sinister manner, 'You know how well I can keep people off.' He seemed to enjoy it as a joke.

The shopman thought it best to join in and laughed nervously, preparing to close the doors of the shop. His nerves were taut lest Sriram should suddenly change his mind. He added, in order to safeguard himself against this possibility, 'You must write your letters, sir, without fail, however busy you may be. I'll be back in a moment.' He felt happy when he gave a tug to his brass lock and jumped down. He felt like a free man. This was his first taste of absolute freedom in all his life. 'I will be back, sir, I will be back, sir,' he cried, running away jingling his bunch of keys. It was an amusing sight to watch the portly man run.

Sriram enjoyed it for a while, leaned back on the door of the shop decorated with enamel plates advertising soaps and hair-oil, and composed in his mind the letter he would write when the paper arrived. His eyes were watching the swaying lanterns dangling from the tree branch over the shrine, and the people assembled for the meeting under it. His mind was busy with the letter: 'Revered Mahatmaji, I don't know why we should bother about these folk. They don't seem to deserve anything we may do for them. They sell and eat foreign biscuits. They are all frivolous-minded, always bothering too much about a young scamp who has climbed a tree. I don't know if he has come down; I don't care if he falls down; it'll be a good riddance for all concerned. They will thank us for leaving them alone, rather than for telling them how to win *Swaraj*. They simply don't care. At this very moment I find them engrossed in preparing for a Loyalists' Meeting. What I want to know, my revered Mahatmaji, is – ' He wondered what it was that he wanted to tell the Mahatmaji. What was really the problem?

478

He lost sight of the problem. He felt suddenly that he was too tired and unhappy. He was hungry and homesick. He wanted to go back to his Kabir Street home, preferably with Bharati, and forget all this. The banana and soda-water were hardly adequate for the strain he was undergoing. He wished he could ask the man for more if he came back and opened the shop door. He was seized with such inertia that he watched without stirring the proceedings of the meeting ahead of him. His conscience pricked him all the time. Something told him: 'You are here to counteract this meeting, but you are doing nothing about it.' He merely told himself, 'I can't do anything. I want to suspend everything till I have guidance from my leader. There is no use rushing along without a point.' He saw without emotion a set of people arrive in a jeep. A gramophone ground away, with amplifiers, producing some film songs to which the public marked time. And then someone came up with a harmonium, and accompanied it in a loud voice. Sriram shut his ears at the sound of the harmonium: 'Damned instrument,' he muttered to himself. His nerves were a jangle with its raucous cry. 'I hope when Mahatma Gandhi becomes the Emperor of India, he will make it a penal offence to make or play this instrument. This too is a British gift, I suppose,' he told himself.

After the music someone presented a scene from Ramayana, with music and narration. The public enjoyed the show. Right in the midst of it all, the two officers occupying the iron chairs suddenly got up and delivered a speech in very bad Tamil. They explained the importance of the war, how Britain was winning, how it was India's duty to help, and how India should protect herself from enemies within and without. There were policemen in plain clothes, made less plain by their broad belts and khaki shirts, civil officers in tweed and bush coats, with sleek hair; somebody was distributing toffee out of a tin to all the children in the assembly. Sriram said to himself, 'I'm here to stop it, but – but – let me first write to the Mahatma and get his advice – ' He looked about him. He had an excuse to wait for the promised letter-paper. But he spotted the shopman in the crowd. 'Oh, liar!' Sriram commented: 'He is probably going to pretend that he is a child, ask for toffee and sell it at black market rates tomorrow at his shop.'

As if in answer to his unwritten letter he received a communication from Mahatmaji. It was enclosed in a note to Bharati and said: 'Your work should be a matter of inner faith. It cannot depend upon what you see or understand. Your conscience should be your guide in every action. Consult it and you won't go wrong. Don't guide yourself by what you see. You should do your duty because your inner voice drives you to do it. Look after Bharati as well as she looks after you, that's all. God bless you both in your endeavours.'

The message had given Bharati an occasion to come up and see him. It was one of his off-days, a day of soldier's leave, as he thought. He had sat at the portal of his ruined temple resigning himself to doing nothing for the day, going through an old issue of a paper he had picked up. It was full of dead news – of the Maginot Line and the like. But that was enough for him. The mail carrier had stepped off the boulder down below long ago on his return journey, and had gone back to the plains. The evening train had crawled in and out of the landscape. The sun stood poised over the western horizon.

Sriram brought out his rush mat, spread it out and threw himself on it, and was presently absorbed not only in reading all the stale news in the paper, but also in all those jokes, tit-bits, and syndicated cartoons which filled the bottom of its columns. He had picked up the paper on the highway, when returning from his expedition at Solur village. It had blown across the highway and hugged a tree-trunk. He unwound the sheet from the tree-trunk, flashed his torch on it and saw that it was an up-country paper which was well known for its reactionary views and carping references to Gandhiji, but still it contained some interesting Sunday reading. He felt irritated for a second at the thought that someone should have been scattering such an imperialistic paper in these parts, but he carefully folded it and put it into his bag. He had been the victim of certain moments of extreme boredom, when he felt that the huge teak trees and bamboo clumps and the estate trees covering slope upon slope would destroy his mind. They got on his nerves and made him want to shout aloud in protest. He once tried talking aloud to himself in order to get over the tedium. He asked himself, 'Hallo, what are you doing here?' and told himself, 'I am fighting for my country.'

'What sort of fighting is it? You look like a vagabond, with no uniform, no weapon, and no enemy in sight, what sort of fight is this? Are you joking?' and he laughed aloud, 'Oh, oh, oh!' He spoke at the top of his voice till the hills echoed with his voice, and one or two birds sitting on a tree nearby took off in fright. This exuberance had greatly relieved his mind. Now he hoped to be provided against boredom with this sheet of newspaper. Here at least was something to read instead of watching endlessly those tree-tops and valleys. It was his lot to be here. He could not kick against it.

He stretched himself on his mat. He had rolled a block of stone over to serve as a back-support for his couch. He had found it a couple of days before lying about in the grass and weeds, and had moved it up with difficulty. It had taken him nearly an hour. There were smoothed-out lettering and ornamental carvings on the stone. He had speculated what they might signify, they were circular letters which looked familiar but eluded study; probably a message carved thousands of years ago by some king or emperor or tyrant one found pictured in history books. History books were full of ruffianly-looking characters, according to Sriram. He had often wondered what good purpose could possibly be served in reading and allowing oneself to be questioned about side-whiskered *goondas*? Reclining against his tablet he thought that if he had at least passed his examinations normally, he needn't have got into this present life. He might have settled as a good-natured clerk in an office, as his friend Prasanna had done. It was only yesterday he had been a champion street-footballer, but already he was in harness, slaving at the Treasury desk several hours a day.

Sriram reclined comfortably against the ancient tablet, and read a joke in which a 'He' and a 'She' indulged in a four-line dialogue. 'When am I going to get my tie pressed?' To which she gave the smart reply: 'Exactly an hour after I get that gown.'

Sriram read it over again and again, and felt irritated. What was the joke? Where lay its humour? He looked it over and examined it minutely, but failed to spot any sense in it. It was accompanied by a grotesque-looking couple, fat about the waist. Sriram thought: 'One can't tell what humour Englishmen will enjoy!' He put away the paper and its corners rustled in the wind. Now it was as if he heard the anklet-sound of his beloved, and there she was down below. Bharati was coming up the road half a mile away. She had never been more welcome. He got up and ran to her with a wild cry of joy. He saw her as an angel come to relieve him of his tedium. She carried a bag in her hand, as usual, and she strode on with such assurance and happiness. She was taken aback, when turning a bend, she was accosted by Sriram.

'Hallo!' he cried at the top of his voice: 'Here is my *Devata* come!'

She slowed down her pace and said: 'What has come over you? What will anyone seeing us think!'

'Who is there to see and think?' he asked haughtily. 'As if a big crowd were milling about!' he said, putting into his expression all the venom he felt at his lonely existence. She detected his tone of bitterness but preferred to overlook it.

'What do you want? A big fair around you all the time?' she asked light-heartedly, walking on.

He asked, 'Where are you going?'

'I'm going to meet you.'

'Here I am!'

'I won't take official notice of your presence here, but if you want me to state my business, I will say it and go back. I have come to you with excellent news.'

'What is it?' he cried anxiously, following her.

She went on, saying, 'Come and hear it at your own place.'

At his place, he ceremoniously showed her the mat, and begged her to recline with ease against the tablet. She obeyed him. She stretched her legs, leaned back on the tablet, and while her figure was rousing wild emotions in Sriram, she picked up the letter from her little bag and gave it to him. 'Here is a letter from Bapu for you. How do you like it?' He read it and remained thoughtful. Owls were hooting, the sky had darkened; crickets were making a noise in the dark bushes. He sat beside her on the mat. He could see her left breast moving under her white *khadar sari*. She seemed to be unaware of the feelings she was rousing in him.

She said, 'Do you know what it means? Bapu wants you to stay on and do your work here. He feels your work here is worth while and that you will have to go on with it.'

'How do you know he means that and not something else?'

'I know it because I can read what he writes and understand it.'

'I can also read what he writes,' said Sriram with pointless haughtiness.

'Did you write anything to him?' she asked.

He didn't like the cross-examination. 'Perhaps or perhaps not,' he said with anger in his voice.

'Why should you be angry? I'll write to Bapu next time that you are a very angry man.'

In answer he suddenly threw himself on her, muttering, 'You will only write to him that we are married.' It was an assault conducted without any premeditation, and it nearly overwhelmed her.

He gave her no opportunity to struggle or free herself. He held her in an iron embrace in his madness. He lost sight of her features. The hour was dark. He felt her breath against his face when she said, 'No, this can't be, Sriram.'

Sriram muttered, 'Yes, this can be. No one can stop me and you from marrying now. This is how gods marry.'

Her braid laid its pleasant weight on his forearm. Her cheeks smelt of sandalwood soap. He kissed the pit of her throat. He revelled in the scent of sandalwood that her body exuded. 'You are sweet-smelling,' he said. 'I will be your slave. I will do anything you ask me to do for you. I will buy you all the things in the world.' He behaved like an idiot. She wriggled in his grasp for a moment and at the same time seemed to respond to his caresses. He rested his head on her bosom and remained silent. He felt that any speech at this moment would be a sacrilege. It was a night of absolute darkness. The trees rustled, crickets and night insects carried on their unremitting drone. He wanted to say something about the stars and moonlight, but he felt tongue-tied. The only thing that seemed to be of any consequence now was her warm breathing body close to his.

He murmured: 'I always knew it. You are my wife.'

She gently released herself from his hold and said, 'Not yet. I must wait for Bapu's sanction.'

'How will you get it?'

'I shall write to him tomorrow.'

'If he doesn't sanction it?'

'You will marry someone else.'

'Don't you like me? Tell me – tell me – ' he said in a fevered manner.

She felt the trembling of his body, and said: 'I shouldn't be coming here or meeting you if I didn't.'

'Wouldn't Mahatmaji have known?'

'No. His mind is too pure to think anything wrong – '

'What is wrong with what?'

'This is very wrong – we – we should not have – I – I – ' she sobbed. 'I don't know what Bapu will think of me now. I – must – write to him what has happened.'

He had never seen her so girlish and weak. He felt a momentary satisfaction that he had quashed her pride, quelled her turbulence. He said aggressively: 'Bapuji will say nothing. He will understand. He knows human feelings, and so don't worry. There is nothing wrong in loving. You and I are married.'

'When?'

'On the very first day I saw you.'

'That's not enough. I can't marry without Bapu's sanction.'

He became positive and dynamic. He swore: 'We shall marry this very moment.' He dragged her by the hand into the inner sanctum. He ran hither and thither feverishly doing things. He lit the lamp and placed it before the image, whose nose and arms were broken, but whose eyes still shed grace. He ran out and came back with a few leaves and flowers, and placed them at the foot of the pedestal. He took out a thread from his spinning wheel saying, 'You cannot have a *thali* more sacred than this, nor a priest more holy than this god.' When he attempted to place the thread round her neck, she gently drew herself away from him.

A sudden firmness came in her voice, as she said: 'Know this, Sriram. If I had not trusted you I'd not have come here again and again.' He did not understand why she was saying it. He felt bewildered. Why was she talking like this? Perhaps she suddenly remembered that she ought to marry Gorpad or someone else. Yes, now it flashed across his mind there used to be some significant exchange of looks between her and Gorpad. What a fellow to marry, rough as emery paper! A stab of jealousy shook him for a moment and he said, 'Will you swear before this god that you will marry only me.'

'Yes, if I marry at all, and mark this, if Bapu agrees to it.'

'Bapu! Bapu!' It filled him with despair. He wailed: 'He is too big to bother about us. Don't trouble him with our affairs.'

She said, 'I won't marry if he doesn't sanction it. I can't do it.'

'If he asks you to marry someone else,' he asked pathetically, checking at the last second the name 'Gorpad'.

'Bapu has better things to do than finding a husband for me,' she said clearly, unequivocally.

He blinked for a moment. The excitement made his throat parched. He wanted to ask something again. But even in his confused state, he was aware that he was saying the same thing over and over. He blinked pathetically. The broken-armed god looked on. Sriram had never bargained for such an inconclusive love-making. It had begun with such spirit that he had felt he would be shot into elysium next moment, but here he was, standing before a god immobilized and listening to an obscure speech. The girl would probably take him for a fool to leave so much space between them. He tried to remedy it by approaching her again and attempting to storm her as he did a moment ago. The first time he had the advantage of a sudden impulse. But now it didn't work. She just beat down his outstretched arm: 'No. You will not touch me again.' She said it with such authority that he felt foolish.

'I didn't intend to if you don't want it. I know you hate me,' he said childishly.

She simply said, 'Why should I hate you?'

'Because I am bothering you.'

'How?' she asked.

'By, by – asking you to marry me. It's wrong, perhaps wrong.'

'It wouldn't be if Bapu agreed to it.'

He resigned himself. 'All right,' he said. 'As you please – '

'We shall marry,' she said, 'the very minute Bapu agrees.' She was very considerate.

He felt it was time for him to ask again: 'Do you – like me?'

'Yes, when you don't misbehave.'


Days of listlessness and suspense followed. Sriram lost sight of her for a considerable period. He thought he had lost her for ever. It made him so paralysed that all day he did nothing but lounge in front of his cottage going over in mind again and again all that had happened that night. He had suspended his usual round of lecturing, agitation, and demonstrations; he didn't seem to think he owed any duty to the country. He ate and stayed in his den all day, he had read the joke about a 'He' and a 'She' two hundred times already. He saw the train arrive and depart. He saw the postman stop on the boulder and go away to the estates. He lounged against the corner tablet and brooded endlessly.

After all, one day she turned up. She came at noon. It seemed significant that she should avoid the dusk. The moment he sighted her on the bend, he gave a shout of joy and wanted to ask, 'Are you coming now, because it is a safe hour?' But he checked himself. He ran to meet her at the usual bend of the road. He asked: 'What news?' She didn't speak till they were back in their place. She sat down, leaned back on the tablet, took a letter out of her bag. Sriram snatched it hungrily and glanced through it:

'Blessed one, not yet ... I am going to ask all workers if they are underground to come out. I want you to give yourself up at the nearest police station. Take your disciple along too. God bless you both.'

Sriram felt stunned. He read the letter over and over, trying to make out its significance. He tried to interpret it. ' "Not yet," he says. What does he mean?'

486

'He just means that and nothing more,' she replied. 'It is never hard to understand what Bapuji says.'

Sriram felt amazed at the hardihood and calmness of the girl. She didn't seem to possess any feeling. She spoke of it with such indifference. He was appalled at her calmness. She was probably feeling relieved that Bapuji had vetoed their plans. It suited her very well – Gorpad. And of course, in his sick imagination he felt that probably Mahatmaji was also in favour of Gorpad, he'd naturally prefer to marry her to a grim and dry-as-dust worker like Gorpad. But why couldn't she be plain with him?

'Why can't you be plain?' he asked her all of a sudden.

'What do you mean?'

He felt tongue-tied, and asked: 'Why should Bapu not want us to marry?'

'He doesn't say so.'

He sighed: 'I thought he would send us his blessing, but he has only turned down our programme.' In his disappointment, he felt sore with the whole world, not excluding Bapu. He suddenly asked her: 'Don't you feel disappointed that we are not married?'

'I have other things to think of,' she said.

'Oh!' Sriram said significantly. 'What may they be?'

'I am going to gaol ...'

The full significance of the whole thing dawned upon him now. He cried, 'Bharati, you just can't do that, what do you mean?'

She replied, 'You will have to come too ...' She opened the letter and glanced through it again. 'Bapu has also given instructions as to how I should occupy my time in gaol. "This is an opportunity for you to learn some new language. I wish you could read Tulasi Das Ramayana without any assistance; you speak Hindi well, but your literary equipment will also have to be equally good. You may ask the gaol superintendent to give you facilities if you are going to be classed as B to take your *charka* along. I would like to hear that you are spinning your quota in gaol. Don't for a moment ever feel that you are wasting your time. Wherever you may be with a copy of Ramayana and Gita, and a spinning wheel, there you are rightly occupied. Anyway look after your health. Very mild exercise may be necessary, you may get it by walking around the compound if you are permitted ... If you would rather not be in B class but would like to be an ordinary class prisoner like others, you will have to ask for it. All that I am saying to you applies to your disciple too." '

Sriram pleaded, 'Don't. Please tell Bapu ...'

Bharati looked at him with wonder. 'After all these months of association and work, how can you speak like this? How can we do anything other than what Bapuji asks us to do?'

Sriram had no cogent answer to give. He hung down his head. For the moment he seemed to have forgotten that he was a soldier in the struggle for freedom.

She said resolutely, 'I ought to be there already. I am reporting to the police station at ...'

'How long will they keep you in gaol?' he asked pathetically.

'How can I say?' she replied. 'Are you coming too?'

He said, 'Not now. I want to think it over. But I will readily come if they will keep me in the same prison, preferably in the same cell.'

'It won't be possible, the government won't keep us together,' she said.

This enraged Sriram. The whole universe seemed to be organized to defeat his purpose, even the government which differed from the Mahatma on most matters seemed to be in accord with him where it concerned him and Bharati. The worst of it was that Bharati herself seemed to rejoice in the arrangement. He became wild at the thought and said, 'Why is everyone opposed to my loving you?'

She took pity on him and said tenderly, 'Poor fool. You have lost your wits completely.'

'How dare you say that?' he shouted.

'There is no point in your shouting,' she said. 'Don't let us quarrel. I will be gone in a moment ... I want to report myself before it strikes four. If they want to send me to the Central or some other gaol they must have time to catch the evening train.'

'What shall I do without you?' he wailed.

'That is why Bapu has asked you to report too.'

He shook his head. 'I have a lot of things to do outside ... Bapu has given everyone freedom to carry on the *Satyagraha* in his own manner. He doesn't really mean me,' he said dolefully.

In answer Bharati seized the letter and held it open under his nose. ' "This applies to your disciple also," he says.'

'But that doesn't mean me. It may mean anyone,' said Sriram.

'I thought he always understood whom he meant by "disciple",' she said grimly. 'Anyway the choice is yours. You may do what you think best. I am doing what seems to me the right thing to do.'

'How do you know it is the right thing to do?'

'I need not answer that question,' she said irritated. 'If I had known that you would treat Bapuji's word so lightly – '

Sriram felt crushed by her tone. 'Oh, Bharati, don't add to my troubles by mistaking me so completely. I revere the Mahatma, you know I do. Why do you suspect me? Have I not followed every word of what he has been saying? ... Otherwise I should not have been here. I should not have left the comfort of my house. All that I want is some more time to think it over. I am ...' he brought out his masterpiece on an inspiration. 'I am only thinking of my grandmother. I want to see her before I am finally gaoled. That is why I asked you how long we should be in prison. She is very old, you know. I will surrender myself after I have seen her once. I must manage to see her.'

This idea seemed to soften the girl. She thought it over, leaning back on the tablet. She seemed to appreciate his tender feelings for his grandmother.

'That is all right, Sriram. I am sorry I mistook you.' He wanted to touch her arm, but he felt afraid to do so. She would surely say, 'Keep off, not until,' and that would irritate him again and make him speak nonsense.

She got up. He asked, 'Must you go?'

'Yes, it is late for me.'

He followed her sheepishly, 'When we meet again after the gaol, and wherever we may meet ... will you not forget me?'

'I will not forget you,' she said, catching her breath ever so lightly.

He loved her as she drew herself up, more than at any other time in his life, but he also felt afraid of her more than at any other time. He simply said, 'If you will not be angry with me, Bharati, I wish to ask one thing.'

'Yes?' she said, stopping and looking at him. He noticed beads of perspiration on her upper lip and wanted to wipe them off with his fingers. He was seized with desolation at the thought that he would not see her any more coming round the bend of the road. He wanted to seize her in his arms and take a stormy leave of her, but he had to content himself with asking, 'Will you marry me after we are out of all this, will you promise, if Bapuji permits?'

'Yes, I promise ...' she said and hurried off before he could talk to her or follow her. He stood where he was and saw her raising her hands to her eyes once or twice in order to wipe off the tears gathering there.

# PART THREE

A person called Jagadish dropped in one day very casually and introduced himself as a national worker. He said he was a photographer in Malgudi by profession, and claimed he had a formula for paralysing Britain in India. His studio in Malgudi with its dark interior served as a meeting ground for a group who were bent upon achieving immediate independence for the country. Jagadish came because he was in need of an out-of-town lair for his activities, and he was looking for a place where he could instal a small radio set which could also transmit code messages.

He came trudging uphill while Sriram was reclining against his stone tablet. He came with a haversack on his back and wore a *khadi* dress. Sriram had been reading his old newspaper. Bharati's exit from his life had created a vacuum, which he found it hard to fill. He felt somewhat confused as to what he should do with himself now.

Jagadish set down his haversack, sat beside Sriram and asked, 'You are Sriram?'

'Yes.'

'I am Jagadish. I used to know Bharati also. We are all doing more or less the same work.'

This was enough to stir Sriram out of his lethargy. He sat up and welcomed the other profusely with a great deal of warmth and asked, 'Where, where is she?'

'In detention ... We don't know where, but one of our boys met her just before she surrendered herself to the police.'

Sriram asked, 'Where is this man?'

'He too has surrendered to the police; before that he came and saw me.'

'Are you going to court imprisonment?'

'No, I have other things to do. That is why I have come here.'

Sriram was happy to find a kindred soul and at once poured into his ears his own feelings. 'I told Bharati not to be a fool ...'

'Don't say that. In this matter we all judge and act individually. Those who cannot follow Mahatmaji's orders are free to act as they think best.'

'How right you are,' Sriram cried, feeling he had blundered into the right set.

The other said, 'This is a war in which we are engaged, we are passing through abnormal times, and we do what we think best.'

He began to unpack his haversack. Sriram, always hungry and rather tired of the monotonous food he was eating, hoped childishly that something nice to eat would come out of it. He hoped it would be chocolate or fruit or biscuits. Oh, how long it was since he had eaten anything like *idli*, those white sensitive things made by his granny on most Sundays. Why Sunday and not on any other day, he had often asked. Now Jagadish took from his bag a small box, unwrapped the paper around it and brought out a tiny radio set.

'You will have to keep this,' he said. 'It can transmit as well as receive. I had it in my studio all these days ... but the police have become very watchful nowadays.' He installed it behind the god's image, and camouflaged it with some bamboo leaves.

From then on the god with the eyeless sockets saw a great deal of Jagadish. He was of short stature with a brown wrap around his shoulders. He had a shaggy crop of minute, springy curls, which spread out parallel to the earth, projecting several inches beyond his ears. He parted his shaggy crop in the middle and applied a vast quantity of oil over his curls so that the top of his skull was always resplendent, and often Sriram saw the midday sun shining back from his head in a thousand colours. He was a very dark man with a large bulbous nose, but there was a fire in him that consumed everything before it, and Sriram felt afraid to oppose him. It seemed incredible that an elegant slender creature like Bharati should ever have spoken to this bear-like personality.

A stab of jealousy passed through him. Could it be that she had ever toyed with the notion of marrying him? God knew what he did with himself when he was out of sight. How did he make a living out of photography? Sometimes he didn't appear for days, and when he turned up he explained, 'The wedding season, you know. More fools getting married, and they drop in to get themselves photographed. I can't afford to waive all the business.' Or he explained, 'The jasmine season, and this is a heavy time for a photographer. What a lot of young girls come with jasmine buds knitted in their braids – the problem for the photographer is to photograph a girl's face and the back of her jasmine-covered head simultaneously, which is what they demand. Poor things, they sit up all night when they have the jasmine in their hair, for fear of crushing it on the pillows. They arrive at the rate of two a minute. When they are in the darkness of the studio, I try to find out their politics and give them our cyclostyled circulars and the latest news. The studio is a help for us in this job. When anyone comes there he is more responsive than he is anywhere else. People generally come to a studio with a cheerful mind, ready to oblige the photographer by being agreeable and responsive, and by listening to all he has to say, the same as being with a barber. They have a feeling that they are obliged to the photographer in some vague way and readily listen to his talk, and I make use of this for our national cause. That's why I keep the studio going, although it's so difficult, without a proper supply of materials. When our country gets independence, if I have anything to do with things, you will see what I shall do to the beggars who are black-marketing spools now!' He ground his teeth at the thought of them.

He was soon converting the temple into a fortress. He explained: 'The advantage of this place, do you know what it is? Except for a few antiquarians, no one knows of its existence. And it is not visible from outside. I've observed it from various points. It cannot be seen from the road down below. I wonder why anyone built a temple here at all. I believe it must have been used as a place for conspirators a thousand years ago,' and he laughed grimly. Sriram laughed. He began to like him.

'Don't think this is always going to be safe,' said the other. 'Sooner or later they will find it.'

'There is an underground chamber,' began Sriram.

'Yes, where I know aged cobras live, if you prefer them to the police. But we have to manage somehow between the cobras and the police.'

'Yes, yes, with so much to do – '

Jagadish handed him a small axe and told him to cut the bamboo foliage, large branches of it, and drag them up. Sriram went at it till the skin on his palm smarted and peeled off. Jagadish induced Sriram to climb the rampart of the old temple and stick the foliage here and there according to his directions. He was shouting energetically. Standing in the sun all day, his face shone like mahogany with sweat. He said, 'I can screen this whole mountain if it comes to that.' Sriram felt tired and indignant. He wondered, 'Why should I let this fellow order me about, when he does nothing but stand around and instruct?' Probably it would have been more pleasant to have gone to gaol. But Jagadish never gave him much opportunity to dwell on such thoughts. He said: 'We are waging a war, remember. Mahatmaji in his own way and we in our own. All our aims are the same.'

'But I thought we were all working out the Mahatma's orders.'

'We are, we are,' he said vaguely. 'I used to be a devoted follower too. I'm still one, but he is no longer there to guide us. What can we do? He permits us all to carry on our work to the best of our abilities.'

'But strictly non-violently,' said Sriram.

'Of course, this camouflaging is not violence. It doesn't hurt anybody. It's done only that we may be left alone to work out our plans without interference. I don't want even that postman to see too much of this place. After all, he is a member of the Imperial Government.'

Sriram's next assignment was more complicated. He found he had become a blind slave of Jagadish, and a word of encouragement from him pleased him to the depths of his soul. He felt proud of his position. He thought that perhaps the other associates hardly ever got a good word from him. All day long, he sat up with the radio behind the god, with a writing-pad on his lap, and a pencil between his fingers, taking down the news and messages coming from Rangoon, Singapore and Germany, which purported to give the hour-to-hour progress of the war in Europe and the Far East. Sriram worked far into the night. His pencil wore out every three days. He had never worked so hard in his life. The only reward he got was Jagadish's 'Very good! Excellent job. More of our troops have joined the Indian National Army, they will soon be marching into India.' He sat by the lamp and went over the reports with concentration as Sriram sat chasing out the gnats and beetles that were trooping in towards the light. Jagadish made several markings on the messages, and carried them off to be cyclostyled and distributed from his studio at Malgudi.

The radio said: 'This is Tokyo calling. Here is Subhas Chandra Bose, your own leader at the mike, addressing you on a special occasion.' A few seconds later the message said, 'This is Subhas Chandra Bose speaking.' Sriram sat up respectfully. 'What good fortune that I should hear his voice!' At the sound of it, Sriram felt reverence for this man who had abandoned his home, comfort, and security, and was going from country to country, seeking some means of liberating his Motherland. With what skill he had managed to slip away from his home in Calcutta in spite of police vigilance, disguising himself as a Sadhu! Sriram felt he was peculiarly fortunate to be hearing the hero's voice.

Subhas Chandra Bose's voice said, 'Men of the Indian Army, be patriots. Help us free our dear Motherland. Many of your friends are here, having joined the Indian National Army which is poised for attack on your borders. We are ready. We shall soon be across, and then you can join the fight on our side. Till then don't aim your guns at us, but only at the heart of our enemy.' And then followed a ten-point programme of National Service that the men of the Indian Army should undertake. Sriram wrote at breakneck speed. He felt as if the commanding presence of Subhas Chandra Bose itself was at his elbow dictating. He filled up several sheets of the pad in respectful silence. He was overawed by the look of the radio now as its lamps burned red. Outside crickets chirped, a train rattled away somewhere, and the bamboo clumps rustled. The radio went on and on. Its red eyes glowed, and threw a red glare on the ankle of the god on the pedestal. Sriram lost count of time. He had never written so much in his life. That the broadcast came through in English was a great trial, for his spelling was none too good.

Subhas Chandra Bose was saying: 'And now stand by for a most important message. Be attentive.' Sriram wanted to catch it without fail, without any possibility of a mistake, but just at that moment a contrary noise began to emanate from the radio. It was as if a bee had started buzzing in time with the Great Message. Sriram felt distressed. If the thing went on undisturbed for a few seconds more, the message would be over. He strained his ears, but the other noise was becoming too loud. He ground his teeth. His left hand strayed towards the knob of the radio, and turned it. It only seemed to irritate the radio further. He lifted his eyes from the paper and glared at the radio. He saw on the dial on the outside of the glass sheet, illuminated by a small light inside, a very small cockroach, its pale body quivered with the battery of noise from the radio. Sriram felt revulsion at the sight of its white belly pressed against the glass dial. He could see but not reach it. He felt sick and angry. He cried, 'You cursed creature, how dare you come and interfere with this most important message! Get away.' He tapped the glass with his finger. He felt indignant. 'Am I here to wear out my pencil, taking down your stupid loathsome noises!' His tapping was so furious that whether it affected the insect or not, he tapped the light away, and all noise from the machine ceased. The radio was dead. Sriram laid aside his pad and pencil and shook the radio, but nothing happened. He turned the knobs, shook his fist at it, and cursed and cried, but nothing happened. He asked pathetically, 'Couldn't you have waited for five minutes more!' Why should this have happened just when the most serious part of the message was coming through? What would Jagadish say about him now? Sriram looked at the radio and realized his utter helplessness. He had seen youngsters who could take any mechanism to pieces and assemble them again. He wasn't fit to turn even a screw. His own limitations came back to him with a good deal of force, and he said, 'I am a fool, I have been brought up as a fool by that granny of mine. It is a wonder that a girl like Bharati cares for me at all!'

This note of self-reproach was fully endorsed when Jagadish turned up at two a.m. After putting the radio out of commission,

Sriram sat for a while wondering what to do, blew out the lamp, kicked open his mat and lay down on it. When Jagadish arrived and struck a match to look for the lamp, Sriram woke up and cried excitedly, 'Who are you?' A sleepy vision of the very dark man illumined by a match-flare was unnerving.

'Hush, it is myself, get up.'

Sriram sat up, rubbing his eyes. The lamp was lit. Jagadish gave him a slight shake in order to wake him fully; he sat beside him and asked, 'What is special today?'

Sriram triumphantly held out his pad to him. He snatched it, crying excitedly: 'Ah, a message from Subhas Babu! How lucky you are to have heard him. Good boy! Good boy! You shall be a big man when our country becomes free and independent.' He ran his eyes down it, muttering, 'These are men who are gods on earth; whose deeds must be recited in odes to posterity. I'll have a *lavani* composed of Subhas Babu's life, his sacrifice, patriotism, courage, and make it compulsory to sing it every day in every school in this country.' He went on reading aloud, ' "My countrymen, heroes of our Indian Army" – ' in a sing-song manner, interlarding it with appreciative comments of his own, such as, 'Very good!' 'Precisely', 'It is a great mind speaking!' 'Listen and learn, all ye good folk,' and so on and so forth. Till he came down to: ' "Now be attentive. In the first place all of you who" – ' He turned the paper over in his hand and asked, 'Where is the continuation?'

'There is no continuation, the message stopped there. Someone has been tampering with the broadcast.'

'What do you mean? Let us see.' He dashed to where the radio was and turned the knob. There was no sign of life. He shook it and cried, 'What has happened to this blessed radio?'

'How can I say? Am I a radio engineer?'

'Don't get into an argument with me about it. It'll not take us anywhere. Subhas Babu must have said some very vital things, and you have chosen to choke the radio.'

'No. You are wrong. It choked itself. Probably a cockroach I saw there must have done it.'

Jagadish clenched his great fist and remained silent. Sriram feared he would hit him. If he did, he wouldn't go down without a fight. He looked at a corner where he kept a bamboo staff for cobras and scorpions. He wondered for a moment whether he should make an immediate dash to it. Would the other give him the necessary time?

After many moments of grim silence the man said, 'Well, let us not bother about it any more. As soldiers, we must learn not to brood over what is definitely past, mind you, what is definitely past.' He said, 'Give me that pencil.' Sriram passed the pencil to him. Jagadish adjusted the lamp, read the message carefully, and after spending one minute thinking, filled in the rest of the sheet briskly. 'You must, you must and you must.' He wrote with inspiration. It took him nearly an hour to complete the writing of the message, he looked over it and shook his head with satisfaction. He gave the pad to Sriram and commanded, 'Now read it, young man, this is exactly how he would have gone on if the cockroach had not stood there acting like a censor.' After this triumph a sudden sorrow assailed him. He was reminded of the radio. 'The last battery set – you could have spoken back to Subhas Babu, if you had only been careful. It was a two-way radio ... I suppose I'd better take it back with me and repair it. As a soldier I will not cry over split milk.'

'Is it split milk?' Sriram asked nervously.

'Of course it is,' asserted Jagadish, 'when milk goes bad, it splits into water and solid, you know. It's no use crying over split milk,' he repeated.

Next afternoon, a little while after the train blew its whistle, Jagadish arrived with a bundle of papers hidden under his shirt. For the purpose of carrying that quantity of paper he wore an inner shirt with an enormous pocket and over it another large cloak-like shirt, and looked so big with all this literature hidden about his person that Sriram sometimes wondered if the impressiveness of his personality might not be due to excessive padding.

Jagadish unwound his robes and took out a bundle of papers, and once again Sriram childishly as ever expected him to produce some nice eatables. 'Come on, sit down,' said Jagadish. Jagadish first went to look up and down and assure himself that no one was watching. He dramatically attempted to close the large door

498

which creaked on its mighty hinges, but could be moved only half an inch forward. Sriram watched him without a word. After these preparations, he pulled Sriram to a seat beside him on the mat. He pressed a sheet of cyclostyled messages into his hand, and said, 'Read it.' Sriram read aloud, ' "Men of the Indian Army, etc., etc.," ' all that he had monitored on the previous day, but it continued for several paragraphs more. ' "First, don't co-operate with our enemy Government. Lay down your arms and lay down your lives, if necessary. You will be the heroes of the day when the Indian National Army marches into Delhi and flies its flag on the Red Fort, the very place where our men are now imprisoned." ' And it went on and on, giving precise directions to the army as to what it should do, for the liberation of the country. Sriram felt a profound admiration for the man. 'How did you manage to get the rest of the message?' he asked innocently.

'Don't bother how,' replied Jagadish, 'where there is a will there is a way. All out of this,' he said proudly touching his forehead. 'I could easily guess how the rest of the message would have run. It is just a matter of thought-reading, more or less,' he declared proudly. 'It is an extremely important message for our army at this moment. It is very vital to us. And it is to your honour that you got it first, although (never mind, let us not think of what is past) you couldn't get the full message; nothing is lost, and so don't bother about it. Furthermore, it should be your honour to see that the message reaches those for whom it is intended.'

Sriram was somewhat confounded. He asked, 'What should I do?'

'Listen to me carefully. I will give you fifty copies of this and you will take them to the army camp at Belliali. The poor fellows there cannot have any notion of what is happening in the world since they are not allowed to listen-in to truth, but only to the cock and bull stories that the British War Department issues. Our boys must know the truth. They must know where Subhas Babu is, where the Indian National Army is stationed, and what is to be done. It is our duty to propagate truth wherever it may be. Has not Mahatmaji told us so?'

499

'Yes, yes,' agreed Sriram, to whom this argument appealed. 'What will you do with the rest of the copies? Why don't you let me carry some more?'

'No, I can spare only fifty. I have made one hundred and fifty copies in all. These are days of paper shortage, remember. I am going to send fifty copies to Lakshi camp, and take fifty myself to the third one at —. You will have to go up tonight and complete the task allotted to you.'

'Agreed,' said Sriram.

Before parting Jagadish said, 'We shall probably all three of us get shot in this enterprise. But don't bother. Our lives are not very important. Our work is more important.'

'I don't care whether I live or die,' said Sriram, remembering the frustrations he had experienced with Bharati. What was the use of dragging on one's existence with this girl always inaccessible? Probably this national fight would never be over, and if over, might probably involve her in further activities. She was bound to be pursuing something else all her life ... This thought caused him so much weariness that he declared with all sincerity his readiness to die. He added, 'If I fail to return, will you tell Bharati what I think of her?'

'What do you think of her?' asked the other with amusement.

'That if she had married me I should probably not have died or something like that.'

'Well, I will tell her that. If I am shot, you can take charge of my studio. It is yours for the asking.'

Sriram felt too moved to speak. 'You are kind,' he murmured. 'How good you are.'

The other just twirled the end of his fancy scarf. 'But I am afraid you will find it hard to run it with the position of chemicals being what it is! Anyway, I wish you luck.'

The pamphlets were written in a convenient size which could easily be carried concealed on one's person. Sriram placed them neatly in a small bundle in a long strip of a towel, brought together its corners and tied them, put the towel around his waist and knotted it; over it he put on his *khadi* vest, and over it his *jiba*. The messages pressed his stomach uncomfortably, but he bore this with fortitude. He went down hill at nightfall. Jagadish had given him precise directions.

Sriram walked down the road and waited under a tree for a bus. There were one or two villagers sitting under the tree, waiting too. It was dark, and beyond the horizon there was the glow of Malgudi town. He sighed like an outcast. 'What a wretched hour it was when I set out to face life! Granny!' he addressed her mentally, 'I want to be back but I can't be, don't worry. All troubles must end. I wish they would release Mahat-maji. As long as he is in prison we will fight this devilish government. How dare they lay their hands on him? If they hadn't done that, Bharati would be out and happy, and Mahat-maji would have given his consent to her marriage.'

'Eh? What do you say, sir?' asked one of the villagers, peering at him curiously.

Sriram became cautious and asked, 'Who is there?' He looked closer, and asked, 'What are you waiting for?'

'The bus is late today,' they said by way of conversation, and Sriram agreed, 'It should have been here long ago, isn't that so?'

'How is the war going, sir?' asked one of them, the usual question that any villager would put to any man who looked informed.

Sriram suddenly became very cautious. He asked, 'Why?'

The other said, 'Because if it is over soon, we shall all be free from troubles.'

'I don't know,' Sriram drawled. In the darkness he could not make out the features of the man to whom he was talking. It might be a police spy or a constable himself.

'How is the war going, sir?' persisted the man.

'Well, the papers say this and that, and that is all I know,' replied Sriram.

'But someone says that it is all false! My brother knows a lot of people and he said that the English are being defeated every-where. He said that the Germans are already in Madras. If they come, will they release our Mahatmaji from prison?'

Sriram wished to divert the question and asked, 'Have you seen Mahatma Gandhi?'

'Yes, sir, he passed through our village,' began the man, and the headlights of the bus became visible far off. The man picked up his bundle, ran to the middle of the road crying, 'Unless we stop the bus, he won't stop.' By the time the bus arrived he stood right in the middle of the road gesticulating wildly.

'You will be run over!' cried Sriram.

The driver jammed on his brakes and cursed: 'What are you doing? Do you want to kill yourself? Why don't you join the army and die if you want to die?' he asked and laughter came from the bus.

The villager cried, 'I wish to go to — .'

'Clear off and don't stand there talking. There's no place even for an ant in this chariot.'

'Let him in,' cried the conductor, to whom this meant extra income. Such passengers were unaccounted for at the end of the day.

'I will sit on the floor,' pleaded the villager.

'Five annas,' cried the conductor.

'Three annas,' cried the passenger. 'Last week you took me for three annas.'

'Last week is not this week,' cried the conductor.

Sriram, who had watched the proceedings with detachment till now, suddenly came forward. 'Take him for three annas if you did so last week.'

'Yes, sir,' said the conductor, awed by Sriram's manner.

'And drop me at — . How much?'

'Three annas, sir.'

'I will stand on the footboard if there is no space inside,' said Sriram.

The conductor became officious. He said, 'You may come in, sir. I'll make room.'

All the passengers craned their necks out of the bus; the engine was hissing like a serpent. 'No, I will stand on the footboard,' said Sriram and clutched the handrail when the bus moved. 'He probably thinks I am a bus inspector off duty,' reflected Sriram, clutching the cold handrail as the night breeze blew on his face. Within the bus someone was snoring, someone was explaining the war and its progress on all fronts, someone was talking about God and Fate, a child was crying, a woman was yawning, the driver and conductor exchanged private jokes and giggled. 'They are probably enjoying the thought of their ill-gotten money,' thought Sriram. The bus ached and groaned under its load. He feared that its bottom might fall out. Unfortunately, he was not a bus inspector.

All the same, he assumed a voice of authority and asked, 'Conductor, what is your limit of loading?'

The conductor replied with humility, 'The Government have set aside the rule, sir. We may take in as many as we can hold. This is wartime, sir, otherwise how many poor folk would get stranded on the highway.'

Many murmurs of approval came from the passengers. 'What with these air raids and troubles, it would be most dangerous to get stranded on the road,' someone ventured.

The bus rocked past sleeping villages. The lights were shaded according to the wartime rule, and the headlights threw a faint patch of light ahead. Someone was humming a tune; all these human sounds were welcome to Sriram's ears, which had grown atrophied through his lonely existence. He revelled in the music of human voices.

The bus slowed down and he jumped off at a village called Sangram. The time was about eleven at night and the entire village was asleep. He waited on the road till the bus was out of sight, and then patted his person to see if his material was intact: a wire-cutter in his inner pocket, and the precious message at his waist. When he stooped, a lump in the belly pained him. 'If only to be relieved of this pain, I must scatter the message,' he reflected. Turning down a road to his left, he walked on the extreme side of the road since one or two military lorries were passing, and he did not want to be noticed. He came up against a vast jungle of barbed-wire entanglements, enclosing a group of bamboo and mud huts, with a private road winding through. The main entrance was on the other side. This was a military depot and training centre, and from here all day the rattle of convoys agitated the silence.

Presently he found himself cutting a portion of the barbed-wire fence. The snap resounded through the place; he feared somebody might machine-gun him. He heard the footsteps of the patrol sentry, and lay low. He thought, 'Well, this is my last moment. Suppose I am sent to hell?' He remembered all the details of hell that his grandmother had given him in childhood, and shuddered. 'There is no sense in getting shot by an unknown sentry,' he reflected. 'One unknown man shooting another unknown man, a ridiculous thing to happen.' On the strength of this, he put away the cutter. He took out a little glue, sat down and applied it neatly to the back of a few sheets, pasted the notices on the pillars supporting the wire and facing the inner barracks. The barb scratched the skin of his forearm. 'Blood is drawn, and this is the utmost I'm prepared to shed on Jagadish's orders.' After this, he rolled up his sheets into one mass, and flung them into the enclosure. He saw under the star-lit heaven the notices fluttering down. 'The boys may pick up and read the messages at their leisure tomorrow morning,' he reflected, and turned back.

Jagadish said, 'Why that lacklustre and far-away look in your eyes, young man? You do a lot of service to the great cause. But your heart is not really in it. May I know why?' Sriram had nothing definite to reply. 'I should have said, "Look pleasant, please," or "Smile please," as becomes a photographer. You must put your heart into your job, my dear young man, otherwise you will not help our country. We are passing through crucial times, as our statesmen say, and we have to do something. I have a suspicion that you let your thoughts play too much around a certain person. Am I right?'

'Yes.'

'Well, that's a futile occupation, since it's the government who think it would be in your best interests to keep you two apart. You don't even know where they are keeping her.'

'That's true,' said Sriram dolefully.

'But I know where she is,' said Jagadish. 'I've my own agents. She is not actually in any regular prison, all gaols being full now. She is in a hurriedly made up one ... You know the Old Slaughter House? She is in it, along with a number of other women prisoners.'

'How do you know?'

'I know a guard who works there. He likes me because he is an old customer, whose photograph in my stock helped him in some family litigation. He will help you to meet your friend if you are inclined that way.'

Sriram's heart palpitated. This was as if the dead had come to life, or at least were promising to come to life.

'A nice fellow, he will help you, at the risk of his own life, to meet and talk to Bharati for about half an hour.'

'When? When?' Sriram asked anxiously.

'As soon as you have done your job smartly. Some business about chrome ore, and I need your assistance.'

'You mean I shall be rewarded for my services.'

'Yes, that's what I mean. One good turn deserves another.'

'Who is going to be benefited by my good turn?' Sriram asked.

'Well, the country. A train load of chrome ore is leaving a certain railway station for England. It should not reach the port. If it reaches the port, it will return to us in the form of triggers and what not and plague us ... I can't think of anyone but you to assist me in this job.'

It was inevitable that soon the police should publish Sriram's photograph and announce a reward for anyone giving information of his whereabouts.

Sriram had a racking fear that Jagadish might be playing a practical joke. 'If he is playing a joke, heaven help him,' he told himself. 'I will crush his skull with a big stone,' and he revelled in visions of extraordinary violence. He pulled his mind back sharply when he realized how Bharati would react. The thought of Bharati softened him. He told himself he would not hesitate to fall at the feet of any villain if Bharati desired him to do so. Anything to please her and earn her approval. His whole being acquired a meaning only when he was doing something in relation to Bharati. He wondered how he should conduct himself when she came out and the photographer too was there. He hoped that his jealousy would not drive him to do wild things. Anyway, he hoped that the photographer would mind his business and leave him alone in order to pursue his life as he liked, he hoped the fight with the British Government would end soon, he hoped Britain would leave India, so that he might return to Kabir Street and live in peace with Bharati and Granny! Ah, that was the trouble. What would Granny do about it? She would probably nag Bharati night and day and compare her with her brother's granddaughter in looks and competence in household duties, but he hoped Bharati would turn round and challenge her to say whether that village niece of hers would have faced a charging police force or spoken to Mahatmaji. As he reclined on his couch at the entrance to his cave and looked at the top of the blue gum trees his mind roamed unchecked.

In a moment Jagadish had come up and was standing by his side. He said, 'Very unsafe, young man. If it had been a police-man instead of myself, you would still have been sitting there, day-dreaming, and he'd have put a nice collar round your neck and led you along to the gaol.'

Sriram, rather irritated, asked, 'What's wrong with day-dreaming?'

'There is much that is not right. You must be more watchful. Our cave is probably not visible from outside, but someone may think of exploring these parts. You are probably not seen but don't imagine that can last for ever. You should always watch, even through the camouflage. Be careful.'

'All right,' Sriram said, cowed by the other's manner, very much like a tiger in the circus ring which subsides on the spot indicated by the ring-master with a rolling growl.

Jagadish sat down beside him with the remark, 'And if you imagine that it's better the police come after you so that they may detain you at the Old Slaughter House, you are mistaken. They will do nothing of the kind: it's reserved for women prisoners.'

At the mention of the Old Slaughter House, Sriram softened. The associations of the Old Slaughter House might not be pleasant for everyone, but for Sriram the name produced the happiest associations and a very profound sense of peace.

'Old Slaughter House? Old Slaughter House?' Sriram said, adopting a playful attitude for the first time these many days. 'Old Slaughter, the sound is familiar! What has that to do with us?'

'It's virtue is that it is an Old Slaughter House, and not a new one,' said Jagadish. 'Many a goat trembles when it passes that building, but it makes you smile and joke. All the slaughter of the place is forgotten ... Yet it's still a place that attacks the heart, doesn't it?' he said.

Sriram felt completely happy. He would have gone on talking of the Slaughter House for the rest of his days: it was an opiate which made him forget politics, history, the police, and his own loneliness.

'If you wish to visit the place, you will have to make certain alterations to your good self,' Jagadish said. He explained, 'First you must look unlike the photo the police have published. If someone wants to make money by informing, you should not help him to do so. I fear the police have published your photo far and wide, and any street urchin may denounce you. It shows the evil of leaving one's photos about. I have an advantage in this respect — there is no photo of me and they have only described me: having been so busy photographing others, I had no time for myself. You have been scattering your portraits about like a film star.'

'Yes, yes,' Sriram had to agree dolefully. He recollected the cheap four-for-one-rupee quick photos that he had indulged in some time after he came into his wealth. Often Sriram had seen his pictures displayed on the advertisement boards of the photographers; and the walls of his house were full of his own pictures. He remembered his grandmother saying: 'In our days people hung up portraits of gods and ancestors, you have nothing but your own! I wonder why you do it?'

'Does it mean the police have taken the photos from our house in Kabir Street?' Sriram asked, assailed by a sudden thought.

'Definitely. That's the first thing they will have done.'

'I wonder what Granny said.'

'She will repeat it all when she sees you next. Don't worry,' he replied. He studied Sriram closely and said: 'You will have to change your appearance. You will have to undertake some drastic changes. First and foremost grow a nice small moustache, a little one that droops at the ends will make you look slightly like a mongol, but don't let that weigh on your mind, they are looking for you, not for a mongol. And then, do you think you could shave off your crop in order to complete the picture?'

Sriram's heart quailed at the suggestion, remembering all the heartaches he had undergone in order to get rid of his old tuft and grow his present crop. His granny would not hear of it at first. She was certain that it would spoil his appearance, but one day he had just slipped away to the temple-tank on whose steps barbers sat and shaved their customers. He induced an old barber to cut off his tuft and run the machine over his ears, and on his lap he emptied all the pocket-money he had purloined from his own sealed money-box. He had widened the slit of the money-box and shaken out the coins, when his granny was in the kitchen. To disguise the rattling he had muffled it with a piece of cloth and carried the operation on till it shed eight annas in small coppers. His granny kept shouting from the kitchen, 'What is that noise?' 'Which noise?' shouted back Sriram, and had gone on with his job. He had had no clear idea how much a barber would demand for a crop-cut. He put it down at six annas, and two annas extra for any unlooked-for expense. But the barber at the tank had demanded a rupee to cut off the thick curly tuft Sriram had possessed. By haggling Sriram brought it down to six annas; and the barber went on muttering disappointed remarks to the tune of snapping scissors. Sriram saw himself in a small mirror produced out of the barber's tin box, and was delighted. He felt he had rid himself of a couple of pounds of tuft: it lay on the stone steps of the tank; and Sriram remembered how he shivered at the sight of the appendage, for no known reason. They were long and curly tresses, and he said: 'Sell it and you will get ten rupees for it.' The barber lost his temper at the suggestion: 'You take me for a hawker of hair. Mind how you speak, young gentleman. I should have cut your throat if it hadn't been yourself but someone else. Look, I don't want anything, but give me the *dhoti* you are wearing: that's the usual custom under these circumstances.'

Sriram was aghast: 'And how shall I reach home?'

'Bathe in this tank and run before anyone notices. Anyway, haven't you got your piece-cloth under your *dhoti*? That'll do for a young man of your age.' So saying he almost tugged the ends of Sriram's *dhoti*, and Sriram had to dodge him desperately. 'Oh!' cried the barber in great surprise. He made queer faces to indicate his feelings. 'Do you mean to say that you go about with – ' He described vividly the under-clothes of respectable and honest citizens, and the habits of the modern generation. The topic was so below-the-waist that Sriram blushed and finally, wrenching himself free, ran off.

All this flashed across his mind now. He put his hand to the top of his head, ran his fingers over it and said to Jagadish: 'I can't sacrifice this crop. I like it.'

Sriram spent a sleepless night wondering how he could change his appearance. He even thought that he might disguise himself as a purdah lady and not show his face at all. Jagadish laughed all his propositions away. He seemed intent on disfiguring him in his own manner; bent upon shaving him like an egg, and making him as ridiculous as possible. Perhaps he wanted to make him the laughing-stock of the world and ruin his chance once for all with Bharati. She would refuse to take a second look at his face for the rest of his life. He wondered why he did not refuse to do anything that Jagadish suggested. Even the Slaughter House might be a huge practical joke or turn out to be a real slaughtering place after all! But his fears had no value. Whatever he might feel or fear the fact was always there that Jagadish was inescapable, and one had to do what he ordered.

Jagadish granted a period of three weeks for a respectable moustache to develop on Sriram's upper lip. He bought him a small bottle of coconut oil for massage to help a quick growth. 'How many things I have to do before I can see Bharati!' Sriram reflected. Jagadish checked the growth on the other's upper lip day after day. He nodded his head discouragingly each time. 'Very slow, very slow, too slow,' he said as if Sriram himself were responsible. Sriram clicked his tongue apologetically.

The period of three weeks was by no means wasted. In association with Jagadish and under his expert guidance, Sriram did a variety of jobs which he hoped would help the country in its struggle for freedom: he set fire to the records in half a dozen law courts in different villages; he derailed a couple of trains and paralysed the work in various schools; he exploded a crude bomb which tore off the main door of an agricultural research station, tarred out 'V' for Victory and wrote 'Quit India' over the emblem. He became so seasoned in this activity that a certain recklessness developed in him. He had no fear of the police: they seemed to him a remote, theoretical body, unconnected with his affairs. He knew he could always slip through. They were looking for him everywhere, except where they could find him. Jagadish kept repeating: 'Britain will leave India with a *salaam*, if we crush the backbone of her administration.' He was always talking in terms of backbone. Sometimes he said: 'Britain's backbone is, you know where?'

'At her back, I suppose?' said Sriram facetiously.

'Do you know where her back is?'

'Behind her front, I suppose,' said Sriram, still facetiously. He was beginning to enjoy these bouts, which were a relief in his lonely, drab life, isolated from all human association.

Jagadish forgave him his tricks. He explained: 'The prospect of the Slaughter House makes you sharp-witted, doesn't it?' He explained with a good deal of tolerance, 'Britain's backbone must be smashed, and it lies in the courts and schools and offices and railway lines, from these she draws the strength for her survival.'

It was an intricate logic which Sriram could not easily grasp. He asked pathetically, 'Why don't we smash her front also?'

'Because it's far away, and we can't reach so far.'

Jagadish dragged him about and made him his instrument and agent. Sriram was actually beginning to enjoy the excitement and novelty and above all the game of hide and seek with the police. It gave him a feeling of romantic importance. He felt that he was a character out of an epic, and on his activities depended future history. But now and then some kind of misgiving assailed his mind, when sitting concealed in a ditch in Jagadish's company, he saw the flames rising from a railway station or a government building and lighting up the night. Once he whispered, 'Do you think Britain will be affected by this fire?'

Jagadish declared unequivocally, 'Churchill will already know of it. It will make him groan. It will make him sit up. It must go on and on every hour of the day, all over the country, until Britain tells us, "We are bundling ourselves out tomorrow, do what you like with your country." '

Sriram asked next, 'I wonder what Mahatmaji will say about all this!'

'I don't know,' replied Jagadish. 'It is not his line. But when the results turn out satisfactorily, I am sure he'll say, "You did well, my boy." '

Sriram felt doubtful. He shook his head. 'I'm not sure. Only Bharati knows exactly what Mahatmaji will say or think ...' And then his thoughts went off to the Slaughter House.

Jagadish seemed to weaken slightly at this point: 'We have not wilfully caused anybody's death. I'm always careful to see that no life is lost, but if in spite of our precautions, some people are accidentally caught in a mess and killed, we can't help it.'

'A lot of people are also shot down by the police when they disperse the mobs that gather to help us.'

'But that is none of our concern,' said Jagadish, and added, 'In a war lives are bound to be lost. However, the job of the moment is more important than any amount of theoretical speculation. Mahatmaji taught me this philosophy when I was with him at Wardha. Anyway, don't bother too much about these questions. He has asked us to work for the movement according to our individual capacities.'

On a certain day Jagadish examined Sriram's face and declared, 'The most satisfactory moustache that I ever saw in my life.' With a razor and scissors he helped Sriram to give its end a downward turn. He produced also some old silver-rimmed spectacles, and mounted them on his nose. He provided him too with an ill-fitting, close-buttoned coat, and a white turban for covering his head. He ordered him to tie up his *dhoti* bifurcated, like all respectable men. After all this, Sriram looked into a mirror, the very tiny one which he used for his shaving; it did not reveal a full picture but it showed enough for him to remark: 'I look like a wholesale rice merchant.'

Jagadish nodded appreciatively and said with considerable delight in his tone, 'True, true ... If I could only put a dark caste-mark on your forehead, that'd indeed complete the picture.'

Sriram as he sallied forth at about seven, after sunset, felt so different that he wondered why he should expect Bharati to admit him at all. He chuckled at the thought, 'Bharati may wonder why a rice merchant has taken a fancy to call on her, all of a sudden.' The spectacles gave him a dull ache on the bridge of his nose, and kept constantly slipping down, pestering him with a dull, misty vision. 'This is what comes of not surrendering oneself to the police when Bharati advises one to do so!' he reflected. At the little station he climbed into the train going towards Malgudi. There were a few sleepy passengers in his compartment. He ignored the whole lot. 'It's no business of a self-respecting rice merchant to speak to these folk,' he reflected and sat looking at his fellow passengers with indifference. Jagadish had proved himself a genius: the moustache was a tremendous asset; it was as if Sriram had worn a mask over his face, the transformation was so complete.

From Malgudi station it was an hour's walk southward through Market Road to the Slaughter House. As he passed along the familiar roads, Sriram felt sentimental and unhappy. It seemed as if he had left this world ages ago. Beyond those rows of silent and darkened shops was the house of his grandmother.

Jagadish had given precise instructions. The rice merchant crouched behind the eastern wall of the old Slaughter House. Bharati would come to the lavatory at that corner, stand up on a large stone, rolled into position for the purpose, look down and talk to him. Sriram was wondering if Bharati would notice his moustache in the darkness, he wondered if he could reach up and touch her hand. He patiently waited. The Taluk Office gong sounded two in the morning. He felt sleepy. He remembered Bharati asking him to meet her at three a.m., when the Mahatma came to Malgudi. 'She seems fond of spoiling other people's sleep,' he reflected. He sat there on the ground. The Taluk Office gong struck the next hour. 'How long am I to stay here?' he reflected. 'Has someone been playing a prank?' Angry thoughts were rising in his heart.

'Hey,' cried a voice.

He looked up hopefully. Over the wall a head appeared, but it was not Bharati's. It was one of the wardresses.

'Where is ... ?' Sriram began, stretching himself up on his toes.

'Hush, listen. She won't come.'

'Is she not coming?'

'No. Catch this.' She dropped a letter. 'Read it,' said the head, 'and be off.'

The rice merchant moved away clutching the piece of paper in his hand, his head buzzing with a thousand speculations.

Under the first street lamp, he spread out the note. It was a piece torn out of a memo pad. On it was a hurried pencil scribbling: 'I cannot bring myself to see you today. It seems degrading to have a meeting under these conditions. Bapu has always said that it is dishonourable to assume subterfuges. In a gaol we must observe the rules, or change them by *Satyagraha* openly, if possible. Forgive me. We shall meet again. But before that, please go and see your granny. A detenue who came in here told me that she was very ill. It is your duty to risk your life to see her. Go before it is too late.'

Not many people were able to recognize him when he ascended the steps of 14 Kabir Street. He saw Kanni, the shopman, coming out of the house. He was softly closing the door behind him. He didn't recognize Sriram, who for a moment forgot that he could not be recognized, and called 'Kanni!' almost involuntarily. His voice betrayed him. Kanni halted and suddenly cried, 'Oh! it's our young master. O, Ram, what is it you have been doing to yourself, deserting your house and the old lady who was your father, mother, and cousin and everything. Have you no heart? Thank God you have come now anyway. But you are too late.'

'Why? Why?' screamed Sriram. 'What has happened?'

'She is dead. She died at ten o'clock last night.'

Sriram ran past him into the house. There, in the old familiar place, under the good old hall lamp, lay the old lady. A white sheet was drawn over her. A couple of women from the neighbouring houses were sitting beside her, keeping vigil.

Sriram was sorrow-stricken: the familiar household, the old almanac still there under the roof tile: the copper vessel in which she kept drinking water still on the window-sill. The easy-chair which he had bought for her with his first money was still where he had put it. He had a glimpse of a past life. He went up to the corner of the house which used to be his and examined his books, pens, clothes, he opened the lid and looked into his old tin trunk. All the articles with which he had grown up were there, kept safe and intact. The vigil-keepers followed his movements with dull, sleep-filled eyes. Sriram wept. But he could not wipe away his tears; he realized that his spectacles were a nuisance: he suddenly plucked them off and flung them down, feeling: 'I'm answerable to Jagadish for this. I'm betraying myself.'

Kanni stood in the doorway, respectfully watching. 'How imperious she looks! Even now!' he cried. 'A great Soul.'

'I can't believe she is dead. She looks asleep! How do you know that she is dead?' Sriram asked.

Kanni merely laughed grimly. 'You had better telegraph to all your relatives. I'm sure many would want to have a last look at her face.'

Sriram sat down on the floor beside the old lady, quietly sobbing. The women looked at him for a moment, and lapsed into mournful silence. One of them turned to Kanni and asked, 'Is he the only relative to arrive or should we wait for some more?' Kanni preferred to ignore the question. The night was absolutely still and silent. Even the street dogs were asleep. Except the low voices conversing under the dim light, the entire world was asleep, following the example of Granny herself. Sriram suddenly rose to his feet, went to Kanni, put his arm round his shoulder, and whispered, 'Kanni, I am very hungry. Can't you open your shop and give me something to eat? There is nothing in the kitchen.'

'How can there be anything? She was ill so long; those ladies were bringing her milk and gruel.'

'I'm very hungry, Kanni,' Sriram said again pathetically.

Kanni jingled his keys and said, 'Come with me.'

They crossed the street. Kanni unlocked the door of his shop and lit a lamp. Sriram climbed the platform and went in, then bolted the door again from inside. The shop was hot and stuffy. Bananas hung down in bunches, buns and biscuits filled various glass containers; all, of course, were presided over by the European queen with apple cheeks. Sriram complained that it was stuffy. Kanni explained, 'I don't want anyone to suspect your presence. Though handing you over and collecting the reward might prove a better proposition than running a business in these difficult days!'

Sriram had not realized how hungry he was. He demanded and ate everything that he saw. Kanni took out a paper and calculated: 'That will be two rupees and four annas. I will put it down on your account.'

Now he was no longer hungry Sriram said: 'Tell me about my granny. What was wrong with her?'

Kanni paused for a while before answering. 'Ever since the police came asking for you in this house, she lost, if I may say so, her original spirit. She was always feeling that you had betrayed her. You may know all about Mahatma and so on, but all she knew was what people told her, that you had run after a girl. The old lady was much hurt. She hardly ever came out after that, and when the police came to take away your photograph, she was very much upset. She felt that she could not hold up her head in public again. She was always saying that you had betrayed her. The police came and questioned me too about you. I said, "You are merely wasting my shop time. I am not to be bothered about every scapegrace in the town because I have the ill-luck to have a shop opposite his house," and that satisfied them. I wish you had not gone away without telling her. It worried her too much. She kept saying, 'What can a little cobra do even if you have brought it up on cow's milk? It can only do what its breeding tells it to do." '

Sriram was visibly annoyed at this comparison. 'She was a very bitter-tongued person, that's why I preferred to go away without telling her at all. What chance did one have of talking to such an unreasonable character?' He forgot for a moment that he was talking about someone dead.

'People came and told her hair-raising tales about you. She was alarmed by your activities. What was the matter with you? I never thought the young master I had known so long ago could ever grow up into a Zigomar.'

Sriram felt hurt by this comparison with an old classical bandit. He said with a lot of self-pity, 'I wouldn't have come if I wasn't eager to see my granny.'

'That's true,' said Kanni. 'The Market Road doctor attended her often; even last evening he was there with his tube and needle and stayed till she passed away.'

'Was she talking all the time?' asked Sriram.

'She wasn't, but she might have been. Why think of all that now?' Kanni said. 'Let us think of what we should do next.'

'Yes, what is to be done?'

'The funeral. Get through it quickly. Are you going to wait for relatives?'

These were tough and complex domestic questions to which he was unaccustomed. He brooded over them. The word 'relative' brought to his mind only his grand-uncle whose dark descendant he was expected to marry; and a batch of miscellaneous folk who dropped in for a meal or two occasionally from their village, and always spoke of lands and litigation. Granny used to find their talk fascinating and forgot to notice Sriram's arrivals and departures, while he generally sneaked out to a nearby cycle-shop and learnt to balance himself on the pedal of a bicycle taken on hire. Sriram had a sudden vision of being responsible for gathering that entire crowd again: they might stand around the corpse and lament over their lands and litigation. He was aghast at the thought. He said: 'I don't care for anyone.'

'Yes, I know. I too think you should not keep the body too long. Better hurry through the funeral. But at least let the lady have the satisfaction of having her pyre lit by her grandson. That may assuage her spirit.'

'I don't know what to do about such things,' Sriram wailed.

'I will help you,' said Kanni.

'One thing. I can't go with the funeral procession,' said Sriram. 'I will manage to come at the end if you will manage the other things.'

'Even the police may not interfere now. After all, they are also human,' said Kanni.

Sriram went back into his house and took another look at his granny. The two vigil-keepers were asleep. They sat hunched up with their heads on the floor, curled beside the body, 'They look more dead than Granny,' thought Sriram. A cock crowed somewhere. Sriram went out, softly closing the door behind him.

Meanwhile Kanni had locked the shop, and had returned. 'She is in your charge,' said Sriram. 'Will you be there at eight? Do everything nicely. Don't bother about expense.'

'Yes, I know. I can always get my debts. I have kept your account in full detail. You should have no misgiving even about an anna. I have even put into the account what I have been paying the doctor from time to time. Are you sure her relatives will not be angry with us later?'

'What do you care whether they are angry or pleased? What have we to do with them? A set of useless rustics,' said Sriram with a certain amount of unnecessary bitterness in his voice.

At about eight Sriram was on the cremation ground beyond the Sarayu river. A couple of pyres which had been lit on the previous day were still smouldering. Bamboo and discarded pieces of shroud were scattered here and there. A funeral procession was crossing Nallappa's Grove. The bier was decorated with flowers and some men wearing white shirts and rings on their fingers were shouldering the corpse. 'Must be devoted relatives,' he thought. 'They are bearing the burden. But poor Granny has no one to carry her.' Once again he felt angry at the thought of those village relatives. The heat was intense although it was not even eight in the morning. 'This is a very hot place,' he reflected. Bullock-carts were crossing the river, villagers on their way into the town with baskets on their heads chattered incessantly. He noticed people coming to the river for a wash. His mind made a dull note of all that his eyes saw. His main job now was to await the arrival of Granny. Why were they taking all this time? Probably priests were holding up the body so that they might get a higher fee for funeral citations. Or could the police have held up the procession? For a moment a fantastic fear seized him lest the police should have suspected foul play and held up the body for a post-mortem. The other, the pampered body carried by the devoted relatives, was now brought in through the gate and laid down on the ground. They were going through a lot of ceremonial activity ... Granny's pyre was also being built up, with dried cowdung cakes, on a small platform: all the arrangements were supervised by Kanni's shop assistant, who was haggling with fuel suppliers and ordering the graveyard assistants about. They obeyed him cheerfully, which made Sriram wonder why they obeyed him at all. 'It is in some people's blood to be respected by all kinds of people,' Sriram reflected, watching with a certain amount of envy all the fuss that the rich were making with the body in their hands.

Led by Kanni, who bore in his hand a pot of fire, a couple of neighbours, the manager of the Fund-Office, and two priests, Granny arrived on a bier made of bamboo, carried by four grim sub-human professional carriers. Sriram rushed to the small wooden doorway to meet the procession. Kanni was the first to step through. He held the pot of fire to Sriram saying, 'Really it is your duty to carry it.' Sriram took charge.

Granny's face was uncovered and faced the sun. Sriram felt a pang of fresh sorrow at the sight. The bier was laid on the ground. 'Sriram, bathe in the river and come back soon with wet clothes on you. She is at least entitled to so much consideration.' The words came from the old family priest. Sriram realized that he was still in the garb of a wholesale rice merchant, and felt ridiculous. The old priest had officiated at festivals and domestic ceremonies ever since Sriram could remember, including the grand ceremony of his first birthday. The old man was several years Granny's senior, but remarkably wiry and alert, with his greenish eyes and hook nose and greed for ceremonial fees.

He asked Sriram, 'Have you two rupees in coins?'

While Sriram fumbled for an answer, the ever watchful Kanni descended on him wrathfully, 'Why do you ask that? Haven't we agreed on a lump sum for everything?'

The priest who was squatting beside the body turned and said, 'Whoever said the lump sum included this? This can never go into that. This is a separate account. Our elders have decreed that the Dear Departed should have two silver coins on his or her chest from the hand of the nearest and dearest. It is said to smooth out the passage of the soul into further regions. I am only repeating what the *shastras* say. Our ancestors knew what was best for us, I am merely a mouthpiece.'

'And what happens to the coins?' asked the Fund-Office Manager. The priest pretended to ignore the question, but

Kanni said, 'It goes the way of other coins, that is into a priest's money-box.'

'Yes, it does. Do you expect the soul to carry the silver with it? You must view it all in the proper light, you must take only its philosophical meaning. We carry nothing from this earth,' said the priest and quoted a Sanskrit verse. He suddenly looked across at the other part of the ground where the rich men were conducting their ceremonies. 'See there. They are devoted and very correct. They are not omitting a single rite.'

'We are not omitting anything either,' said Kanni angrily.

His tone cowed the priest, who mumbled, 'Don't think I am after money: I only do things in order to satisfy a great soul known to me for several decades now.' He looked up at Sriram and said, 'Now go and bathe quickly. Nothing can begin until after that.' He paused and added, 'You will find a barber there. You will have to shave off your moustache and the top of your head. Otherwise it would be very irregular. The *shastras* say ...'

'I will not shave my moustache nor my head,' said Sriram emphatically.

'All right,' said the priest. 'It is my duty to suggest what the *shastras* say, and it is left to you to follow it or modify it in any manner. Of course modern life makes it difficult to follow all the rules, and people have to adjust themselves. There are even people who like to perform their funerals with European hats on, nowadays. What can one do about them? "It is wisdom to accept what has come to pass," say the *shastras*, and we bow our heads to that injunction.'

Sriram presently returned from his bathe in the river, dripping wet with his hair sticking on his head and his clothes stuck to his body. They had now laid the corpse on the pyre. The pyre beyond was already aflame and the party was leaving the ground. 'They are very business-like,' said the priest. He seemed to admire everything they did. Sriram felt piqued, and Kanni said, 'Don't go on talking unnecessarily.'

The rites before the lighting of the pyre started. The old lady lay stretched out on the cowdung fuel. The priest placed a small vessel in Sriram's hand and asked him to pour the milk in it over the lips of the dead. Sriram poured the milk, chanted some *mantras*, and finally dropped the fire over Granny's heart, which was actually below a layer of fuel. The fire smouldered and crackled. 'Now it is all over with her,' Sriram said.

The Fund-Office Manager suddenly cried, 'See there, see there.' He was excited. They looked where he pointed. The big toe on the left foot of the lady was seen to move. 'Pull off the fire, pull off the fire ...' Someone thrust his hand in and snatched off the burning piece. The old lady's *sari* was already burning at one end. Sriram flung a pail of water on it and put it out. Now with the fire out, they stood around and watched. The toe was wagging.

'She is not dead, take her out,' cried Sriram.

'I've never heard of such a thing, you can't do that,' the priest cried. People seemed to have suddenly lost all common sense.

'You want us to burn Granny alive, do you? Get out of our way, priest,' cried Sriram. He kicked away the pile of fuel, lifted the body and placed it down again on the ground. 'I knew something was wrong. I knew Granny wouldn't die,' said Sriram. He sprinkled water on her face, forced some milk down her throat, and fanned her face. The priest stood aside with a doleful expression. Kanni seemed too stunned to speak. The shop assistant was running in circles announcing the glad tidings and collecting a crowd.

The Fund-Office Manager cried, 'Let us not waste time. I will fetch the doctor.' He started running towards the city.

Kanni cried, 'Oh, what doctors, these days! They don't even know whether someone is alive or dead! If we had failed to notice in time ... oh, what doctors.'

Under their nursing, the movement in the toe gradually spread. All the toes showed signs of revival, then her leg, then her arms. The old lady seemed to be coming back to life, inch by inch. Her eyes were still shut. Sriram murmured, 'Granny, Granny, open your eyes. I am here.' At this moment all politics were forgotten, all disputes and wars, Britain, even Bharati. 'Get up Granny, you are all right.' Now her heart began to throb, her breathing returned, ever so faintly. Sriram let out a cry of tremendous relief. He called the shop assistant, 'My granny will not die, she is not dead. God bless her.' He dragged Kanni by his hand and said, 'Kanni, Granny is alive.' He nursed his granny with one hand and put the other around Kanni's shoulder and sobbed. His face was wet with tears.

Kanni patted his back and said, 'Don't, don't. Be brave. You must not break down. She may open her eyes and she must see a happy face.'

The rattle of an old car was heard far off. Everyone cried, 'Doctor's car.' Presently a little car with a flapping hood was struggling over the sand and pebbles at the Nallappa's Grove crossing, and on through the rough sandy track leading to the southern door of the crematorium. The doctor was a puny man wearing an enormous white overall, with a straggling crop of hair resembling Einstein's; a small man above whom everyone seemed to tower. He jumped out of his car, followed by the Fund-Office Manager. 'Is this true, is this true?' cried the doctor running forward. He stopped suddenly and said, 'Someone go and fetch that bag from the car.' Presently he knelt above the old lady, took her wrist in his hand, pulled out his watch, held his fingers under her nostrils, and smiled at Kanni. 'Yes, she is not dead.'

'Oh, Doctor, can't you even say whether a person is dead or alive?' asked Kanni.

'Why go into all that now? Let us be happy that she is back from the other world.' The doctor brooded. This was the first situation of the kind in his experience. Previously he had known only one-way traffic. He rubbed his chin thoughtfully.

'How is she, Doctor?' asked Kanni.

'Her pulse is good. She is all right. She will need some rest and recuperation.' He took several things out of his bag. He sterilized a syringe needle, picked up a phial, and injected Granny's forearm. She twitched at the touch of the needle and groaned slightly. The doctor looked at her with approbation. 'Well, freaks like this just happen. We can't say why or how. Last night she was practically dead. I don't know. This is enough to make one believe in the soul, *Karma*, and all that.' He stood looking at her and biting his lips. 'I read about a similar thing in a medical journal years ago but never thought it would come within my view.'

Granny was reviving little by little. Her breathing was becoming normal. The doctor said, 'It is not right to keep her here when she becomes fully conscious. She must be moved. Why not take her back home? Take her in my car.'

The priest interrupted, 'How can you suggest such a thing? No one who has been carried here can ever step into the town bounds again. Don't you know that it will … it will …'

'What will happen?'

'Happen! The whole town will be wiped out by fire or plague. It is very inauspicious. Do anything you like, but she can't come back into the town.'

This point of view gathered a lot of support. The news spread to the town. People began to throng into the cremation ground. Everyone who came said, 'This is a big problem. What are you going to do with her?'

In deference to this view she had to be carried to one of the small abandoned buildings on the river-bank, which had once been used as a toll-gate station, and since the river was between her and the town, she was out of bounds. She was kept at the Toll Office, and nursed by the doctor. Her world hummed round her, Kanni, the Fund-Office Manager, Sriram, the old hook-nosed priest, and the two mournful women who had kept vigil. They nursed and fed the old lady as she lay on a bed in the old building. The doctor's little car drove up half a dozen times a day and Kanni practically abandoned his shop in order to conduct the operations. A vast concourse began to arrive in order to witness the miracle. Some close relatives of Granny who had not seen her for years came and cried, 'Oh, sister, how good to see you. No one sent word to us that you were dead.'

'Word was not sent because there was nothing to send.'

'But when a close relation is dead, is it not … ?'

'But she was not dead, so why send word?'

'How did you know that she was not dead?' asked the relatives, and the conversation flowed on in rather bewildering channels. Sriram feared all along that this crowd and publicity would ultimately lead to trouble. He tried to keep himself aloof. When too many people arrived he went away to the back of the building, while Kanni and the others managed the visitors. He overheard people ask, 'Where is that grandson of hers?'

'Oh, that ne'er-do-well adventurer is probably in Burma,' said Kanni.

But none of this helped. A police inspector in plain clothes and two constables arrived on the third afternoon as Sriram, having fed his granny and eaten a meal brought in a vessel by the Fund-Office Manager, was enjoying a siesta in the shade of a tree behind the toll-gate building. Granny and her attendants were peacefully sleeping. The inspector looked down at Sriram and said, 'Get up.'

'Why?' asked Sriram, rising. 'What do you want?'

'You are under arrest,' said the inspector. 'We have been looking for you for a long time now.'

'Who gets the reward?' asked Sriram with heavy cynicism.

The inspector did not reply. He said, 'We know the special occasion which has brought you here, and we don't want to make any fuss, provided you make none. That is why we have stationed our jeep over there. I have some more men in it. You may come with us as soon as you are ready. Don't be too long.'

Sriram said, 'Yes, give me a little time.'

'I am armed and will shoot if you try to escape,' the inspector said.

Sriram went to take a look at Granny. He found her sitting up and conversing with the two people near her. The moment she saw Sriram she cried, 'Oh, boy, when did you come back? They told me that you were here, but with a moustache. Whatever made you grow one, my boy? Take it off, don't come before me with that, whatever else you may do.'

'Yes, Granny,' he said obediently. He was so happy to find her old spirit revived. One could not doubt that it was Granny speaking. There was the genuine ring in her tone. Her personality seemed to have returned from the other world unscathed by the contacts there. He sat down on the edge of her bed, took her arm into his hands, and stroked it. She looked at him closely and said, 'You are down and out, no doubt about it.' She shook her head dolefully. 'Whatever induced you to get mixed up with all those people, I can't say. I tried to bring you up as a respectable citizen. If you didn't go up for your B.A., it wasn't my fault. No one can blame me for it. But is it all true, all the things people say about you?'

Sriram thought and replied slowly, 'Don't believe a word of anything you hear. People talk falsehoods, remember.'

Granny's face puckered in a happy smile. 'Vile-tongued folk,' she cried. 'May all those that talk ill, think ill, slander you, or mislead you, or tempt you out of your way ...'

At this point Sriram had a slight misgiving that the old lady might mean Bharati. He tried to divert her attention. 'Don't exert yourself, Granny, lie down.'

'Why should I? There is nothing wrong with me. You believe that doctor! Let him come before me. I will tell him what I think of him. He would have burnt me alive if he had had his way!' She laughed grimly. Presently she recollected the interrupted curse she had intended to hurl on someone. 'Whoever has been responsible for taking you away, whether it be man, woman, or whatever, may they perish and suffer in the worst hell!' After uttering her imprecation she felt both relieved and happy. Sriram thought of the police waiting outside, and said, 'Don't exert yourself, Granny, you must not talk too much.'

'Why not? And who says that?' she asked. 'I will speak as much as I like and no one shall stop me.'

At this point one of the policemen peeped in at the doorway and Granny asked, 'Who are you?' so authoritatively that he withdrew his head immediately.

'Who is he?' asked Granny.

'Someone to see me,' said Sriram.

He went on stroking her arm so soothingly that she presently felt drowsy. He gave her a few ounces of milk. She said, 'I am glad to see you. Good boy, don't let people tempt you out of your way. Be with me. Don't leave me again.' Sriram helped her to stretch herself on her bed, and she was soon asleep. He walked over to the police officer and said, 'Let us go.' Kanni followed him to the jeep. Sriram said, 'Kanni, look after Granny till I am back. I don't know how long they will keep me. Try to see me and tell me how she is. I think the Collector will let you see us in gaol. I don't know what you are going to do about her.' He stood with bowed head for a moment, and then as though the problem was beyond any solution, he stepped into the jeep.

Kanni said, 'Don't be anxious. She is like a mother to us. We shall take care of her.'

# PART FOUR

He was in detention at the Central gaol. He occupied a cell with a few others and slept on the hard cement floor. They woke him up at five in the morning. This irked him most. He sometimes wished that they wouldn't pull him out of his retreat in a soft dream into the harsh reality of the prison world. And then the hurried getting up and washing at the dribbling water-tap, and the public toilet; this sickened him at first. He prayed that they might let him wait at least till the others had gone, but that could not be; the warder stood over him and the others and hustled them.

Sriram once attempted to approach the Most High of this world, in regard to it, when he came to inspect the prison. The superintendent of the prison lagged behind the Most High respectfully, with all the other officials trooping after them. Sriram had been in a file awaiting inspection at the central yard which was surrounded by the horrible slate-coloured barracks; the great man was marching by throwing a haughty glance at the file. The prisoners had been advised to stand stock still, and not to utter a word or move a muscle when the man passed; they were not to speak unless spoken to. But when Sriram saw the great god approach his part of the file, he could not resist the impulse to step forward and begin: 'I have a complaint and a request to make, sir.' At once several people seized him and pulled him out of the way; and the great man passed on, pretending not to have noticed anything. After he was gone, Sriram was summoned to the superintendent's office. The guards held his biceps and kept him standing at attention before the superintendent's table. The superintendent looked up and said: 'You have violated gaol discipline and you are liable to receive punishment.'

'What punishment?' Sriram asked.

The man, who had trailed like a meek puppy behind the visitor an hour ago, stamped his foot under the table and shouted, 'I will not have you talk to me in that manner, understand?'

Sriram felt cowed. He feared the other might go mad and kick him: he was the overlord here and was entitled to kill people if he chose. People might talk of monarchy being abolished, but here was absolute monarchy. This was his world, ruled by his authority, and no one could do anything about it, so Sriram said meekly, 'Yes, sir,' the very first time in his life he had adopted a tone of meekness.

The other was pleased with his submission and asked, 'Why did you step out of the line? What did you want to say?'

Sriram felt it would be better to speak plainly. 'I wanted to ask if something might not be done to provide us some privacy for our toilet.'

The superintendent sniggered, 'So you thought you might get things done over my head? Eh?'

'Not that, sir, but it hadn't occurred to me earlier, that's all,' Sriram said.

The other said, 'You saved yourself by not talking more, understand? If you had spoken to him, you would have been put in chains. Remember, we don't want indiscipline in this prison, understand?'

'Yes, sir,' Sriram said, completely crushed by his manner.

The other softened a little at this and said, 'Ask me for anything you may want.'

'Yes, sir.' Sriram found that this was the best way of talking to the man; the only idiom that didn't upset him.

The superintendent asked, 'What did you say you wanted to tell the I.G.?'

'I wanted to ask about the privy arrangements,' he said, feeling tired of all the repetition and publicity.

'Oh, is that so?' the other asked, and added, 'Here is the reply to your representation.'

'What, sir?'

'You will not be getting any arrangements other than what you have already got, understand?'

'Yes, sir,' said Sriram, uttering the soothing word. 'But may I know why?'

The guards pinched his biceps, alarmed at his impudence. But the superintendent did not seem to mind. He merely replied, 'If it had been any other time you would have been shot without a word, remember. You are not our guest, but our prisoner. You are not a classified prisoner, but one in custody under the Defence of India Rules, remember.'

'But there has been no trial. How long am I to be here?'

'There is no need for a trial in cases such as yours. The whole world knows why you are here.'

'I was only trying to do my duty,' Sriram said.

The superintendent kicked the table and said, 'I'll not have you fellows talking politics here.' The word 'politics' seemed to sting him.

'Yes, sir,' Sriram said, and this again soothed the man's temper.

He said as a concession, 'You are neither Gandhi's man nor an ordinary criminal, but more dangerous than either.'

Sriram could express no opinion in the matter himself. The word 'Gandhi' brought to his mind the memory of Bharati and he heartily wished that he had surrendered himself to the police with her. They would probably have treated him as an honourable political prisoner. 'Where is Bharati? Is she by any chance in this gaol? If so won't you let me see her? Is she keeping well?' Questions by the score buzzed in his head, as he stood staring at the wall.

The superintendent said, 'I'm glad you are paying close attention to my words. But let me say at once, it won't pay you to be troublesome within these walls. What are you thinking?' he demanded suddenly.

'I was only wondering how long I shall be kept here. It's already several months. I have lost count of the months.'

'It is unnecessary for you to keep count of anything, it's not going to be of any use to you. Your stay here will be as long as His Majesty wishes you to be here, that is all. We're instructed to keep you not very differently from your other friends here, under sentence of various terms of rigorous imprisonment. That's all, dismiss.'

The guards clicked their heels, saluted, and turned Sriram round. As he was going the superintendent threw after him the remark, 'You will ask me for anything you want.'

'Yes, sir.'

'That's all, dismiss.' And the guards marched him off.

The days, weeks, and months, that followed were similar, one day following another without much distinction. Sriram began to feel at home: he looked forward to the little excitements that came to him in the course of his existence. When he was taken to break stones in the quarry behind the gaol, he welcomed it as a change: the rocks that he hewed were hot under his seat, the sun scorched his body, the iron hammer with which he broke the stones peeled his skin, but still he liked the job because it took him, though under surveillance, outside the gaol. He was with a gang of men, miscellaneous criminals, who were there for any-thing from murder down to confirmed pocket-picking. Most of them were planning what they would do at the end of their term. Some of them were planning to return again and again, and spend the rest of their lives here. Sriram felt uneasy in this rough company, who laughed at the soft-handed, soft-headed man. They simply could not make out why he should have courted all this trouble from the police because someone wanted him to do something, and not because such exploits as derailing a train brought him a share of profit. This was a fresh outlook that had not occurred to Sriram in his self-centred political existence. He had a feeling that he was running up against a new species of human being, speaking like monsters, but yet displaying sudden human qualities; they were solicitous that he should not undernourish himself; they pitied him for his inability to relish the food: a tough ball of boiled millet with very watery butter-milk. (The buttermilk was a recent addition because somebody had agitated for it in the press and in the assemblies, and the butter-milk content was just enough to satisfy the technical needs of all agitators in general.) While he ate he thought of all the good things that his granny had made for him and remembered how even during his very last visit to her, at their house, she had offered him something that a neighbour had sent. He felt agony at the memory of the crunchy, ghee-flavoured rice; he could almost hear the music of his bite, while he held up his aluminium platter to receive his quota. The very manner in which he munched made his fellow prisoners comment.

'You still think of *Badam Halwa*?' asked the Culpable Homicide not amounting to murder. They were sitting side by side during the break for food at midday.

'If ever I leave this place, I am going to spend a hundred rupees on *Badam Halwa* at the corner shop, you know Krishna Vilas, the shop is small but it is a wonderful place; he serves on clean banana leaves and not on plates. You know his *idlies* are almost as if made of the lightest ...' Sriram was at a loss for a comparison, and his companion helped him with similes of jasmine, rose petals, soft butter, and so forth. Sriram added passionately, 'And you know he gives free chutney to go with it, you can't see the like of it anywhere else on the globe. You must have known the corner hotel?'

'No,' his companion shook his head. 'I am from Bellary, I am not familiar with the town.'

'I know that hotel,' the guard added, joining in their conversation. 'It's a good place, but I go there rarely. I haven't much chance of getting out of this place.'

'You are like us?' said one of the prisoners and all of them laughed happily at the joke.

Meal times were the best. Sriram's neighbour, a veteran forger, whispered to him, 'Don't tell anyone. I am getting some good things to eat and drink next Thursday. I will give you some when I get them.'

'What are you getting?' asked Sriram, unable to control his curiosity.

'Some *vadai*, and the nicest chicken *pulav*.'

Sriram retched at the mention of the chicken. He made a wry face: 'Chicken! Chicken! Oh! I can't stand the thought of it!' he said, his face twisting with disgust. 'I don't eat those things!' he cried. 'I have not even eaten cakes because they contain eggs.'

The forger was amused. He rolled with laughter till the guard, who had been friendly hitherto, objected: 'Stop that, where do you think you are!'

The central tower threw a welcome shade. The afternoon was languid, though warm. The superintendent would be snoring in his quarters, enjoying his afternoon siesta: there was really no one to object to anything, and this was the only hour when the prison ceased to be a prison for a while and gained a human and habitable atmosphere; the warders themselves acquired a friendly mellowness, and all conversation flowed on the human level. This was the hour at which it was impossible to continue the rigours of the gaol atmosphere – it was almost like the midday recess at Albert Mission School of Sriram's younger days.

The forger pleaded with the warder: 'Don't bother us for a while, please. A man needs some rest after all the labour of the day. Please leave us alone for a while.' And then he turned his attention to Sriram: 'I know they will use the purest ghee and nutmeg leaf and cinnamon bark for the *pulav*. If you scoop a handful of it, ghee will drip down your fingers; it's so rich. Don't say that you won't have it. You must accept it. It will do you good. Once you taste it, you will keep demanding it every day. That's the worst of it. It'll be impossible to get it into the place every day, though once in a way we can do anything. Our friend here and his friends will not mind what we do. He knows he will get his share.'

A gong struck the hour. The warder jumped to his feet and said: 'Get up and march,' and he led them back to their quarry at the back of the gaol.

At night, Sriram had companions in his cell. Before lying down on their cement beds, wrapped in their blankets, they sat up talking. The sentry at the corridor cried, 'Hush! Don't talk.' One fellow, the one who had committed house-breaking and murder, took it into his head to sing a hymn and insisted upon all the others joining him. *Rama Rama, Sita Rama*, he sang musically, and urged all the others to follow the chorus. He said, 'This is the only thing which is real,' in a very philosophical manner. 'You must know what is real and what is unreal. You must know the nature of the world in which we live. You must repeat the name of the Lord ceaselessly.' And he began a sing-song devotional recitation of the Lord's name. Others followed. If they stopped, he shouted in the dark, 'What Satan's offspring is in this room with me? I will cast him out.'

Sriram could not help asking, 'If you were so religious, why couldn't you have remained outside and led your followers?'

'It's because the police would not let me be, that's all,' he said.

'Of course, but for the police we would all be happier men,' someone said.

After this they all started their chant again. The sentry came and peeped at them. They guffawed. He muttered something and went away. The leader said in the dark, 'I am not afraid of anyone, I am not afraid of any gaoler.'

'It's because you are so experienced,' said another admiringly.

'I would have been swinging in that shed long ago, but the judge understood I didn't kill because I wanted to. I only wanted to break the bones of that ill-fated fool.'

'Which ill-fated fool?' asked Sriram, unable to check his curiosity. Here were men who formed a new species. He might have to spend the rest of his life as a member of this family.

The other answered: 'I only wanted him to give me the keys, as so many others had done, but he suddenly ran to the window, shouted for the police, and when I tried to run away he jumped on me and held me down. What could I do? I had to do something. I thought I might crack his legs and – but he pushed me, and that didn't work. These people force us to do unhappy, unpleasant things.' He ruminated for a while and sighed, 'No use thinking of it, but the magistrate understood, and when I leave the gaol I shall take him some fruits, oranges, plantains, things like that. Let us not waste our time.' And he began his chant with the others joining in. Sriram wanted to speak to them about politics, Mahatmaji and non-violence, and the British rule. He began to speak, but he was cut short by the man saying, 'Who cares who rules? We don't belong to that world. I've seen all those Gandhi followers in prison, and they think they are honoured guests! If you had been careful you could have enjoyed that too. They'd have put you in a bungalow with a cook and pocket-money and they would have given you books to read and sherbet to drink.'

Sriram's blood boiled at his words. 'How dare you speak like that of those who are suffering for the country's cause? You are mistaken. You are completely mistaken.' He wanted to get up and hit him, but he remembered that Bharati would have labelled him a traitor to the non-violence creed of Mahatmaji. Perhaps she would have said, 'I don't want to look at your face again. Get out of here.' And so he merely mumbled, 'Don't talk in that utterly ignorant manner of our patriots.'

The other growled, 'Who are you to talk to me in that tone?'

There was a pause. The forger at his side nudged him and said, 'Say you regret it. Don't rouse him. He is very strong.'

Sriram heard heavy steps approaching him from the other end of the cell. The man stood over Sriram and growled: 'I insist upon saying that your political prisoners are no true prisoners, do you understand? I've been in ten gaols so far. I have seen a lot of them. They feel they are in their father-in-law's house, visiting for *Deepavali*. I know what I'm talking about. I won't have you correcting me, do you hear?'

'I don't agree with you,' said Sriram. 'They are great patriots. They put themselves through much suffering.'

'I will knock your teeth out if you contradict me. Am I clear?'

'I will say what I please,' said Sriram defiantly. 'Even the British Government could not make me do what I didn't want to do!'

The other sneered: 'H'm, this is what comes of reading and writing. You don't know obedience of any sort, let me tell you. People should never go to school. They talk too much.'

'If I had been out, I'd have made you prostrate yourself before Mahatmaji, and confess your crimes,' said Sriram with passion.

At the mention of the Mahatma, the other brought his palms together and said, 'Don't drag his name in here; that great saint.'

'He is also in prison, I suppose you know that,' said Sriram.

'He may be, but what is that to you? Do you think you are also Mahatmaji because you are here?'

'Go back to your bed, man,' commanded Sriram. 'You don't know what you are talking about.'

'You call yourself the Mahatma's disciple, and you have derived no good from it. What business have you to come in our midst?'

Sriram said in disgust, 'Go back to your bed, man, I won't talk to you.'

The gangster swung his arm to hit Sriram. Sriram felt the rush of air in the dark, and ducked his head, and the other went back to his bed. Sriram felt happy and relieved only after he heard him stretch himself out and utter a long noisy yawn, which he prolonged into a song, till the sentry cried through the bars, 'Hush! Silence. No more talk.'

During the day the various duties he had to perform and the variety of derelict humanity he watched in the prison kept his mind from too much gloom. But when the last of the prisoners in his cell fell asleep and snored, loneliness came down on him and he became a prey to introspection. He was seized with a desire to meet and talk to Bharati. Where was she? Dead? Married to someone else? Or hanged in the prison? There was no way for him to know. He was amazed at the isolation that had been devised – inhabiting the same planet people were completely cut off from one another. States and their police minions seemed capable of devising any torture for human beings. Bharati had probably married Gorpad and gone to North India. It was months and years since they had met. He had lost count of time. The only reckoning they had was morning, midday and night punctuated by meal hours, drudgery, and occasional excitements such as that caused by the bully in his cell. He wondered if Bharati would ask, 'Who are you?' if he appeared before her. He was seized with the obsession that day by day he was deteriorating so much that he wouldn't be fit to be seen by her. He was losing his identity. He had lost his patriotic aim. He wondered what he had done to warrant anyone calling him a political sufferer. But for Jagadish he would not have done things that he wouldn't wish to enumerate before any decent person now. If it had not been for Jagadish he would probably have gone on living in his ruined temple until the police forgot him. And then he might have been worthy of associating with Bharati.

The thought of her produced in him a certain uneasiness: he heartily wished that she had not been such an uncompromising zealot. Everything that she thought or said or expected was set in grooves and hard to practise. For all practical purposes he was a back-number now, nothing better than the associate of forgers and homicides: their world was his world. Why should he be thought of differently? The longer he stayed here the more likely he was to drift away from Bharati. It was imperative that he should get away. How? He revolved in his mind all the things he had read in story-books – of files and hack-saws, being smuggled into prisons and people working their way out. The more he thought of it, the more unhappy he became. The sheer helplessness of the whole business weighed him down. He became silent and glum. All night he was racked with dreams of being caught while escaping, taken out and shot, the shooting party being directed by Bharati. He woke up in a cold sweat and was greatly relieved to find that after all he was still in the solid and homely prison. Why was Bharati causing him worry even in his dreams? Why couldn't she make herself agreeable and amenable like any other normal sweetheart?

The Fund-Office Manager sought special permission to meet him.

The call came to him when he was at work in the weaving shed. A warder came to say, 'You are allowed to see a visitor today, between three and four in the afternoon.'

Sriram felt excited. 'What visitor?' he cried. 'Man or woman?' He had a wild hope that his visitor might be Bharati. Could it be? What would he say to her? How was he going to talk to her? How could he tell her all that he wanted to within the time? Perhaps she would spurn him when she saw him. Better not see her. Could he send word back that he would not see anyone? All this passed through his mind in a flash. He asked: 'What sort of a person?'

But the warder said, 'See for yourself. The interview is in the Chief's room. If you don't waste too much time asking questions, you can have a few minutes with the visitor.'

Sriram followed the other meekly, dropping his job. His neighbours muttered: 'Your mother-in-law has probably come to see you with sweets!'

At the entrance to the Chief's office, the warder halted for just a second to look him up and down, flick off a cake of dirt on his jacket, and pull up his dress in general: he murmured: 'Remember how you should behave before the Chief. If you make any trouble, he will have you whipped.'

Sriram answered, 'I don't like whipping,' to which the other retorted, 'Don't talk back. It is enough if you do what you are told.'

It was only after Sriram had mumbled an unqualified affirmative that he would behave properly that the warder pushed him in. He saw the Fund-Office Manager waiting for him. He looked intimidated by his surroundings; he sat on a stool, his legs dangling, afraid to cross them.

The Chief looked up briefly and said, 'Prisoner, you have special permission to meet a visitor today.'

Sriram felt abashed to stand there in that uniform and face the Fund-Office Manager. He stared at the manager, who stared back at him. The Chief was busy looking through the papers on his table.

'You may speak,' he ordered. 'I can't allow this interview to be prolonged beyond four p.m. If you have anything to say to each other, go ahead, and don't waste time.'

Sriram felt like a fool. He thought that the manager should break the ice and begin the conversation. But the man seemed bereft of speech.

The Chief tried to ease the situation again by interrupting his study of the papers to order, 'Guards wait outside.'

Two men who had mounted guard over Sriram saluted, clicked their heels, and went out. This brought a slight improvement, but still the interview did not proceed beyond the stage of mutual staring. The Fund-Office man seemed to be stunned by the sight of the Sriram he saw before him now. He seemed to doubt whether this lank, sallow, close-cropped man in striped knickers and jacket could be the one he had come to see. Sriram noted his surprise and hesitation and said to himself: 'When even the manager is so reluctant to admit my identity, what will Bharati do? Perhaps she will say, "Get out, you *budmash*. Who do you think you are?" '

The Chief looked at his watch and fretted. He said: 'You may talk about anything except politics and other banned subjects.'

Sriram suddenly found his voice to say, 'How is everybody, Manager?'

'Very well, very well,' the man said, swinging his short legs, still afraid to cross them.

'Tell me about Granny,' said Sriram.

'That is why I have come here,' said the manager. 'We had a communication from her today.'

'Communication! Where from?'

'Don't you know? She is in Benares now.'

'When did she go there?'

'Don't you know the story? When she revived at the cremation ground, some orthodox people said that she could not come back into the town because it was inauspicious and might blight the city. She respected their wishes and stayed in the toll-gate house for some days, and then said she would go to Benares. We helped her to take the train at Talapur.'

'Benares! What is she doing at Benares?'

'She is with a number of others, who spend their last years there, old persons who are waiting to die. They cheerfully await their death, and look forward to the final fire and the final ablution in the sacred Ganges.'

'Did she ask for me?'

'Oh, she was so – ' the manager began, and at this point the Chief said, without looking up from his papers, 'Not allowed. Talk of something else.'

'But it is not politics,' began Sriram.

'Don't argue. Talk of something else,' ordered the Chief.

Sriram helplessly glared at him and said to the manager: 'And then what happened?'

'She is quite well in Benares. There is a whole street of them, old people who have retired there to the banks of the great Ganges, awaiting their end. Some have been there for years. That's as it is enjoined upon old people in the *shastras*. No one could wait for a happier end.'

The man from the Fund Office seemed to be so impressed with this that he became very eloquent, and Sriram could not help asking, 'You too want to retire there?'

'Yes, in good time. If God wills it. Everyone can't be as fortunate as your granny!' He paused to reflect, gently swinging his short legs. He had respectfully left his sandals outside the office and Sriram noted how dirty his feet were, and blackened with dust and wear. When he came back to the sordid world again, the manager said, 'She has given instructions regarding the disposal of the rent of her house. She wants the amount to be sent to her.'

'Is someone living in the house?'

'Of course, of course. Didn't you know?'

Sriram seemed to be hopelessly out of date, he knew nothing of what had happened anywhere. 'It was her instruction that a tenant should be found for the house, and accordingly we found one to pay a rent of forty rupees only, which they are crediting to the old lady's account in the bank.'

It was an appalling thought for Sriram that someone else should be living in the old house, shutting and opening its doors.

'Who are they?'

'Some yarn merchant.'

'Yarn merchant! I never thought we would have to surrender our old house to a yarn merchant!' he said with disgust.

'It's no surrender, they will vacate at a month's notice.'

This information filled Sriram with uneasiness. 'Where am I to live?' he thought. 'Where am I to accommodate Bharati, when I marry her?'

Although he had lived away from the old house for so many years, he still had a feeling that everything was all right so long as Grandmother lived there and so long as he could think of it as a home. He was filled with nostalgia for its brass-bonded, slender pillars, the pyol over the gutter, and the coconut-tree tops beyond the row of buildings.

'This is the point,' said the manager. 'She wanted me to tell you about it, and if you didn't want this money – it's been accumulating, as I have already told you, into a considerable amount – she said it might be sent to her. She seems to have exhausted all the cash she had taken with her. This can be done, I suppose?'

'Of course, why not?'

'I am merely carrying out her instructions. She wants me to consult your wishes in the matter.'

'Do anything she asks you to do. If she needs more money, don't hesitate to take it out of my funds. Poor Granny! I wish I had more time to give to her affairs. She has done so much for me. How is she? Does she feel very lonely?'

'Far from it. A friend came from Benares today. She is keeping very well; bathes thrice in the Ganges, and prays in the temple, cooks her food, has good company. A sublime life; it's this friend who has brought the letter.'

Sriram thought of his house again and felt unhappy.

'They are probably driving nails in all the walls, and what has happened to all my books and other things?' He gave a list of articles he possessed, and the manager said soothingly, 'Don't worry about all that. They are all safely kept. In that end room, which we have reserved for your own use.'

'What other news? How is the war?'

'Don't talk of that,' said the Chief.

'How is everything else?'

The man got up to say something, but Sriram interrupted with: 'I don't even know what year or month it is.'

'Nothing on those lines,' said the Chief. 'No politics, no war.'

Sriram in the solitude of midnight in his cell developed the notion of escape. He revolved in his mind all the techniques of escape that he had read or heard about. Smuggled files and rope formed, of course, the staple points in the whole business. Scaling the walls and crawling through ventilators were an inevitable feature. He dwelt on reminiscences of Monte Cristo's escapades; it was all very interesting and kept his mind busy planning. His admiration for the old prisoners became genuine; his sympathies were really widening. He realized how impossible it was to do anything within the walls of a prison except what the gaoler permitted. The warders seemed to take a personal pleasure in carrying out their duties, they were incorruptible and could not in any way be influenced. And yet how did people smuggle in hack-saws and things like that? While his hands were busy digging the earth or turning a wheel, his mind revelled in dreams of filed bars and nimble ascents up dangling ropes, escapes which story and film writers presented so slickly. This dream became so troublesome that he could not contain himself any longer. Lying on his cement bed at night he was busy weaving a rope that would go up to the ventilator in the ceiling, through which the night sky was visible, the only glimpse of a shining free world.

His only consoling thought, perversely enough, was that perhaps Bharati herself was languishing similarly within the bounds of the Old Slaughter House. It was not that he wanted to see her suffer, but the idea of her suffering established a community of interest. If he succeeded in escaping from the gaol, he would smuggle the tip to Bharati, wherever she might be, so that she might climb out of her prison, meet him outside its formidable walls, and hug him as her hero. But she might insist upon going back to her cell, refusing to walk out of it unless they opened the gates for her in a right royal manner. She might spurn him for his labour. She was incalculable in her behaviour. She would want the sanction of Bapuji, perhaps. Bapuji would probably applaud the proposal, if it could be proved that Sriram's technique would enable all prisoners to climb out of gaols; they would at once understand its national implications: how the British could be driven to despair if they were made to realize that their prisons could hold no one. It might drive them mad and make them decide, 'Well, we will quit. We can't hold India any longer.'

It was wishful thinking on a very big scale, but that could not be helped. It was the only excitement that he could ever conjure up. In his desperation he consulted the bully in his cell when an opportunity occurred. One evening he was unusually friendly, and Sriram slipped over to his cement bed and sat there. He whispered: 'Why don't we all escape from this hell?'

The other laid a clammy sympathetic hand on Sriram and said, 'It's usual to get that feeling. But nowadays I don't get it. I just do my *Bhajan* and feel all right. You must also join us in our *Bhajan*.'

'Well, we will speak about that later. But now let us discuss how we should escape.'

'How?' asked the other.

'You must help us. You are experienced. Have you never escaped from a prison?'

'Yes, twice, that's why I'm doing my seven years now.'

'You should not have allowed yourself to be caught.'

'Well, these things just happen, we can't help it,' said the other philosophically.

Sriram was interested in the method and asked, 'How did you escape?'

'Easy,' said the other, looking up at the ventilator. 'We were just six in a cell. We spun out the blanket strands, raised ourselves on each other's shoulders, tied up the rope, and climbed out: it didn't take much time. We were crossing the *cholam* fields in about an hour. No one would have found us again, but a fellow who had come out with us broke the lock of a house on the way and was caught.'

'Shall we do something like that and get out of here?'

The other thought it over and said, 'Why should I? What have I to do outside?'

'But I wish to get out. I can't stand this place any more,' said Sriram.

'If you didn't like this place, you should not have done things to bring you here, that's all,' said the other. 'Even if you manage to get out, they will bring you back in no time, it's not worth all the trouble. You can't hide your face.'

'I will grow a beard.'

'They will pluck out your beard just to see how you look. That is how you bring dishonour on even holy Sadhus, who have beards.'

'I promise I will keep out of the way of the police.'

The other shook his head. 'What is the use of going out if you can't move about freely?' He seemed to take pleasure in teasing him and to disapprove of people who didn't appreciate their life in gaol.

Finally, Sriram took out his trump card and said, 'I want to escape because a girl I want to marry is out there.'

'Where?' asked the man ruthlessly.

Sriram was afraid to give the reply, but he blurted it out before he could hold it back. 'She is in gaol too.'

'Oh! Oh!' the other cried amused. 'Do you mean to say you are going to slip into her gaol and ask the gaoler to officiate at your nuptials?' he asked coarsely.

Sriram felt angry and regretted that he had ever mentioned his angel to this coarse man. God knew what terrible things he would say now. He remained silent, afraid to open his mouth. And the other said: 'If she is the kind to go to gaol, listen to my advice, leave her alone. You can't bring up your children in gaol.

There must be someone to look after the house. It's not at all right that both a man and his wife should be the gaol-going sort.'

'How is it with you?' Sriram asked.

'I have three wives, here and there, and they run the homes in my absence: if they didn't I wouldn't hesitate to put sense into them. That's the way. You are not going to be here all your life. When you are let out, go and marry a good girl, I tell you. This gaol-bird will be no good for you.'

'She is not a criminal, she has gone to prison on Mahatmaji's command.'

'Oh! Oh! Oh!' the other sneered. 'Why do you drag in that great man's name here?'

Sriram grew annoyed. Somehow the mention of Bharati seemed to rouse in the other the worst ideas. Sriram abruptly rose to his feet and went to his bed muttering, 'Go on and sleep. Let us not talk any more.'

'You are afraid I shall tell the Chief, aren't you?' the other sneered. 'If you don't join me with gusto in our *Bhajans*, I will report you to the Chief.'

'I'm not afraid,' said Sriram defiantly.

'Well, we will see, don't be surprised if they lock you up in a solitary cell. You will have only the walls to talk to,' said the other. He took a fiendish pleasure in promising hell to Sriram.

Sriram paused for a moment and said, 'I have not wronged you. Why do you hate me?'

The other said sulkily, 'I have no sympathy for those who don't believe in God. I don't like fellows who speak ill of God.'

'I have not said a word against God,' Sriram said, wondering at the turn the subject was taking. 'What have I said?'

'I won't repeat it,' the other replied. 'If you don't respect God, you will be whipped in gaol, remember. That's my experience. You should listen to a man with experience, that's all.'

'I am in need of no advice from anyone,' said Sriram haughtily.

The forger turned in his sleep and swore, 'Are you going to sleep or keep on talking all night? A wretched place, it's becoming worse than the market place. No peace for a man who wants to sleep. I will call the guard if you fellows don't shut up at once.'

In answer the bully let out a loud, challenging song in a stentorian voice, enough to wake the whole town. There was a sound of running feet outside. Sriram sneaked back to his bed. The guard asked through the bars: 'What's going on here?'

'People are chattering and chattering. This has become worse than the market place,' said the bully from his bed.

A friendly warder brought them the news of the outside world: 'Mahatma Gandhi is becoming the Emperor of India,' he said one day. 'I heard it today from a person who knows these things. Some men have come by plane from England with the proposal.'

'Don't be silly. How can they want the Mahatma to become the King of India when they have put him in prison for fear that he may become one?'

'Didn't you know? It seems he is out of prison.'

'I don't believe it.'

'I swear he is. They released him long ago because he was ill and his wife died. A woman who comes here to cut grass told me so.'

'It is not safe to have any transaction with grass-cutting women. They will get you into trouble,' said a veteran prisoner.

'How do you know?'

'It is because I have suffered. They are sirens. They will seduce you before you know where you are. And then you will have trouble everywhere. They don't like such goings-on in a gaol.'

'But this is an old woman who cannot seduce anyone. She is a grandmother, so don't fear.'

'Then it is all right. Go on.'

'Her son is in the army. Her grandson sells newspapers in the market and he tells her what goes on in the world.'

Every one of the prisoners and their guards as well eagerly crowded round him to ask, 'What is happening? What is happening? Tell us.'

'It seems that some men have come from England and they want to make Mahatma a king.'

They clapped their hands in glee. 'Oh, how good to hear this!'

'Why does it make you so happy?'

'Because if Mahatmaji becomes the king of our country he will not allow anyone to be kept in prison. He doesn't like it. It's because he is a very good man. It seems the British don't like him because he says such things.'

'They like him now, all right.'

The indulgent warder looked on as the prisoners discussed these matters among themselves, while going through their various duties. The warder didn't however like the idea of a prison-less state. He said: 'How can there be no prisons? There will always be prisons whoever may become the king.' This was a ticklish technical point. The best thing was to consult the political expert in their midst. They turned to Sriram for guidance.

Sriram was breaking the stones unmindful of what they were saying. He was listening to their discussions, but he chose not to display any enthusiasm. He said, 'I don't know anything about anything.'

They plied him with questions: 'Is it a fact or is it not a fact?'

'How should I know? I am in your midst.'

'Will they release us all from prison?'

'All? I don't think so; they are likely to release only political prisoners.'

The warder seemed relieved to hear it. 'Ah, you say so. Political prisoners are different. There are some in the other block. I have heard that some of them are leaving every day. That is a different thing altogether. But you are not all political prisoners.'

They all said, 'What if we aren't? We are also human beings. Why should we not be treated well too? Whatever you may say, Mahatma Gandhi will help us. Do you mean to say that Mahatmaji will not care for us? He is a kind man.'

Their curiosity could not be contained. Night and day they worried about it, until one day a newspaper was smuggled in through the good offices of the friendly warder, and put into Sriram's hand for perusal and explanation. While his audience sat round him, and the guard watched over them, at the quarry outside the gaol, Sriram read out to them the *Daily News* from the first line to the last. It was as if he had been given a sudden vision of a broad and active world. He read of the impending

political changes, of the proposed division of India into Hindu-
stan and Pakistan, of Mahatmaji's firm refusal to countenance the
proposal, of the Cabinet Mission, and the endless amount of
talking that was going on at Delhi, of death, disaster, and con-
vulsive changes. The greatest triumph for Sriram was that the
British were definitely quitting India. He said proudly, 'I myself
wrote on all the walls "Quit India", and you see it has taken
effect.'

People looked at him with wonder. He became a hero in their
midst. 'Will they give you some reward for all your work now?'

He read, and this was heartening, of the release of political
prisoners from all the gaols in the country; but he could not hope
to come under this category. He was not classified as a political
prisoner.

The Chief sent for Sriram. His tone was suddenly friendly. 'I
don't know what the Government order will be about you. But
we have received a number of names for release this week. I am
glad to do it, because it will reduce our pressure of work.
However,' he said, looking through the list, 'your name is not
on it.'

Sriram's heart sank. He had a feeling that he was being kept in
a cage when all the others were roaming the wide earth freely.
He thought unhappily that someone was discriminating against
him. It was a cruel and sadistic world. The Chief noted the pain
in his face and said, 'Evidently you have not been classified as a
political prisoner. All those who have done what you have done
are under the consideration of the Government. If you like, you
may send in a representation, with an undertaking, and I will
forward it.'

'What representation and what undertaking?' asked Sriram.

'You will have to give an undertaking to report your movements to the police for some time till all the papers are scrutinized
and your classification is settled.'

Sriram thought it over. 'Is this a New India or are the British
still here?'

The Chief answered, 'I cannot tell you anything about it. That
is politics. I am merely carrying on as per the rules.'

In a moment it flashed across Sriram's mind that all the difficult, hazardous things he had done would be set at naught by this undertaking. If he met Bharati she'd probably say, 'You sneak out of prison, do you? You have degraded yourself beyond description. Get out of my sight.' He told the Chief: 'No. I can't give any such undertaking.'

'All right, please yourself. Right, dismiss.' The warders tugged his biceps and he turned and walked out of the room, more depressed than ever.

After all there came a day when he went into the office adjoining his Chief's room, a spacious office in which there were a number of racks. He was led in there by his usual warders without much ado; he handed a slip of paper to a uniformed man sitting at the table; there were a number of others standing around him, to each of whom he was passing bundles of clothes. Sriram waited patiently till his turn came; the man took the slip from his hand, looked him up and down, and cried, 'Number six seven,' at which one of the attendants ran up a ladder and brought out a bundle, and placed it on the table. The man scrutinized the bundle, looked at Sriram and asked, 'Are these yours?' Sriram looked at the clothes; he had been made to take them off long, long ago and change into gaol uniform. He was thrilled at the sight. He hugged them close to his breast and said, 'Yes, these are mine.'

'Wait,' said the other, snatching them back from his hand. 'Sign here.' He held a sheet of paper; there were numerous sheets of papers to be signed. Sriram was irked by the number of hurdles he had to cross before going out of this hateful place. At last the man was satisfied. He handed him the bundle, his old close-collared coat, shirt, and *dhoti*, in which he had been arrested ages ago at the cremation ground.

'Change into your own clothes now. You are no longer a prisoner.'

Sriram proceeded to strip his gaol dress before everybody. Life here had toughened him. The man said, 'You can go behind that shelf and undress.'

When Sriram emerged from behind a shelf loaded with old

discoloured bundles of papers and documents, he felt he was back in his old shape. He rolled up his striped shorts and jacket, and shoved them into a corner. The man said, 'You are free, you are discharged.' Sriram stood still unable to decide which direction to take. 'Go this way, the door opens out,' said the man. Sriram saluted him vaguely, and muttered, 'I am going,' and opened the door; it gave on to a small yard which was closed with a barred gate at the other end; an armed sentry paced in front of it. Sriram's first instinct was to turn back at the sight of him, but he told himself, 'I am no longer a prisoner,' and walked on haughtily. The man opened the door at his approach. He said as Sriram passed, 'Going out! Very good, try not to come back, unless you like this place very much.'

'I hate it,' said Sriram with feeling. 'I never wish to see a prison again.'

'That is the right spirit,' said the man, 'keep it up.' He was evidently used to uttering this formula to every outgoing prisoner. It was a sort of convocation address.

When the barred gate closed behind him Sriram could hardly believe that he was free. He felt weak and faint, and inexplicably unhappy. The memory of his cellmates who had become sullen and gloomy when it became known that he would be leaving was painful.

The bully had said, 'You are a selfish sort. I don't like your type.'

The forger said, 'If you can be released, why not we? Tell Mahatmaji that we want to come out.'

Another one said, 'If you become a big minister or some such thing, don't forget me.'

The bully had added, 'When I am released I will break into your house some night, and teach you good sense. I don't like selfish fellows like you.'

The warders had trooped behind him for tips. There was a little money that had accumulated as his wages, which the Gaol Accountant had handed over to him, and his old warders followed him muttering, 'We have been together so long. I would like you to remember us.' 'This is my child's birthday. Give me something to remember you by.' 'We cannot come beyond this block and please give anything you like.' 'We have looked after you all these months.'

Sriram gave a rupee to each of the crowd that followed him importuning, and that took away fifty per cent of his earnings.

PART FIVE

He walked on as in a dream. It was difficult for him to move about without a guard following him, and without being told where he should go. He found the evening light dazzled his eyes, the wide open spaces were oppressive. He turned back to cast a look at the building which he had occupied for years now. It looked in its slate-grey colour innocent enough, but what a tyrannical world it had contained: a fellow there could not do anything he wanted, even the calls of nature had to be answered as per regulations! The gaol was outside the town limits at the Trunk Road end. He had never gone so far before; he had been living all along on the Trichy Trunk Road, not knowing where he was.

He walked down the road towards the town, wondering where he should go now. A few buses passed him. He hoped people would not recognize him. There was a policeman sitting in one of the buses and Sriram turned instinctively away from the direct line of his vision. He walked on along the edge of the road. 'This is an independent India into which I am walking now,' he reflected. What was the sign that it was independent? He looked about him. The trees were as usual, the road was not in the least improved, and policemen still rode on the footboard of highway buses. He felt tired and hungry. He had not more than a few rupees left after the warders had had their claim. He wished that some sort of transport was provided for prisoners let out of gaol: it was very inconsiderate, even in a free India to have to face this! He hoped that some day they would make him a minister and then he would open a canteen, and place station-waggons at the disposal of prisoners at the gaol gate so that those that came out might not feel so lost.

It was dusk when he got into the Market Road. Nobody seemed to notice him. Here and there he saw buildings hung with the tricolour flags, the *charka* in the middle. He saw that there was less traffic than formerly. Shops were lit and crowded as ever. He felt a pang of disappointment. He had a gnawing hunger inside him. There were still a few rupees in his pocket, hard-earned, literally earned by the sweat of his brow. He put his hand into his pocket and jingled the coins, and remembered the axe he had wielded, and all the undreamt-of tasks that he had performed. He had a feeling of pride at the thought of all he had earned by his hard labour: no one could say that he was one who lived on the fat of the land. Even his granny could feel proud of his achievement and ability. He sat on the bench of a small park that had been formed at the traffic junction of New Extension and the Market Road. He sat there in order to think clearly how he ought to manage. There was no use trying to settle things while walking. This was a free country and no one was going to demand why he sat there and not somewhere else. It was difficult to get used to the idea, it was a luxurious idea worth brooding over. But he felt startled again and again as he thought from habit that he was exposing himself to the public gaze too much, and that he might have to slip swiftly into a hiding place. Sitting there on the cement bench beside a potted fern, he told himself: 'I'm free. No one can come after me now. No one will bother whether I have a clean-shaven face or a hairy one.' He felt hurt at first that the pedestrians went by without noticing him and the traffic without pausing to say, 'Hallo, hero!' But he soon realized the blessedness of being left alone after all the years of being hunted and looked for everywhere.

He realized that his first business was to eat something. He could do the clear thinking while sitting on a hotel chair instead of a park bench. He got up and moved briskly off down the road; the first hotel that showed itself in sparkling bulbs was 'Sri Krishna Vilas'. He turned in. Most of the tables were empty. It was long past the rush hour. He sat at a marble-topped table and waited for someone to come and ask what he wanted. A man sat at the exit on a raised seat with a cash box. The waiting-boys were all in a group chattering among themselves. 'They don't care,' Sriram told himself. 'I suppose I look like a gutter-rat.

They will drive me out.' He looked around him. He recognized one of the waiters: he used to come here often in other days.

'Hey, Mani!' he called, and the waiter turned. 'Come here,' he commanded.

The other came up. He recognized Sriram, and cried, 'Why, it's you! Where have you been all these years, sir? It's a long time since we saw you.'

'I was away on business. Give me something good to eat.'

At the word 'good' the boy puckered his face in worry.

'There is nothing very good now, sir, what with the present difficulty of getting rice and any pure food. Our government do not do anything about it yet. Do you know how hard it is to get any frying oil? Most of it's adulterated stuff, I tell you.' He started on a long narrative about the situation in the country, the food shortage, the post-war confusion, and the various difficulties and hardships that people experienced. All this was a revelation: it was the first report that Sriram was getting of the contemporary world. But he had no patience to listen to much of it.

'What have you?'

The boy cast a brief look at the shelf on which trays of edibles were on display and started, '*Kara sev, vadai*, and *potato bonda* ...'

Sriram said sharply, 'I can see all that from here. I want to know if you have anything fresh inside, on the oven, something more solid.' The thought of *idli*, soft and light, and of *dosai*, was alluring. It seemed as if he had tasted them in a previous birth. While he spoke he was racked with the thought that he had probably lost the necessary idiom to get on with ordinary folk. Perhaps he only had the ability to talk to gaolmates. He said, 'Something very g– ' he avoided the word 'good' lest it should start the other off again analysing the world situation. He said, 'I want something heavy, just made, I am very hungry.'

'There's nothing inside, sir. This is closing hour, and the kitchen department is the first to shut up. While our proprietor wants *us* to work till ten, those who sit at the fireside – '

Sriram lost his patience. He didn't want to spend the rest of the evening listening to shop-talk. He said sharply, 'All right, all right, get me something, anything to eat, now run and get me coffee, *good* coffee,' and he felt sorry that he had again blundered into the word, for the boy began to say something about the difficulties of making good coffee: milk-supply difficulties, the sugar racket, and the general avarice of black marketeers of various kinds. Sriram didn't know what to do. He lost his patience completely, 'Why do you tell me all that?'

'Because it is so.'

'All right,' he said callously, 'I'm hungry. If you are going to give me anything look sharp. If you stand here and talk, I shall get up and go away.'

'What shall I give you, sir?' the boy asked officially, for the first time giving an impression that he was on duty.

'Two sweets, one savoury and a large quantity of hot coffee,' commanded Sriram. This was the first time in many months he was able to order anyone about. He was surprised at his own voice, almost fearing that someone would say that he was to be put in solitary confinement. But it worked. The boy ran off with alacrity and interest.

He felt elated after his tiffin, and after chewing a betel leaf and nut he felt as if he were back in the times when there was no war, no political struggle of any kind. He was himself, grandson of a grand old lady, with no worries in life, shuttling between a free reading-room, the market place and Kanni's shop, living in a world with well-defined boundaries, with set activities, no surprises or worries, everything calculable and capable of anticipation.

He hurried on to Kabir Street. It was a fine home-coming. It was seven o'clock, but as usual children were playing in the streets, and the space in front of every house was washed and decorated with white flour. Why could he not have lived like these folk without worries of any kind or any extra adventures; there seemed to be a quiet charm in a life verging on stagnation and no change of any kind. The lights were on in most of the houses. He ran down the street with his eyes wide open. He stopped in front of his house. He looked through the doorway. Some strangers were moving about. He felt angry and cheated. What right had they to usurp his place? Some unknown children were chasing each other in the front hall under the lamp – that old lamp where Granny had taught him so many things in life!

He wanted to run up the steps and tell the children: 'You can't run around here, I can stop you if I want to.' They were probably knocking holes in the wall, banging the doors and shutters, only leaving wreckage behind for him to occupy when the time came.

He turned round to see Kanni and talk to him. But the shop had gone: the portrait of Maria Theresa was no longer there to brighten up the surroundings. In Kanni's place, a new cement structure rose without windows, probably a godown. He felt pained and cheated again. He walked up and down the road. None of his neighbours noticed him. He saw a few of them in their houses, sitting by the window reading an evening paper – comfortable folk. He felt like going up and talking to them, but they'd probably reprimand him for various lapses and he felt diffident about his ability to talk to anyone! He was obsessed with the thought that he had lost the idiom of communication with these people. The street remained very much unchanged since he saw it last – only Kanni's shop was gone, and there was no one of whom he could enquire.

Suddenly he felt that he had nowhere to go that night. In the prison at least, one had been assured of a place of retirement for the night.

The photographer's establishment was brightly lit, and threw its illumination on the road. It was a low-roofed shop with the usual glass front displaying a variety of enlarged portraits of children, pretty girls, and important men.

There was no one in the front parlour with its coir carpet and a small stool with a decorative potted plant on it. There was no sign of anyone living there. Sriram stepped into the next room, which was also empty. He cleared his throat and made sounds with his feet in order to indicate his presence.

'Who is there?' came the call. It was the photographer's voice. Sriram replied: 'A gaol-bird.'

He felt happy that after all there was someone he knew to meet him in this world. The other came out of the innermost chamber and advanced, trying to find out the identity of the visitor. He had evidently been working close to a light and could not see clearly. When he came near enough, he cried, 'You!

When were you released? What a pity I didn't know. I was wondering what you had done with yourself. Where were you? They would not tell us where you were. If I had known you were coming out today, I'd have arranged a grand reception for you at the gaol gate with flowers and garlands. The trouble is that things are still disorganized. But I blame no one. Ours is an infant state, still a baby, many things have still to be done, we must be happy that we are our own rulers and no foreign nation rules over us. We must be happy that things are being done and not spend the time finding fault with anyone.'

'We ought to rejoice that it's our own people that are blundering, isn't that so?' Sriram asked, some of his irresponsible spirit returning.

'Fancy Nehru and Patel and the rest sitting there where there were haughty Viceroys before. Didn't Churchill call Mahatmaji "The Naked Fakir"? The "Naked Fakir" is everything now, think of it ...' He was excited. 'There are bound to be mistakes, bound to be blunders everywhere, but we must not make much of them.' He was wildly incoherent and happy. 'If you had been out of gaol, you would have been garlanded and carried in a procession on Independence Day. What a pity you missed it. It was a grand affair.'

Jagadish seated Sriram on a large sofa, put a great album on his lap, took a seat by his side and turned its leaves. He remarked, 'As a photographer, I am proud of this. Future generations can never blame me for being neglectful. I have done my best. Here is a complete history of our struggle and the final Independence Day Celebration.' He had put various pictures of himself into the album, subscribing himself as a humble soldier. There were even photographs of the ruined temple, where Sriram had lived and worked. The photographer had entitled it: 'One of the secret headquarters of the Independence Army.' Sriram looked through the album which in effect was a documentary of the independence movement.

Jagadish had even stuck in photographs of gaols and their exteriors. He had pictures of barbed-wire entanglements. It was a completely romantic picture. Nor could he be said to suffer from modesty in any way. He was the chief architect of

Independent India, the chief operator in ejecting the British. He had included several pictures of Malgudi street scenes. Flags flew from every doorway and shop, crowds were moving in procession with people singing and playing musical instruments. Flowers everywhere. Great masses of men moving down the roads. Jagadish looked at the scenes with great pride. He felt he had striven to give people a good time and had succeeded. He said, 'After all, what do I get for all the trouble I took and the risks I ran? Are they going to make me the Minister of this and that? Not a chance, sir, there are others waiting for the privilege. Even if I stand for election, who will know who I am? Will the parliamentary board choose me as their candidate? Not a chance, sir, that is the reason why I have held fast to my camera and studio all through my various activities. Nobody can take it away.' There was a tone of regret in his voice which Sriram did not understand.

'After all, as you said now, we are an infant nation.' The word was very convincing, it had a homely and agreeable sound, nobody need worry what it meant or why it was mentioned.

'True, true,' said the photographer, 'I'm not complaining or grumbling. What I have done, I have done with the utmost satisfaction. I am not worried about it at all. What I say is I have got these photographs to record all that we have done, that's all.'

There were hundreds of pictures to wade through. Sriram began to turn the leaves fast. He felt bored. They were monotonous to see. More and more processions. More and more people. Flags. Pictures carried in the procession of national leaders and others, and more and more people. There was a sameness about the whole thing; he simply could not stand any more. He briskly turned the leaves of the album and came to the last page of the sequence in which Jagadish was seen hoisting the flag at some public gathering. Sriram put away the album and asked, 'How did you manage to photograph yourself?'

'Ah, a pertinent question, who could photograph the photographer? Guess how it was done. Do you imagine I attached a camera to my back to follow me and take the pictures?'

'Possibly, possibly,' said Sriram, losing interest in the whole question. He didn't want to look at any more pictures or hear about them. The sight of the Independence Day Celebrations irritated him. He almost said, 'If only I had known that people would reduce it all to this. I didn't go about inscribing "Quit" and overturning trains just to provide a photographer with material for his album.' He decided that he wouldn't look at any more pictures.

The photographer said, 'I have three more albums. They present another phase of our struggle.' He attempted to reach them down from a shelf.

Sriram held his hand, saying, 'No, not now. I have a headache. I won't look at any more pictures.' He was terrified at the prospect of having to look through more crowds, flags, and assemblies.

The photographer said: 'Good photographs are a sure remedy for headache. That's what an American scientist has recently found out.'

Sriram said defensively, 'I will examine them again tomorrow.'

'Very well. You know what my greatest regret is?' He paused to give him time to guess, and added, 'That I haven't a cine camera. If only I had had one I'd have shown you all the scenes you have missed as if you were seeing them before your eyes. That's the stuff. If I had charged as much as other photographers, I'd have had the biggest movie camera there is. But oh, this troublesome conscience with which some of us are burdened!'

Sriram felt disappointed with the man: he had looked so imposing as an underground worker: so precise and clear-headed and purposeful. Now he seemed woolly-headed and vague. The atmosphere of peace did not suit his nature. Sriram wondered for a moment why he had ever carried out his orders at all. He was disappointed that the other showed so little interest in his own gaol existence. Sriram asked, 'Did the police get you?'

'Me! Oh, no! How could they? They didn't know my whereabouts. It was possible for me to evade them completely. I lived in that temple after you left; didn't you see it in the first picture? Didn't you notice how I labelled it?' He again tried to reach out for the album.

Sriram said hastily, 'Yes, yes, quite right. It was very apt,' although he could not clearly recollect what it was.

'Moreover,' concluded the photographer, 'there was no occasion for the police to get me. My grandmother did not start dying at a wrong moment. If it hadn't been for your grandmother, you would not have gone to gaol at all.'

Sriram said nothing in reply. This was a subject which he did not wish to brood over. He had a hope they might have something to talk about in common, some diversion from the photographs. He asked point blank, 'Where is Bharati? Did she come out of gaol?'

'Oh, yes, I was wondering why you hadn't asked anything about her. I thought perhaps you had forgotten her!'

'No, never! Not even for a moment!' cried Sriram passionately. 'Have you seen her?'

'Of course,' said the photographer in a tone which made Sriram anxious and jealous. While he had been having social intercourse with homicides, she seemed to have come out of prison, been received and garlanded by the photographer and his friends, and probably they had all had a good time. She must have wondered why he was not there! He hoped that the others had had at least the goodness to remind her that he was still in gaol.

'Did you receive her at the prison?' he asked suddenly.

'We should have, but it was impossible to meet her. She was in one of the earliest batches to be released and she immediately took the train that very evening for Noakhali.'

'Noakhali; what is her business there? Where is it?' His geography was poor.

The photographer ignored the geographical question and said, 'Are you aware of what has been going on in East Bengal? Hindus versus Muslims. They are killing each other. Are you not aware of anything?'

'No. How could I be?' said Sriram. 'I was not kept in a municipal reading-room or the public library. I'm not aware of anything or of what you are talking about.'

'Whole villages have been burnt in inter-communal fights. Thousands of people have been killed, bereaved, dispossessed, demented, crushed.'

'Who is doing what and why?'

'Don't ask all that. I am a man without any communal notions and I don't like to talk about it. Somebody is killing somebody else. That is all I care to know. Life is at a standstill and Mahatmaji is there on a mission of peace. He is walking through villages, telling people not to run away, to be brave, to do this and that. He is actually making the lion and the lamb eat off the same plate. And Bharati seems to have had a call.'

Sriram was seized with cold fear. This was a new turn of events for which he had not bargained at all. Noakhali, Calcutta, Bengal, what was the meaning of it? What did she mean by going so far away from him? Did she do it by design? Did she try to make good her escape before he could come out of prison?

'What did she mean by going away?'

The photographer simply laughed at the question.

'Couldn't she have come and seen me in prison? She must have known I was in prison?'

'How?' asked the photographer.

'By enquiring, that is all, it is simple,' said Sriram with feeling. He said, 'Probably she has no thought of me. Perhaps she has forgotten me completely!'

Jagadish became serious on seeing his gloom. 'Don't let all that disturb you so much. Did you think of her often?'

Sriram began to say something in reply, but could not find the words, spluttered, remained silent and began to sob. The photographer patted his back and said, 'What has happened now that you feel so bad about it?' Sriram had nothing much to say in reply. He merely kept on sobbing. The photographer said, 'You are a fool! What have you done to keep in touch with her?'

'What do you mean? What could I do, chained and caged?'

'Now, I mean. What are you going to do about it now? Now you are not chained or caged. What are you going to do about it?'

'She is so far away, thousands of miles from me,' Sriram wailed. The thought of Noakhali was very disturbing.

'But there is such a thing as a postal service. You don't have to employ a special runner to carry your mails. Why don't you write to her?'

'Will you see the letter addressed and despatched properly?'

'I promise. Give it to me. I will send it off.'

This brought a ray of hope to Sriram. He suddenly asked, 'What shall I write to her?'

'H'm, that is a thing I can't tell you. Each man has his own style in these matters.'

It was clear that his mind was in a complete fog. To think or plan clearly was beyond him. Prison life showed its damage only now.

The photographer took pity on him. He said, 'Please rest a while. Close your eyes and relax.' He went to a small table and took out a pen and a sheet of paper, and started writing. The traffic on the road outside had ceased.

'Don't you wish to close your shop?' Sriram asked.

'Don't let that bother you. I can look after myself. I'm not much good at writing this sort of stuff. Anyway, I will try. Meanwhile, shut your eyes and switch off your thoughts, if you can.'

He sat and faithfully wrote a long letter which began:

'MY DARLING, – Who keeps slipping away like this! I might as well be in gaol. But in gaol or out of it – there is only one thought in my mind, that's you. I have been thinking of you night and day, and not all the gaol regulations could prevent me from thinking of you. And today I came out of the prison and my good friend Jagadish (he is a very fine man, let me say) told me about you. The prison bars kept me away from you so long, and now all the miles between here and there, but that is of no consequence. This distance is no distance for me. May I come and join you, because I will gasp and die like a stranded fish unless I see you and talk to you? Give me your answer in the quickest time possible.'

Jagadish got so lost in writing the letter that he forgot how long he was taking, and Sriram began dozing in his seat and snoring gently. Jagadish looked at him and hesitated for a moment. He put the letter under a paperweight and wrote a covering note: 'If approved, this letter may be signed and sent first thing in the morning, though preferably it should be copied in your own hand.' He got up and shut the front door of the shop. He switched off the light, and went into his living apartments, softly closing the door behind him.

Ten days of anxious, desperate waiting, and then Sriram received a letter:

'Happy to hear from you. Come to Delhi. Birla House at New Delhi, if you can. Our programme is unsettled. We are going to Bihar with Bapu, where there is trouble. There is much to tell you. We shall be in Delhi on 14th January. After that come any time you like. We shall be happy to meet you.

BHARATI.'

The Grand Trunk Express in the end arrived at New Delhi station. Sriram struggled to reach a window in order to have the first glimpse of Bharati. The men near the window would not let him near it. It was no use speaking to them: they seemed to live in a different world. He spoke Tamil and English, and they understood Hindi, Hindustani, Urdu or whatever it might be. He could now realize the significance of Bharati's insistence that he should learn Hindi. Just to please her he had looked through readers and primers, but that took him nowhere. He had been isolated for the last thirty-six hours. He had sat brooding, gaol life had trained him to keep his own company. His greatest trial had been when two men appeared suddenly from somewhere when the train was in motion, and scrutinized all the people in the compartment; when they came to him, they stopped in front of him and asked him a question. He could catch only the words 'Mister' and 'Hindu' with a lot of other things thrown in. They were rowdy-looking men. He said something in his broken Hindi, and Tamil and English, which seemed to make no impression on them. They came menacingly close to him, peering at his face; Sriram was getting ready to fight in self-defence. He sprang up and demanded in the language that came uppermost, 'What do you mean, all of you staring at me like this?' As he rose, one of the two pulled his ear-lobe for a close scrutiny, saw the puncture in it made in childhood, and let go, muttering, 'Hindu'. They lost interest and moved off. After they were gone, a great tension relaxed in the compartment. Someone started explaining, and after a good deal of effort in a variety of languages, Sriram understood that the intruders were men looking for Muslims in the compartment: if Muslims were found they would be thrown out of the moving train: an echo of the fighting going on in other parts of the country. Sriram lapsed into silence for the rest of the journey.

It was a most uncomfortable journey: he was crushed, could not find the space even to stretch his length or swing his arm: people came crowding in and sat on him. Sometimes he could not even extricate his legs. When he felt sleepy, he leaned his head back on the window or on the shoulder of a total stranger. When he felt hungry, he called to someone selling tea outside, and drank it. He could not get coffee. The people here seemed strange men who could swallow the very sweet *jilebi* and wash it down with bitter tea the very first thing in the day: this only confirmed his feeling that he was in a strange, fantastic world. He yearned for coffee, his favourite, like a true South Indian, but coffee could not be had here. He had to content himself by dreaming of it as he used to do in gaol. In fact this seemed only an extension of prison life: this life in a crowded, congested compartment, with a lot of strangers. He felt more uncomfortable here than he had felt in the prison. There at least he could say something or hear something from others' lips, but here the human voice conveyed nothing but jabber. The compartment was full of people who smoked *beedis* and filled the air with it, spat on the floor without a second thought, and the closet was nearly always inaccessible. He managed by jumping out of the train when the train halted and rushing back to the train when it whistled.

At ten-thirty or eleven on some day or other the train came to New Delhi. '*Nav Dheheli*,' people in the compartment cried and bustled about. He tried to run to the window or door to catch a glimpse of Bharati. She had written promising to meet him at the station. He felt ashamed of his appearance: he combed back his hair with his fingers: it was dishevelled and standing on end. He knew he was grimy, grisly, and unsightly. He wished he could tidy himself up before Bharati set eyes on him after all these years. He caught a glimpse of her through a number of heads and shoulders jammed at the window, and, in his anxiety he pushed and bumped into people rudely, and the train moved past before coming to a halt. He saw her standing, gazing earnestly at the window. For a brief second he caught a glimpse of her figure, and his heart sank. He wished he could improve his appearance before facing her. He wished he could skulk away with the crowd and see her later. He had great misgivings as to what she might think of him if she saw him in his present state. But even in that desperate state, he knew, by his experience in the train itself, that he could never ask his way again and go in search of her. She might be lost to him for ever.

When he got down from the train, carrying a roll of bedding and a trunk, Bharati's searching eye picked him out in the crowd. She waved her arms and came running to him. She gripped his hands and said, 'Oh, how good to see you again!' and in that tone of spontaneous affection Sriram lost himself, forgot his own appearance and griminess, and acquired self-confidence. He looked her up and down, and cried, 'You look like a North Indian, yourself. You look like a Punjabi. I hope you understand our language.'

She took charge of him immediately. She picked up his bedding and said, 'You carry your trunk.' He snatched the bedding from her hand, and took the load on his own shoulder. She said, 'Don't be silly. You haven't four arms, re-member.' And she snatched back the bed from his hands. Sriram lost his bewilderment. The proximity of Bharati gave him a sense of homeliness. It was as if he were back in Malgudi with her. He didn't notice the strange surroundings, the strange avenues, and buildings, the too broad roads, the exotic men and women, and the strange shops they were passing. He had not time to notice anything. His attention was concentrated on Bharati. She looked darker, and more tired, but her tresses were as black as ever. She looked tired, as if she had undernourished herself. He could not get over the novelty of meeting her again. He was always on the point of disbelieving what he saw and felt. Perhaps, he was going through a fantastic dream. Perhaps he was dead. Or dreaming from his confinement. For the first time these many months and years he had a free and happy mind, a mind without friction and sorrow of any kind. No hankering for a future or regret for a past. This was the first time in his life that he was completely at peace with himself, satisfied profoundly with existence itself. The very fact that one was breathing, feeling, and seeing, seemed sufficient matter for satisfaction now. She kept looking at him, and asked, 'When did they release you?'

He gave a summary of his gaol existence and a résumé of all that had happened to him since she saw him last. The *tonga* ran smoothly. The extreme sympathy with which she listened to his story pleased him greatly. It gave it a touch of importance. As he spoke, he was impressed with his own doings. He was on the point of asking himself: 'Am I the one who has done all this or is it someone else?' He was filled with a sense of extreme heroism. 'I never thought I could put up with all this sort of trouble. I was very keen that the man in the street − ' he began, and puffed with his own importance. The listener, Bharati, gave his whole life a new meaning and a new dimension. When they arrived at a colony of huts somewhere in New Delhi, he was completely satisfied with all the things he had done in his life.

'This is my present headquarters,' Bharati explained. She had taken him to her own hut. 'Yes, this is my home.' There was a spinning wheel in one corner, and her clothes hung on a rope tied across the doorway.

'After all, she is going to be my wife, that's why she doesn't mind my staying with her,' he reflected.

She said, 'You will have your "room" ready in about an hour, till then you may rest here. There is another block, where you may wash yourself. Make yourself comfortable.' As she was speaking a group of children came running in crying, '*Moi, Moi* − ' and they said something that Sriram could not make out. They came and surrounded Bharati and dragged her by her hand. She stopped and said something to them in their own language. They left her and went away.

'Who are they?' asked Sriram with a touch of jealousy.

'Children, that's all we know about them,' she said.

'Where do they belong?'

'Here at the moment,' she said, and added, 'They are refugee children, we don't know anything more about them. I will be back in about an hour. Make yourself comfortable.' And she went out.

She was gone a long while. By the time she returned he had explored his surroundings. He had discovered the bathroom and the tap, and washed and tidied himself. He went back to her hut and spent a long time combing back his hair and studying himself in the mirror in order to decide whether he was worthy of Bharati. Bharati's kindness had restored his confidence in himself. He had never hoped that she would treat him with such warmth and kindness. The years that had separated them did not seem to make the slightest difference. It was as if they had separated only an hour ago: all the moments of loneliness and hankering and boredom that had made life a hell for him within the last few years were gone as if they had not existed.

He saw one of her *saris* hanging up, a white one with yellow spots. It was of course made of *khadi*, hand-spun; the rope sank under its weight. He pulled it down to take it in his hands and gauge its weight, reflecting, 'She ought to wear finery, poor girl. I will give her everything.' He took it in his hand and weighed it; 'It seems to weigh twenty pounds.' He stretched it and held it before his eyes. 'It's like a metal sheet. She must feel stuffy under it. I can't see any light through it.' He rolled it up and pressed it to his breast. It had a faint aroma of sandalwood which pleased him. 'It has the fragrance of her own body,' he reflected, closing his eyes. As he sat there the door opened and Bharati stood before him.

'What are you doing with my *sari*?' she asked in surprise. 'One would think that you were trying to wear it,' she said with a laugh. Sriram reddened, and put it hastily away.

'It does not try to ward me off,' he said, 'when I take it to my heart.'

'Hush!' she cried. 'Don't try to be silly. We are all very serious people here, remember. I see you have tidied yourself up. If you have any clothes for washing, give them to me.'

Sriram handed her a small roll that he had brought back from his bathroom. 'They are terribly soiled,' he murmured apologetically.

She snatched the bundle from his hands and went out. He reflected, 'She is almost my wife, she is doing what a wife would do, good girl! God bless her. If I tie a *thali* around her neck somehow, when she is asleep, things will be all right.'

She returned in a moment saying, 'Your clothes will come to you in the evening. Here in this camp everyone is expected to wash his or her own clothes and not employ others to do the job, but you are new and I have got a *dhobi* to wash for you as an exception. Are you hungry?'

'Extremely,' he said. 'I am longing for something to eat.'

'I don't know what you mean by something,' she said. 'You can't expect all our South Indian stuff. It is months and months since I tasted anything like that. You will have to learn to eat *chappati*, and vegetable and curd and fruit, and not ask for rice or *sambar*.' She led him to a shack where some people were eating and children were sitting with plates before them. There were two platters laid for her and Sriram, side by side. 'This is how husbands and wives sit together,' Sriram reflected as he sat beside her and tried to work his way through wheat *chappatis*. He longed for the taste of the pungent South Indian food and its sauces and vegetables, but he suppressed the thought. Gaol life had trained him to eat anything offered him. 'I am really still in a gaol,' he reflected.

She was extremely busy all through the day. She seemed to have numerous things to do. She was always attending on children, changing one's dress, combing another's hair, engaging another group in dance or play, and continuously talking to them; besides this she had a great deal to say to a lot of miscellaneous men and women who came in search of her. Hers was a full-time occupation. She gave the children a wash, fed them, put them to sleep on mats in various sheds, drew their blankets over them, said something to each one of them, and finally came back to her own room, sat down on her cot, and stretched her arms. Sriram followed her about for hours but could not get in a word of his own. He tried to smile at the children, thinking that that might please Bharati, but she hardly noticed his presence when she was with them. It infuriated him. After a time, he turned on his heels, and went back to his hut. It was furnished with a rope cot and a mat and had no door. There was a common bath at the end of the alley which he shared with a number of others. He had felt indignant when he was transferred here. It seemed to dash his hopes to the ground. 'Did she put me in here in order to get rid of me?' he reflected. 'Was it because I picked up her spotted *sari*? If I had not done so, she would probably have let me sleep in the same room. I have probably destroyed her trust.' He reflected ruefully. 'Trust! Who wants her trust! I only want her.'

He had switched on the light and was sitting on his bed. The entrance darkened. The low roof of the hut made it stuffy, although it kept the place warm in winter. She came in bearing his clothes which he had given her for washing. Sitting in his hut, Sriram had been seized again with the feeling that he was still cooped up in a cell. 'My gaol seems to be on my back, all the time,' he reflected. The fatigue of the journey had begun to affect him, the intense cold air, and the gloomy and novel surroundings depressed him and made him feel unhappy – a gloom and unhappiness without any cause. The brief spurt of happiness he had experienced seemed chimerical.

Bharati put his clothes on his bed and said, 'Are you comfortable?'

'Yes and no. I feel happy when you are with me, and miserable when you go away.' She looked at him, startled. He continued, 'Won't you sit down here?' and he made a space for her. She sat down. He moved close to her, and laid his arm on her shoulder.

She said, 'Not yet,' and gently pushed away his arm. 'What a strange man!' she cried. 'You have not changed at all.'

He sat away from her and asked, 'Am I still an untouchable?'

She said, 'Bapuji alone can decide.'

'Have you spoken to him about it?'

'Yes, more than once, but he has not given an answer yet.' She sat with bowed head when she said it, her voice was low. She looked subdued.

There was an uneasy silence for a while, then he asked, 'Why? Doesn't he want us to marry?'

'It may not be that,' she said. 'But he really did not have the time to give it a thought, there were other things to do.'

It was a relief for him to know that Bapuji was not against the notion of their marrying, but it was not enough. He held his breath and listened without speaking. He had a fear that his slightest word might spoil everything. This was an occasion for speech in the most delicate of whispers. Anything more harsh might destroy the whole fabric. He wanted to be on his guard. He wanted to do nothing that might scare her and take her away from him, nothing that might make fruitless all the thousands of miles he had come. So he refrained from speaking. He wanted to shout at her and demand if it was only for this that she had wanted him to come all that way, he wanted to tell her that he regretted ever having set eyes on her. He wanted to threaten her that he would seize her by force and carry her back to South India.

'More than anything else,' she said, 'the thing that pains Mahatmaji now is the suffering of women. So many of them have been ruined, so many of them have lost their honour, their home, their children, and the number of women who are missing cannot be counted. They have been abducted, carried away by ruffians, ravished or killed, or perhaps have even destroyed themselves.' She appeared to be on the point of breaking down at the thought.

Sriram felt he must say something in sympathy. 'Why do these things happen?' And he felt ashamed of the utter inanity of his question. She didn't notice his question, but just went on speaking.

'On the 15th of August when the whole country was jubilant, and gathered here to take part in the Independence Day festivities, do you know where Bapu was? In Calcutta where fresh riots had started. Bapu said his place was where people were suffering and not where they were celebrating. He said that if a country cannot give security to women and children, it's not worth living in. He said it would be worth dying if that would make his philosophy better understood. He walked through villages barefoot on his mission. We followed him. Each day we walked five miles through floods and fields, silently. He walked with bowed head, all through those swamps of East Bengal. We stopped for a day or two in each village, and he spoke to those who had lost their homes, property, wives, and children. He spoke kindly to those who had perpetrated crimes – he wept for them, and they swore never to do such things again.

I have seen with my own eyes aggressive rowdy-looking men taking a vow of non-violence and a vow to protect the opposite faction – don't ask what community they were: what one community did in one part of the country brought suffering on the same community in another part of the country. I have seen what has happened both at Noakhali and Bihar, and then at Delhi. How can one choose? Human beings have done impossible things to other human beings. It's no use discussing whether this community committed greater horrors or the other one. Bapuji forbade us to refer to anyone in terms of religion as Muslims, Hindu, or Sikh, but just as human beings. He said one day that he sometimes pitied those who committed acts of violence – he advised some women in a village that they should sooner take their lives with their own hands than surrender their honour ...'

'You must have gone to many places,' said Sriram, not having anything else to say.

'Yes, for about a year I have been with Mahatmaji. He was at first unwilling to take me to all those places but I bothered him again and again after I was released from gaol. I don't know how many villages I have seen. We followed the Master through burning villages. Of course, anything might have happened to us anywhere. There were a few places where they showed their anger even against Mahatmaji. They held up placards threatening Bapu's life unless he turned back and left them. But in such places he stayed longer than in other places. And ultimately he held his ground.'

'Were you at any time in danger?'

'Of what? Of being assaulted? Yes, sometimes, but Mahatmaji had advised women as a last resort to take their lives with their own hands rather than surrender their honour. There was no sense of fear where Mahatmaji was. But ... if any unexpected thing happened, I was always prepared to end my life.'

'No, no,' said Sriram horrified.

'It seemed quite a natural thing to do in those places, where one saw burning homes, children orphaned, men killed, and women carried away. I felt we were in some other country. My special charges were children wherever I saw them.

I gathered them and brought them here. All those children you saw here, we don't know anything about them. They escaped death, somehow, that's where providence has shown its presence. They are all gathered from various villages in Bengal and Bihar. We had more, but some were reclaimed in Calcutta itself. But the ones we have now with us, we don't know anything about them. If their parents are alive, they will know they are here and come for them: otherwise we will bring them up. We have collected toys and clothes for them. Don't ask whether they are Muslim children or Hindu children or who they are. It is no use asking that; we don't know. We have given them only the names of flowers and birds. Bapuji said once that even a number would be better than a name, if a name meant branding a man as of this religion or that. You see one child was called Malkus, that's a melody: a girl is known as Gulab, that is a rose. These children must grow up only as human beings.'

Sriram shivered a little, and Bharati said, 'I'll give you some warm clothes and blankets out of what we have collected for refugees. For this purpose, we'll count you as a refugee, no harm in that.' She laughed slightly. He was frightened of her. She seemed too magnificent to be his wife. 'You now understand why I could not talk to Mahatmaji about our own affairs. It would have been sacrilegious. Even so, I mentioned you to him one day in a village in Bengal. He was about to say something, when someone dashed in crying that he had been stabbed, and then another time in Calcutta I was telling him about you, and he asked when you were coming out of gaol; it was late at night. I had waited for our opportunity when there would be no one about, and suddenly some big men, ministers of the place and others, arrived for urgent consultations. I never got a chance again.'

'Will he remember me?'

'He never forgets anyone. I felt that the time was not yet −. Tomorrow, let us go together and see him at Birla House, and if there is an opportunity, we shall ask him together.'

'If he says no?' asked the anxious lover, with a shudder.

Bharati rose saying: 'I will send you the blankets in a minute.'

* * *

Next afternoon, Sriram, before setting out for Birla House, tidied himself, looked into a mirror, and suddenly decided that he was probably looking too smart for the occasion. He rumpled his hair a little. His mind was buzzing with numerous doubts. Bharati had gone ahead to arrange an interview with the Mahatma. She had left a guide behind to conduct him to Birla House. He picked out a *khadar* shirt and vest, wrapped a shawl round his shoulder, and satisfied himself that he looked unostentatious. His greatest fear was that Mahatmaji would be reduced to saying, 'Marry you? Bharati marrying you! Begone, you presumptuous worm!'

Bharati took charge of him at the gate of Birla House. She said: 'He is terribly busy, but he will see us both for a moment. He knows we wish to see him urgently.' A lot of people were going in and out, people in *khadi* and white caps, foreign correspondents in European dress, and motor-cars passed on the drive. Sriram was blind to his surroundings. He asked Bharati: 'If he asks me about anything, what shall I say?'

'Say anything, he will not mind it, as long as you speak the truth.'

Sriram was amazed at the ease with which she moved about the place. He was confirmed in his view that she was too good for him, that he had no right to expect her to become his wife. All kinds of people stopped to have a word with her. She spoke English, Tamil, Hindi, Urdu, and God knew what else. She spoke with great ease to men, women, young boys, and old men of all nationalities. She had a smile or a word for everyone.

'What a lot of people you know!' Sriram said with admiration. She acknowledged the compliment with a smile that charmed him.

'Yes, but I don't know the names of most of them,' she said. They went through the drive and the garden.

'What a mansion!' he cried. They had to speak mechanical trifles: both of them were preoccupied with one thought: the impending interview with the Mahatma. If he said, 'Yes,' what should they do next? To Sriram it was entirely unbelievable. It meant that he needn't dwell in a separate hut, that he could touch her, take her, he would have rights over her person, and he could always be with her. He took her aside on the lawn.

'Just a moment, Bharati,' he whispered, 'if Bapu permits us to marry, shall we go through it immediately?'

Her breath blew on him warmly as she whispered: 'Yes, without doubt.'

'How could we do it immediately? How could we make the necessary arrangements?' he asked.

'What arrangements? Are we going to have pipes and drums and a dowry and feasts?' she asked.

'Don't we have to buy flowers at least? Where am I to buy them in this place? I don't know anyone. I don't know my way about. How can I ask my bride to undertake all this for me? If only it were Malgudi, instead of Delhi, you would have seen what I would do.'

'Don't worry about all that. Bapu himself will tell us what to do.'

They crossed a small stretch of ground on which already some people were sitting. There was a dais at one end.

'This is where Bapu holds his evening prayers every day,' she said.

She entered the main building through the back. They reached a small veranda, crossed a passage, and stopped just ten yards from a window. She hushed her voice and pointed through the window. 'There he is!' There he sat with spectacles on his nose, with his legs folded under him. He was earnestly listening to the talk of two people sitting with him. 'That's Nehru, that's Patel,' the girl whispered. There were a number of others also in the room – very busy men. 'We must not disturb them,' she whispered, and flattened herself against the wall. Sriram followed her example. The men inside were talking in low whispers. Someone came out of the room and smiled at Bharati. Bharati told her something in Hindi.

'She is Bapu's grand-niece, she looks after him.'

'Won't they mind our being here?' Sriram asked. 'They seem to be talking over important things.'

'But Bapu has asked me to wait here for him and take a chance. I'll peep in at the right moment and show my face at the window. He will call me in, or he may come out for a moment.'

'I tremble at the thought of his coming out!' Sriram confided to her.

'This is the only way we can have a word with Bapu. He is always busy and surrounded by people.'

'He is looking somewhat weak,' Sriram ventured, peeping through the window for a moment.

'Yes, his last fast has completely fatigued him. Sometimes, he lay there without moving, unconscious.' She stopped talking as a couple of girls passed. Someone with a shorthand notebook and pencil hurried off. A liveried government-house servant went in bearing a glass of water.

Seeing all this, Sriram wanted to postpone his meeting with Gandhi. 'Should we disturb him today? He may not be free.'

'He is always busy. This is the way. He has told me to wait for him and meet him today. I just told him that you were here and he said, "Bring him along *today*." "Sometime tomorrow, Bapuji, you are busy today," I said, knowing that he was going to have important conferences with the Prime Minister and others. "I *mean* today," he emphasized. He even indicated the spot where we should wait. He said when he had a moment to spare he would see us.'

'I know you are waiting there, come in, come in with your friend,' came Mahatmaji's voice. 'You may come now, all the dreadfully serious business in life is over. Come, come my daughter.'

'That is Bapu,' said Bharati, clutching Sriram's hand and leading him. His heart palpitated. Just before stepping into the room, she whispered, 'Be natural and truthful. And tell him about the marriage.'

'Yes, yes,' Sriram gulped. They stepped in.

The Mahatma was seated on the floor. He looked up from a paper. Bharati brought her palms together and saluted. Sriram said, '*Namaste*, Oh, Revered Master!' The Mahatma returned their salutations with a smile. He indicated a place near him and said, 'Come and be seated here. I have postponed meeting you too long. Now tell me about yourself. Bharati, I hope your children are flourishing: you are a mother to thirty already, what a blessing!'

'Yes, Bapu,' she said. 'They are all fine. There was a little one who was down with a cold, that little girl whom you named Anar.'

'Oh, yes, I remember her, you know what *Anar* means, pomegranate bud; what a beauty! God reveals himself to us in the shape of children. I have collected a lot of fruit today, you know the fuss people make when I fast: they always seem to think that it must always be followed by a feast! Well, I have kept them for you: take them to the little ones and let them enjoy the feast.' He indicated in a corner a heap of bright oranges and apples.

'Yes, Bapu.'

'And don't forget to take them the flowers too.' The Mahatma now turned to Sriram: 'Now tell me about yourself.' Sriram hesitated for a moment. 'What have you been doing in your part of the world?'

'They kept me in prison till a week ago,' he said.

'Why didn't they release you earlier?' Gandhi said.

'I was awarded an ordinary sentence,' he replied, putting into it all the poignancy he felt at the thought.

'That's very good. What did you do?'

Sriram hesitated for a moment and remembered Bharati's injunction to be truthful. He said, 'For some time I preached "Quit India", but later I was overturning trains and – '

Mahatmaji looked grave. 'You have done many wrong things. It's no comfort to think that worse things have happened since.'

'Bharati went away to gaol, and there was no one who could tell me what to do: no one who could show me the right way.'

'That is an excellent confession,' Mahatmaji said with a smile. 'Yes, the mistake was hers in leaving you behind.'

'No,' said Sriram: 'The mistake was mine. I refused to go with her to the gaol, when she told me about it.'

'Indeed, is that so, Bharati?'

'Yes, Bapu, he said he was – '

'Very well, when all this stress is over, you will tell me in detail all you have done as a political worker, and we will decide what we should do.' He laughed. 'We will hear if there has been anything so serious as to warrant my going on a fast again. Do you know how well a fast can purify?'

'I will fast if you order me to,' Sriram said.

'I hope you have done nothing to warrant it. We will go into the question later.'

'If it is decided, I'll be prepared to go through a fast myself,' Bharati added, her face all flushed and red.

'You!' said Mahatmaji, 'for your friend!'

At this point, at the farthest end of the hall someone was moving. The Mahatma said: 'There is my conscience-keeper dangling a watch, telling me it is time to get up.' He held up five fingers and said, 'Give us five minutes more.' He turned to his visitors: 'I'm sorry I have to leave you in five minutes. Already people must have assembled on the prayer ground. Don't you hear their voices?' Sriram was seized with anxiety at the thought of time running out. Every minute counted. Already, even as he was thinking he was losing precious moments. Only three and a half minutes more. He must speak before the watch was dangled again. He threw a side-glance at Bharati in the hope that she might at least seize the precious hour. But she turned on him what seemed to him a look of silent appeal. The Mahatma kept looking at them with an amused look. Sriram suddenly heard himself saying, 'We are waiting for your blessed permission to marry.'

Mahatmaji looked from one to the other with joy. 'Do you like each other so much?'

Sriram burst out, 'I've waited for five years thinking of nothing else.'

'What about you, Bharati, you are saying nothing.'

Bharati bowed her head and flushed and fidgeted.

'Ah, that is a sign of a dutiful bride,' said the Mahatma and asked, 'Does this silence mean yes?' Sriram looked at her with bated breath. Mahatmaji observed her for a moment and said, 'She'd be a very unbecoming bride, who spoke her mind aloud! Good, good, God bless you. When is the happy occasion, tomorrow?'

'Yes, if you bless us so.'

'Very well. Tomorrow morning, the first thing I do will be that. I will be your priest, if you don't mind. I've been a very neglectful father; I'll come and present the bride. Tomorrow, the very first thing; other engagements only after that. I already have here all the fruits and flowers ready, and so after all you can't say I have been very neglectful.'

When the man with the watch appeared again, the Mahatma said, 'I'm ready for you.' He rose to his feet. Sriram and Bharati also got up. The Mahatma said, 'You have already a home with thirty children. May you be their father and mother!' He went into an ante-chamber and came out after a minute. Bharati waited at the door for him. He passed her with his eyes on the floor. Bharati followed him out with Sriram trailing behind her.

Mahatmaji suddenly stopped, turned round and said: 'Bharati, I have a feeling that I may not attend your wedding tomorrow morning.'

'Why? Why, Bapu?' she asked.

'I don't know.' His voice trailed away: 'I seem to have been too rash in promising to officiate as your priest.'

'Bapu, without you  – '

'Tut, tut,' said Gandhi. 'You don't have to say all that. I want to be there very much, but I don't know. If God wills it I shall come. Otherwise, know my blessing is always on you both. Anyway you are not to put off your marriage for any reason, remember,' he said, with a new command in his voice, and Bharati replied, 'Yes, Bapu.'

The Mahatma patted her back, threw a smile at Sriram, and hurried down the passage. He walked leaning on the shoulder of his granddaughter. Sriram and Bharati followed, their heads full of their plans. Mahatmaji took out his watch and said, 'I hate to be late ...'

As they stepped on to the lawn, Bharati said to Sriram, 'Let us attend the prayer today. There is a place for two of us.' They stepped aside.

As the Mahatmaji approached the dais, the entire assembly got up. At this moment a man pushed himself ahead of the assembly, brushing against Bharati, and Sriram cried petulantly, 'Why do you push like that?' Unheeding, the man went forward.

'I'm sorry to be late today,' murmured the Mahatma. The man stood before the Mahatma and brought his palms together in a reverential salute. Mahatma Gandhi returned it. The man tried to step forward again. Mahatmaji's granddaughter said, 'Take your seat,' and tried to push him into line. The man nearly knocked the girl down, and took a revolver out of his pocket. As the Mahatma was about to step on the dais, the man took aim and fired. Two more shots rang out. The Mahatma fell on the dais. He was dead in a few seconds.

# A GLOSSARY OF INDIAN TERMS

| | |
|---|---|
| *Ahimsa.* | Hindu ethical idea advocating non–injury or kindness to other creatures. |
| *Badam halwa.* | A sweet made of almonds, sugar and ghee. |
| *Beeda.* | Betel leaf, folded and ready for eating. |
| *Beedi.* | Popular Indian cigarette, with the tobacco wrapped in a leaf. |
| *Bhai.* | Brother. |
| *Bhajan.* | Collective prayer at which devotional songs are sung. |
| *Bharfi.* | A sweet made of sugar and milk. |
| *Bonda.* | A fried, hot food. |
| *Chalak.* | Captain of a volunteer corps. |
| *Chappati.* | Pancake made of wheat flour. |
| *Charka.* | Spinning wheel. |
| *Deepavali.* | Popular Hindu festival at which fireworks and crackers are set off. |
| *Devata.* | Celestial being, friendly to man. |
| *Dhoti.* | Length of cloth worn round the body below the waist. |
| *Dorai* | (literally 'King'). Common way of referring to Europeans. |
| *Dosai.* | Pancake of rice and black–gram flour – very popular in South India. |
| *Gita.* | Usual way of referring to the *Bhagavad-Gita.* |
| *Goonda.* | Hooligan. |
| *Himsa.* | Cruelty. |
| *Hindi.* | Language of a great part of North India and the official language of the Indian Republic. |
| *Idli.* | Popular steamed cake of South India. |
| *-ji.* | Honorific suffix to names like Gandhiji, Mahatmaji. |
| *Jiba.* | Shirt–like Indian garment. |
| *Jilebi.* | Popular sweet of North India. |
| *Karma.* | Hindu theological idea meaning desert or destiny. One's actions continue to have their effects in another incarnation. |

| | |
|---|---|
| *Khadar or Khadi.* | Hand–spun cloth popularized by Mahatma Gandhi. |
| *Khara sev.* | Fried savoury. |
| *-ki – jai.* | Victory to – |
| *Lavani.* | Bardic song. |
| *Mahatma.* | Great Soul. This was what the people of India called Gandhi. |
| *Mantra.* | Sacred verse, chanted on certain occasions. |
| *Mull.* | Thin translucent cloth much liked by Indians as clothing. |
| *Namaste.* | Word uttered while greeting another with folded palms. |
| *Peepul tree.* | *Ficus religiosa*, considered sacred by the Hindus. |
| *Pooja.* | Worship. |
| *Pulav.* | Famed Islamic dish of rice and meat. |
| *Pyol.* | Elevated and roofed veranda in front of a house. |
| *Raghupati Raghava*, etc. | Devotional couplet mentioning the name and attributes of Rama. |
| *Ramayana.* | Hindu epic, narrating the adventures of Rama. |
| *Ram Dhun* or *Ram Nam* | Chanting of the name of the Hindu *avatar*, Sri Rama. |
| *Sadhu.* | Religious mendicant. |
| *Sambhar.* | South Indian vegetable curry. |
| *Sari.* | Hindu women's dress. |
| *Sewak Sangh.* | Social Service Association. |
| *Shastras.* | Scriptures. |
| *Sircar.* | Government. |
| *Swaraj.* | Home Rule. |
| *Subedar.* | Revenue official of pre-British days. Also a non-commissioned officer in the Indian Army. |
| *Thali.* | Sacred marriage-badge tied by husband round wife's neck at wedding. Symbol of wifehood. |
| *Tonga.* | Horse-drawn vehicle. |
| *Zamindar.* | Big landowner. |
| *Zigomar.* | Popular name for highwayman, robber, etc. |